Harlequin is proud to present
four complete novels from four fabulous series

Looking for...

Upbeat romances about the pursuit of
love, marriage and family?
Choose

Rich and vivid historical romances that
capture the imagination?
Choose

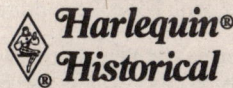

Breathtaking romance combined with
heart-stopping suspense?
Choose

ROMANTIC SUSPENSE

Sensuous stories and sexy men?
Choose

Muriel Jensen is the award-winning author of nearly fifty books that tug at readers' hearts. She has won a Reviewer's Choice Award and a Career Achievement Award for Love and Laughter from *Romantic Times Magazine,* as well as a sales award from Waldenbooks. Muriel is best loved for her books about family, a subject she knows well, as she has three children and eight grandchildren. A native of Massachusetts, Muriel now lives with her husband in Oregon.

Kelsey Roberts's first novel, *Legal Tender,* was published by Harlequin Intrigue in January 1994. Since then, she has published sixteen novels and garnered numerous award nominations for her talents in writing romantic suspense. Before turning to writing as a full-time career, Kelsey worked as a paralegal, a profession that has provided wonderful fodder as well as technical expertise for the type of stories she loves to write. Kelsey makes her home outside Annapolis, Maryland, with her college professor husband.

Heather MacAllister has written almost twenty-five books, and her unique ability to mix sexiness and humor in a love story has made her a reader favorite. She has also been nominated for a RITA Award for Best Short Contemporary Romance by Romance Writers of America. A former music teacher, Heather traded in her grand piano after deciding a computer keyboard was a *lot* quieter while her children napped. It's the perfect career for this Missouri native now living in Texas with her electrical engineer husband and two live-wire sons.

Deborah Simmons began her professional career as a newspaper reporter. A voracious reader and writer, she turned to fiction after the birth of her first child, when a longtime love of historical romances prompted her to pen her first book, published in 1989. She lives with her husband, two children and two cats on seven acres in rural Ohio, where she divides her time between her family, reading, researching and writing.

Muriel Jensen
Mommy on Board

Kelsey Roberts
Unspoken Confessions

Heather MacAllister
Bride Overboard

Deborah Simmons
The Squire's Daughter

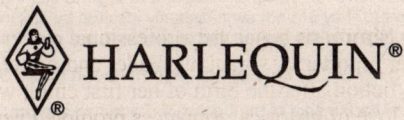

TORONTO • NEW YORK • LONDON
AMSTERDAM • PARIS • SYDNEY • HAMBURG
STOCKHOLM • ATHENS • TOKYO • MILAN • MADRID
PRAGUE • WARSAW • BUDAPEST • AUCKLAND

If you purchased this book without a cover you should be aware that this book is stolen property. It was reported as "unsold and destroyed" to the publisher, and neither the author nor the publisher has received any payment for this "stripped book."

ISBN 0-373-83433-0

HARLEQUIN SERIES SAMPLER

Copyright © 2000 by Harlequin Books S.A.

The publisher acknowledges the copyright holders of the individual works as follows:

MOMMY ON BOARD
Copyright © 1995 by Muriel Jensen

UNSPOKEN CONFESSIONS
Copyright © 1995 by Rhonda Harding Pollero

BRIDE OVERBOARD
Copyright © 1997 by Heather W. MacAllister

THE SQUIRE'S DAUGHTER
Copyright © 1994 by Deborah Siegenthal

All rights reserved. Except for use in any review, the reproduction or utilization of this work in whole or in part in any form by any electronic, mechanical or other means, now known or hereafter invented, including xerography, photocopying and recording, or in any information storage or retrieval system, is forbidden without the written permission of the publisher, Harlequin Enterprises Limited, 225 Duncan Mill Road, Don Mills, Ontario, Canada M3B 3K9.

All characters in this book have no existence outside the imagination of the author and have no relation whatsoever to anyone bearing the same name or names. They are not even distantly inspired by any individual known or unknown to the author, and all incidents are pure invention.

This edition published by arrangement with Harlequin Books S.A.

® and TM are trademarks of the publisher. Trademarks indicated with ® are registered in the United States Patent and Trademark Office, the Canadian Trade Marks Office and in other countries.

Visit us at www.romance.net

Printed in U.S.A.

CONTENTS

MOMMY ON BOARD   9
Muriel Jensen

UNSPOKEN CONFESSIONS   225
Kelsey Roberts

BRIDE OVERBOARD   441
Heather MacAllister

THE SQUIRE'S DAUGHTER   615
Deborah Simmons

Muriel Jensen
Mommy on Board

Mommy on Board originally appeared in the Harlequin American Romance® line, a series of lively romances that feature tough and tender men, confident and caring women, falling in love in the backyards, big cities and wide open spaces of America. Four new Harlequin American Romance® novels appear at your bookseller's every month. Don't miss them!

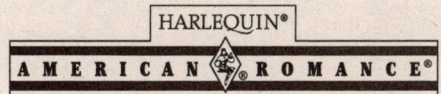

PROLOGUE

THERE ARE NINETY-ONE more days until I am born—at least, I hope so. Mom's been out since early this morning shopping for a desk chair, and that was after eating mocha macadamia cake for breakfast. Her indigestion sounds as bad as mine. If she isn't careful, I'm going to be born right now with my eyelids half-open and still wearing this tacky lanugo mink coat that I was promised would be gone if I make it full term.

But, you gotta love her. She's explained to me about my father. He's been out of the picture for three months, and though she insists it isn't going to matter, I have my own thoughts about that. But if she's willing to give it a shot, so am I. I mean, he wanted me out of the picture, and in order to keep me, she gave up everything—including him, her job in New York, her rent-controlled apartment—that place on Forty-second Street with the cheese and onion bagels. It's like I owe her.

Whoa. What was that? Ouch! Oh, no. I knew this would happen.

Hey, not yet! No! Mom? Mom, I'm not going anywhere 'til I have toenails! Mom!

CHAPTER ONE

"SOMETHING WRONG, ma'am?"

Nancy Malone concentrated for one more moment on the vibrating echo of the pain in her abdomen that had made her gasp. The fisting sensation was gone now, but it had left an unsettling discomfort in its place. She rubbed the spot worriedly, then returned her attention to the burly, bearded man in coveralls, who was loading the old upholstered desk chair onto the back of her truck.

"I'm fine, thanks." She smiled reassuringly at him and raised the tailgate into place.

He did not appear convinced. He frowned at the mild but definite swell of her stomach. "You sure? Pregnant ladies shouldn't be hefting furniture. You got someone to help you unload this at home?"

No, she thought defensively. *And I don't want to talk about it.* But aloud she said, "I'll manage. Thanks," and offered her hand. "Good doing business with you, Sam. If you come across an old-fashioned wide-top desk, you'll call me?"

He delved into the bib pocket of his coveralls and produced the note with her telephone number, which Nancy had handed him just before the pain hit. "Right away. Want me to keep an eye out for baby furniture, too?"

No. She wanted to buy one of those pristine oak-and-white sets with five matching pieces and fluffy bunny decals all over them. But she'd priced one at Hobbs Furniture, and unless she won the lottery, it was far beyond her means.

She nodded and hauled herself into the truck, pleased that

at almost six months pregnant, she still had a measure of grace. "I'd appreciate that."

Sam tipped his dusty baseball cap and walked back to the old hipped-roof barn that sat in the midst of a sea of appliances, automobile parts, and old furniture in various stages of stripping and restaining.

Nancy waved and turned the key in the ignition. At the same instant—as though it, too, had been controlled by the turn of the key—her abdomen cramped and tightened.

She fought momentary panic. "No," she told herself firmly as the sound of the tubercular truck engine filled the cloudy, early summer morning silence. "This is not going to happen. I have overdone it a little, but I've felt so *well*. It'll go away when I get home and put my feet up."

The knot of pain in her abdomen loosened and she drew a deep breath. She put the truck in gear and moved to the exit of Sam's Super Seconds parking lot. Traffic was light on the road that connected the small Columbia River town of Heron Point with coastal Highway 101 and Nancy let the truck idle for a moment, considering her options—north to town and Riverview Hospital, where her obstetrician had an office, or south to her beachfront cottage and the blissful solitude she so enjoyed.

With the rationale developed over a lifetime of depending on herself, she turned south. The little pains were a reaction to the tiring move across country; to bringing her small cottage into order; to feeling generally so well that she'd forgotten she had a problem.

Nothing was wrong. All she had to do was go home, leave the chair on the truck until later, settle down with Dashiell Hammett and a cup of herbal tea, and put her feet up. Or she could watch Oprah. It was always comforting to know how many people there were in the world in more bizarre situations than her own.

She cranked her window down, turned up the volume on Michael Bolton, and headed down the beautiful, meandering, tree-lined highway that bordered the turbulent ocean.

The next pain brought a small scream from her and made her yank the wheel instinctively toward the grassy shoulder. She came to an abrupt stop. She panted, waiting for it to abate. It didn't.

She suddenly experienced a profound revelation. She may have needed only herself in the past, but she was carrying a new life now. She was dealing with Mother Nature at her most forceful, and when the lady flexed her muscles, she was a most powerful opponent.

"All right!" Nancy conceded aloud, her voice breathless with the pain in her abdomen. "I'm going. But don't try to get tough with me. I've done almost everything else in my life alone. I can do this, too! And I'm uninsured, remember? Pick on someone with total coverage!"

THE PAIN WAS GONE. Nancy tried to relax as she waited in the darkened room for the radiologist. She'd taken in so much water in preparation for the test that lying still was difficult. But she'd done this once before in New York. She knew the drill; a stomach filled with water provided an acoustical window for sound vibrations.

The emergency-room doctor had called her obstetrician, who had prescribed a drug whose name she couldn't remember at the moment. All she knew was that it had stopped her premature labor. She said a silent prayer of thanks and promised God that she would turn over a new leaf, make a point of putting her feet up and eating better. And even if she needed no one else, she would reach for Him more often.

Meanwhile, she'd been admitted for several tests and a night of observation.

The door opened and a tall man in a lab coat walked into the small room. He kicked a rolling stool aside and came to stand over the gurney. His features were in shadow, but his form was tall and broad. A fresh-air fragrance wafted toward her.

"Good morning," he said, glancing up from her file to

smile at her. She saw white teeth in the dim light. "Contractions stopped?"

"Yes." She heard the relief reflected in her own voice. "Scared myself there for a few minutes."

He nodded. "Bet you did. Okay, let's have a look at this baby and see how he's doing."

"He's a girl," she said, removing her hands from atop the blanket as he tugged her gown up and out from under it, folding it back above the small bulge of her stomach. He folded the blanket out of the way just below it.

He looked into her gaze, his eyebrow raised in question. "Just a guess, or do you know for a fact?"

Nancy opened her mouth to reply as he moved closer. That placed his face and upper body in the feeble glow of the room's only light—a gooseneck lamp placed over his equipment. Her reply stopped in her throat as she stared. He looked just like Harry Boeneke, Portland, Oregon police lieutenant. Considering Boeneke was entirely a figment of her imagination, the resemblance was doubly remarkable.

His hair was that same golden brown, his eyes a level, steady hazel. His nose and chin were angular and well-defined, his mouth nicely shaped. He even had a small scar on his chin, along with that same air of competence allied with danger that provided alternating states of fantasy and ecstasy for Geneva Frisco, Private Eye—the fictional heroine in Nancy's mystery novel in progress.

"Ah...no." Nancy forced herself to concentrate on his question. "I mean, yes. I did have an ultrasound at four months in New York, but I didn't want them to tell me the sex. I just know."

His eyebrow rose in surprise, arched in curiosity. The name tag on his lapel, she noted, read J. V. Nicholas, M.D.

"Then, if you *know*," he asked, "why don't you want it confirmed?"

She laughed softly. "I want being right to be a surprise."

And that was about as much sense as pregnant women made sometimes, Jave thought as he powered up to perform the test. He guessed this woman was single. After ten years in radiology, he prided himself on being able to see inside his patients almost as well as his equipment did.

He could tell single mothers by their eyes. It wasn't that the excitement wasn't there; many of them were more thrilled about their pregnancies than married women were. But beneath it all, he could see the fear—particularly with first-timers. They were worried about the delivery—worried about having to do it alone.

And he'd be the last one to fault them. By the nature of his work, and because one of his sons had been a preemie, he knew a lot could go wrong.

And this one, Malone, Nancy R., had that look in her eyes. And with good cause after the morning she'd endured.

"You told the ER nurse," he said as he squeezed out a few inches of gel, "that your mother took DES when she was pregnant with you." Diethylstilbestrol was a drug taken by many women several decades ago to prevent miscarriage. Jave knew that studies of the female children born to those women revealed a tendency to disfiguration of the reproductive system, which sometimes resulted in problems ranging from an inability to conceive to difficulty carrying a baby full term.

"Yes," she replied, her head turning toward him in the darkness. Her voice was calm. "My mother called me when she first heard about the effects of DES. I saw my doctor right away. He said my problem was relatively minor. I had a slightly weakened cervix, and he warned me that I might have to deal with preterm labor."

He nodded. "I'm going to put coupling gel on your abdomen. If you've had an ultrasound before, you'll remember that it's cold. Here it comes."

She lay absolutely still as he rubbed the icy solution over her rounded stomach.

"So, you've been taking it easy, remembering to nap every day, to stop before you're tired?"

"Well...I did before the move."

He wiped the gel off his hands. "The move?"

"From New York," she replied. "I bought a cottage on the beach a couple of miles out of town. I've been working a little too hard trying to get things in order. I guess it's a nesting frenzy or something."

Her obstetrician was McNamara. That was good. He'd take good care of her. Probably already chewed her out for overdoing it.

"I bought a desk chair today," she said in a jovial tone that sounded false despite the smile that accompanied it. "I'm going to write a bestselling mystery novel and win the Edgar."

He couldn't tell if her chattering meant she was relaxing or growing more nervous. "Is that anything like the Nobel?"

"Not *quite* as prestigious. It's like the Oscar of mystery novels." She heaved a deep sigh and closed her eyes. "That way I can work from home after she's born."

Jave placed the convex probe on her abdomen and fine-tuned the picture on the screen. He saw the baby—a black-and-white form about a foot long in the windshield-wiperlike swath of the echoes' image. At the center, the tiny heart beat steadily. He felt a sense of relief.

"Okay," Jave said, concentrating. "Here it is."

"Where?" She propped herself up on an elbow to look, holding on to the gurney's rail, her eyes alight with excitement and trepidation. Jave and the machine were slightly behind her and to her right.

Jave moved back to the gurney to reposition her. "This generally goes better if my patients don't try to climb into the machines." Her eyes, wide and whiskey brown, locked with his. Her small-fingered hands clasped his forearms as he eased her back to the pillow. She clung to him for one protracted heartbeat, then dropped her hands and relaxed.

"Sorry," she said, turning just her head to look this time. "I got a little excited. Do you see her?"

"I do." He pointed to a movement in the image. "Has

its back to us," he said, grinning as he traced the image with the tip of his pen. "Probably upset with you for all you've put it through today."

Nancy laughed. "Oh, dear. Mother-daughter disharmony already. Does she look all right? Can you tell if this morning hurt her?"

"Dr. McNamara will explain everything to you," he said, studying the image. "But the heartbeat's good, movement's normal. Looks like everything's developing all right." A tiny hand, digits clear and visible, moved on the screen. "Whoa. There's a wave. Let's get a Polaroid of that for the baby book." He pushed the button that would give him a photograph. "We can label that one, 'Hi, Mom.'"

MOM? HI! It's me! Didn't know this thing lets me see you, too, did ya?

We got lucky today, didn't we? Whew. Had me worried there.

I like the man on the machine. Nice eyes. Nice touch, too. Ask him if he's married.

NANCY WAS GIDDY with relief. "Thank God," she whispered. "I was so afraid she was having a problem."

Jave changed her position slightly and fine-tuned the machine again. "*She* doesn't seem to be having a problem," he said, obviously concentrating on the image, watching for the details he knew her doctor would want to see. "But you'll have to remember that *you* do. The baby's counting on you to keep it safe."

Nancy felt a stab of irritation at the suggestion that she was being careless with her baby's life. It quelled the euphoria of a moment ago. "I've been feeling so well that I overdid it. I wasn't deliberately behaving irresponsibly."

"You moved," he said evenly, ignoring her indignation as he repositioned her. "We'll have to reshoot that one. Lie still."

Irritation deepening, Nancy cooperated.

When he'd taken the shot, he explained quietly, "I wasn't impugning your sense of responsibility. I was just reminding you that what seemed like a normal range of activities to you before your pregnancy has to be curtailed now, or you'll get both of you in trouble."

Nancy propped herself up on an elbow, not caring if she ruined his shot. For the past few months she'd had everyone telling her what *they* thought she should do, and no one listening to what *she* wanted for herself and this baby.

"Look," she said firmly. "I am not being careless with this baby, so don't lecture me. You're not my doctor."

Jave turned on the stool to face her, resisting the urge to smile. It was good that she was pugnacious. It was a quality she'd need.

She was right. He wasn't her doctor. But he couldn't help himself. Single mothers made him feel protective.

"No, I'm not," he said gravely. "When Dr. McNamara explains the results of the pictures to you, I'm sure *he'll* lecture you. I just don't want to see you back in here with pictures that might not look so good next time." She drew in a breath to fling a heated reply when the telephone interrupted her. Jave stood and reached across the machine for it. "Nicholas," he answered.

Nancy looked away from his neat form in gray slacks. The fabric molded itself to his slim hips as he leaned forward to accommodate the short telephone cord. Men had a way of looking wonderful, she thought, and being far less than that when you needed them.

And this one had some kind of a messianic complex. Well, she wasn't going to be her mother's rehabilitative project, and she certainly wasn't going to be his.

Not that that would ever even be within the realm of possibility. She just had a bad habit of considering every man she met in terms of his husband potential even though she never wanted another one. It was a quality she'd inherited from her mother, who was currently planning wedding number four.

He turned to look at her, the telephone still to his ear. "Almost finished. Five minutes. All right, I'll ask her." He grinned. "Yeah. You can use my office if you promise not to disturb my careful filing system." He listened a moment. "Right. Bye."

He leaned forward to hang up the phone, and this time Nancy let herself look. She sighed, grateful she wasn't having her blood pressure taken. He had long legs, a wonderful backside and a long-armed reach. She closed her eyes. Not for her. Never again.

Her eyes flew open when his hands settled gently on her shoulders and guided her onto her side. "One more shot and we'll have it," he said. He went back to his machine. "Take a breath and hold it. One more. Hold it. Okay. All finished." He made adjustments on the machine and shut it down. Then he came to the gurney to pull up her blanket. "That telephone call was for you," he said, crossing the room to turn on the light.

Nancy blinked against the sudden brightness as she sat up, holding the blanket to her. "For me?"

"Amaryllis Brown from public relations wondered if you'd mind talking to her in my office for a few minutes before I take you back to your room."

Nancy blinked, waiting for the message to make sense. "Public relations? Wants to see me? Why?"

He grinned. "I didn't ask. But Amy's an experience. I'm sure you'll enjoy the interview." He went to the corner where the nurse who'd brought her down had stashed the requisite wheelchair.

"She must have me confused with another patient," Nancy insisted as she slid into the wheelchair.

"She had your name and your due date," he said as he began wheeling her down the corridor.

"My due date?"

J. V. Nicholas turned into a tiny, narrow office that reminded Nancy of her crowded galley kitchen in Manhattan. He pushed the chair farther into the room, blocking in the tall blond woman who stood at his cluttered desk.

Nancy took in the confined space, most of its room taken up by file cabinets and a desk, all of which were covered with papers and storage boxes. She decided that his remark on the phone about disturbing his filing system had been a joke.

Then her attention was redirected to the woman who turned a nuclear-powered smile on her. "Nancy Malone?"

Nancy nodded.

"Amaryllis Brown, public relations coordinator for Riverview Hospital. Everybody calls me Amy." She offered her hand, then smiled at the man standing behind Nancy's chair. "Thanks for the use of your office, Jave. I brought a pot of tea. You don't mind, do you?"

"Not as long as you leave some. Don't keep her too long."

"Ten minutes tops."

Jave closed the door behind them. Despite the flicker of antagonism that had grown between her and the radiologist, Nancy almost hated to see him leave. The woman now seating herself in the desk chair had a friendly but curiously predatory air about her, which filled Nancy with foreboding. She couldn't imagine why, but she had a feeling she was going to regret agreeing to this meeting.

Amy Brown began to talk about how Riverview was a small hospital, always seeking to solidify its patient base by trying to provide as many of the refinements to quality care as big city hospitals offered. Unable to see how that related to her, Nancy allowed herself to be distracted by Amy Brown's appearance—a fashion nightmare.

Her dress was pale pink with full, puffy sleeves, a nipped-in waist too high for her long body and a flared hem that hung to midcalf. There were bows down the front and on the sleeves. She wore patterned white stockings and pink flats. Her hair was silvery blond, but was caught back in a lank ponytail. Clear-framed glasses sat on the bridge of a pretty, straight nose in the middle of a pleasant face completely devoid of makeup.

"...anyway, we're all very proud of the project. The Riverview Foundation picked out the wallpaper, our designer made everything look as much like home as possible while still keeping everything required for a safe, conventional delivery at the doctor's fingertips. Wait until you see it. It's like a bedroom out of *Town and Country*."

"Oh?" Nancy brought herself back to the conversation, confused that she still couldn't figure out how all this related to her—or even to the hospital. A beautiful bedroom in *Town and Country* magazine? She wished she'd been paying closer attention.

Amy went on, frowning over Nancy's tepid response. "Birthing rooms!" she said with a sweep of her hand. "Here in little old Heron Point. Now you don't have to go to Portland for the amenities of a home-style delivery. We'll have it right here. No more hard labor in a dingy little room. No more having to separate the mother-to-be from her husband or any other family member who wants to be part of the birth."

Nancy smiled, delighted and relieved to finally grasp the issue. Birthing rooms. Of course. She'd read about them in women's magazines, and several of her New York acquaintances had talked about having used them.

She nodded enthusiastically, compelled by Amy's passion. "That's wonderful. I've read about them. They seem like an intelligent and sensitive innovation."

That remark seemed to please Amy. She beamed. "I'm so glad you think so. Because...guess what!"

"What?" Nancy asked warily.

"Ours are under construction even as we speak, and they'll be ready...guess when!"

There was a trap here somewhere and Nancy thought she could see it yawning, waiting to spring. "When?"

Amy spread both hands, palms up, in a sort of ta-da gesture. "Two days before your due date!"

"Oh." Nancy proceeded cautiously. "So...I'll get to use one?"

Amy placed both hands on the arms of the wheelchair, her smile widening even farther. "Not only that, but I've picked *you* out!"

Uh-oh. "Me? For...what?"

"To be the very *first* to use one! We're planning a big *extravaganza*—" she made a wide, exploding movement with her hands to underline the word "—for the opening of the rooms, and our auxiliary has gotten the entire community involved! There'll be newspaper and radio coverage, saturation advertising, merchant parti—"

"Wait. Wait." Nancy spoke gently, almost reluctant to stop the woman's excited spate of information, but this was beginning to sound like the kind of thing she hated. She was basically shy and always resisted anything that attracted attention to herself. And since Jerry's defection, she found herself even more reclusive. All she wanted to do was hide out in her little beachfront cottage, help this baby grow big and strong, and raise her quietly amid the serenity of one of the most beautiful spots on earth. She did not want to be part of Amy's extravaganza. "Thank you," she said politely, "but I'm really kind of a...a private person. I—"

"But the timing's perfect." Amy looked stricken. "You'll have your picture in the paper. You'll be famous."

"Thank you but I..." Nancy searched her mind for something to say besides the truth. Then she was suddenly inspired. "Don't you think it would be safer to wait for a mother whose due date is more reliable than mine? I mean, I have this cranky cervix that could—"

"That doesn't matter. One of the smaller rooms is within a couple of weeks of being ready. We'd like you to use the biggest room, but if you did deliver early, we could still put you in the smaller one." She leaned an elbow on the desk and heaved a sigh. "To be honest, I knew you'd be perfect the moment I saw you. You're attractive, probably photogenic, it's your first baby, and…" She patted Nancy's hand and said softly, "And I'll bet you'll be able to put the gifts to good use."

Nancy was sure the woman meant well, but she wasn't anxious to be patronized or pitied. She tried to smile but look firm at the same time. "Thank you, but I don't need gifts. I—"

"Most of the gifts are for the baby," Amy interrupted.

Nancy stopped in the act of searching for the wheelchair's brake. She let a heartbeat pass while she reconsidered. "Gifts for the baby?"

"Yes." Amy picked up a typed sheet from the cluttered desk and read from it. "Silver cup and spoon from Anderson's Jewelry Company, chocolate cigars to announce the birth from Columbia Chocolates, a two-hundred-dollar gift certificate from Falmouth Toys, new shoes for you and the baby from Isaac's Bootery, linens for the baby's room from Lillith's Boutique, free passes to the movies for you and your husband from the Liberty Theatre." Amy made a show of gasping for breath. "An outfit from Lolly's, a dress from Dine and Dance, lingerie from Magic Moon, an outfit a month for the baby's first year from Catering to Kids, and…" She glanced up from the sheet to assure herself of Nancy's attention. She needn't have bothered. Nancy was now hanging on her every word. "Are you ready for this?"

Nancy couldn't speak. Clothes for the baby's first year? Shoes for the baby? Toys? It would be like winning the lottery. She nodded and whispered, "I'm ready."

Amy cleared her throat, then announced, like Bob Barker at his best, "A complete set of top-of-the-line furniture for your baby's room, complete with crib, chest, dressing table, three-way teddy-bear lamp and night-light, windup musical mobile and bumper pads for the crib and dressing table." She dropped the sheet of paper to her lap and finished with a flourish, "And a glider rocker with ottoman for you to rock the baby to sleep. All from Hobbs Furniture."

Mom! Chocolate cigars! A teddy-bear lamp. Say yes! Please, say yes!

Nancy stared at her, eyes glazed with avarice. Her baby would have everything she'd despaired of being able to provide. Everything! More than she'd imagined in her wildest dreams. All she had to do was agree to be part of Amy's extravaganza. Deep down, she shuddered at the thought. But closer to the surface, right under her heart where her baby lived, she knew that she had to do it.

"All right," she said, smiling brightly and trying to inject sincere excitement into her voice. "I'll do it."

Amy looked stunned by her own success. "You will?"

"I will."

"All *right!*" Amy whooped excitedly, then poured tea from a hot pot into two institutional white cups on the desk. "Let's toast the deal. You're going to love this, Nancy. I know you are. I appreciate your shyness, but having a baby tends to kill that in the average woman anyway." She rolled her eyes expressively, then added seriously, "But I promise to keep anything you consider too personal out of it, and just make you, the mother-to-be, the symbol for all mothers in the county who now have a comfortable, cheerful place to have their babies with their families close at hand."

She handed Nancy a half-filled cup of the aromatic tea, then tapped her cup against it. "To babies!"

"To babies!" Nancy toasted, refusing to acknowledge the little niggles of doubt and conscience that prodded at her.

Amy's extravaganza was a gift to her and her baby from the heavens. She wouldn't question it, wouldn't doubt it. When Jerry had walked away, she had vowed she wouldn't infect her baby with bitterness. She would be serene and hopeful and a firm believer in the glass-half-full, silver-lining theories.

"Okay." Amy put her cup down and lifted another sheet of paper off the desk. From Nancy's vantage point, it appeared to be a form of some kind. "I just need a few more details from you that weren't in your file."

Nancy, too, put her cup down, prepared to provide them. "Right. What do you want to know?"

Amy poised her pen expectantly and glanced at her. "Husband's name?"

CHAPTER TWO

NANCY blinked. Husband? So the extravaganza *was* too good to be true. She didn't have a husband, and she understood with sudden clarity that the hospital wouldn't want her to represent "all mothers in the county" without one.

"I really wasn't snooping in your files," Amy explained quickly. "But I happened to be in Dr. McNamara's office talking to him about this project when he put the ultrasound order on your chart."

Nancy nodded, buying time by letting Amy talk.

"Dr. Mac had sent to New York for your files when you had your first appointment with him. They were sitting on his desk. I glanced at it to get your name so we could talk, and I noticed your husband's name, but I can't remember it." She leaned over the form, ready to fill in the name, and confided intimately, "It wouldn't matter to us if you were single, but I think the foundation and many of the old-guard contributing merchants will be pleased that you aren't. And it's appropriate for what we're trying to do. Birthing rooms are for everyone, but particularly for loving couples who want to share the experience of giving birth to the child they've created together, the child they intend to nurture together."

"Jerry," Nancy heard herself say with detached fascination. "Gerald W."

GOOD WORK, MOM. Stay calm. We can do this.

NANCY WAITED FOR the next question in a kind of panic, her cheeks warming, her hands fidgeting nervously.

"His occupation?"

This was going to be tricky, Nancy foresaw. Next, she'd be expected to produce him. Then inspiration unexpectedly struck again, and she wondered if the drug that stopped her labor had somehow managed to multiply her gray matter.

"He's in the Coast Guard," she said with convincing ease. "Aboard the *Courageous*."

Amy looked up, apparently thrilled by the news. "Heron Point's own *Courageous*? Oh, this is getting better and better."

Nancy blessed the fact that the ad for Sam's Super Seconds in last night's paper had been placed directly beside the story about the *Courageous* leaving on a three-month patrol. She'd perused the article, thinking about the wives of the men aboard the vessel being separated from their husbands that long—never imagining that she'd be fictionalizing herself among their number.

"It just left, didn't it?" Amy asked as she hurriedly made notes.

Nancy nodded, then imparted further information in a convincingly knowledgeable tone. "They're heading south on a standard law-enforcement patrol. You know, watching for drugs, enforcing fishing regulations. That sort of stuff."

Amy's eyes widened. Nancy guessed she was hoping the father of her birthing room's first occupant would somehow distinguish himself and return home a hero. She let herself smile. Amy didn't know Jerry.

"He'll be home in time to be with you for the birth, won't he?"

It would be safer to say that she doubted that and eliminate the need to produce him. But she felt a very real fear that Amy would withdraw the offer if it didn't look as though she'd have every member of the family available for her extravaganza.

"He's due in the week before," she said with a broad

smile. She was *not* giving up the baby furniture—or the chocolate.

"What's his rank?" a male voice asked from the doorway.

Amy looked up with a smile. Nancy, her back to the door, didn't like the tone of the question. It sounded suspicious. She looked over her shoulder to see that the radiologist with the messianic complex had been eavesdropping.

What was worse, she didn't know a private from an admiral. She smiled at Amy hoping to distract her with other details. "He's been in since right after college. About ten years."

"Really?" The PR coordinator made hasty notes. "And what does he do aboard the *Courageous?*"

"Well..." Making him the captain would have been overplaying, but that was the only title Nancy could come up with. She prayed that her newfound extra gray matter wouldn't fail her now. "He...ah...oh, you know. He keeps everything running. Motors...all that stuff."

"And what is that called?" Amy insisted.

Nancy was about to either pretend renewed contractions or tell all and abandon this hospital and this scheme while she was able, when the male voice behind her spoke up. "He must be the engineering officer."

Nancy gave him a drop-dead smile over her shoulder. "That's it. He's the engineering officer."

WHEW! HE SAVED OUR SKINS, Mom. Not that mine's much to look at right now. Let's take him home.

JAVE DIDN'T KNOW WHETHER to trust Malone, Nancy R.'s, word, or his own usually reliable instincts. He'd have sworn she was single. But he'd been about to step into his office when he heard her reply to Amy's request for her husband's name. He had two young boys. He knew lies when he heard them.

But he also knew the innocent could sometimes *look* guilty.

Yet, a woman should know her husband's rank. And she should be ready to boast about his duties with his formal title. But then the world—and male-female relationships in particular—weren't always what he thought they should be.

So the pretty dark-eyed woman, who pretended courage but appeared lost and frightened, was married. Or wanted them to believe she was.

He decided to reserve judgment. That array of gifts, along with Amy Brown's intimidating enthusiasm for her first solo PR project, were enough to encourage a single woman to produce a husband.

"Time's up," Jave said, reaching over the back of the wheelchair to disengage the brake. His cheek brushed her cool, silky hair for a moment, and he inhaled the fragrance of a floral shampoo.

Nancy looked up with a frown at his abrupt interruption...and found her eyes looking directly into his. She felt two things simultaneously—sexual awareness and the suspicion that he could see right through her. Both alarmed her.

"Sorry," he said to Amy, pulling the chair backward toward the door. "McNamara wants her to rest tonight. If all's well and she goes home tomorrow, the two of you can talk before she leaves."

"Of course." Amy stood to follow them to the door. "You just sleep well, Nancy, and dream about all the wonderful things you and your husband and baby are going to get."

"I will," Nancy promised, then added for effect, "I can't wait to tell Jerry when he calls."

She glanced up at J. V. Nicholas, giving him an innocent look, daring him to question her. His expression was neither accepting nor challenging, but simply steady and deliberately neutral. She felt her wide-eyed sincerity wilt just a little.

With a wave, Amy turned left down a side corridor. Jave

pushed Nancy past a plate-glass window against which rain slashed at a deep angle.

"Rain!" Nancy exclaimed, suddenly faced with a new dilemma. She pushed upward in her chair with every intention of getting out of it.

"No, you don't." A firm hand pushed down on her shoulder. "What are you doing?"

She pointed to the window. "Rain!"

"Yes," Jave said, continuing to push the chair down the hall. "I recognized it right away."

"Ohh," she groaned. "How long has it been raining? My chair will be ruined."

"What chair?" He stopped the wheelchair and came around in front of it to push open the double doors that separated the obstetrics wing from the rest of the hospital.

Nancy leaned back in the chair, looking grim. "The desk chair I bought for my home office. It's sitting in the open bed of my truck. It's secondhand, but it was high backed and upholstered. It'll be drenched!"

"You're supposed to keep a tarp in the back of your truck," Jave said, turning into room 221. "It's an Oregon rule. Otherwise, everything you try to transport will get soaked or moldy, or blow away."

Nancy sighed as he stopped the wheelchair beside her narrow hospital bed and leaned over her again to set the brake. He didn't touch her, but she absorbed his nearness. There was something...solid in it. She pushed herself up, reaching for the back of her gown, annoyed with herself for being so aware of him.

"Well, I haven't been here long enough to know the *rules*." She climbed into the bed and frowned at him as he pulled the covers up for her. "What kind of a state is this anyway? It's like living in Atlantis. The sun hasn't shone since I've been here."

"Oregon's rainfall is notorious all over the country," he pointed out. "Why'd you come if you don't like rain?"

She sighed again and gazed grimly out the window. "It was a long way from New York."

"That's interesting," he said. "I'd have thought you came because your husband was transferred here."

HE'S ON TO US, MOM. But don't panic. I'm already doing that. Just think of something!

NANCY SWORE SILENTLY, but had her expression composed by the time she turned away from the window to look into J. V. Nicholas's eyes. "We were. But Jerry had a choice of several places. We decided on Heron Point because it's a long way from New York."

"What didn't you like there?"

"The snow," she replied with an icy tone that defined the word and discouraged more questions.

But he'd never been easily discouraged. He smiled. "Are you a hothouse flower, Mrs. Malone?"

"No." She pulled the blankets up to her chin. "But I could do with a little less rain—and a lot less interrogation."

He acknowledged her complaint with a grin and turned the chair around. "Describe your truck."

She was puzzled by the non sequitur. "What? Why?"

"Maybe there's something I can do about your chair."

She was quiet for a moment, completely surprised by his reply. "It's an early seventies blue pickup with a dented right front fender," she said finally, then added in a dry tone, "You can't miss it among the Mercedeses and the Blazers in the parking lot."

"All right." He pushed the chair toward the door, then turned to offer her a quick smile. "Rest well," he said before pulling the door open.

Nancy fell back among the pillows with a mighty yawn. This day had not gone at all the way she'd planned. She'd expected to have her office chair in place by now, to have her curtains up in the kitchen and dinner in the oven.

Instead, her office chair was probably underwater, her curtains were still folded over the sewing machine, waiting to be hemmed, and there was nothing for dinner but a container of strawberries and a plastic tub of nondairy topping in the refrigerator.

And she'd made an enemy—or a friend. It was difficult to gauge at this point the status of her relationship with Dr. J. V. Nicholas. She had a feeling he didn't approve of her, didn't believe her story about Jerry, and yet he said he'd do something about her desk chair. He probably had the requisite tarp in *his* truck and would toss it over her chair.

She watched the rain drive against the windows and wondered if anything would help her chair stand up against this monsoon.

She settled into her pillows, thinking he'd simply reinforced her theory that men were the complex gender, while women were the ones falsely accused of being so—by men.

The door opened and a candy striper walked in with a tray of food. It smelled wonderful.

"Hi!" the girl said cheerfully. She was all of sixteen, with curly masses of bright red hair and gleaming braces. "Chicken pot pie, salad and ice cream. I brought this by twice, but you weren't here. I was hoping they'd sent you home and I'd get to eat this."

The girl, whose badge said April, balanced the tray on one hand, expertly positioned the bed table, then placed the tray on it. Everything looked as good as it smelled.

"I was having an ultrasound," Nancy said, realizing for the first time in hours that she was hungry. "I'll tell you what, April. You can have the salad."

April laughed. "Gee, thanks, but can we do a deal on the ice cream?"

NO! KEEP THE ICE CREAM. It's the salad, or nothing.

NANCY SHOOK HER HEAD. "Not a chance. Vanilla's my favorite."

April pretended disappointment. Then she smiled with genuine warmth. "I'm glad your baby's okay. I was taking coffee to the ER staff when you came in."

Nancy forgot the food for a moment and enjoyed sharing her good fortune with someone. She felt truly lucky that all was well. "Thank you. It was pretty exciting to see a strong heartbeat on the ultrasound."

The quality of April's smile changed, became unmistakably female. "Did Jave do it?"

Nancy nodded, recalling how Amy Brown had also used that name—Jave for J.V.

April rolled her eyes and sighed. "Isn't he just too cool?"

Nancy presumed that was a compliment and wasn't sure she felt inclined to give him one. Of course, all the remark required, really, was a clinical assessment. And that was easy.

"He's gorgeous, yes," she admitted, turning her attention to the pot pie. She savored the crisp crust and succulent chicken and vegetables in expertly seasoned sauce. It was five-star quality.

"Oh, it's more than that," April corrected earnestly. "Don't you think? I mean, some guys are hunks, but they're like so—" she considered the word, her turned down mouth saying what she couldn't seem to describe "—and I mean, like you'd die before you ever let them touch you. But Jave..." Her bright green eyes glazed over. She joined her hands together and drew a gusty breath. "I keep hoping I'll get a gallstone or something and he'll have to do an ultrasound on me."

Nancy was appalled. "I understand gallstones are very painful."

"It'd be worth it."

Nancy shook her head at the girl's unfocused gaze. "He's probably not the marrying kind."

April came out of her dreamy spell. "He was once. He has two little boys."

That surprised Nancy into stopping a forkful of chicken pie halfway to her mouth. "He does?"

"Yeah. And a dog."

In the girl's eyes, that apparently made him a family man. "Well, you have to beware of men other women have divorced. There's usually a good reason."

April nodded. "There was. She ran off with Dr. Templar, the orthopedist. A year ago. I wasn't here then, but my mom volunteers afternoons. Everyone was talking about it. Specially 'cause she left the boys."

Nancy put her fork down, feeling sympathy—even empathy—for Jave Nicholas *and* his children. Her husband had also walked away. And when she'd been a child, her mother, too, had left her and her father and struck out on her own.

Nancy rubbed the gently moving mound of her stomach and wondered at the wisdom of bringing a new life into a world filled with such undependable people. Her only comfort was that she had enough love for this baby to make up for any shortfall in their tiny family of two.

April glanced at her watch, then excused herself. "Gotta go. I'm supposed to help with stories in pediatrics. But tomorrow's Saturday. I'll be here bright and early with your breakfast."

WHEN HER TRAY had been taken away and a watery dusk began to settle in beyond the louvered blinds at her windows, Nancy closed her eyes and concentrated on relaxing. It wasn't difficult with her stomach full and with the knowledge that her baby was healthy and strong.

But what must the evening be like for Jave Nicholas? she wondered. Was he lonely and bitter, or grateful to be single again? And how were his children dealing with their mother's abandonment? She had always pretended that she'd adjusted, and she guessed in some ways she had, but there'd always been an emptiness, a curious feeling of inadequacy. And there'd always been that question in the back of her mind. If she'd been different, would her mother have stayed?

Well, she could empathize all she wanted, but ultimately it wouldn't matter. If she remembered to curtail her activities and follow Dr. McNamara's directives to the letter, she need never see Jave Nicholas again. She curled into her pillow, the baby moving lazily inside her, and drifted off to sleep.

"WHY DO WE WANT to save this chair?" Pete asked, holding the roaring blow dryer to the blue-and-gray-tweed contoured seat. He was seven, and it was very important to him that the colors of things matched or coordinated. It was an inheritance from his mother. "It's old. It's even kind of ugly."

Eddy, three years older, took after his father. He chose things for comfort, not for style. "It isn't ours," he explained with an impatient lack of grace as he dried off the legs with a rag. "It belongs to some pregnant lady at the hospital. It was outside in the rain all day."

Jave and his boys were sitting on a carpet remnant in the middle of their garage, doing their best to salvage the chair after its amphibious experience. Jave had unscrewed the back of the chair and now propped it up a safe distance from a space heater. He would turn the heater off before going to bed, but hoped the few hours of heat would begin to dry the thick wadding inside.

Pete transferred the blow dryer from hand to hand as he pushed up the sleeves of his *Lion King* sweatshirt. "How come *we* have to do this? She's not *our* mom."

Jave's head came up at that, and he focused on the disgruntled expression on his younger one's face. He felt the stab of worry that had plagued him since Bonnie had walked away. Pete had cried for two days, then had emerged from his room on the third day and simply pretended that it didn't matter.

Yet under it all was something that worried Jave more than the tears—a curiously insidious dislike for other people's happiness, a selfish unwillingness to give or share or otherwise participate in anyone else's life. Jave thought he understood the reaction; it wasn't that different from his own feelings for the first month or so. However, having to cope with important work, two little children and a mother and a brother who simply refused to let him be lonely, he'd snapped out of it and found a way to cope.

But he didn't know how to make that happen for a seven-year-old. He'd explained clearly and honestly to both boys that their mother was gone, but that didn't mean she didn't love them. It just meant she couldn't find a way to be with them at this point in time. And he'd done his best to make them believe that he'd stretch himself as far as possible in any direction to see that they had everything she would have provided.

That was impossible, of course, but they didn't know that. And he'd done his best.

Eddy had understood, and though he, too, had been devastated when his mother left, he was coming out of it and functioning well. He had all the aggressions and sweetness of a normal ten-year-old.

But Pete was another story—he showed all the signs of becoming a problem.

Jave opened his mouth to offer a reply, but Eddy beat him to it. "Because she doesn't have any kids, stupid. Didn't you hear me say she was pregnant? That means she hasn't had kids yet." Eddy stopped rubbing the chair legs and sat back on his heels to fix Jave with a look of complete disgust. "I thought when he turned seven, he'd start getting smarter. But he's just getting worse."

"*You're* stupid!" Pete turned the blow dryer toward Eddy's face, sending his longish, already dusty and play-tossed blond hair flying every which way. "A lady can have kids and still be pregnant for another baby. Darren Bolger's mother is."

With a cry of rage, Eddy leaped at his brother, intent on doing him bodily harm.

"All right, that's enough," Jave said quietly. He always tried that calm, authoritative tone first. It had yet to work. "Enough!" he shouted, injecting an undefined threat into the single word.

The boys sprang apart, glared at each other with utter loathing, then went back to their tasks.

"This particular pregnant lady," Jave said, getting to his feet to check his shelf of paint and stain cans, "just moved here from New York. And she doesn't have any other kids but the one she's carrying."

Pete shouted over the blow dryer, "She has to have a husband, doesn't she? A lady can't have a baby unless she has sex. And she has to have a husband for that."

"No, she doesn't." Eddy's tone changed from scornful to instructive. He turned the rag over and lay on his back under the chair, rubbing at the wood that braced the seat. "She can have sex with any guy and get pregnant. It doesn't have to be her husband. Right, Dad?"

"Right." Jave pulled a can of gold oak stain off the shelf and went to join the boys on the floor. "But most women don't do that because having a baby's too important. It all works better if she does it with someone she loves. Like a husband."

"Well, doesn't this lady have one?" Pete asked.

Jave nodded, running his fingertips over the wood Eddy had wiped off. "She does," he said. There was no point in sharing his doubts with the boys. "But he's in the Coast Guard and his boat's gone for a couple of months. She needs help, and because she's new here, she doesn't know anybody yet."

Pete made a face. "This is a dorky chair."

"It's an old-fashioned desk chair," Jave corrected. "She's making an office in her house because she wants to write books."

Pete's interest was piqued. He had an extensive, eclectic library of children's books, and he loved every one. "You mean like *Cat in the Hat* or *Goodnight Moon?*"

"Sort of. Only she wants to write books for adults. Mystery books."

Now Eddy looked interested. "Like the Hardy Boys grown up, or something?"

Jave smiled at him and decided to give the chair a few more hours to dry before sanding and restaining the battered legs. "Close. You guys know what Grandma's fixing for dinner?"

"Something with noodles," Eddy replied. "And you'd better be careful, 'cause her arthritis is kicking up again and she's grumpy."

"I am *not* grumpy." A formidable presence in a gray sweat suit appeared in the doorway from the kitchen. A wonderful aroma wafted past her into the garage. With it came a very large, long-haired black-and-brown dog of indeterminate heritage. It ran straight for Eddy, barking excitedly, and wagging its tail. "But when two boys and a dog run through the house, collide with me, and dump an entire bowl of chocolate cake batter onto the floor, it tends to diminish my sense of humor."

Jave looked from one boy to the other. Both were suddenly very interested in the dog.

"Pete had my ball glove," Eddy explained simply. "I wanted it back. Mo was helping me get it."

Pete made a scornful sound that suggested his brother overdramatized. "I just borrowed it."

Jave focused on Eddy, then on Pete. "There is no running in the house, and no borrowing what doesn't belong to you. Now, go get washed up for dinner."

Their grandmother stepped aside as the boys hurried past her, shoving each other, the dog behind them. She fixed her son with a grin as she came toward him. "You know, I could stay home and watch my soaps, visit the senior center and paint greenware with Hazel and Betsy, or I could find political causes to picket for in front of the post office. But, no. I come here every afternoon at two-thirty—not to mention all day, every day, during the summer—so I can be here when your boys come home from school and put your dinner on, and what does it get me?"

"Your lawn mowed every Saturday and your groceries picked up on Wednesday evenings." Jave got to his feet and kissed his mother's cheek as he passed her to check on the chair back drying in front of the space heater.

"Besides that."

"I offered to pay you, but you refused."

Agnes shook her head, impatient with his faulty replies. "Aggie Nicholas gets knocked on her keister, that's what. At sixty-seven years old, that's not a pleasant experience."

Jake hooked an arm around her shoulders and led her toward the door. "What I want to know is, did the dessert survive?"

Aggie elbowed him in the gut. "I managed to put together an alternative. So, what's with the chair?"

"I explained when I carried it in, Mom," he said, flipping the garage light off as they stepped up into the kitchen.

"You said an emergency patient had bought it this morning and left it in her truck out in the rain all day. But you didn't say how it became your responsibility."

He went to the kitchen sink to wash his hands. He could hear the boys laughing and splashing in the utility room down the hall. "Her husband is at sea. She's young and alone and six months pregnant," he said, making every effort to sound casual. His mother read him like an X ray. "She was worried about the chair. I was just trying to be a Good Samaritan." He glanced at her over his shoulder as he rinsed his hands. "You're the one who taught me that we have to care about each other."

"Single men," she said, lifting the lid on a pot and giving the contents a stir, "should let someone else care about married women."

He dried his hands on a dish towel and crossed the room to look over his mother's shoulder and into the pot. "Come on. Someone has to provide healthy scandal to this staid and proper community."

Aggie snickered. "This family's already done that once."

Jave laughed mirthlessly and crossed back to the sink to hang up the towel. "True enough, but that time was no fun for me. I was the victim."

"You get involved with a married woman," she warned, "and you'll be the victim again."

"Mom." Jave opened the refrigerator and pulled out a beer and a carton of milk. He frowned at her as he bumped the door closed with his elbow. "I'm not involved. I saw her all of half an hour. She was worried about the chair, her husband's on the *Courageous* on his way south, and she's only been here a couple of weeks. She doesn't know anybody. So I thought I'd help."

Aggie carried the pot of chicken noodles to the table. "That's probably what Lancelot told *his* mother when he got involved with Guinevere. 'Mama, she's new here from Cameliard, her husband's always at the office, and I'm just gonna show her around because she doesn't know anybody at the castle.'" She straightened and placed both hands on her hips. "And look at the tragedy that resulted."

Jave put a hand over his eyes and summoned patience. It was futile to fight her logic, so he fought her facts. "Guinevere was at Came*lot* some time before Lancelot arrived."

She swatted his arm with a pot holder. "That's not the point!"

Jave opened his mouth to counter his mother's portent of doom when the back door opened and his brother walked in, a grocery bag in his arm. He looked from Jave to his mother and grinned.

"She's got you on the ropes again, huh?" he assessed. "What is it this time? Your diet? Your poker night? Your celibacy?"

Aggie went to take the grocery bag from her younger son. "He's in love with a married woman," she said.

Tom raised an eyebrow at Jave. "You are? Does she have a sister who could fall in love with a master carpenter with no money but great prowess in the bedroom?"

Jave placed the beer and the milk on the table, then went back to the refrigerator, asking over his shoulder, "Prowess at *wallpapering* the bedroom, you mean?"

"Ha-ha," Tom replied without the smile to accompany the words. He pulled out a chair at the table and sat down. "Now, what's this about a married woman?"

Jave returned with a second beer and handed it to him. He briefly related the story of the young woman and the chair. "That's it. I am not in love with her. I hardly know her. I was trying to be a good guy."

"Well, stop it," Tom said. "You'll hurt yourself."

"Ha-ha," Jave mimicked him in return. "I thought you were finishing that roof tonight and wouldn't make it for dinner."

"So did I. But I found dry rot when I put a leg through it. I have to back up and rebuild before I can go on. Hey, guys. How's it going?"

Eddy and Pete ran into the room and converged on their uncle, delighted to see him, and Tom quickly shifted his attention to his nephews.

"Don't try to tell me you don't feel something for this woman," Aggie said under her breath as Jave reached into the cupboard over her head for the bowl beyond her grasp.

Jave slapped the bowl into her hand. "Mom," he said, also under his breath, "if you mention Nancy Malone or the chair one more time, I'll hire a *real* nanny for the boys."

She dismissed the threat with a wave of her hand. "Right. Like anyone other than the CIA could deal with them." She put the bowl aside and grasped his elbows—that was as high up as she could reach. Her dark eyes were earnest and concerned. "I can see it in your face," she said. "You care. Oh, I know you're not in love—at least not yet—but I know you. You did this before. You loved a woman who wasn't good enough for you, and you thought your love could cover everything. It can't. You have to get love back or it doesn't work. I know you're lonely, but I don't want you to get hurt again, Jave."

Jave held her shoulders and leaned over her until they were eye-to-eye. "Now, listen carefully," he said in a voice just louder than a whisper. At the table, the boys were busy putting a head on their uncle's beer. "I am not lonely. I do not want another wife. I have no interest in this woman other than to fix her chair. And the last thing on earth I will do is allow myself to be hurt again. I learned a lot from the divorce. Trust me. Now can we have dinner?"

Aggie sighed. "Certainly. If you want to take my concerns so lightly. Who warned you that Clinton had no skill in foreign policy, that Wynonna Judd *could* make it on her own, and that the queen should have been tougher on her children? Who, huh? Who?"

CHAPTER THREE

"Hi, Mickey." Jave stirred the oak stain with a thin stick while cradling the cordless phone on his shoulder.

"Hi, Dr. Nicholas," the bright voice of the switchboard operator on night shift replied. "Nothing for you. Bingham's on call tonight."

"I know. I'm checking on an O.B. patient in 221. Can you connect me to—"

"Hold on."

Jave dropped the stick into the can. "*Not* the room, Mickey, the nurses'—"

"Hello?"

Jave closed his eyes as he heard Nancy Malone's voice. He had intended simply to ask the night nurse for a progress report. He put on a brisk, professional voice. "Mrs. Malone. It's Dr. Nicholas."

There was a moment's surprised silence. "Hello, Dr. Nicholas," she said finally. Then her voice took on a panicky edge. "Did you find something wrong after all? Is the baby...?"

"No," he assured her quickly, firmly, regretting the impulse to call. He should have left well enough alone. "Everything's fine. I just...wanted to make sure you were comfortable."

"I'm fine," she replied, sounding vaguely confused. There was another small silence, then she added, "I'm watching 'Mystery' on public television."

He heard sinister music in the background and smiled to himself. "Research for an Edgar-winning book?"

"Simple entertainment," she said on a yawn. "Sorry. It's been a long day."

"Well, sleep's what you need right now, so I'll leave you to it." He found himself suddenly anxious to get off the line. Her voice was soft and drowsy and did curious things to his ability to concentrate. "Good night, Mrs. Malone. I'll see you tomorrow."

"You will?" Nancy asked. But the line was already dead. She looked at the receiver in her hand and wondered why the radiologist had called to check on her progress, and not her obstetrician.

She smiled wryly to herself. Probably because the radiologist didn't trust her. It was too bad, she thought as she yawned again. Hearing his voice made her feel less lonely.

She chided herself for the thought. It was nighttime, she was vulnerable, and the whole thing was too complicated for her sleepy state. She cradled the receiver, turned off the television, and closed her eyes.

It occurred to her as she dozed off that she should have asked him if he'd found her chair.

JAVE PUT THE PHONE ASIDE and recognized Tom's paint-and-putty-spattered shoes directly in front of him.

He frowned up at him, then dipped his brush in the can of stain. "What are you doing back? You took Mom home three hours ago."

"She's crocheting and watching Letterman." Tom came to crouch beside him. "I thought you might have something to tell me that you don't want to tell her."

Jave groaned and concentrated on staining the chair leg. "Don't start with me, Bro. Mom manufactured the whole thing. You know her policy—if there's no news, make some."

Tom nodded and sat on the floor beside the chair, one knee drawn up, his elbow resting on it. "But you deal with dozens of women, young and old, every week of your life.

And you've never repaired a chair for one of them before. Who was that on the phone?"

"A patient," he replied without looking at him. The nearest leg finished, Jave lay on his stomach and propelled himself on his elbows to the one on the far side. "I felt sorry for her, and that's the sum total of my feelings in the matter."

"So, she goes home tomorrow?" Tom absently rubbed at his knee.

"Right."

"And you're going to put the chair in the back of her truck and that's it?"

There was a moment's silence. Jave had been thinking about this for the past few hours. And the sound of her voice had decided him. "Not exactly."

Tom leaned back on an elbow. "What, then?"

Jave answered with another question. "What are *you* doing in the morning?"

Tom appeared to consider what the question could mean, then asked hopefully, "She *does* have a sister?"

Jave gave him an impatient glance then leaned around the back of the chair to reach the inside of the leg. "I thought I'd drive her home. She doesn't have anyone to pick her up, and if she goes home on her own, she'll never get the chair out of the truck by herself. The wet upholstery weighs a ton, and it'll probably take days to dry. I'll drive her, and you can follow in my truck. We'll unload the chair for her and place it where she wants it. Then she's out of my life."

The chair leg finished, Jave straightened from under it, capped the can of stain and gave the lid one solid whack with the side of his fist. He looked up to find Tom watching him.

"What?" he demanded.

Tom sat up. "I just wondered if it's really going to be that easy."

"Yes," Jave said, wiping his hands on a rag. "It will."

"Then I'll be available to help you. What time?"

"Nine. I think she'll be released right after breakfast."

"All right." Tom stood and pulled something out of his hip pocket. He handed it to Jave as he, too, stood and tossed the rag into a metal can in the corner of the room. "*Oregonian*'s classifieds. I've circled the boat that could change our luck. No more buying burgers on the way home from fishing."

"Really." Smiling, Jave unfolded the page Tom had torn out of the newspaper's classifieds. "I've kind of gotten used to the supermarket folks laughing at us."

Tom started for the door and Jave looked up in time to note his limp. He put the paper aside and caught his arm.

"What's the matter?" he asked. "Leg acting up again?"

Tom flexed his knee and winced. "It's been pretty good, but that episode on Wilkins's roof this afternoon set me back a little. It'll be all right."

Jave noted the carefully concealed pain in his brother's eyes, but was careful not to comment on it. "Maybe you should consider a Jacuzzi instead of half a boat."

Tom made a face. "A Jacuzzi is for old guys."

Jave laughed. "Yeah. And pro athletes, and playboys."

"You just want to buy the boat by yourself so you don't have to share it with me."

Jave walked with him through the house to the back door he always used. "I wouldn't know what to do with something I didn't have to share with you," he grumbled good-naturedly. "It's been the story of my life since I was five and you were eighteen months old and took my favorite fire truck."

Jave hadn't thought out the remark before he'd said it. He'd thought he'd simply been reminiscing, then the word "fire truck" came out before he could stop it.

There was a moment's silence, a deepening of the pain in Tom's eyes. Then Tom smiled and pulled the back door open. "If you'd given it to me," Tom said reasonably, "I wouldn't have screamed and Mom wouldn't have punished you. Live and learn."

Jave gave him a fraternal shove into the driveway. "I'll read the ad and tell you what I think. I'll meet you in the hospital parking lot at nine."

"Why not in your office?"

"Because it's my weekend off, and if I show up, someone will find something for me to do. See you tomorrow."

"Right."

Jave waved his brother off, then turned back into the house, wanting to kick himself for the fire-truck remark. It wasn't that Tom required they walk on eggshells around him, but the road back from the fire that had killed Tom's best friend and put him in the hospital for three months had been long and slow.

In the intervening year, he'd started his own business and learned to cope with constant pain. He'd made major strides forward. Tom had been a rock for him when Bonnie left. He hated to be the one to set him back, even in a small way.

Jave locked the back door then walked back into the garage for a last look around before going to bed. Satisfied that all combustibles were put away, he flipped the light off and locked the garage door. He went through the house, turning lights off as he went, creating shadows in his wake as he climbed the stairs.

This vague disquiet in his gut had nothing to do with Nancy Malone. It had to do with...loneliness. It had to do with a longing for some nameless something that was always just beyond his reach.

He'd seen that same longing in her eyes—that's what was forming this strange connection he felt toward her.

Well, he didn't need it, he told himself firmly as he pushed soundlessly at Eddy's half-open door. What would be the point of developing a relationship with a woman who also lacked what he lacked? The man/woman covenant was about *providing* what each other needed, wasn't it?

He suddenly found his foot entangled in a pile of clothes. He shook his head over Eddy's slovenly habits and reached down to scoop up what felt like jeans and tossed them at the laundry basket near the door.

He approached the bed and found his elder son lying on his back, arms spread wide, Mo lying beside him, his big head resting on the boy's chest. The dog's thick tail slapped against the bedclothes as Jave rubbed between his ears.

Jave gently folded the boy's arms in and pulled the blankets up. Mo lifted his head to allow the adjustment, then settled back down again, tail still thumping. Jave leaned down to kiss the boy's cheek, patted the dog, then left the room, leaving the door partially open.

Pete's door was closed. The floor of his room was clear of debris, and his war-worn sneakers were lined up neatly in front of the nightstand. The boy was curled up in the middle of the twin bed, the covers pulled over his head and tightly gathered in.

Jave frowned at the picture he made. It was so indicative of what was happening inside him, as well. He was hiding, closing himself off, making neatness an obsession at seven years old. Jave fought an impulse to rip the blankets off him and throw on the light. To make Pete share all the tumultuous feelings he shouldn't have to deal with alone.

But the situation was delicate; he knew that. He just didn't know what to do about it. His pediatrician had seen him and told Jave to try to relax about it—to keep the lines of communications open, to simply be there. This was just a normal reaction to his mother's departure, and when he was over being angry, he would find a way to cope.

Jave patted the roundest part of the bump under the blankets and left the room, pulling the door closed. Then he walked into his own bedroom and left the door slightly ajar.

Jave deliberately turned away from the skillful contrast and coordination of green and berry fabric patterns that composed the curtains, bedspread, pillow shams and dust ruffle, and went into the bathroom.

He peeled off his old jeans and sweatshirt, wondering if there was a psychological connection to his abiding hatred of his bedroom. Bonnie had redecorated it several months before she left. He'd come home from a three-day radiology convention in Seattle and walked into this bower of saccharine country charm.

There were layers of plump coverlets, deep lace trims and enough pillows for a harem. And his desk was gone. In its place was a small round table covered with a cloth that matched the curtains. It held two small carefully placed books and a candle.

Bonnie's cheeks had been flushed and she'd greeted him with a fervor that had surprised and flattered him after months of lukewarm response.

Then he'd come home several months later while the boys were at summer camp, to find her side of the closet empty and a note propped up against the philodendron on the dining-room table.

"We no longer want the same things," it had read. "You could move to a metropolitan hospital and make a fortune, but you have no ambition. Well, I want more out of life. I'm moving to Houston with John Templar to help him open a clinic." She'd gone on to explain that the boys related to him better than they did to her, so she thought it best to leave them with him. "I know it's cowardly to do this while they're away, but tears and recriminations wouldn't help anyone." She'd finished with "I made over our bedroom, but I couldn't make over our lives."

He'd been dumbfounded that a relationship that had been founded on a genuine passion, and that had developed so comfortably, was simply over.

Then he'd overheard a conversation between a young woman from payroll and one of the ER nurses that suggested something had been going on between Bonnie and Templar for some time. "She wasn't even discreet," the payroll clerk had said. "Bringing lunch to Dr. Templar's office, picking him up at the hospital when Dr. Nicholas was at the convention. *Everyone* knew."

"Except Dr. Nicholas," the nurse had replied with a pitying tone in her voice.

Then he'd become angry. He hated being stupid. And he hated missing important details. His work required meticulous attention to everything visible to him, and constructive understanding of everything that wasn't. How could he have failed to notice an affair between his wife and his colleague being conducted right under his nose?

Standing under the spray of a hot shower, he let the anger wash over him anew, then drain away like the water. It was over. It didn't matter how it had happened, or how he had missed it. The important thing was that he had two boys to raise who required his complete attention. He had a job that demanded his dedication. And if that left nothing for the man inside him who longed for something he couldn't name, that was life. God didn't make any promises. Even the constitution only promised an individual's right to the "pursuit" of happiness. It never said you'd catch it.

He climbed into bed, telling himself that in the morning, he'd rip everything off the bed and scour the boxes in the garage for the old blue quilted bedspread. Who cared if it didn't match the curtains? And he'd move the round table into the garage and put his sander on it, then find his desk and put it back in front of the window.

Those decisions made, he closed his eyes and tried to relax. The image of Nancy Malone's face floated across his mind's eye. He could hear her sleepy voice. He tried to dismiss them. She was married.

Then his brain re-created the picture of her as he'd first seen her, lying on the gurney, waiting for him to conduct the test. Her eyes had been dark and defiantly nervous, as though she was impatient with herself for being unable to control her early contractions.

Then he saw her as she'd looked when she'd told him she knew she carried a girl. He had to smile at that, remembering when the image on the screen had turned.

Jave turned onto his side and let himself remember the

confusion on her face when he'd taken her back to her room and asked her to describe her truck so that he could save her chair from the rain. She'd looked confused. He'd enjoyed that.

So, he'd take her home tomorrow, carry her chair in for her so she could write her mystery novels and make enough money to stay home with her baby, and he'd feel as though he'd done his good deed.

Then, unbidden, the moment when she'd strained to see the ultrasound image flashed in his mind. He'd caught her arms, and she'd clutched his. He'd felt a desperate need in that grip.

He felt something prod at his heart and somehow change him from clinical radiologist to interested male. And once he admitted that, he felt a twinge in his groin that was a clearly sexual reaction.

He groaned aloud, and pushed his face into his pillow. Come on, man, he told himself. She's six months pregnant and she claims to be married. What's wrong with you?

The answers were too numerous to contemplate, and probably too alarming. He thought about the description of the boat Tom had clipped for him from the newspaper, and tried to imagine the two of them, alone on Willapa Bay in some sleek motor boat with salmon nibbling at their lines.

He drifted off to sleep.

CHAPTER FOUR

"NANCY!" April rapped on the bathroom door. "Telephone for you!"

Nancy pulled her blue sweatshirt on over her stretched-out black sweatpants and determined she would never leave the house again in her grubbies, even to go to the second-hand barn. She pulled the door open, her expression clearly surprised. "I don't know anybody here. Is it Dr. McNamara?"

April shook her head, her eyes wide. "Not unless he's moved to Greece," she whispered, and pointed to the telephone she'd left off the cradle on the table beside the bed. "The call's from Athens."

"Oh, no," Nancy whined. She hated herself for it, but couldn't help it. Only her mother could reduce her to whining. She sat on the edge of the bed and picked up the receiver.

"Hello," she said, as though she were answering the switchboard for General Motors. There was more business than warmth in her tone. "What is it, Mother?"

"Thank *God!*" The exclamation on the other end of the line was delivered in a deep, throaty voice. Nancy could imagine the roll of large, velvety brown eyes that accompanied it. "Are you all right? What happened? I can be there in twenty-four hours!"

Oh, God. Anything but that. "I'm fine, Mother," Nancy replied, trying to inject her voice with brightness and conviction. "I just overdid it a little. I had an ultrasound and half a dozen other tests and I'm fine."

"But Dr. McFarland said you went into labor!"

"Dr. McNamara," Nancy corrected. Then as April pushed her gently back against the pillows and pulled her feet up onto the bed, she asked, "How did you know to call him? How did you know I was here?"

"I called you at home all afternoon yesterday," her mother replied, "and when I couldn't reach you last night, I began to panic. I *knew* you'd get into trouble with that move. I wanted you to meet me in Laguna and let me take care of you, but nooo, you had to go to some pine-tree, flannel-shirt, salmon-stew outpost in the middle of the northwest wilderness to have your baby. Honestly, I—"

"Mom," Nancy interrupted, rolling her eyes at April, who was obviously straining to listen.

"Well, I called Dr. Carmody in New York, and he told me that an obstetrician in Seagull Point—"

"Heron Point."

"Heron Point, had called for your records. Well, I called *him,* sure you were in trouble and, well, there you are *in* trouble!"

"I'm not in trouble, Mom," Nancy insisted, rubbing her forehead where a small pain was beginning to grow into a major one. "I'm fine. I was given medication to stop the contractions. It worked, and all I have to do is continue to take it easy until delivery time. And everything will be fine."

"I'm coming out there."

"No!" Nancy shrieked the word so loudly that April jumped. There was a profound silence on the other end of the line.

MOM, YOU'RE SHOUTING! Don't do that. Water carries sound, you know.

"MOM." NANCY DREW a deep breath and tried to collect herself. She spoke in a reasonable tone now, though she still felt the panic that had prompted her desperate negative. "You're vacationing. There's no need for you to leave Athens to come here. I'm fine. April, tell my mother I'm fine." Nancy raised the receiver to April, who backed away, then took it reluctantly when Nancy scowled at her.

"She's fine, Mrs....um...?"

Nancy couldn't hear the exchange, but guessed by the expression on April's face what had happened. The Denise DiBenedetto magic had reached halfway across the world.

April swallowed. Her eyes, large as lily pads, went to Nancy. Nancy reached up impatiently for the phone. April took a step back with it, and turned protectively away from her.

"*You're* Denise DiBenedetto?" she asked in an awed tone into the receiver. "Nancy's mother is the Country and Western star!"

There was more conversation Nancy couldn't hear. She crossed her ankles and closed her eyes, thinking this was the story of her life. Upstaged by her mother when the woman was thousands of miles away.

"She's really doing very well," April was saying. "Dr. McNamara was in this morning and told her he wants to see her every two weeks, and she's to call him if she feels the least little twinge." Then April giggled. "I *loved* your 'Denise in Devon' video. You looked excellent in that silver, off-the-shoulder thing, and Willy Brock is *so* cool."

There was a moment of silence while April listened, then her eyes grew even wider still and her tin-tracked mouth flew open.

"*You are?* You're *marrying* Willy Brock?"

April placed a hand over the receiver and whispered loudly to Nancy as though certain she didn't know, "Your mom is Denise DiBenedetto and she's *marrying* Willy Brock!"

Then she put the phone back to her ear, and nodded. Nancy could hear her mother's voice giving directions.

"Ah, no," April said. "Jave Nicholas is going to take her home. He's our radiologist."

"What?" Nancy pushed herself carefully off the bed, torn between concern about the threat her mother posed from thousands of miles away, and that posed by Jave Nicholas, very close by. She pulled the phone from April and held her hand over the mouthpiece. "What are you talking about?" she demanded.

"Jave…" April said, obviously perplexed by her dismay. "He's going to drive you home. I saw him and his brother in the…" She pointed vaguely in the direction of the parking lot.

Nancy didn't want to hear any more. "Mother," she said firmly, "I am fine. There is not a thing wrong with me or the baby that rest and the medication won't take care of. Now, do *not* come to Oregon. Do you hear me? That would upset me, and you don't want to do that, do you?"

"Nancy—"

"Mother, I mean it. I was fine by myself for all those years, and I will be fine…" Nancy suddenly remembered that she'd created an elaborate charade about a husband and that April was listening intently. She placed her hand over the mouthpiece again and turned calmly to the very interested aid. "April, would you go ask the nurse if I can have another pair of those footie things to take home with me?"

April began looking around on the floor for the little sock-like slipper the hospital provided. "But I put them right…"

Nancy kicked the visible one out of sight under the bed. "I know, but I misplaced them somehow, and I'd love to take a pair home. Would you mind?"

"No. Of course not." April headed for the door, then turned back to grin with delight. "Say bye to your mom for me," she whispered.

The moment April was out the door, Nancy returned her attention to her mother. "I will be fine alone!" she said, trying to imbue her voice with the sincerity she felt over her solitary stand.

"No one should be alone," Denise observed quietly.

"Really." Nancy's voice became flat. "Curious that *you* forgot that when I was eight."

Another silence. Nancy closed her eyes, hating herself for sinking to petty barbs and old grievances.

"I've explained that many times," Denise said, her tone husky but controlled.

"Yes, you have," Nancy replied, "but it doesn't excuse it. So let's just forget that, and let me say for the last time that I feel wonderful this morning, and I know I'll be fine as long as I'm careful."

"Who is Jave...?"

The man walked in the door pushing a wheelchair, as Denise posed the question. Nancy decided to rid herself of both problems immediately.

"Have to go, Mother," she said. "Thanks for calling. I'll be in touch." She hung up the phone and turned to Jave as she grabbed her purse from the chair. "Hi," she said. "I...ah..." The dismissal on the tip of her tongue was stalled by a weird little warmth that formed in her chest and stole up her throat into her face. She remembered his call the night before and how the sound of his voice had dispelled her loneliness.

J. V. Nicholas was truly gorgeous in "civilian" clothes. He wore a mossy green cotton sweater this morning instead of his lab coat, and an old pair of jeans faded to the contour of his long thighs and spare hips. The color of the sweater darkened his hazel eyes, and his casual appearance destroyed whatever distance his professionalism had placed between them.

She felt suddenly very vulnerable. And very interested. And then she remembered she was supposed to be married.

"No need for the wheelchair," she said, offering her hand. "Thank you for your help. I'll just be—"

He took her hand and pulled her gently down into the chair. "Hospital rules. You have to leave the grounds in a wheelchair."

April reappeared with a pair of Footies in a plastic bag. Behind her was Amy Brown, hugging her clipboard to her chest.

"Did you know that her *mother* is—" April began in wide-eyed excitement, eager to share her news with Amy and Jave. Nancy shook her head discreetly but quickly. She didn't want her mother to intrude on her new life in Oregon, and the way Amy ferreted out information, her mother could be on her doorstep by morning.

April stopped, looking confused.

"My mother called from Athens," Nancy said to Jave and Amy, who waited for April to go on. "She's traveling with a friend. April got excited about getting such an exotic phone call."

Amy nodded heartily. "I can relate. Athens conjures up images of whitewashed buildings, beautiful ruins, blue sky and bluer water...." She sighed longingly.

"Greek men," April breathed.

"Mmm," Amy purred.

Jave made a scornful sound and turned the wheelchair in a tight circle. "What is it about foreign men that's so appealing to women anyway?"

"Their foreignness." A short, square nurse with a cap perched on a bun of dark hair planted herself firmly in the doorway. "They're over there and not over here, so they can't bother us." She placed both hands on her hips. "Where are you going with my patient?"

Nancy had been visited by Nurse Beacham several times in the past eighteen hours, and had quaked in her "footies" every time. The woman had an Attila-like bedside manner.

"She's Dr. Mac's patient," Jave said, returning her authoritative glare, "and he's released her. I'm taking her home."

"But I don't need..." Nancy began.

Beacham folded her arms. "He didn't tell me."

"That's because you never listen to anyone, Beachie," Jave said amiably, and headed for her with the wheelchair.

April and Amy leaped out of his path. "Now get out of my way before I mow you down."

Beacham stood her ground. Nancy thought she saw amusement invade her glare. "Do that and you'll find yourself on the fracture table, Dr. Nicholas." Then she stepped aside. He pinched her chin as he passed and Nancy watched in shock as the woman fought a blush.

Nancy tried to protest again that she didn't need the wheelchair and was capable of driving herself home, but no one was listening to her.

Amy and April walked them to the double glass doors.

"Remember," April said, holding one of the doors open for them, "when the baby comes, I'm an excellent sitter."

Nancy waved as Jave pushed the wheelchair across the parking lot in the direction of her battered blue pickup.

"Bye," Amy called after them. "I'll keep in touch, Nancy!"

The day was gray and windy, late June feeling more like a blustery March. Nancy rubbed her arms against the chill.

"My chair!" she groaned as they approached her vehicle. The bed of the pickup was empty. "Where's my chair?"

"Relax, Mrs. Malone," Jave said quietly, pointing to the elegant red-and-silver GMC parked beside her truck. A man about Jave's age smiled and waved at her from behind the wheel. Something was covered by a tarp in the back. "I told you I'd take care of it for you."

Jave helped her out of the wheelchair, then gave it a roll toward April, who waited and waved.

He turned back to Nancy, holding a hand out, palm up. "Keys?" he asked.

Nancy squared her shoulders. This was going no farther. "Thank you," she said again. "But you're not driving me home. I feel fine. If you'll just put the chair in my—"

"Tom's going to drive it home for you."

"Tom?"

"My brother."

She looked up toward the cab of the fancy truck again and returned the driver's warm smile with a polite wave.

"That's kind of you, but unnecessary," she insisted. "If you'll put it in my truck—"

"You'll be faced," he cautioned reasonably, "with unloading the chair by yourself when you get home. Or leaving it in the truck until someone comes along to help you. And it's going to rain again. Even the tarp won't keep it dry forever. Now, will you give me your keys?"

Nancy knew it was critical that she make this stand and hold it. She didn't know why, she just knew.

"No," she said with quiet firmness. She walked around the truck to the driver's-side door, then took hold of the mirror when she got there. Her knees were wobbly. She wasn't quite as strong as she'd thought. But she was strong inside. She always had been. She looked into Jave Nicholas's steady hazel gaze and lied. "I have a neighbor who can help me with the chair."

Jave saw that touching toughness in her. Something about that desperately brave look reminded him poignantly of Pete. "I know your box number," he said candidly. "You're two miles from your nearest neighbor. Now, it's my weekend off, but my brother has a business to run, and he came to help me this morning out of the goodness of his heart. Are you going to give me your keys, or am I going to keep your chair?"

Nancy opened her mouth to suggest that that would be theft, but he probably had a point about his brother. And she couldn't wait to get back to her comfortable little cottage and put her feet up. She reached into her brown pouch bag and took out her keys. "All right," she relented. "You can unload my chair for me, but *I'll* drive."

He considered a moment, then accepted the compromise. "Fine. But let me help you climb into the seat."

Before she could agree, he literally lifted her up into it, then locked and closed her door. As he loped around to the passenger side, she sat immobile, completely flustered.

As he leaped in beside her, she turned the key in the ignition. The engine coughed asthmatically.

"Doesn't sound very healthy," he said, buckling his seat belt as she put the truck into gear and headed across the parking lot toward the road.

Nancy patted the dash affectionately. "Well, it climbed so many mountains coming here. I think it gave me its all." She pulled jerkily into the light traffic and headed for the coast highway.

"I'm surprised your husband left you alone for three months in your condition, living that far out of town, with a truck that's on death row." Jave responded to her quick glance with an innocent expression, hoping to catch her in a look that would reveal the truth about her husband.

But she quickly turned her attention back to the road. "He knows I'm competent. He doesn't worry about me."

There was a moment's silence in the cab of the truck.

"Does he love you?" Jave wasn't sure why he asked that, unless it was that he wanted very much to catch her off guard. She'd placed a barrier between them, and he didn't like that. It made no sense, considering that he intended to drop off the chair at her place and drive away with Tom. But he'd found that much of life didn't make sense. So he followed his instincts.

Nancy gasped indignantly. The exclamation was completely false, but she thought it sounded good. "What a question! Of course he loves me. He loves me enough to know I can handle myself in an emergency."

As the road widened, Nancy turned into the right lane. A glance at the rearview mirror showed Jave's brother falling in behind her.

"When a man loves a woman," Jave said, remembering the early days with Bonnie, "he never considers her completely capable without him. It isn't that he doesn't trust her competence, but he feels so necessary to her every breath that if he can't be there with her, he usually makes certain he's cleared all the obstacles from her path."

Nancy entertained that philosophy for a moment and even emitted a dreamy little sigh over it. She'd never known a relationship like that. She was content to be responsible for herself, but it would be nice to be so cherished.

"He has to keep the boat running," she said, straightening in her seat and dismissing futile longings. "He forgets about the truck."

Jave wasn't sure he believed in the husband, but if he did exist, he was a jerk.

HER COTTAGE WAS WHITE where the paint remained, and square and solid looking despite its cosmetic disrepair. It had a deep front porch, a picket fence that closed it in on three sides and a grassy hillside that hemmed it in from the road. Along the front of the property, bright pink tea roses cascaded in full bloom all along the fence, making the cottage look like a plain woman in a beautiful dress.

Nancy opened her door to leap down before Jave was out of the truck. He turned to caution her to wait, then saw that Tom was there to help her.

"Hi." Nancy smiled into the warm brown eyes of the man who held both her hands until she eased herself to the sandy ground.

"Hello," Tom said with a courteous dip of his head. He was darker than his brother, Nancy saw, and possibly an inch taller. His smile hid something, she thought, but when she looked more closely, he looked away toward the cottage. "I'm Tom Nicholas," he said, freeing her hands. He angled his chin at the house. "Pretty cottage. Needs some work."

She nodded. "I'm trying to make the inside livable before the baby comes. Then I can have the roof repaired, along with a few other things."

Tom looked up at the roof with a critical eye. "Then it'll be fall. The time to fix a roof is *before* the cold *winter* rain."

"She's not from here," Jave said with a grin, coming around the truck to lower the tailgate. "She doesn't understand about the rain. She doesn't even keep a tarp in the bed of her truck."

Tom shook his head. "Bad, Nancy. Gotta be prepared."

Even as they spoke, rain began to fall. It was thin but strong, and Nancy hunched her shoulders against it as she watched the men pull the chair to the edge of the gate.

"I know," she conceded. "Your brother gave me the lecture yesterday. I just didn't expect there to be this much rain. I feel as though I'm living an episode of 'seaQuest.'"

Tom laughed and pulled the chair toward him to lift it off the truck. Jave stopped him with a hand on the tarp. "The upholstery's still a little wet, it weighs a ton, and you're favoring that knee." He added reasonably but authoritatively, "Let's do it together."

Tom looked heavenward in supplication. "I'm not helpless, all right?"

"Neither am I," Jave retorted. "I asked you along to help me, not to do it for..."

He stopped as Tom ignored him, lifted the chair, and headed for the house with it. Jave took Nancy's hand and pulled her out of the way.

"*You* can explain to Mom why the limp's worse," he shouted after Tom.

"Oh, stow it!" Tom shouted back at him.

"House key's the round one next to the car key," Nancy said, pushing Jave toward the house. "Go ahead. I'll be right behind you."

Nancy pulled her hand from Jave's and watched him lope past his brother and up the few porch steps to the door. He opened it and stepped inside to hold it out of the way.

Nancy went up the walk, trying to recover from having her hand held. That was such a simple gesture, one of the more innocent steps of courtship, yet it had always been one of the most appealing to her.

It represented a sense of security, of belonging, that she'd never experienced—except for those first few months with Jerry. And Jave Nicholas had a good grip, a strong hand that was hard and gentle and felt rather wonderful wrapped around her much smaller fingers. She flexed them, trying to dismiss the impression. He'd meant nothing by it. She was alone, she reminded herself. She wanted it that way.

When Nancy reached the living room, the men had the still-wrapped chair between them and were placing it in front of the table she'd put near the window to serve as a desk. Her computer and printer sat on it, and a neat row of reference books stood up between two simple metal bookends.

Tom untied the rope that held the tarp in place and pulled it off. Nancy's gaze narrowed on the chair as she approached it. She ran a hand over it, thinking it appeared considerably better than it had yesterday morning when she'd bought it. And cleaner. And the legs looked less rough, almost as though they'd been...

She turned to Jave with suspicion in her eye. "What did you do? It looks fifty years younger than it did yesterday morning."

Jave shrugged. "My boys and I shampooed it since it was drenched anyway, but it's still pretty wet. We put a little stain on the legs. It could use a few more coats, but there wasn't time."

My boys and I... That was the first time he'd mentioned his children to her. Warmth tugged at her unexpectedly. She could imagine him with children. He had the kind of quiet, autocratic demeanor that made young children feel secure.

"That was very thoughtful," she said, feeling suddenly indebted—and just a little awkward. She laughed softly. "I thought you were just going to throw a tarp over it."

He studied her with frank masculine interest for a moment, and she found herself desperately wanting to make a friend of him. To tell him that she had no husband. That she was competent but just a little afraid. That she needed someone.

But for the sake of her baby, he had to believe she was

married. And what appeal could she have for him anyway? She was beginning to look like she'd swallowed the moon.

She lowered her eyes. No. She had to do this alone. Thousands of women did. She could, too.

Jave saw the small step toward him that had taken place in her eyes—then the two steps back. He had to admit to feeling disappointment. And more than that, he felt a fascination he couldn't simply turn off. Not until he understood what was going on. Not until he understood her.

"Well," he said, thinking she was beginning to look pale. "You can't win an Edgar in a moldy old chair. Anything else we can do before we go?"

"No," she said, both relieved and upset that he was leaving. "But, thank you. And thank you, Tom."

Nancy turned to Jave's brother, who stood in the middle of the kitchen, looking up at the ceiling. Each room on the bottom floor meandered into the other so that living and dining rooms and kitchen were all connected, separated only by artfully placed screens and tall plants.

"You're welcome," Tom called back, still looking up. "This ceiling tile's going to fall on your head from the leak in the roof."

"I know," she replied. "It's on my list of things to take care of."

Tom wandered into the living room and handed her his business card. "Call me when you're ready. I'm pretty good. And my rates are reasonable."

Nancy read the card aloud. "Nicholas Carpentry and Repair. Roofing, Siding, Painting, Papering." She smiled up at him. "Do you have an easy payment plan?"

"You bet."

Nancy accompanied the brothers to the front porch steps, then leaned against the pillar and watched them walk away, two tall, impressive physiques, one limping slightly.

Jave took the tarp Tom carried and tossed it into the back of her truck. He turned and shouted over his shoulder, "Now you're an Oregonian!"

She laughed and waved. They climbed into the red-and-silver truck and drove away. Her world fell suddenly silent, except for the sound of the surf in the background.

She put her hand to a flutter of feeling in her upper abdomen. Almost as though she'd been patted.

Don't feel sad, Mom. I'm here. And we're going to have baby furniture and chocolate and movie passes. We're gonna be okay.

Nancy went back into the house and locked the door.

CHAPTER FIVE

Boenecke caught a glimpse of her across the fog-shrouded bridge. He ducked behind the limo, afraid of what she'd do if she knew he'd followed her. Temper would overtake good sense, he was sure, and she'd probably blow her cover. He hunkered down and waited.

NANCY REREAD THE PARAGRAPH, considered it passable for the moment, and reached for her glass mug. She put it to her mouth, trying to decide whether to let Geneva notice Boeneke or not, then was completely distracted from her plot plans by the disappointing taste of lukewarm tea.

BLECH! Nuke that stuff, Mom.

SHE PUSHED HER NEW CHAIR away from the computer and went into the kitchen to brew another cup. The room was shadowy this morning, despite the daylight, and she turned the small old-fashioned light on over the sink. She filled the kettle and put a fresh tea bag in her glass mug and the spoon that tradition insisted absorbed the heat from the boiling water and prevented the glass from cracking. Tea in a glass was an eccentric indulgence, but she liked it. And of all her cravings, it was one of the more harmless and easiest to satisfy.

Outside, the sky was pewter again and threatening more rain. The grassy slope behind her cottage rippled beautifully in the wind and Nancy watched it, rubbing her stomach absently as she waited for the water to boil.

Thanks, Mom. That makes up for the cold tea.

Then she saw the cat. He was black with eyes so light they were almost silver. He'd been coming to the back door every day since she'd moved in, but he wouldn't let her near him. She guessed he'd been wild for some time. He'd plumped up a little in the weeks she'd been feeding him, but he still ran away every time she opened the door. He would stop halfway up the slope, then turn and watch her put out the food. He never came down until she'd gone back inside.

She called him Shaman because he was like a mystical, mysterious shadow with connections to another world.

She took a plastic butter tub full of dry food, filled a glass with water, and carried both outside to the corner of the porch. Shaman ran halfway up the slope and turned to watch her. She poured the water into the other bowl she always left out, then placed the dry food beside it.

She turned to look at the cat before going inside. She was patient with him, understanding his suspicion. But she felt the need to make contact with another life today, and for some reason her fictional characters simply weren't doing it for her.

"You know I won't hurt you," she called to him.

He sat unmoving, an eerie stillness in the waving grass, his eyes intense.

Nancy thought she could read them. "I'm not worried about physical pain," they said. "I'm worried that I'll trust you and you'll move away and I'll be hungry again."

With a last wry look at him, she went inside and closed the door. No matter how much she would have liked contact, he preferred not to have it, and she could relate to that.

She went to the whistling kettle, accepting that she and the cat would coexist along parallel lines.

That had more or less been the story of her life anyway. She hadn't connected with anyone in a long time, except Jerry, of course, and he didn't count because he was gone.

Nancy dunked the bag up and down in her mug, watching the rich redwood color darken. She rubbed her stomach with her other hand. A small kick met her palm and she felt suddenly less lonely.

She carried her mug to the table-cum-desk in the dining room, patting where she'd felt the kick. "Hi, Malia Rose," she said. "I was wondering if you were up. We're writing pretty well today. Listen to what Boeneke discovered about Geneva."

"Hi, Mom. I'm glad the work's going well. Could you send something down? Not that lumpy white stuff with the raisins and the milk, but something cold and creamy, maybe with chocolate in it? Oh, good. I'm glad we're sitting down. I felt like I was swimming against the current."

NANCY HEARD THEM before she saw them. She was so engrossed in Boeneke's pursuit of Geneva, who was in pursuit of the killer ambassador, that she thought the sound of the engine came from Boeneke's Cherokee. Then she heard children's voices and the bark of a dog, and knew she'd written neither into *Death on the Danbury Bridge*.

She looked over the top of the computer screen and saw what almost constituted a crowd, coming through her gate and up the walk. There were three adults, two children and a dog. And one of the adults, an older woman, stopped to lean over and admire the profusion of roses on the fence.

Nancy felt a little jolt of...alarm?...excitement?...when she recognized Jave Nicholas. His brother Tom followed.

Whoa. There's foaming adrenaline in here.

EVERYONE WAS CARRYING something. The boys had grocery bags, the woman, a box she balanced carefully on both hands. The men carried a ladder between them, and Tom had a toolbox.

Nancy pushed open the front door and stepped out onto the porch, a confused smile on her face.

"We invited ourselves over to fix the roof," Jave said from the bottom of the steps. He held the ladder upright now, one hand leaning over a rung to support it. She saw his eyes go over her with one quick assessing glance before settling on her face. "How do you feel today?"

There was something intimate in the question, something that isolated them in the little crowd.

"I'm fine," she said, ensnared by his gaze. He wore a blue shirt this morning that complicated the color of his eyes. She finally pulled hers away in self-defense.

The two boys stood on his other side, the taller blond one studying her with interest, the smaller dark one looking as though he'd been torn away from his favorite cartoons. "This is Eddy..." He touched the head of the taller boy. "And Pete."

"Hello," Nancy said, coming down the steps. Eddy came toward her, holding out the bag. Pete shrank against his father and kept a firm grip on his sack.

"This is from the Farmers' Market," Eddy said. "Dad and Grandma went shopping and got too much stuff."

Nancy peered into the bag. It was filled with half a dozen tasseled ears of corn, several enormous golden onions and a pint box each of strawberries and raspberries.

"Well...thank you!" Nancy looked from the boy to his father, touched by the kindness.

"You're welcome." Jave indicated the woman. "And this is my mother, Agnes Nicholas."

"Aggie," she corrected. She gave Nancy a polite smile that didn't quite conceal suspicion and disapproval. She held out the box she was carrying. "Chicken enchilada casserole," she said. "We've also invited ourselves for lunch."

The implication was that she didn't think that was such a good idea, but had been forced into compliance. "Can we put this in the refrigerator? Do you have a microwave?"

The dog stayed out with Jave and Tom while Nancy led the way inside. She placed the bag of produce on the counter, then placed the casserole in the refrigerator. Pete continued to clutch his grocery bag.

Aggie wandered slowly around, studying Nancy's eclectic collection of furniture odds and ends and framed advertising prints from early in the century. Eddy followed Nancy from the refrigerator to the stove.

"Do you have hot chocolate?" he asked.

She picked up the kettle and carried it to the sink. He followed her again.

"No, I don't," she said, "but I have Russian tea."

He frowned as they retraced their steps to the stove with a full kettle. "What's that?"

"It's tea made with orange juice and lemonade. It's sweet. I think you'll like it."

"Tea?" he asked doubtfully. "That's kind of for old ladies, isn't it?"

He had deep blue eyes, Nancy noted, and the spark in them of a bright and well-loved child. She prayed her baby would have that look in her eyes.

Nancy laughed. "I drink it, and I'm not old. Well, not *too* old."

Eddy considered. "Okay," he said finally. "As long as there aren't any girls or dolls or anything. Usually when there's tea, there's a bunch of old ladies or girls dressed up all fancy with their dolls."

"That's a tea *party*," Nancy said, pulling mugs down from the cupboard, deliberately searching out those without teddy bears and cutesy patterns. "This is just tea—without the party."

"It is too a party," Pete said, joining them at the counter with his bag. "There's cake in here. And ice cream." He handed it over. "That makes a party."

Nancy accepted it. Both boys followed her to the freezer. "I guess you're right, Pete," she said, putting the half gallon of strawberry ice cream away. "This does look like a party. Would you like to try some tea?"

"Yes, please," he answered politely.

Nancy turned toward Aggie. The woman's smiling but remote good manners filled the space between them with tension.

"Can I make you some coffee?" she asked.

Aggie studied her a moment. Nancy refused to let herself squirm. "I'll try the Russian tea," Aggie said finally.

Nancy put on the television in the living room for the boys, and blessed her foresight in contracting for the Disney Channel with her cable hookup. A cartoon feature was in full swing and immediately absorbed the boys.

She made the tea, adding cold water to the boys' mugs. It met with their approval.

Aggie, sitting at the kitchen table, sipped it and nodded. "A tad sweet, but good."

Nancy explained that it was made with ingredients for instant juice drinks and instant tea. "An old neighbor of mine in New York used to make it and got me hooked."

"I've never been to New York," Aggie said. Her tone suggested that was something she didn't intend to rectify.

"It's a wonderful place," Nancy said charmingly, smilingly defensive. "I grew up in a neighborhood in Queens that was just like any small town in the Midwest. Then I lived in the Village when I was trying to be a playwright, and that was very exciting—full of actors and artists and dancers. I loved it."

"Is that where you met your husband?" The question was asked conversationally, but as Nancy looked into Aggie's eyes, she understood what the hostility was all about. Aggie thought she was married. And she probably didn't approve of her son showing such care and concern over a married woman.

Well, Nancy didn't, either—though for different reasons.

"Yes," she replied. It was the truth. "He was an actor, and we were working together on a small, low-budget play a friend of ours was producing."

Aggie's gray eyebrows came together. "I thought your husband was in the Coast Guard."

Nancy didn't even blink. "He was. He is. But he's always involved in community theater in his free time." She had to remember, she told herself sharply, that the honest elements of her story only stretched so far.

"How long have you been married?"

That was safe. "Four years." Divorced for four months, but who's counting?

The sound of ripping and prying apart came from overhead. Several roofing tiles went sailing past the kitchen window to land on the ground.

"Jave was married for ten years," Aggie said, glancing toward the boys, then lowering her voice. Eddy and Pete were completely entranced by the television and unaware of their conversation as they sipped at their tea. "She ran off with an orthopedist a year ago."

Nancy nodded. "I heard about that. It must have been very hard on everyone."

Aggie fixed her with a level gaze. "Bonnie was a nice girl, who was a good enough wife and mother, but she got bored with small-town life and didn't have the character to realize that what she needed was more substance within herself, and not another man. Jave married her because he loved her. She married him because he got her pregnant. She never gave as much as he did, so it didn't work. I don't ever want to see him hurt like that again."

Nancy heard the message there, but replied as though she didn't. "No one should ever be hurt like that. Unfortunately, life isn't as protective as we'd like it to be."

"But *I* am," Aggie said in a distinctly militant tone. "I'd die for my family. I'd even kill for them."

Nancy heard that message, too. Exaggerated or not, she felt lucky she and Jave Nicholas weren't romantically involved. She had no desire to be on the other end of Aggie's weapon of choice, whatever it was. She drew on the acting skills she'd acquired by watching her ex at work. Naturalness was the key.

She nodded gravely and leaned across the table toward Jave's mother. "That's how I feel about my husband," she said, telling herself it wasn't really a lie. She'd often thought of killing and Jerry in the same context. Then she added with genuine sincerity, "And my baby. Nothing had better ever get between me and mine."

THAT'S telling her, Mom.

THE SUSPICION IN Aggie's eyes seemed to waver. Then Pete appeared at the table, requesting a refill on his tea, and Nancy stood to fill his order, leaving Aggie to reevaluate her impressions.

There was more pounding from the roof, and Nancy looked up as she handed Pete his tea. The soggy tiles were looking more and more precarious. Maybe she'd better hire Tom to take care of that as soon as she could manage it.

JAVE BRACED HIMSELF against the gutters that ran around the rim of the roof and studied the seamless patch. Except for the brightness of the new tiles, it would have been impossible to tell that the roof had been repaired.

"Damn, you're good," Jave praised Tom. His brother, braced for balance as he was, gathered tools into his box.

Tom gave him a superior glance. "I hear that all the time," he said with feigned arrogance. Then his eyebrow arched. "Usually from women."

Jave groaned. "Save it, please. I don't believe you for a minute. If you were in such demand, you'd be off in your Jag this weekend with some blonde instead of here with Mom and me and the kids."

Tom gave him an affronted look as he edged carefully

toward the ladder, guiding his toolbox along the tiles. "I'm here because you asked for my help. I'm only doing the brotherly, charitable thing."

Jave laughed as Tom backed down the ladder. "You're doing the geek-without-a-date thing." Then Jave toed his way toward the ladder—only to find it pulled away from the side of the house beyond his reach. Fifteen feet below on the grass, Tom balanced it carelessly with one hand.

"The what thing?" he asked.

"The geek-without-a-date thing!" Jave shouted at Tom fearlessly, turning carefully to crouch down and brace himself on the edge. "The workaholic-small-businessman, spare-time-couch-potato-baseball-freak thing!"

Tom tilted his head sideways. "You know, I like the way you look there," he said, still holding the ladder away. "Sort of like a contemporary gargoyle. The nose and the fangs particularly."

"Daaad!" The front door slammed and Pete's voice preceded the child into the yard. He ignored his uncle and looked around frantically for his father.

"Up here," Jave called. "What's the matter?"

Pete looked up, his eyes wide. "Hurry, Dad. The ceiling fell on Grandma!"

"Oh, God." Tom leaned the ladder back in place and ran inside.

Jave rode the sides of the ladder down with hands and feet and raced to follow.

"I'M *FINE!*" Aggie insisted, though in a faintly pathetic voice that suggested otherwise. "Good heavens, the tiles are only cardboard."

Nancy dabbed at a small cut on Aggie's forehead with a damp cloth, and the boys stood by, one holding a tube of Neosporin, and the other a tin of Band-Aids. Tom examined the tile that had fallen.

Jave leaned down to inspect the injury. "You okay, Mom?" he asked.

"There's hardly any blood," Pete said with obvious disappointment.

Aggie angled him a glare. "I'm fine. But I'm enjoying the attention. Please don't spoil it."

As Nancy folded the cloth and prepared to reapply it, Jave caught her hand and held it away so that he could inspect the cut more closely. "It's hardly more than a scratch, Mom," he diagnosed. "But, by all means, make the most of it. Want me to call for oxygen, or shock pants, or something to make it look more dramatic?"

Then suddenly, without warning, he became sharply aware of Nancy's knuckles in the palm of his hand, of the bite of the topaz in her ring against the pad of his index finger, of the nail on her little finger digging into his.

He turned to her and found her soft, dark eyes on him filled with a message he couldn't interpret.

Nancy knew if she didn't withdraw her hand in a minute, the moment would grow heavy with significance. *Everyone* present would become aware that they were gazing into each other's eyes. But for now, Aggie's eyes were closed and the boys were studying the ceiling with their uncle, so she did a foolish and dangerous thing. She allowed herself to enjoy the sturdy grip, the quiet, fathomless hazel eyes, the fascinating paradox of strength and gentleness that was a kind man's touch.

Then Tom's voice brought her back, and she drew her hand away. "A few of the other damaged tiles are going to be right behind that one," he said. "I'm afraid my hammering worked them loose. I can pull down the bad ones until you have it taken care of. It won't look very good, but at least they won't fall on you."

Nancy nodded, striving for a steady, even tone. "I'd like to hire you to replace them. But first, I insist on paying you for the work you've done today."

Tom shook his head. "No, thank you. This is a sort of 'welcome to Heron Point' gesture. I'll be busy on another job until Friday, but I could work on your tiles the following week. Will that do?"

She nodded agreement. "Whenever you can fit it in would be fine. And thank you for the welcoming gift. That's very generous."

He'd come at Jave's request, she knew. She felt oddly disoriented, thoroughly upset by her reactions to Jave. She was pretending to be married, and here she was playing patty fingers with a man who *must* believe her performance.

She thanked Tom again, then handed Jave the wet cloth and went to microwave Aggie's casserole.

After lunch, Aggie insisted on cleaning up and drafted the boys to help. She grumbled at the spare contents of Nancy's cupboards, and the frozen yogurt that was the only other item in the freezer half of her refrigerator.

"I haven't done any serious food shopping in a week or so," Nancy explained. "I've been busy making the house livable and working on my book."

Aggie lectured her on the importance of nutrition to pregnant women. "Don't be afraid of a little weight gain," she said, taking a last look around the kitchen before closing the dishwasher. "You'll be such a slave to that child forever after that you'll work it off."

Aggie then looked down at her own plump form in a casual black-and-white pants outfit and smiled fondly in Jave's and Tom's direction. Tom stood atop the ladder removing the loose tiles, and Jave stood at the bottom to receive them.

"Until, of course, they begin to take care of *you*. By then, you're entitled to a few extra pounds."

Aggie's manner had changed subtly, Nancy noted, over the course of the past few hours. The woman seemed no longer hostile, but friendly, even warm. She congratulated herself on her convincing portrayal of a married woman.

As Tom carried the ladder back to his truck, the boys trailing him, Aggie gave Nancy her telephone number. "Tom and I live in a house about this vintage on a hill above town. I'm at Jave's house most of the time, so please call me if you need anything. I can imagine how lonely it must be for you way out here with your husband gone. Do you still have your parents?"

"My father passed away," Nancy replied. "My mother is very much alive and living on a yacht in Greece at the moment."

Aggie's eyes widened. "How wonderful that must be. Will she come when the baby arrives?"

Nancy shook her head and walked Aggie to the door. "We don't get along very well. She called to check on me when she heard I was in the hospital, but I asked her not to come. I...just don't want to get involved again at this point in time."

Aggie put a sympathetic hand on her arm. "But, Nancy, you are involved. She's your mother. And you're about to have her grandchild."

Nancy shook her head, patting the hand on her arm. "This baby belongs to me alone."

Aggie frowned. "And your husband, of course."

"Yes," Nancy said quickly. "Of course."

Aggie gave her a quick hug. "Well, call me if you find yourself needing motherly advice after all. And you have Tom's business card."

"Yes. Thank you."

As Aggie walked out to the truck, Nancy returned to the kitchen. Jave had carried the old tiles out to the trash and now returned through the back door, pushing it closed and dusting his hands on the thighs of his jeans.

Nancy felt a deep, sharp, alarming awareness of him. She deliberately kept the table between them. She saw his smoky hazel eyes note her careful distance and ponder what it meant.

She assumed her role of married woman. "Thank you so much for bringing Tom by to fix the roof. That was very kind and...neighborly."

It hadn't been neighborly at all, Jave admitted to himself.

It had been something else altogether. Something she apparently understood, judging by the panicked look in her eyes every time he came within ten feet of her.

There were confusing messages here, and he was just beginning to get his life straightened out after Bonnie. Confusion was something he didn't need. So they could call it neighborly and let it go at that.

Curiously, it hurt to accept that.

"Take care," he said, picking up Tom's toolbox and keeping to his side of the table as he headed toward the living room.

Nancy found herself wanting to call him back, to grab his arm, to hold him somehow. "Wait!" she called.

Jave turned near the front door, his heart giving an uncomfortable kick. "Yes?"

She took a jar off the countertop and secured the lid as she walked toward him with it. She stopped in front of him and handed it to him. "Your boys liked my Russian tea," she said softly. "Two teaspoons in a mug of hot water." He accepted the tall jar of powdery orange stuff in his free hand. Her fingertips brushed his, lingered for a moment, then she dropped her hand and said firmly, "Goodbye. Thanks for all you've done."

"Sure," he replied. "Good luck."

She waved them off from the porch, feeling a sharp pinch of loneliness when the red-and-silver truck disappeared from view.

She went back into the house, found the kitchen more pristine than she usually kept it, and brewed a cup of black tea. She had to get back to Boeneke and Geneva. The story had been going well before the Nicholases arrived.

She carried the tea to her desk where a midafternoon sun had broken through the clouds and brightened the view of sea grass and ocean from her window. Perfect working conditions, she told herself as she sat down to work.

An hour later, she was still staring at the flashing cursor

on the screen. It sat at the end of the last sentence she'd written before Jave and his family had arrived.

Impatient with herself, she went into the kitchen, wondering if Shaman was ready for his evening meal. She refilled his bowl and looked for him on the slope where he always watched and waited. He wasn't there. She called, then chided herself for it. Of course he wouldn't come. He never came when she called.

She looked left and then right, and saw the same view in both directions—miles of empty beach. Even the sea gulls and the sandpipers were somewhere else this afternoon. The sun dipped back behind its tufty pewter screen and everything around her darkened subtly.

Nancy turned her face into the west wind and admitted to herself that she was lonely. She'd valued her solitude until it was invaded by a host of loud and cheerful people who gave her a glimpse of another kind of life, then disappeared—leaving a gray crater in the middle of her day.

MOM. IT'S GONNA BE OKAY. I can feel your grim vibrations. And your spine's a little tight. You're pinching my backside.

Come on. You told me the first time we saw the doctor and he told you I was coming that everything would be all right. That we just had to have faith and believe in each other.

I know that's not easy for you right now because frankly— I wouldn't trust anything that looked like me, either. But I have faith in you. I know we're going to be fine.

Mom? Yo! Are you listening?

"WHOA." NANCY PUT A HAND to the sharp kick on her ribs and rubbed. "Easy, baby. It's all right. Everything's going to be fine. It's just you and me, but we're already a pretty good team. We can do this. Go back to sleep. I have it handled."

CHAPTER SIX

"DO NOT PICK UP THAT MAGAZINE while I'm standing here with you," Jave warned his mother. "Or I'm out of here and you can drive yourself home and carry in your own three tons of groceries."

Aggie, standing in front of the shopping cart behind which he waited in the checkout line, gave him a look of complete disdain as she picked up a tabloid magazine and tossed it into her cart.

"Don't be such a stuffed shirt, James Victor Nicholas." She perused the rack filled with other publications of the same type and asked absently, "Where else can you read about things that never happened?"

Jave opened his mouth to answer that and realized the danger. There was no answer. In fact, the question itself was just a little out there.

"You know..." Aggie tossed another magazine into her cart and moved forward with it as the line moved. "Tom missed his last appointment with the therapist."

Jave nodded. "He had a big job that day so he couldn't leave. The principal's new home office, remember? I helped him lay the carpet. He told me he'd make another appointment."

"Well, he hasn't," Aggie said, moving to the back of the cart where he stood and lowering her voice. "And he won't take Judy Taft's phone calls."

Jave nodded again. "I know that, too. And I don't blame him. When he was hurt and there was a chance he might not have use of that leg, she made a token visit to the hospital, left a few messages on the answering machine, and that was it. Now that he's more like himself again, she's willing to give him her time. That stinks, Mom."

Aggie sighed, and for a moment Jave thought she looked like she had that week after the fire when Tom had teetered between life and death. He put an arm around her shoulders and squeezed.

"He's going to be all right—inside as well as out. You've got to stop worrying about every little move he makes—or doesn't make."

"But he never goes out—except with you and the boys." She leaned into him and looked up, her usually wise, dark eyes filled with worry. "I want him to be happy again. I want him to find a nice girl and get married and have babies. When I'm gone, he'll be all alone in that house."

The line moved again and Jave pushed the cart up against the grocery conveyor and began unloading.

"If you want him to be happy," he reasoned, "you have to let him come to that in his own time. What he went through was hard on all of us, but think about how hard it was on him. And we can't make him push it all aside because we're tired of seeing him suffer. He has to get through it his way."

Aggie held a three-roll package of paper towels against her and looked at him over it. "And what about you? When are you going to be ready?"

Jave sighed. He knew she would work her way around to him sooner or later. He had less patience and understanding there. "I'll get to it."

"It's been a year."

"That's not so long."

"It's too long to grieve over a selfish woman who left you and two wonderful little children."

Jave fixed his mother with a warning glance. She didn't comprehend subtlety. "I'm not grieving over her. And I don't want to talk about it."

She considered him another moment while he tried to

dispel more conversation by concentrating on pulling the heavy items out of the bottom of the cart.

"I think—" she began again.

Jave interrupted under his breath. "I know what you think. You think you can decide how Tom's and my life should be and make it happen. But you can't. There's a lot of you in us—well, more of you in Tom than in me, but you..."

She smiled, first considering his remark a compliment. Then her expression changed and she asked suspiciously, "What do you mean, there's more of me in Tom?"

He pushed the now-empty cart forward and pulled his checkbook out of his hip pocket. "Well, you know. He's hardheaded, opinionated, quarrelsome, hard to—"

She hit him with the rubber divider bar that separated grocery orders on the conveyor.

"Mrs. Nicholas!" The checker, a tall young woman Jave had gone to school with, pretended shock at Aggie's behavior. "I saw that, Jave," she said. "If you need a witness to parental abuse, I saw the whole thing."

Jave took the bar from Aggie and dropped it into the slot near the register. "Good. I'll send my attorney by tomorrow. And I want to make it clear that the scandal sheets, the praline chocolate drizzle ice cream and the disposable security undergarments are hers and not mine."

"Jave!" This time Aggie hit him with her hand, then dissolved into hearty laughter.

JAVE AND TOM WALKED along the service dock to which the boat described in Tom's newspaper clipping was moored. They stopped at the stern, where a landing net was propped against the rail, and stared quietly.

"Does this look sixty-three feet long to you?" Tom asked in a whisper.

Jave ran his gaze from stem to stern. This was a cabin cruiser from the twenties or thirties, and looked as though it hadn't been scrubbed or painted since it was built. "I think it's an exaggeration," he returned wryly. "By about thirty feet."

Tom frowned as he reread the clipping aloud. "'63' Bertram Int'l '72/89. '89 major remodel/update. Charter potential, 3 staterooms, low hours, been loved."

Jave snickered. "Looks more like 'Canoe with two oars, comes with unimpeded view of passing traffic through missing windows. Depth may be sounded through hole in deck.'"

Tom leaned forward to run a hand along the old lapstrake hull. It had been primed in preparation for paint, and the name had been obliterated. "Oak," he whispered reverently. "Jave, this boat has character."

Oh, no. Jave knew that tone. "Tom, if by some miracle this didn't sink and got us out to where the fish are and we caught any, they'd have to swim back beside the boat because no self-respecting fish would want to cruise on this—alive or dead."

Tom gave him a pitying glance. "You medical types are too sophisticated for your own good. This could be a good boat."

Jave humored him. "It probably was when the Vikings used it to raid the English coast, but we need…"

Tom patted the hull. The gesture had a more proprietary air than the previous stroke. Jave began to get nervous. "We need something to replace the *River Lady*. I think with a little love and effort, this could do it."

The *River Lady*. Jave thought longingly of the fifty-five-foot fiberglass motor boat he and Tom had bought together before he was married and when Tom had just been promoted to battalion chief. It had been a fisherman's dream. They'd spent all their spare time on it, then Jave had gotten married, and for him that time had been reduced to several weekends a year and one week-long trip every summer.

Tom had tended it like a doting parent, and almost lived on it from June to October. Then Bonnie had left and Jave had needed money for a divorce settlement. And Tom had finally gotten out of the hospital and was anxious to settle growing debts. So they'd sold the *River Lady*.

"Tom," Jave said reasonably, "that was a sleek..."

Tom walked up the ramp and stepped aboard. Jave knew he'd lost him.

The galley was small and ancient but efficient. The two staterooms were minuscule but neat. So was the head.

A gruff voice interrupted their perusal. "Interested in the *Mud Hen*, are you?"

"The *Mud Hen*," Jave repeated flatly. He turned to his brother. "It's called the *Mud Hen*, Tom. Do we really want to own something called the *Mud Hen*?"

A small man, who looked almost as old as the boat, appeared in the doorway of the tiny room into which the men were crowded, heads tucked into their shoulders as protection against the low ceiling.

He offered a hand to Tom, then to Jave. "Captain Wolfe," he said. He wore a baseball cap emblazoned with the insignia of the USS *Kearsarge*. His eyes were sea blue, his skin as leathery as his name would suggest. "Been on the sea for sixty years."

Tom waved the newspaper clipping at him. "Pardon me," he said politely, "but the ad says—"

Wolfe laughed heartily. He had a gold tooth. "That was the *Stormwind*. Sold her yesterday to a lawyer from Portland. This is only..." He named a price that was half that listed in the clipping. Jave thought it could have been cut in half again. "Wasn't gonna sell her, but the missus is in a nursing home and...well...it costs."

Tom turned to Jave. And Jave saw something in his eyes that hadn't been there since he'd gotten out of the hospital. It was enthusiasm.

A love deeper than he even understood won out over financial good sense. And then there was the thought of the captain's lady in a convalescent home.

He smiled at Captain Wolfe. "Would you mind if we look around a few more minutes?"

Wolfe shook his head. "Help yourselves. Price includes the paint job and the repairs already underway. I'll be at the Scupper, tossing down a cold one."

The moment he disappeared, Tom sat down on the bunk—and sank in as though it were a beanbag chair. Jave leaned a shoulder against the doorway and watched his brother laugh. It brought a catch to his throat that he coughed away.

"This is nuts," he said, intending to put on a good show of resistance.

Tom patted the mattress on the bunk that was now even with his underarms. He looked like a man in an inner tube. "I think it's great. Sleekness isn't everything, is it? I mean, I could redecorate this and make it very comfortable." He looked around him with sincere interest. "Think about all the fishing trips this thing has seen, think about the men who've lived on her, and the—"

"Okay," Jave said.

Tom stopped in surprise. "'Scuse me?"

"Okay," Jave repeated. "I'm in. On one condition. Two, actually."

Tom's gaze narrowed and he pushed himself out of the bunk. They moved into the galley, then out onto the deck. The weather had turned, and summer seemed finally to have made its appearance.

The homes of Heron Point were scattered over a hillside that sloped down to the river. In the late-afternoon sunlight, windows gleamed and tall evergreens stood out against the bright blue sky.

Jave and Tom carefully skirted the hole in the deck and leaned elbows on the rail to look away from town and out at the blue river that separated them from Washington State.

"Why do there have to be conditions?" Tom wanted to know.

"To get Mom off my back," Jave admitted.

Tom groaned and put a hand to his face. "Let me guess. I have to start going out."

Jave gave him a congratulatory pat on the back. "Good so far."

"And...clean the garage?"

"No."

"Put up her new shower curtains?"

"Nope."

"Install the Casablanca fan in her bedroom?"

Jave shook his head and turned to look him in the eye. "No. You have to reschedule your appointment with the therapist. And you have to promise not to miss any more."

"I was working," Tom said with an indignation that wasn't entirely honest. Jave recognized it immediately. "You were with me. We were supposed to be done by—"

"I know, but *you* were supposed to make another appointment and you didn't. So do it."

Tom pushed up from the railing and turned his back to lean a hip on it. "I'm tired of hearing myself blame myself, and hearing *him* tell me to consider why I want to cause myself that pain."

"Why do you?" Jave asked.

"Because I left Davey!" Tom screamed at him. It was a loud roar that seemed to come out of nowhere. Tom had been the personification of calm since he'd come out of the hospital. But Jave thought he understood. The rage was finally working its way through the pain. That seemed like a good sign. At least he hoped it was. "I..." Tom made a strangled sound that he had to swallow before he could go on. "I left him."

Jave, still facing the hillside, backed up a pace to be able to look into Tom's eyes. They were miserable. They made him miserable. "You thought you heard a woman cry out, and you went to look for her. And the floor gave way on Davey. I know you'd been friends forever. I know he once dug you out from under a wall and saved your life, but that doesn't make you responsible for *this*. Who in the hell do you think would ever blame you for that?"

Tom drew a deep, ragged breath. "I'm sure the Porters

do. If I hadn't told him to stay there, it wouldn't have happened. Or if I'd sent him instead, he might—''

"Tom, you can second-guess every move you made, but it'll never make you responsible for Davey's death. And his parents don't blame you. They've asked you to go see them several times. I think you should. It might give you some peace."

Tom turned away from him to frown at the hillside. "I don't want peace."

Jave decided it was time to let that go for the moment. "Well, I do," he said briskly. "So you agree to reschedule your appointment, and you get a date within the next two weeks, or you can buy this rust bucket on your own."

Tom turned back, his expression still tense. It was now also mildly aggressive. "Maybe I *should* buy it alone," he said.

Jave held his glare. "Maybe you should."

The tension hung between them for a moment; then Tom relaxed and pushed away from the rail. He placed an arm around Jave's shoulders and led him toward the ladder. "You own both fishing poles," he said with a feigned whine.

Jave nodded. "Wise of you to remember that."

TOM AND JAVE FACED each other at a small table in a quiet corner of The Scupper Tavern. Between them on the table was the *Mud Hen*'s registration slip and maintenance record.

Tom toasted Jave with his tankard of dark ale. "Thanks. To bringing home the fish."

Jave raised his Guinness. "Just make certain we're well insured."

They drank quietly for a few moments as the waterfront establishment's clientele began to thin out. With dinnertime approaching, the rowdy after-work din began to dissipate, and the bartender busied himself drying glasses and hanging them up on the overhead rack.

"Okay," Tom said, pushing his ale aside and folding his arms on the table. "I'm going to do one for *you.*"

Jave smiled thinly. "Thanks. The *Mud Hen*'s enough to last a lifetime."

Tom pulled the Guinness out of his hand and put it aside. "Will you shut up about that? It's a great boat. Now listen to me."

Jave turned in his chair to lean his back against the wall and took a peanut out of the bowl holding down the *Mud Hen*'s papers. "All right. What?"

Tom grew suddenly serious. But it wasn't the troubled seriousness of earlier. He seemed to be more remote from this particular concern. Jave could only conclude that it was because they were about to discuss one of his, Jave's, problems.

"I've done two jobs for Nancy Malone in the past three weeks," Tom said. Jave's interest was instantly sparked. "A couple of weeks ago I replaced her ceiling tiles." Jave nodded. "Last Wednesday, I replaced a broken window in her bedroom."

"Yeah?"

"Yeah." Tom paused significantly. "It's pink."

Jave raised an eyebrow. "The window?"

"The bedroom!" Tom huffed impatiently. "Will you pay attention? Her bedroom is pink. And you know what's in her closet?"

"What?"

"*Her* clothes."

Jave tried desperately to put the facts together. "Her bedroom is pink," he repeated flatly. "And *her* clothes are in *her* closet. Well, call a cop. She sounds like a threat to national security to me." At Tom's groan, he demanded, "What? What am I missing?"

Tom dropped his forehead onto his folded arms. After a moment, he raised his head again and spoke slowly. "To think that you're entrusted with people's lives. How many men do you know who would be willing to sleep in a pink bedroom? Would you?''

"No,'' Jave replied, but then he even hated the green one.

"Neither would I,'' Tom said. "And I mean it's serious pink.''

"It was probably that color when she moved in.''

"It wasn't. She did it herself. She told me. And there are no men's clothes in the closet. Zip. *Nada.*"

Jave considered what that could mean. "Well...her husband's away for three months....''

"I know, but would he take every old tennis shoe he owns? Every tie? Every belt? Every—''

"They just moved in. I mean, a lot of that stuff could still be packed.''

Tom rolled his eyes. "All right. Consider this. There is not one family picture on the walls. Nothing. Do you figure she'd wave goodbye to a husband who's going to be gone for three months and not prop up one photo of him on the bedside table? Or on that table she uses for a desk? Wouldn't she even stick one to the refrigerator with a magnet?''

Jave felt a certain vindication of his initial instincts in the matter of Nancy R. Malone. Of course, his brother's suspicions didn't prove anything, but they posed some interesting questions.

Tom watched his carefully controlled expression. "I'm telling you I don't think she's married, Jave,'' he said finally. "And don't give me that stoic look like it doesn't matter to you.''

Jave picked up his Guinness and took a long pull. "I suspected she wasn't married when I did her ultrasound.''

Tom frowned. "Then why do you suppose she's pretending? The world's full of single mothers today.''

Jave explained about the hospital's grand opening and Amy Brown's extravaganza.

"Amy Brown?'' Tom asked.

"PR coordinator. It's a new post with the new administration. She's the administrator's niece. Nice girl, but disgustingly cheerful and with ideas more appropriate to Long Island than Heron Point. I think she's kind of an ugly duckling in a family of swans, trying hard to make good."

Tom grinned. "You probably understand her so well because you relate to her situation—being the Nicholas ugly duckling and all."

Jave rolled his eyes. "Tommy, I don't know how to tell you this, but Mom's been lying to you all these years. You're not the cute one, I am."

Tom sighed with great drama. "How our standards have fallen. So, you mean you think Nancy's doing this for the gifts?"

Jave had given it some thought. "Is that so selfish? If she is single, she doesn't seem to have all that much, and setting up a nursery is a pretty expensive proposition, particularly when there are no friends around for those showers and things women give each other to help prepare. I imagine the prospect of having all that handed to her was very appealing."

Tom drank his ale and leaned back in his chair. "And the hospital wouldn't want to use her for the publicity if they knew she was single?"

Jave shrugged. "The way Amy explained it, the hospital foundation preferred that she find a candidate who fits the conservative American image."

"That of having a husband."

"You got it."

"Hmm. But what made this Amy think she *was* married? Is it on her hospital records?"

Jave inclined his head in perplexity. That was a detail he'd forgotten. "Apparently the records transferred from New York said she *had* a husband." He remembered suddenly her reply to his question about why she'd come to Oregon. "It was a long way from New York," she'd replied. "Maybe," he speculated, "something's changed in the meantime."

"You going to check it out?" Tom asked. "I got the impression you were...interested."

Jave stared into the corner, his gaze unfocused. She'd haunted his thoughts from the moment he first saw her. And though he'd resisted all emotional tugs in her direction for the past three weeks, telling himself he didn't need the confusion or the aggravation she presented hadn't diminished them. What he felt was something that required action. Where it would lead, he hadn't the vaguest notion. All he knew was that he had to find out.

And he remembered her soft dark eyes looking into his—looking for something she seemed to want desperately. He had the damnedest feeling that whatever it was, he had it somewhere.

He brought himself back to Tom's question. "You doing another job for her some time soon?"

Tom nodded. "Yeah. Next...Friday, I think. I'll check the calendar at home to be sure. I'm cleaning out the gutters and replacing the one on the north side that's hanging."

Jave nodded, his eyes taking on a devious gleam. "That's a two-man job, isn't it?"

"No. I can usually— Oh." Jave's tactic suddenly dawned on him and he halted his denial. "Well, sure. Your day off. You can do the work, and I'll sit in her kitchen and eat dessert. She claims she can't cook, but she loves to bake. Last time, she sent cream horns home for Mom and me."

Jave heaved a long-suffering sigh. "Great. I save the chair and you get the cream horns."

Tom clapped his shoulder. "Builds character."

"I'LL GET STARTED," Tom said quietly as Jave helped him position the ladder. He gave him a conspiratorial grin. "You can tell her we're here."

"Want me to get the gutter out of the truck for you first?" Jave asked.

Tom shook his head. "I don't need it yet. Hey."

Jave had turned away to head for the porch steps and turned back.

"If you get a cream horn," Tom said, "I want my half."

"Oh, right. At what you're paying me an hour, the cream horn's mine."

Jave loped up the steps and knocked on the front door. There was no answer. Tom had parked behind the blue pickup, so he knew she had to be home. And he could hear the sound of the television beyond the door.

Suddenly alarmed that something might have happened, he tried the doorknob. It turned, and he pushed the door open. He peered around it and saw her on a blanket on the floor in front of the television. She lay very still in leggings and a baggy sweater. His heart gave an uncomfortable lurch.

"Nancy?" he called quietly. She did not respond.

From the television came instructions given in a gentle voice by a middle-aged woman in nurse's whites. Jave recognized the routine demonstrated by a young couple as a relaxation exercise in the Lamaze program.

He knelt down beside her and noticed with relief the gentle rise and fall of her breasts. She lay on her side, her head on a pillow, a pillow also between her knees.

Jave smiled as he listened to the instructions from the film she'd apparently borrowed from the hospital. It encouraged complete relaxation. It seemed Nancy had mastered that. She was asleep.

Nancy heard voices, but the images she saw didn't necessarily relate to the words being spoken.

"Take a moment to scan your body," the gentle voice said, "for a part that remains tense."

But the artfully misty pictures she saw were of herself in something long and white and silky in the arms of a man in a white uniform. He stroked her as the soothing voice suggested, but his movements were long and erotic and she moved even more closely into his arms.

He whispered her name. She twined her arm around his neck and pulled him closer.

Jave had no idea what was happening. He knew only that it jangled his nerves enough to scramble thought.

Eyes still closed, dark lashes fanned against cheeks slightly pink with sleep, Nancy curled an arm around the one he'd braced across her to assure himself that she was breathing. With it, she pulled herself up higher and curled her other arm around his neck. She smelled of that floral shampoo and baby powder.

He might have handled that with aplomb, but then she touched her parted lips to his cheek and ran them in a series of little kisses from his ear to the corner of his eye.

He held tightly to his fraying self-control. Did she truly have a husband? Did she think he was him home from sea?

Then she did the one thing that could have snapped his control. She whispered his name.

Nancy felt the firm, smooth cheek under her lips, the strong arms holding her securely, and leaned back to look into his eyes. They were shadowy with the green and gold of all that was precious in nature—all that was becoming precious to her. "Jave!" she whispered.

When she moved her lips to his, Jave was lost. He bent a knee to brace her as he held her firmly in the crook of his arm and helped her have her way with him. Her lips nipped at his then kissed him, angled as she inclined her head and nibbled gently. Then he felt the tip of her tongue dip into his mouth and met it with his own.

They sparred, explored, withdrew, then tangled again to finally draw apart and lean forehead to forehead, gasping for breath.

Nancy knew instantly that something was wrong. It wasn't that it felt wrong—it felt wonderful. But it was a flaw in the pattern she'd grown used to. She felt warm, secure, cosseted. Something was out of tune.

Then she became aware of sinewy arms around her, of a strong shoulder under her head, of flesh against the flesh of her cheek—smooth, suedelike male flesh!

She shoved Jave away with such force that he would have

fallen backward if he hadn't been so determined to keep a firm grip on her.

"What are you doing?!" she demanded as she struggled awkwardly to get to her knees. He tried to help her and she shook him off. Her cheeks were crimson now, her eyes blazing. "Don't touch me!"

Jave's instincts told him her response wasn't from the indignation she pretended, but from anger at herself for being caught in such a vulnerable position.

"Easy, Mrs. Malone," Jave said, on his knees a mere foot from her. "It was all your fault."

"*My* fault!" she disputed. "I was asleep. You took advantage—"

"I did no such thing," he denied. "You didn't respond to my knock. I looked in to check and found you on the floor—not moving. I came over, you...must have been dreaming...and the next thing I knew..." He grinned unabashedly. "You kissed me."

"I—did—not!" she insisted in breathy denial.

"I'm afraid you did."

YOU DID, MOM. I heard you. And I shared the dream. It was him. He's got you.

NANCY COULD FEEL the heat in her cheeks. She remembered the dream very clearly, the absolutely vivid reality of it. And little wonder. She'd apparently been living it at the same time. And in her dream she'd been very much the instigator.

She tried desperately to explain herself. "I...I haven't been sleeping well," she said, trying to balance her awkward weight as she pushed herself up. "I must have mistaken you for...for Jerry."

Jave stood lightly and supported her unsteady rise to her feet. The grin vanished and his eyes were deadly serious. "You called me Jave," he said.

She had no idea how to explain that she'd been dreaming

of him. Feeling completely off balance, and needing desperately to regain precious ground lost in her "married woman" fiction, Nancy did the only thing she could think of—she made it clear she considered this all his fault.

"You invaded my home!" she accused. "What are you doing here anyway?"

"It's my day off," he replied calmly. "I came to help Tom clean the gutters and put up the new one."

So he did have a good reason. Sort of. She folded her arms over the mound of her stomach and tried to look imperious. She could feel that her hair was atumble and her cheeks warm. "The gutters," she said coolly, "are located *outside.*"

Neither her tone nor her manner seemed to impress him. He continued to look amused and somehow pleased. "Tom asked me to tell you we were here."

"Very well," she said. "Thank you. I'll have coffee ready when the two of you take a break."

Jave's eyes swept the living room as he walked to the door. Tom was right, he noted. Not one photograph.

He had an opportunity to check the kitchen an hour and a half later when she invited them inside for coffee. She made a point of chatting cheerfully to Tom and excluding Jave from the conversation. So he let his gaze wander around the room. No pictures. Not a single sign that a man lived here.

The wall of the mudroom was visible from where he sat, and he could see a small pair of grubby sneakers, several non-gender-specific gardening tools and a very large sack of cat food.

No men's sneakers, no baseball cap, no black umbrella.

He caught a glimpse of the pink bedroom when Tom suggested he change a weak light bulb in the hallway before they left. No photos there, either. The closet door was slightly ajar, but the interior remained shadowy, its contents indistinguishable.

He thought, though, that he'd seen enough to give credence to Tom's theory. No man lived here.

Tom was packing up the truck when Jave carried the step stool back into the kitchen, then headed for the front door. He found Nancy on the blanket again, doing the exercises according to the video's instructions. She continued, unaware that he watched.

He approached her and squatted down just behind her. "Excuse me," he said. "But you're not doing that quite right."

Nancy jumped in surprise, then sat up in annoyance. She clearly hadn't forgiven him for that kiss, which pleased him inordinately. "How do you know?" she asked. "Don't tell me radiology also teaches Lamaze classes."

He put a hand to her shoulder and pushed her gently back to the pillow again, repositioning her so that she lay on her side, her knees tucked up so that she was almost in a sitting position.

"Of course not." He touched the base of her spine. She felt heat fill her face and was grateful she was turned away from him. "You're not relaxing completely," he cautioned, "and it's essential to the method. I went through the classes with my ex-wife before Pete was born. Classes are held in a hospitality room at the hospital, you know. I think that would be easier for you than trying to figure it out from a video."

"Participation in classes," she said, "requires a partner. And mine is somewhere down the coast."

"The important thing here," he said, running a fingertip gently from the base of her neck to her waist, "is to learn to relax completely to ease the pain."

Nancy felt that deceptively innocent fingertip touch every vertebra in her spinal column. Feeling rayed in every direction and she fidgeted, thinking it was no wonder it was called the "nervous" system.

"A friend can serve as your coach. Or stand in for your

husband so that you at least can get the benefit of the classes."

He spoke casually—too casually, Nancy thought. He knew she didn't have any friends. He was the one who'd brought her home from the hospital, seen that her roof was repaired, saved her desk chair. She didn't know what to make of his suggestion. Actually, she thought she did, but it seemed safer to deny it to herself.

She pushed herself to a sitting position and then had to prop herself there with a hand to the floor. "Thank you, Jave. I'll see about it."

He got to his feet and offered her both his hands. She could struggle up on her own; she did it often. But at almost seven months along, it wouldn't be pretty. And there was something about the simple, solid pleasure of his hand wrapping around hers that she couldn't deny herself.

She placed her fingers in his and felt his tighten around hers as he brought her effortlessly up. The protrusion of her stomach bumped lightly against the waist of his jeans as he steadied her. The baby kicked. She blushed. He grinned.

"Jave Nicholas," she said with a scolding frown. She tried to imbue her voice with displeasure, but its high breathlessness negated the effort. It sounded husky and flustered. His watchfulness had unsettled her from the moment she'd answered Amy's questions about a husband and discovered him standing in the doorway.

But there was something about him today that betrayed more than simple suspicion. He seemed to think he knew something. And he was enjoying taunting her with the possibility.

She had to prove him wrong. Even though he was right.

"Your behavior," she said with a tilt of her chin and what she hoped was frosty, matronly displeasure, "is inappropriate."

The arm he'd cupped around her to steady her remained in place. "You mean your husband would disapprove?" he asked.

"Of course he would," she replied, pushing at his chest. "But what's more important to your physical health at the moment is that *I* disapprove. Now remove your arm."

He smiled amiably. "Can't do that."

She continued to brace his chest away from her with the flat of her hand. "And why is that?"

"Well, it's attached to my body," he replied with bland innocence. "You know, tendons, muscles, messy stuff. I could ampu—"

She closed her eyes, drew a breath for patience, then opened them again. "I mean, remove your arm from around *me*."

He looked into her glare, his suddenly gentle, amusing mood filtering through her determined solitude, reaching inside her. She stiffened, resisting its effect.

"You know," he said quietly, "I'm beginning to think you're attached to me, too, in a very similar way. No muscles or tendons, of course, but stuff that seems to be just as hard to sever. I think I'm going to stop trying."

Excitement and panic grappled with each other in Nancy's chest. Even the baby must have felt the conflict. Nancy felt a kick to her side.

Then she thought desperately of her five-piece Thomasville nursery set, her chocolate, her movies, her clothes...the hospital's reaction should anyone there ever suspect what Jave suspected.

I DON'T KNOW, MOM. Do we really need furniture and chocolate if we could have him instead?

SHE HAD TO TURN the suspicion aside firmly once and for all. "If you don't unhand me this minute," she said, thinking absently that she sounded remarkably like Bette Davis, "I'll call my husband tonight, then I'll call the hospital administrator and report your conduct."

The ruse might have been convincing, Jave thought, if

she'd been drawing away from him instead of leaning into the arm she claimed to find so offensive. If the hand at his chest had been pushing him away instead of clutching at his shirt.

"Where is your husband?" Jave asked conversationally.

Her jaw firmed and her eyes flashed. "I told you. He's off the California coast."

"Where?"

"Southern California."

"Long Beach?"

Nancy knew he was trying to lay some kind of trap for her and she found herself less mentally nimble than she wished.

"I'm not sure now," she said, careful to meet his eyes and keep her own level. "He hasn't called me in a few days. They must be some distance from port."

"Well, what if you go into labor? Certainly there's some procedure to follow to get in touch with him."

Before she could dredge up a convincing lie, Tom appeared in the doorway. "All done, Nancy. Ready, Jave?"

Nancy pulled away from Jave and raised a finger at Tom, indicating that he should wait. "I'll send some bread pudding home for you and Aggie."

Tom mouthed a ha-ha in Jave's direction when Nancy disappeared into the kitchen. She returned with two square plastic containers. She handed one to Tom and the other to Jave.

"These are for your boys," she said, a dark glance making it clear she'd included none for him.

He suddenly remembered a last minute request from Pete when he'd left that morning. "The boys wondered if you'd give me the recipe for the Russian tea. They're addicted and we've run out."

She nodded. "Of course. I'll send it to you so you don't have to wait for me to copy it down." She smiled at Tom. "Thank you. That's all the budget will allow for a while, but when that changes, I'll call you about replacing the kitchen floor covering."

"Great. Thanks for the bread pudding."

"Sure. Say hi to your mom."

Jave let the door partially close as Tom headed across the grass toward his truck. Then he turned to face Nancy.

Nancy didn't like the look in his eye. Her threats about her husband and a call to the hospital administration didn't seem to have affected it. He still appeared indulgently superior.

"Is there anything you'd like to tell me, Nancy?" he asked gently. "Last chance."

She smiled sweetly. "Why, yes. Get out."

He gave her a tolerantly scolding look. "I meant anything about yourself. Possibly something that would save us undue embarrassment later."

"There *is* something you should know about me," she said, reaching around him to pull the door wide. She placed a hand on his chest and began to push him backward. Considering her condition, he chose not to resist. "I've read everything Stephen King ever wrote, even the *Bachman Books*. My mother is neurotic, my great grandfather spent time in Taunton—"

"Taunton?"

"It's a state hospital in Massachusetts." They had reached the porch steps and she clutched the front of his shirt in a fist. "And centuries ago, I had an uncle who was an executioner in the Tower of London." She stood on tiptoe until they were nose-to-nose. "In a nutshell, Nicholas, it isn't safe to mess with me. Now, I've been nice about this because you saved my chair and you have a wonderful family. But don't push it. I do not want to see you again, but if our paths should cross, don't you ever touch me again, or when my husband returns, he will make a puree of your arms and legs—and anything else that offends me." She released his shirt and stepped back. "Now, goodbye!"

Jave smiled to himself all the way to the truck. By the time he climbed inside, he was laughing.

Tom, who'd watched the scene from behind the wheel, looked worried. "What in the hell was that all about? It looked as though she was chewing you out royally."

Jave buckled his seat belt, still laughing. "She did."

"What brought that on?"

"She kissed me."

"What?"

"It's a long story."

"I want to hear every word. Did you ask her about her husband?"

"She insists she has one," Jave said, rolling down his window and taking a deep draft of warm, sunny afternoon. "And told me never to darken her door again."

Tom frowned. "So that's it? It's over?"

Jave leaned an elbow on the open window and looked at his brother with a broad grin. "Hell, no, Thomas. It's just beginning."

CHAPTER SEVEN

THE DAY AFTER the...episode with Jave—she wouldn't call it a kiss because she'd been asleep when it had begun and infuriated when it was over, and that didn't seem to fit within the parameters of what a kiss should be—Nancy received a call from Amy, another pair of footlets from April and a basket of goodies from her mother.

"I just thought you'd like to know," Amy said, enthusiastically breathless, "that Atkins Auto has donated a top-of-the-line infant seat to our program, and Heron Point Fitness is giving you three months' free use of the facility after the baby's born. Isn't that great?"

Nancy tried to project several months ahead to a time when she would be enthusiastic about exercise. She couldn't quite do it. She was now beginning to feel seriously ungainly and unattractive, and was happy to simply walk slowly up and down the beach, where she wouldn't be seen.

"How nice," she replied, forcing interest into her voice. It was easier when she thought about the infant seat. "How's the work coming on the rooms?"

"Good. The curtains are lost somewhere between here and the warehouse in Buffalo, but we can't put them up for another month and I have faith the freight company will find them by then. How are you feeling?"

"Wonderful," she said. Generally it was true. She attributed a fairly new lethargy to...well, she wasn't sure what, but she was sure she could talk herself out of it as soon as she had the energy.

"Is your husband excited about being married to the Riverview Hospital Model Mommy, so to speak?"

"Oh...he's delighted." Nancy worked harder on the enthusiasm now. She could remember clearly Jave's skeptical face when he'd held her to him the day before and wondered if he'd shared any of his doubts with Amy. It didn't sound as though he had.

"Do you think we'll be able to get a picture of him before he comes home for the birth?"

Nancy winced. "I doubt he'll be able to put in an appearance before the *Courageous* comes back in the middle of September."

"Do you have a snapshot we can use?"

Nancy's heart lurched. She thought fast. "I'll try to find it, Amy, but you know, some of our stuff is in storage, and a lot of things I haven't unpacked yet, and I'm not supposed to move anything too heavy...."

"Of course," Amy said quickly. "Don't do anything to endanger yourself, for heaven's sake. We'll manage just featuring you and *talking* about him."

"That...would probably be best."

The footlets from April had arrived in a manila envelope with a note shaped like a teddy bear. "Hi, Nancy!" it said. "Housekeeping found these under your bed after you left, so I took them home and washed them, thinking you'd like to have an extra pair. Don't forget that I'm a *great* babysitter. Love, April. P.S. If your mom and Willy Brock ever come to visit, please find an excuse to invite me over."

Nancy smiled as she folded the note away and studied the enormous basket from her mother. It was typically overdone—a huge, ornate affair decorated with patterned tissue paper within embossed cellophane with a giant pink bow tied to the handle.

Contained inside was every kind of gourmet treat to nibble on—from smoked oysters to sugar wafers. Attached was a card. "Since you won't let me come and 'mother' you, I'm sending this in my place. Love, Mom."

Nancy felt guilt and aggravation in equal measure, and wished she was enough her own woman that neither would affect her. She dug around in the basket until she found a very large gold-foil-wrapped chocolate truffle. She stood in the middle of the living room, staring at the chair Jave had rescued for her, and ate the sweet. Then she found another one and ate it, too.

ALL RIGHT. *More?*

SHE WAS FEELING PURSUED. Even cornered. How had this happened to her? she wondered. She'd moved thirty-three hundred miles across the country to start over on her own, and somehow, a brief two months into it, she was hearing from her mother more than she had in years, she had acquired an unusual collection of nice but nosy friends, and she'd backed into a place in the spotlight that promised great things for her baby, but might still prove to be her undoing.

And then there was Jave. She didn't know what to do about him except hope that he went away. And that was hardly likely. He was a definite fly in the ointment of her role as the hospital's model mommy. That was bad. But it got even worse.

Nancy had to dig out a package of genuine Scottish shortbread cookies and make a cup of tea before she could even let herself consider this part.

THAT WASN'T BAD, but what happened to the chocolate?

SHE THOUGHT ABOUT Jave Nicholas all the time. He seemed to be everything she'd thought she was getting when she'd married Jerry. Despite a tendency to unsettle her, he was kind and thoughtful, and a man who was apparently willing to go the extra mile for someone else in need. And he made her smile, though she usually didn't give him the satisfaction of doing it in front of him.

She ran a hand over her desk chair and thought about the abuse it had taken in the back of her truck exposed to the rain. Yet he'd practically restored it.

He was kind to his mother, helped his brother, and his children seemed to love him.

But those weren't the qualities that had kept her awake last night and occupied her mind this morning.

She remembered in minute detail what it had been like to awaken in his arms and feel his lips on hers. In fact, with very little effort, she could reconstruct the moment with all its confusion and wonder and sense of deliciously dangerous security.

She understood that thought for the paradox it was. She didn't know how danger could make her feel secure, but it did. His warm, mobile lips on hers had made her feel open and vulnerable, yet the tender competence with which he used them, the gentle strength of the arms that held her, told her with absolute certainty that she could entrust herself to him and be safe—physically, if not emotionally.

And that was at the heart of her anxieties today. She'd come to Oregon to be alone with her baby. To trust herself to bring this baby to life and good health without having to depend on anyone. To raise it alone without the interference or the support everyone else seemed to crave.

She didn't want to be tempted to trust. It never worked out for her.

Well, it was time to do something about it. As a step toward the life she envisioned alone with her baby, she picked up the stack of neatly printed pages on her desk and inspected them one more time. They contained a complete synopsis of her novel, the first three chapters and a cover letter to a Los Angeles agent whose name she'd found in the Northwest Mystery Writers' newsletter at the library.

Confident that this was her best work, that her letter was intelligent and coherent and hopefully witty enough to stand out in the glut of mail the agent probably received, Nancy placed everything in the envelope she'd addressed, placed her palm on it and said a small prayer, then went out to the truck to drive to the post office.

She stopped in her tracks halfway across the yard. Shaman sat on the hood of her truck, dozing lazily in the sunlight. She'd never seen him in the front of the house before; he'd always stayed on the slope in the back. Did this mean he was beginning to feel at home? He was the only one with whom she'd consider sharing her environment besides the baby.

"Shaman?" she called softly, taking small, slow steps.

He sprang tensely to his feet, eyes wide and alarmed.

"Shaman," she chided gently. "Come on. Hasn't this gone on long enough? I've been feeding you for weeks now. Isn't it time...?"

Apparently he didn't think so. He leaped to the grass in a swift and graceful arch and disappeared around the back of the house.

Nancy sighed and climbed into the truck, shaking her head over the sandy pawprints on her hood.

"CAN I HAVE ANOTHER Frosty?" Eddy asked.

Jave and Eddy sat side by side on the Heron Point Park bleachers, watching the Turner Plumbing Turtles take the field against the Roundhouse Restaurant Rattlers. Jave frowned into the late-afternoon sun, trying to spot number 23 as the tiny athletes ran out to distribute themselves in the fragrant, manicured grass.

The father who coached the team, a saint in Jave's estimation, placed them all carefully, talking and laughing as he worked his way around the bases, then pep-talked the pitcher and the catcher.

"No," Jave replied. "You've already had two and the game hasn't even started yet."

"There he is." Eddy pointed to his brother, who appeared to be all ball glove and hat.

"Right field," Jave said.

"Yeah," Eddy said with a snicker. "Where nothing ever happens."

Jave remembered that he'd once reacted to Tom with the same older-brother superiority, so he admonished gently, "You know, he could really use your support in this, Ed. You've been on a winning team three years running. He admires you. I think he'd like to know you come to cheer him on and not to criticize him."

"He's a dweeb, Dad," Eddy said with no particular condemnation, but simply as though it were a fact. "And look at that. How can you cheer for someone who isn't even thinking about the game?"

Jave choked back a laugh at the sight of his youngest, twirling with arms outstretched like a whirling dervish. He seemed to be in his own little world, fielding the ball apparently the last thing on his mind.

Around the field, various itches were being scratched, shoes were being tied, imaginary foes being swung at with imaginary weapons.

Eddy shook his head with a veteran's concern. "I hope the other team's not any good."

At that the first of the Rattlers took the plate, shouldered his bat, then adjusted what appeared to be a very aggressive pair of underwear.

Eddy collapsed in giggles against Jave, who struggled valiantly not to join him.

"THE OTHER GUYS WON," Pete said later, "because they had a better name. Rattlers are tougher than Turtles."

The boys sat at the kitchen table in their pajamas while Jave made the last two servings of Russian tea.

"You better not let Michelangelo and Leonardo hear you say that," Eddy said. "They won because they have more nine-year-olds. You guys are shrimpy."

Pete seemed too depressed to argue. Jave remembered that Eddy had taken his first loss in much the same way. Life was full of hard lessons.

"I'm gonna watch 'The X-Files,'" Eddy said. He took his tea and reached up to kiss Jave good-night.

Jave leaned down to hug him and caught a whiff of the tea the boys had come to like so much. "Can I have a sip of that?" he asked.

"Sure." Eddy offered up the mug. "It's good stuff."

Jave sipped, found it flavorful if a little sweet, and handed back the cup. "I asked Nancy for the recipe. She promised to send it."

"Oh, yeah." Eddy delved into his pocket and produced a crumpled envelope. "We met her at the post office today, and she gave me this instead of mailing it." He handed it to Jave, picked up the package of cookies they'd been sharing, tucked it under his arm, and headed for the stairs. "Night," he said.

Jave grabbed the back of the cookie package and pulled it neatly away. "Good night," he replied.

Eddy gave him a good-natured grin and went on.

Jave turned his attention to Pete, who leaned his chin on one hand and hooked the index finger of the other in the handle of his cup. He looked for all the world like a Wall Street financier faced with a repeat of Black Friday.

"It's bad to lose," Pete said. "Mr. Walker says it doesn't matter, but all the guys say it's bad."

"It's only bad to lose," Jave corrected, sitting in the ladder-back chair beside him, "if you lost because you didn't try. But that's not what happened tonight. You guys tried really hard. But this summer is the first time you've all played together. It takes time to become a team—sometimes a couple of seasons. Everybody knows that."

Pete sighed deeply and loudly. "That ball came right to me and I couldn't catch it, so that other big kid made a point. I didn't do very good."

"That was a pretty big kid," Jave said. "The ball was coming hard. You'll learn to be ready, to stand so that you're loose when you catch a ball and ready to throw it back."

Pete sipped his tea and rubbed his bare feet together. Jave was reminded of a cricket—one in a brightly striped bathrobe.

"Maybe I don't want to play anymore."

Jave hated working out win-and-lose issues with the boys. He had a laid-back attitude about the whole business himself, but though he didn't care if they won or lost, he wanted to raise children who were willing to compete.

"Then you won't lose anymore, but you sure won't win, either."

There was a moment's heavy silence, then Pete took a big sip of tea and changed the subject. "I know what's going to happen when Nancy has her baby."

Interested, Jave asked, "What?"

"If her truck doesn't start, she's going to call a taxi to take her to the hospital."

"She is?"

"Yup. That's what she said. But Grandma said she should call *us*."

Jave waved the envelope he held. "Did you talk about this when you saw her at the post office?"

Pete nodded. "This afternoon. Grandma was sending back her Publisher's Clearing House thing. She's going to buy me a motorcycle if she wins."

Doubting seriously that she *would* win, Jave felt confident in sharing his enthusiasm about the motorcycle. He propped the envelope up against the cat-shaped napkin holder in the middle of the table.

"Want a ride up to bed?" Jave asked. Before Bonnie left, he used to carry Pete up to bed on his shoulders every night. It had been a small but important ritual. But Pete had refused it since then.

Pete thought about it. "When the big kids play," he said gravely, "sometimes the guys who win get carried off the field."

Jave confirmed that with a nod.

Pete stood and carried his cup to the sink. "But nobody carries the losers."

A mild rebellion had been brewing in Jave most of the day. He'd been walking a careful line with many facets of his life. He'd been trying not to push Pete regarding his feelings about his mother; he'd been trying to let him unfold slowly and find his own feet in his adjustment.

And a similar situation had developed with Nancy. He'd found himself attracted to a woman who by all indications was pretending to have a husband, while still reacting to him, Jave, in a decidedly sexual way—and there seemed to be no pretending *there* at all. So he'd been acting like a man in a fog, afraid of losing himself with the wrong move.

Well, he was suddenly tired of it all.

He swept Pete off the floor and dangled him by his feet for a full ten seconds while the child first screamed, then giggled with unbridled hilarity. Then he turned him and swung him up onto his shoulders and walked upstairs with him.

"Anybody who tries is a winner," Jave said as they reached the landing and angled toward the top of the stairs. "And I love you. To me, you'll always be a winner."

Pete leaned over Jave's head as they ducked under the top of the door to his room. "Mom said I was too little to play baseball," he said.

Jave kept his surprise to himself. This was the first time Pete had brought up the subject of his mother.

"Well, that was last year," Jave observed, "when you *were* too little."

"I wish she could watch me play," he said wistfully. "I mean, if I could play better."

Jave tipped him onto the bed, then sat on the edge of it, looking down into the pensive brown eyes. "I'm sure she'd like to see you play. Only she's kind of far away right now."

"With that other guy."

"Yes."

Pete drew a deep breath and reached over to his bedside table for a Matchbox fire truck Tom had given him for his last birthday. He toyed with it while he thought.

"Do you think she'll have other kids?" he asked. "You know, like Nancy? Will she get...?"

"Pregnant?" Jave asked. Curiously, he could find no jealousy in the thought. What he'd had with her seemed to be well and truly gone. "She might. But that doesn't mean she would love you any less."

"But she isn't *with* me," he said with what seemed to Jave to be eminent reasonableness. He found it difficult to argue. So he leaned on what he was sure to be true, though he couldn't really reconcile it to her actions.

"But she still loves you."

Pete put the truck down and gave him that very direct, adult look that told him he wasn't making sense.

"It's a little like you and the ball," Jave said, bracing himself on an arm on the other side of Pete's body. "You want to hit it. In your mind, you know what to do. But it's just hard to make it all come together. So you just do the best you can."

"But she quit, didn't she? You said you only lose if you quit."

This was the true parent trap, Jave thought. Snared by your own rhetoric.

"Well, sort of. She quit living with us. But she didn't quit loving you."

Pete frowned over that logic, then gave a mighty yawn. Jave pulled the covers out from under him then drew them up and tucked him in.

"Next game," he promised, "you'll do a little better. And the next one, you'll be better yet."

Pete turned onto his side, his eyelids growing heavy.

"You think Mom'll do any better?" he asked.

Jave knew it wouldn't be fair to tell him what he wanted to hear. "I don't think so," he said.

Pete settled into his pillow without another word. Jave stayed until he knew he was asleep.

JAVE'S OFFICE DOOR OPENED and Nurse Beacham walked in. She handed him the department's copy of the *Heron Point Herald*. "I know you'll want to read the sports page before I cut out the recipe on the back. Make it snappy. I'm off in ten minutes."

He smiled at her. "Such a gracious offer, Beachie. Thank you."

"No time for graciousness, Doctor," she said with a theatrical tilt of her head. "I have to save lives and stamp out disease."

He nodded gravely. "You're absolutely right. I'll have this back to you in ten minutes."

"That's a good doctor."

Jave covered the files on his desk with the small daily newspaper. National and local news, sports, comics and classifieds were all covered in twelve pages. He subscribed to the newspaper at home, but his mother usually commandeered it, so he enjoyed perusing the department's copy before he went home.

And this evening there was a very interesting item in it. Very interesting indeed. News that made him fold up the paper, reread the item, then pick up the phone while a small, calculating smile played at his lips.

It had been two weeks since he'd seen Nancy and convinced himself Tom was right—she had no husband. Since then, he'd been biding his time, waiting for just the right moment. And this was it.

"MRS. MALONE?"

"Yes." Nancy didn't recognize the voice on the other end of the telephone, but it had a professional telephone-voice sound. She braced herself, certain she was dealing with an operator somewhere who was about to connect her with her mother.

"This is Serena Borders. Your Lamaze classes are scheduled for Monday, August 15, from 7:00 to 8:30. I was asked to remind you."

Nancy frowned at the receiver. "But...I haven't enrolled for Lamaze classes."

The voice sounded puzzled. "Are you Nancy R. Malone?"

"Yes, but I haven't—"

"Of Box 73, Heron Point Road?"

"Yes."

"Your fee's been paid, Mrs. Malone, and you and your coach are scheduled to start next Monday."

Then a niggle of suspicion began to form in Nancy's mind. She remembered the Lamaze tape she'd borrowed from the library and Jave's suggestion that she take the class in person instead.

"What is my coach's name?" Nancy asked.

"What is your...?" the voice began to repeat, as though unable to imagine why Nancy was asking *her*. Then there was the sound of papers rustling and a terse reply. Now the voice really sounded puzzled. "J. V. Nicholas."

"Thank you," Nancy said. "I'll get back to you about this."

Temper, confusion and genuine concern billowed inside Nancy while she changed out of the sweats in which she'd been writing in all day. She glanced at the clock and decided she had time to shower and change and still be on time to give Jave Nicholas a piece of her mind.

What's happening, Mom? It feels like we're gearing up for battle. Please calm down. You're pinching my backside again. Why are we rocking? Whoa. Tights? Gasp! What happened to our sweats? Where are we going? Can you send down some Dramamine?

CHAPTER EIGHT

JAVE WAS CONCENTRATING on his options for the evening as he walked out to the hospital's parking lot. Tom had taken the boys to Portland with him to pick up supplies and didn't expect to be home until late. His mother, free for the day, had gone to visit a friend on the Long Beach peninsula.

He could pick up dinner at the deli and rent a movie—something with sex and violence that he wouldn't want the boys to see, but that would remind him that somewhere deep inside he wasn't as civilized as his mother and his children thought he was.

He could go to the Y where there was usually a pickup basketball game in progress.

He could lie in the hammock in the backyard with a gin and tonic and remember the *River Lady*.

Each idea had something to recommend it, but it was another lady altogether whose plans changed his.

"You, James Victor Nicholas, can go to hell!" Nancy Malone delivered that suggestion quietly but with apparently heartfelt conviction. She was leaning against the driver's-side door of his truck in black tights and a crisp, long black-and-white top, her arms folded over her ample stomach.

She straightened and assumed a sort of battle stance, her arms at her sides, her fists clenched.

He'd never been quite so pleased with a reaction in his life.

"Nancy," he said, walking around her to open his door, toss in his jacket. The evening was breezy and fragrant, and he swore he could feel the life in it. "How nice of you to come to see me."

"I'm not here to *see* you," she corrected stiffly.

He grinned. "Then you'd better close your eyes, because I'm here."

She firmed her stance. "Don't play games with me, Nicholas."

The very words conjured up many fascinating mental images. His grin widened. "I guess we'll have to save those for a few months down the road. But we could still enjoy planning them."

She studied him a long moment, her eyes snapping and troubled, her cheeks pink, her nicely molded chin dimpled in consternation. He saw her struggle to remain calm. She folded her arms again.

"What are you doing?" she demanded.

He indicated the open door of his truck. "I'm going home. What are you doing?"

She closed her eyes impatiently. When she opened them again, she said with exaggerated quiet, "No. I mean what are you trying to do—to *me*."

He gave her an innocent look. He'd learned it from the masters of the craft—his sons.

"Well, I've done a few things *for* you, but I wasn't aware of having done anything *to* you."

Her mouth slanted to a cynical angle. "Really. And who enrolled me in a Lamaze class?"

"I did," he replied readily.

"And who enrolled himself as my coach?"

He was quick and ingenuous again with his answer. "I did. But I don't understand—"

"Why did you do that?"

"You weren't doing very well with trying to teach yourself at home. So, I thought—"

She jabbed a finger at his chest, patience apparently deserting her. "And what gave *you* the right to think on my behalf?"

Several nurses walked by on the way to their cars. They turned their heads at her raised voice. Recognizing Jave, they smiled and moved on.

"Would you like to discuss this in my truck?" he asked Nancy politely.

"No, I would not," she replied curtly. "Just answer my question."

"All right." He reached into the truck to roll down the window and hooked an arm over it. "Well, there were several things," he said amiably. "First, I knew you'd get more out of the class. I mean, let's face it. You tried to do it with the tape at home and first you fell asleep, and then you had the position wrong. I'm a doctor after all. I'd like to see you do this right."

"Right," she echoed dryly. "Hippocratic oath and all that."

"Yes. That, and I hate the thought of you squishing your baby and getting me called in in the middle of the night."

She shifted her weight, her eyes dark with disbelief. "You listed yourself as my coach."

"That's right."

"Why?"

He gestured broadly with his free hand. "Your husband's somewhere off the California coast, remember?"

She looked into his eyes for any betrayal of duplicity. She couldn't find it. He was good.

"How do you think he'd feel about my lying in such intimate positions with my radiologist?" she demanded candidly, hoping to shake his ingenuousness.

"Probably much the same as your radiologist feels," he said quietly, "about you lying about your husband."

THERE GOES the furniture and the teddy-bear lamp. Don't admit anything, Mom. Maybe we can still save the chocolate.

So there it was. The words were out, right there in the parking lot, between her battered old truck and his shiny new model. She stared at him openmouthed for a moment as control of the conversation, the whole situation, began to slip away from her. But she grabbed for it and held on.

"What are you implying?" she demanded defensively.

Several visitors walking by turned interestedly in their direction.

He looked back at her evenly. "Why don't we talk about this in the truck?" he said. Then he walked around to the passenger side to open it for her without giving her an opportunity to refuse.

Insistently maintaining her pose, she stood her ground.

"I can't step up that high," she resisted. "And there isn't anything to say that can't be said in..."

As she spoke, he reached under the tarp in the back of the truck and removed a plastic kitchen step stool. He placed it on the ground on the passenger side and waited wordlessly for her to walk around.

She did, surprised despite herself by the amenity.

"My mother has difficulty climbing up that high, as well," he explained, "and I take her shopping regularly." He clasped Nancy's hand to help her up. With little alternative but to stand there holding his hand, she climbed inside.

Jave dropped the stool in the back then climbed behind the wheel.

With him beside her, confined in the small space of the truck cab, Nancy felt suddenly surrounded and strangled by the lie. But her baby had so much to gain from it that she would otherwise never have. So she took the offensive.

"What are you suggesting?" she asked, her eyes steady, her jaw set.

"I'm suggesting, Mrs. Malone," Jave replied, turning in his seat to face her, "that you come clean."

She angled her chin. "Whatever do you mean?"

Jave leaned a wrist on the steering wheel and sighed good-naturedly. "Where *is* your husband, Nancy?"

She replied in the same tone. "I've told you. They're off the Southern California coast somewhere."

"And when was the last time he called?"

She shrugged. "A week. They're often out of touch on that kind of a trip."

Jave inclined his head in a gesture of regret. "If that's true, you might want to examine the status of your relationship."

She frowned. "Why?"

"Because tonight's paper says the *Courageous* is at the San Diego shipyards. Been there for four days."

She tried quickly to save herself. "Oh, right. That problem with the engine. Jerry mentioned it."

Jave shook his head, almost apologetically. "No. It was the electrical system. Story was in the *Herald*."

Nancy stared at him for a full ten seconds while she absorbed the untenability of her position. She swore to herself, then simply sat in the corner of the richly upholstered seat and steamed.

"You set me up," she said finally, accusingly. "That was calculated entrapment!"

He nodded without apparent remorse. "And if lying about having a husband was the kind of thing that went to trial, this evidence might prove to be inadmissible. But it isn't."

"No," she said morosely, seeing the five-piece nursery set, the infant seat, the chocolate, slipping away. "It's just the kind of thing that'll go to the hospital administration and beat my baby out of her freebies."

Jave put the key in the ignition. "Not necessarily."

Nancy turned to look at him, tension high in her attitude and her eyes. "What do you mean?" she asked, warily.

Jave placed an arm on the back of the seat and leaned toward her until only inches separated them. "I mean," he said with theatrical menace, "that I'm willing to be quiet, but you'll have to be my personal slave, to fulfill *all* my desires, both practical and sexual, then agree to be sold at auction on the back streets of Marrakech when I'm finished with you, and promise not to write an exposé about me or discuss me on 'Geraldo.'"

Her eyes widened, first in horror, then in indignation at his audacity as she realized he was putting her on. And that glimpse of humor in him, coupled with the very real threat his knowledge of her deception presented, succeeded in completely confusing her.

She slapped his arm. "This is no time to be funny!"

He pushed himself back behind the wheel and laughed softly at her over his shoulder. "Actually, it's time to have dinner," he said. "Do you have plans?"

She reached for the door handle. "Like I would have dinner with the man who just threatened to sell me on the back streets of Marrakech."

He turned the key and the engine growled smoothly—not at all like her old truck. He grinned boyishly. "I'm sure you know I wouldn't do that."

She pushed open the door.

"Unless you try to get out of the truck," he amended.

She looked back, slanted him a dry glance, and tried to calculate the best way down without the stool.

"But I *would* tell Amy that your husband doesn't exist," he said. "Or at least that you're no longer married to him. And she'll have to tell administration."

Nancy's heart thumped. When she turned to look at him, he was staring through the windshield, then he turned to meet her eyes, and she wondered what had ever made her think she'd seen humor there. He looked deadly serious.

"You wouldn't," she challenged.

He shrugged a shoulder. "You can believe that if you prefer."

She considered a moment, then pulled the door closed. There seemed little sense in tempting fate if there was an alternative.

"Good," he said, reaching around her to pull out her seat

belt. "I appreciate a reasonable woman. Do you like pasta?"

"What about your family?" she asked, feeling the graze of his knuckles across her belly as he reached to tuck the belt into its lock.

"Mom's gone," he said, "and the boys are with Tom. It's just you and me."

Jave backed smoothly out of the parking spot, turned the big truck easily in a very narrow area, and turned toward the small road behind the hospital.

Nancy felt as though her life had taken a sudden and dangerous turn. She wanted to run away, and she wanted to run toward it. She settled quietly in her corner, seriously depressed. It wasn't like her to be indecisive.

CHEZ PASTA WAS HOUSED in a converted cannery on the waterfront. Distressed board and batten gave a trendy look to the walls of glass that looked out on the river, and the railed-in patio that was built over it. The decor was green and white, and a tall, barrel-chested man wearing a white apron over a white shirt and tie and black slacks was there to greet them.

"Jave!" The man gave Jave a hearty handshake then looked with undisguised interest at Nancy, obviously noting her condition.

"Nancy," Jave said, "this is my old high school buddy, John Barstow. John, Nancy Malone, a newcomer to Heron Point."

"Well..." John hesitated, obviously hoping for more of an explanation. When one wasn't immediately forthcoming, he bowed politely and said, "Welcome to Chez Pasta. Follow me. I saved Jave's favorite table." He took two menus from a rack near the door and led the way inside.

"I can't believe you did that," Nancy said under her breath as they trailed John to a table in the corner on the patio. "I came here looking for unsophisticated, small-town life and what do I find? Dinner reservations made on a car phone."

Jave took her elbow as they walked down three shallow steps. "But you didn't want an unsophisticated, small-town man, too, did you?" he asked.

"I didn't want *any* man," she muttered, then smiled a thank-you to John as he pulled out her chair.

"The usual cabernet?" John asked.

"No." Jave raised a questioning eyebrow at Nancy. "Mineral water?"

She nodded. "Please."

John went off and Jave smiled knowingly across the table. "I realize designer water is also a disappointment to you, but what can I say? Try as we do to keep it out, the modern depravities invade our idyllic—"

"All right, all right." She cut him off with a condemning look over the top of her menu. "I didn't mean that the way it sounded. I suppose a doctor has to have a cellular phone. It just made me forget where I was for a minute."

But not who she was, or the pickle she was in, she thought. She saw his eyes note that change in her expression.

"Relax," he said. "Dinner first, then you can confide in me over dessert."

"I don't want to confide in you," she said, looking back at her menu.

He smiled. "I know. But you probably don't want to lose all that baby stuff, either."

Nancy looked around, found that they were relatively isolated from the rest of the diners, and put her menu down. "You know," she said, anxious, desperate even, to regain the upper hand here. "*That* is blackmail. *I* could tell on *you!*"

He agreed without apparent concern. "If you were willing to give up all that baby stuff."

"You..."

John arrived with their water, interrupting her heated response. Jave calmly made suggestions from the long list of entrées that included every kind of pasta imaginable with a wider range of sauces than she had ever seen, even in Manhattan.

She finally ordered the more familiar pasta *Primavera,* while Jave ordered *Chichiglia* in marinara sauce.

She couldn't help her curiosity. "What is that?" she asked. "I didn't notice it on the menu."

"It's a very large shell stuffed with several cheeses," he explained, toasting her with his water. "I'll let you try one."

She did not toast him back. Sharing from another person's plate was an intimacy. She struggled against that recurring feeling of losing her grip on things.

"I'll spare you the need to worry about squealing," she said. "I'll call Amy Brown myself and tell her everything."

Jave looked into her eyes and saw through the heroic, vaguely martyred expression. He said cynically, "Right. And my mother's going to give up bingo."

Nancy's temper began to blow. "Nicholas, what century are you from? You think you can calmly threaten me with blackmail, and I'm going to sit by and—"

This time John interrupted with Caesar salads. He looked in concern from one to the other. "Is everything all right?"

Nancy smiled up at their host. "They would be better if you'd move Mr. Nicholas to another table."

John winced at Jave.

"Isn't she charming?" Jave asked with a forbearing grin. "Everything's fine, John. Thank you."

John walked away with a concerned look at them over his shoulder.

Jave pushed a bowl of freshly grated Parmesan cheese in Nancy's direction. "Considering your position," he said, "you might try to be more courteous."

"Blackmail," she replied, spooning cheese onto her salad, "doesn't inspire courtesy." But he was right. Unless she truly was willing to tell Amy the truth and risk everything, she had to know what he intended to do. She picked up her fork and measured him with a look. "You said you might be willing to be quiet," she reminded him.

He had unsettled her. He could see it in her eyes, and he was pleased about that. He maintained a neutral expression, trying to keep the upper hand.

"I might," he confirmed. "But I would need to be assured of your cooperation."

Nancy studied him another moment, trying to see beyond the courteous distance he maintained between them. She had no idea where this was going, and she was more than a little uneasy. So far, except for a little mild teasing and a kiss she'd precipitated, he'd been the epitome of kindness and gentleness.

But his willingness to be quiet about her single status suggested that all that could change—depending on what he wanted in return. She had to make a few things clear—and risk losing the precious gifts in the process.

She put her fork down and pinned him with grave, dark eyes. "Let me assure you of a few *other* things first," she said quietly. "You're right. I am single. But I was married when I conceived this baby, and even though the baby and I have been thrown over for a role in a sitcom with a thirty share, I still have a high opinion of myself and big plans for this baby." She drew a deep breath as though that had taken courage. She pushed the cheese back toward him. "So, don't think I'd be willing to do anything foolish or… stupid, just to keep the gifts. Because I wouldn't."

He knew precisely what she meant by foolish and stupid, and nothing like that had crossed his mind. Well, it had, but not in relation to the issue of Amy's extravaganza.

"I was kidding," he said, "about using you as a personal slave and sending you to Marrakech."

A little pleat formed over the bridge of her nose. "Then what do you want?"

"I want you to eat your salad." Forestalling her with a shake of his head when she would have insisted on an answer, he pointed to her plate. "We'll talk about it over dessert. Eat."

But John joined them for dessert and regaled Nancy with tales of Jave in their high school days.

"He'd gotten a job bussing tables at the Elmore Pier Restaurant in our junior year. In the meantime, he got a date with Ginger Busfield—" he waggled his eyebrows expressively "—so he sent me to work in his place."

"What happened?" Nancy asked, having difficulty imagining Jave as young and irresponsible.

"He was fired," John said, laughing, "and I was introduced to a restaurant kitchen." He waved a hand toward the crowd of diners inside. "And it's become my life. As far as I'm concerned, Jave owns this table personally." John slapped the edge of the table with the flat of his hand and all the crockery shook. He looked at the last few crumbs of Nancy's sour-cream cake. "Another dessert?"

She groaned and shook her head. "Please. The baby's begging for mercy."

WHO, ME? No, I'm not. Send down more, but skip the mineral water.

JAVE PUSHED his chair back. "Well, maybe we'd better take her for a walk." He handed his credit card to John and pulled out Nancy's chair.

Nancy pushed herself up, and Jave reached an arm around her waist to help her the last few inches. She had to lean into him to slip out of the small space between table and chair. Attraction crackled, but she pretended otherwise as she thanked him and excused herself to visit the ladies' room.

The evening was balmy and blue as they crossed Chez Pasta's lawn to the narrow path that ran most of the length of the river from one edge of town to the other.

Jave took her hand and looped it through his arm, then

put his hand in his pocket. "Your husband was an actor?" he asked without preamble.

She'd never wanted to talk about him again, but she knew Jave was finally getting down to business about his keeping-quiet offer, and that she *did* want to settle.

"Yes," she replied, letting her eyes rove the wild, weedy grass that bordered the bank of the river. There were no freighters on the water tonight, just the beautiful arch of the bridge that connected Heron Point to the Long Beach peninsula. Its undulating lines were soothing somehow. "I was writing for 'New York Nights.' Have you ever seen it?"

Jave shook his head. "Sorry."

She shrugged a shoulder. "Doesn't matter. It's a late-night television show about celebrities and New York lifestyles. Anyway, I was trying to write for sitcoms on the side, and Jerry was having auditions every other day."

Jave glanced down at her profile and saw its usual softness stiffen with anger—or was it pain? He wasn't sure.

"We both had high hopes and had decided not to have children for a while so that we could devote ourselves to these careers we wanted so much." A glistening cormorant stood on a piling with its wings outspread and Nancy stopped to admire it. "Why do they do that?" she asked, distracted from her memories. "Are they preening or something?"

He laughed softly. "Nobody seems sure, but there are a couple of theories. One is that they're drying their wings, which are not waterproof. Another is that that's a resting pose that helps their digestion after they've gorged on fish."

"They look like something out of a science-fiction story. Like that's really a cape and they're part man, part bird."

"Must be that imagination that makes you a writer. Far as I know, they're all bird. No man involved."

Nancy gave him a wry smile as she started off along the trail again. "Sometimes I feel that way about myself. All dodo, no man involved."

He pinched her fingers punitively. "You put me more in

mind of a goose when you talk like that," he said. "And the 'no man involved' element is about to undergo a change. You were telling me about Jerry."

"Change?"

"Jerry," he prompted. "Finish the story."

With a sigh, she continued. "He got the part of Drago in 'Delta Diary' the same day that I learned our birth control failed and I was pregnant. He told me he loved me, but he couldn't love 'it' when it got in the way of his choices."

The wind began to pick up as the sun slipped toward the horizon. Jave moved his arm to put it around her, suspecting she needed support as well as warmth.

"And you?" he asked.

"I," she said, her voice reflecting surprise, "was already sure I was carrying a girl and felt this weird disassociation from everything else I'd ever wanted and suddenly wanted only her...." She splayed her hand over her stomach and rubbed in a circular motion. She shook her head, feeling as though that had all been a century ago. "I'd made a lot of concessions in our marriage because I thought, deep down, we both wanted each other more than we wanted anything else. But, when Jerry couldn't accept this baby, when it was not only part of him but part of me, it occurred to me that maybe he didn't love me as much as he claimed. Anyway, here I am."

WAY TO GO, Mom. Thanks.

NANCY LAUGHED SOFTLY and glanced up at Jave. "She just rubbed against my hand. I wonder if she knows I'm talking about her?"

"I think you should pick out a boy's name, too," Jave warned indulgently. "Just to be on the safe side. Bonnie was sure Pete was a girl and he's definitely not."

She shook her head adamantly. "That would be hedging

bets and an indication of weak faith. I'm carrying Malia Rose."

Jave remembered the ultrasound again and smiled. "All right. But don't say I didn't warn you. Pretty name anyway."

She stopped to look up at him. He stopped, too, expression bland.

"Did the baby turn around while you were testing me?" she asked, her eyes bright with that possibility. "Do you know?"

It drew a smile from deep inside him. "Yes," he replied.

"And I'm right, aren't I?"

"You said you didn't want to know."

"That's right. I don't." She hooked her arm in his of her own volition this time and drew him along. "I know. I'm sure."

"Nothing is ever sure," he said. "That's what makes life an adventure."

"That's why you have to believe in *yourself*," Nancy insisted. "I'm sure. It's a girl."

"Or a boy who's not going to be happy being called Malia." Jave smiled and walked alongside her around the point that had given the town its name, then up the bay. "Getting tired?" he asked.

"No." She was discovering that she rather liked walking arm in arm with him, even when she had no idea what he intended to do about her married-woman deceit. "In New York, I walked this far from the subway to the office. But the view wasn't this spectacular, of course." Then she said brightly, "Oh, look! A marina."

She began walking a little faster.

"You like boats?" he asked.

"I *love* them," she said. "Well, I mean, I love to look at them. The only boat I've ever been on is the Staten Island Ferry. But I've always thought I'd love to lie on the deck in nothing at all and soak up the sun." She looked up into his speculative expression and added quickly, "Unpregnant, of course, and far away from shore."

He smiled. "Tom and I have a boat here."

"You do? Where?"

They approached the docks where several dozen boats bobbed at their moorings. The harbormaster waved from his shack and Jave waved back. "At the other end. We just bought it. A fixer-upper." As they walked the length of the dock he told her about the *River Lady*. "And we've missed her ever since. Now, we're both getting ahead enough to get something economical. Frankly, it was more economical than I had in mind, but Tom forms these attachments to things.... There she is. The *Mud Hen*."

Nancy looked in the direction Jave pointed and spotted the boat—and felt her heart melt. It reminded her somehow of a seagoing version of *The Little Engine That Could*. She'd just bought the book and several others for the baby in the used bookstore. The story of the little engine that struggled valiantly against impossible odds and *won*, seemed important to own.

When she'd been living in New York and competing with the literary world's clever and sophisticated minds, she'd eschewed such philosophy as saccharine. But now that she had a little life inside her, she had a different perspective. She wanted very much to believe that the human spirit could triumph over all obstacles.

She went toward the platform to board the boat, and Jave loped ahead to help her on.

"We can't go below," he said, stopping her as she headed for the stairs. "Tom has it all torn apart and you might trip over something." He pointed out the large tear in the deck's planking. "And watch the hole."

"It's beautiful," she said with a sincerity that surprised and touched him. Then she asked almost apologetically, "But is it seaworthy?"

He made a so-so gesture with his hand. "Valid concern. It will be by the time Tom's finished. You really like it?"

"Yes," she replied, surprised that he seemed surprised. "Don't you?"

He leaned against the rail to look at the hillside and the lights just going on in the homes that dotted it. "Well, sort of. Because Tom loves it, and working on it is starting to bring him back."

She leaned beside him. "Back from where?" Her voice was quiet. She knew there was a story of some kind attached to Tom.

Jave explained about the old hotel fire, about the loss of Tom's friend and about the girlfriend who'd abandoned him and was only now trying to reenter his life.

"There was no woman crying?" Nancy asked quietly.

Jave shook his head. "He didn't find anyone. But I guess a fire can cause a lot of strange noises. Anyway, the floor also gave way under him, but he was able to catch himself. His right leg is badly burned and hard to look at," he said. Then he added with a quick glance at her, "Not because it's ugly, but because it hurts to know he suffered that. He thinks no woman will want to live with a limb like that. And, though he's built another career for himself, he was a fireman at heart. He thinks he's lost a lot of things that make him less than he was."

Nancy responded to his brotherly concern. She'd longed for a sibling throughout her childhood, but only now, as an adult, was she beginning to realize how much comfort and support a brother or sister could be as one faced life with parents gone and lovers fled.

"The right woman will make him see that isn't true," she said encouragingly. "A year isn't very long to recover from something so traumatic."

Jave nodded. "I'll explain to my family. My mother wants him married and his wife pregnant by Christmas."

Nancy giggled. Maternally aggressive Aggie was such a cheerful thought.

Silence fell between them. Dusk began to settle over the harbor, darkening the quiet water and turning the gentle slope of the hillside purple. The antique globed lights that marked the road and rimmed the marina bloomed to life, and a small green-and-white fishing boat turned off the river into the marina, coming home.

"Are you divorced?" Jave asked.

She nodded. "It was final just before I moved here."

He was quiet a moment, then he turned to look down at her. "Are you heartbroken?"

"No," she replied without needing time to consider. "At first I felt abandoned and betrayed and simply hurt." She sighed and gave him a wry look. "But being alone isn't new to me. When I was a child, my mother left to pursue her own life, and my father was kind but busy, so I learned to fend for myself. I became very good at managing on my own. And I'm getting better all the time. No. I am not heartbroken." Then she smiled. "Unless it would gain your sympathy and make you reconsider your threat to tell on me?"

He folded his arms and leaned a hip on the railing. "The hospital's success and good image means my success," he said. "It's too important to take lightly."

She looked into his eyes, trying to gauge just how serious he was about the issue. One moment he was warm and teasing and she was convinced he'd never do anything to deprive her of this boon. Then that no-nonsense look would come over him and she suspected she wouldn't even be able to guess what he was capable of if he was determined about something.

"Then what's the solution?" she asked.

"I'll be quiet about your husband," Jave said finally, looking up as the fishing boat pulled into a slip at the next pier, "if you'll agree to see me."

Nancy, who'd also been watching the boat, turned to look at him in bald surprise. "'See' you?" she quoted him. "You mean...like...go out?"

"Yes." Jave returned her stunned gaze, his own eyes steady. "Dinner, theater, picnics." He slapped the *Mud Hen*'s railing. "Boating."

"But, I…" She took several agitated steps and stopped, both hands spread in stupefaction. "I'm…seven and a half months pregnant!"

He nodded. "I noticed that. I'm the one who enrolled you in the Lamaze classes, remember? But that's not a problem, is it?"

"Well, yes," she said, apparently amazed he didn't see it. "It's several problems. First of all—I'm ugly." She said it with such conviction, he straightened with a frown. "Secondly, in about six weeks, this is going to be a living, breathing, probably screaming baby who won't give me or anyone near me a moment's peace! And thirdly—I'm supposed to be married to someone else. Are you crazy?" She turned in a complete circle, looking just a little wild, then asked again with a broad sweep of both arms, "Are you *crazy?*"

He caught her hands in his and pulled her to a stop. "Easy," he said quietly. "You've got the picture out of focus, Nancy." He tucked a strand of wayward hair behind her ear in a gesture so gentle she even stopped breathing. "You're beautiful," he corrected, "not ugly. And I know all about demanding babies. I had two of my own, remember? And we can be discreet about spending time together until we figure out what to do about your hospital image."

GO FOR IT, MOM. Are we going to find anyone more perfect than this? He knows about demanding babies. Just make sure there's chocolate in the deal.

SHE STARED AT HIM for a moment, mouth open but incapable of forming words. She paced away from him to the rail, then turned back to him, finally pulling her thoughts together.

"Jave," she asked, "what would be the point?"

"What's the point of any relationship?" he countered. "To learn about each other. To see where it leads."

"But where *could* it lead?" she demanded. "I mean, certainly you realize…we can't…I'm not…"

Jave watched her struggle with the issue she seemed to be sure must concern him, and enjoyed it enormously. As she stammered, he waited with interest, making no effort to help.

Nancy decided she could not deal with this delicately. He was obviously going insane from exposure to ultrasound rays or something and it was her responsibility to be brutal—for both their sakes.

"Jave," she said, "you did my ultrasound. You know that I have a…a…"

He nodded. "An incompetent cervix. Yes, I know."

"Then you have to realize that…" She gestured frustratedly. "Even if I *did*…appeal to you in this condition…that we couldn't…"

He was tempted to force her to fuddle through the explanation she seemed to think had eluded him. It would serve her right. But she was growing more pink, more agitated, and the helpless, frustrated waving of her arms and hands was about to create its own weather system.

"We couldn't have sex," he said for her. He noticed the sag of her shoulders in relief.

"Not that that would be an immediate consideration," she said quickly, chattering now that the words were spoken. "But if it *did* come to that, I'm a month and a half from delivery and then it'd be six weeks before—"

Jave shook his head and placed a hand over her mouth. "You know," he said, "I'm beginning to think that other parts of you are also incompetent." Then he rapped lightly on her head to indicate the specific area. "Is the power on in there? What makes you think I choose my relationships based on how quickly I can get a woman to bed?"

Her wide brown eyes softened with regret, and her lashes brushed his thumb as she closed her eyes. He lowered his hand to allow her to answer.

"I'm sorry," she said, putting a hand to his arm. "I know

that wasn't fair. But I only...mentioned it because..." She hesitated, parted her lips as though to speak, then shook her head and dropped her hand.

Jave took hold of her arm and pulled her back to him. He'd seen a glimpse of something in her eyes, a flash of honesty that reached right inside him and set his whole world on edge—and he wanted to hear it in words.

He applied the slightest pressure to her arm. "Because of what?" he asked.

Nancy knew there was little point in swallowing the words. She was sure he'd read them in her eyes. And she wanted very much to say them.

"I mentioned it," she whispered as the fragrant river breeze wound around them and stirred her hair, "because *I've* thought of making love with *you*." She smiled thinly in self-deprecation. "It must have been guilt transference or something."

"Maybe," he suggested very softly, "it was the desire to make a wish come true." His mouth inched slowly down to hers while his eyes seemed to chart every millimeter of the way.

The hand that held her arm pulled her closer still, and the other wound itself in her hair and tipped her head back. He leaned down and, over the interfering protrusion of her baby, kissed her.

Nancy felt herself dissolve into his tenderness like so much butter on warm bread. His arms were strong but tender, his lips gentle in their exploration of hers. He nibbled and caressed, moving from her mouth to follow the line of her nose, her eyebrows, her cheekbones. Then he nipped at her earlobe and traced kisses along her jaw until he found her mouth again.

Jave was keenly aware of her substantial roundness in his arms, and felt her resist the inclination of her weight against him. He tipped her a little farther to the side, until she was slightly off balance and had no choice.

"I'm too heav—" Her attempt to protest about her

weight was lost as he held her easily and opened his mouth over hers.

She clung to his shoulders, the strong muscles there giving her confidence and allowing her to forget her precarious suspension and concentrate on him.

Her tongue met his, teased it languorously, then explored his lips and the line of his teeth as he touched hers.

She felt his hand moving on her, tracing the line of her spine, shaping her hip, then using it to pull her closer. Her belly was wedged against him and the sensation startled her. Since the day she'd discovered she was pregnant, there'd been no one with whom to share the wonder, no one to hold and enfold her and her baby.

Wow. TIGHT SPOT, MOM. But I like it. I like him. And I can tell you do. It's hot in here.

JAVE FELT HER SLIGHT START and straightened, pulling her securely up and into his arms. "What?" he asked in concern. "Are you all right? Does something hurt?"

"I'm fine," she assured him breathlessly. But she continued to cling to him as she struggled for composure. "It was just...the baby moved."

He splayed his large hand over the mound of her belly, drawing the breath from her like a gust of wind.

Jave felt strong movement against his palm, then at the tips of his fingers as the baby probably flailed an arm or kicked. He felt Nancy's tension, too, and liked the notion that his touch energized her.

"Feels busy," he said. "You might have to rock her to sleep tonight."

He removed his hand and she was able to draw breath again. A little giddy with relief, she mimicked him teasingly, "'Rock *her* to sleep'? So you admit it's a girl?"

He rested his hands on his hips. "So you admit you'd really be more comfortable with a supporting opinion?"

She vacillated for one moment. He waited it out, realizing her decision would probably set the tone for the months ahead.

She finally shook her head. "No. It's a girl. I know it's a girl."

He placed an arm around her shoulders and drew her with him toward the ladder and the ramp, accepting within himself that he'd already known she was not going to make this relationship easy.

"Well, more power to you," he said, climbing the steps and reaching back to pull her up behind him. "Most of us are more comfortable with a confirming opinion."

"Some of us," she said, balanced precariously at the top of the ramp, "have found that you can't trust support. You can only trust yourself."

Jave, halfway down the ramp, turned toward her. She reached out her hand, certain he intended to help her down the rest of the way. But, she realized, she'd just denigrated the very thing he was ready to offer. Accepting it now would mean a compromise on her part.

His hazel eyes challenged her, his hand, loosely resting on his hip, beyond her reach.

Nancy studied the expanse of unsteady board with its crossbars intended to provide footing that only seemed to confuse hers.

It was on the tip of her tongue to ask for his hand; she knew that was what he was waiting for. But it went against deeply ingrained personal training, and the fact that she even considered it proposed a new possibility that held its own terrors. She decided to go it alone.

She took several sure steps and Jave had just turned to walk the rest of the way down, when the sole of her sandal caught on the next crossbar. Without the bulk of her pregnancy, she would have easily recovered, but the weight pitched her forward and she shouted Jave's name at the same moment that he heard her misstep and turned to help.

He caught her against him. He looked into her eyes and

let her feel for a moment that his muscle supported her. Then he lifted her in his arms and carried her the rest of the way down. He set her on her feet at the bottom.

Without a word, he took her hand and started back up the trail. Of course, there was no need for an I-told-you-so, Nancy realized wryly. That look had said it all.

"Okay," she conceded voluntarily. "There are times when it's good to have support. Even for me."

He didn't seem impressed with her admission.

"There are times," she added, "when I can trust you."

"You could *always* trust me," he corrected, "if there were times when you could let yourself believe it."

"That's the hard part," she said candidly. "If you want to see where this relationship goes as you said, that's something you should understand about me. It's hard for me to put my faith in someone else."

That, he guessed, he'd have to allow her.

"You screamed for me when you slipped," he reminded her.

She remembered that clearly. His name had been on her lips before she'd even formed the thought. "That was instinct," she explained lightly—mostly because she didn't feel light about it at all.

"That was trust," he corrected. "And to be sure your baby doesn't come into this world with the same skewed suspicions you have, you're going to agree to see me."

"I didn't say that."

"I know. You can say it now."

She wanted to. It would be dangerous to her peace of mind, foolish and irresponsible in her condition, and generally ill-advised. But she wanted to.

He fell into line behind her to let a pair of lovers coming from the other direction pass by. They appeared to be in their teens and oblivious to everything but each other until they were right upon Jave and Nancy. They laughed as Jave and Nancy stepped out of their way. They continued down the trail, gazing into each other's eyes in the encroaching darkness.

Nancy smiled after them. "Summer romance, do you suppose?" she asked Jave as he moved beside her again. "Or the real thing?"

"Hard to tell," he said. "They usually look the same. You'd have to overhear a discussion of life-and-death issues to know for sure. And don't try to change the subject."

Nancy grinned. "I thought I was pretty slick."

Jave shook his head. "Pete and Eddy make you look like a rank amateur. So what's it to be? You keep company with me? Or you lose your status as Amy's model mommy?"

"Jave," she said reasonably, "there are a few pitfalls here you haven't thought out. What will your mother think? And your children? The afternoon you fixed my roof, Pete spent a little time telling me about his mother. How will he react to his father dating a pregnant woman? Seems to me he'll feel threatened on all sides. And what about our being seen together? How can you be my Lamaze coach at the class held at the hospital when everyone there is supposed to think I'm married?"

Jave nodded. He'd already thought that through. "I'll explain to my family. My mother loves to offer her opinion, but she knows I do what I want to do. And she's always after me to reactivate my social life. Truth is, she'd be thrilled to know I was interested in a woman."

Nancy could guess that might be true. Aggie seemed ever watchful of her boys and her grandchildren.

"Eddy's pretty well adjusted," Jave went on, "and generally accepting of everyone. Pete is another story, but he has to come to terms with his life the way it is, not the way he wishes it still were."

She gave him a softly scolding look. "That's a lot to expect of a little boy."

He admitted that with a nod. "It's a lot to expect of anyone. But it's required if you're going to live a normal life."

"And what about appearances? It'll really kill my chances of being Amy's candidate for the gifts if I'm seen with another man while my husband's supposed to be away."

They'd reached Chez Pasta and turned across the broad expanse of lawn toward the truck.

"We'll establish at Lamaze class that I've become a friend, helping to coach you until your husband gets back. Beyond that, we'll be discreet." He grinned at her as he unlocked the door, then reached into the back for the step stool. "Or you could admit the truth in the interest of being able to conduct our relationship in the open."

She looked at him as though he were crazy. "And lose everything?"

He took her hand to help her up. "Maybe there's another way to acquire all that stuff."

She didn't see it. She even shook her head against the possibility.

There'd be no advantage, he realized, in explaining that to her at this point in time. He locked and closed her door, tossed the stool in the back and walked around to the driver's side.

Nancy looked doubtful. "It all sounds dangerous."

"The whole deceit," he said frankly, "is dangerous. But you started it."

She buckled her seat belt and suggested quietly, "You could just forget what you know and let me carry on as I've been doing."

"Then what'll you do at delivery time when you can't produce a husband?"

"Dating you," she said, pointing a finger at him, "isn't going to help me there, either."

He met her eyes, the hazel of his darkening in the dim interior of the truck to some turbulent and mysterious shade of gold. "You're sure about that?" he asked.

"Well...I...um..." His look debilitated her. She couldn't think, couldn't form a coherent sentence. Her mind was too busy wondering what that question meant, what that look would mean if it could be formed into words. "Jave…I…"

He turned the key in the ignition. "I'm going to be working most of the weekend, but I'll pick you up Sunday afternoon for the arts festival down the coast."

Protest would be useless. He was determined, and her resistance was halfhearted at best. There was trouble here, she knew, but it was all very complex, very convoluted, and she wasn't sharp enough to think about it. She was just a little intoxicated on the fresh, early August air and the look in Jave's eyes.

She nodded and settled back in her seat. The baby seemed to do the same, only she swore she could feel tiny toes wriggling in between her ribs. Was she needing more room? Was she thinking about making a break for it?

ROUGH EVENING, MOM. How're we doing? You know, the walls are shrinking in here.

NANCY WRIGGLED to get comfortable. Six more weeks and the life inside her would become the life in her arms. Excitement warred with terror. Was she ready? She wasn't sure.

As Jave turned the truck out of the parking lot and onto the road, she shifted again as the baby continued to squirm.

Jave glanced away from the road. "You okay?"

"The baby's stretching," she explained, sitting up to relieve sudden pressure against her back. "I feel as though she's redecorating in there, moving my spinal column to make more room."

He kept an eye on the road while reaching behind the seat for a pillow. "Here," he said, glancing away from the road again to hand it to her. "Try that in the small of your back."

She did and felt a little relief—in her back, and in her thoughts.

"I THOUGHT THIS was supposed to be art stuff," Pete announced querulously at high volume as Nancy stopped at a quilt display. The Coast Arts Festival took up all the grounds of a high school, including a standard-size football field. And so far they'd encountered everything from crocheted doilies masterfully created by a ladies' church club, to fine oil, acrylic and watercolor paintings done by some of the West Coast's most renowned artists.

"These are just old blankets," Pete went on.

"Art isn't just pictures," Nancy explained patiently. "Art can be anything that someone works hard to make pretty. Like these blankets."

"They're patched," Pete disputed scornfully.

Nancy glanced up at Jave, whom she suspected was listening while pretending not to. He studied a leather vest at a booth behind them while keeping an eye on Eddy, who was watching an artist hand tool a belt.

"They aren't patches," she said, taking Pete's hand and drawing him to a particularly pretty quilt in shades of pink and blue that was displayed at his eye level. "Quilting is an old art," she said, leaning over as much as her bulk would allow to point out the pattern, "but pioneer women used it because in those days they didn't have big pieces of fabric, so they put together all their little pieces to make what they needed." She pulled the quilt close so that he could see all the tiny stitches. "And for a long time they didn't have sewing machines, so they made all these little stitches by hand."

Nancy traced a fingertip across the width of the quilt, then into every repeated pattern to call his attention to the work involved.

"Wow!" he said, his dark eyes widening as they followed the path she traced. "There must be a million of 'em!"

She smiled. It was a gross exaggeration, but she had his interest.

"Sometimes ten ladies would all work on a quilt at the

same time to make the work go faster. They would talk about what was going on in town and tell stories while they sewed."

Pete looked up at her, his eyes brightening. "I like stories."

Nancy nodded. "Me, too. Sometimes a quilt tells a story." She led him to a friendship quilt hanging on a special rack beside the other. Her finger traced the names and dates embroidered on the panels. "This one was given to a lady who moved away from friends she'd had for a long time. And they wanted her to remember them, so they all quilted a square for her and signed it with embroidery. Then they sewed all the squares together."

Pete studied all the names, then he looked up at Nancy. "My mom moved away from us," he said, his big eyes troubled at the thought. "David Fuller's mom *died,* so she *had* to go away, but mine didn't even die. She just moved. Now she can't see me play baseball."

Nancy experienced a mild sense of panic. She felt her own baby tumble around inside her and wondered if she didn't like what she was hearing, was afraid, perhaps, that it could happen to her. She wanted desperately to comfort both of them.

"I'd like to watch you play," Nancy said, wishing she hadn't started this, wishing she'd simply let him dislike the "old blankets" and not brought up an obviously painful subject.

Pete shook his head. "I'm not very good."

Nancy caught his hand and walked farther up the display to quilted clothing, hoping to find something to distract him. "I'll bet you will be," she said. "It just takes time to learn everything."

"Eddy plays really good."

"He's bigger."

Pete sighed, obviously considering the plight of being little. Then he pointed to a display of quilted bags and backpacks. "That's cool," he said, reaching on tiptoe to touch one that was made from denim squares and tied with a bandanna cord. "Do you think a bunch of ladies made that?"

Nancy studied the perfect, even stitches. She knew there were museum-quality quilters who could produce such stitches by hand, but the seams had been shop sewn, she felt sure, and a manufacturer's label was tucked inside the flap.

"Well, I think it was a bunch of ladies in a shop. Would you like to have it?" She began to delve in her purse for her wallet.

"Yeah!" Pete said excitedly, then he quickly shook his head. "But I'm not supposed to ask for stuff."

Nancy gestured for the owner of the display. "You didn't ask, I offered. And if your father complains, we'll just tell him that."

Jave appeared suddenly from behind the rack of bags. "Tell me what?" he asked.

Pete already clutched the bag possessively. "Nancy wants to buy me this," he said, then assured him quickly, "and I didn't even ask her."

Jave reached into his hip pocket for his wallet, and Nancy gave him a look that threatened mayhem if he tried to prevent her from buying the bag herself. He thought it might be interesting to try it just to see what developed, but the clerk was waiting patiently.

"That's great," he said instead. "Let's see." He squatted down before the boy to examine the purchase.

Pete related in detail everything Nancy had told him about quilting. "But this one was made by a bunch of ladies in a shop."

Eddy came to peer over his father's shoulder at the bag. "Cool," he said.

"Would you like one?" Nancy asked.

The clerk, in the act of ringing up the sale, stopped as she raised a halting finger at him.

Eddy shook his head. "No, thanks. I have a Harley one. Black leather. It's *really* cool."

Sure it wasn't politic to buy for one child and not the other, Nancy spotted a baseball cap, also quilted out of denim. She snatched it off its rack and placed it on his head. The clerk raised a mirror behind the counter and they all went to it, Nancy, Pete and Jave peering down behind Eddy to see his reflection.

"I like it," Eddy said with a broad grin.

Nancy smiled at the clerk, who rang up both items while Pete regaled Eddy with his newly acquired quilting information.

They settled down with sausage dogs on a grassy area, where a country and western band played familiar tunes. Jave helped Nancy sit with her back against a mountain ash full of plump red berries, and he and the boys formed a semicircle around her.

Eddy rolled his eyes over the music. "They need some drums or some electronic stuff," he said.

Jave pulled the bill of Eddy's cap over his eyes. "Just listen to the sound. This is good music—written before you could plug in an instrument and mess electronically with the sound it made. This is *real* music."

Eddy blinked at him. "Don't stroke out on us, Dad. I just thought they could do with a little...metal."

"This is sound that's unenhanced," Jave said patiently. "When the ladies were quilting in the old days like Nancy explained, their husbands were probably on the front porch, making just this kind of music."

"Un-en-hanced," Eddy repeated, obviously trying to make sense of the word.

"Nothing fancy added to it," Nancy contributed. "Pure stuff."

"And that's good?"

She considered that, remembering that today's child was accustomed to things that were electronically, medically or psychologically augmented or reduced. It distracted her for a moment with thoughts about the world into which her child was about to be born. Then she looked at Eddy and Pete and decided she'd be in good company.

"Sure it is," she said. "They're making beautiful music without the help of anything but a little wood and string. There has to be more satisfaction in that. And it's an easier sound to listen to."

Eddy listened as though evaluating that remark, then tilted his head from side to side in a so-so gesture that reminded her sharply of his father. "I guess. But I'm more into Guns 'n' Roses."

He picked up his soft drink and took a long swig, apparently considering the discussion over. He took a huge bite of sausage dog, his sneakered foot tapping unconsciously to the music.

Nancy looked up at Jave over the boy's head to commiserate over failing to reinforce his point. Humor was alight in his eyes as he rolled them to express his frustration. She laughed softly.

Pete struggled with a plastic packet of mustard. She took it from him, tore the end off with her fingernails, and handed it back. "Mmm," she said, studying her sausage dog. "I forgot mustard."

Jave began to get to his feet to go back to the stand for another packet. But Pete walked to her on his knees and handed back the packet. "You can have half," he said, sitting with his knees curled to the side so that he could lean against her, "and I'll have half."

Jave sat down again, marveling at the little victory. No one else would have recognized it as such, but he did. For the first time in a year, Pete was offering to share, making an effort to enjoy something. Though he suspected the boy felt as he did—sharing with Nancy didn't require much of an effort.

Nancy ruffled his hair to thank him. Jave saw the boy glance at her, his dark eyes soft with adoration. Jave smiled to himself, liking the turn things were taking.

They attended an art auction in the evening, and drove

home with a three-by-four-foot oil painting of a cubist face sharing the back seat of Jave's second vehicle, a blue LeBaron. Pete was belted in between Jave and Nancy, fast asleep against Nancy's bosom. Eddy shared space with the painting.

"How come his face is so weird?" Eddy asked lazily. He leaned far into the corner, studying the painting in consternation. "It's like a profile, only you can see his other eye and his other ear."

"It's a style of painting called cubist," Jave explained. "It allows you to see things in a way you wouldn't ordinarily."

"But why would you want to?"

Jave slanted Nancy a grinning glance. "'Cause it gives you a different perspective. It makes you think."

"But it's...like...wrong."

"It's not wrong," Jave corrected. "It's just different."

"Why'd we buy it anyway?"

"Because Nancy liked it. It reminds her of Boeneke."

They'd argued over the purchase for fifteen minutes. Well, Nancy had argued that she didn't want him to buy it for her, that it was too expensive, and that her carelessly spoken "I wish I had that for my office" had been simply wishful thinking. Jave had listened patiently, then bought it anyway. Nancy had protested but was secretly delighted. Because Boeneke reminded her of Jave.

"That's her police guy," Eddy said. They'd discussed him on the ride down the coast and planned several solutions to her current plot problems.

"Right."

There were a few moments of silence, then Eddy said sleepily, "Policemen shouldn't be cubist."

Jave smiled into the rearview mirror. "Why not?"

"'Cause you shouldn't be able to see all of them at once like that. Shouldn't they have secrets? You know, things that are hidden, so that the bad guys can't figure them out? Otherwise, they'll know how to get away."

Jave glanced at Nancy, an eyebrow raised in amazement. "Is my kid brilliant or what?" he asked.

Eddy had fallen asleep and missed the compliment.

JAVE WALKED NANCY into her house and hung the painting over her desk while the boys slept in the car. Then he took a cellular phone out of a bag he'd also brought in and placed it on her coffee table. He plugged the battery into a charger.

"What...where did you get that?" she asked.

"Through one of the hospital's suppliers." He gave her a few rudimentary instructions, then showed her how to install the battery in the morning. "This is already programmed," he said, "and the battery has to charge for twelve hours. I want you to take the phone to bed and in the truck with you. You'll have help at the tip of your fingers."

She opened her mouth, a protest forming out of habit. But he caught her upper arms and pulled her close. He kissed her slowly and soundly.

Though she had no idea how this relationship had come about or where it was going, she understood clearly at that moment what it was like to be cared about—and cared for. Tears stung her eyes as she parted her lips to respond with the heartfelt adoration of a woman who felt cherished.

Jave studied her one protracted moment, then blew a frustrated breath and left, locking the door as he closed it.

She went to the window and watched him pull out of her front yard, his headlights arching through the darkness. It was getting more and more difficult, she thought, her nose and her belly pressed against the window, to watch him drive away.

WASN'T that sweet, Mom?

"NANCY'S GOING TO COME and...watch me play," Pete told his father, the news interrupted by a big yawn as Jave tucked him into bed.

"You'd like that?"

Pete opened heavy eyelids and nodded. "I like *her*."

"I know," Jave said. "So do I." He kissed the boy goodnight and turned out the light, thinking as he closed the bedroom door how much he missed her.

THE PHONE WAS RINGING as he walked down the stairs to breakfast. He picked up the cordless in the kitchen, opening the refrigerator as he pushed the On button with his thumb.

"Hello," he said, reaching for a peach.

"Hi. It's Nancy."

The soft voice brought him upright even before she identified herself. He kicked the door closed and put the fruit on the counter, his heart beating fast.

"Nancy," he said. His voice sounded breathless. "Anything wrong?"

"No, I'm fine." He felt relief, but his heart continued to pound. "I wanted to test the phone. The best way seemed to be to call and thank you for it."

"You're welcome," he said. The bones in his legs seemed to turn to butter. He leaned back against the counter for support. "Did you get any sleep last night? Your baby ate sauerkraut."

She laughed. The soft sound over the telephone wire turned the bones in his upper body to liquid. "We slept beautifully. She's going to be an eccentric gourmand with widely varied ethnic preferences. She loves chili, Szechuan, moussaka and anything that reeks of garlic and onions." He was drinking in the sound of her voice, the fact that *she'd* called *him,* when she added with quiet gravity, "And thank you for the painting. Did I ever tell you about Boeneke?"

"You explained him on the way down yesterday afternoon," he replied. "Remember?"

"I mean about him and you," she said.

He had a connection to this character with whom she

spent part of every day? And the nights when she couldn't sleep? He tried to sound nonchalant. "Me?"

"You look just like my image of him," she explained.

He heard a disarming vulnerability in her voice. What he wouldn't have given to have the freedom to jump into his truck and cover the miles that separated them.

"Same hair, same eyes. I saw it that first day, when you were doing my ultrasound. The room was dark and you stepped into the light...." She paused. The silence was heavy. "You're him."

He waited as he heard her hesitate again, possibly wondering whether or not to say more. He wanted to hear that that was why she'd liked the painting. That she'd called to tell him she was staring at it now and pretending he was there. But he knew what he was up against. The lady couldn't bring herself to believe in anyone.

"Well...thank you again," she said. "For the phone, for the painting, and for the wonderful time. You have great kids."

"Yes, I do," he said. "Thank you for noticing. I'll pick you up for Pete's game on Thursday night."

"Wonderful," she said.

Had he heard a vague edge of disappointment? Had she hoped she'd see him today? He wasn't one for games of intrigue, but this seemed like an important one. She had to see for herself that she was coming to care for him, coming to need him, coming to want to believe in him. And nothing would underline that like a little absence.

"Have a good day, Jave," she said finally.

He fought down the urge to forget his scheduled appointments at the hospital and drive over to her.

"You, too, Nancy," he replied. "Don't forget to take the phone with you in the truck."

He heard her sigh. "Right," she said, the sound heavy and wistful. "Bye."

Jave punched the Off button on the phone and slapped the antenna down. All *right*. Points were stacking up on his side.

CHAPTER NINE

JAVE RAN INTO HIS OFFICE for a quick sip of coffee between patients and found Tom turning idly from side to side in his desk chair, sipping from the hot cup he'd left on the desktop.

"Moocher," Jave accused mildly. "Now you have to go to the cafeteria and get me another one."

Tom remained in the chair but handed back the cup with a grimace. "Actually, I saved you from a fate worse than motor oil. Who makes that stuff?"

Jave took an appreciative swig. "Patients get the good stuff. The cafeteria saves the bad food for the staff."

"It tastes like a stagnant pond."

"That's where we grow the penicillin. The coffee's a by-product." Jave perched on the edge of the desk and put the cup aside. He studied Tom's rather natty attire of beige Dockers and a blue-and-beige silk shirt. "What are you doing here?"

Tom picked up a marking pen, removed the cap with studied casualness, then recapped it. "Keeping my appointment with my therapist."

"Are you coming or going?" Jave asked.

Tom grinned at him. "I don't know. That's why I'm seeing a therapist."

Jave kicked at the chair, sending it backward a few inches until it collided with the wall. "Very funny. I meant, have you had your appointment, or are you headed there now?"

Tom used his feet to walk the chair back to the desk. "I've had it. Came to see if you wanted to go to the Scupper for lunch and see how the boat's coming."

Jave nodded. "Got one more patient scheduled in five minutes. Then I'm free until three."

"Good. I'll be out in the—"

"Jave! Here's the guest list for the birthing-room dinner. We're—" Amy Brown walked into his office, waving a sheet of paper and clutching her ever-present clipboard to her. She stopped dead three steps inside as her gaze fell on his brother, leaning back in his chair.

Jave looked on in surprise as Amy's eyes widened and darkened, and a quickly indrawn breath fluttered a lacy ruffle that ran across the front of her dress.

A blush, instant and thorough, rose from her throat to her hairline.

Tom got to his feet with an uncertain glance at Jave.

"I'm sorry," Amy said, her voice high and broken. She cleared her throat and nervously shifted her weight. "I didn't realize you had a patient." She backed toward the door. "This can—"

"No, it's all right," Jave said, straightening off the desk. "This isn't a patient. Although one has to be patient to deal with him. Amy, this is my brother, Tom Nicholas. Tom, meet Amy Brown, Riverview Hospital's publicity and PR coordinator."

Amy offered her hand and dropped her clipboard. The guest list she'd intended to hand Jake fluttered to the floor.

With an apologetic exclamation, she bent down for it at the same moment that Tom made a grab for the sheet. He hit her glasses and knocked them off. She reeled backward and her head collided with the corner of the office door. She sagged against it, bleeding profusely.

"Oh, God! I'm sorry." Tom pulled her toward the chair as Jave, unable to believe that he'd seen what he'd seen, called the ER to see if they could handle another patient.

"It might be a good idea," Jave said to Tom two hours later over his bottle of Guinness at the Scupper, "if you didn't date for another year. Or at least get the women you meet to sign their insurance over to you first."

Tom leaned back in his chair, a baseball hat pulled down low over his eyes. "She looked so nervous, she made me nervous. Thank God I didn't break her nose."

Jave nodded dryly. "Yeah. Ten stitches in her scalp isn't half that bad."

Tom drew a deep breath. "All right. It wasn't my finest hour. I don't ever have to see her again."

The merest outline of a notion had formed in Jave's mind several hours ago when Amy had walked into his office and blushed after one glimpse of his brother. It had been even too small to consider a thought, but it had been growing ever since and was now a full-fledged idea.

"Yeah, you do," he said. "Remember the rest of our boat deal?"

Tom frowned, thought, then shook his head. "Oh, no. No, no."

Jave shrugged. "Well, do you have another candidate for a date? You don't want to see Judy Taft and I don't blame you. Who else do you know? As far as I can tell, the only women you're acquainted with are clients—mostly married ones—except for Nancy, and she's mine."

"No."

"The two-week deadline we made is long past. I think you should ask Amy for a date."

Tom shook his head adamantly. "Not a chance. I'll buy out your share of the boat first."

Jave downed the last of his ale. "I don't want to sell."

"Then you can buy *me* out."

"You're the one who knows how to find the fish."

Tom was looking desperate. He pushed his hat farther back on his head. "Like she's going to want to go out with the guy who socked her in the nose, broke her glasses, and sent her to the emergency room."

Jave shrugged as though that was all of no consequence. "She knows everybody there. It was no big deal. Why don't you ask her?"

"Jave," Tom said, leaning toward him on his forearms.

"She seemed nice enough. I mean she didn't even shout at me or anything, but she's...you know...she's not really my type."

"She's a fine, good-hearted woman," Jave said firmly. "With a cheerful nature and a kind word for everyone."

Tom fell moodily against the back of his chair. "Yeah, well, I'm not exactly Pollyanna myself. We have nothing in common. I won't do it."

"I'll do it for you."

"I'll remove your spleen with my crowbar."

"YOUR COACH WILL PROVIDE emotional support and companionship at a time when you'll need him or her more than you've ever needed anyone in your life."

Serena Borders, the American Society for Psychoprophylaxis in Obstetrics-Lamaze-certified trainer, stood in the center of the carpeted room and smiled at the half-dozen couples distributed around her on the floor with their pillows.

Nancy leaned a little self-consciously against Jave, who bracketed her with his knees and quietly awaited instructions.

She shouldn't be nervous, she reasoned, as the instructor gave a brief history of the Lamaze program, and explained that its purpose was to teach relaxation, breathing and expulsion. Nancy, who'd borrowed several books from the library on the subject and watched the film several times, let her mind wander.

Though it refused to wander too far. It seemed to be concentrated, along with every sensory receptor in her body, on the man who supported her weight.

That wasn't so surprising, though, she figured. They'd spent a lot of time together in the past week and she was feeling a closeness to him that was really very strange. She'd been to one of Pete's games and one of Eddy's, she'd helped Aggie make Sunday dinner, and she'd spent yesterday evening on the *Mud Hen* with Jave and Tom deciding on fabric and paint colors for the galley, the head, the small salon and the staterooms.

His family liked her. She liked them. She found herself beginning to want something that couldn't possibly happen here. How *had* she gotten into this? Greed, she reminded herself. Simple, unvarnished greed.

"Effective relaxation," Serena was saying, "will diminish fatigue and pain. Now the first step is to get comfortable. Lie down on your sides."

Serena demonstrated with a handsome couple who appeared either to have never seen each other before, or come to class straight from a sizzling argument. Since the former possibility seemed highly unlikely, Nancy found herself wondering what they had argued about. The man, broad-shouldered and dark-haired, looked vaguely familiar.

Jave told her he managed the Heron Point branch of the First Coastal Bank, that they'd worked on several community projects, and he'd helped him and Tom with a loan for the boat.

The woman was tall, slender and very blond. She had masses of tightly curled hair that fell forward when she lay down. He smoothed it gently back for her, despite his tight-lipped frown. Serena had him lie down beside his partner, close but not touching.

She made shooing motions toward the other couples. "You do the same. Coaches, I want you close, but not touching. It's important for you to learn to relax, too, because when the time comes, our mothers won't respond to tension and fear. At least, they won't respond in a positive way."

Nancy felt Jave's hands on her as he helped her tip onto her side. Then she felt his presence behind her, though she could no longer feel his touch. The skin prickled on her neck, while sensation rayed out from her spinal column like the day she'd tried these exercises by watching the videotape and he'd run a finger down her vertebrae to make her straighten.

To distract herself, she watched the other couples. Beside the demonstrating pair, there was a plump couple who couldn't stop laughing, a very young couple who gazed adoringly into each other's eyes, an older man and woman who had confided they were expecting their first child after fifteen years of trying, and a very pretty young woman whose coach was her best friend—another woman. She was very serious, Nancy noted, and followed every instruction to the letter and with grave intensity. Nancy guessed she was an accountant or an IRS auditor.

"Now, I want you to listen to the rhythm of your own breathing." Serena walked among them, peering down at them as though they were under glass. "Relax your hands, relax your face, relax your shoulders, relax your knees."

She waited a brief amount of time between instructions. Nancy tried desperately to relax, but guessed the effort involved was negating the outcome.

Serena leaned over her and opened the fist into which her hand had clenched. "Relax, Nancy. Relax. Having this baby is going to be a wonderful experience. You're going to enjoy it. Relax."

As Serena walked on to the next couple, Nancy felt Jave's breath against the back of her neck, then his hand. He kneaded gently. "What's the matter?" he asked in a whisper. "You're tight as a drum."

"In case you hadn't noticed," she turned to whisper irascibly, "I am *carrying* a drum. It's big and round enough and it's always beating on me."

That wasn't the problem, of course, but it was the best she could do in front of eleven other people.

She wished he wouldn't touch her, and breathed a sigh of relief when Serena went to the front of the room to deliver more instructions and Jave dropped his hand.

"All right, coaches. I want you to change the level of your awareness now. Notice your 'mother' as she begins to become aware of her surroundings."

For Nancy, who hadn't relaxed in the first place, her

awareness of her surroundings was doubly sharp. And it was comprised entirely of Jave.

She'd never been a particularly sensual woman. She'd made love with Jerry, of course, and, before her pregnancy, it had been nice. But it certainly hadn't been everything literature and Hollywood purported it to be.

But, suddenly, it was always on her mind. She wanted to make love with Jave. She fantasized about it. Alone in her bed at night, she swore she could even imagine it happening. His hands on her sensitive flesh, his breath against her breasts, pearling their tips. His fingers and his breath moving down her body, forming a molten pool of sensation that finally forced her to get up and make a cup of tea.

"Now, coaches, I want you to touch your mothers. Touch is a very effective technique in releasing tension. It has to be gentle, of course, but firm. When her mind is occupied during the birth process, your touch will have to be firm to get through. Now touch her head."

Nancy felt Jave's large hand cup her scalp, palm against her crown, fingertips against her temples and her forehead. She felt his energy jolt into her, his calmness imbue her with peace.

She let herself drift along as the technique began to make headway against her tension.

Serena went on. "Touch her side and press lightly inward."

Nancy felt Jave's hand on her ribs on her left side. It stroked lightly forward over the mound of her baby, then back again. His touch was confident, even possessive. She let herself float off on her favorite little fantasy and pretended that they were like most couples here—that he was her husband and this was his baby.

But that was a mistake. As she let reality slip away, she lost her frail grasp on the relaxation technique and tension came back into play. It was rife with awareness of every one of Jave's fingertips moving over her swollen belly in gentle, proprietary circles.

AHHH. TOTAL BODY MASSAGE. I like it. Can we do it again? Watch the ribs, though. And the soles of my feet. Hee! Hee!

SHE BARELY RESISTED a moan. Her body didn't seem to know it was required to be celibate. It did all the things she imagined at night in her lonely bed. It squirmed and pooled with warmth and filled with a desperate longing. Only now she was in a room filled with people, and she was supposed to be concentrating on the little life inside her.

She was suddenly swamped by selfishness. She was going to be a terrible mother. She'd suspected it all along. Here she was supposedly concentrating on her baby and all she could think of was herself and how she wanted this man.

She survived Jave's execution of the rest of Serena's instructions, though she didn't know how. Resolved to endure it, she lived through his massage of her shoulders, the circles he made with his thumbs and fingertips down her spinal column. But she almost lost it during the whole hand press and the scalp massage. "Use a rotating motion on the scalp, as though you're washing hair."

As they all filed out of class with Serena's beam of approval, Nancy noted that the handsome couple looked as tense as she felt. The woman caught her eye, and for just an instant, she felt a curious and inexplicable kinship.

"Bye," she said quietly. "See you next time."

Nancy nodded. "Bye."

She remembered when they'd all introduced themselves at the beginning of class that the pretty blonde's name had been different from her coach's. Had she just chosen to retain her maiden name, or were they not married? Was it one of those designer relationships where couples had a baby but chose not to marry? She knew many couples did that successfully; it just seemed to her like such an uncertain way to run a family. She found herself worrying about them as well as herself.

"Are they married?" she asked Jave.

He shook his head, frowning. "No. She was acting as

surrogate for her sister, Ryan's—the banker's—wife. But Cassie died, and now they're working together to get this baby born."

"It doesn't look," Nancy said, watching them walk away, "as though they're happy in their work."

Jave placed a hand at her back and pushed her gently toward the car.

"You don't look very happy, either," he noted as he drove away from the hospital and toward the coast road. "Something you want to tell me?"

Nancy was primed for just that question. After that interminable evening of torture following on the heels of the weeks of anxiety laced with lust and burgeoning dreams that could be nothing but trouble, she forgot the beautiful blonde's problems and rounded on him, eyes turbulent with her own difficulties.

"No, there's nothing I want to tell you!" she said, her voice breaking. "That's what got me into this in the first place."

He pulled over to the side of the road and into the sheltering branches of a row of shaggy cedars. He removed his seat belt and turned to her. His eyes went over her in quiet analysis. He'd had his hands all over her body for more than an hour. He seemed completely unaffected, while she was one raw, raging nerve. That annoyed her beyond description.

"No," he reminded gently. "Claiming to have a husband is what got you into this. You feeling blue?"

"Blue? Blue?" She slapped his hand away when he tried to touch her. "No, I feel Red! Red with a capital *R!* Wildfire, fire engine, gushing blood Red! And don't *touch* me. I've *had* it with your tender pat and stroke, as though you have every...as though..."

She heard herself sounding like a deranged fishwife dealing with issues of id confusion, and stopped. She stared at him while emotion mounted and all her options for backing out of the conversation with dignity intact seemed to disintegrate. She couldn't walk home. Heron Point had no bus system. She didn't have cash for a cab.

She leaned the side of her head against the back of the seat and dissolved into tears. Emotion rolled over and over her, confusing how things were with how she would like them to be, and leaving her feeling jealous and short-changed.

She couldn't understand herself. She'd never been into self-pity. Of course, she'd never wanted Jave Nicholas and been sure she couldn't have him before.

Jave felt severely battered by physical and emotional frustration and repression. Despite all his noble claims to the contrary, he wanted to make love to her every time he saw her, and was forced to remind himself that her condition dictated it would probably be Thanksgiving before that could ever come about. And it was only mid-August now. Three months. God. He expected to implode before Labor Day.

It was going to be hell to hold her, but she needed him.

Nancy felt Jave's arms come around her, and she allowed herself the luxury of leaning into him, of wrapping her arms around his middle and holding on, forgetting that she'd just insisted he not touch her.

He stroked her hair, her back, the mound of her baby cradled between them. "As though what?" he asked.

She shouldn't say it aloud. It would reveal her vulnerability. It would show him what she wanted. And it had always been her policy to keep what was in her heart to herself.

But not only did she have new life in her, that life seemed to be changing her own. Sometimes she didn't recognize herself anymore. She *wanted* him to know what she felt.

"As though this were your baby," she whispered, tipping her head back to look into his eyes. "You touch me as though...this were your baby. And I wish she were. I wish she were."

Jave felt every frustration within him melt into insignificance. She could not have said anything that would have firmed his resolve to withstand the physical and emotional tyrannies of this relationship more than those few words—"I wish she were."

"The solution to that," he said calmly, combing his fingers through the sides of her hair, "is very simple."

She sighed softly against him. "Nothing in this entire situation is simple," she denied.

He kissed her pessimism away. "When you become mine," he insisted, "the baby becomes mine." She blinked at him, obviously needing that clarified. He did it readily. "Marry me."

She reacted precisely as he'd known she would. She pushed herself upright and pressed her hands against his chest to force a distance between them. "That would never work," she said, her voice soft despite the firmness in her hands. But that defined her, he knew. A heart and a body always at odds.

But understanding her didn't make it easier to deal with her. "Why not?" he asked pointedly. "It's what you want. I can see it in your eyes. It's there now."

Nancy abruptly turned her face and focused on the world beyond the windshield, as though that gesture alone could deprive him of what he knew. It was dusk turning to darkness, a single pair of headlights coming from the west.

"I know nothing about families," she said, rummaging in her purse for a tissue with one hand, eyes still focused on the windshield. "I could no more take on two little boys than I could..." She turned impatiently toward her purse, further frustrated by her inability to find a tissue. She pulled out her wallet, her makeup bag, her keys, her calendar.

Jave reached over the back of the seat into a fabric organizer attached to it by a loop around the headrest and produced a small travel pack of tissues.

Nancy accepted it with a sodden glance. "Thank you," she said, then dabbed at her eyes and finished her statement.

"I could no more do that than I could win the Edgar," she said.

He frowned. They were mere inches apart in the front seat and he fought parallel eruptions of lust and temper.

"Do you approach everything with such lack of resolve?" he asked quietly.

She finally focused on him, obviously offended. Her eyelashes were spiked with tears, her lips still vaguely atremble. "I know my limitations."

He nodded, leaning back slightly to put a little distance between them. It was difficult to be merciless with a woman when he could smell her fragrance and feel the warmth radiating from her body.

"I'm sure that's a good thing," he said, "if you're a tightrope walker or a sky diver. But if you're going to be a parent, you'd damn well better understand that your limits are going to be stretched beyond anything you thought you could handle. Most of the time you're working without a net or a chute, and it's all too important for you to fail to come through."

She angled her chin. "That's precisely what I mean. No one ever came through for me. I'm not sure I could come through for you."

"You're looking forward to your baby," he remonstrated. "How do you expect to come through for her? Why is that different?"

"Because it'll just be her and me," she retorted, her voice rising a decibel. "One-to-one. I can do that. She'll be part of *me*."

He shook his head and grimaced. "So this impressionable little baby is going to learn all her lessons from a woman who can't trust anyone?"

Nancy opened her mouth to protest his assessment of the situation, then hesitated, unable to produce a convincing response.

While she thought it over, Jave swept a hand gently down her cheek, then pinned her chin between his thumb and forefinger. He felt her stiffen, knew she concentrated on his touch with her entire being.

"And do you really think," he asked softly, "that I don't belong to you every bit as much as she does? I'm not living in your belly, but I know I'm in here." He moved that hand down to the inside of her left breast, right over her heart.

Nancy felt its delicious weight there and closed her eyes against it, swallowing.

"If you walked away from me now, you'd spend the rest of your life wondering what lovemaking between us would have been like. You'd dream about falling asleep in my arms and waking up there. And you'd remember all the things we've done together, and imagine everything that remains undone."

He leaned down and kissed her lightly, just to remind her what they had shared—and all the promises it held.

"Most lovers," he said, "are tied by the memories of nights of tenderness and passion. You and I..." His hand moved back to her chin and he ran his thumb lightly over her bottom lip. It was trembling again. "You and I are connected by all we know we can have when there's finally time for us. That moment is out there like a light, waiting for us in the distance."

Nancy felt herself being pulled toward him as if she were magnetized. Everything he said was true. She felt as close to him as though they'd been lovers for years, and yet, when she indulged her fantasies, she felt excitement in the dream that somewhere, someday, there would be their first time.

Then her cellular phone rang.

Jave and Nancy stared at each other, unable to surface from that shared thought. Then the telephone rang again, and Nancy delved into her purse for the phone. She raised the antenna, pushed the button, and cleared her throat, groping for a normal tone.

"Hello?" Even as she answered, she wondered who could be calling her. Jave was usually the only one who used the number, and he was sitting beside her.

"Nancy? It's Mother. Where are you?"

Nancy frowned in surprise. "I'm on the road on my way home from Lamaze class. How did you get this number?"

There was a sigh of impatience on the other end of the line. "Just once I'd like to talk to you without having to answer research questions on how I've located you. Jave gave me the number."

Nancy gaped at Jave for a full ten seconds while all the ramifications of the situation came home to her.

"Jave" gave it to her? Not J.V. or Dr. Nicholas, but Jave?

"Mother, how do you know Jave?" she asked, her voice deadly quiet.

Jave thought a definitive, four-letter word and abandoned all hope of Nancy falling into his arms tonight with admissions of trust—however frail—and undying love. He returned her glare with a look of defensive unrepentance.

Another sigh from the other end of the connection. "The aide who answered your phone the day I called you at the hospital mentioned that someone named Jave was taking you home. When I wanted to know how you were, I simply called the hospital, asked for Jave and was connected with the doctor in Radiology."

"And when was this?" Nancy asked.

"Oh, let's see. Three or four weeks ago."

The O shape of Nancy's mouth rounded further and Jave rolled his eyes at her and moved back behind the steering wheel. He should have told her. But Denise had asked him not to. Deceptions weren't safe, but his relationship with Nancy was built on them. He was growing more and more comfortable with them.

Suddenly the most critical question of the moment occurred to Nancy.

"Mom, where are you?" she asked.

"On your front porch," her mother replied, "talking to you on *Willy's* cellular phone. And we're being stared at by a very malevolent-looking black cat. When are you coming home?"

Nancy felt panic begin to close her throat. No. Oh, no. Her mother was here. She fixed Jave with her deadliest look, but he was staring out the windshield, the wrist of his right hand resting on the steering wheel.

"I'll be right there, Mother. Goodbye."

Nancy hit the Power button, pushed down the antenna, and slammed the phone back in her purse.

"What *right* do you have to talk to my mother behind my back?" she demanded.

Jave turned to her with a look of weary forbearance. "Every right in the world. This is a free country. Or don't you *trust* that notion?"

Nancy ignored his sarcasm, too incensed by the thought that her mother and Jave had been in touch without her knowledge.

"She said you gave her this number three weeks ago," she accused.

"That's right," he said, nodding. "She was concerned about you and asked me about your condition. I told her you were doing fine, that your obstetrician and I were keeping a close eye on you, and I gave her your cellular phone number. She got upset when she couldn't reach you at home."

Nancy huffed in indignation. "If I'd wanted her to have the number," she said loudly, "I'd have given it to her."

"She's your mother, Nancy," he said reasonably. "She was worried. You wouldn't let her come to you and you wouldn't go to her, so it made her feel better to have another way to keep in touch."

Her tears were dry now, her vulnerability of a few moments ago well and truly hardened. She donned her wronged-daughter persona like a suit of armor.

"Years ago," she said stiffly, "when I wanted her, she went off to become a star. Well, now I don't need her. Only she's here, thanks to you." She put a hand to her forehead and groaned, the thought of having to cope with her mother more than she could bear. Then she pulled herself together and turned to narrow her eyes at Jave. "This is all your fault. So you're going to get me out of it."

He tried to imagine what she had in mind. He couldn't. "Really," he said. "And why would I do that?"

"Because *it's all your fault!*" she said again at full voice. Then she drew a deep breath and seemed to be counting. When she'd finished, she said in even tones, "And she and Willy Brock are sitting on my front porch."

Jave turned the key in the ignition.

"You're going to do what I tell you," she said, her tone threatening.

He gave her a lazy-lidded look over his shoulder as he pulled onto the quiet road. It was flat and clear for a distance, so he floored it. All the love he'd felt for her moments ago was still there, but was temporarily sealed off by exasperation. "You have a lot to learn about negotiating with a man," he said.

"This is not negotiable," she said firmly and a little desperately. He'd never seen her this frightened, even the day he'd done her ultrasound. He wondered if she was concerned as much with seeing her mother as she was with how she would *feel* when she saw her. "You owe me this," she declared. Then she said quickly, crisply, "I'm going to tell her that you're living with me."

He neither agreed, nor disagreed. "Do you ever handle a problem," he asked, "without lying about it?"

It was a valid question, she realized. That was all she'd done since she'd met him. "I write fiction," she said with a helpless wave of both hands. "Making something up is what comes to mind."

"I think it's becoming a crutch you should take time to deal with."

"I will. As soon as she's gone. Will you do it?"

He considered it. He'd go to the bowels of hell for her, but it didn't seem prudent at this moment for her to know that. "What's in it for me?" he asked.

She let her head fall back against the headrest. "I'll let you live. Only because I'm fond of your children."

The road began to wind and he slowed the car, glancing in the rearview mirror. They were alone on the road.

"And I'll do it," he said, "because your baby needs someone to think of it. And if you get any more distressed, you're going to induce labor."

"It is a *she*."

"If you say so."

YOU TELL HIM, MOM. I'm with you. But I'm excited about meeting my grandmother.

CHAPTER TEN

DENISE DiBENEDETTO did not look fifty. Jave watched her unfold gracefully from the porch steps as he pulled up to Nancy's front lawn. She wore jeans and a sweatshirt with the St. Tropez logo emblazened on it, and simple white tennis shoes. Hair a little lighter than Nancy's was caught back with a broad silver clip.

She had Nancy's brown eyes, a warm smile and a solid handshake. Jave knew he was bucking the tide, but he liked her.

She embraced Nancy the brief two seconds that was all Nancy would allow, then smiled at Jave. "Thank you for looking out for her," she said. "I wasn't a very good mother and it seems I'm not going to get a second chance, so I appreciate all you've done."

"My pleasure," Jave said. He read something in her eyes that he often saw in the faces of terminal patients. It was a brave acceptance mingled with wild recklessness, a sort of nothing-left-to-lose attitude.

She turned with a smile to the tall, loose-limbed man beside her who appeared to be about her own age. He wore jeans, a well-worn chambray shirt and a gray Western hat. Jave had seen his face on CD covers and on videos. He was nice-looking in a Marlboro Man kind of way, but his gentle voice and manner belied the chiseled features.

"Willy Brock," he introduced himself. "Friend of Denise's. How are ya?"

Nancy shook hands politely with him and led the way

inside. She disappeared to make coffee and left Jave to entertain them. Instead, they entertained him.

He understood that Nancy's mother had walked away from her family, and that that had had a lasting and traumatic effect on Nancy. He could relate. Bonnie had done the same to him and their children, yet he couldn't find it in him to hate either of them.

Bonnie was on a search for something he doubted she would find in a new man and a new relationship. He pitied her. But Denise seemed to have such vivacious energy, and he remembered what Nancy had said about her father being there but never available. He imagined it must have been difficult for a personality like hers to live unnoticed, unacknowledged.

Nancy fussed with filters and coffee and heard the sound of her mother's girlish laughter. She wanted to feel annoyed. She didn't. She felt nostalgic instead.

She remembered lying in bed and hearing the sound of it carrying up the stairs and into her bedroom. She remembered that it had soothed her and made her feel safe. But she remembered also how bereft she had been when it was gone.

Nancy pushed the thought from her mind and slammed the lid on the coffee carafe. She placed it on the coffeemaker and turned it on.

She went into the living room to find Jave and her mother laughing together on the sofa, and Willy carrying in two large bags.

Nancy smiled casually, taking the chair opposite the sofa. "Mom, I'm afraid you can't stay here," she said, thinking as she heard the sound of her own voice that that was probably as far from courteous as one could get. "You see…" She indicated Jave with a wave of her hand and fixed him with a look that warned him not to contradict her. "He's living here with me and…well, there just isn't enough room. There's only one real bedroom. The other one's full of all the things I couldn't unpack in my condition."

Denise nodded as though she understood, then patted the sofa on which she sat. "This'll do fine for Willy and me. We're used to hotel rooms and the back of a tour bus. We'll be fine."

"No...you see..." Nancy thought fast. "Jave has two little boys, and that's where *they* sleep."

Denise nodded again. "Pete and Eddy. He was just telling me about them."

Nancy turned up her glare over the forcedly sweet smile she sent Jave. "They're wonderful, but they're pretty rambunctious and I don't think..."

Jave propped his elbow on the back of the sofa and smiled into Nancy's glare. "I think we could stay at my mother's for a few weeks so your mother can be with you when the baby's born."

"No!" Nancy said, inching forward in her chair, her face going pale. She had expected his cooperation. She felt panicky without it. "Jave," she said, an underlying plea in the words she spoke, "I need you here. Mom can't help me if anything goes wrong."

Denise sat up a little stiffly, looking from Nancy to Jave. "I thought you said you were doing fine. That everything was all right."

"Well, it is," Nancy said quickly, "but...you know how these things are...it could change at any moment." She focused narrowly on Jave. "Darling, please," she said, accentuating the endearment, lending it a lethal quality, "I need you with me."

The thought of facing her mother alone was debilitating, even though the alternative was facing her with the man who could ruin her life—in more ways than one.

Jave raised an eyebrow at her little scene, then went to sit on the arm of her chair and put a comforting hand on her shoulder. "All right. All right." She sagged in relief. Then he added, "The boys will stay with Mom, and your mother and Willy can have the sofa." He squeezed her to him as she looked up at him, her eyes ready to ignite. "I'll stay right here. Don't worry."

Denise looked a little troubled. "I hate to part you from your children, Jave."

"It's all right," he assured her. "My mother's about to take them with her to Bend for a week to visit my uncle, then it'll be just about time for them to go back to school. They spend a lot of time with my mother while I'm working anyway."

Nancy thought the evening would never end. Her mother and Willy regaled them with stories about their life on the road. She told herself that there was nothing she could do about this now. Her mother had insinuated herself into her life until the baby was born, and the best thing for all concerned was for her to cope with it graciously.

I like her, Mom. I have a grandmother!

But she didn't feel gracious. She felt resentful and angry...and as though she might erupt emotionally at any moment like an egg in a microwave. She hadn't quite recovered from her Lamaze class and her discussion with Jave about their relationship. He'd asked her to marry him. And she'd been about to *consider* it. Then he'd admitted moments later that he'd been in collusion with her mother for weeks.

Jave excused himself just before ten to "check with the hospital," but Nancy guessed he was calling home and explaining the situation to Aggie.

She wanted to run away. But she was getting to the point where all she could manage was a sloppily navigated waddle. No. She had to stay.

Jave helped Willy bring in some more of their bags while Denise helped Nancy make up the sofa bed.

"I'll make you cinnamon French toast for breakfast," Denise said, smoothing the sheets in place. "You used to love that."

"I don't have any cinnamon bread," Nancy said, hoping to dampen her maternal enthusiasm.

Her mother smiled brightly. "That's what supermarkets are for."

Nancy knew there was little point in arguing. Her mother would do what she wanted to do. Then a critical detail in all this occurred to her. "Mom," she said, straightening to put a hand to her back. It was beginning to ache. "I have to explain something to you."

Her mother shook a blanket. "Of course. I'm listening."

Nancy drew a deep breath. "No one knows you're my mother, so...please don't mention it to anyone."

Hurt flashed briefly across Denise's eyes, but she nodded and continued to smile. "I know you're not proud of the fact. I promise not to bring it up."

"It isn't that." Nancy explained about the hospital's birthing-rooms extravaganza, about Amy Brown's enthusiasm and all the gifts involved, about her pretense that Jerry was still around and in the Coast Guard.

Her mother listened quietly, though her eyes widened as the story progressed. "What are you going to do when it's time to have the baby and it's Jave holding your hand instead of the phantom husband? And the hospital staff knows Jave. Won't they be...surprised?"

Nancy nodded, afraid to think about that too closely at the moment. She could deal with only one crisis at a time. "I don't know. But I'll think of something."

"Nancy," Denise said, walking around the sofa bed to place an arm around her shoulders, "when the time comes, your mind will be on anything but explaining yourself. All you'll want to think about is getting the bowling ball out of your stomach. If you're going to come up with a good story, you'd better think about it now. You know..." she said, her tone deliberately casual. Nancy suspected what was coming. "I'd be thrilled to buy all those baby things for you."

"No," Nancy said firmly, moving out from under her arm on the pretext of rearranging pillows. "I'll do it myself."

"Nancy..."

Nancy smiled stiffly. "Good night, Mother." She called a good-night to Willy as he and Jave walked in with the last of the luggage—two guitars.

Nancy stood in the middle of her bedroom in her long cotton nightgown and waited for Jave. He walked into the room a moment later with the brisk confidence of a man who had every right to join her.

"Sorry," he said quietly after the door was closed. "I'd have knocked, but I didn't think it would fit in with your scenario."

She squared her shoulders, trying to look in control of the situation. But all the action did was make her stomach protrude farther and accentuate her vulnerability. Still, she played the role.

"Thank you for your assistance and support," she whispered harshly. "You promised to help me!"

"I did," he said. Hands loosely on his hips, he leaned over her until they were nose-to-nose, he, too, whispering. "That's your mother, and she came a long way to be with you. I know you have grievances against her, but maybe some things have changed since those days. She seems like a sweet and giving lady. Maybe you could learn something from her."

Nancy was too angry and frustrated for speech. She pointed to the old four-poster. "We have to share the bed," she said. "I know that. I wouldn't ask you to sit up all night. But you keep to your side, Nicholas. We may have to sleep together, but we're no longer 'seeing' each other, so don't you *touch* me!"

Nancy went to the far side of the bed. Jave disappeared into the bathroom. Nancy climbed under the covers and listened to the rushing sound of the shower. Jave was out in a few minutes wearing a white T-shirt and a pair of white cotton briefs.

Nancy watched him walk to the light switch, shoulders broad under the thin cotton, back straight and narrowing to tight, muscular hips neatly contoured in the briefs. His legs were long and moved with easy grace. Lust raged in her like a hungry black bear.

She pulled the sheet up over her head and turned to the window. "Good night," she muttered, in the tone one might use to say "Drop dead."

She felt the mattress take Jave's weight and tried to relax, telling herself she could get through this if she just remained calm.

Then he made that impossible by reaching around her, dipping a hand under the bulk of her baby and pulling her back against him. She gasped a startled little cry, but his enveloping arms were too comfortable and comforting to encourage protest.

"We agreed..." she began to grumble because she felt she had to.

"No, we didn't," he corrected quietly in her ear. "You dictated. Now you know how I react to that."

"This is all your fault," she said lazily. This bed had never seemed so cozy. With his solid warmth to lean against, she felt all the gnarly concerns of the day smooth out into inconveniences she'd probably be able to handle when she had time to think clearly. She snuffled sleepily, unable to completely abandon the need to be quarrelsome. After all, it *was* really his fault. "I'll never be able to sleep. And you probably won't, either. I toss and turn a lot...."

From the living room, the sound of a country tune blossomed. It floated on the quiet night, her mother's husky, vaguely anguished voice joined by Willy's deep, lighthearted sound. The strum of a guitar provided soothing accompaniment, and Nancy found herself nuzzling into the shoulder Jave had eased under her and drifting off to sleep.

MMM. THIS IS NICE. Cozier than usual tonight, huh, Mom? Nice to lean on somebody who isn't always moving me around.

SHAMAN WAS SITTING on the slope when Nancy went out the following morning with white turkey meat from a can. This was bribery, she knew, but she was beginning to worry about him. It was almost fall. She hated the thought of him stubbornly living out in the wind and rain and eventually even snow.

"He doesn't like me," Denise said from behind her. Nancy turned to find her mother standing in the open doorway.

"He's suspicious of everyone," she said. She tossed out the water in his dish and refilled it from the hose. While she worked, she told her mother about her history with Shaman. "He stays around because he knows I'll feed him. And he comes a little closer than he used to. But he still won't let me touch him."

"Maybe he was abused," Denise suggested. "Or has lived on his own for so long, he's forgotten how to relate to other creatures. You just have to let him work it out in his own time."

Nancy nodded reluctantly, watching the cat refuse to move until she went back inside. "I know. I won't push. I just worry about him, stuck outside the circle of warmth and security because he's afraid to believe I won't hurt him."

Nancy missed her mother's wry perusal of the back of her head. When she turned, Denise had gone inside.

BY MIDMORNING, Nancy had Boeneke and Geneva tied up together on the second floor of a warehouse in which the antagonist had placed a bomb. They had eleven minutes to free themselves and run to safety.

But she couldn't for the life of her come up with a plan that didn't sound like everything she'd ever seen on prime-time cop shows.

She contemplated the monitor and listened to the quiet. Jave had left early for the hospital, and her mother and Willy had gone to town to get groceries.

"Cantaloupe and kielbasa and..." Her mother, doing an

inventory of supplies had leaned into the refrigerator for a closer look. Then her head had appeared above the refrigerator door, her eyes wide with surprise. "Napoleons? You still love to bake?"

Nancy, pouring tea, had nodded. "Yes. But I still don't cook very well."

Her mother had fluttered her fingers greedily. "Can I have it?"

"What?"

"The napoleon."

"Yes. Of course."

She'd reached into the refrigerator, pulled out the sweet, and offered a bite to Willy, who stood behind her with a pad and pencil, taking down the grocery list.

He chewed and swallowed. "Delicious."

Her mother took a bite, chewed, and made a sound one would usually associate with the arms of a lover.

"Is this the last one?" she asked.

Nancy nodded. "Jave's mother loves them, too, so I sent some to her."

"Well, tell Willy what goes into them so you can make some more!" And nibbling on the napoleon, she'd moved on to an inspection of the cupboards.

Nancy smiled as she remembered her mother's ingenuous greed. Then she shook off the thought and tried to concentrate on her work.

HER MOTHER AND WILLY returned at lunchtime with a dozen bags of groceries and takeout from the deli.

By then, Boeneke and Geneva had made a daring escape from a second story window before the explosion, thanks to a Swiss army knife in Geneva's purse and the fortuitous arrival of a sanitation truck.

TOM AND AGGIE and the boys arrived at about the same time with several casseroles and a watermelon. Aggie greeted everyone politely but slid suspicious glances toward Denise.

"Jave said he'd pick up some things on the way home from the hospital tonight," Aggie said, stopping in the middle of the kitchen and studying the ample stores that surrounded her. "Maybe," she added, "you should call and tell him not to bother." She went to the refrigerator as though she had every right to. "In any case, I know how you love my pasta *bolognese,* so I've brought enough that you won't have to cook tonight."

"Pasta *bolognese?*" Denise was beside Aggie at the refrigerator. "May I taste?"

Aggie looked from Denise to Nancy, then back again, obviously unsure whether or not the request was for purposes of criticism.

Denise produced a fork, and after a moment's consideration, Aggie elbowed a grocery bag aside, placed the casserole on the counter, and removed the lid. "By all means," she said, her tone aggressive.

Nancy waited a little nervously. She didn't know what she'd do if her mother suggested the dish needed more of something or other and the women began feuding in her kitchen.

But her mother tasted and made that orgasmic sound again. Then she dipped her fork in a second time, cupped one hand protectively under the dangling noodles, and offered the bite to Willy.

He took it and quickly agreed that it was delicious. "That's better than Abrogazzi's in Milan," he said.

Aggie beamed.

"Can you join us for lunch?" Denise asked. "We have cold cuts, cheeses and salads from the deli."

The boys, staring at Willy in his snakeskin boots and his hand-tooled belt with its buckle fashioned out of gold nuggets, followed him eagerly when he suggested they create an assembly line to put the groceries away.

Denise and Aggie worked companionably, pulling down

plates and setting out lunch, shooing Nancy back to her computer until it was ready.

Aggie and the boys were still there when Jave came back that evening. Aggie called Tom at home and told him dinner was being served at Jave and Nancy's. Nancy overheard that comment and caught Aggie's wink. She seemed perfectly willing to play her part in their little scenario and had apparently coached the boys to do the same. Both children took the opportunity to hug her, laughingly straining around her bulk and telling her they missed her.

They ate pasta and salad and watermelon until everyone groaned, then they moved out onto the porch, and Denise and Willy played their guitars and sang while the sun set and dusk turned to velvety darkness.

Nancy sat with Jave on the glider, crowded close to him as the children joined them. Pete leaned his weight on the mound of her stomach, leaving her little choice but to lean against the support Jave provided. He placed an arm behind them on the back of the glider and kept it moving lazily with the toe of his Nike on the porch floor.

Eddy leaned over the other corner, mesmerized by the movement of Willy's fingers on the guitar.

Aggie took the wicker chair at an angle to the glider, and Tom sat on the floor, his back against the balusters on the railing. Mo was stretched out beside him on his back, his rear legs pointed, his forelegs curled in a hedonistic display of contentment.

Nancy, gazing into the darkness and concentrating on the music, saw a shadow move in the vicinity of her truck. She sat up, startled.

Jave eased her back against him, his hand soothing her hair. "It's all right" he said quietly. "It's only Shaman."

He was drawn by the warmth, Nancy knew, just as she was. She relaxed, and for the first time that she could remember since her mother left home, she tried to look at her with unbiased eyes.

There was a bittersweetness about her, Nancy noted, and

for all the loving glances she sent Willy's way, she often looked away after the contact, effectively shutting him out of whatever lay behind her thoughts. Nancy saw Willy's disappointment, then the loving gaze he invariably returned, followed by a smiling persistence that said more effectively than any words that he was there for the duration.

Denise sat in the crook created by the banister and the porch column, and Nancy had to admire how slender she'd remained. In jeans and a simple pink camp shirt, she looked feminine and supple and somehow eternal. Nancy felt like a walrus on a rock, large and braying, and unable to do anything but occasionally slide off her perch to her next duty.

She wondered idly if she'd ever look like her old self again. This pregnancy seemed to be going on forever, probably because suddenly so much in her life had developed around it—the gifts from the birthing-room extravaganza, her mother's insistence on visiting, her relationship with Jave and her resultant connection with his family.

But the connections grew as she grew, and she couldn't dispel the feeling that the impending birth of her baby girl would just be the beginning of an enormous disruption with far-reaching consequences.

And all at once everything frightened her—childbirth, children, love, reestablishing a relationship with her mother. She considered running and hiding, but at eight months along she could barely waddle, much less run, and she doubted that anything short of the pyramids could hide her.

Nothing was going according to plan. Claiming to have a husband was supposed to secure her position as the hospital's model mommy, but Jave had discovered that it was all a lie and blackmailed her into a relationship to secure his secrecy. So—she'd taken on a boyfriend to convince the hospital that she had a husband. Or something like that.

She finally excused herself, pleading a backache. She kissed the boys—a sincere gesture, not one for the benefit of her deception—and waved a smiling good-night to everyone else, insisting that they stay and enjoy the evening. Then she pecked Jave on the cheek for the sake of appearances and went inside.

In the dark bedroom, she stood at the foot of the bed, listening to the strains of the guitar and wishing things were different. Wishing *she* could be different.

"I can help with that backache." Jave's voice preceded the soft click of the closing bedroom door.

Tension inched up her back to the base of her neck. She put a hand to it, rubbing unconsciously.

"I'm fine, really. You should be entertaining…"

He wasn't listening. He took a small straight-backed chair from the corner and placed it directly in front of her, advising her to straddle it. Then he took two pillows from the bed and placed them between her and the back of the chair.

"Lean into the pillows," he said, pushing her gently with a hand between her shoulders.

Nancy opened her mouth to insist once again that she was fine, but her protest was muffled by the pillow.

"Concentrate," he said, placing his hands on her shoulders, "on putting all your worries out of your mind. Pretend you've just handed them all to me, and you don't have to be responsible for them anymore."

She leaned into the pillows and closed her eyes. "For how long?"

His thumbs began stroking circles down her spinal column, his long fingers working down her shoulder blades and her ribs. "You have to pretend it's forever, or you won't relax."

"Mmm." She was succumbing already to the strength in his hands. She remembered that moment during her ultrasound when she'd moved and he'd come back to the gurney to reposition her. His grip had felt as though it could keep her safe forever. "So you're going to have to raise this baby?" she asked, suddenly relaxed enough to feel playful.

He laughed softly. "That's right. Don't examine the details. Just operate on faith."

Her sigh went a little deeper, her relaxation becoming a little more complete. "I know you're a good parent."

"Thank you."

"Where are you going to send her to college?"

"Oregon State."

"Good school?"

"Great. Produced me."

She smiled into the pillow as his hands repeated their down-and-up journey. "You won't let her date too early?"

"Not until she's twenty."

Her sigh was deep now—all the way to the heart of her real concerns. She exhaled and sloughed them off. "She should have a fussy wedding."

"Of course."

"Since you're dispensing with all my problems," she said lazily, "I can just assume I've gotten my figure back, right?"

Jave rubbed at her shoulders and the base of her neck. "Every delicious curve."

She turned her head. It now felt as though it rested on a springy stem. "Actually, when I'm not pregnant, I'm kind of...flat."

"Since we're operating on faith," he said, "consider that you retained a certain...ripeness just where you want it."

"Mmm," she murmured again. She hadn't the energy for words.

"There." He peeled her gently from the pillows. "Now, let's get you to bed while you're still relaxed enough to sleep."

Nancy accepted his hand up, then turned to lean on him as far as the bed, but found that once she got there, she didn't want to let go of his solidity and all it represented at that moment. She'd shed concerns and responsibilities and he represented everything she longed for with all her heart.

Jave's first instinct was to resist her tug onto the bed. He'd lain there all last night, able only to hold her while his body rioted for closer contact. He didn't know how he was going to deal with that night after night until her baby was born and her mother left.

But her lips were already on his, her hands under his shirt, and he simply hadn't the character to pull away.

They strained together over the obstruction of the baby, and finally pulled apart laughing when the baby's kicks and rolls protested their strong embrace.

Jave pushed himself up, knowing this could safely go no farther.

"The baby objects to being sandwiched between us," Nancy said as Jave lifted her to her side of the bed and pulled the light blanket over her.

No. YOU'VE got it wrong, Mom. I'm happy. That was applause. I like *the way things are going!*

"I'M GOING BACK OUTSIDE," Jave said, leaning over her to plant a light kiss on her lips. She tried to prolong it, but he drew away. "Do me a favor," he said firmly, "and be asleep before I come back."

Nancy was drifting off when the door closed behind him. She was deep-down mellow, and slipped into a dream of back rubs and babies and strumming guitars.

JAVE SLAMMED THE HANDBALL back with a vicious swipe. Tom barely dodged its ninety-mile-per-hour return and sank to the court floor as it hit the back wall and ricocheted with almost the same ferocity. He covered his head with his hands as it whistled past him. It finally slowed on the next rebound and settled harmlessly in a far corner.

Jave, dripping sweat, leaned forward on his knees and gasped for breath. He angled his head sideways as Tom unfolded carefully from his crouch.

"Had enough?" he laughed.

Tom rolled his eyes as he got to his feet. "I quit three games ago, but you haven't even noticed." Tom grabbed their towels off the bench and tossed one to Jave. "So who is this phantom opponent you're playing tonight? Shall I guess?"

Jave wiped his face. "Don't start with me, Tom," he said as he wrapped the towel around his neck and headed for the showers.

Jave washed under a hot spray. He did not feel better, he thought. Exhausted, maybe, but not better.

Sleeping with Nancy in his arms for a week had his frustration level at crisis point. She was warm and affectionate, but carefully distant whenever the conversation turned to the future. And he'd *had* it. He was determined to have it out with her tonight. He just wanted to defuse his temper by ridding himself of pent-up frustration and exasperation.

He wasn't sure it was working.

"Turn off the hot water," Tom advised from the neighboring stall. "Cold showers really do work. I've done it a lot myself in the past year."

CHAPTER ELEVEN

SHE WAS TRYING on clothes when he got home. There was no aroma of dinner underway, no television blaring the evening news, no soothing guitar as a background to everything.

The house was empty, except for Nancy, who stood in front of the mirror on the closet door, studying the simple blue dress with white buttons.

"Where is everyone?" he asked.

"With your mother and the boys gone," she replied, smoothing the line of the dress, "and you going to the gym with Tom after work, Mom and Willy decided to go exploring. You hungry?"

"I'll fix something. You going somewhere?" He leaned a shoulder against the doorway.

"No." She turned toward him with a casual smile before peering over her shoulder into the mirror. "I'm trying to decide what to wear for the photo session tomorrow."

All the hopes he'd carefully cherished deflated and died. The photo session. Amy had mentioned it over lunch in the hospital cafeteria several days before. The newspaper was coming to do a special foldout section on the remodeled O.B. department, and would feature Nancy's tour of the facility. Riverview Hospital was beginning to gear up for the opening of the birthing rooms.

"You're going to go through with it?" he asked, his voice tight.

She raised an eyebrow as she held on to the closet door

and toed off the sandals she wore. "Of course I am. Isn't that the point of all this?"

He studied her for one long disappointed moment, and wondered if it was worth a confrontation after all. The time they'd spent together that made him fall in love had apparently had little effect on her.

Careful not to touch her, he tossed his athletic bag into the bottom of the closet.

Nancy fluffed her hair, pretending not to notice his temper. She could guess what prompted his mood, but she didn't want to deal with it now. She'd been fighting tooth and nail for the past week to stay with the plan.

She was beginning to feel a desperate but dangerous need to come clean with everyone, but it was all too entangled now and she no longer knew how to sort it out. Instead of securing her position, the lies had trapped her.

And she had to think of the baby. She was the reason she'd done all this in the first place.

Jave left the room and went to the kitchen in search of something tall and cold. He found iced tea in a pitcher and poured a glass.

He walked out the back door with it, letting the screen door slam. Shaman, about to approach thinking he was Nancy with his food, ran away up the slope. Jave called him back to no avail.

He finally raised his glass to the cat. "Congratulations," he said. "You hold the number two place for emotional holdout, Nancy, of course, being the champ. I imagine you just haven't been at it as long. But don't think you'll ever take the crown. Her technique is too skillful."

Jave heard the squeak of the screen door behind him and turned to see Nancy standing there, holding a can of tuna and a spoon. He judged by the glower on her face that she'd heard his little self-satisfying lecture to the cat.

He was tired of pussyfooting around the issue, he thought, then berated himself for the pun. Gallows humor, he told himself, was the only humor he had left.

"I'd apologize," he said, watching the cat stiffen alertly at the sight of Nancy and his food, "but it was all from the heart. It would be a lie."

"It's quite all right," Nancy said coolly, trying to lean over the bowl. She'd done it the day before, but she didn't seem to be able to today. That confirmed it. She knew she'd gained fifty pounds overnight. She gave Jave another glower then looked down at the dish again, wondering if she could hit it from this height. She'd also lost all eye-hand coordination in the past few weeks. "Just because you've been calling the shots all this time, you think you actually understand what's going on. But you didn't get it when you intruded into my life, and you don't get it now. Still, that's no reason to pick on the cat."

Jave took the can from her, yanked the spoon impatiently from her other hand, and squatted down to scrape the tuna into Shaman's bowl. Then he straightened and handed the can and the spoon back to her.

"I wasn't picking on the cat," he said, temper rising despite his efforts to tamp it down. "I was just telling him how it is—that he was the king of panhandled love until you came along."

He stalked back into the house, letting the door slam again.

With a growl of anger, Nancy followed him. She tossed the can and the spoon into the sink. She grabbed Jave by the arm as he walked away.

He faced her, hands going impatiently to his hips.

"Panhandled...love?" she asked, separating the words distinctly. She didn't know what he meant by that remark, but she didn't like the sound of it.

"Love that's begged from people so that you get a handout," he explained. "You don't want to give anything to get it, so you just hold your hand out. You did it to me. You do it to your mother."

Nancy's anger swelled to rage. "I never did any such thing!" she denied, her cheeks crimson. "In fact, I didn't want any part of this relationship. You're the one who insisted—"

"Nancy," he said, tipping his head back in exasperation as he interrupted her, "that's so much crap and you know it. You were lonely and frightened before I came along. You responded to me and accepted what I was willing to give—as long as you didn't have to do anything for it."

"That's not—"

"Yes, it is. But I didn't care, because I thought you were a normal and intelligent woman. I thought you would see the advantages of love in your life and that would turn you around."

"I told you," she said, her hands clenching in the folds of her dress, "I don't trust easily."

He shook his head, unmoved by her quietly spoken reminder. "That's just more bull. You trust me. That's not the issue here."

She raised an eyebrow imperiously. "The issue is that you found out I hadn't been entirely honest about my husband and confused a situation that could have—"

He shifted his weight and made an exasperated sound. "Not entirely honest? Don't dress it up, my love. You're a liar! You lie about everything. But what's most important—you're lying, even to yourself, about how you feel about me! And about how you feel about your mother. You love us both. But you've figured out that if you hold yourself apart, if you never admit to anything, you don't have to give anything in return. So you figure you can just sail through life without being beholden to anyone, and that you can have this baby and not *share* it with anyone—and that'll protect this rarefied atmosphere you've created in your own little beachfront kingdom."

The verbal onslaught paralyzed Nancy where she stood, and the incisive accuracy of at least some of it punched her below the belt—and that had become a very large target.

"I don't *have* to share," she said defensively, tears burning behind her eyes. "I'm not married to you, and my mother walked away from me. I don't owe either of you anything."

"Oh, come on." He turned away from her impatiently, then turned back. "So the baby you're carrying is going to have no one in its little life but you, who tells lies all over the place, claims not to trust anyone, and carries grudges for a lifetime? What's that going to do for her development?"

"I don't—" Nancy began a heated reply, full of anger and indignation. Then a sharp pain ripped across her lower abdomen, and she stopped, reaching down with a gasp to cradle the weight of the baby in both hands.

Jave caught her arm. "What?" he demanded.

She ignored him, wondering for a moment if she was imagining pain. This argument did have all the qualities of torture. But the pain continued, holding strong—strong enough to frighten a cry out of her.

MOM! WHAT IS THAT? Is it time? I'm not ready. I mean, it's not like I have a lot to pack, but—ah!

"A...CONTRACTION, I think," she said, fear for her baby crowding everything from her mind. "Jave, I don't understand. I've been taking my medication...."

He placed a kitchen chair behind her and eased her into it. "Relax," he said calmly. "It could just be Braxton-Hicks contractions, but with your history we'd better be sure. And they shouldn't be breaking through your medication anyway. Where's your cellular phone?"

She pointed to her purse on the table as the pain seemed to work its way down and begin to fade.

Jave went for her sweater, dropped it over her shoulders, and led her out to the car, calling the ER on the phone as he helped her in.

"Jave was right," Dr. McNamara told Nancy half an hour later. "It was just Braxton-Hicks contractions."

Nancy nodded, feeling everything inside her relax, including the baby. She'd read about the false labor pains in her mother-to-be book. They were sort of a muscle flexing, a warm-up for the real contractions at delivery time.

FELT LIKE THE REAL THING to me. You know, I was excited about doing this, but after that, I'm beginning to wonder. You're sure there's not another way out?

"EVERYTHING'S STILL all right?"

McNamara nodded. "Everything's fine. I'll just up your Tributilene dose a little bit. You let me know right away if this happens again. We don't want you delivering this baby until that wandering husband of yours is home to help."

Her relief was slightly deflated by the intrusion of reality—and the many falsehoods she'd created in it.

If her obstetrician was curious about why it was Jave who brought her in, and what the circumstances were that resulted in their being together when the contractions had begun, he didn't let on. He simply handed Jave the new prescription and teased that cellular phones should be required for all pregnant women.

"Jave has become a…a good friend…." she felt compelled to explain. It sounded lame and unconvincing.

Again, McNamara did not let on. "Everyone needs friends," he said. "Take care. I'll see you next Friday. Unless you have another problem, then call me right away."

Jave drove straight to the drugstore and had her wait in the car while the prescription was filled.

Denise and Willy were back when they arrived. Jave explained what had happened, and Denise immediately put Nancy on the sofa, covered her with an afghan, and positioned Willy nearby to play something relaxing. Then she left to make a pot of tea.

Jave went to take a shower.

After a few moments, Denise brought the pot and a Garfield mug to the coffee table and set them within Nancy's reach. Then she insisted on pouring for her.

"You're sure everything's all right?" she asked.

Nancy nodded. "The obstetrician seems to think so. And I feel fine now."

Denise sat on the edge of the table and put a hand to Nancy's forehead as though her daughter had a fever rather than a very ripe pregnancy. "I feel so responsible," she said with such genuine guilt that Nancy frowned at her over the rim of her cup. She could think of a few things her mother should feel guilty about, but the baby wasn't one of them.

"Why?" she asked.

"Well..." She gestured toward Nancy's swollen stomach, her movement nervous. "It's my fault that *you* were born with a defective reproductive system."

"Oh, Mother." Nancy didn't like her mother's big-eyed concern. It made *her* feel guilty. "That's hardly your fault. DES was given to lots of women. No one knew what it would do. And my case isn't that extreme anyway. It's just a little troublesome right now."

Denise shook her head. "I don't want the baby to grow up hating me for having caused both of you problems."

Nancy caught her eye. Her mother had meant the immediate problems of preterm labor, Nancy knew. But as the words hung between them, they suggested all the other problems to which Nancy assigned blame to her mother.

Denise held her gaze, apparently willing to discuss it if she wanted to. But she didn't. She lowered her eyes and drank her tea. Denise went off to make coffee for Willy and herself.

JAVE PRETENDED TO BE asleep when Nancy came to bed, and was up and dressed by the time she stirred awake the following morning. He saw Nancy's gaze go to the small bag he'd packed and placed by the door. It contained most of the clothes he'd moved over unobtrusively since her mother had arrived.

She sat up slowly, her eyes regretful but resigned. He didn't know whether to be pleased or angry that she, too, understood there was no other alternative.

He came to sit on the edge of the bed. It hurt abominably to be that close and know it would be foolish to touch her, that nothing would come of what had seemed to hold such promise. But she couldn't let him in, and he couldn't live on the outside, looking in. There was no other way.

"I know you hate the prospect of being alone with your mom," he said softly. Sun shone through the long bedroom window, but the rest of the house was very quiet, as though no one was up. "But we can't do this anymore. It's too hard on both of us. There's no way to know if our argument brought on your contractions, but I don't want to take the chance that the tension between us is going to compound your problems."

She opened her mouth to deny that that was the problem, but felt sure it was—only not for the reasons he thought. She'd been fighting herself over her feelings for him for weeks. And the internal struggles grew as strong as the baby's kicks.

And she couldn't deny a sense of relief. The prospect of opening up to him had been scary. Seeing how much she'd needed him the night before had been just as scary. Feeling the abysmal loneliness that stretched ahead of her without him and his children and his family was terrifying. It was so much easier not to have to deal with it.

So she ignored the tears that slid down her cheeks and nodded.

"You can tell your mom I'm working long hours at the hospital," he said, turning his gaze away from her tearful face to the window, "and that it's easier for me to stay there as long as someone's here with you. Then maybe you can think up some…fiction…to explain why I don't come back." He looked up at her then, his eyes that could have been condemning, teasing instead. "Maybe…an alien abduction, or the girls from 'American Gladiators' kidnapped me for their mascot. I kind of favor that one.''

She tried to laugh, but it came out as a sob. She swallowed it and smiled. "Then we'll go with that."

"If you do have any trouble," he said, "and you need me for whatever reason, call. I'm just twenty minutes away."

She nodded. Her throat was too tight, too painful to permit sound.

"Bye, Nancy." He kissed her cheek, then he was gone.

MOM? SHOULDN'T WE be doing something? Like going after him? We don't want to lose him, do we?

NANCY SAT PERFECTLY STILL, ignoring the baby's kicks as she heard the front door close quietly, then the sound of Jave's car pulling out of the driveway. He could go back to using the truck now, she thought irrelevantly. Now that he no longer had to accommodate her graceless bulk.

As the sound of his car engine drifted away, the relief she'd felt at not having to deal with their relationship dissolved completely. In its place, a cold loneliness planted itself and took firm root. She wrapped her arms around her baby and told her in a strangled whisper that it would be all right.

Food, she thought. Food would make her and the baby feel better. She slipped on a robe and padded out to the refrigerator. She opened the freezer in search of the Nutri-Grain waffles she used to pop in the toaster before her mother arrived and started making frittata for breakfast— and her eyes fell on a half pint of Columbo frozen yogurt— Chocolate Cappuccino Twist. It hadn't been there yesterday. Jave must have bought it last night when he filled her prescription.

She burst into helpless sobs, unaware of her mother's concerned voice as she raced out of the living room toward her.

NANCY THOUGHT SHE LOOKED a little like a *T-rex* who'd just had her hair done. She caught her reflection in the glass that surrounded the nursery, and saw the unfamiliar swoosh and spiking of her bangs, the elegant upsweep of her hair. The topknot, she felt, made her head look like a grape with frightened hair, placed atop a watermelon.

"Are you feeling all right?" Nurse Beacham barked out as though it were an order rather than an expression of concern. "I heard you came into the ER the other night with contractions."

Nancy drew a breath and forced a smile. She knew she had to have one somewhere, even though she felt empty of anything remotely resembling cheer. It didn't have to be spontaneous. She could do it.

"False labor," Amy said before Nancy had to. She rolled her eyes dramatically and pretended to wipe her brow. "Don't think she didn't terrify the entire committee." She placed an arm around Nancy's shoulders and squeezed. "Our model mommy having her baby three weeks early in ER would have ruined *everything*. But here she is, safe and sound and ready to be the spokeswoman for Riverview's new birthing rooms. And in just two weeks, Jerry Malone will be back with the crew of the *Courageous* and at Nancy's side as the countdown begins."

The photographer raised his camera and framed the two heads close together. Amy grinned broadly, and Nancy dug deep for a similar expression. He snapped the shutter.

The tour continued, and Nancy made more of an effort to appear enthused and excited. And she *was* enthused and excited about the baby, but another part of her was barely able to function because she missed Jave so desperately.

Now she couldn't even recall all her arguments about why they couldn't stay together. They'd seemed so logical once and now paled in importance beside the emptiness his absence created in her life. And he'd been out of it only three days.

She found herself wondering how he was doing, if Aggie

and the boys were having a good time at her brother's, how Tom was.

The tour ended in a conference room where Amy had collected and artfully arranged all the gifts the merchants had donated to Riverview's model mommy. As her entourage looked on, Nancy walked slowly into the room and into the midst of all the riches any new mother and baby could ever imagine. The gifts sparkled like a mound of treasure in some Ali Baba nursery.

Everything was there—the furniture, the silver cup and spoon, baby shoes, lingerie, chocolate cigars, elegantly monogrammed envelopes that probably contained gift certificates.

She went straight to the crib. It was made of oak with painted white details and baby animal decals decorating the flat surfaces. It matched the dresser beside it, the chifforobe, the toy trunk. Attached to it was a mobile in patterns of black and white, the only colors a baby could see for the first few months.

And Nancy felt nothing. She couldn't quite believe it. She picked up the colorful baby quilt folded at the foot of the crib and brought it to her cheek, trying to inspire feeling, to renew the maternal avarice that had once raced through her at the thought of all these treasures. Nothing.

She felt herself go pale with panic. She touched the shade on the teddy-bear lamp, the state-of-the-art infant seat, the hand-embroidered infant carrier from a local craft shop. Nothing.

Her heart began to beat faster. She put a hand to her forehead, suddenly feeling unsteady.

"Okay, that's it." Nurse Beacham pushed her way through the group, took Nancy firmly by the arm, and pushed her into the Boston rocker placed near the crib. She shooed everyone toward the door, including Amy, who tried to stay, pleading friendly concern. Beacham was firm. "You've had this poor woman on her feet for two hours.

Give her a few minutes to herself, then I'm going to see that she has lunch and a nap."

"But..."

"Out!"

"NANCY, YOU SHOULD TALK about this." Denise placed a cup of tea on Nancy's bedside table and sat on the edge of her bed. Beacham herself had driven her home at the end of her shift, and had April follow with the truck. Then they insisted on walking her to her door.

Nancy had tried to persuade them that she was fine, certain disaster would result if Beacham saw and recognized her mother or Willy Brock. She was already looking askance at the black Lincoln in the driveway.

"Second car," Nancy said.

Beacham opened her mouth, probably to ask her why she hadn't driven it to the hospital instead of the truck that now required three men and a crane to place her behind the steering wheel, but Nancy stepped into the house and immediately placed the screen door between herself and her Good Samaritans.

"Thank you," she said, her tone more perfunctory than grateful, but she was desperate to be alone and give in to a primal scream.

Beacham and April disappeared in Beacham's car, just as Denise and Willy walked in from the back porch. Denise was dirty from head to toe, and Willy seemed to be acting as her beast of burden, carrying odds and ends of wood, a bag of potting soil, a trowel and a toolbox. "We put in a window box outside your bedroom win—" Denise began.

Nancy excused herself, claiming a long, tiring session at the hospital.

She now repeated the excuse to her mother, who was perched on the edge of the bed.

Denise shook her head and folded her arms, looking very much as though she had settled in. "Nancy, please," she said quietly, "I've been there. You don't have what you need to get from day to day—I can see it in your eyes. Tell me why Jave is suddenly gone."

"I told you." Nancy took a sip of tea and scraped up a small quantity of patience. "He's working long hours this week at the—"

Denise cut her off with a nod. "But that's the result of your problem, not the reason for it. Why did he leave? What did you do?"

"What makes you think it was *my* fault?" Nancy grumped.

Denise seemed to consider her for a moment, then she took a breath, as one would before jumping off a cliff. "Because there's a lot of your father in you—the good and the not so good."

Nancy turned accusing dark eyes on her. "Daddy was there when you weren't," she reminded brutally. "Whatever my problems are, they're probably more from what *you* didn't give me than from what *he* did."

Denise faced her attack with a steady gaze. "Your father *was* tenacious," she said. Nancy couldn't decide if it was an admission or an accusation. Then her mother leaned toward her, her blue eyes urgent. "For you, the child, that… that…permanence…was a good thing. For me, the woman, his inability to let go of antiquated notions and personal prejudices was like being imprisoned. He didn't want me to sing, even in church. He wouldn't hear of my joining a band when the opportunity came because he was convinced everyone who worked on the road lived lives of depravity. He didn't want me doing anything he couldn't control. So I left."

"You left *me!*" Nancy shouted, the sound ringing with resentment and a child's anguish. She put one hand to her baby and the other to her mouth, unable to trust what else might emerge if she made no attempt to hold it back.

Denise closed her eyes, then heaved a deep sigh. When she finally opened them again, a tear spilled over and she said huskily, "So you *do* care."

Nancy saw the same vulnerability she'd seen in her the other night when she'd blamed herself for her problems with the pregnancy. It wasn't that easy to ignore this time because she understood what it was to want what you couldn't have and to feel the need to run away.

"I loved you," she accused weakly.

Denise brushed away the tear, her voice still a little high. "You still do, darling. That's why you think you hate me."

"Mother, don't be cute."

"I'm not. I'm trying to be honest." Denise placed a hand over the one on Nancy's stomach and smiled grimly. "I did a purely selfish thing that I can't explain away, except to tell you that I felt I would die if I couldn't sing. Your father wouldn't hear of it, so I did what I had to do to save myself, knowing I'd be no good to you otherwise."

Nancy heard that calm explanation and tried to understand. But remembered pain got in the way. "You ruined my life, Mom."

Denise shook her head, rubbing a hand gently over Nancy's. "No. I may have ruined your childhood, but your *life* has a potential bigger than even you realize. And so does everyone's. I didn't know that until I got away from your father and had a chance to live mine."

Nancy thought back to the empty routine of her father's life. Work, home, golf, work, home, golf. Year after year.

"He wasn't a bad person," Nancy defended stiffly.

"No, he wasn't," Denise said. "I couldn't have left you with him if he had been. And you needed all the things at that age that I couldn't guarantee when I started out on the road—good food, health insurance, school and a comfortable routine. Your father *wasn't* bad. The trouble was, he wasn't anything. He wasn't good. He wasn't wicked. He wasn't kind. He wasn't hurtful. He *wasn't*. And life shouldn't be made up of negatives. It should be filled with positives." She sighed wearily and brought her hands back to her lap.

"It took me two more marriages to figure that out. I married my second husband because when I was with him, I wasn't lonely. But I wasn't happy, either. I married my third one because he owned a club, and when I was with him, I wasn't without work. But I wasn't happy, either.'' She sighed again, and this time it had a restorative sound. She smiled. It was the smile of someone who'd been very unhappy and knew a smile didn't have to be wide to be genuine. "So I was alone again when Willy walked into that recording studio in Nashville. He listened to me sing, then came and asked me who had broken my heart.''

Tears began to flow as she went on. "I told him I'd broken my own heart because I'd left you so I could find myself. And I couldn't get you back.'' She swiped at her tears and recounted grimly, "This wasn't long after that week you came to stay with me and husband number three. It was like Dante's Inferno on fast forward, remember?''

Nancy smiled thinly at her mother's description of events. It was pretty accurate.

"Anyway, Willy reminded me that every day is a chance to turn your life around, to try to set things right, to make amends, to do good instead of nothing.''

Nancy shook her head, her emotions in a turmoil, her world revolving in a faulty orbit. "Mom, I've tried to just forget, but...''

"I don't expect you to forget,'' Denise corrected gently, "just to try to understand. To imagine, if you can, how I felt, and see if you can forgive me. But mostly...'' She caught one of her daughter's hands and held it between her two. "Your father believed only in himself. And what he had, he didn't want to share. Do you remember him as a happy man?''

Nancy remembered a man who provided all of life's physical necessities, but none of its magic.

"No,'' she admitted, "I don't.''

Denise squeezed her hand. "Then love his memory, please, but don't be like him. Don't be afraid to share what you are and what you have, and don't be afraid to trust, even if you find that it's misplaced."

Denise lowered her gaze to their hands and held Nancy's so tightly that she barely resisted crying out.

"I know you trusted me, and I failed you," she whispered, looking up. Her eyes were profoundly sad. "And you trusted Jerry Malone, and he failed you. Well, I don't know where he is, but I want to make that up to you. I like to think that I'm different from him. He chose his career over the baby because he didn't want to have to consider what was best for it over his career. I did what I did because I was weak, not because I was selfish. And I knew if I didn't get my own life together, I could never be anything to you."

Her voice was tight and breathy. She swallowed and smiled tentatively. "A woman is never too old to have a mother, is she? Let me be your mother now. Let me be the baby's grandmother. Let me be nosy and call you with advice, and send you cartoons out of the newspaper and gaudy souvenirs from our travels. Let me buy T-shirts from everywhere for the baby."

She dropped Nancy's hand and wrapped her arms around herself, as though she'd suddenly grown cold—or prepared herself for a rejection.

"But, if you can't trust me again," she said, "don't let what Jerry and I did stop you from trusting Jave. I know Aggie isn't exactly impartial, but she makes him sound like something pretty special. And you can just tell that his boys adore him." She smiled grimly. "Children are tough critics." She stood abruptly. "Well...I guess I've lectured you long enough."

Nancy caught her wrist before she could move away. Denise stood immobile. Nancy tugged her back onto the edge of the bed.

"He doesn't live here," Nancy admitted on a broken sigh. "I asked him to say he did so that you wouldn't want to move in with me." She made a self-deprecating grimace.

Denise's eyes widened. She turned the wrist Nancy held

and caught her hand. "What is your relationship? I'd have sworn you were lovers."

Nancy groaned and explained about the early relationship that had never been simply professional—about him saving her chair and bringing Tom over to fix her roof. She told her about Jave guessing she had no husband, that she was lying for the sake of the gifts. "He literally blackmailed me into a relationship."

Denise said interestedly, "Define 'relationship.'"

Nancy shrugged, embarrassed. "Well, my condition doesn't allow anything physical." She gave her mother a blushing side-glance. "Though he does kiss very well and gives the most delicious body massage." She grew serious suddenly and laced her fingers nervously. "And he asked me to marry him."

Denise blinked. "You mean you've never made love and he proposed? I can't believe you let him walk away!"

Nancy shook her head, her eyes wide and wounded. "I didn't. He decided to go. And now nothing means anything. I sent a book proposal to an agent, and I got a letter from her yesterday saying she thought it was very good and she was sure she could sell it for me."

"Nancy." Denise squeezed her hand. "That's wonderful!"

Nancy shrugged, her gaze unfocused. "It should be, but it isn't. And you know what else?"

"What else?"

The pain she'd been suppressing all day to keep smiling for the camera suddenly overcame her attempts to hold it at bay any longer. It pummeled her.

"Today they took me into the room where all the baby furniture is being held for us, where they're keeping all the wonderful things that I thought Malia needed...." Her eyes brimmed as she concentrated on that moment and the reaction she simply couldn't understand. "And I didn't feel anything. I mean, that was why I did all this—lied and pretended, and lied again." She sighed and narrowed her gaze on her mother as though she held the answer. "I didn't even care." She leaned toward Denise's shoulder as tears began to fall. "I'm going crazy, Mom," she wept.

Denise wrapped her arms around her and squeezed, relishing the feeling for a moment before laughing softly and answering, "I don't think so, darling. I think you're going sane."

CHAPTER TWELVE

"JAVE. Have you heard the news?"

Jave looked up from paperwork to see Amy Brown standing just inside his office, clutching her clipboard. Her eyes behind her glasses fairly gleamed, and she smiled from ear-to-ear.

He hadn't heard anything in the past few days that warranted that kind of excitement. In fact, most of the news in his life this week had been bad. He wondered idly if Tom had asked her out.

"Unless you're talking about the new frozen yogurt machine in the cafeteria," he said, beckoning her to the chair beside his desk, "I haven't." He glanced at his watch. "But you've got to make it quick. My mother and the boys are coming to pick me up. We're taking Tom to dinner for his birthday."

"Tom." She folded into the chair, her cheeks growing pink. "How is he?"

Well, that answered his question. If Tom had asked her out, she needn't have asked after his health.

"He's fine," he replied, putting his pen aside and turning toward her. "What's up?"

She gave a toss of her head and tapped her pen against the clipboard on her knees. "The *Courageous* is back!"

Uh-oh. Nancy. The problem in the San Diego shipyard must have changed the ship's plans. What would she do now?

That question was answered for him the next moment when Amy leaned closer and said excitedly, "I called

Nancy and she said she's bringing her husband in to meet me."

Jave maintained a studiously neutral expression. "Bringing him in...to meet you."

"Right. Isn't that great? Just in time for our big publicity push. We can even reshoot the special-section pictures we took the other day to include him, and still have everything out in plenty of time. I can't believe I got this lucky!"

Jave stared at her a moment, trying to decide what this could mean. Then it occurred to him. Nancy must have found someone else to plump out the lie. How she'd done it didn't concern him. He just hoped it all worked out for her.

Then an even more distressful thought struck him. Had the *real* Jerry Malone come back, deciding he'd been a fool to leave Nancy and their baby? That, unfortunately, didn't concern him, either.

He smiled at Amy. "Great. I hope it all goes beautifully and that you get a bonus."

Amy sprang to her feet. "I only hope I get to keep this job. My sister Jane's a lawyer, Peggy's a model, and I'm kind of plain and really not genius material. I'm sort of the family..." She bobbed her head from side to side, then shook it briefly, apparently deciding against a description. "Well, I need to do well."

Jave nodded. "Don't we all."

"If you wander by my office in about fifteen minutes," she said conspiratorially, "you can see Jerry Malone."

Something that had been tightening inside Jave for almost a week now yanked painfully. "No, thanks," he said. "I've got a lot of work here."

She frowned. "But I thought he was your friend. I mean, you went to her first Lamaze class in his place."

No, he didn't, he thought. He went to that Lamaze class for himself. But Amy wouldn't understand that.

He smiled offhandedly. "I'll see him later. Right now, the three of you have a lot of plans to make."

She accepted that and left his office with a cheerful wave.

Jave stared unseeing at the pile of work on his desk. In his mind's eye, he saw Nancy standing on the back porch steps, trying to lure Shaman toward her. He pictured her walking hand in hand with his younger son through a maze of colorful quilts, talking excitedly as Pete listened with big-eyed adoration. He remembered how she'd lain in his arms, the bulk of her baby between them, obstructing their closeness, yet somehow intensifying it. And he vividly recalled the feel of the baby's movement against his hand, against his stomach, when Nancy curled into his body in sleep.

But that was over. He concentrated for one moment on the sense of profound loss that inhabited and surrounded him, then tried to keep in mind that his family would be here at any second. He had to shake off the dark mood. But he'd been living with it for days, and he suspected it would be with him for a long time to come.

WILLY PULLED the black Lincoln into the hospital parking lot. He glided to a stop near the side entrance, then turned to Nancy, seated beside him.

"This okay?" he asked.

She nodded. She felt remarkably calm. "Fine."

"You're sure you want to do this?" Denise, seated in the back, leaned over the front seat. "There might be another way."

Nancy shook her head firmly. "No. This is the way it has to be. You're sure you don't mind doing this for me?"

Denise shook her head. "Of course we don't. But you're sure it'll work?"

Nancy sighed philosophically. "I'm not sure of anything, but if you two can distract the photographers long enough for me to talk to Amy, this might all end as just a minor disaster rather than a major one."

Willy grinned that calm, gentle grin Nancy was beginning to truly appreciate. "Disasters are our specialty, minor or major. Let's go."

He came around to help Nancy out of the car, then followed behind with Denise as she walked into the hospital.

The corridors were quiet, Nancy noted. Dinnertime. She just prayed she wasn't too late.

She rounded a corner, calm slipping away. Her heart began to beat a little fast as she picked up her pace. She turned into the radiology department, not surprised to find the reception area dark, the office staff gone for the day.

But there would be a technician on duty during the night. And Jave would still be here, finishing up the day's paperwork. In the brief time they'd "lived" together, he'd seldom been home before seven.

But there was no one in Jave's office. Nancy stood in the doorway, staring with a sense of disappointment that felt fatal. The little cubbyhole seemed suddenly cavernous in its emptiness. An emptiness even larger opened up inside her. Tears burned her eyes and she made a small sound of distress. Jave was gone.

BREATHE, MOM! I'm not getting any air. Where is he? I don't hear him. We haven't lost him, have we?

SHE JUMPED AT THE SOUND of a loud squeal behind her and turned to see that a crowd of nurses, volunteers and candy stripers had clustered around her mother and Willy, cutting her off from them.

It was ironic, she thought, that that part of the plan was working, when its major element had just fallen apart.

With a little sigh of despair, she turned back toward the office, thinking she would sit in Jave's chair and try to plan containment of the disaster—when she saw him coming in her direction from an open door across the room. He was pulling on a summer-weight mossy green sports jacket over a shirt with a thin stripe, open at the neck. As he stopped several feet from her, she noticed that it affected the color of his hazel eyes.

Air seemed to be trapped in her lungs. She stared at him for a moment, unable to say anything.

Jave had hoped he'd be spared this. In fact, he'd dressed quickly, planning to be out of the building before she arrived. If his family wasn't here yet, he'd have waited for them in his truck.

But now that she was standing there, he was glad he hadn't escaped. It was good to see her again. She wore a soft shade of pink and reminded him of a very plump bouquet of rhododendrons. Her longing eyes reminded him how much they'd enjoyed together, even though all he felt now was sadness.

He drew a deep breath and tried to be bigger than his grief. "Hi," he said. "It's good to see you."

"Yeah," she whispered after a moment. "You, too."

They stared into each other's eyes, then, unable to stand it another moment, he said conversationally, "I hear your...*husband*'s home." He emphasized the word, hoping she would explain it—hoping he could take it.

She nodded. "I'm going to Amy's office right now. Will you come with me?"

He thought that was a lot to ask. "It's Tom's birthday tonight, and the family's coming to pick me up for a party at Chez Pasta."

Chez Pasta. Nancy had such sweet memories of that night.

She studied Jave's eyes for some sign that she wasn't crazy to do this, that her instincts were on target. But except for a flare of emotion in his eyes when she'd first seen him standing there, his expression was carefully remote.

She rubbed a hand over her baby, looking for comfort and support, and felt a firm kick. That was it, she decided. Confirmation. There was nothing to do but do it.

She smiled, took Jave's hand, and drew him out of the office. "I promise not to keep you very long. Come on."

Jave had little choice but to follow. There was a squealing crowd around Denise and Willy. They skirted them skillfully and headed for Amy's office. The *Heron Point Herald*'s photographer was taking pictures of the celebrities, and a reporter was shouting questions from the back of the crowd.

"How come," he asked as he was tugged along, "you brought your mother here? I thought—"

"To distract the photographer," she said over her shoulder.

"Why? Isn't that why you're here? To be photographed with your 'husband'? Where is he, by the way?"

Amy's office was three times the size of Jave's and contained an oval-shaped conference table. Amy stood at the head of it when they walked in, and gathered around it were the hospital administrator and his assistant, Nurse Beacham, and several other members of Amy's committee.

Nancy stopped just inside the room. She hadn't counted on anyone being here but Amy. Whatever confidence she'd had that this might work abandoned her completely. She was certainly in for a very public humiliation if it didn't. Not that she didn't deserve it after all she'd done.

All the men around the table stood, and Amy smiled as she approached her, though she seemed obviously confused.

"You look wonderful," she said to Nancy, then her eyes passed over Jave and peered behind him. "Where's your husband?"

Nancy drew a deep breath and decided some things were more important than pride—or safety. She lifted the hand she still had linked with Jave's. "Ladies and gentlemen," she said, "I'd like to present my *future* husband, Dr. Jave Nicholas."

There was a long, pulsing silence. Then there were frowns of confusion, wary glances exchanged. Nancy looked up at Jave.

Jave, accustomed now to her dramatic schemes, remained calm. Not that he could have done anything anyway. He had no idea what the hell was happening.

Then he looked into her eyes and saw the pleading there.

Only this time it wasn't pleading for his compliance with her scheme. She was pleading for his love.

He stared down at her, unable for a moment to believe what he saw.

"Tell me," she whispered, hope naked in her eyes as the committee began to grumble among themselves, "that you haven't withdrawn the proposal."

Before he could answer, Amy asked, "But where's the father of your baby?" Then apparently realizing the indelicate nature of the question, she began to stammer, "I mean...well, you know..."

Nancy didn't want to bring Jerry into this conversation. This was about truly starting over for herself and the baby, about love and trust and the kind of generosity Jerry had never understood.

But Jave hadn't said anything yet, and there was a good chance she'd been all wrong about the outcome of her brave confrontation with the truth.

She opened her mouth to try to clarify the situation when Jave said clearly, "*I'm* the baby's father."

With those few words, Nancy felt a lifetime of loneliness wash away, a world of love and trust open up. She squeezed Jave's hand, and thought she would have died for him at that moment.

Amy glanced hesitantly at the committee and smiled nervously. Then she turned back to Jave. "I don't get it," she said candidly. "You didn't know each other then. She was in New York. You were here."

Jave nodded, unable to remember one grim moment of his past. All he could see, all he could feel, was sunshine.

"No, I wasn't there at conception. But we all know that's not what fatherhood is about."

Nancy held his arm in her two and faced the committee. "I was married, got pregnant, and was abandoned. I came here with very little money to start over, and when Amy proposed that I be the star of your birthing-rooms event, I pretended Gerald W. Malone was still in the picture so that

I could acquire for my baby all the things you were offering, things I could never get otherwise."

Jave leaned down to kiss her upturned face, basking for a moment in the adoration there. Then he picked up the story. "But I suspected the truth, fell in love with her, and a lot of things have changed for both of us in the past couple of months. This woman and this baby are now mine."

"But..." Amy began, hands spread helplessly.

"I know." Nancy reached out to touch her arm. "Of course you'll need a new mother for your project. I relinquish any claim to the gifts. And I apologize sincerely for the trouble I've caused."

Amy made an effort to pull herself together. She tugged on the ruffly sleeves of her mint green dress. "But we promised them to you. And while we like to think that the model family is composed of mother and father and two point three children, that doesn't really apply..."

Nancy shook her head. "Thank you, but I want you to pick another mother. None of the photos you've taken has appeared yet, and our Lamaze class had several couples who'd be perfect candidates."

Then Amy said for her ears alone, "But I know how much you wanted the nursery set and the—"

Nancy gave Amy a hug, her heart feeling suddenly as swollen as her belly. "I think what I really wanted for my baby was a father, and because I knew I couldn't give her that, I wanted to give her everything else." She beamed at Jave. "But I don't need that now."

The administrator came forward, followed by Nurse Beacham. "The decision is yours, Mrs. Malone," he said. "But please don't think we'd reject you because the situation isn't...traditional." He smiled at Jave. "We're all, of course, very fond of Jave."

Jave nodded. "Thank you, Frank."

"All those wonderful gifts," Nancy said firmly, "should go to some mother who needs them as much as I thought I did."

"Very well," he said. "Amy?"

Amy squared her shoulders. "Yes, Uncle Frank."

"Back to the drawing board."

She breathed a sigh. "Yes. Right away." Then her attention seemed to be caught by something beyond them. "Isn't that...?"

Everyone turned to look.

Nancy smiled at the woman in the doorway. "Mother," she said.

Beacham gasped in girlish disbelief, "Denise DiBenedetto and Willy Brock!"

The office was suddenly filled to capacity with the celebrities, followed by Aggie, Tom, Eddy and Pete.

"What's going on?" Aggie asked Jave as the boys ran to Nancy.

"Lots of things," he replied, hugging his mother, and laughing as he held her close. "I'm getting married, you're about to have a third grandchild, and we have to haul all the baby things up from the basement."

She pushed against him to look into his eyes. "You're kidding."

"I'm not."

"Oh, my God." She fell against him again, wrapping him in a stranglehold. "One down. One to go. I can't believe it."

Hugs were distributed with emotional abandon. Jave found himself holding Beacham, who had tears in her eyes. "Good work, Doc," she said with a sniff. "Didn't know you had it in you to make such an intelligent decision."

Tom squeezed the breath out of him. "All *right!* A house in constant need of repair in the family. I like it." Then he grew serious, the rough year they'd weathered together right there in his eyes. "Good going. Be happy."

Then Jave found himself looking down at his boys. Eddy's grin was broad, his eyes bright. "This is cool, Dad. Russian tea anytime we want it!"

But Pete's eyes were incredulous. Jave lifted him into his arms. "Is it true?" his son asked.

Jave nodded. "Nancy and I are getting married."

"Yeah, but I mean about the baby. It's gonna be ours?"

"Right."

Nancy, who'd been passed from hug to hug and now found herself beside them, overheard the question and leaned into father and son with concern. "Is that okay, Pete?" she asked.

His smile was sudden and wide. "Yeah. It's cool. And now you can come to all my games."

ME, TOO. I'll be there.

NANCY LEANED HER HEAD against him and kissed his small hand. "Every single one."

She felt a jab at her elbow and found Nurse Beacham standing beside her. She pointed toward the crowd gathered around her mother and Willy. The group of nurses and candy stripers from the hallway had also spilled into the office. "Could you introduce me?" Beacham asked with uncharacteristic shyness. "I have all her CDs and I've taped all her videos. I stood in line all night when she came to Seattle."

Nancy hugged the nurse, thinking life was full of the most delightful surprises. She'd never have taken Nurse Beacham for a country and western fan.

"Of course." She took Beachie's arm and used her pregnancy as a method of parting the crowd. People moved away as she smiled apologetically. "Mother," she said into Denise's smile of surprise. "This is one of your biggest fans. Nurse...Beachie, what's your first name?"

"Medora." Beachie held out her hand and smiled widely when Denise took it.

"Medora," Nancy said formally, "I'd like you to meet

my mother, Denise DiBenedetto and her fiancé, Willy Brock."

"Aren't you lucky, Nancy," Beacham said, her expression clearly star-struck, "to have Denise DiBenedetto for a mother?"

Nancy gave her mother a wink. "Yes," she said firmly. "I am."

Denise smiled, her eyes brimming. "Thank you, darling," she said. "I needed that."

The crowd eventually dispersed and the Nicholases and Nancy and Denise and Willy collected in the hallway, preparing finally to go off in celebration of Tom's birthday.

As everyone else drifted toward the parking lot, Nancy remained in the hallway, frowning in concern at the sight of Amy Brown, sitting alone at her desk, wondering, probably, what had happened to all her brilliant plans for the birthing-room extravaganza.

"I feel so bad about Amy," Nancy whispered to Jave, who'd remained beside her.

"Everything's in place," he said, pulling her into his side. "All she has to do is find another mother. I can't believe it'll be that difficult."

"I know," Nancy said. "But she wanted so much to do this well. And she's so...sort of...vulnerable. I don't know what it is, but she makes you want to take her home and take care of her."

Jave smiled wryly. He'd had that feeling about a woman before, and it had gotten him into no end of trouble.

"Why don't you just invite her to my party?"

Both turned in surprise to find Tom standing behind them.

"Why don't you?" Jave challenged.

Tom studied him for a moment, looked with an uncertain frown at the young woman now leaning back in her chair and fiddling forlornly with her pencil, then drew a breath. "All right," he said, "I will," and disappeared into Amy Brown's office.

Nancy stared up at Jave, wide-eyed with surprise. "Tom and..." She pointed toward Amy.

"Don't even say it aloud," he cautioned. "Or Mom will think she's got two down."

"Two... What?"

He kissed her temple as he walked her to the parking lot. "I'll explain later. We have to have something to talk about on our honeymoon."

JAVE WALKED NANCY DOWN the aisle on Labor Day weekend, then took her for a two-day honeymoon at a bed and breakfast on the river.

He'd been reluctant to take her any distance from the hospital at that late date, and she wanted to be home on Tuesday to see the boys off to school.

"I don't ever want them to think," she explained to Jave, "that they're less important to me than the baby is."

They lay wrapped in each other's arms on their wedding night in an upstairs room decorated in crisp yellow and white. The windows were closed against the change-of-season chill and the gauzy fog blanketing the ship channel.

His hands moved slowly, endlessly, over her, then over the baby, who seemed to rise against his touch in response.

Nancy concentrated on the wonder of their unique threesome—and the utter frustration that that third party imposed on them.

She sighed against Jave's shoulder, her fingertips exploring the strong lines of his chest. "Some way to spend a wedding night," she grumbled.

He kissed her soundly and drew away with a groan of reluctance. "I'll settle for it. I've got you and you're not getting away. I can live with knowing that *one day,* I'll finally be able to make love to you."

"Oh, Jave." She rubbed her cheek against his shoulder and stroked his chest, following the jut of his ribs to the flat plane of his stomach. "There's no reason for you to spend *your* wedding night this way." She stroked lower, planting kisses on his chest. "Let me make love to you."

He caught her hand before it could make his denial any more difficult. "No," he said.

She propped up laboriously on an elbow to look down at him in surprise. "No?"

It had been hard enough to say the first time, but he made himself say it again. "No." Then he cupped the back of her head in his hand and smiled. "Our first time is not going to be without your pleasure."

She kissed his shoulder. "I'll enjoy doing my part, Jave. I promise you."

He shook his head. "No. Six weeks after this baby is born, it'll be you and me and a night that's twelve hours long. Until then—" he pulled her down into his arms "—I'll be happy just to hold you."

"For eight more weeks?"

"For as long as it takes."

Nancy hugged him fiercely and laid her cheek against the steady beating of his heart. Despite her bulk, she felt lighter than air. This is what it is to be cherished, she thought. Every worry halved, every happiness doubled—and everything shared.

They lay quietly, listening to the quiet thrum of a freighter going upriver. Nancy asked in a whisper, "Jave? Are you still awake?"

"Barely," he replied lazily.

"*Is* our baby a girl?"

He hesitated. "Are you sure you want to know? I mean, you've been convinced it's a girl all this time."

She looked up into his face in the darkness. She could see his loving eyes and his indulgent smile.

"You said," she reminded, "that when I trusted you as much as I trust myself, you'd tell me. And I do. So is it?"

He laughed softly and raised his head to kiss her. "Yes," he said. "It is."

CHAPTER THIRTEEN

MALIA ROSE was born at 2:32 a.m. September twenty-third in the back of Willy's Lincoln on the way to Riverview Hospital. She was delivered with terror and great excitement by her father and her maternal grandmother.

Wow. MOM. Hi! Well, here I am. What do you think? I hope you're not disappointed. I'm not. You're beautiful.
And that's him *touching my hand. Wow. Hi, Dad. I heard it all, you know, and I love you, too. I am so glad to be out. What are those lights up there? Stars? So that's what they look like from this side.*

NANCY WAS ASSIGNED a birthing room, though she'd already accomplished what the room was intended to encourage.

"I'm so glad," she told Amy, who leaned over the bed to admire Malia's thick dark hair, "that circumstances made you choose another couple. It would have been awful if your model birthing-room occupant didn't even arrive at the hospital in time to do what she was supposed to do."

Amy laughed. "That's all right. One day Malia will be able to flaunt her birth in a Lincoln Town Car."

Riverview Hospital's shower of gifts had been bestowed three days before on a young couple from Virginia who'd just moved to Heron Point a month earlier—ironically, with the Coast Guard. It was their first baby and they were thrilled beyond description. Everyone, including the hospital's administration and birthing-room extravaganza committee, was delighted.

Denise spent hours watching Malia. "I helped deliver her," she said over and over. "I can't believe I helped deliver my granddaughter."

Willy sat by strumming lullabies.

Denise presented Nancy with a pile of tissue wrapped in a pink bow. Nancy opened it and discovered a slightly frayed pink blanket appliquéd with kittens and sailboats. Someone had sewn on a new silk binding.

Nancy squealed, old memories bubbling to the surface of herself at a very early age holding it, wrapped in it, dragging it. "My blanket!" she breathed.

Denise emitted a laugh that sounded like a sob. "It was one of the few things I took with me when I left. I made it for you when I was carrying you, and now it's Malia's."

Nancy pulled the hospital blanket from around the baby and wrapped her in the relic from her own childhood. She pulled her mother close so that the three of them shared an embrace. Then she kissed her cheek. "Thank you, Mom."

TOM HELD MALIA with remarkable ease. "She is the prettiest little thing." He turned to Jave and said brutally, "You can tell you had nothing to do with her looks." Then he sighed and brushed the thick hair back with the tip of one long finger. "But I suppose she'll grow up to be honorable and responsible and charming and we'll have to admit your influence after all."

"Speaking of charming," Jave said, "have you thought about asking Amy out again?"

Tom walked across the room with the baby to show her her reflection in the mirror—and to dodge the question, Nancy guessed. She caught Jave's eye across the room.

"You seemed to have such a good time at your party," she said.

Tom nodded. "She's very nice. But...you know. I'm not...I don't want to get serious about anybody at this point.

The business takes most of my time and...that's not fair to a woman."

"She asks about you all the time," Jave said.

Tom kissed the baby's cheek and handed her back to Nancy. "Gotta go," he said. "I'm picking up lumber this afternoon to start on your addition to the beach house. When's your Mom leaving?"

"Tomorrow," Nancy replied, feeling genuinely sad at the prospect. "She and Willy have to be in Houston for a concert."

He nodded. "Neat lady," he said, then leaned down to kiss her cheek. "You, too. See you when you get home."

"Do you think," Nancy asked Jave as the door closed behind his brother, "that he didn't enjoy that evening with Amy?"

Jave shook his head. "No. I think he enjoyed it too much." He smiled speculatively. "He's a man with a heart. He'll come to realize he can't live alone forever. We just have to be patient."

"Speaking of which," Nancy said with a frown, "when my mother leaves, there won't be anyone around to feed Shaman regularly. We'll have to bring him home to your house."

Jave winced at the thought. "And I get to catch him, right?"

She smiled winningly. "My hero."

Mine, too!

Aggie crooned promises of extravagant dishes "worthy of such a princess," and the boys simply stared in wonder. Eddy held her briefly, then handed her back, obviously uncomfortable, but Pete sat with her in a rocker near the window. Eddy leaned over the back of it to supervise.

"You're going to come to all my games," Pete said

softly, "and I'll make you Russian tea and read you my favorite books."

Deal. Can I play with your toys?

Jave, sitting on the bed with an arm around Nancy, watched his sons and daughter in the chair and felt peace settle inside him and take root. He knew the scene wouldn't always be this idyllic, but under the quarrels, big and small, that were bound to come, there would be the bond of a family formed by something even stronger than blood—love that was the result of conscious choice and determination and devotion.

"Did you ever see anything more beautiful?" Nancy asked on a tearful whisper.

He hugged her tightly. "It ties," he said, "with the look in your eyes."

Shaman came home to Jave's house two days later in a live trap Tom had fashioned out of oak and wire mesh. It had been baited with tuna, and he was freed in the kitchen, where a bowl of the same waited for him. Mo was temporarily closed in the backyard.

Jave, Tom, Aggie and the boys watched in disbelief as the trap's door was raised, and the cat walked out and went straight to the dish as though he'd been doing it all his life.

"I thought he'd run and hide," Tom said.

"Yeah," Eddy agreed. "I thought he'd freak!"

Pete knelt beside Shaman and petted him. The cat continued to eat. Pete looked up at his father with a big grin. "He knows he's home."

Nancy, who'd just fed Malia and couldn't seem to make herself put her down, came to observe Shaman while absently patting the sleeping baby.

Jave reached out to pull her into his arm. "He's acting," he said in surprise, "as though he's always lived here."

"Of course." Nancy leaned into him and gave him a teasingly superior look. "Even a streetwise—or a beachwise—cat, knows he can't live on handouts forever. Sooner or later he has to move in somewhere, be willing to do his part as a member of a family."

Jave turned his attention to her, the smile in his eyes acknowledging her conviction. "Is that a fact?"

"It is. I have it on good authority." She kissed his chin and said for his ears alone, "I'll be soooo glad when six weeks are up."

He nodded grimly as he squeezed her close. He put a gentle hand to Malia that almost covered her completely. "That'll be November fifth, but who's counting?"

CHAPTER FOURTEEN

November 5

JAVE AND NANCY climbed aboard the *Mud Hen*, carrying a picnic basket between them. It was the evening of November fifth, and rain fell in torrents. They wore roll-neck sweatshirts Denise and Willy had sent from their Southwest tour.

The marina's lights ringed the darkness like moons, and several boats with live-in owners were brightly lit against the night.

"Let me find the light in the galley," Jave said, leaving Nancy at the top of the ladder with the basket.

A small glow appeared below and Jave reached up to take their overnight fare.

Nancy handed it down then followed, holding on to the overhead, still careful of the almost perpendicular steps.

Jave lifted her off the last few steps and into his arms. She clung to his neck, drunk with the freedom of being alone with him and of having passed her six-weeks' checkup with flying colors.

Jave held her against him and felt the love and the trust in her embrace. During their four-and-a-half-month relationship, conducted without the distraction of sex, they'd learned more about each other than he guessed most couples learned in the first five years of marriage.

They were now irrevocably connected by thought, emotion and yearning. But he was anxious to finally share the passion.

He tightened his grip on her as he thought about how long and how forcefully he'd capped his desire for her.

She bit his earlobe and dipped the tip of her tongue into his ear.

He groaned and hunched his shoulder. He'd wanted to approach this slowly, to show her that despite the endless longing, he could be patient and tender and remember that this was their first time.

"There's...ah...champagne in the basket," he whispered, moving the few steps toward the table, still holding her.

She planted kisses along his jawline. "I'm not thirsty."

"Pâté and—"

"Not hungry," she said against his mouth. "Except for you." Her eyes smoldered as she looked into his.

His resolve toppled and he carried her through the elegantly renovated salon and the beautiful blue-and-grey stateroom without even noticing Tom's hard work on their behalf.

Jave placed Nancy on the queen-size bed that took up the entire space. She pushed at his sweatshirt and he yanked it off, then drew hers up over her head.

Nancy was delighted to see his impatience. In the two months they'd been married, she'd had evidence over and over of his strong character and personal discipline. Now she was thrilled to know that though he'd made restraint look easy, it hadn't been—and that he was as desperate for her as she was for him.

He reached under her to unhook her bra, freeing her swollen, blue-veined breasts.

She resisted an urge to cover them. The mother in her appreciated their function, but the vain woman in her longed to retain the size they'd become while smoothing them to alabaster.

"They're ugly," she said.

Jave's eyes concentrated on them a moment, then he kissed each one with a tenderness that negated her claim.

"They're like Carrara marble," he said, looking up into her eyes. "Only warm and silken, like Malia's skin."

Vanity restored, Nancy lifted up as he tugged her leggings off. They brought her panties down, too, and he tossed both out into the salon.

He expelled a ragged breath as he stared down at her lean hips, her stomach still slightly, charmingly rounded by the pregnancy, her long, slender limbs.

"I can't believe I can finally make love to you," he said, his eyes reverently perusing every plane and hollow. "Even yesterday, I wouldn't have believed this, but I almost want to just sit and stare and savor the moment."

Nancy braced herself up on an elbow, caught his shoulder, and traded places with him.

"Tell you what," she said, leaning down to kiss his lips. "You savor while I undress you."

He relaxed, willing, at least for the moment, to let her take over.

She unzipped his jeans and inched them down, prepared to tease and tantalize him. But as she uncovered every formidable inch of limb and masculinity, she found herself as awed as he had been.

"You're magnificent," she whispered, clutching the jeans and briefs to her. Then she added on a note of wonder, "And you're *mine!*"

Jave swallowed a lump in his throat, humbled by her expression. He took the clothes from her, tossed them aside, pulled her down to him, and wrapped her in his arms.

They moved against each other, silky skin to suedelike flesh, muscle to soft curve, angular limbs to supple arms and legs.

Nancy felt her heartbeat quicken and her breath fail. Jave felt his mind go—all thought and control lost to sensation too long suppressed.

He tucked Nancy into his arm and braced himself on his forearm to reach down to her knee. She raised it for him and he stroked gently from it to the juncture of thigh and body.

She sighed against him, her small hand exploring his back and over his hip.

Jave's hand covered her femininity. He applied a small amount of pressure, as though making a claim. Mine.

Nancy rose against him, offering an admission. Yes. Yours.

He dipped a finger inside her and every receptor in her body relayed the sensation. It was an affirmation of rightness, an acceptance of truth, life and love just as she knew it was intended to be.

She moved restlessly against him.

"Hurt?" he asked in concern.

"No," she whispered, reaching between them to touch him, enfold him. Inside her, pleasure was already blossoming, expanding, ticking out of control. "Come to me," she pleaded. "It's been *forever*."

He rose over her, the only coherent thought in his head calling for care. But she banished even that with the nimble artistry of her touch.

He entered her in self-defense, but carefully, intent on withholding his pleasure until he'd prolonged hers. But her body closed around him and the sensation surpassed everything he'd imagined even in the darkest depths of his frustration. Pleasure stormed over him, touching every hidden corner of his being. Yet, at the heart of what he felt, there was something spiritual—a satisfaction so complete it seemed to come from the depths of the universe.

Nancy took Jave deep inside her, startled for an instant by a mildly painful pressure on still-sore stitches.

He made to withdraw, but she held him to her, taking him deeper until the simple perfection of their connection eased her discomfort. She felt as though they were lovers in a fine sculpture, destined to embrace for all eternity.

Then he began to move within her, reminding her that

they were not only a work of art, but also one of genuine flesh and blood.

She clung to him, moved with him, and felt herself reborn as they climaxed together. Passion confined for so long reacted like dynamite at the end of a long fuse. Flame burst, sparks flew, and their entire personal terrain was changed forever.

They lay wrapped in each other's arms, legs entangled, comfortably cocooned in the small space of the stateroom. Rain fell rhythmically overhead as the *Mud Hen* rocked gently in its slip. The darkness felt magical.

"What time is it?" Nancy asked.

"Ah..." Jave raised the arm with which he held her to him so he could check the illuminated dial of his watch. "Eight twenty-one," he replied.

She snuggled against him, pulled that hand to her lips and kissed its palm, marveling that anyone could feel this wonderful. "At 8:21 on November fifth, Jave and Nancy Nicholas finally made love for the first time. Do you believe it?" She tilted her head back to look into his eyes, her voice suddenly grave. "Did you feel everything I felt? Could you possibly be as happy as I am?"

"Nancy." Her name on his lips said everything. The sound was filled with all the tenderness and the passion with which he'd made love to her. "I've never known what I feel at this moment. I can't imagine what the boys and I did without you and Malia." He kissed her soundly to underline that truth. Then he added wryly, "And had I *known* what it was like to make love to you, I'd have died of the frustration long ago."

She sighed and kissed his throat, very satisfied with his reply. "Eight twenty-one on November fifth," she said. "We'll have to celebrate every year."

He reached under her to lift her atop him. "And 8:59, 9:32, 10:06, 11..."

Kelsey Roberts
Unspoken Confessions

Unspoken Confessions originally appeared in the Harlequin Intrigue® line, a series of dynamic stories that combine breathtaking romance and heart-stopping suspense. Four new Harlequin Intrigue® novels appear every month.

HARLEQUIN®
INTRIGUE®
ROMANTIC SUSPENSE

CHAPTER ONE

"HAVE YOU CALLED the police?"

Shelby nodded as she gulped in air. "They're on their way."

"Where's Cindy?" Rose asked, placing her hands on Shelby's trembling arms.

"I think she went into the kitchen," she answered. "As soon as I realized the baby was gone, I really lit into her."

"I should hope so! What was she doing? How did they get in?" Rose thundered.

Shelby glanced over her shoulder and saw the teenager hunched over the kitchen table. The muffled sounds of her crying filtered into the living room.

"She put him to bed around nine. She said she never heard so much as a peep."

"Peep, my foot!" Rose huffed. "You mean to tell me someone waltzes in here and snatches our baby, and *that* one didn't even feel a draft from the door?" She waved her thumb in the direction of the girl.

"The window was open when I went in to kiss him goodnight." The memory of that horrible moment brought with it a renewed flood of warm tears for Shelby. All at once, her mind filled with so many possibilities—none of them good. "What am I going to do?" she managed to choke out.

"I don't know," Rose answered with her usual candor.

The police arrived then. A virtual army of men and women, in all ranks, shapes and sizes. Rose brought one of them over to Shelby, who stood next to the window, peering out at the bustle of activity. She couldn't stand the thought of Chad being out there. With God only knew what kind of stranger.

"I'm Detective Greer, Mrs. Hunnicutt."

"Shelby," she said automatically.

"Shelby," he repeated in a soothing voice. "I need to get some information from you as soon as possible."

"Anything," she told him.

He smiled wanly and touched her elbow, directing her to the table in the center of the room. He reached into his pocket and pulled out a small notebook. As he flipped it open, he pushed the vase of cut flowers on the table off to one side.

She was only vaguely aware of what was happening in her own home. Rose was on the sofa, talking to one of the female officers. There was a man in the kitchen with Cindy. Still others moved past her toward the stairs, stopping only long enough to ask about the rooms on the second floor.

She tasted the remnants of salty tears as she moistened her lower lip.

"The FBI will be here soon, so I'll need to get some background."

"Chad is nine months old. He weighs twenty-two pounds and has some dark hair just beginning to grow. His eyes are blue, but not the same color as mine. He—"

"We'll get a recent picture," Greer said gently, interrupting her.

She nodded and said, "I just had some done at the mall. I'll get them."

"No." Greer placed his hands over hers. "Just tell me where they are."

"On the kitchen counter," she said.

"Do you live here alone?" he asked.

"Yes."

"And your husband?"

"I'm not married."

"Then the baby's father?"

"Isn't involved."

One of the detective's brows arched in an unspoken question.

"He isn't," she insisted.

"Give me his name and address," he stated as he poised his pen above the page.

She looked around then. There were at least a dozen people in the house. Judging from the beams of bright light flickering in the window, several officers were positioned outside, as well.

"His father couldn't have had anything to do with this," she insisted.

"We won't know until we talk to him," Greer pointed out.

"It isn't like that," she said. "Chad's father doesn't even know about him. I left without ever telling him I was pregnant."

The detective leaned back in the seat. His head tilted to one side as he regarded her for several long seconds. "If you're keeping information from us..."

"I wouldn't do that! My son is gone!"

"Will you at least tell me the guy's name?"

"I—"

A young uniformed officer came over and whispered something to Greer. He then placed a small plastic pouch in the detective's hand before retreating back out the front door.

"Do you recognize this?"

She reached out and took the bag. Inside was a small, round silver medallion on a broken chain. Instantly, she remembered....

"THIS IS VERY NICE," she murmured.

She could smell the faint traces of his cologne. The medallion was between his thumb and forefinger. Her eyes remained transfixed as she watched him absently run the silver object along its chain.

She sensed the change in him. The knowledge brought with it a flood of anticipation that swirled in her stomach. Her nerves were electrified; her awareness was acute. All these weeks of waiting, wondering, dreaming, seemed near an end.

"What are you doing?" she asked through a smile when he moved around behind her.

"Protecting you," he murmured against her neck. His hands wound around her waist, his large fingers splayed against her abdomen.

"Is this part of your job description, Dylan?"
Her fingers laced with his.

"I know someone who wears one like this. His name is Dylan Tanner. He's an agent with Alcohol, Tobacco and Firearms. But I haven't seen him for a long time," Shelby finally answered. She retained her hold on the medallion, remembering all too vividly what it had looked like nestled in the dark mat of hair on Dylan's chest.

"Is this Tanner guy the baby's father?" Greer asked pointedly.

Shelby's only response was a faraway look that seemed to quiet the detective's inquiry—at least for the present. The front door burst open, and Helen Hopewell was ushered in by a pair of officers. Cindy, her eyes rimmed by damp red circles, went running to her.

Helen clutched the girl, but she was looking at Shelby. "I don't know what to say," Helen began, her expression pained.

"I never heard a sound!" Cindy wailed, and then dissolved into another fit of loud sobs.

Helen explained to Greer that she was the sitter's mother, and that she lived in the house three doors down the street. The officer who had been talking to Cindy was furiously scribbling notes as she spoke.

Greer motioned to one of the officers, whispered a directive, then dismissed him. Shelby watched him leave, the shock of what had happened to her baby slowly evolving into a sort of numbness tinged with a certain amount of denial. The room was filled with the telltale scent of baby powder, and other small reminders of Chad. Part of her mind insisted on believing that this was all some sort of nightmare. Eventually she would wake up, and he would be there, smiling, drooling, even crying.

Sometime later, an officer poked his head in the front door and said, "He's here."

"Chad!" she screamed, looking in the direction of her front door. A flood of bright lights projected the long shadow of a man.

"Is it Chad?" she asked anxiously as she jumped to her feet.

Rose, who had been standing with her supportively, shoved one of the officers to one side to allow Shelby a unobstructed view of the door.

"I'm sorry, Shelby," Greer said.

She actually swayed when he came into the room. He was wearing jeans and a pale blue polo shirt. His federal identification badge hung from one of his belt loops. He looked exactly as she remembered, tall and distractingly handsome. He walked with such arrogant authority that he was able to reach her in two long strides.

"Shelby," he said softly as his hands gripped the bared flesh of her upper arms.

"I'm Detective Greer, Agent Tanner," the smaller man asserted as he thrust his hand forward.

Dylan didn't take the hand, but simply said, "Greer." His eyes were trained on her. "You have a son?" Dylan asked.

Shelby nodded, then lowered her eyes. Why was he here? Who had decided to bring Dylan into this? She couldn't deal with him now. Chad had to be her only concern.

"Do you recognize this?" Greer asked as he passed the bagged medallion to Dylan.

He turned away from her and accepted the item. His dark brows drew together as he turned the bag over in his palm.

"I did have one like this. I lost it about six months back," he told the detective. "It does look like mine."

Greer nodded and took back the evidence bag. "We found it in the bushes below the nursery. Can you think of any way it could have gotten here?"

"You thought I might have had something to do with this?" Dylan asked Shelby.

She was standing so close that he could smell the faint scent of her perfume. But it wasn't like the last time they'd been together, he thought as his hands balled into fists. Her contagious smile was gone, replaced by a tormented expression clouding her blue eyes. The hair framing her face was as dark as his own, but unlike his, it fell in soft waves to her slender shoulders. Even in grief, Shelby was beautiful.

Rose piped up. "Of course she doesn't."

"Who are you?" Dylan countered, bracing his feet as he crossed his forearms over his chest.

"Rose Porter," the woman responded. "I'm Shelby's business partner."

Dylan turned away from Rose's narrowed green eyes and gave his full attention to Shelby. "Business partner? So you did break with Nichols?"

"He bought me out," she answered, moving fractionally closer to Rose as he watched her.

"Hey, Greer!" Rose bellowed. "Are you still in charge here? Or have you decided to let this guy run your investigation?"

The police official bristled at Rose's decidedly sarcastic tone. "What is it you'd like me to do?" Greer retorted.

"Find the kid," Rose volleyed back.

"That's what we're trying to do," he said defensively. "That's why I sent a car for Mr. Tanner."

"You're wasting time and resources," Shelby insisted. "You heard Dylan. He didn't even know I had a son."

"No," Dylan agreed quietly. "I didn't."

Shelby felt his eyes on her, and she held her breath.

Would he put it all together? How long would it take for him to realize the obvious?

"Have you wasted the last couple of hours tracking him down instead of looking for Chad?" Rose demanded. Her arms flailed at her sides, dislodging her animal-print blouse from the thick black patent-leather belt cinching her waist.

Her loud, distinctive voice garnered the attention of the officers and technicians. Greer blanched, and a red stain seeped up from the neck of his rumpled white shirt.

"I'm following up on the only lead we've got. That's how we do things, Mrs. Porter. We look at every detail."

A flash of something passed between the two of them that Shelby wasn't able to decipher. While she considered Rose her dearest friend, she also recognized that her outspoken tendencies didn't always endear the raucous woman to strangers.

"What leads *have* you got?" Dylan asked the other officer.

Greer shrugged and said, "The neighbor across the street thinks he may have seen a strange car parked up the street. We're showing him catalogs now, to see if he can come up with a make or model year."

"Have your men checked out Nichols?" Dylan barked.

"Nichols?" Greer repeated.

Dylan turned to Shelby again, and his eyes bored into her. "Ned's the father, right?"

Shelby shifted her weight from foot to foot. She wanted to scream the truth, but something told her now was neither the time nor the place. Her only answer was her silence. She couldn't lie to Dylan. Not directly, at least.

"Ned Nichols was her business partner. ATF's been investigating him on and off for almost two years," Dylan explained.

"Why the hell didn't you tell me this?" Greer bellowed at Shelby.

She started at the harsh question, and was grateful for Rose's hand on her shoulder. "I haven't seen or spoken to

Ned in more than a year," she answered stiffly, careful to keep her eyes averted and fixed squarely on one of Chad's stuffed elephants.

"Where can we find him?"

Shelby hesitated, then said, "Ned could not possibly be involved in this."

"He's slime," Dylan countered. "If you think being the kid's father would make a difference to a guy like Nichols, you're dead wrong, Shelby. Christ," he muttered. "The guy's old enough to be *your* father."

"Where can we find this Nichols?" Greer asked.

"Charleston Import Company," Dylan supplied, then rattled off the address.

Greer took the information and moved away.

"Would you mind leaving us alone for a minute?" Dylan asked Rose.

Shelby could sense her friend's misgivings. "It's okay, Rose," she said.

"Chad means everything to Shelby," Rose warned Dylan before she turned toward the kitchen.

The scent of coffee lingered in the air between them. Her entire body tensed under his close scrutiny. At any second she expected the light to dawn. *What then?* her mind screamed.

"You look tired," he said, guiding her to the chair. "Do you want to go up and lie down for a while?"

"I couldn't," she insisted. "The FBI told me that kidnappers usually make a ransom demand in the first few hours."

"I'm sure they'll find him, Shelby."

"He's only a baby!" she cried in a choking voice. "What if he's hurt? What if—"

"Don't do this to yourself," he said soothingly, kneeling in front of her. His square-tipped fingers rested on top of her knees. "I'm sure they'll have him back here before morning."

She looked into his eyes, hoping to draw on his confidence. His angled features were set in what she suspected was an artificially optimistic expression.

"Ned wouldn't take Chad," she told him.

Dylan's handsome features immediately hardened. "I know you've always wanted to believe the best about that guy, but—"

"He doesn't even know about the baby," she admitted, carefully watching for his reaction.

It wasn't good.

"You mean to tell me you never told the man he had a son?" Dylan demanded in a harsh whisper.

"I didn't tell Ned about the baby," she stated simply, feeling her face warm under the weight of her evasiveness.

"I thought the way you dumped me was cold," he observed. "I never would have thought you were capable of doing something this dishonest."

"My son is missing, Dylan! The last thing I need from you is a lecture on my decision making. You don't have the first clue what you're talking about. And besides, this doesn't really concern you."

"What is going on here?" Rose asked, in time with the rhythm of her spiked heels hitting the floor.

"Nothing," Shelby answered quickly.

"Well, it doesn't look like nothing," Rose muttered. "Just what did you say to her?" she asked Dylan. "Her hands are shaking, and she's crying again."

"Sorry," Dylan mumbled.

"I'm sorry your mother didn't eat you when you were born," Rose spit at him. Placing her hands on her rounded hips, she arched one neatly plucked brow toward the pile of coiffed blond hair that added height to her small frame.

"Look, lady," Dylan said, rising slowly, "I didn't mean to upset her."

"You did," Rose told him pointedly.

If his size intimidated her, nothing in her expression gave it away. Rose simply squared her shoulders and offered him one of her wilting looks. Shelby had seen it work magic on the most unruly patron. It didn't seem to be having much of an effect on Dylan.

"I really am sorry, Shelby," he said to her. "I was way out of line."

"Forget it," she breathed as she picked up one of the dozens of photos strewn across the table. A lump formed in her throat the instant she looked at the big eyes smiling back at her from the picture. They were nearly the same shade of electric blue-gray as those of the man standing just a few inches away. She felt the wetness of tears that flowed soundlessly.

"They'll find him, Shelby honey," Rose said. "You gotta have faith."

"I do," she lied. What she had was a deep, consuming pain in her chest. It was hard to keep her mind from wandering into those unspeakable places. Hard to keep her imagination from producing horrible scenarios.

"I know most of these guys, Shelby," Dylan said as he again knelt in front of her. "They'll find your little boy."

She nodded, afraid to speak, for fear of what she might say.

She lifted her head when she heard her front door open. One of the plainclothesmen walked in and whispered something to Greer. The detective's head moved fractionally, and it appeared to her that his guarded expression lightened just a bit.

Dylan rose and placed a hand on her shoulder as Greer strode over.

"I don't want to get your hopes up..." he began.

"What?"

"Ned Nichols isn't at his house *or* his business. One of his neighbors saw him leave his house around midnight."

Shelby held her breath and swallowed.

Greer continued, "He was carrying something wrapped in a blanket."

CHAPTER TWO

DYLAN WATCHED as her mouth dropped open. He should have expected it. Shelby had a definite blind spot where Nichols was concerned.

His gut knotted, and he rammed his fists in his pockets. She looked so shocked and scared that it took every ounce of his self-control for him to keep a level head. How could Nichols do this to her? How could *she* have had his son?

He looked away then. The thought of Shelby and Nichols together still rankled. More than it should. But it was because he remembered....

HIS LIPS BRUSHED against the sensitive skin just below her earlobe. The silky feel of her skin drew his stomach into a knot of anticipation. His grip tightened as his tongue traced a path up to her ear. He heard her breath catch when he teasingly nibbled the edge of her lobe.

His hands traveled upward and rested against her rib cage. He felt her swallow, heard the moan rumbling in her throat.

"You smell wonderful," he said against her heated skin.

"Dylan..." She whispered his name. "I don't think this is such a good idea."

His mouth stilled, and he gripped her waist, turning her in his arms.

"I've kept my hands off you for five weeks," he said. He applied pressure to the middle of her back, urging her closer to him.

"I know," she managed to say above her rapid heartbeat.

"I've never done this," he said.

Shelby's eyes flew open wider, and her expression registered obvious shock.

His chuckle was deep.

"I mean, I've done this,*" he went on. "I've just never been so attracted to a woman that I've been willing to compromise my professional responsibilities."*

"Will this affect your job?"

"I hope so," he said as he claimed her mouth. The kiss lasted for several heavenly moments. "I just wouldn't want you to think I make a habit of this sort of thing."

"I don't think I am *thinking," she admitted as she rested her cheek against his chest.*

"I CAN'T BELIEVE Ned would take Chad," she finally said in a soft voice. "There's no reason for him to want to hurt either one of us."

Dylan snorted. "I can think of one." Turning to Greer, he continued, "Nichols knows that Shelby can put him away."

"But he's known that for more than a year!"

Dylan ignored the conviction in her tone. "For the past six months, I've been working it from the other end. My agency has reliable information that another shipment is due any day. Nichols's suppliers are about to make their move."

"Back up," Greer told him. "Shipment of what?"

"MAC-10s," he answered. "A large shipment of those guns, along with a hefty amount of ammunition, was stolen from an Israeli depot last month."

Greer let out a low whistle. "I guess it's too much to hope that you guys had him under surveillance?"

Dylan shrugged. "I've been working with a contact at the port, but I can call my superior."

"I'll keep my fingers crossed," Greer said.

"I still can't believe that Ned would be involved," Shelby said, wrapping several strands of her deep ebony hair around one finger.

Dylan remembered all too vividly how soft her hair was. How it had felt fanned out across his chest.

Shaking his head, he told himself he needed a breather. He was no good to Shelby when he couldn't stay focused. The kitchen offered the safe haven he needed. *What kind of man was he?* he wondered as he lifted the telephone receiver and dialed. Her kid was missing, and all he could think about was the memory of that one night.

A groggy male voice answered on the third ring. "Yeah?"

"Jay, it's Dylan. We've got a serious problem."

In the other room, Shelby was quickly losing hope. It had been nearly five hours. "Where could he be?" she asked.

"I know they'll find him," Rose answered. "And when they do, I'll arrange for a little justice for the dirtball that's responsible. Southern-style."

"That kind of talk won't help," Greer cautioned.

She watched as Rose leveled the man a pointed stare. While her partner was a small woman, Rose was an imposing person, with an impressive vocabulary of fierce looks.

"Well, what are *you* guys doing?" Rose demanded of the officer.

"We're following leads, Mrs. Porter," Greer answered. Then, rather ominously, he added, "All of them."

"Right," Rose muttered derisively.

Greer excused himself and wandered over to a small collection of men huddled in the corner of the living room. Some were busy connecting some sort of reel-to-reel tape machine to the telephone outlet. Others were occupied covering every inch of the room in a bluish black dust.

"We'll need your prints," a woman announced to Shelby as she placed what looked like a tackle box in the center of the table.

"What for?" Rose asked.

Shelby merely blinked.

"We need to print everyone who has had access to the

house. Then we can eliminate friends and family when we begin to run comparisons."

"Why don't I go back to the Tattoo and bring whatever desserts are left for these folks?" Rose suggested.

Shelby felt her mouth drop open at the uncharacteristic suggestion. Not that Rose wasn't kind—she was. But she wasn't normally given to attacks of hostessing. Maybe she needed some way to deal with her emotions, Shelby speculated. Rose was definitely nervous. Perhaps a trip to their restaurant would do her some good.

"You can do my prints when I get back," Rose told the technician.

The uniformed woman simply shrugged as she began taking ink pads and file cards from inside the tackle box. "Give me your left hand first," she instructed Shelby.

Numbly Shelby complied, her eyes searching for Dylan. She found him in the kitchen, talking on the telephone. His eyes, which were neither gray nor blue, but a devastating combination of the two, were thickly lashed and hooded. A lock of his jet black hair had fallen forward to rest just above his brows. His chiseled mouth was pulled into a tight line.

"Give me your right hand now, please."

"Sorry," Shelby mumbled, starting. The woman looked down at her with compassion, and that was almost enough of a catalyst to set her tears off yet again.

Crying wouldn't help. She could cry later, once Chad was home.

Cindy was fingerprinted next, and then allowed to leave in the comfort of her mother's supportive arms. Shelby felt a pang of envy, followed by a dose of anger. Intellectually she knew she shouldn't blame the sitter, but she needed a hate object until the kidnapper was found.

"No," she whispered as her head dropped forward. "I need Chad."

"We'll find him," Dylan said.

She looked up at him through her unshed tears. "Why haven't I been contacted?"

He shrugged his broad shoulders. "The ball's in his court. You've just go to keep it together until Ned decides the time is right."

"It still doesn't make sense to me. Ned has no reason to take my son."

"His son, too," Dylan countered. "You know," he began as he slid into the seat next to her, "maybe that's the reason."

"What?"

"Maybe Nichols found out he had a son and just decided to make himself the custodial parent."

"That isn't possible," she told him.

"Why not? I'll admit I had a similar thought when the officer showed up at my house tonight."

"What thought?" she asked, in a barely audible tone.

"Before he told me how old your son was, I wondered if I was..."

"Chad is nine months old," she asserted.

"I know. And I can add and subtract."

"Your math skills aren't going to bring my son back," she pointed out stiffly.

"Did you know you were pregnant when we were together?"

"Dylan," she began as she rose, "I don't want to get into all this with you. Not now."

"You're right," he said quickly. "I'm sorry."

Greer came over then. His forehead was wrinkled into a series of deep lines. He spoke to Dylan first. "Did you get in touch with Special Agent Williams?"

"He's on his way."

"Your boss is coming here?" Shelby interjected.

His dark head dipped slightly. "He's alerting the unit."

"But I thought the FBI was in charge of handling kidnappings."

"Jay spoke to them and offered to spearhead things because we already have so many agents in place."

"In place where?" she asked.

"We've got agents undercover at the import company. People already on the inside of Ned's organization. We've got wiretaps, some surveillance, the whole nine yards. It would be a waste for the FBI to duplicate everything we've done."

The creases in Greer's forehead became shallower. "I think you're lucky in this respect, Shelby. Having Alcohol, Tobacco and Firearms in on this will save time. Time is important when you've got a missing kid."

The phrase *missing child* conjured up all sorts of unpleasant images in her brain. Milk cartons and posters. Billboards and grim news footage. She swayed.

Dylan's hands went to her shoulders, steadying her.

"Are you sure you don't want to lie down for a bit?"

"I'm sure," she answered.

"Actually," Greer began, "there's something I'd like you to consider."

Shelby's eyes flew to his face. "What?"

"The morning news shows start in about forty-five minutes. I'd like you to think about making an appeal for Chad in front of the cameras."

"Go on TV?"

Greer nodded.

"The exposure might do some good," Dylan suggested.

His hand touched her shoulder as she looked from man to man. "Will it help?"

"It'll get his face out there. It will make it hard for the kidnapper to hide him if the whole city of Charleston is looking for him."

"I don't think I can do it," she said, in a quavering voice.

"Sure you can," Dylan insisted with a weak smile.

"I'll be there with you," Greer offered.

"So will I," Dylan added.

"No," Greer said, with a slight shake of his head. "If it is Nichols, seeing you might not sit too well."

She saw the reluctance in Dylan's eyes. She felt an unexpected flash of disappointment. *What is wrong with me?*

her brain screamed. *I need to get him away from here!* Letting him see pictures of Chad was one thing. But how could she keep her secret if Dylan saw her little boy up close? Surely he'd discover her deception.

"Greer is right." She looked directly into Dylan's arresting eyes. "In fact, there's no reason for you to even stay here."

She saw him flinch.

"I want to stay here until I find out why my medallion, if it is mine, was found here."

"It couldn't be yours," she argued. "You said yourself that you lost yours a long time ago."

"It isn't exactly a one-of-a-kind item," Greer pointed out.

"Right. See?" Tension stretched between her and the tall man.

"No," Dylan answered firmly. "I don't see."

"We're getting off track," Greer said. "Are you willing to go on camera?" he asked Shelby.

"If you think it will help find Chad."

"Good," he said with a nod. "I'll set it up."

When Greer went to the front door, he was greeted by Rose, her arms weighted down by a large box filled with foil-wrapped packages.

"I brought everything I could think of," she said as she placed the box on the edge of the table and slid it toward the center. "Keith left the kitchen in a mess. Remind me to give him hell when this is all over."

"Who is Keith?" Dylan asked.

Rose unpacked items as she spoke. "He's our cook. No," she added with a smirk, "he's our chef. He gives me one of those snotty looks if I call him a cook."

Greer and several of the other officers came over to the table. Shelby stepped back, nearly sickened by the smell of the food. Dylan moved with her.

"Does Keith always leave your kitchen a mess?" he asked.

"Not usually," Shelby responded, without really giving

the matter much thought. "He's a character. Rose isn't fond of him, because she thinks he puts on airs."

"And what do you think?"

"I think he's trying to overcome his past."

"His past?"

"Keith learned to cook in Europe."

"That's impressive."

"He learned to cook on army bases in Europe."

"Oh."

"Rose doesn't much like airs. It has something to do with her marriage."

"She's married?"

"Was," Shelby said. "She rarely talks about it, and I learned early on not to ask."

"Aren't the two of you friends, as well as partners?"

"We're very good friends." She glanced up at him, meeting his gaze directly. "Part of being friends is respecting each other's privacy."

"Nice to see you're still willing to turn a blind eye where your friends are concerned."

"Don't start with me, Dylan," she warned him. "I'm worried sick about my son, and I certainly don't intend on allowing you to take potshots at me now."

"Shelby," he said, gripping her upper arm, "I'm sorry. Really. I don't know what possessed me to say something so stupid."

She waffled as her emotions warred with her common sense. Now would be the perfect time to tell him to take a hike. *So why don't I?* she wondered.

"Forget it," she managed.

The grip on her arm loosened. "I'm not going anywhere, Shelby."

"But there's really nothing—"

"Shelby, honey, eat something," Rose said as she passed a croissant forward.

"I can't."

"You've got to try," Rose insisted. "You aren't going to do the baby any good if you starve yourself."

"Maybe later," she said, offering her friend a forced smile.

"It's already morning." Rose inclined her head in the direction of the window.

"Maybe coffee," Shelby suggested, and she infused lightness into her voice.

"You won't have time for coffee," Greer said as he joined them. "The television people are all set up. They're waiting for you outside right now."

"What do I do?" Shelby asked the officer.

"We've given them a picture of Chad that they'll show when the piece airs. All you need to do is ask for the safe return of your son."

"Then what?"

"Then we wait," Dylan answered.

The lights were hot. And they were so bright that she couldn't see beyond the porch. She knew there were people out there, because she could see several pairs of feet radiating out from under the harsh white glare. It took several protracted seconds for her eyes to adjust to the brilliant light.

"Miss Hunnicutt?" someone shouted. "Can you lift your chin a bit?" Then: "That's good. Look straight ahead, toward the red light."

She found the small glowing dot and stared at it until her tired eyes began to burn.

"Anytime you're ready," the faceless voice called.

"I...um... If you're listening to me, please bring my son back. I don't want to see you punished. If you're afraid of being caught, please take him to a hospital, or to a firehouse. He's all I have. Please, please, let him come home."

She was shaking by the time she went back inside the house. Rose immediately appeared at her side, as did Dylan.

"Do you think that will do any good?" she asked no one in particular.

"Of course it will," Rose said firmly. "If nothing else,

Chad's face will be all over the morning news. He's bound to be noticed by someone. He's too cute to fade into the woodwork."

Shelby smiled then. "I hope so."

"Jay's here," Dylan noted, turning away from them.

She watched as the man entered the room. He was the type of person who naturally commanded attention. He had that air of authority, that stoic sort of focus, that Shelby had always found intimidating. Now, however, she found the determined set of his squared chin comforting. Jay Williams would be a definite asset in their hunt for Chad.

"Miss Hunnicutt," he said as he approached.

His nondescript dark brown suit matched his eyes and hair. In fact, everything about him was so neat and perfectly matched that Shelby had the keen sense that she was in the presence of a Ken doll. His shirt was straight and white, as were his teeth. His shoes were polished, their laces perfectly spaced and knotted, so that each lace ending precisely matched its twin.

"Agent Williams," she said by way of greeting.

"Miss Hunnicut. And you must be Rose Porter," he said to a visibly surprised Rose.

"That's right."

"You and Miss Hunnicutt own the Rose Tattoo, on East Bay?"

"Yep," Rose answered.

Shelby noticed a guarded look fall over her friend's face.

"Any other investors?"

The agent's attention was fully on Rose.

"No," Shelby answered.

"Is that right, Mrs. Porter?"

She watched as Rose looked down and then began to tap her thumbs against her thighs. "I'm the owner of record."

"Then you deny having any other investors?" Williams went on in a badgering tone.

"What is this—?" Shelby's words were cut off when Dylan reached out and gave her hand a pointed squeeze.

"I'm carrying a note," Rose said softly.

"With a bank?" Williams demanded.

Greer and one of the ATF agents appeared then, apparently drawn by the heated interrogation.

"Not with a bank. No."

Shelby looked at her friend. Rose refused to make eye contact with her.

"Do you know Mitch Fallon?"

"Mitch Fallon?" Shelby repeated. She recognized the name from various newspaper reports.

"I know Mitch," Rose reluctantly answered.

"Doesn't he hold your note?"

"I borrowed money from him."

"At twenty-five percent?" Williams hammered.

"Look." Rose's voice had risen an octave. "Mitch lent me money when the banks wouldn't touch me."

"He's what's commonly referred to as a loan shark, isn't he, Mrs. Porter?"

"I suppose."

"And he has a reputation for collecting interest in some rather violent ways, does he not?"

"He's never been anything but straight with me," Rose shot back.

"Everything on the up-and-up?" Williams asked.

"You bet."

"Never had any trouble from Fallon?"

"Never."

"Then he doesn't mind that you're three months behind on your payments?"

CHAPTER THREE

"YOU OWE MONEY to a loan shark?" Shelby gasped.

"How do you think I kept the Tattoo going before you?" Rose countered in a subdued tone. "Mitch couldn't have anything to do with this, Shelby," she continued. "I know he's got a bad—"

"So you don't deny that you are indebted to Fallon?" Williams asked.

"Of course not," Rose shot back. "Mitch and I are old friends. He lent me money because of that. He knows Shelby and I have been spending a fortune trying to build the business. He agreed to let me slide for a while."

Agent Williams's face dissolved into an expression of guarded concentration as he listened to Rose's explanation. Shelby looked from Rose to Jay, then to Dylan.

He appeared to be mulling the revelation over. His eyes were clouded and unreadable. "When was the last time you talked to Fallon?" he asked.

Rose shrugged, then said, "Week ago. Maybe ten days."

"Check it out," Williams barked to one of the other officers gathered in the dining room. "Withholding information in a kidnapping is a serious offense," he warned Rose.

"I didn't withhold squat," she told the stiff man.

"Really?" he asked, in a tone Shelby thought sounded strangely like a taunt.

"Really."

"You'd better be telling me the truth, Mrs. Porter."

"And you'd better find the kid," Rose responded.

"This isn't getting us anywhere," Shelby said. "First you

start screaming that it has to be Ned. Now you're leaning toward some loan-shark person I've never even met. Instead of attacking my friends and grabbing at straws, would you please do something constructive to find my son?''

"We are." Dylan spoke close to her ear. "I'm sure we'll have him back as soon as we find Nichols."

Pivoting on the ball of her foot, Shelby angled her body so that she faced Dylan. "Just humor me," she pleaded. "Don't waste all your energy and resources on Ned. I know he wouldn't take my baby."

"Then give me an alternative that makes sense," he said in a soft tone.

"How am I supposed to know?" she wailed. Her hands flew into the air, then slapped against her thighs before dangling helplessly at her sides.

"Other than Nichols, do you have any enemies? Anyone that would want to hurt you?"

She shook her head. "I don't have any enemies. Not even Ned."

He let it pass, even though it pained him to keep his thoughts on the subject to himself. She looked rough. There was strain around her eyes, in her voice. And it was getting to him.

"What about the bar?" his boss asked.

"Restaurant and bar," he heard Rose say.

"Whatever," Jay muttered.

Shelby hugged her arms against her body and let out a breath. It looked to him as if she was losing the battle to keep her tears at bay.

"We're just getting off the ground. We cater mostly to young professionals, but we get a few neighborhood folks," Shelby said.

"Employees?" Dylan asked.

"We gave all this to Greer!" Rose fairly shouted.

He saw the slight tremor in Shelby's hand when she touched her partner's forearm. He wanted to reach out to her, promise her everything would work out. Only he wasn't sure he believed it. Not when they had so little to go on. *And what?* he wondered for the umpteenth time, *was my medallion doing at her place?*

"Detective Greer will no longer be directly involved, so you'd better give it to me," he told Shelby. "ATF will be handling the investigation."

"There's Keith," she began. "He's the chef. Then we have Tory—Victoria Conway. She's a waitress and tends bar on and off. Josh Davis is our regular bartender. And Erica and Kelly wait tables."

"What about you?" Jay asked Rose.

"I own the place," she answered. Dylan noted that the Porter woman's spine had gone rod-straight but she still wasn't making eye contact with his boss. He decided to file that bit of information away for the time being.

"Do you work, as well?" Jay asked.

"We both do whatever is necessary, Agent Williams."

It was Shelby's soft voice, with its cultured Southern drawl, that answered the question.

Being from New York, Dylan often found the slow Southern way of speaking annoying. But not hers. Not Shelby's. The cadence of her speech wasn't slow, it was seductive.

"Something wrong?"

He was pulled back to the present by the sudden jab of Jay's elbow into his side.

"What?"

"Your expression," Jay said, prompting him. "Think of something?"

Dylan shook his head and said, "No."

"Shelby, honey," Rose said quietly, "go up and rest for a little while. I'll stay here."

"I can't."

"Sure you can," she insisted.

Shelby felt herself being pushed toward the stairs. "I need to be here in case—"

Rose cut in. "Don't be stupid. I'll be upstairs in a split second if anything happens. I promise."

"I'll walk you up."

Shelby froze at the base of the steps when she heard Dylan's offer. She couldn't very well insist that he stay away from her, not without a lot of explaining.

"That isn't necessary," she said, in a voice she hoped sounded aloof.

"I know it."

"Go on," Rose urged.

The handrail, which had been carved by a previous owner of the house, was covered in a thin film of blue fingerprint dust. But Shelby noticed only the marks on the walls. They weren't from the forensic team. They were small gouges and scratches from Chad's toys. She felt her chest fill with weighted guilt. How many times had she admonished him for scraping the wall with a toy? What she wouldn't give to have him home, crawling precariously up the stairs with a toy in each hand—that defiant smile on his round face.

Stopping at the top of the stairs, Shelby turned and looked into the shadowy room. She felt Dylan's fingers fan against her back as she reached for the wall switch.

Light flooded the small space. A clown smiled at her from above the crib, which had been pulled away from the wall and left at a strange angle. The window was covered with the blue dust, as was the top of the dresser. Only the neatly organized changing table appeared to have made it through the onslaught undisturbed.

"This doesn't seem real to me," she said in a near whisper.

"I can't imagine how you must feel."

She turned then, and lifted her chin in order to meet his gaze directly. "Numb."

She watched as his dark head lowered and he pressed his lips together.

"We'll find him," he told her as his fingertips found the underside of her chin.

"I hope you're right."

"Believe me."

"I have to," she said as she bowed away from his touch.

Flipping the switch, Shelby backed out of the room and headed down the narrow hallway toward her room. There, in the golden rays of the morning light, she saw it.

"What on earth?" she exclaimed. "What is that doing here?"

"Jay!" she heard Dylan call as she moved to the foot of her bed.

Resting just on the edge was an odd rectangular black item. She went to pick it up when Dylan's hand clamped over her wrist.

"Don't touch it!"

"But what if—"

Jay, with Greer on his heels, hurried into the room. Someone turned on the overhead lamp.

"What is it?"

"A videotape," Dylan answered.

"Is it yours?" Jay asked her.

"I don't think so," Shelby said after she looked on the side for a label. "No. It's not one of mine."

"Get the lab boys up here," Jay said.

Shelby looked down at her wrist, suddenly realizing that the warmth was from Dylan's viselike grip. His skin tone was darker than her own, despite the similar coloring of their hair and eyes. Using her free hand, she tapped the back of his hand with her fingers, without ever meeting his eyes or saying a word. She didn't dare let him know how his touch still affected her.

A small swarm of men crouched around the videotape, photographing, measuring, fingerprinting, mumbling. It felt as if hours had passed by the time they finally relented and allowed her to place the tape in the machine in her room.

Shelby and the others stood in a semicircle at the foot of her bed. She stared at the screen, watching as the static slowly organized itself into an image.

"Oh, God," she whispered through the fingers of her trembling hand.

"Is that him?" Dylan asked.

She nodded as she felt his fingers gently move to her waist. "That's the outfit I left for Cindy to put on Chad after she gave him his bath."

"Do you recognize anything else?" Jay asked. "Any of the surroundings?"

Shelby concentrated on the television screen. Chad was asleep on a small blanket, guarded by a collection of plush stuffed animals. When his small body moved involuntarily, a hand appeared in the frame.

"Looks like a woman," she heard someone remark.

"What's that?" Jay asked.

"Maybe a ring," Dylan answered.

The tape ran out then, leaving Shelby feeling shaken and more confused than ever.

"He looks like he's being well cared for," Dylan said against her ear.

"If you can call being kidnapped well cared for."

"Run the tape again," Jay told one of the officers as soon as it became apparent that there was nothing else on the video.

They stood in silence and watched the tape for a second, then a third time. She was surprised when her chest knotted with a sudden burst of anger. Who was the woman on the tape? And why had she taken Chad?

"See if you can get a blowup of the ring," Dylan said before the lab technicians spirited the tape away.

"And have the report sent directly to me," Jay added.

Shelby was left with only Dylan and the tall, slim Agent Williams in the room with her.

"Has anyone been around your restaurant lately? Anyone ask you about your son?"

Shelby shook her head. "No one."

"Is it common knowledge that you have a son?" Dylan asked.

"Yes," she answered defensively. Dylan was treading dangerously close to an area Shelby resented being questioned about. "I quite often take Chad to work with me."

"To a bar?"

She leveled Dylan an angry stare. "The Rose Tattoo is more than just a bar, Dylan. It's a restaurant, *and* my place of business. Stop saying it like you're implying I run some sleazy truck stop out along I-95."

"Okay," Dylan said, raising his hands in mock surrender. "I wasn't criticizing you."

"Not much," she muttered under her breath.

"Let's get back to the issue," Jay suggested.

Shelby guessed the man had picked up on the tension in the air. She wondered how long it would be before someone put it all together. *Then what?* her brain cried.

"What about at the market? Or shopping?" Jay continued. "Anybody approach you recently? Maybe say something about the baby."

"No," she said on an expelled breath. "Nothing like that has happened."

"Think, Shelby," Dylan urged, in a slightly raised voice. "Maybe someone commented on how cute he is? Something like that?"

Shrugging, she began to pace in the small area between the two men and the now silent television set. "I get compliments about him all the time. Chad's an adorable child."

She glanced at the two men and felt her face redden at the same time. Jay was stoic, but Dylan seemed to have allowed a small smile to penetrate his rigid facade.

"Maybe someone found him more adorable than normal?" The suggestion came from Jay.

"Nothing jumps out at me," she said. "I can't think of anything."

"Okay," Dylan said, shoving his hands into the front pockets of his jeans.

Shelby was distracted for a fraction of a second. For just that instant, she allowed her mind to fix on the outline of his well-muscled thighs. On the way the soft denim hugged his tapered hips.

"What about the woman on the tape?" Dylan continued. "Judging from the weathering of her skin, I'd say she was probably over fifty. Definitely spends time outdoors."

"Right," Jay agreed as he stroked an imaginary beard with his left hand. "We can assume she's local, since the tape showed up here so quickly."

"I don't see how she got it up here," Dylan added. "This place is crawling with cops."

"I think we can assume we're dealing with a very resourceful individual," Jay said.

"And it's not Ned," Shelby stated. Her remark was greeted with resistance from both men. Dylan's reaction seemed more pronounced than Jay's, but then, everything about Dylan left a strong impression on her.

"The tape doesn't exonerate Nichols," Jay said in a paternalistic tone.

"But we all agree that it was a woman's hand that pulled the blanket over Chad."

"Which simply could mean that Ned has an accomplice. Maybe she's the elusive ex-wife we were never able to track down."

She met Dylan's eyes and read the conviction there. "Dylan," she began reasonably, "isn't it possible that you are so convinced that Ned is evil that you're twisting things to make them fit?"

Dylan's dark head shook vigorously. "Hardly" was his derisive reply.

"He's right," Jay agreed. "It still appears as if Nichols is our best suspect."

"How can you say that?" Shelby asked. "There's nothing to indicate Ned is in any way involved in all this."

"Nothing except the fact that your son is gone," Dylan told her.

"A man, most likely Ned, has to be involved. I don't think a fifty-plus-year-old woman scaled the side of your house, not once, but twice," Jay told her. "Once to take the baby, and once to plant the tape."

"Why leave a tape?" Shelby asked. "Why would someone want to torment me like this?"

"Maybe it isn't to torment you," Jay suggested.

"Right," she heard Dylan say.

"I don't understand."

Dylan took two steps that brought him right in front of her. His breath washed over her face in warm waves. Shelby struggled with her strong urge to take a step backward.

"Maybe this is Nichols's way of letting you know Chad is all right."

"That's crazy!"

"Not necessarily," Jay said. "Nichols always did have a soft spot for you. And besides, since he's the baby's father, maybe in his sick little mind, he's trying to be humane."

Shelby sidestepped Dylan and turned toward the window. Wrapping her arms around herself, she tried to make some sense out of their farfetched assertions. "Ned would not do this to me," she breathed.

"He's an arms dealer, Shelby. Do you really think he's above kidnapping?"

She stiffened at Dylan's question. She had never wanted to believe that about Ned. He'd been good to her, and she owed him a debt of gratitude. But she and Dylan had been over this ground time and time again. She knew he would never understand her feelings, any more than she could understand his obsessive need to continue with the accusations.

"He wouldn't do this to me," she said again.

"How can you be so sure?" he thundered from behind her. "I know you don't want to accept that Ned is less than perfect, but be real, Shelby. The man finally realized you were a potential hazard. When he found out you'd had his kid, it was like playing right into his hands."

"You're reaching," she said, without turning toward him. She could almost feel his intense eyes boring into her back.

She didn't dare risk facing him, not while Chad's parentage was being discussed.

"I'm not reaching, and you know it, Shelby." Her name came out as a husky whisper. "No one else has any reason to take your baby. Nichols has to be behind this."

"No. There has to be some other explanation," she said as she bowed her head.

She felt his hands move to her neck. He began a gentle kneading massage of the tense muscles between her shoulders. She was reminded of the magical way he had touched her. It seemed like a lifetime ago.

"Don't fight us on this," he said. "We aren't out to crucify Nichols. Jay and I only want to help you get your son back."

Shelby turned then, drawn by the soft invitation in his deep voice. She looked up at him through the veil of her thick lashes. "I'm not fighting you," she told him. "I just want to make sure that nothing goes unchecked. I'm just afraid that if Ned isn't guilty, we'll have wasted too much time and effort when—"

The shrill sound of the telephone split the air. Shelby jumped at the unexpected sound before brushing Dylan aside and running toward the nightstand.

When she reached the table, her hand seemed to freeze in midair, hovering just above the receiver.

"Pick it up," Dylan instructed.

Shelby looked to Jay, who gave a reassuring nod of his head.

With trembling fingers, she lifted the phone off the cradle and placed it at an angle near her ear. Dylan leaned against her, pressing his head next to hers.

"Hello?" she managed in a small voice.

There were some muffled sounds, followed by a raspy voice that said, "Cute kid. It'd be a shame if something was to happen to him."

CHAPTER FOUR

"WHO IS THIS?" she shouted into the receiver.

"Now, Shelby. If I told you my name, it would take all the fun out of it."

"Where's Chad? Is he all right?"

She heard the faint sound of cruel laughter. Her hand went up to brush the strands of her hair away from her eyes. Her heart pounded against her chest, making it nearly impossible for her to hear the muffled voice.

"He's fine. And he'll stay that way, as long as you do what I tell you."

"Anything," she promised. "Just don't hurt him."

"Shelby...Shelby... You've got to have some faith."

"Please let me talk to him. Hold the phone against his ear so that he can hear my voice—"

"There'll be time enough for that later," the voice said. "I'll be in touch."

"Wait! Please!" she yelled into the phone.

"He's gone," Dylan said. She could feel him move away from her. "It wasn't long enough for a trace."

She slammed the phone down with the full force of her frustration. Warm tears welled up in her eyes, but she refused to crumple. *Not yet,* she told herself.

"Was there anything familiar about the man?" Dylan asked.

"No," she answered softly. Shelby sat on the edge of the bed and cradled her head in her hands. She desperately wanted to scream.

"I'll go and check with the guys downstairs," Williams said. "Maybe they got lucky."

When she lifted her head, Shelby found Dylan staring down at her. His shoulders were slumped forward, and he appeared to share her dejected mood. The corners of his chiseled mouth moved slightly, lingering somewhere near an apology.

"He didn't ask for anything," she finally managed to say.

Dylan shrugged. "He could have been feeling you out. Or..."

"Or what?"

"Or—" Dylan shoved his hands into his pockets "—he could be fronting for someone else, who might make his demands known at a later date."

"I presume you're trying to tell me that you think the caller is somehow connected to Ned."

He nodded. "Nichols can't very well call. He knows you would recognize his voice."

"Why are you so convinced it's Ned?"

"Because nothing else makes sense," he told her. "Crimes are very rarely committed by strangers."

"Is that where we get the expression 'random act of violence'?" she shot back at him.

"I didn't say it doesn't happen," he stated reasonably. "I'm just trying to explain to you that it's rare."

"Why would anyone I know want to take my son?" she asked. "I'm hardly in a position to pay a sizable ransom. And I don't have any power. Nothing makes any sense."

"You have power over Nichols."

She looked at the ceiling and let her breath out slowly. "I explained the situation to you more than a year ago, Dylan. I never had any firsthand knowledge of Ned's dealings outside the import company."

"But you could have gotten it, if you'd continued to work with me."

"That wasn't an option," she said softly, careful to avoid his eyes.

"And I guess now I know why."

She watched in nervous silence as he began to pace back and forth. His muscular shoulders pressed against the fabric of his shirt with each intake of breath. Then his hand went up to rake through his thick mass of black hair, which he wore to a length just below his collar.

"I brought you up some herbal tea."

Shelby had been so busy studying Dylan's profile that she hadn't heard her friend come up the stairs. Rose expertly balanced the tray in one hand while she cleared a space on the nightstand with the other.

"You didn't have to do that," Shelby told her.

"You need to get some rest," Rose returned as she patted Shelby's hand. "There's nothing for you to do until that bozo calls back."

Rose's green eyes shimmered with a kindness at odds with the thick layers of makeup that were part of her image.

Shelby managed only a small smile in response.

"You," Rose said, turning in Dylan's direction, "go on downstairs and see if you can muzzle that boss of yours."

Dylan's expression lightened considerably. "I don't think Shelby should be alone."

"That's why I'm here, Sherlock. I'm the friend, you're the officer. The friend offers support and companionship. The cop investigates." Rose planted her hands firmly on her hips. "Go down and see if you can discover if Williams is thinking with both lobes of his brain."

"You shouldn't talk about Agent Williams like that," Shelby said as soon as Dylan had left the room, grumbling under his breath.

"He's not *doing* anything," Rose snorted as she began to pour tea from the small pot.

"They're convinced Ned has Chad."

After filling the cup, Rose took a breath and patted her stiff blond curls into place. "It's not really any of my business, but are you sure you're going about this the right way?"

Shelby felt her brows draw together. "What do you mean?"

"Well," Rose said slowly, "are you sure it's such a good idea to let Williams handle this, instead of Greer and the FBI?"

"No," Shelby answered quickly. "But I'm not sure I have a choice. But I know Agent Williams is a very capable, driven individual."

"How do you know him?"

Shelby smiled then. "Wait a minute. Doesn't this violate our 'don't ask about the past' agreement?"

"That was before Chad was kidnapped," Rose answered. "You don't have to tell me anything," she continued. "I just never figured you to have been involved with the cops, is all."

"I wasn't involved," Shelby said. "Not really, anyway."

"That isn't how I see it."

Shelby's head came up, and she met Rose's inquisitive stare.

"Look, Shelby," Rose began as she took a seat next to her on the bed. "I saw the way you reacted to Dylan Tanner. And while I have always thought Chad was the spitting image of you, after seeing—"

"Enough!" Shelby interjected. She didn't want Rose to say it aloud. "I think I'll take your advice and try to rest for a while."

Rose hesitated, and Shelby feared her friend might press the issue. But, Rose being Rose, she simply nodded and quietly left the room.

Shelby stared at the door long after it had closed. If Rose had figured it out, how long would it take Williams? Or, worse yet—Dylan?

"Wake up, Shelby."

She did more than wake up. Shelby leapt to her feet with her heart pounding. Dylan was next to the bed, his face a mixture of anticipation and anxiety.

"What is it?" she asked as she vigorously rubbed her hands over her burning eyes. "Have you found Chad?"

"You've got to get to your restaurant," he said, gently nudging her toward the door. "Keith called and said the kidnapper called you. He's going to call back in—" Dylan paused and checked his watch "—less than twenty minutes."

"Oh, Lord," she moaned as she hurried down the stairs.

Her living room was no longer a hub of activity. Williams and two other officers were seated by the reel-to-reel machine, their faces expressionless.

"We'll wait here," Williams said to her. "Dylan can take you over. Mrs. Porter is already there, waiting by the phone. She said she'd stall if the call comes before you get there."

Shelby noticed a strain in Williams's voice. She wondered if this development had ominous overtones that no one was willing to admit to.

"Keys?" Dylan asked, offering his palm.

Shelby had to think for several seconds before her dulled brain recalled where she had left her purse. Shaking away the few remnants of sleep, she grabbed her bag off the side table and pulled her key ring free from the pocket.

"I'll drive," Dylan said.

She squinted against the bright afternoon sunlight. The pleasant scent of the flowers seemed an unkind intrusion into her grim thoughts. She followed Dylan across the lawn, sidestepping gouges in the turf that she guessed had been left by the television crews early that morning.

"What's the fastest way?"

She gave him directions by rote, her mind still not fully functional. It wasn't the result of the fitful few hours of sleep she'd had. No, Shelby was distracted by the sight of her son's empty car seat. And the brightly colored plastic rings abandoned on the floorboards.

She shut her eyes and summoned strength from her dwindling reserves. "Why the restaurant?" she asked.

Dylan gripped the wheel tightly and said, "Maybe he knows we've got a trace on your home phone."

"Can't you put the same equipment at the Tattoo?"

She saw him shake his head.

"Not enough time. But Jay's making the necessary arrangements to have that taken care of ASAP."

"Drive around back," she said, pointing toward the alleyway next to the Rose Tattoo.

The scraping of the car's underside drew the attention of the few patrons scattered along the restaurant's porches. She could see their curious expressions as she looked past Dylan.

He brought the car to an abrupt halt between the building and Keith's black Chevy. Shelby quickly forced open the door and stepped onto the weathered stone drive. Her heels echoed in the cavernous space as she walked toward the back entrance.

Almost immediately, her senses were assaulted by a barrage of odors from the kitchen. Dylan was right behind her as she slipped past the bustle of the work area and headed up the back stairs.

She had to turn sideways in order to pass by the stacks of boxes lining the small hallway. She found Keith and Rose waiting in their office.

Keith was tall and slender, with straight blond hair that he shaved just above his ears. A cubic-zirconia stud sparkled in his left earlobe. It seemed an appropriate accessory for his starched white chef's ensemble.

As she entered, Keith pulled himself up to his feet, wiping his hands on the fronts of his trousers. His eyes fluttered from her face to an area near her feet.

"Has he called back?" Dylan asked.

"Not yet," Rose answered. Then she turned to the chef and said, "You go on back downstairs. Take care of anything that comes up."

Keith's head bobbed slightly, and his lanky form began to move toward where Shelby and Dylan stood in the doorway. He was a few feet from her when he said, "I'm really sorry about little Chad. It shouldn't have happened."

She had to strain to hear his soft voice. When she reached out to acknowledge his sentiment, Keith nearly flinched at the contact. It was his usual response. Whenever he was around Shelby, Keith acted like some sort of shy teenager.

A sudden burst of laughter floated up from the room below as Shelby crossed the thickly carpeted floor and took her place behind the cluttered desk. Rose was to her left, leaning against the credenza near the far wall. Dylan lingered at the edge of the desk, his hands resting on the surface.

"Tell me what happened."

Rose's head tilted to one side. The action allowed the harsh rays of sun spilling in from the window to glisten off the lacquered layer of hairspray. "Keith was the one who actually answered the phone. He turned it over to me when the guy said he was calling about Chad."

"And?"

Rose rubbed her upper arms and said, "His voice gave me the creeps. He said he was going to call back in thirty minutes, and you'd better be here. After he hung up, I called your place and told Williams."

Shelby glanced at the small oval clock on her desk. Any minute, she thought. But the minutes passed without the phone call. She began tapping her thumb against the desk, her fingers just inches from the receiver. *Come on!* she mentally pleaded. But still nothing.

When the intercom buzzed, Shelby nearly had to peel herself off the ceiling.

"What?" Rose barked into the small speaker.

"There's a new delivery guy here," Keith said. "He says he has to speak directly to one of the owners."

"Tell him I'm coming," Rose said, then moved toward the door, mumbling some rather unkind words under her breath.

As soon as Rose was gone, Dylan moved over to the other desk in the room.

"What are you doing?" Shelby demanded. He didn't respond. "That's Rose's desk."

"I figured that out for myself," he said as he slipped into the seat and opened the top drawer.

"You shouldn't be going through her things," she admonished.

"Under the circumstances," he began as he opened the second drawer, "I don't think she'll complain."

"You could have asked first," Shelby said. She looked again at the clock, then to the phone, then back to Dylan. Her patience was wearing thin. "Why doesn't he call?"

"He will," Dylan said. His attention remained on his task.

He hadn't even bothered to look up when he spoke. She could hear the rustle of papers, and she could just imagine how her partner would respond if she returned to find him elbow-deep in her private affairs.

"Why is this locked?"

She stood, her curiosity slowly edging out her impatience. "I don't know," she said as she walked around to where Dylan had rolled the chair back from the desk.

"Let's see what we have here."

She felt her eyes grow wide when he reached into his hip pocket and produced a small packet of long, thin metal picks. "You can't be thinking of picking the lock!"

He turned and looked up at her, his eyes sparkling with challenge. "Do you have a key?"

"No," she admitted quickly. "But you could show Rose the courtesy of asking her permission. She's just downstairs, for heaven's—"

The telephone came to life then, causing Shelby to jump.

"Are these connected?" Dylan asked as he pointed to the phone on Rose's desk.

"Yes."

"Grab the one on your desk. I'll listen in."

Shelby made a dash for the phone and grabbed it on the third ring. The cord tangled as she turned to watch Dylan as she spoke.

"Hello?"

"Nicely done, Shelby," the cryptic voice said. "You follow directions real good."

"Is Chad all right? Please let me talk to him."

"Patience, Shelby," he replied. "He's fine. So far."

She swallowed the lump of fear clogging her throat. Dylan nodded encouragingly when she made eye contact. She interpreted the motion as a sign of his support.

"Please don't hurt him."

"I'm not going to. Not unless you screw up."

"Just tell me what you want me to do," she said as she gripped the receiver in both hands. It was getting difficult to hear him over the sound of her pulse pounding in her ears.

"We're going to help each other, Shelby."

"Fine," she said quickly.

"I like saying your name, Shelby. Is it a family name?"

"My name isn't important!" she snapped. "Tell me what you want me to do to get my son back!"

She could hear him breathing, but it felt like several minutes before he said, "I want you to tell me about your name, Shelby. If you won't, I'll hang up."

"No! Please don't hang up," she breathed. "Shelby was my mother's maiden name."

"Fine Southern tradition, don't you think?"

"Yes."

"And what about Chad? Is Chad a family name, Shelby?"

"I named him after my father," she answered, without hesitation.

"He must have been proud."

"He's dead," she said flatly.

"I'm sorry about that, Shelby. Do you miss him?"

She bit her lip in an attempt to fend off the tears of frustration welling up in her eyes. "Yes, I miss him. We were very close."

"Like you and Chad?"

"Yes."

"Then I suppose we should do something about that, Shelby. How about it?"

"Anything."

"Then I'll be in touch."

"No! Wait!"

When she heard the distinctive click, Shelby closed her eyes and held the receiver to her chest.

"He's toying with you," Dylan told her as he quickly moved in front of her. "You did a good job, though. You were calm and cooperative. That'll almost guarantee he'll call back."

Her eyes opened, and he saw raw emotion in their blue depths. The pain ripped through his gut as he tried to think of something comforting to say. But there wasn't anything he could say. Nothing that could even come close to erasing the anguish he read on her face. Why the hell hadn't the CPD found Nichols yet? he wondered.

When she didn't move, he debated his next action. Swallowing once for courage, he reached out and placed his hands on her shoulders. He waited, not sure how she would interpret his actions. Hell, he wasn't even sure of his own motivations. But he decided it didn't really matter. Nothing mattered but his fierce need to protect her from Nichols and whoever his pathetic accomplice turned out to be.

With very little pressure, he eased her toward him, fully prepared for resistance. There was none. She fell against his chest, her hands still clasped around the telephone. He reached up and stroked her silky hair, wondering if she would fall to pieces. He'd been expecting tears since the beginning. At first he'd thought it was admirable that she'd been able to retain her composure. Now, however, he wasn't at all sure that stifling all her emotions was such a good idea.

"You can cry, you know."

She jerked back, out of his arms. Hard as it was, Dylan didn't do anything to counter her. He watched, almost helplessly, as she fell into the chair and leaned her head back against the cushion. Her body shuddered only slightly as she took in several large gulps of air.

"Did you recognize anything this time?"

"No," she answered in a small voice.

Nodding, Dylan moved back to the other desk and called Jay to fill him in.

"I don't like this," Jay said as soon as Dylan had recounted the gist of the conversation.

"Shelby wasn't real thrilled, either." He looked across at her as he spoke. She had picked up a framed photograph from her desk and was staring at the image of her child.

"This guy could be a kook," Jay continued. "All that stuff about her name—"

"It was weird," Dylan said, interrupting him. "I got the feeling the guy was out in left field, but we don't have much else to go on."

"There's Nichols," Jay countered.

"So why haven't we been able to find him?"

"His boat's gone from the marina. We've got men up and down the Ashley River looking for him."

"Find him fast," Dylan said in a near whisper. "I don't know how long she's going to be able to take this."

"Keep her there for a while," Jay instructed. "The guys from Southern Bell should be out there soon to set up the tap."

"Will do," Dylan said, and then hung up. She was still looking at the picture, and he had the feeling he should leave her alone with her thoughts.

He decided to busy himself by continuing his search through Rose's desk. The Porter woman wasn't the neatest female he'd run across. Her desk was filled with all sorts of interesting, though unimportant, things. He'd discovered an envelope filled with cereal-box tops, a pad of notepaper in the shape of a man's behind, and a whole collection of half-eaten rolls of antacids.

Nothing important, really—until he jimmied open the bottom drawer. His fingers ran across the faded label on the top of a bulging accordion file. He didn't recognize the name on it, but the word *Esquire* jumped out at him like a bright red flag.

Pulling the file from the drawer, he slid his thumbnail beneath the seam and ripped open the seal. He looked inside.

"What's that?"

"I don't know yet," he answered as he shook the papers out onto the desk top.

Shelby came over then, standing on the opposite side of the desk, with her arms crossed in front of her chest.

"Why don't you have Rose come up and go through that stuff with you?"

"You're one of the owners, so technically—" he lifted his eyes to hers "—unless you tell me I can't go through the desk, there's no legal expectation of privacy."

She shrugged, though indecision and uneasiness shone in her eyes. "It doesn't seem right...."

Her voice faded in his ears as he began to read the captions and skim the text of the documents. He felt his stomach knot with foreboding as he continued to read. Shelby began to speak, but he raised his hand in order to keep her quiet until he'd had an opportunity to finish.

When he finally looked up at her, he hoped his expression didn't reveal his true feelings. "We do need to get Rose up here."

"Why, Dylan?"

"Because she got three years from a Florida court for kidnapping."

CHAPTER FIVE

"WHERE'S ROSE?" Shelby demanded as she grabbed a handful of Keith's shirtsleeve.

The lanky young man's eyes flew open, but he remained mute.

"I asked you where—"

"She ran out of here about fifteen minutes ago."

Shelby turned away from the chef and peered around Dylan's rather imposing shoulders.

Tory Conway stood with her foot holding the shiny metal door at an angle. An empty tray was balanced against her nearly nonexistent hip.

"Where did she go?"

Tory entered the kitchen and shoved an order ticket into the chrome carousel before automatically giving the thing a spin. "I don't have a clue," she said on a breath. "She just ran past me as I was coming in for my shift."

"Who are you?" Dylan asked in a deep voice.

Shelby watched as Tory's dark blue eyes roamed over Dylan's handsome face. The younger woman's head angled to one side, and her expression seemed to cloud defensively.

She told him her name and added, "I work here. Unless that's a problem."

Dylan seemed taken aback by the challenge in the tiny woman's tone. Shelby could almost feel him stiffen in response to the defiant tilt of Tory's chin.

He turned and looked to her for verification. Shelby nodded and said, "Tory works evenings as a waitress."

"Tory is working harder this evening, because it doesn't

seem as if anyone else around here does squat," Tory grumbled.

Keith piped up. "Because of what happened to Chad."

Tory's features softened instantly, and she immediately made eye contact with Shelby. "Chad got hurt?" she asked, moving a few steps closer.

"Someone took him," Shelby managed. Saying it out loud was amazingly painful. It had a certain finality to it that sent a shiver of renewed fear the full length of her spine.

"God! Shelby!" Tory ran a hand through her stylishly short blond hair. "I had no idea."

"I tried to tell you," Keith whined, in a tone reminiscent of sibling one-upmanship.

Tory cast him a withering look before she asked, "How? When?"

"Last night," Dylan answered. "Sometime after nine."

Tory leaned against the countertop and abandoned her tray with a loud clanging. "This is terrible."

"Yes," Dylan agreed, "it is."

"What can I do?" Tory asked.

"You can start by telling me where you were last night between eight and midnight," Dylan said.

His question seemed to take Tory by surprise. She blinked twice before beginning to speak. "I was right here until two this morning."

"I can vouch for that," Keith chimed in.

Shelby could have sworn something passed between her two employees, but whatever it was, or wasn't, it hadn't lasted long enough for her to give it a definition.

One of the swinging doors flew open and banged against the wall.

Erica, one of the other waitresses, leaned forward and yelled, "Hey, Tory! The deuce by the door wants you, now!"

"Shelby, I—"

"Go on," Shelby said, interrupting her.

Tory gave her a weak smile, and she was vaguely aware

of the fact that the woman squeezed her arm before racing out into the dining area.

Dylan turned to face the cook. Keith was on the opposite side of the long stainless-steel counter that spanned nearly the entire length of the kitchen. He saw a thin sheen of moisture on the man's upper lip. He noted the slight tremor in the guy's bony hand.

"You need anything, Shelby?" Keith asked in a small voice.

Dylan saw her shake her head in his peripheral vision.

"When did you say Rose left?"

Keith looked up at him then. His pale eyes were surprisingly angry. "About twenty minutes ago, now. Just before the phone rang."

"And she didn't say where she was going?" Dylan pressed.

Keith shook his head. "Nope. She just read the note and bolted."

"*What* note?"

Both Keith and Shelby started at the harsh edge in his voice, which he couldn't manage to keep in check.

"From the delivery guy."

"She ran out of here because of something the deliveryman gave her?"

Keith shifted his weight from foot to foot and bowed his head. "I think he was one of them."

"Well?" Dylan slapped his hand on the counter in front of him. The bustle of activity in the kitchen came to a sudden halt. "Was the note from a delivery person or not?"

Keith slowly raised his head and looked pleadingly at Shelby before giving Dylan his reluctant attention. "He came in with them, so I thought he was with them."

"And then what?" Dylan prompted.

"He told me he needed to speak with Mrs. Porter. Said she was the only one he could speak to."

"What did he look like?"

Keith's forehead drew together beneath his chef's hat as

he thought about his answer. "He was just a kid. Maybe fifteen or sixteen."

"Height? Weight?" Dylan asked, pulling a small notebook from the back pocket of his jeans.

"About your height."

Dylan made a note. Six feet three inches.

"Thin, like me."

He added an estimated weight of 180 to his note. "Anything special about this kid?"

"No."

Dylan flipped the cover closed with a flick of his wrist, and let out a breath of frustration. He turned to find Shelby leaning against the wall. The black hair framing her face reflected the afternoon sunlight, much as it had that afternoon so long ago....

"ARE WE ALLOWED to take picnics on government time?"

Shifting the basket to his other hand, Dylan reached out and caught her around the waist. He loved the feel of the soft fabric of her blouse. His mind instantly began to wonder about what was beneath the material. It was a path his thoughts had taken over and over during the course of their time together. He was fascinated by everything about her— her delicate features, the way her eyes grew large when she laughed, the shy way she smiled when she caught him looking at her.

"Just think of this as your tax dollars at work," he teased, bending low enough to catch the scent of her perfume on the warm breeze.

"Does this mean I'm responsible for the unchecked growth of the deficit?"

She looked up at him with those stunning blue eyes, and he nearly tripped over his own foot. He felt like some sort of overgrown teenager caught in the throes of first love. He had all the signs—sweaty palms, the inability to keep that simpleton's grin off his face. And then there was the matter of his jeans, which grew increasingly more uncomfortable the longer he was in the company of Shelby.

"Is this okay?"

She stopped suddenly as she asked the question. Dylan couldn't stop quickly enough, and found himself plastered against her. It wasn't exactly an unpleasant predicament, but he cleared his throat and regained his balance.

"Excellent choice," he told her as he placed the basket on the ground, and made a production out of scanning the nicely secluded spot she'd chosen for their lunch.

When she leaned over to smooth out the blanket, Dylan was treated to a view of her backside. He found it far more interesting than the topography of the park. Her jeans clung lovingly to her shapely hips and hugged her slightly rounded derriere. Her blouse had worked its way free from the waistband, revealing just a hint of creamy white skin.

"Start grabbing things," she said.

"WE HAVE TO FIND ROSE," Dylan said as he slid onto one of the high stools at the bar.

"I can't believe Rose would do anything like this to me."

The bartender placed a cup of coffee in front of her, then somberly took Dylan's order. The din of voices gave Shelby an odd sense of comfort. She supposed it had something to do with her emotional connection to the bar. The Rose Tattoo had given Shelby a sense of belonging when she desperately needed security.

Elvis Presley's voice crooned softly from the jukebox, which was audible above the faint crackling of the logs burning in the fireplace.

"She has a lot of explaining to do."

"You saw her, Dylan," she said as she angled herself on the stool, crossing one leg over the other. "Rose has a few rough edges, but she isn't capable of doing anything like kidnapping my son."

"You have an incredible knack for only seeing the best in people."

"And you always seem to look for the worst," she returned.

His jaw tensed, but he still didn't take his eyes off her. The pleasant scent of his cologne reached out to soothe her frazzled nerves. *Why am I jumping down his throat?* she wondered as she gripped the warm ceramic mug full of coffee with both hands.

"I called Jay and told him about the papers I found."

She felt her mouth drop open. "Why did you do that before we've had an opportunity to talk to her?"

"Because I thought—"

The chirping sound of the phone cut him off in midsentence.

Josh reached beneath the bar and brought the extension to her reach. Shelby grabbed it on the second ring. "Rose Tattoo."

"Hi, Shelby."

The icy fingers of fear gripped her throat, and she waved her hand in front of Dylan to get his attention. "It's him!" she mouthed.

Dylan swiveled on his seat. Shelby braced herself, placing her free hand on the bar.

"Is Chad all right?" she managed, in a deceptively calm voice.

"Of course he's all right, Shelby," the male voice replied. "I told you nothing would happen so long as you followed my instructions."

Dylan leaned close enough that he, too, could listen to the tormenting voice.

"You haven't given me any instructions."

"I suppose you're right," he said after a short pause. "But I'm ready now."

"Anything!" she gushed. "I'll do anything to get my son back!"

"You really love that kid, don't you?"

"Of course I do."

"How much?"

She blinked and said, "What do you mean? He's my child! I love him more than my own life!"

"No, no, Shelby," he said with a humorless laugh. "I don't mean philosophically. I'm talking dollars here."

"Dollars?" she repeated.

Dylan gripped her wrist and gave a squeeze. She met his gray eyes and watched as he signaled her to agree to whatever the demand might be.

"N-name your price."

She could almost hear a satisfied smirk as he said, "Good, Shelby. I always thought you were an exceptional businesswoman."

"What made you think that?"

"You always treated folks decently."

"At the Tattoo?"

His snort of laughter frightened her. Had she pushed him too far? Asked too many questions?

"I've really enjoyed our time together."

"What about my son?" she demanded. "Has he been well cared for?"

"I told you the kid was fine," he shot back impatiently. "And he'll be home before bedtime, if you do exactly as I say."

"I will."

"Do you know the Tennison Packing Plant on River Road?"

"Yes."

"Bring fifty thousand dollars cash there at eight o'clock tonight."

"Fifty thousand dollars?" she repeated.

Shelby looked up to see Dylan nodding furiously.

"Is that a problem?"

"No," she assured him. "No problem."

"And, Shelby?"

"Yes."

"No cops, or you'll never see your little boy again."

She stared at the silent phone for a few seconds before

replacing it on the cradle. Dylan reached out and placed his hand on her thigh. She felt the heat of his touch as she fought to keep from crumbling then and there. She actually considered blurting out her secret. She wanted someone to share her pain and her fear.

"Do you think he was telling the truth?"

As usual, he only shrugged his broad shoulders. "We'll know tonight at eight." He took his hand away and used it to lift his glass of cola to his lips. "We've got just about enough time to make the arrangements for the money—"

"How am I supposed to get my hands on fifty thousand dollars in a little over four hours?"

The muscles in his face relaxed then.

"We'll take care of that."

"But what about what he said?" she all but screamed. Then, realizing she was attracting the attention of some of the patrons, she lowered her voice. "If he sees any police, he'll hurt Chad!"

"He won't see us, Shelby."

"How can you be so sure?"

He looked at her then. Turned those intense eyes on her without warning. "You'll just have to trust me."

His words were still ringing in her ears when Jay Williams entered the dining room. He and a handful of other officers weaved through the early dinner crowd and joined them at the bar. Josh acknowledged them by placing napkins in front of each man.

"Where's Mrs. Porter?" Jay asked them, his elbows resting on the bar.

"She hasn't come back yet," Dylan answered.

Jay's expression soured at the news, and he slapped one hand against his leg in frustration.

"I made arrangements for a couple of the city boys to wait at your house in case she shows up there."

"Do you have the papers you mentioned on the phone?"

Dylan shook his head, causing some of his ebony hair to

spill across his brow. Shelby fought the urge to reach up and brush it back into place.

"I left them upstairs. I didn't think we'd need them."

Jay's expression went past sour, all the way toward hostile. "I would like an opportunity to—"

"I got another call, just a minute ago," Shelby said, interrupting. She didn't like listening to Jay berate Dylan.

"Another call?"

She nodded at him and said, "He called to let me know he wants me to meet him at Tennison's tonight."

"With fifty grand," Dylan added.

"And I have to go alone."

Jay slowly slumped against the back of one stool. Both hands came up to rake through his neat pile of wavy brown hair. His eyes clouded over, as if he were totally perplexed. Shelby wondered what he knew that he wasn't telling.

"Oh, thank God!" Rose bellowed.

Rose burst into the room, clutching something to her chest and struggling for gulps of air.

Dylan was the first to reach her. Without preamble, he pulled the brown paper sack from her hand and roughly tugged her toward the group.

"What do you think you're doing?" Rose barked as she steadied herself.

Shelby couldn't stand to see her friend being badly treated, so she tried to move past Dylan. He wasn't having any of it.

"Where did you disappear to?" he demanded.

Rose blinked once, and then the expression in her eyes grew wary. "I was doing you a favor."

"How so?"

"That!" she yelped as she waved her hand in the direction of the paper bag.

Williams grabbed the bag from Dylan and reached inside. She watched him slowly pull a videotape from inside.

"It looks like another one," he said after a brief examination.

He was in the process of handing it to Dylan when Shelby stepped up and snatched it away. "You can analyze it to death—*after* I've watched it."

With the lot of them on her heels, Shelby led the procession to her office. The tape was placed in the machine connected to the small television set behind her desk, and in a few seconds the image began to appear.

As Chad's smiling face filled the small screen, Shelby felt Dylan's hand close over her shoulder. Rose lowered herself onto the edge of the desk, next to her. They all stared silently at the television.

"That's Waterfront Park!" Shelby exclaimed when she recognized the area where the stroller her son sat in was parked.

"That's less than three blocks from here," Rose added.

Suddenly a hand came into the shot. It was the same woman's hand as in the first videotape. At least the ring looked the same. The hand placed a newspaper in front of the baby. The camera zoomed in for a close-up of the date.

"Today's *Centennial*," Dylan said.

The baby managed to get hold of a corner of the paper. His squeal of delight at his accomplishment was both reassuring and heart-wrenching for Shelby.

The camera angle widened, giving her a full view of the baby. He was dressed in what she could only have described as an adorable outfit—one she knew wasn't his. His broad smile was contagious and she felt the corners of her mouth curve upward.

"Da, da, da, da."

The tape ended on the sobering sound of Chad's babbling.

"Did you hear that?" Dylan asked excitedly.

Lifting her chin, Shelby looked up at him, confused.

"Was he saying 'daddy'?"

She averted her eyes and said, "Of course not."

"But you heard him say—"

"He's a baby, Dylan. Babies speak gibberish like that all the time."

"A lot like you guys," Rose said in a stage whisper.

Jay cut off the set, and he and Dylan stood in front of them. Dylan crossed his arms in front of his chest, and glared down at Rose.

Shelby turned to see that Rose was glaring right back.

"It's come to our attention that you were involved in a kidnapping in Florida," Jay began.

Rose flinched, and her shoulders slumped forward slightly. "I guess I should have told one of you about that."

"It isn't true, is it, Rose?" Shelby gasped, placing her hand to her open mouth.

"It isn't what they've no doubt led you to believe," she answered quickly. "It's not like I'm some sort of criminal or anything."

"A Florida court didn't see it that way," Jay countered.

"I got three years probation," Rose told him. "It wasn't any big deal."

"Kidnapping is usually considered a big deal," Dylan suggested rather snidely. "Parents like to know where their children are."

Rose got to her feet and stood toe-to-toe with Dylan. Placing her hands on her hips, she tilted her head back and said, "But they were my children."

CHAPTER SIX

"YOUR CHILDREN?" Shelby queried through her confusion.

Rose's head bobbed furiously up and down. Shelby was only vaguely aware of the others in the room as she silently struggled to overcome the shock of hearing such an incredible revelation.

"It wasn't like they're making it out," she insisted.

When Shelby looked into her friend's eyes, she discovered they were wide, almost pleading in their intensity. "But you took—"

"I didn't do anything wrong!" she insisted. "Listen," Rose said, tugging on the sleeve of Shelby's blouse. "I had my kids young. Too young." Her head dipped fractionally, and her expression clouded, as if she were actually traveling back into the memories.

"Joe Don and me, we just sort of drifted apart."

"But the children?" Shelby prompted.

"Two boys," Rose said softly. The small smile that curved her bright fuchsia lips was bittersweet and tight.

"You're divorced?" Dylan asked.

For the first time in several minutes, Shelby lifted her head and looked in his direction. He leaned against the bar, his massive arms crossed in front of his equally impressive chest. Fatigue registered around the corners of his gray-blue eyes. More of his dark hair had fallen forward on his forehead. Rich rays of golden sunlight spilled in from the window, creating shadows that softened the sharp angles of his features.

"Of course I'm divorced," Rose said on a sigh. "Joe

Don Porter became Joseph Porter. And Joseph Porter became an architect who didn't need or want me as a wife.''

Shelby patted her friend's hand. ''It happens,'' she said, then instantly felt foolish for having said something so trite.

''This is all very interesting, Mrs. Porter,'' Jay said. ''But your marital woes don't explain the circumstances of—''

''I'm getting to it!'' Rose snapped.

Shelby could feel the other woman's slight body tense as she shifted her weight from foot to foot. The sound of the heels of her shoes scuffing the carpet preceded her words.

''Joe Don and me used to be a lot alike.''

With thick, sluggish movements, Rose began to pace. For the first time, Shelby noted that Rose's normally confident shoulders had slumped forward. That almost defiant wiggle was gone from her walk.

''He went to night school while I waited tables,'' Rose continued as she fingered a small pile of pale pink napkins embossed with the rose logo of the restaurant. ''J.D. and Wesley were just out of diapers when Joe Don decided he needed a change.''

Rose turned then, her eyes narrowed and full of long-held fury. ''Of course, part of the change included a young, pretty coed he'd met.''

''That's terrible,'' Shelby managed.

Rose snorted. ''Not really. After the initial shock wore off, I was just as glad to be rid of him.''

''Could you get to the part about the children?'' Jay asked, without bothering to disguise his impatience.

''The boys and me were fine. I was working, making decent tips.'' Rose turned her back and began rubbing her hands along the sides of her arms. ''The manager let me keep the boys in a playpen on the top floor during my shift.''

''You kept two toddlers at a bar?'' Dylan asked.

His question earned him a sharp look from Shelby. She wondered if the man had any earthly idea what it was like to be a working mother.

''I kept food in their mouths and clothes on their backs,''

Rose answered. "We didn't hear a peep from Joe Don until nearly two years later. He'd married his coed. They had a successful architectural firm in south Florida. And they wanted my kids."

Shelby swallowed and closed her eyes for a brief second. She knew instantly how Rose must have felt all those years ago.

"He and the coed took me to court."

"You lost custody of the boys?"

Rose's mirthless laugh sent a chill the full length of Shelby's spine.

"Hell, no, I didn't lose custody. At least not here in South Carolina."

"You were charged in Florida," Dylan put in gently.

"The judge here said I had to let them have the boys for summer visits. I did. The kids were with them for almost three months. Joe Don and the coed used their influence down in Florida to pull some fancy legal stuff. The next thing I knew, some weasely process server shows up on my doorstep with papers that say I have to appear in court for a custody hearing."

"What happened in Florida?" Jay asked.

"I wouldn't know," Rose answered. Her shoulders fell forward another fraction. "I ran right down there and got my boys."

Shelby felt the muscles in her face relax.

"I didn't even get as far as the Georgia border before the cops pulled me over and arrested me."

"How awful," Shelby moaned.

"It took months for all the court stuff. By then, the boys had been with Joe Don and the coed for so long that this psychology woman told the courts that it would be harmful for them to be returned to me."

"Did you fight him?" The question came from Dylan.

Rose nodded and said, "At first. Then I went and saw them at their father's place." She grew silent for a few minutes, her fingers nervously twisting the chain of plastic beads hanging from her neck. "They each had their own room. They had nice clothes, a house with a yard and a pool."

"So you decided to leave them with your ex-husband," Jay concluded.

"Joe Don and the coed were...persuasive," she admitted. "They wouldn't take my word that I'd leave the boys with them. That's why they didn't back off the kidnapping thing. But I would have done what was right for the boys even without their threats."

The last statement was delivered in a barely audible whisper. Sucking in a deep breath, Rose went through a remarkable transformation, right before Shelby's eyes.

Her posture straightened, and that air of belligerent confidence returned, as Rose spun and faced her. The chain of beads dangled from the tip of one long red fingernail.

"So you see," she said, only to Shelby, "there's no way I could be involved with little Chad's disappearance."

"I know that," Shelby said as she moved to hug her friend. "I never believed you were involved, Rose."

"DAMN IT!" Dylan yelled as he jumped away from the stream of hot water spewing from the shower head. His skin burned where he had stupidly allowed the water to scald him. He let out a few additional expletives as he adjusted the knob.

"Lack of sleep," he told the mixed-breed that came bounding around the corner.

The dog's nails slid and scraped the tile just before he caromed into the side of the tub. Dylan snickered at the dog's stupidity. "No wonder I've kept you all these years, Foolish," he said as he patted the stubby hair on the top of the animal's head. "We have something in common." He slipped into the shower and pulled the vinyl curtain closed. "Neither one of us can do two things at once. I can't think and turn on the shower, and you can't walk and...do anything."

Foolish barked once before insinuating his elongated snout on the edge of the tub. Dylan looked down and tried to keep a straight face, the way his neighbor, Miss Dog Expert, had instructed.

"Get down. You're getting water on the floor."

The dog looked up with his eyes, but no other part of him moved.

He searched his memory to recall what Miss Dog Expert had told him to do when Foolish ignored his command. He couldn't remember a damned word, so he improvised.

"I said, get down." He punctuated the remark by spritzing the dog with just a few drops of water.

It worked—sort of. Foolish shook his head and left the bathroom, but not before he captured the towel in his teeth and dragged it off to God knew where.

"Your life has gone to hell," he muttered as he allowed the water to massage the stiff muscles between his shoulder blades. He had pretty much resigned himself to the fact that Shelby was a part of his past. Until he had seen her again.

His hands reached up to lather the shampoo. "She has a baby," he muttered. "*And* she has a life."

Dylan continued to mentally berate himself as he showered. That sick, selfish part of his mind had always hoped that she was as miserable without him as he'd been since the night she'd told him it was over. He wanted to believe that Shelby had regretted ending their short-lived relationship and was secretly longing for him.

"It turns out that's about as likely as you learning to behave," he told the dog as he walked, naked and dripping, toward his dresser. "I don't suppose you'd like to cough up the towel?"

Foolish barked loudly, and his tail thumped against the floor.

"Thank you," Dylan said with a sneer. "The next time I run, you stay home."

The dog barked again.

"I'm threatening you," he told the dog as he began pulling clothing from the dresser and the closet. "I'm taking away your privileges. You're grounded."

The dog's tail beat more enthusiastically.

"You're supposed to look humble, and slink off into a corner and wait for me to forgive you."

Foolish sneezed.

"Thanks," Dylan said, patting the animal. "Obviously I have as much luck with animals as I do with women."

Foolish followed him into the kitchen and made a general nuisance of himself as Dylan tried to put together something that resembled a sandwich. He had to be quick, though. The dog believed in self-service, so nothing was safe. Not the cheese, not the bread, not even the condiments.

Dylan sat at the small round table that fit awkwardly into one corner. The dog was just a few inches away, poised and ready.

Reaching into a bowl in the center of the table, Dylan plucked up a few grapes. He ate one, then tossed the other in the air. Foolish snagged it as it arced.

"She looked incredible, even under the circumstances," he said as he alternated between eating and tossing grapes to the dog. "None of this makes any sense, pal."

He carried his half-eaten sandwich with him when he went to the refrigerator for a bottle of water.

"That's why it has to be Ned. He must have found out about the baby. It's the only possible explanation."

Foolish whined, apparently in protest against the interruption in his feeding. "But the medallion is what gets me," he continued, thinking aloud. He could feel deep lines of concentration gather between his brows. "Why would a medallion, that looks like the one I lost, suddenly turn up at the scene of a kidnapping? If it had to turn up, why there? Why at Shelby's?"

He pushed the plate away from him and leaned back in the seat. The thin wooden slats creaked in protest against his size. The clock above the stove told him he had less than an hour to pick up the cash and meet Shelby back at her place for the drop.

"If Ned took the baby, then Ned planted the medallion," he reasoned. Shaking his head, he said, "But Ned didn't have access to my medallion. Which means it can't be mine. If it wasn't mine, then Ned fits."

But nothing else does, he thought. *Not by a long shot.* As he pulled a pair of black jeans, Dylan was still trying to make some sense out of what he knew. Unfortunately, the image of Shelby kept interfering with his ability to think clearly and precisely. Even at the worst possible time in her life, she was the most beautiful woman he'd ever seen. She had the ability to tie his gut into a knot just by making eye contact. He'd never reacted to a woman the way he reacted to her, and he didn't like it.

His long-suppressed feelings for her were clouding his ability to use his brain effectively. He should be thinking about motives and opportunity, but he was still stuck on the issue of the baby. He knew it was wrong, but he felt something far too much like betrayal when he allowed himself to acknowledge that Shelby and Nichols had created a child together.

"You're being stupid," he cautioned himself as he pulled a black sweater over his shirt. "It wasn't like you were engaged to her," he told his frowning reflection.

"Things just got out of hand," he said, mimicking Shelby's voice as he repeated the words she'd said to him.

After brushing his still-damp hair, Dylan grabbed his keys and took the dog out for a quick walk. Then he headed out.

With the money safely tucked inside a nylon bag on the seat next to him, Dylan weaved his way through the city traffic, toward Shelby's place. His mind kept volleying between thoughts of her and his analysis of the crime. Part of him wanted it to end, and end quickly. They'd pay the ransom, pick up the kid and arrest Nichols, then they could part company for good.

Another part of him hated the thought of walking out of

her life for a second time. Even more, he hated the fact that in both instances Ned Nichols had been the catalyst. His grip tightened on the wheel as he fantasized about what he'd like to do to the slime when they finally tracked him down.

Jay was waiting for him when he turned onto the street. He would have preferred Shelby.

"We've located Nichols," Jay announced as soon as Dylan emerged from the car.

CHAPTER SEVEN

LATE AFTERNOON had brought with it a series of dark, moisture-ladened clouds that Shelby watched from the window as a sense of foreboding settled over the room. Her eyes were drawn to Dylan, who stood in the driveway, engrossed in animated conversation with Jay.

There was a time when she had dreamed of him walking back into her life. Her fantasy had never included any of this. "Why is this happening?" she whispered as her eyes closed to fight off the threat of tears.

There wasn't any answer, just as there was no explanation for so many things. Why Chad? Why now? And why had a medallion that looked like Dylan's turned up in the bushes?

Now that she was adjusting to the situation, her mind was beginning to function, despite the numbness. She had some private misgivings about Ned. But they had nothing to do with his supposed connection to arms deals. "And they certainly don't have anything to do with Chad."

Moving away from the window, Shelby picked up her brush and began the process of gathering her hair into a barrette at the back of her neck. Her hair was still damp from her hurried shower, and she wasn't in any frame of mind to do much with it.

Her thoughts kept analyzing what little she knew. Desperation slowly gave way to determination as she pulled on a pair of jeans. It couldn't be Ned. No way.

Dylan and the rest of them were convinced it was Ned acting on some surge of parental emotion. Shelby felt herself frown as she acknowledged the many flaws in that conclusion. First, Ned had no reason to think he was Chad's father. Second, in spite of Dylan's delusions in that area, Ned had never treated her with anything other than professional interest. Until she'd opened the purchase orders by mistake. Maybe she should have told Dylan everything. Now that wasn't even a possibility.

A succession of rapid knocks interrupted her thoughts. She was pushing the bottom edge of her sweater into the waistband of her jeans as she went to the door.

The sight of Dylan dressed head to toe in black was enough to still the breath in her throat. He loomed in the shadowy hallway, his broad shoulders diffusing the light from the first floor.

"There's been a new development."

Shelby reached out and grasped his forearm, her eyes meeting and holding his.

"Nichols has been located."

She didn't react. He wasn't sure what he had expected, but it hadn't been this bland poker face. *God,* he thought as he battled to keep a sneer off his face. Her feelings for Nichols were obviously strong enough that she was willing to accept the kidnapping of her son as just another of the guy's minor character flaws.

"Don't you want to know where he is?"

He saw her expression stiffen in response to the anger he seemed incapable of keeping out of his tone. Her eyes widened with astonishment, almost making him regret the derision in his voice.

"Where is he?" she asked after a long silence.

"Istanbul."

"Turkey?"

It wasn't really a question, so he didn't bother with an answer.

Actually, he was more distracted by watching her move than he was by the lack of emotion in her voice. He hated himself for noticing the flattering fit of her clothing, but that didn't stop him from looking. When she turned her back to him, Dylan allowed his gaze to slide slowly over every inch of her. He tried to tell himself that he was just doing his job. Just making sure she'd chosen an appropriate outfit to meet the caller.

It was crap, and he knew it. There was no such thing as a dress code for paying off a kidnapper. He lowered his eyes and swallowed some of his guilt.

"Ned goes to Turkey several times a year."

He looked up to find her taking things out of her handbag, and placing them in a black leather fanny pack on the bed.

"Does he usually go by way of Savannah?"

She turned and faced him then, her perfectly shaped brows drawn together in a question. "S-Savannah?" she stammered.

Dylan felt himself relax. He was most comfortable when he had control of the situation. It was an elusive concept whenever Shelby was around, so he savored the moment. "Apparently he took his boat down to the Atlantic, sailed to Savannah. Took a flight to Heathrow. Then on to Istanbul."

This new information had taken her by surprise. He could tell by her body language.

"What about the package he was supposed to have had when he was seen leaving his house?"

Dylan cleared his throat and shifted his glance to a collection of brightly colored glass bottles on top of her dressing table.

"He didn't have it when he went through customs in London."

"So he can't possibly have Chad," she said with conviction.

"He didn't when he went through customs," Dylan admitted. "But that doesn't—"

"And if he's been on boats and planes and heaven only knows what else since before midnight yesterday, then he can't be the one sending the tapes and making the calls."

"Shelby," he said as he moved next to her. Cautiously he placed his hands firmly on her shoulders and forced her to make direct eye contact. "We've assumed all along that there's more than one individual involved. Everything about this case indicates that there is more than one individual pulling the strings."

"How do *we* know that? And why are you so sure one of them is Ned?"

His hands gave a gentle squeeze and he said, "Well, Ned is your only enemy—plus, there's too many jobs for just one perp."

"Jobs?"

Dylan withdrew his hands and used the fingers of his left hand to count off each point. "Access was gained through the nursery window. We found impressions of a ladder in the soil beneath the window."

"How does that tell you there were two kidnappers?"

"The indentations were of approximately equal depths."

"Meaning?"

"Meaning that, in all likelihood, someone was holding the ladder on the ground."

He watched the faint flicker of pain flash in her blue eyes, and began to question the advisability of getting into all this with her.

"What else?"

"It isn't really important, Shelby."

"It is to me," she told him quietly, her eyes pleading for his cooperation.

"The videotapes require at least two people—the camera operator and the mysterious woman with the ring."

"Couldn't they be taken using a tripod?" Shelby asked.

Dylan shook his head and said, "The lab guys say no. They say the movement of the lens position is inconsistent with the use of a stable base."

She smiled at him. He found it contagious.

"They like it when you quote them exactly," he admitted with a sheepish grin.

"You're very good at it. You sounded just like some boring report."

"Boring, huh?" he teased, feigning great indignation.

Her smile grew wider, and he noted just the palest tinge of color appear on the flawlessly opaque skin near her high cheekbones. Her lashes fluttered just before she lowered her eyes.

"I didn't mean it like that."

"I know it," Dylan responded.

"What else?" she asked as she returned her attention to packing items into the largest of the compartments of the fanny pack.

"There's the problem of the tapes and the calls."

"Problem?"

"It's not exactly the standard in cases like this."

"There's a standard?" she asked.

He felt a tug in his chest at the almost pitiful sentiment behind the statement. "It's like overkill, Shelby. Neither I or Jay have ever heard of a case where so much contact was initiated by the perp. You can expect calls. You can expect tapes. But never both."

Her expression clouded over with uneasiness. "And you think this is a bad sign?"

"No," he said on a rush of air. "I'm not saying anything of the kind." He placed his hand on her arm, silently wishing there was some way he could comfort away the shimmer of tears he saw pooling in her eyes.

"Personally, I think it's a good sign that these people are so hell-bent on proving to you that Chad is doing okay."

She held on to his words as if they were some sort of lifeline. It was far superior to allowing her own thoughts to wander.

"But why have you and Jay decided that no matter what the evidence, Ned has to be one of the individuals involved?"

She could see his expression darken in her peripheral vision. At least he's consistent, she thought as she buckled the leather pouch around her waist.

"Motive, Shelby. That, and the fact that we haven't been able to come up with a single lead in any other direction. It would appear that you've managed to live your life without making any enemies."

Except you, she thought dismally. "I've been telling you that from the beginning."

"What about when you and Ned were working together?"

"What do you mean?" she said as she brushed past him.

"Did you ever have it out with a customer? Pad the markup?"

She stopped just short of the door, her back stiff. "Of course not, Dylan. We sold imported items, and the occasional antiquity. They were all big-ticket items, and our customers were educated and informed. We sold many items to museums and universities."

"Thanks for the résumé," he muttered.

Shelby ignored the sarcasm in his tone. She'd accomplished her mission. Dylan's anger was preventing him pressing the issue any further.

"We have everything in place," Jay announced as soon as they reached the landing. "I've verified that everyone's in position, and we've decided to kill the radios, just in case our man is listening in."

"Are you sure he won't know you're there?" Shelby asked for the hundredth time. "I couldn't live with myself if anything happened to my baby because I didn't follow his instructions to a T."

"Don't worry," Jay said, placing a fatherly arm across her shoulders. "We've done this more times than I'd like to remember. There's no way this fruit will know we're within ten miles of the packing plant. He'll show for the goods. We'll nab him, and he can spend the rest of his useless life in some stinking prison cell."

Shelby looked up, and nearly flinched at the hostility she

read in the man's eyes. "Didn't you forget something?" she asked cautiously.

"What?" Jay snapped.

"Getting him to tell us where he's hiding Chad?"

Jay's dark eyes narrowed, and the small smile of reassurance he offered failed to reach his eyes. "Of course we'll find the baby, Shelby."

"Are you sure he won't be able to see *him* in the car?"

Dylan made some sort of unflattering noise. She guessed he didn't like being referred to as "him."

"He'll be in the back seat. Tanner knows the drill. He won't compromise the situation."

I'm still worried about him, she thought. Just being around Dylan was unnerving. Shelby wasn't at all sure she could function with him literally at her feet.

"The money is in the gym bag," Jay said. "All you have to do is park and wait."

Nodding, Shelby pulled out her car keys and placed her slightly trembling hand on the cool doorknob.

"Relax, Shelby."

She turned to take one final look at Jay. His face was impassive, only his dark eyes hinting at something more. Her throat constricted. There was something about Jay's demeanor that wasn't right.

The smile he offered was weak, and did nothing to alleviate her budding misgivings.

"We'll be right there with you," Jay assured her. "No matter what."

"Will you explain Jay to me?" she asked after backing her car out of the drive.

"Jay's beyond explanation" came Dylan's muffled reply.

"Is it me, or did he seem less than enthusiastic about all this?"

Dylan didn't respond immediately, which only added to her growing insecurities.

"That's just his way. He's reserved."

His voice had an oddly immediate soothing effect on her

nerves as she steered out of the city, toward the appointed drop site. A thick layer of clouds obscured the sunset, bringing on a premature darkness.

Bohicket Road, a winding strip of macadam in dire need of repairs, was all but deserted. Each pothole was tallied by Dylan's grunt of discomfort. She could only imagine how cramped he must be, his large body folded into the small space between the front seat and the back seat.

"Are you sure you wouldn't be more comfortable up here?" she asked. "At least until we're closer to Tennisons?"

"Too dangerous."

"How so?"

"This guy may be watching. It's better to play it safe."

Shelby immediately checked the rearview mirror. Not a car in sight. She told Dylan.

"He could be watching from the roadside. Or come from the opposite direction. I don't think you want to risk annoying this guy."

"Definitely not," she agreed. "I just want my son back."

Dylan fell silent. Her only indication that he was in the car was the gentle rustling of the blanket whenever he shifted his position.

"Why'd you do it?" he asked, in a deep, soft voice.

"Do what?"

"Decide to have the kid."

Her hands tightened on the wheel, her knuckles turning white. "It wasn't a decision."

"An accident?"

There was an edge to the question that only added to her apprehensions. "I prefer to think of Chad as a surprise. *Accident* carries the connotation that he wasn't wanted. He was."

"So why not do it the traditional way?"

"It didn't happen that way," she returned shortly. "I'd appreciate it if you'd drop it."

"Sorry."

But she could tell he wasn't. Was he beginning to put it together?

"I hope not."

"You hope not what?" he asked.

Realizing she had spoken her fears aloud, Shelby cleared her throat anxiously and said, "I hope I haven't made a mistake by involving all of you in this. I meant what I said, Dylan. I won't be able to live with myself if anything happens to Chad."

"I won't let anything happen to him. I promise."

God! she thought as she flipped the turn signal and prepared to turn into the lot. He sounded so sincere, so concerned. *How will he feel if he learns the truth?*

She banished such thoughts as she eased the car across the uneven gravel lot. The air was thick with the scent of damp cardboard and rotting produce. It was fully dark now, her headlights the only source of illumination.

A chill danced along her spine. "We're here."

"See anything?" he asked in a whisper.

"Everything's dark. I can barely make out the buildings."

"Turn your lights out," he instructed. "Let your eyes adjust to the dark."

Following his directives, Shelby blinked against the darkness until the formless shadows began to take shape. A loading dock, three Dumpsters, and several towers of packing crates lining the parking area.

Her eyes darted in all directions, trying to find some evidence that her tormentor was there.

"Roll down the window, see if you can hear anything."

"Like what?" she whispered.

"A baby crying."

Depressing the button, she lowered the window, then cut the engine. She listened intently for some sound to emerge over the chorus of insects. She held her breath. Nothing.

"I don't hear anything," she whispered.

Dylan's hand snaked between the door and the seat to rest on the side of her hip. The contact was equal measures comforting and disturbing. She swallowed some of her dread.

"What should I do?"

"Wait."

She could hardly hear him above the sounds of the crickets.

There was a rustling sound to the left of the car. Shelby whipped her head around and held her breath.

Her eyes fixed on something—movement in the thick brush at the edge of the parking area.

Her heart drummed in her ears, and she didn't blink. She didn't dare. It felt as if years passed before the bushes swayed a second time.

"There's someone out there," she whispered.

"Stay in the car," Dylan warned. "Let him come to you."

She heard a snapping sound from the rear seat, followed by several metal clicks.

"What are you doing?"

"Gun."

The single syllable hung in the air between them. Several more minutes passed with nothing happening. She was about to explode.

The sound was so faint that she almost missed it. And it came from the opposite side of the building.

"I think I see something," she whispered, her eyes fixed on the far corner of the loading dock.

"Sit tight."

Leaning forward, she stared hard at the shadows. *Is that him?* she wondered silently, trying to determine whether she had actually seen a form in the darkness.

The shadow moved. She was certain of it.

"He's leaving," she cried softly as she tracked the shadow toward the edge of the building.

"Stay put!" Dylan said between gritted teeth.

He's leaving! her mind screamed. Ignoring Dylan and all

their well-intentioned plans, Shelby grabbed the satchel of money and yanked open the door.

"Wait!" Dylan yelled from his hiding place.

The money was heavier than she had anticipated, and she nearly stumbled getting out of the car. Without thinking, she ran blindly in the direction of the retreating form.

"Hey!" she yelled as she rounded the front of the car.

The form kept moving.

"I have the money!" she announced as she picked up speed.

The person appeared to look back, then broke into a dead run toward the back of the building. Without giving thought to her action, driven only by her fierce need to be reunited with her child, Shelby followed.

She was only vaguely aware of the sound of footsteps behind her. She watched as the person ahead of her reached the edge of the woods.

"Please!" she called in a raspy, winded voice. "I've got the money!"

She reached the spot where he had disappeared. After just a brief hesitation, Shelby ducked her head and leapt forward. Her front foot settled in the mossy ground just as she felt an explosion of pain in her forehead. There was a flash of bright light, a ringing in her ears, and then nothing.

CHAPTER EIGHT

"SHELBY?"

She heard his voice above the whooshing of helicopter blades. Opening her eyes, she immediately squinted against a beam of bright light. Her hand came up to shield her eyes. That's when she felt it.

"What?"

"It's a cloth," Dylan answered.

He was so close that she could feel his breath wash over her face.

Slowly she became aware of her surroundings. Her head was resting against something warm and solid. It was a sharp contrast to the damp ground she could feel beneath the rest of her. Her hand moved to the right, and she felt the unmistakable soft ruggedness of denim. She tried to open her eyes again. Dylan's face was the only image she saw.

"Sorry about the light," he offered with a weak smile.

"My head?" she managed.

"Tree branch," he explained, as the wail of a siren echoed in the distance. "I don't think you need stitches, but you've got one hell of a gash."

"Chad?" she asked, leaning to grab a handful of his shirt in order to pull her sluggish body upright.

"Sorry, honey," he said quietly. "No sign of him."

"But we brought the money..." Her voice trailed off, her eyes closed, and she slumped back against him.

His arms wrapped around her, holding her against him as an ambulance skidded onto the lot, spewing gravel.

Two attendants emerged and moved to where Dylan and Shelby sat at the edge of the woods, their bodies illuminated in the glow of the headlights. It was only then that Shelby realized just how many people were gathered around them.

"Who?"

"Other agents," Dylan said, as he relinquished his position to one of the corpsmen. "She was out for about ten minutes."

A young man crouched next to her, shining a small penlight in her eye. It hurt, and she winced in response.

"Sorry," he mumbled. Then, turning to look up at Dylan, he asked, "Any other injuries?"

"She snapped her neck pretty good."

"We'll strap her."

"Strap her?" Shelby yelped. "Strap her to what?"

"Backboard," he explained as the item suddenly appeared by his side, thanks to the other attendant.

"I don't think that's ne—"

"Precaution," he said, interrupting her.

Shelby suffered the indignity of having herself rolled on to the hard board. She was then held in position with a series of leather-and-Velcro straps before being hoisted onto a waiting stretcher. It seemed like overkill, but she had neither the strength nor the inclination to argue. Her mind screamed for answers. *Why hadn't he stayed to collect the ransom? And where was her baby?*

HE FOLLOWED the ambulance in her car. He'd used the time to run it all back in his mind. Dylan had a feeling in his gut. A really bad one. Something wasn't right. It was like he was missing an important fact or bit of information, and he couldn't for the life of him figure out what it was.

He slammed his clenched fist against the steering wheel once before leaving her car in the hourly lot. Luckily, they had taken Shelby to one of the smaller hospitals, so he'd be spared that gory task of sitting among the battered and bloody while she was being examined.

He sucked in a deep breath before passing through the double sliding glass doors. Immediately he was assailed by the scent of disinfectant, poorly masked by some fruity deodorizer. He hated hospitals.

Scanning the area, he found the two ambulance attendants leaning against a tall counter. They were laughing with a little redhead who looked more like a cheerleading captain than a nurse. The observation made him feel old.

"Agent Tanner," the taller of the two corpsmen said.

"Thanks for responding so quickly." Dylan looked to the nameplate pinned above the man's shirt pocket, "Burns."

"No probs," he said with a shrug. "I think she'll be fine once they get her vitals stable."

He felt as if he'd been kicked in the stomach. "Her vitals?"

"Pulse was way up there. So was her pressure."

Dylan mumbled some additional words of thanks and asked the nurse to let him know when the medical team was finished with their evaluation.

He followed the signs to a bank of pay phones. While he waited for the phone to be answered, he rearranged the collection of half-full coffee cups and wondered why the hospital failed to provide a trash can for the waiting area.

"Hello."

"Jay? Dylan."

"How is she?"

"She's still in the ER. I think there's a problem with her blood pressure."

He heard the other man let out a breath before saying, "Understandable, under the circumstances. What about the injury to her head?"

"She took a pretty good hit, but I don't think it did any permanent damage."

"But the guy did show?"

Dylan shifted his weight as he processed the surprise in his boss's voice. "Why wouldn't he have?"

"Right." Jay's laugh seemed forced, almost nervous.

"Hang in there for her, make sure she has everything she needs."

"I think the only thing she needs is her son."

He placed the receiver on its cradle and looked down the hall, hoping to catch a glance of Shelby. The corridor was deserted, as was the small waiting area, which was enclosed by a row of dusty plastic palms in large plastic pots.

Selecting a seat on the end of a tattered vinyl sofa, Dylan tried to get his mind off her by staring at the static image on the muted television. He lasted about five minutes, before leaning his head back and closing his eyes.

He remembered vividly what it had felt like to watch her crumple and fall to the ground in the cool, dark woods. If only he'd gotten to her sooner. If only she'd stayed in the car. What, he wondered, had happened to that cautious side of her that had been the beginning of their undoing...?

"DEFINE SLOWLY," he asked, leaning his palms against the smooth surface of the kitchen counter. He felt as if all the breath had been knocked from his body, and he struggled not to let it show.

"Everything's happening so fast, Dylan," she told him, in careful, measured syllables.

"We're not kids, Shelby," he countered, hoping he didn't sound like some sort of groveling high school kid about to be dumped by his girl.

"I know." She smiled then. The action was almost enough to make him forget that he was being brushed off.

"I'm not saying I don't want to see you," she continued. "I just want us to get to know each other a little better before we...again."

He liked the fact that her cheeks burned red when she tried to give a name to the intense passion that sizzled between them. "I'm not sorry it happened," he told her.

"I didn't say that I was," she assured him, lowering her eyes.

"Then why are you putting the brakes on?"

She spun gracefully and moved over to the window. She was wearing a skirt that billowed out from her small waist. It might have looked dowdy on another woman, but not Shelby. She had the poise and posture of a dancer. She looked good in everything, but he liked her best in nothing.

"Last night shouldn't have happened."

She wasn't looking at him. Not a good sign.

"Why not?"

"There's too many unresolved issues between us."

"Such as?"

"Ned."

His mood took an immediate trip south. "I'm not asking you to do anything but help us get a dangerous man off the streets."

When she met his eyes, the pain he read in her expression did even more damage to his deteriorating mood.

"I've already told you," *she complained.* "I don't know about any of the shipments y'all are interested in. I've never seen any guns, or anything remotely lethal."

"But you can get us the information, Shelby. We need someone on the inside."

"Do you know what you're asking me to do?" *she wailed, her small fists balled at her sides.* "You're asking me to help you build a case against a man who has never been anything other than kind and nurturing to me."

"Really?" *he asked as he shifted his feet to shoulder width apart.* "Exactly how nurturing is Nichols?"

"For heaven's sake," *she groaned as she snatched her jacket and purse off the sofa.* "You sound more like a jealous lover than an investigator."

"Maybe that's because I am," *he muttered, just as she slammed out the cabin door.*

"AGENT TANNER?"

He opened his eyes to find a portly man in a signature white coat staring down at him over the edge of a metal clipboard.

"I'm Tanner."

"Dr. Harrison," he said as he thrust one hand forward.

Rising, Dylan accepted the hand, and was surprised by the firm handshake. Doctors usually treated their hands like their most prized possessions. Especially trauma surgeons, which was the description embroidered beneath the doctor's name on his coat.

"She's resting comfortably now. I'm going to keep her here overnight."

"Is there a problem?"

"All her films were negative, but I'm concerned about her overall health. Her vital signs aren't at all normal for a woman her age. She's extremely upset."

"That's understandable, don't you think?"

The doctor's response was a confused frown.

"She didn't tell you?"

"No."

Dylan spent the next several minutes explaining the crisis that was the underlying cause of Shelby's emotional state. The doctor nodded quietly as he listened, his face impassive. It was obvious that this man was no stranger to horrific events. Dylan envied the man his detachment. It would be so much simpler if he'd never known Shelby. If somehow he could get through all this without tripping over the past.

"I want to alter my orders for her," Harrison said as he scribbled something on the chart. "I think it's advisable that she get some rest."

"What about her head injury?" Dylan queried.

"Minor," the doctor answered. "I'm much more concerned about her emotional state. And now that I fully understand the situation, I can act accordingly."

"Thank you." It was Dylan's turn to offer his hand. "I'll call my superior about arranging for additional security."

Harrison nodded with a resigned sadness. "We have an excellent security staff here, Agent Tanner. I'll instruct the nursing staff to assist you in coordinating your efforts with them."

"They're keeping her overnight," he told Jay a few minutes later. "I'll stay with—"

"You're going home."

"C'mon, Jay."

"Home," came the terse command. "I'll send a unit over now. I want you to leave the moment they arrive."

"But—"

"But nothing," Jay interjected. "Look, Dylan. I know you have an interest in this woman that goes beyond your usual conscientious attention to detail. It's not a problem now, but it could be."

Anger churned in Dylan's stomach. "Meaning?"

"Meaning you need to distance yourself. At least for a while. Take the rest of the night off. Get some sleep. I'll tell the unit you'll be back to relieve them around ten tomorrow morning. Until then, I don't want you anywhere near that hospital. Understood?"

"Yes," he hissed. "Later," he added, just before slamming the phone down.

His reluctance to leave her only increased when he slipped into her darkened hospital room. Soundlessly he moved to the edge of the bed, careful not to disturb her. She looked so frail just lying there, her black hair fanned out against the starched white pillow.

Careful to avoid the wires from the blood-pressure device cuffed around her upper arm, Dylan brushed her bangs away from the small bandage taped to her forehead. Her lashes fluttered, and he actually stopped breathing. Her eyes didn't open.

The silence was disrupted by the automatic inflation of the nylon sleeve. After several seconds, the cuff deflated and a green readout flashed on the monitor above the bed. The numbers were high. Still Shelby didn't move.

Just as he was about to leave the room, Dylan acted on impulse. With utmost care, he leaned forward and brushed a kiss against her lips.

He meant for it to be brief, comforting. It wasn't. He left

the room with his fingers pressed to his mouth, her scent still lingering in his mind.

"YOU BLEW IT."

She was dreaming. It had to be a dream. No one actually spoke in that raspy, hoarse whisper.

"You shouldn't have called the cops."

It was a dream, but she could feel the hot breath against her ear. She tried to turn away, but her body wouldn't cooperate. Next she tried to open her eyes, but they were slow in responding. She managed to force her lids open a fraction of an inch. She smelled something. What was it?

"You were supposed to do exactly as I said, Shelby."

"What?" she said through the thickness of her own tongue. She managed to open her eyes a bit farther. The dream was wearing white.

"You'll regret crossing me, Shelby."

CHAPTER NINE

DYLAN TOOK THE STEPS two at a time, a sudden and unexplainable rush of adrenaline fueling his progress. It took a few seconds to work through the series of locks securing his door.

Foolish greeted him by skidding into his legs, nearly knocking him to the floor.

"Hi there," he said as he patted the dog's head. Scooping up the mail, Dylan moved toward the kitchen, battling Foolish all the way.

Flipping on the light, he began to sift through the stack of envelopes, but then his attention was drawn to the table. Or, more accurately, a suspicious-looking paper bag leaning against the bowl of wilting fruit on it.

"What—?" he said as he bent closer to examine the object.

The top of the bag had been twisted, but not secured. He could see inside the bag.

Grabbing a pen from the counter, Dylan tossed aside his mail and used the flat end of the pen to ease open the folds of brown paper.

"Holy hell," he muttered as the contents became clear. Dylan dropped the pen and grabbed the phone.

Jay answered on the first ring.

"I've got another videotape," he said, without preamble.

"You?" Jay asked.

"It was sitting on my kitchen table when I got home."

"How?"

"No kidding, how," Dylan barked. "How in the hell

would this guy know to leave a tape here? I haven't exactly been high-profile in this investigation."

"Nichols," Jay responded, without hesitation.

Dylan lowered himself into a chair, his mind working furiously. "This is getting more weird by the minute."

Foolish moved and placed his muzzle against Dylan's thigh. His tail thumped loudly against the tiled floor.

After trading theories with his boss for several minutes, Dylan hung up. He wanted to look around before the forensics guys showed.

The front door showed no signs of tampering. Anger simmered just below the surface as the realization kicked in that his home had been violated by some dirtball.

"Obviously you were a big deterrent," he said to the dog, not bothering to mask his disgust. The dog's ears lifted, and his tail wagged furiously. "I'm criticizing you," he pointed out as he weaved his way through the living room. Foolish followed, apparently undaunted by his master's harsh tone.

The sliding glass door was closed. The lock had been drilled out, a domino-size hole left in the metal framing. Dylan turned to face the dog, hands on his hips, feet braced threateningly apart.

"I don't suppose you barked, or anything?"

Foolish whimpered.

"Dogs are supposed to protect property. Someone comes in here, your job is to bite them, deter crime."

Foolish barked.

The sound was followed by a rapid, insistent knocking on his front door. Automatically Dylan glanced at the clock above the fireplace. Twelve-fifteen. Before he answered the door, he stopped in the hallway and retrieved the small-caliber gun from his ankle strap.

"Yes?"

"Mr. Tanner!" came a painfully familiar, shrilly grating female voice.

He groaned, replaced the gun, and tugged open the door.

Miss Dog Expert was angry. He could tell even before she opened her lipless mouth.

"Your dog is a problem."

He leaned against the wall, watching the spongy pink curlers in her hair bob and wiggle as she spoke.

"I'm sorry if Foolish disturbed you."

"Disturbed me?" Her hands moved to the vicinity of her hips. Dylan wasn't actually sure she had hips. The Expert was given to wearing layer upon layer of clothing, none of it related by color, texture or pattern. He supposed her fashion sense was meant to be eclectic. It was just god-awful, if you asked him.

"That dog barked for a solid hour after you finished fixing your door. I would have thought—"

"When did you hear this, Miss James?"

"Johns."

"Excuse me?"

"My name is Johns, not James," she told him tartly. Her bland brown eyes narrowed significantly. "And it was around eleven-thirty."

"Are you sure?"

Red blotches appeared on her thin neck. "Of course I'm sure, Mr. Tanner. I was trying to watch television, but I couldn't—thanks to you."

"What made you think I was fixing the door?" he asked.

She looked heavenward and let out a loud, annoyed breath. "I saw you."

"You did?"

"I looked over my balcony railing and saw you fiddling with the lock."

"How did you know it was me?"

"Well..." she breathed, perplexed. "Who else would have been on your patio at that time of night?"

"Someone breaking in?" he suggested sarcastically.

Her eyes grew wide, and she began shaking her overly large head. "Not in this neighborhood, Mr. Tanner. We don't have a crime problem here."

"Right."

"But we *do* have a problem with your dog."

Dylan fought the urge to slam the door in her face.

"If you don't curb his barking at this stage, it will be impossible to train him properly. Now, take a spray bottle and fill it with one part white vinegar to two parts water..."

She droned on for a full five minutes. All he could think of was Foolish, dripping with vinegar, smelling like some sort of decomposing Easter egg. He thanked the Expert and mumbled something about taking her suggestions under advisement. The woman—if she actually was a woman—annoyed him beyond belief.

"Eleven-thirty, huh?" he said to the dog as he moved back to the place where the intruder had gained entry. Foolish attempted to help Dylan examine the hole. His efforts earned him a gentle shove.

"This was a professional job, pal," he said as he ran a pen around the smooth metal edge where the lock had once been. "And it wasn't me," he muttered, adding a few colorful curses for his less-than-observant neighbor.

The forensics team spent more than an hour examining the scene. As expected, there was no trace evidence left behind. That annoying sense that he was missing something nagged at Dylan as sat at the table, passing the videotape from one hand to the other. "Something isn't right."

"No kidding," Jay said as he joined him at the table.

Looking up, Dylan noted that his boss was looking rather ragged. In fact, it was the first time in a long time that he had seen a case get to Jay like this one. Must be the kid, he concluded as he accepted the mug of instant coffee Jay handed him.

"We gonna watch the tape?" Dylan queried.

"I watched it in your living room while you were being printed. It's basically the same."

"So the kid's still alive?" Dylan said, feeling an incredible relief. He was beginning to see Chad strictly as Shelby's son, not Ned's. He couldn't stand the thought of something happening to the little guy. He could pretty much guess what would happen to Shelby if the outcome was bad.

"Why drop one here?"

Jay toyed with a chip in the rim of his cup and shrugged his shoulders. "Maybe Nichols is taunting you."

"If he's in Turkey, how would he know I was working this case?"

"He's managed to orchestrate things flawlessly so far. I mean, he's made sure Shelby receives news of the kid at amazingly regular intervals."

"Then why the low ransom demand?" Dylan dumped some sugar in the coffee and stirred it quickly with one finger.

Jay's expression darkened. His brows drew together in a continuous line. "I can't say. The calls are...unusual."

"Someone was here," Shelby insisted as soon as Rose had closed the door.

"Of course, lots of people were," Rose stated, patting the perfect curls emanating from her large, teased mass of white blond hair. "Nurses, doctors, orderlies."

"No, someone in white."

Rose slapped her forehead with her palm and clicked her tongue. "That's suspicious. A person dressed in white, roaming around the hospital, must have caused quite a stir."

"I'm telling you—" Shelby let her arms flop down on the hard mattress "—I think it was the kidnapper."

"Shelby, honey," Rose said, comfortingly as she sat on the edge of the bed, "why would the kidnapper come here? They said they gave you something to calm your nerves. You probably just imagined it."

Shaking her head, Shelby persisted. "I know it was him. He was really mad at me for bringing the cops. I think he might hurt Chad because of it."

"If he was going to hurt the baby, he'd have done it by now," Rose stated firmly.

Shelby wondered whether her friend actually believed that. She hoped so.

"I don't know what I'll do if I—"

The phone rang. Shelby reached over and picked up the receiver. "Hello."

"Hi, it's Dylan."

"Hi," she returned hesitantly.

"I'm going to come by and pick you up around—"

Shelby cut in. "Rose is here with me. She's going to give me a lift home."

"Did you get any rest?"

She considered telling him about her visitor, but decided not to. "I slept."

"You okay?" When she didn't respond immediately, he said, "I mean, I know you're not okay. I just wondered how you were doing, what with the botched..." His voice trailed off.

"Has there been any news?" she asked, then held her breath as uncertainty gripped her throat.

"As a matter of fact, there has."

"What?" she demanded, sitting straight up and grabbing Rose's arm as she waited.

"We got another tape."

"Another tape? Is my son all right?"

"He was sleeping."

"Where?"

"It looks like a hotel room."

"Any idea when it was taken?"

"Apparently it was long after the fiasco at the packing plant."

"How could you tell?"

"There was a television on in the background. 'Early News at Ten.'"

"From last night?"

"We've verified it with the station."

"That means he's still alive."

"Of course he is."

Shelby's spirits were much higher after Dylan's call. She had definite cause to be optimistic, and she latched on to that thought in order to retain her sanity.

"Is your smile only about Chad?" Rose asked as Shelby pulled on her dirty clothing from the night before in the minute bathroom.

"What do you mean?"

"C'mon, girl. I know that look. I've had it a time or two myself."

"What look?"

"You and Tanner," Rose explained, in a slow, deliberate tone. "In spite of everything that's happening, the two of you are something to watch."

"I don't know what you're talking about." But she did. Merely being in the same room with him had an odd effect on her. She would never forget her first encounter with the tall, mysterious man....

The buzzer forced her from the relative security of her office to the darkened shop. Annoyance quickened her step and straightened her spine.

Pulling aside the small curtain covering the window, she spoke through the painted name of the Charleston Import Company.

"We're closed!" she yelled as she tilted her head to see the face of the late-evening caller.

His eyes were incredible, brilliant, almost too pretty to belong to a man. But they did, and what a man he was. Dressed in a tailored suit the same ebony color as his hair, he had an air of authority that was apparent long before he pressed his identification against the glass.

"I'm Agent Tanner. Alcohol, Tobacco and Firearms."

Shelby unlocked the door and gazed up at the man. "Yes?"

He looked from side to side in a very clandestine fashion before saying, "May I come in, Miss Hunnicutt?"

She eased the door opened and allowed him to enter. A

scent, masculine and compelling, clung to him as he brushed past her.

"What can I do for you, Agent Tanner?"

"I'm here in reference to a telephone call you made to the customs office."

She smiled nervously.

"That was just a misunderstanding," she explained. Did that high-pitched voice belong to her? she wondered as a blush warmed her cheeks.

"You didn't call customs?"

"I did, but—" Shelby began hesitantly. "My partner returned the crates to the carrier. They were delivered here by mistake."

"Did you open the crates?"

His tone was her first indication that this was something more than just a bureaucratic field trip.

"I started to open one, which is why I called."

He fished in his suit coat and produced a small notebook and then a pen. She noted that he was left-handed, and wondered why she would notice such an inconsequential detail.

"Can you describe the contents?"

"It looked like gun barrels," she answered, feeling the first stirrings of a problem seep into her mind. "Look," she said as she rubbed her hands together. "I told all this to the customs guy who showed up here to take the crates."

"Can you describe this individual?"

Shelby blinked once, and her eyes grew wider as she gaped at the man. "He looked like a government official."

Her answer earned her a smile from the big man. It was the most attractive, appealing and sexy smile she'd ever seen, and her heart responded by skipping a beat.

"Like me?" he teased, his head tilted to one side.

"Not exactly like you," she admitted, after clearing the lump from her throat.

"Then humor me, Miss Hunnicutt. Describe him."

Shelby lifted her arm with the intention of brushing her

hair back off her face. The small act of vanity cost her dearly. Her elbow tapped the edge of a small cloisonné plate, which went crashing to the floor.

Numbly she looked down at the hundreds of shards. Bits of porcelain were glistening in the light filtering down the hallway from her office.

"I'd better get a broom," she mumbled.

"Let me," he said, one large hand coming out and gripping her shoulder.

Small sparks emanated from his touch, singing her skin wherever his squared fingers made contact.

"Don't be silly," she countered with weak smile. She was so embarrassed she wanted to crawl away on her stomach, slither off into obscurity.

"You'll hurt yourself," he insisted.

"Sweeping?"

"No," he said as he tucked his notebook away and placed the pen between his perfectly straight, brilliantly white teeth.

Shelby made a small noise when he scooped her up in his arms and carried her in the direction of the light.

"What do you think you're doing?" she gasped. She was afraid to move, afraid of experiencing any more of his solid body.

"Protecting your feet," he said between clenched teeth.

"My feet?"

"No shoes," he said, as if she were dense. "I'd feel terrible if my visit resulted in an injury. I'm supposed to be one of the good guys."

He placed her gently on top of her desk, but he didn't slide his hands away. His face remained just inches from hers, so close that she could feel his breath. She watched as his eyes roamed over her face, lingering on her slightly parted lips. It was so innocent, and yet so blatant that Shelby gulped in air. Her body grew warm, and she wriggled against him.

He smiled as his hands fell away. His expression was so

pleasant, so relaxed, that Shelby wondered if she hadn't imagined those few seconds of interest.

Ignoring her protests, Dylan took a broom and dustpan and cleaned the shards off the floor. She spent the time lecturing herself on decorum.

The first nice-looking man I see in a while, and I go to pieces, *she chided herself as she fanned her face.*

By the time he came back from depositing the remains in the Dumpster, Shelby had managed to compose herself sufficiently. It helped that she had slipped behind her desk, donning her professional persona.

"So," Dylan said as he unbuttoned his jacket and took the seat across from her. "You were going to tell me about the guy who took the shipment."

She again spoke to his tie. "He was young, early twenties or so. His name was Conners or Collins, I think."

One dark brow arched questioningly. "You asked his name?"

Shelby shook her head. "No. He had identification."

"Like this?" he asked, pulling out his badge and passing it across her desk.

As she brought the black leather case toward her, Shelby was struck by two things. First, the wallet had the same pleasant scent as its owner. Second, it carried his body warmth. She swallowed, trying not to think about how hard and warm his body had been when he held her against him.

"Is it?"

"Is it what?" she said, her voice choked.

"Like his?"

She finally got around to looking at the badge and the accompanying identification card. His picture was amazingly flattering for one of those official photographs. It gave his height, weight and date of birth. She read them slowly.

"Well?"

"No," she admitted, after really studying the emblem on the badge and the layout of the card. "It wasn't anything like this."

She looked up to find him nodding, as if he'd expected her answer.

"Is that because he was with customs?" she asked as she handed back the wallet.

His fingertips brushed hers, sending a small jolt through her system.

"Nope." He leaned forward and met her eyes. "It was because he wasn't with customs. They have no record of any of their men coming out to pick up the guns."

CHAPTER TEN

SHAKING OFF THE MEMORIES, Shelby pulled on her jeans. "What on earth?" she mumbled as she fingered the crisp white envelope tucked in the front pocket.

Carefully she extracted it. Her eyes were wide as she read the neat block print.

CHAD'S MOM.

Slipping her nail beneath the flap, she broke the seal and peered inside. She braced herself, fearing the unknown.

A small square of paper was folded into the corner. She pulled it out and read.

BE IN YOUR CAR AT 2:00. NO COPS THIS TIME.

"You okay?" Rose hollered through the door.

"Um…" Shelby quickly folded the envelope and the cryptic note and stuffed them in her pocket. "Fine!" she called back. Panic caused her hands to tremble as she ran her fingers through her mussed hair. He *was* here, she thought as she stared at her reflection in the small mirror above the sink. The note also explained the video delivered to Dylan. The kidnapper had provided proof that her son was still fine. She knew at that very instant that she would follow his instructions to the letter. She wasn't going to risk her son's well-being—not again.

It was just before noon when she and Rose emerged from

the hospital. The day was gray and dreary, much like her mood. When, she wondered, would this nightmare end?

"I don't mean to harp," Rose said as she slid behind the wheel of her battered car, "but how long do you think it will be before Tanner puts it all together?"

Shelby flicked at the Elvis Presley air freshener dangling from the rearview mirror. "I don't know what you mean."

"Look," Rose said as she angled herself in the seat. "Chad is the spitting image of that man. Obviously you didn't tell him you were pregnant. I'm just wondering how long you think you can keep this charade going."

She leaned back in the seat and closed her eyes. Rose was right. "Once Chad is safely home, there will be no reason for Dylan to stick around."

"Right," Rose muttered as she turned the key in the ignition. "Except he doesn't impress me as the type to just walk away. Not the way he looks at you."

"That was the problem," Shelby admitted in a tired voice.

"I don't know. Man looked at me that way, I'd be tickled pink."

Shelby felt the corners of her mouth twitch. "Dylan and I had chemistry."

"I think you still do," Rose offered.

"Not possible now," Shelby said, surprised by the amount of regret she heard in her own words.

"Why is that?"

She thought for a few minutes before answering. "Dylan and I never really had a relationship."

"But you had a son?" Rose asked. The question wasn't the least bit judgmental, and Shelby was grateful for that.

"Believe it or not, it was only one night."

"That's all it takes."

"Yes," Shelby agreed. "I know."

"There had to be more to it than one night."

"I wanted there to be," Shelby admitted. "There might have been, but we'll never know."

"Did you ever think of giving the guy a shot? I'm telling you, Shelby, the man is smitten."

She cringed. "How smitten do you think he'll be when he finds out Chad is his? You should have heard him when he found out I had a son."

"I heard what he said," Rose told her. "I got the impression he was more upset because he thought Chad was Ned's son."

Rose let it drop, leaving Shelby alone with her guilt and confusion. How would Dylan react if he discovered the truth? Would he understand her reasons? Her fears? Probably not, she decided as they turned into the drive.

She was surprised to find Dylan and Jay huddled in the living room. Several color photographs were scattered across the coffee table in front of them.

When she walked in, Dylan looked up at her, his expression hopeful.

"You look better," he said as he rose. He'd changed into jeans and a short-sleeved silk shirt in a pale gray. The contrast to his dark coloring was flattering—too flattering.

"I feel better," she acknowledged. Absently she felt for the folded envelope and considered sharing the note with them. The words *No Cops* flashed against her brain, and she said nothing.

"Has there been any word?" Rose asked.

Both men shook their heads. Shelby felt a stab of pain in her heart as the realization that her son was still missing banished all other thoughts from her mind.

"What are those?" Shelby asked as she picked up one of the photos. It was a blowup of the woman's hand from the first videotape. Every detail of the ring was visible. It was some sort of signet ring, maybe from an organization.

"So far, Jay hasn't been able to match this to anything," Dylan explained as he moved next to her and tapped the picture. He smelled woodsy and soapy, and it reminded her of the cabin he'd taken her to just after they'd begun the investigation of Ned.

Refusing to allow the memories to haunt her again, Shelby nodded and moved away from the heat of his presence. "What about the new tape? Was it a hotel?"

"They're still going over the tape," Jay answered. "But we're absolutely sure the second tape was made at Waterfront Park."

The first rays of hope filtered through her mind. "If the kidnapper had my baby at the park yesterday, maybe someone will remember them."

"I'm going to work on that today," Dylan said. "The lab boys said that they were probably in the park around lunchtime, based on the shadows."

"I'll go with you. Then we can canvass the area. Hopefully someone saw them," Shelby volunteered.

All three of them looked at her as if she'd just confessed to killing Reverend Martin Luther King.

"Don't you want to stay here?" Rose asked. "What if he should try to make contact?"

Shelby glanced at the clock. It was already after one, and the note was explicit. She needed to be in her car at the appointed time. If she accompanied Dylan, she would be spared the task of trying to think of some plausible excuse to sit in her car, waiting for the contact.

"I...I think I'd like the fresh air."

Dylan was staring at her. Every nerve in her body was aware of his eyes on her, the intense scrutiny as he quietly studied her face. She noted that his expression had darkened.

"Mrs. Porter has a point," Jay interjected. "It might not sit too well with the caller if he tried to reach you."

"The cellular in my car is portable," Shelby explained. "I gave the caller that number in case he needed to reach me while I was out. I'll keep the phone with me while we look for signs of Chad or the woman."

Her reasoning didn't totally convince Jay, judging by the deep furrows etched in his brows. Thankfully, he didn't argue.

"We'd better go," Dylan said as he placed several photos of Chad in his shirt pocket.

Shelby nodded, not trusting her voice.

"I'm going to the Tattoo," Rose said. "Call me there if you need anything."

Shelby smiled at her friend and gave her a hug before preparing to leave. She quickly changed into fresh clothing and ran a brush through her hair, careful to avoid the small bandage on her forehead.

Taking a deep breath, she joined Dylan at the foot of the stairs. She nearly jumped when his fingers splayed across her back as he gently steered her in the direction of the door. Her brain was swimming with conflicting thoughts and emotions. She reminded herself to stay focused on finding Chad. She'd wait for the kidnapper to call and follow instructions, and then she'd have her son back. She clung to that scenario as she slid into the passenger seat.

"We'll park near the customs house and do it street by street," he explained.

"Fine."

She fixed her eyes on the dash, silently willing herself not to think about the fact that she was alone with him. Trying not to focus on the man dominating her peripheral vision. The interior of the car seemed to grow smaller with each passing second—until she was aware of little more than Dylan's broad shoulders, or the sculptured muscles of his upper arms, wrapped in the soft fabric of his shirt.

Shelby closed her eyes, hoping the awareness would fade. It worked. The image her mind produced instantly returned her to the present. She closed her eyes and saw Chad. Only Chad.

"Here," Dylan said, after he pulled into a metered space and handed her one of the pictures.

Shelby ran her fingertip across the image of her son's cheek. Chad liked it when she did that. It always made him laugh, or drool. The tightness in her chest was almost unbearable.

"We'll start on the east side of the street and work our way toward the park."

Shelby disconnected the telephone, slipped in the battery pack and stuck the phone in her purse. She checked her watch. It was a quarter to two.

"Why don't you do the east side, and I'll take the west?" Dylan's brows arched questioningly.

"It'll save time," she stated, without meeting his eyes.

"Can you handle it?"

His voice was so deep, so full of concern, that it almost inspired tears. She didn't want his kindness or his sympathy—not when she felt certain it would eventually turn to contempt.

"I think so," she said, hedging.

"Here's a stack of my cards. Give one to each person you talk to. Tell them to call if they see anything later on."

They had reached the corner. Their shadows were splashed on the walkway in front of them in perfect silhouettes. Shelby checked her watch again—five of two.

"Maybe we should do a couple of these together first."

"No!" she yelled, then instantly regretted it when she noted the surprise and curiosity on his face.

"I can handle it, Dylan. I'm just anxious to get started."

He looked as if he wanted to protest. He hesitated before shrugging his shoulders and crossing the street. Shelby let out a breath she hadn't realized she was holding. Moving quickly, she ducked into the first business.

It was one of those bath-and-fragrance places. She was inundated by the scents of vanilla and lavender. The shop was small, with narrow aisles stacked high with a full variety of soaps and lotions. She frowned when she realized there was no place in the store that would provide privacy. It didn't help matters much when she saw the woman behind the register staring at her with open suspicion.

Shelby smiled at the blue-haired woman and pretended to browse. The heavy scents wafting upward from a bin of carved soaps made her stomach churn. She glanced at her watch and discovered it was a few seconds after the hour. Her anxiety level intensified. "Come on, call," she pleaded as she checked the price on some potpourri.

The woman behind the register followed her every move. Shelby smiled again. The gesture wasn't returned. She moved on to a display of body lotions. Her hand trembled slightly as she feigned interest in one of the bottles. Her toe nervously tapped against the worn floor in time with the agitated beat of her heart. Three more minutes crept by.

Shelby checked the window, searching the opposite side of the street for any sign of Dylan. She was relieved when she saw no sign of the big man. At least she didn't have to worry about him.

"You need help?" the woman asked.

Only it wasn't a question, it was an accusation.

"Just browsing," Shelby returned, as aloofly as possible.

"Let me know if you ne—"

The shrill chirp of the phone sent her digging through her purse. She had the handset to her ear in record time.

"I'm here," she said in a whisper.

"Good job, Shelby."

"I'm sorry about last night. They've been listening to my calls, and I couldn't—"

"Shut up!" came the terse command.

She was instantly silent.

"I told you no cops."

His voice was so angry, so full of menace, that Shelby felt tears well up in her eyes. "No cops this time," she assured him. "How's my baby? Please, tell me he's still all right."

"He's fine," he answered. "So far."

"Please," she begged, turning away from the watchful eye of the shopkeeper. "Please don't hurt him."

"Give me one reason why I shouldn't."

"He's a baby!" she wailed, gripping the phone with both hands. "I'll do whatever you say. Just please, please don't hurt him."

"How do I know you'll follow instructions, Shelby?"

"I will," she promised. "I'll keep the police out of it." The ensuing pause was so long that Shelby feared he might have hung up. "Are you still there?"

"I'm thinking," he growled.

"Just tell me when and where to meet you. I'll bring you the money."

"It won't be that easy."

"What?"

"You have to be punished."

"Taking my son has been punishment enough," she said, without thinking.

"Don't take that tone with me."

"I'm sorry," she said hastily. "I'm just very upset. You can understand that, can't you?"

She heard a noise on the other end. It was the sound of ice tinkling in a glass.

"Of course I understand, Shelby. But that doesn't give you the right to talk down to me."

"I wasn't trying to give you that impression," she insisted.

"Well, you did. And I didn't like it."

She bit her lip, not sure how to respond.

"I think I might know how we can resolve this," he said after a brief silence.

"Anything."

"We'll double the amount. Yes," he said, in an obscenely cheery tone. "One hundred thousand dollars should take care of my inconvenience."

"That's a lot of money." Shelby swallowed. Without the participation of the ATF, she had no earthly idea where she could get her hands on that kind of money.

"Isn't getting your son back worth that to you?"

"Of course," she told him. "But it might take me some time to get that amount together."

"That's fine," he said. She heard him raise a glass to his lips. "I'm a reasonable man, Shelby."

"Then let me talk to Chad."

His laugh was low and completely mirthless. "Not right now."

"Then will you continue to send me tapes?"

"What?"

"The tapes. They are the only thing keeping me sane."

"We need you to stay sane while you get the payoff together," he said after a brief delay. "I'll tell you what, Shelby. I'm feeling generous, so I'll give you forty-eight hours to get it together."

"That's two days!" she nearly shrieked. "I can't stand another two days without Chad!"

"I'll be in touch."

"No!" she whimpered as the line went dead. Fighting both tears and the urge to smash the telephone against the nearest wall, she closed her eyes.

"This isn't a phone booth, honey," the woman announced.

"Sorry," Shelby mumbled as she slipped the portable into her purse. She turned and headed toward the door.

She pushed out of the shop and ran smack into Dylan's solid form. She looked up at him through unshed tears.

"What happened?" he asked as his hands gently gripped her shoulders. The compassion in his voice moved her closer to the edge.

She just shook her head and averted her eyes.

"I don't want to get your hopes up."

Her head whipped up and she noted the small spark in his eyes. "What?" she asked, grabbing handfuls of his shirt.

"I found a guy who thinks he saw Chad and our mystery woman."

CHAPTER ELEVEN

DYLAN STARED DOWN AT HER, his eyes moving over every inch of her face. Something was wrong. The remnants of tears had left her lashes moist, and the tiny lines around her mouth appeared to have deepened.

It took a few seconds for his brain to register the fact that she was touching him. He could feel the slight tremor in her hands where they rested against his chest. A warm breeze lifted her hair off her shoulders to glisten in the now bright sun. In spite of the circumstances, Dylan was reminded of her subtle beauty.

"I've got what might be our first real break," he told her.

Her lips parted slightly as she sucked in a shocked breath. "Thank God," she managed, in a hoarse, emotional voice.

Allowing his hands to slide down the sleeves of her blouse, Dylan took her hands in his. "Don't get your hopes up until after I check it out," he warned.

"I won't."

But he knew that wasn't the truth. He'd seen the relief bring a glimmer of light into her eyes. Silently he prayed he could find the woman and put an end to this nightmare. Then what? his mind asked. Finding Chad would mean walking out of her life. Again.

He held tightly to her hand as they worked their way toward the Historic District, in the center of Charleston. The streets were thick with tourists and fragrant-smelling street vendor's carts. Dylan noticed little beyond the silky softness of her skin.

"What are we doing?" Shelby asked as Dylan unlatched the ornamental gate of one of the stately homes.

"The guy at the dessert shop said the woman with the baby he thought might be Chad bought a box of those fancy cut-up cakes."

"Petits fours?" she asked.

He responded to her small smile with one of his own. "Whatever," he answered. "He was pretty sure she told him she lived on Market."

"So we're just going to knock on every door until we find this woman?"

"If we have to," he answered as he ushered her into a courtyard garden. "I'll do whatever it takes to find your son."

Shelby gave his hand a small squeeze. It somehow eased her mind to know that Dylan was so committed to finding Chad. It also eased her mind to think they might find Chad before the kidnapper's deadline. The possibility that she might be forced to spend another two days without her baby heightened the knifelike pain in her chest. And, she thought as she ducked under the arm he used to hold opened the gate, she wouldn't have to come up with the money.

Where am I going to get my hands on one hundred thousand dollars? she groaned inwardly.

The first house was structurally just like the Rose Tattoo—a Charleston single house with dual porches and lots of windows. The floor of the lower porch was wide pine plank, covered in layer upon layer of paint.

An oval historical marker was mounted just to the left of the screen door. Beneath that, there was an additional emblem, so tarnished that she couldn't quite make out the inscription.

Dylan yanked open the protesting screen door and lifted the heavy iron knocker several times. The scent of roses floated over from the garden, and she could hear the faint rippling of water from the ornamental pond off in the corner.

"Yes?"

A rotund woman in a domestic's uniform opened the door and eyed them with a mixture of annoyance and curiosity. The annoyance disappeared when Dylan offered his identification.

"Yes, sir. What can I do for you?" She patted the coarse gray hairs that had fallen free from the knot at the nape of her neck.

"We're looking for a missing child," Dylan explained as he handed a picture of Chad to the cooperative woman.

She smiled at the picture. It was an apologetic smile that told Shelby the woman would be of no help. They thanked her and moved on.

For the next several hours, their door-to-door canvass resulted in the interruption of two bridge games, but no sign of Chad. The homes were opulent, standing memorials to Charleston's historic past. She was growing tired of polite dismissals and well-intended wishes for a quick resolution.

"We aren't dead yet," Dylan said as he placed his arm around her shoulder. "Christ," he breathed, his hands closing over her shoulders. "I didn't mean that the way it sounded."

"I know," she said quietly, her head automatically tilted toward his chest. It was a reflexive action, based on her need to be comforted. She tried to convince herself that it didn't matter that it was Dylan's shoulder offering the solace. They walked slowly, without words. For Shelby, it was like taking a much-needed respite. A safe haven from the terrible reality that her baby was in the hands of some stranger. It was getting harder to resist the appeal of having him in her life. Harder to deny that she felt safe whenever he was around.

Their next stop was a large home on a deep corner lot. Again she stood at Dylan's side, reading the historical markers, while he conducted his interview. As her eyes roamed over the various plaques next to the door, something gnawed at her brain. There was something—

"You have?" Dylan was asking in an excited voice.

She looked into the face of the teenage girl who leaned

in the doorway, twisting several strands of her strawberry blond hair.

"Looks like him. They just moved in, but I think I've seen her taking him for walks in his buggy."

"Do you know which house?" Dylan asked.

She leaned out, blocking the screen door with her foot and pointed south. "Third house. The green-and-gray one with the carriage stone in the front."

"Thank you," Shelby gushed as she patted the girl's hands.

"No problem," the girl said with a shrug. "Good luck."

Dylan had her by the hand and was nearly dragging her as they sprinted toward the house. Shelby's emotions boiled up to the surface. Was it possible? Was her baby inside that house?

"I want you to stay by the gate," Dylan said.

Shelby stopped suddenly and jerked his arm. "You've lost your mind if you think I'm going to hang in the weeds while you go to the door."

He lifted his sunglasses and glared down at her. His mouth was a thin, determined line. "If the kidnappers are in there, we have to go about this the right way."

"There is no right way," she insisted as they stepped into the shadows of a live oak. "I want my son."

"But I'm assuming you don't want your son hurt."

Shelby's heart stopped for a brief second at the mere thought of Chad suffering. "Of course I don't want him hurt."

"Then we'll do this the right way."

"Which is?"

Dylan's expression softened somewhat. "I'll scope it out. If it looks promising, I'll call for backup."

"That could take hours," she protested.

"But we need to minimize the risks."

Reluctantly Shelby nodded, and she remained hidden by the tree trunk as Dylan strode boldly to the front door. He knocked.

There was no response.

He knocked a second time, with a bit more force.

His efforts were rewarded. A woman answered, wiping her hands on the front of a starched white apron.

"I'm from Charleston Power," Shelby heard Dylan say. "There's been a report of a possible gas leak in the area."

Shelby wondered if the woman would actually fall for that lame story.

"Oh dear!" she said, her hand going to her mouth.

Judging by her accent, Shelby thought she might be from the Midwest. She also looked to be a decade or so beyond her childbearing years.

"Do come in," she said, stepping aside so that Dylan could enter.

The door closed, leaving Shelby alone on the street with her imagination running wild. Could Dylan simply grab the baby and run out? Were there procedures and protocols that might allow that woman to keep Chad after the discovery?

"Does she even have him?" Shelby wondered aloud as the minutes ticked by.

It was more than twenty minutes before Dylan casually emerged from the house. His expression gave her no indication of what had transpired. She did note that the woman in the apron was smiling. She even waved as he retreated through the garden.

"Well?" Shelby asked, grabbing his solid forearm.

Dylan tugged her down the street, nervously glancing over his shoulder until he apparently felt comfortable and stopped.

"Do you have your phone?"

"Of course!" she snapped, reaching into her purse. "Please tell me what you found out."

"It looks like a possibility," he said excitedly.

Shelby welcomed her tears this time. "Oh, thank you," she gushed, before wrapping her arms around him.

"Hold on," he said, wriggling free and placing her at arm's length from him. "I didn't actually see the baby."

"Then how—"

"That's why I need the phone. I need to have Jay run a check on Mrs. Osburne."

"But you said it was promising," she repeated, unwilling to abandon her first real glimmer of hope.

"And it is," he assured her in a soft tone. "The place didn't check out."

"I don't understand."

He took the phone and quickly pressed the buttons for the connection. "Several things were out of whack. Didn't fit."

He held up one finger to keep her quiet while he spoke to Jay. There was a flash of something in his eyes as he spoke to his boss—something Shelby was helpless to decipher. He was kind enough to keep the call brief, but the suspense had her stomach knotted and her palms damp.

"There were bottles in the sink, and a few other indications that there's a kid in the house."

"That woman has to be in her late fifties," Shelby added. That earned her a bright smile from the handsome man. One she felt all the way to her toes.

"She could be a grandmother, but I didn't see any pictures. But that wasn't what bothered me. I couldn't figure out why her house wasn't like yours."

Shelby peered up through her lashes. "We don't exactly share the same tax bracket," she observed dryly. She couldn't even afford the property taxes in this part of Charleston.

"Not like that," he said with a chuckle. "There weren't any of those childproof things you've got all over the place. No plugs in the outlets, no gates near the stairs."

Shelby felt some of her jubilation draining away. "Not everyone takes those precautions."

"But most parents invest in a high chair of some sort."

She thought of the high-tech model that dominated her small kitchen.

"This woman had rigged a dish towel to a chair. Like

maybe she was securing the baby for his feedings. Kind of strange, wouldn't you say?''

"Wow," she breathed, allowing herself to rest against a tree. "I can't stand it, Dylan. Let's go back, demand to see the baby."

He was shaking his head, moving closer, so that mere inches separated them. "We have to do this right."

Did he realize what he was asking? she wondered. "But I— She has Chad—"

"We'll get him, Shelby. But we can't just go barging in without doing some sort of background first."

"They didn't mind just barging into my home and stealing my sleeping son."

Dylan felt a pang of intuition. It was a common thing with law-enforcement officials. His sixth sense was itchy. Something wasn't right about all this. He thought back to his brief conversation with Jay. His boss was something less than enthusiastic about this sudden break in the case. From experience, Dylan knew that Jay's instincts were as good as, if not better than, his own. Jay's reluctance remained lodged in his consciousness as he looked down at Shelby's expectant face.

How would he feel if he disappointed her? If they didn't recover her son? The possibility infected his thoughts like a festering wound.

"You've got to prepare yourself," he began slowly.

"I'm trying," she admitted on a breath. "I know this could be another false lead. I just don't want it to be."

"We don't always get what we want in life," he said, not at all sure he was limiting his comments to the plight of little Chad.

A city police cruiser arrived, followed by three more. They parked in front of the Osburne home, blocking the residence. A uniformed officer from the first car came over to them.

"Agent Tanner?"

Dylan nodded and produced his identification.

"Sergeant Gilroy," he said as he offered his hand. "We're waiting on a warrant."

"How long will that take?" Shelby demanded. Both men stared at her.

"This is the mother of the missing boy."

The police sergeant, who looked young and rather thin compared to Dylan, offered a weak smile and touched his finger to the brim of his hat. "Sorry, ma'am."

"How long will it take to get a warrant?" she asked again.

"Not too long," the officer said cautiously. "We'll remain in position until it arrives."

Shelby cursed under her breath. Fury seized her small body, and she gritted her teeth so long that her jaw began to ache.

It was another forty minutes before the warrant was delivered to the scene.

"Finally," she muttered.

"Wait here," Dylan instructed.

"Like hell," she shot back. "If Chad is in there, I'm not going to stand by while a bunch of strange men go tromping in, scaring him worse than he's already been scared."

The two men exchanged a look before Dylan made the determination that she could follow behind them.

Three additional officers joined in the trek to the door. They pulled their nightsticks from their belts as they crept up the stairs. They parted at the door to stand on either side. Shelby was tucked behind Dylan, his large body blocking her view and shielding her from harm.

He knocked.

Nothing.

He knocked again.

Shelby could barely hear the sound of muffled footsteps above the pounding of her heart against her ribs.

Mrs. Osburne appeared at the door, balancing the baby on her left hip.

CHAPTER TWELVE

"FEDERAL AGENTS," Dylan announced, dangling his identification in front of the startled woman. "Gleason," he added, nodding to indicate one of the officers.

The man stepped forward and reached for the child. Mrs. Osburne defensively twisted to the side, preventing the man from touching the wide-eyed child.

"What do you think you're doing?" the woman gasped.
"We're—"
"That's not Chad," Shelby stepped forward to say.
Mrs. Osburne's face registered obvious shock.
"This is Bobby," she said, clutching the child closer to her chest.

There were several awkward seconds when no one, Shelby included, seemed to know what to do next. The woman's initial surprise was rapidly deteriorating into anger. Her faded green eyes sparkled with annoyance as they narrowed to accusatory slits.

"What on earth is this all about?" she demanded, her eyes moving past the small entourage on the porch to take in the scene beyond the garden. Many of her neighbors had followed their curiosity into the street. They manned positions just beyond the barricade of police vehicles.

"Sorry, Mrs. Osburne..." Dylan began.
"Sorry for what?"
"We're investigating the disappearance of a little boy."
The woman's expression softened somewhat. "The son of that woman who owns the bar?"
"Restaurant," Shelby muttered automatically, under her

breath. The implication in Mrs. Osburne's tone had put her on the defensive. What did owning the Rose Tattoo have to do with Chad's kidnapping?

"And you thought my nephew was the missing boy?"

"We're checking every lead," Dylan explained.

The baby began to babble happily as he swatted one chubby hand in Dylan's general direction. Dylan surprised her by offering the drooling little boy his finger, which the baby promptly inserted in his mouth.

"I'm sorry we can't help you," Mrs. Osburne said.

Shelby walked away from the house with a very heavy heart. Dylan's warnings about not getting her hopes up hadn't worked. Her ache for her missing son weighted each limp limb.

"It was a shot," he said as he fell into step beside her.

"I know," she managed to choke out.

"We'll find him."

A kaleidoscope of images spun through her mind—Chad's smiling face, the empty crib. Then she remembered the call. She knew then that her best hope of getting Chad back was to follow the kindnapper's instructions. But where was she going to get the money?

"Hey," Dylan said, placing his hand on her shoulder.

She stopped and turned toward him. She could see her reflection in the mirrored lenses of his sunglasses. Looking up at him had the effect of shutting out the rest of the world. Her brain no longer acknowledged the sounds of the city street.

"I'll find him, Shelby," he reiterated softly. "I promise."

She wasn't sure if it was the conviction of his declaration, her tumultuous emotional state, or simply the reemergence of feelings long buried. It didn't matter, really. She leaned into him, without care or thought for the consequences. His body was large and warm, his arms were comforting, protective. Dylan welcomed her, stroking her hair as she rested her cheek against the solidness of his broad chest.

Drinking in the scent of him, she closed her eyes and

allowed her tears to flow freely. He responded by whispering compassionate words against her ear. She cried until the tears stopped of their own accord. When she lifted her head, she felt drained and exhausted, but that wasn't the most telling emotion.

His sunglasses were gone. She found him looking down at her with raw emotion in his eyes. She should have pulled back, out of his arms. She should have apologized and made some distancing excuse for stupidly turning to him for comfort. But all rational thoughts evaporated as his hands slowly glided over her shoulders until they gently cupped her face.

She felt the calluses on his palms as his thumbs made small circles against her face, erasing the remnants of her tears. He bent forward, until his breath washed over her face in soothing waves. The pulse at her throat fluttered as his fingers fanned over her skin. Her head tipped back as her lips parted ever so slightly. Shelby hovered on the precipice of indecision. Rational thought eluded her as she watched his eyes drop to her mouth. Her breath stilled in her throat when he looked at her like that.

Although she'd expected the contact, it still sparked a thousand fires in her motionless body. His mouth was gentle, tentative, the kiss little more than a whisper of a touch. When it was over, he didn't lift his head. Instead, he laced his fingers behind her neck and leaned his forehead against hers. She could hear his uneven intake of breath.

"I'm not going to say I'm sorry," he said. But he was. He was sorry time and circumstances made it impossible for him to kiss her the way he wanted to. For now, he knew, he would have to settle for offering comfort.

"It was nothing," she told him in a small voice.

Reluctantly Dylan allowed her to step away from him, though he managed to retain his grasp on her hand. It felt small, and he thought he detected a slight tremor as his fingers entwined with hers.

"Let's call it a day," he suggested as he tugged her in the direction of the car.

He was content to walk in silence with her at his side. He liked just having her with him again. He was willing to take whatever crumbs she might toss in his direction. His stomach knotted as he realized what was happening. It was like stepping back in time. Back to when he'd first met her, first fallen in love with her.

"Dylan, look!"

He was reaching to unlock the door of her car when his attention was directed to the rear seat. He froze.

Mumbling a string of expletives under his breath, he kicked the tire with enough force to rock the car. A videotape was resting in plain view, in her baby's car seat. The perversity of the scene, and its effect on Shelby, made every muscle in his body tense with a subtle, barely controlled fury.

"We should call and have the car dusted," he explained. When she looked up at him with those sad blue eyes, he almost abandoned procedure. "It's not worth risking the possibility of getting a handle on this guy," he said, in response to her unasked question.

Jay arranged for them to wait at the Rose Tattoo while the car and the video were being tagged, taped and photographed. They arrived just as the early dinner crowd began to fill the tables on the patio. He was impressed by the business.

This place, with its hanging baskets and trendy menu offerings, was a far cry from the overpriced knickknack shop she'd run with Nichols. The mere thought of that slimeball made him grit his teeth. He wondered where Nichols was at that very moment, and whether he knew what he was doing to Shelby.

"Let's go upstairs," she said as they weaved their way through the bar area.

The sound of Elvis singing gospel tunes filtered through the din of conversation. The small blond waitress, Tory, emerged from the kitchen area, balancing a dish-laden tray slightly above her head.

He almost missed the flash of fear he saw cross her face when she saw Shelby. Dylan filed that away, along with some other things that were beginning to challenge his initial impression of the abduction.

"How are you doing?" Tory asked, stopping long enough to give Shelby's arm a squeeze.

"Hanging in there."

"Any leads?" she asked, giving Dylan only a brief moment's attention.

He shook his head and watched as she began to buckle beneath the weight of the tray.

"I'm so sorry," Tory said, before going on about her duties.

This scenario was played out as each of the employees stepped forward for an update and to offer heartfelt words of encouragement.

"You need to buy a few new records for your jukebox," he said as soon as they reached her office.

Her smile was genuine. "Rose would kill me. We only play the King."

"Why?" Dylan asked as he sat on the edge of her desk. Shelby seemed more relaxed now, as she slid into the chair.

"Rose is a *real* Elvis freak. She even makes a pilgrimage to Graceland each year on his birthday. She's a hard-core fan. You should see her house. It's a shrine."

He whistled and chuckled at the image. Rose Porter was a character. He didn't share Jay's reservations about the woman.

"You didn't know anything about her husband or her kids?" Dylan asked.

She leaned back and locked her hands behind her head. He tried not to notice how the action caused her sweater to hug every curve of her body. It was a struggle.

"Not really."

"Meaning?"

She shrugged and said, "She was really helpful when

Chad was born. I never questioned her, but she knew an awful lot about newborns.''

He realized that his image of Shelby was expanding. The knowledge that she was a mother had been a shock. And he still wasn't completely comfortable with the fact that she had this tie to Nichols.

''I'm sure it was nice having someone around when Chad was born.''

Her movements became still, forced. She couldn't meet his eyes. He wondered at the reason for her reaction. It was like watching a door close and hearing the bolt slide into place.

''Tell me about the guy behind the bar.''

''Josh?''

He nodded as he plucked a pen from its holder and began to twirl it in hand.

''Josh came with the place. Same as Tory.''

''You bought people?'' he asked, teasingly.

Some of the small tension lines around her mouth appeared to ease. ''They worked here when Rose originally bought the place.''

''So you and Rose didn't start this together?''

''I invested the money that came from selling my interest to Ned.''

The mere mention of the guy's name produced a sour taste in Dylan's mouth. He was sure he was frowning when he asked, ''Why would Nichols let you buy out, knowing you were—''

Her eyes met his. There was definite challenge on their brilliant blue depths. ''Ned didn't *let* me do anything.''

''Then why the split? Why did you leave?''

Having risen from the chair, she offered him her back as she peered out the window. ''Ned was furious with me when he found out I had been meeting with you.''

''He should have been. We should have nailed that slimeball.'' His words echoed in the still room.

''It was complicated, Dylan.''

"Your business partner was—and still is—an arms dealer."

He noticed a definite stiffening of her spine, but couldn't seem to contain himself on the issue of Nichols. "Okay," he began, as his blood pressure went up a notch or two. "Forget his criminal shortcomings. I don't understand why he'd let you walk out of his life when you were carrying his child."

"For the last time—" she turned, her eyes narrowed and fixed "—it's complicated and personal, Dylan. And not open for discussion. All right?"

Hell, no! his mind screamed. He couldn't stand to let go of it, but he had no choice. She stood her ground, her arms folded in front of her. He could see the rapid rise and fall of her chest as she took each annoyed breath.

"Dylan?"

"Yep?"

"I don't want us to discuss Ned every time we're together."

That small crack in the wall she'd put up against him was all he needed. He moved next to her, taking her small hands in his. She smelled faintly of wildflowers, and looked as if the weight of the whole world rested upon her slender shoulders. Arguing about Nichols had destroyed their budding relationship once before.

"Sorry," he said, lifting her hands to his lips.

Their eyes remained locked as he brushed his lips across the back of each hand in turn.

"You shouldn't do that," she said in a near whisper.

"Why?" he asked against her skin.

"You know why."

"The only thing I know," he said as he turned her hands and placed kisses in her palms, "is that I have a hard time keeping my hands to myself when you're around."

"We knew that," she admitted, tugging her hands from his. Sidestepping him, she moved to the relative safety of her desk.

"Then why didn't it work?"

He couldn't see her face, but he heard her heavy sigh.

"It just didn't, Dylan. There's no need to do a postmortem."

He didn't agree, but he let it pass—for now.

"Why do you think he's sending the tapes?" she asked.

Dylan sauntered back to the desk and perched on the edge. "Good question."

"Do kidnappers usually send videos?"

"Sometimes. Sometimes they send other stuff."

"How did he know you and your men were there last night?"

Dylan's foot tapped nervously against the floor. "There was a mix-up on the far side of the plant."

"What?" she fairly shrieked.

"A couple of the men were out of position."

"And just what does that mean?" she demanded, getting to her feet.

He nearly winced at the sharp edge to her voice. "There was a miscommunication."

"You're beating around the bush," she said accusingly.

"Two guys moved out of position at the perimeter," he explained. It sounded just as lame as when Jay had told him. "They apparently misunderstood their instructions."

"Good Lord!" she cried, falling back into the chair, holding her head in her hands. "You mean I could have gotten my son back last night, but you guys screwed up?"

He raked his hands through his hair, trying to think of something to say. "It was unfortunate."

"Unfortunate?" she parroted. "Why wasn't I told about this last night?"

"You were in no condition."

"How could this have happened?" She rubbed her eyes, then began a slow massage of her temples.

Jay wouldn't be too happy to hear that he had shared this bit of information with her.

"Mistakes happen, Shelby. Two of our men left their positions prematurely."

She looked up at him, her eyes wide with disbelief. Her expression worked like a machete, slicing its way through his gut.

"It was regrettable, Shelby. But we'll get him. Hell," he said as he moved next to her. Swiveling her chair, Dylan knelt in front of her, his hands resting on the tops of her thighs. "We've got a lead on Nichols in Turkey. As soon as he's questioned, I'm sure we'll be—"

"Ned isn't behind this!" Shelby wailed, tossing his hands aside as if his touch appalled her.

"Then give me something else," he nearly pleaded. "He's the only enemy you've got."

"He isn't my enemy," she insisted. "He would never do anything like this to me."

"Who besides Ned Nichols knows so damned much about you?"

"What?"

He jumped to his feet and began pacing, trying to allow his muddled thoughts to solidify.

"Dylan?" she prompted. "What are you talking about?"

"Think, Shelby. This guy knows your home, your place of business. He seems to always be one step ahead of us. Obviously he's no stranger to your daily routine."

Her hand clutched her throat as she absorbed his words. "You're saying it has to be someone I know?"

"And who do you know, besides Nichols, who would be capable of something as low as snatching your son?"

"This is crazy."

"But it's not," Dylan insisted, moving back to capture her face in his hands. "There's too many aspects of this that don't fit the typical kidnapping."

"What does Jay think?"

Dylan took a breath and exhaled slowly. "He is focusing his attention on Nichols."

"And you're not?"

His fingers brushed a few strands of her silky hair away from her upturned face. "I'm leaning toward Nichols. But I'm not closed-minded."

"That's comforting?"

"I'll admit I'm having some trouble fitting Nichols into every aspect of the case."

She reached up, and he felt her fingers close around his wrist. Her hand was as warm as the small smile she offered. He could almost see the thoughts churning through her mind. Her expression stilled and grew serious, almost frightened.

"If we rule out Ned—"

"I didn't say I was willing to go that far."

She pursed her lips. "For the sake of argument?"

"Fine."

"If it isn't Ned, then how would a total stranger know so much about me?"

He hesitated, trained those cool gray-blue eyes on her and said, "What if it isn't a stranger?"

CHAPTER THIRTEEN

"TELL ME AGAIN why we're doing this," Rose muttered as she inserted her key in the lock.

"I need to make a call, and I want it to be private."

"Does this have something to do with Chad?" Rose asked, one brown arched high on her forehead.

Shelby didn't meet her friend's eyes. "I just wanted to get away from Dylan."

Rose flipped a switch on the wall, flooding the small house with yellowish light. A life-size cardboard cutout of Elvis Presley greeted Shelby as she stepped into the cramped living room. The decor conveyed both the taste and the personality of its owner. Every conceivable inch of the room was home to some form of memorabilia. There were street signs, movie posters, coffee mugs, ashtrays. But Shelby's favorite was the Plexiglas-enclosed item resting next to the hound-dog-shaped telephone. An engraved brass plate mounted on the glass announced that the whitish, half-moon-shaped item was one of the King's fingernails. It was so disgusting that it inspired a certain amount of morbid amusement.

"You didn't seem to mind having Dylan around earlier," Rose said.

"What are you talking about?"

Leaning forward through the small space that separated the kitchen from the living room, Rose said, "I saw you two in the office. I don't think he was fingerprinting you with his lips."

A guilty warmth spilled on to her cheeks. "I wasn't—"

"Don't feel the need to explain yourself," Rose interjected. She flipped her hand in the air, causing the vast array of bracelets on her arm to clang and jingle. "Dylan seems like a pretty okay guy. Lord knows he's about as cute as they come." Rose pulled a can of coffee from the freezer compartment. "All that dark hair, and that sorta sexy half smile. Kinda reminds me of the King when he was in *Love Me Tender*. That was the one where he died at the end." Rose's voice took on a wistful quality. "Yes. Your Dylan has that same look."

"He isn't mine," Shelby insisted. "I just hope this ordeal ends soon, so I won't have to be around him anymore."

"Coulda fooled me."

"Rose..." Shelby groaned.

"Well." Rose marched out of the kitchen, her stiletto heels muted by the thick pile carpeting. "Who are you kidding? Not me." Rose loomed over her, brandishing a chrome coffee scoop. "Once your initial shock wore off, you warmed right up to that man."

"Warmed up to him?" Shelby snorted. "I've done nothing of the kind. I'm in a very precarious position. I can't very well tell him to take a hike. Not until I've gotten my son back."

The lines at the corners of Rose's eyes deepened. "I know you're worried sick about the baby, but I also see what's going on between the two of you."

"Now you are being ridiculous."

"Really?" Rose said, her tone taunting. "Honey, you can't be in the same room with that man without your eyes following his every move."

"That's silly."

"Now, I can't say as I blame you. I think he's right easy on the eyes myself."

"Rose!" Shelby whined. "I'm not interested in Dylan like that."

"If you're breathing, you're interested. He's too fine a man to go unnoticed."

"Maybe for you," Shelby mumbled, primly folding her hands in her lap. "But I'm immune."

Rose snorted. "And the King really is alive and living in Hoboken."

Shelby rolled her eyes. "I *am*."

"No," Rose said, her tone somewhat less forceful. "You backed yourself into a corner by not telling that man the truth."

"I did the only rational thing I could," Shelby replied defensively.

Rose sat on the sofa next to Shelby, and placed one heavily jeweled hand on the fabric between them. "Secrets as big as yours always come back to haunt you." Her eyes dropped to the sofa, and she began to trace the outline of the leopard-spot print. "Take me, for example. Look at all the dirt they dug up on me in such a short time."

"I'm really sorry about that," Shelby told her.

Rose shook her head. "Doesn't matter. The point is, a secret like the one you're hiding is bound to blow up in your face."

"I won't let it. As soon as Chad is safely back home, Dylan will be out of my life."

Rose's mouth curved downward. "I think you're deluding yourself, Shelby. How do you expect that man to walk away, when the two of you are joined at the lips?"

"We haven't really kissed," she insisted. "Dylan is only trying to comfort me."

"I want to offer you comfort, too, but I sure as hell don't plan on kissing you."

On that note, Rose went into the bedroom, in order for Shelby to use the phone in private. *Great,* Shelby thought as she dug in her bag for her address book. As if things weren't already complicated enough, now Rose wanted her to reassess the situation.

"It won't happen," she said as she waited for the international operator. "Dylan and I have chemistry. But we have nothing in common. It could never work with us.

We're too different. I knew that when I broke up with him. And nothing's changed.'' Unless you count Chad, her mind added.

Reading off the code on her calling card, Shelby asked for a specific number and listened for the series of clicks and static as the connections of modern technology warred with primitive electronics. Shelby nervously twisted several strands of her hair around her finger.

"Come on," she pleaded.

Her patience was rewarded when a high-pitched voice recited the name of the hotel.

"Ned Nichols, please."

"Nick?"

"Nichols," she repeated slowly.

She allowed her eyes to roam around the room. She could trace the life and career of Elvis from his early childhood to the final months of his life, thanks to the photos, news clippings and other items framed, mounted or otherwise displayed on every inch of wall space. She couldn't imagine being so committed to anything. Especially a total stranger.

"No Nick," the voice said.

"Not Nick," she just about screamed into the receiver. "Nichols. Ned Nichols. Charleston, South Carolina."

"Nichols."

She cursed and fiddled with the orange plastic tail on the base portion of the novelty phone.

"Hello?"

"Ned?" she breathed into the receiver.

"I'm sorry. This is Mr. Chan. I'm with the hotel. I understand you are trying to reach one of our guests?"

"Yes," she said, adding words of gratitude to be rid of the language barrier. "I'm looking for Mr. Ned Nichols."

"Ahh...Mr. Nichols."

Good, she thought. "Yes, Ned. It's very important that I talk to him."

"I'm afraid that won't be possible."

"He isn't there?" she cried, feeling the cool finger of panic tickle her voice.

"Not at present," Mr. Chan answered. "He's expected later this morning."

Shelby stared at the phone for a long time after hanging up, mentally weighing her options. There weren't any, she acknowledged with a sigh.

"Finished?" Rose asked as she stuck her head into the room.

"Yep."

"What's all this about?" her friend queried as she placed two mugs of steaming coffee on the table. "You aren't doing something stupid, are you?"

She couldn't meet her friend's eyes. "Of course not."

DYLAN PARKED in the alley, and made his way to the back door. Keith answered his knock.

"Yes?"

"I need to talk to Tory Conway," he stated.

Keith made no move to step away from the door. "She's busy."

"Yeah, well," Dylan muttered as he squeezed past the man, "I'm busy, too. I'm trying to find Shelby's son."

The kitchen was in a state of chaos. Pots and pans littered the counters; the equipment was in pieces, and various items were soaking in three of the four large sinks. The room smelled of herbs and stale grease, and still held the heat of the now quiet ovens.

"Where is she?"

Keith's eyes narrowed in a mute challenge.

"Look," Dylan said, in his most official voice, "don't jerk my chain, pal. I'm in no mood for it."

Keith shrugged and tossed his head in the direction of the dining area. He then shuffled off to tend to the items in the sink.

The sound of clanging steel followed him into the dimly

lit room. He spotted Tory out on the porch, sitting at a small table, chasing food with a fork.

"Miss Conway?"

She jumped at the sound of his voice, and her light eyes regarded him warily as he turned the chair and fell in next to her.

He could almost sense Shelby out here on this porch. She was the kind of woman designed for soft breezes and sunny afternoons. It was easy to summon an image of her seated on one of the rattan swings, her shapely legs dangling, her silky hair lifted off her long neck.

"Tanner, right?" Tory asked, averting her eyes.

"Dylan," he said. "I need to ask you a few questions about Chad."

"Why me?"

"Just a formality," he answered. He schooled his tone to remain bland, not to react to the nervous quaver in her voice.

She was a petite woman who looked much younger than her mid-twenties. Her light hair, dark tan and curvaceous build made him think of a California poster girl.

"So, what do you want to know?"

She still wasn't making eye contact.

"How long have you worked here?"

"About seven years."

He opted to listen, rather than take notes. He suspected any attempt to record the conversation would only heighten the young woman's anxiety. "Like it?"

She stabbed at a chunk of chicken, but made no move to place the food in her mouth.

"Of course I like it," she told him. "I make decent tips, and my days are free."

"To do what?"

"School."

"You're in college?"

"Graduate school. But I've taken this quarter off."

He noted that some of her tension had abated. "In what area?"

"Historic preservation," she said with a smile.

That small act did wonders for her. Tory was an attractive young woman when she smiled. But not as attractive as Shelby, he thought.

"I'm working on a doctorate. My area of concentration is architectural preservation."

"Sounds interesting," he lied. "Where do you go to school?"

He whistled when she named a prestigious, expensive and exclusive private college on the outskirts of Charleston. "You need those good tips. Tuition alone must run you around twenty grand a year."

"Seventeen-five," she said in a soft voice.

"That's a piece of change."

"Yes," she said, dropping her fork. She made a small sound when the utensil banged against the china. "I'm... um...I'm on a partial scholarship. So that helps."

"And you make up the rest working here?"

"Mostly."

"Married?"

She gave a nervous laugh. "No."

"Boyfriend?"

Gathering up the remnants of her meal, Tory rose, but remained at the edge of the table.

"What does this have to do with Chad being kidnapped?"

"Routine," he said, watching her intently. "We need to know about the people in Shelby's life."

"I don't have a boyfriend," she said quickly. A devilish light sparkled in her eyes. "In fact, I haven't even had a date in recent months."

"I know the feeling," Dylan said under his breath.

"You?"

He actually felt his cheeks grow warm as a result of her question. "Anyway," he said, clearing his throat. "Have you noticed anyone hanging around here? Maybe asking about Shelby or the baby?"

Tory shook her head sadly. "Shelby keeps pretty much to herself. I mean, she's polite, but she usually stays in her office unless we have some sort of disaster. Rose, on the other hand, thinks nothing of busing a table or mixing a drink."

"Speaking of drinks, what can you tell me about Josh?"

"Wow," Tory said as she scratched her head. "Great bartender. Fast. And he's nice, but a real trawler."

"Trawler?"

"Contrary to current advice, Josh has a thing for one-night stands. He rarely leaves here without his nightly trophy."

"Sounds like a real prince."

Tory flipped her bangs back away from her face. "He's not evil, he's just not real big on responsible adult relationships, or the concept of commitment."

"Do I detect a note of bitterness?"

Tory snickered. "He's nice-looking, and we went out a couple of times. Josh was a gentleman, but it nearly killed him in the process. I think he's uncomfortable with women with IQs in three digits."

"How's he feel about working for two women?"

Her brows drew together as she appeared to mull over the question. "I never gave it much thought. He's never said anything nasty about Shelby. Only Rose."

"He has a problem with Rose?"

"Rose can be blunt. Josh doesn't take it well when someone points out his shortcomings. Rose delights in taking him down a peg or two."

Dylan thanked Tory, and walked to his car. All of this was accomplished under the watchful eye of Keith. He drove back to his apartment, with his mind replaying the interview.

"Something doesn't fit," he told Foolish. "There's something I'm not seeing."

HE ARRIVED early in the morning, the videotape tucked under his arm. Shelby tracked his movements from the relative safety of her bedroom. He was wearing jeans and a short-sleeved white shirt. He walked with such authority, yet each lithe movement was relaxed, fluid and confident. She loved to watch him move.

She wondered if Chad would inherit that confident walk. The thought brought the familiar pain to her chest. "He's okay," she said aloud. "Just think about the videotapes."

When Dylan knocked on the door, Shelby felt her heart flutter in her chest. It was silly, futile, but she couldn't seem to stop herself from reacting to this man.

"How are you?"

"Holding up," she lied. She still hadn't reached Ned. The money was weighing heavily on her mind.

"Jay will be here in a little while," he told her as he brushed past her.

The scent of soap and his cologne was incredibly comforting as his massive form filled the small vestibule. He was smiling down at her, his eyes searching her face.

"I can't get over how well you're doing," he said as his fingers closed around the bared flesh of her upper arms.

"I'm not doing well," she told him in a shy voice. "I'm operating on autopilot, and constantly reminding myself that I have to stay rational for Chad's sake." *But I'd love it if you held me,* she added silently.

"He's a lucky little boy," Dylan remarked as their eyes met.

"Yes," she managed to say as she backed away from his disturbing closeness. "Chad and I are lucky to have each other."

An awkward silence ensued. She was aware of everything. His size, his smile, the intensity of those eyes. It caused every nerve ending in her body to take on a life of its own.

"Do I smell coffee?"

"Yes," Shelby gushed, grateful to have something to occupy her mind besides him. "I'll get you some."

She all but ran into the kitchen, chased by the ghosts of her guilty past. "How can I be glad to see him?" she asked as she got cups down from one of the cabinets. It was turning into a dangerous and potentially disastrous situation. One she knew she would have to deal with.

"But not right this instant," she whispered as she carried the mugs into the living room.

Dylan was seated on the sofa, his legs crossed at the knee. He looked relaxed, and quite comfortable. His eyes were her only indication of what he really felt. She saw a sadness mingling with frustration when she met his pointed stare.

"I'm flattered," he said, his deep voice resonating through the still house.

Nervously Shelby took the seat at the opposite end of the couch, allowing as much space as possible between them. "Flattered?"

"You remembered," he said, nodding in the direction of the coffee cup. "Hot and black."

"I guess I did," she admitted, with a small smile.

"I like that."

"Don't make too much out of it," she warned, trying to inject some lightness into her tone.

Dylan slid across the sofa until mere inches separated them. "I'm trying not to," he said quietly. His hand came up, and he captured a lock of her hair between two of his fingers. He silently studied the dark strands, his expression clouded and indecipherable.

"I never thought I'd see you again," he continued, his voice low, almost seductive.

"Let's not do this," she said, swallowing.

"I just don't understand what happened, Shelby. It was like everything was fine one minute, and then you gave me my walking papers out of nowhere."

"Please, Dylan," she pleaded, cowering in the small space he'd allowed. "It just didn't work out."

"But I don't know why."

The sincerity in his voice worked like a vise on her throat.

The lump of emotion threatened to strangle her as the moments of silence dragged on.

"Just tell me why, and I'll leave it alone."

Closing her eyes, Shelby actually entertained the thought of telling him the truth. Getting it all out in the open. *Then what?* her voice of reason asked. The answer was all too clear. She had no way to gauge his reaction. But she wasn't going to risk it, not when Chad's welfare still hung in the balance.

"I told you that night," she stated in a flat tone. Raw nerves propelled her from the sofa. She carefully placed herself on the opposite side of the table, and tried to ignore the desperation in his eyes. "We don't have anything in common. We want different things."

"We never talked about what we wanted," he countered, his voice rising a notch.

"That was one of the problems. Our relationship was too...passionate."

"Worse things can happen between two people, Shelby."

"But there's more to life than sex."

He jumped to his feet and caught her by the arms before she had a chance to react. As he pulled her closer, she encountered the solid outline of his body. His expression was pleading, his mouth little more than a taut line.

"It was more than sex, Shelby. And I think you know that."

CHAPTER FOURTEEN

"WE MADE A MISTAKE early on," Shelby said as she swept her coffee cup off the table. The now lukewarm liquid splattered on the table.

They grabbed napkins and went for the spill in unison. Dylan intentionally allowed his hand to brush hers as his eyes remained fixed on her face, watching. He could tell from her expression that the contact was disturbing, and he was fairly certain he wasn't filtering the observation through his ego. That was the kick of all this, he thought as he dabbed at the coffee. The signals were still there. She was too nervous, and he'd caught her looking at him more than once during the past few days. Her actions and her words didn't mesh. The knowledge only served to sour his mood.

"Don't pout," she told him.

The sound of her soft voice brought him back to the present. "I'm not pouting."

"Then don't frown."

Her eyes were the color of deep, still water. Her lashes were thick and feathery. While he admired her strength, Dylan found her vulnerabilities most appealing. This woman inspired a primitive need to protect, to comfort.

"What would you like me to do?" he asked with a sigh.

Her shoulders lifted in a shrug. The action revealed the slender curves of her body, forcing him to look away. A definite sense of self-loathing enveloped him as he silently berated himself for thinking such thoughts. He needed to get a grip.

"I just don't feel up to sparring with you, Dylan. I can't

think of anything right now but the welfare of my baby." Her voice was low, almost pleading.

"Deal," he said, forcing a smile to his lips. He hesitated before speaking again. "I went to see Tory last night."

Her head cocked to one side. "She's very attractive."

"I suppose," he agreed.

"Most men think so." Her words came out in a rush.

Was this a spark of jealousy? he wondered, hopeful. "She's definitely an asset to your business."

"She's a competent waitress."

He smiled.

"What?" She drew her hands up to rest them against her small hips.

"Competent?" he parroted. "Isn't that a little cold?"

He liked the small stain of red on her high cheekbones. Jealousy was looking more and more like a possibility.

"Okay." Shelby lifted her chin regally and met his eyes. "She's the best waitress in all of Charleston."

Dylan's chuckle didn't sit too well with her. Shelby's eyes narrowed, and her lips pulled into a taunting smirk.

Dylan relaxed against the sofa, his eyes never leaving her face. "Tory definitely has a lot on the ball."

"You actually noticed her brain?" Shelby asked, feigning great surprise.

"Right after I checked out her incredible body. Does she work out?" He tried to make the last remark sound conversational. He was glad to see his teasing was relaxing her a little. God knew she needed a break from the strain.

"No. She's just one of *those* women."

"Those?"

She tossed her hands in the air, her face contorted with exasperation. "She eats like a horse and has never once set foot in a gym."

"A horse, huh?"

"Dylan?" she said. "If you want inside information on one of my employees, I suggest you put your request in writing."

His laughter chased her into the kitchen. Her hand was still shaking as she poured herself another cup of coffee. Turning, she leaned against the counter and gripped the steaming mug in both hands.

Damn him, she thought. He'd been provoking her, and, like a fool, she'd gone for the bait. It would never have happened if he hadn't appeared on her doorstep looking like *that.* She tried to tell herself it was just because she was so exhausted.

Dylan had that unmade-bed, casual-sensuality look about him that left her weak in the knees. Every touch, every look, inspired a definite tingling sensation that began in the pit of her stomach and branched outward until she was consumed with her own awareness of him. The man was as annoying as he was exciting.

And he's the father of your child, her little voice of reason reminded. She felt her whole being slump beneath the weight of her secret. Her mind instantly produced one of the images from the last video. She clung to the memory of her son's happy face. Chad had to be okay. There would be time enough for her to sort through her feelings for Dylan. Right now, she had more pressing things on her mind. One hundred thousand of them.

"Morning."

She jumped at the sound of Jay's voice. Turning, she offered a weak smile. Only then did she realize that she had again sloshed coffee.

"She seems to have developed a drinking problem," Dylan said from over the other man's shoulder.

"Cute," she muttered as she surveyed the damage. Depositing the cup in the sink, she pulled the now splattered fabric of her blouse between two fingers. "I'll just run up and change," she said.

Jay backed out of the doorway. Dylan wasn't quite as generous. He planted his large body to one side, making it impossible for her to pass without brushing against him.

Shelby held her breath and willed herself not to think about the solidness of his thighs, the rigidness of his taut stomach.

The transferred heat of his body still warmed her skin long after she'd shed her blouse. The annoying hammer of her pulse pounded as she surveyed the contents of her closet. After settling on a pale gray sundress, Shelby ran a brush through the unruly mass of her dark hair. Her eyes fixed on the phone, then the clock on the nightstand. She was running out of time.

Taking a seat on the edge of the bed, Shelby reached tentatively for the phone. After a few seconds of internal debate, she dialed the series of numbers and gave her instructions to the international operator.

"Come on," she whispered as she listened to the static on the other end. She forced herself not to think about the possibility that her outgoing calls were being taped. Her body gave an involuntary shudder at the mere thought of Dylan and Jay discovering what she was trying to do.

"Hello."

"Ned. It's Shelby."

Her breathy whisper was greeted by silence.

"Are you there?"

"Yes."

"I need help."

"I know."

"You know?" she asked.

"I've just spent the past three hours being interrogated by two goons from the State Department."

Shelby let out a long breath, and her fingers nervously twisted through the plastic cord of the phone. "I need money."

After what sounded like a snort, he said, "From the kidnapper?"

"I know you didn't take my son."

"Really?"

His voice was strained, angry, much as it had been on that day when he discovered her involvement with Dylan.

"I didn't get that impression when I was dragged out of bed and through the streets of Istanbul."

"I'm really sorry that happened."

"I'm sure you are," Ned shot back. "No doubt your lover set them on me. How am I supposed to conduct business with two bozos dogging me all over the world?"

"I'll see what I can do, Ned. But I need money to pay the kidnapper."

"Have the feds front the money."

Closing her eyes, she struggled to keep her tears and her frustrations in check. "I can't do that, Ned. The man who has my son will do God knows what if I involve the authorities."

"From my vantage point, you've already involved the cops. I'd think they'd do anything to help you out, under the circumstances."

"It's more complex than that," Shelby countered. "I've told them all along that you couldn't possibly have anything to do with this."

"I'm sure you told them everything but the truth." A punishing pause followed.

When Shelby refused to rise to the bait, Ned continued. "Then why are they breathing down my neck?" Ned demanded. His voice had risen, and she could almost see his dark eyes bulging from his angry face.

"They think we're enemies."

"Why?"

"Because of what happened before."

"None of that would have happened if you'd kept your nose out of my affairs."

"I've explained all that to you," Shelby groaned. "I never meant to cause you any trouble."

"Well, you did."

"Ned," she said in a pleading tone. "I know you hold me responsible, and maybe I am. But right now I need your help. I need one hundred thousand dollars."

"What makes you think I have that kind of money? My business took a nosedive, thanks to all the negative press."

"Ned..." she began, then stopped, long enough to muster all her courage. "I know all about your secret account in the Caymans. I saw the bank statements."

"I don't know what you're talking about."

"Please, Ned. Don't make this harder than it has to be."

"Me?" he shouted. "I trained you to be a top-notch antiquities dealer. I tried to do right by you, and how did you repay me?"

"I didn't help them!" she countered in a loud whisper. "I backed out and refused to testify about any of the things I suspected you might be doing."

"But not before you put out for that agent."

"Please, Ned," she begged, feeling exhausted. "Believe me, if I had it to do over again, I would never allow myself to be dragged into their investigation."

"But you did. And you damned near cost me my life."

"I'm sorry," she said for the umpteenth time.

"Did you know that?" Ned was plainly seething. "Do you have any idea how close you came to getting me killed?"

"I've said I was sorry, Ned. I have explained to you time and time again that I only answered their questions and worked with Dylan because I believed you were incapable of leading a double life."

"And now?"

"Now what?"

"You left me because you couldn't stand to be around me after Tanner poisoned your mind. But you don't mind taking my money? Is that right?"

"I'll do anything to get my son back."

"How do I know this isn't just another ploy? Just another trick you're helping them execute?"

"I'm not," she told him flatly. "If I didn't tell them what I suspected a year and a half ago, what makes you think I'd do it now?"

"Tanner is back in your life."

"He is not!" Shelby assured him. "He's helping with the investigation."

"That must be cozy."

"Will you help me?" she asked, trying to ignore his cutting sarcasm.

Silence.

"Please."

"I'll have to think about it."

"I don't have the luxury of time. I'm supposed to make the payoff tomorrow night."

Again, silence.

"Ned, I—"

"I'll call you tomorrow morning with my decision."

"Ned—"

She stared at the phone, battling tears. "If he won't help me, what am I going to do?" The heart-wrenching question came out in a hoarse whisper.

"Shelby?"

"Yes?" she responded as she quickly replaced the phone. Shelby wiped the dampness from her cheeks with the back of her hand.

The door creaked open and Dylan slipped into the room. His face contorted into a series of deep lines as his eyes roamed over her face. In an instant he was at her side, the fingers of his hand splayed against her back.

The small gesture was nearly enough to send her into a fit of sobs. Hopelessness manifested itself in the form of a deep ache in her chest. An ache she felt certain would be lessened if only Dylan would hold her.

"What's wrong?" he asked. "Did you find another tape?"

"No," she answered, her voice choked.

"I would do anything to help you," he said, gently pulling her head against his chest. It felt so good, so right. She needed this, needed his strength, if she was going to make it through this without losing her mind. Closing her eyes,

Shelby reminded herself that Chad was safe, then surrendered to the promise of comfort she felt in his touch.

Cradling her in one arm, Dylan used his free hand to stroke the hair away from her face. She greedily drank in the scent of his cologne as she cautiously allowed her fingers to rest against his thigh. His jeans were well-worn and smooth, a startling contrast to the very defined muscle she could feel beneath her hand. She remained perfectly still, comforted by his scent, his touch, his nearness. Strange that she could only find such solace in his arms.

"You've got to hang in there," Dylan told her. "We'll find him."

"I hope so," she breathed against his solid form. "I can't close my eyes without seeing his face. Not having Chad is killing me. If it weren't for the tapes, I don't think I could handle it. When I think of what might be—"

"Don't," he murmured. He captured her face in his hands, his callused thumbs wiping away the last vestiges of her tears. His gray-blue eyes met and held hers. His jaw was set, his expression serious. "You can't fall apart, Shelby. You have to stay strong."

"I don't feel very strong," she admitted. "I'm teetering on the edge here. I try not to think about what's happening to him, but—"

"Hush," he said. "He's fine. You have to hold on to that thought. We haven't gotten anything that would indicate Chad has been harmed in any way."

Using his hands, he tilted her head back. His face was a mere fraction of an inch from hers. She could feel the ragged expulsion of his breath. Instinctively her palms flattened against his chest. The thick mat of dark hair served as a cushion for her touch. Still, beneath the softness, she could easily feel the hard outline of muscle.

"I'm here for you," he said in a near whisper.

Her lashes fluttered as his words washed over her upturned face. She'd been expecting it, perhaps even wishing for it. Dylan's lips tentatively brushed hers. So feather-light was the kiss that she wasn't even certain it could qualify as such. His movements were careful, measured. His thumbs stroked the hollows of her cheeks.

Shelby banished all thought from her mind. She wanted this, almost desperately. The sensation of his hands and his lips made her feel alive. The ache in her chest was changing, evolving. The pain and hopelessness were being overtaken by some new emotions. She became acutely aware of every aspect of him. The pressure of his thigh where it touched hers. The sound of his uneven breathing. The magical sensation of his mouth on hers.

When he lifted his head, Shelby grabbed handfuls of his shirt. "Don't," she whispered, urging him back to her.

His resistance was both surprising and short-lived. It was almost totally forgotten when he dipped his head again. His lips did little more than brush against hers. His hands left her face and wound around her small body. Dylan crushed her against him. She could actually feel the pounding of his heart beneath her hands.

What had begun so innocently, quickly turned into something intense and consuming. His tongue moistened her slightly parted lips. The kiss became demanding, and she was a very willing partaker. She managed to work her hands across his chest, until she felt the outline of his erect nipples beneath her palms. He responded by running his hands all over her back and nibbling her lower lip. It was a purely erotic action, one that inspired great need and desire in Shelby.

A small moan escaped her lips as she kneaded the muscles of his chest. He tasted vaguely of coffee, and he continued to work magic with his mouth. Shelby felt the kiss in the pit of her stomach. What had started as a pleasant warmth had grown into a full-fledged heat emanating from her very core, fueled by the sensation of his fingers snaking up her back, entwining in her hair, and guiding her head back at a severe angle. Passion flared as he hungrily devoured first her mouth, then the tender flesh at the base of her throat. His mouth was hot, the stubble of his beard slightly abrasive. And she felt it all. She was aware of everything—the outline of his body, the almost arrogant expectation in his kiss. Dylan was a skilled and talented lover. Shelby was a compliant yet demanding partner.

Jay was knocking on the door.

Reluctantly Dylan lifted his head, his eyes fixed on her mouth. He looked at her with such intensity that Shelby found it almost as carnal as his kisses. She should have uttered some reprimand, or possibly apologized for allowing things to get so heavy. She should have, but she couldn't. She wasn't going to lie to Dylan—not again.

"One second," he called through the closed door. He placed one more kiss against her partially opened mouth. Reluctantly he rose, savoring the taste of her lingering on his lips. She hadn't screamed recriminations—or, worse yet, voiced regrets.

Ignoring Jay's questioning once-over, Dylan moved to allow his boss into the room. He turned to find Shelby seated on the bed, looking right at him.

Her eyes were still hooded by her heavy lids. Her lips were slightly red from the imprint of his kiss. He looked again for some negative sign. There was none. In fact, he detected just the trace of a smile at the corners of her mouth.

"I thought we should start by watching this," Jay was saying.

"I suppose it's too much to hope that the lab guys got anything off the cassette?" Dylan asked.

"No such luck," Jay answered.

"Is Chad on the tape?" Shelby asked as Jay bent forward to insert the tape.

"Yep. And he looks like he's in great shape."

Dylan watched as the light in her eyes flickered, then was extinguished, like the flame from a faltering candle. Her small body stiffened as she scooted to the edge of the bed. Dylan wanted desperately to go to her, to take her back into his arms. To protect her from Nichols and his cohorts.

"We've drawn a blank on the location," Jay admitted as he pressed the play button. "We know it's somewhere on one of the islands."

"The barrier islands?" Shelby's voice was tight and even when she formed the question.

"Looks that way. At least that's what I got from the lab boys. Something about the vegetation in the shot."

The blue screen gave way to the image of the smiling baby, which Dylan would have recognized anywhere. Chad was in the same stroller they'd seen in the earlier tape.

He heard Shelby's sharp intake of breath when the camera zoomed in on the child. The baby was pounding a set of keys against the stroller. In the background, he could make out some sort of construction site. Stacks of lumber surrounded elaborate scaffolding.

The baby began to babble—a stream of nonsensical consonants punctuated with a continual stream of drool. The camera pulled back until the frame included the right foot of a person. More specifically, a woman.

"Are we assuming it's the same person?" Dylan asked.

"No reason not to," Jay answered.

There was the obligatory placement of the newspaper in the frame with the baby. This time the woman balanced the paper against the baby's feet. The camera caught the date, and then the tape ended.

"Not much help," Jay admitted apologetically.

"Yes, it is," Shelby said. "I know exactly where that was taken."

CHAPTER FIFTEEN

"You know where it is?" Dylan asked, excitedly grabbing her shoulders.

"It's the Vanderhorst mansion on Kiawah Island."

"Kiawah?" Jay asked.

Dylan smiled down at her, his eyes hopeful. Shelby noted that the senior agent's expression was guarded. She suspected his hesitation was a direct result of the lack of success they'd had thus far. Secretly she thought it was kind of Jay to be so concerned. Perhaps he, too, had recognized the aging building and had said nothing to spare her yet another heartbreak. Or maybe they'd just taped her call to Ned.

"I'll head out there," Dylan announced.

"Why don't you go with him, Shelby?" Jay suggested.

Dylan turned away from her, but not before she saw a frown overtake his chiseled lips.

"I don't think that's necessary," she heard Dylan tell Jay.

Jay simply shrugged. "I do."

"Jay," Dylan began, his hands balled into loose fists at his sides, "there's no point in sending her on what could turn out to be another wild-goose chase."

Shelby felt the first twinges of annoyance. She didn't like being discussed as if she were invisible. "I'd like to go."

Dylan spun around, and his eyes bored into hers. "Do you really think you can handle another disappointment?"

"What makes you so sure this will be a disappointment?"

"I'm not saying it will be. Not definitely," he said. Falling down on one knee, he knelt in front of her, gathering her small hands in his much larger ones. "I know how all this is affecting you."

She cut in. "Do you? I don't think you can even imagine the anguish I feel. Chad is my whole world."

"I understand that," Dylan said soothingly. "That's why I'm not so sure it's a good idea for you to come along. Why not let me check it out first?"

"Because he's my son. Because I want to be there when he's found—to reassure him. But mostly because I can't stand sitting around here, just waiting."

Long after Dylan and Jay had left her alone, Shelby began to reassess her motivations. She believed the argument she had given Dylan, but she was beginning to acknowledge that there might be more to it. "I'm losing my mind," she grumbled as she reached over and allowed her hand to slap the pillow next to her. Just being with Dylan was comforting. When he held her, she actually believed that everything would be all right. That Chad would be returned safe and sound.

The room still cradled the faint scent of Dylan's cologne. She could close her eyes and his image was there, gorgeous and dangerous. "I should be doing everything possible to shut him out of my life," she murmured, her whispered voice full of self-loathing.

It was true. As easy as it was to lean on him now, how easy would it be to say goodbye—again? Turning on her side, Shelby hugged the pillow to her breast and tried to formulate a plausible plan. Nothing seemed to work. Not one of the scenarios she considered was pleasant. Her mind kept going backward in time. Replaying that ugly scene when she'd told him it was over. The image of his seething face was one she would carry for all time. It had been a year and a half, and still she could vividly see the fury behind the stiff set of his jaw. She could still feel the pressure on her arms from where he'd bruisingly grabbed her and kissed her farewell in that hurtful, derisive fashion. The thought of having to experience all that again sent her heart plummeting in her feet. But she had no choice.

"WHAT'S THE PLAN?" she asked as Dylan threw the Blazer in gear.

He laughed softly and said, "We don't have one. We're checking out the possibilities, not conducting a raid."

"I know that," she said, defensively. "I was just asking."

They drove several miles in silence. Shelby was aware of everything. The way his large body filled the small confines of the passenger compartment; the way his thumb kept time with the soft rock tune on the radio; the way the heavy air spilling through the partially open window lifted his black hair off his collar. She wiggled against the soft upholstery, trying to figure out just what had gotten into her.

The low country varied little, mile after mile. Tall sea grasses lined marshy swamps as the various rivers surrounding Charleston converged on the Atlantic. Kiawah Island, she knew from her days selling pricey antiquities, was a posh resort south of the city. The barrier island was essentially divided in half. One portion of the land was devoted to the tourist trade—shops, restaurants, golf courses and tennis courts. The remainder of the island sported some of the largest, most expensive and elegant private properties in the area. Her first trip to Kiawah had been something of a shock. What she originally mistook for a conference center had turned out to be an individual home, all 7,500 square feet of it—facing the gentle surf of the Atlantic.

"Why are we going to the inn?" Shelby asked. "The Vanderhorst mansion is in the property owners' section."

"I know that," Dylan answered as he pulled into a parking spot.

"But you told Jay you were going to touch base with island security."

Dylan turned and lifted his mirrored glasses from his eyes. "I'm taking a different approach."

"Why?"

Clipping the glasses to the front of his polo shirt, Dylan leaned closer. "I'm taking a new tack."

"Which is?"

"Spontaneous investigation." Reaching out with one square-tipped finger, he lightly tapped the end of her nose. "It's a trick I learned in agent school."

He moved from the car in fluid movements. Shelby followed closely on his heels, her eyes fixed on the broad expanse of his shoulders. She made the mistake of lowering her eyes. His jeans hugged his slender hips, outlining his masculine curves. She swallowed, hard.

Reaching back, Dylan clasped her hand in his. His skin was warm, his grip firm. In an attempt to keep her mind focused, Shelby began to catalog the various flowers lining the walkway. A small twinge of emotion tugged at her heart. Chad was just developing a fascination with flowers.

The entrance to the Kiawah Inn was a skeleton of weathered wood framing, decorated with massive hanging baskets of spring flowers. The sweet floral fragrance was carried on the warm ocean breezes wafting through the walkway.

Dylan eased her close to the banister to allow a couple to pass. The pair walked with that bouncy, happy step often reserved for vacationers. Shelby envied them.

As they passed the lobby, the air suddenly filled with the inviting smells coming off the poolside grill. The distant hum of a lawn mower was interrupted by an occasional squeal of pure delight coming from the beach.

"We'll start here," Dylan announced when they came upon a bicycle-rental stand at the end of the ribbon of fine-grained sand.

"Start what?"

"I thought we might want to go in the back door."

Dylan reached into the front pocket of his jeans and peeled several bills off to give to the young attendant. They were directed to a pair of neon-orange bikes at the end of the rack.

"I'm assuming you can ride a bike?"

"I could when I was seven," she muttered under her breath. She looked from the bike to her clothes and frowned. She had abandoned her jeans in favor of a gauzy sundress. The uneven handkerchief hem threatened to be a problem.

"Here," Dylan said, reaching for the bottom of the dress.

"What on earth?" she cried as he folded the fabric and tucked the ends into the belt at her waist. His fingers worked deftly, arranging the garment until it was immodestly short, resting very near the top of her thighs. Shelby remained perfectly still. It was her only choice, since she was firm in her resolve not to react to the feel of his hands brushing the skin of her bared legs.

His head came up, and he wore a decidedly satisfied smile. "That should keep it out of your way."

"And I'll be giving free shots to everyone I pass." Shelby tugged and wriggled until the hemline dropped a couple of inches.

"Ready?" he asked.

"Yes," she answered as she threw one leg over the bike. "Would you mind telling me what I'm ready for?"

"A leisurely ride along the beach."

"Dylan!" she breathed. "We're supposed to be looking for my son. I don't think this is a particularly good time for one of your silly little—"

His hard stare stilled the words in her throat. She sensed his anger long before he lifted his glasses and she saw the harsh glint in his eyes.

"This isn't a silly anything." He forced the words out between nearly gritted teeth. "If you don't like the way I'm handling this, feel free to go on home. I didn't ask you to come along in the first place."

She flinched at the unexpected venom. Not knowing the cause of his uncharacteristic attack, she simply stared at him through wide, confused eyes.

"I'm sorry," he said, after several deep breaths. "All I can say is that I'm on edge about all of this."

"You think something's gone wrong?" she asked, grabbing his forearm.

"No, no. Nothing like that. I'm just bugged."

"By what?" she queried, studying the deep, telling lines around his eyes.

"All of this," he answered disgustedly.

"*Please,* be more specific."

Dylan took his foot off the pedal and stood straddling the bike. Placing his glasses on the bridge of his slightly crooked nose, he raked his hand through his windblown hair. "Something just isn't right," he said.

"Dylan?"

"Like I said before. this guy always seems to be a half step ahead of us." He slapped the handlebars in apparent frustration. "It's like Nichols has a pipeline into my head."

"Dylan," she began, in a purposefully soft voice, "I know you want to believe it's Ned. But he's not even in the country. And he has no reason to want to hurt my baby."

"His baby, too," Dylan said gruffly.

"And what did you mean about your head?"

His shoulders rose and fell in a quick shrug. "I'm starting to feel manipulated."

God! she thought as panic swelled in her chest. *He's finally put it all together!*

"I never meant for you to—"

"Not by you." He patted the back of her hand, where it rested against his arm. "I know you haven't exactly welcomed me on this investigation. It's this perp. I feel like he's pulling my strings."

"Is the sun getting to you?" she asked.

"I'm serious," he insisted, the corners of his mouth curving downward to form the beginnings of a frown. "This is the weirdest case I've every encountered. There's something here I'm missing."

"I think you're allowing your frustrations to cloud your perspective," Shelby said. *Was it possible? Could he some-*

how sense his close connection to the baby? How long would it be before he uncovered her deceptions?

"It's more than that," he insisted with a shake of his head. "First the medallion, then a tape shows up at my apartment. Let's not forget the video left in the car yesterday. I mean—" he paused and ran his fingers pensively across the faint stubble on his chin "—how in the hell did this guy know we'd be downtown? Let alone that he'd have enough time to slip into your car without leaving so much as a loose fiber behind?"

Shelby's relief regarding the issue of her son's parentage was short-lived. Instantly her mind replayed the phone call she'd gotten in the bath shop. He must have followed them into Charleston. After renewing the ransom demand, the kidnapper must have seen them go down Market Street. But she couldn't say anything to Dylan, for to do so would only jeopardize her last hope of remaining in the kidnapper's good graces. She understood how he could have delivered the tape to her parked car in the city. Dylan's medallion, and the other things, weren't so easily explained.

"Shelby?"

She came back to the present with a jolt.

"I'm sorry," he said.

"About what?"

"Obviously, I upset you."

"I'm fine," she lied. "Where to?"

"We'll ride down the beach and then cut over to the mansion."

"Forgive me," she said as she balanced herself on the slow-moving bicycle, "but why can't we just drive up and check it out?"

"You saw all the construction debris?" She nodded. "I think we might have more success if we used the subtle approach."

"The subtle approach to what?"

"Just trust me," he said as his powerful thighs pumped

effortlessly carrying him over the packed sand. "And no matter what happens, follow my lead."

The beach was nearly deserted. Wispy white clouds floated overhead as they rode side by side at the edge of the rolling surf. The sand was flat near the water, and the cool spray coming off the surf kept her from feeling the exertion of keeping up with his pace.

"Doing okay?" he said above the call of a gull.

"For now," she told him. "My legs will probably be screaming at me later."

"What? You don't spend hours in some gym, praying to the god of fitness?"

She laughed easily. "I think the last time I broke a sweat was when Chad was born."

Steering with one hand, Dylan turned and stole a quick glance in her direction. "Was it tough?"

"What?"

"Having him? My sister told me it was like having her lower lip pulled over her skull."

"Just about," Shelby said through her laughter. "I didn't know you had a sister."

"Three."

"Three sisters?"

"And two brothers."

Shelby gaped at him. "Six children? Your mother deserves a medal."

"No argument from me," he said as he slowed his bike. "We didn't give her a moment of peace. Let's take a break."

Following his lead, Shelby brought her bike to a stop, pulled the kickstand, and parked it in the sand next to his. Her legs didn't adjust immediately to the flat ground. Shading her eyes with her hand, she looked back at the inn. "I didn't realize," she gushed, feeling suddenly tired.

"We've come about five miles. I thought you might need a breather."

"I'll probably need physical therapy," she stated as she fell into the sand next to him.

Dylan leaned back, resting his weight on his bent forearms. With his legs crossed at the ankles, he appeared totally relaxed.

"Want me to tell you about my family?" he asked.

"Why?"

He didn't look at her, and she couldn't see anything but her own reflection in those damned glasses.

"You said that we didn't know anything about each other. I figured my family might be a good place to start." He interpreted her silence as acquiescence. "I grew up in a small town in New York—in the Catskills."

"Did you have the largest family in town?"

"Hardly." She could hear the smile in his voice. "Loganville is a staunchly Catholic town. Everyone was fruitful and multiplied."

"Did you have block parties and forts and a carnival that came to town every summer?"

"You bet," he said as his finger began to trace a geometric pattern in the small strip of sand separating them. "We had PTA and youth groups, bake sales and Little League."

"Sounds like a nice place."

"It is."

"Do you ever go back?" she asked.

"Every chance I get. Of course, Thanksgiving is mandatory. My mother has promised to put a curse on any of her children who fail to show up for her favorite holiday."

"Thanksgiving? Why then?"

"I think it has something to do with control. Christmas and Easter were really hard on my folks. Since both sets of grandparents also lived in Loganville, the big holidays were nothing but marathons that began with early mass and ended with one of us kids barfing from eating too many sweets. Thanksgiving was her day."

"I can't imagine getting six kids organized to do anything. I often have trouble managing Chad, and he's a pretty adaptable little guy.''

"I can imagine.'' His expression grew solemn before he asked, "Why did you do it, Shelby? I mean, you didn't have to go through with it.''

"I already told you. Chad was a surprise, but I never even once considered terminating my pregnancy.''

"What do you plan to tell him?''

"About what?''

"You know.'' Dylan paused and sucked in a great lungful of the fresh sea air. "About his father.''

"I'll explain to him that I had the right child with the wrong man.''

"Think he'll buy it?''

Shelby felt herself stiffen under his direct scrutiny. "I don't know. I guess I'll cross that bridge when I get there.'' Sitting up, she hugged her legs with her arms. "Tell me more about your family.''

"Typical big family.''

"Meaning?''

"We fought constantly amongst ourselves, but heaven help the outsider that dared lay a finger on any of us. Especially the girls.''

"Why the girls?''

"You kidding?'' he asked as he joined her by drawing his long legs to his chest. "Would you have wanted three older brothers screening your dates?''

"Probably,'' she admitted in a soft voice.

"No brothers?''

She shook her head.

"Sisters?''

"Nope.''

"Your folks only wanted one child?''

"No, but my father never resented me for it.'' She gathered her hair at the nape of her neck to prevent it blowing on her face.

"Come again?'' Dylan said.

"Chadwick Hunnicutt married my mother when I was two. He adopted me shortly after they got married."

"What about your real father?"

"He was my real father," Shelby told him stiffly.

"I didn't say that right," Dylan said apologetically. "I just meant, do you have any contact with your birth father?"

Shelby swallowed. How had she allowed the conversation to turn to this most unpleasant subject—and with him, of all people? "Not really. I don't really know him."

"Do you speak?"

"Occasionally," she said carefully. "It's very complicated, and I don't really like discussing it."

"How does he feel about Chad?"

"He's about as good at being a grandfather as he was at being a father."

"I can't imagine not having my family," Dylan said, draping his arm lazily over her shoulder. "Thanks to them, I have a whole bunch of great memories."

"Such as?" she asked, hoping a turn in the direction of the conversation might help her think of something other than the feel of his skin touching hers.

"There was the time we wrecked the station wagon."

"That's a great memory?" she asked.

"We rolled the family station wagon coming down one of the mountains. No one was hurt. We rolled it back on its wheels, and then swore to my pop that we didn't have a clue how the car got all banged up."

"Did he buy it?"

"Hell, no!" he recalled, with genuine fondness. "It took us the better part of two years to pay for the damage out of our allowances."

"What does your father do?"

"He's a butcher."

"Then what made you become a cop?"

"I guess it was all those nights I dusted my little sisters for prints when they came home from their dates."

"Cute," Shelby said, swatting him.

"I'm not kidding. My sisters are gorgeous."

"So you thought they were easy?"

"No, but I knew how persuasive young men could be after a few hours in the back of a Chevy."

"From personal experience?"

"I preferred to think of it as research," he said with a devilish grin. "My contribution to the family."

"What a guy," she said under her breath.

"I am a nice guy, Shelby. You just didn't stick around long enough to find out."

"Dylan," she groaned, "let's not beat this dead horse, okay?"

"For now," he said as he hoisted his large frame off the cool sand.

Extending his hand, he helped her to feet. He held her hand a fraction longer than necessary. Shelby was still struggling with her conscience. For the first time, she questioned her decision, thanks in large part to the things he'd said. *Why didn't he tell me of his family before? If he had, would I still have walked away?*

True to his prediction, they pedaled for another five or so miles before they came upon a smooth wooden boardwalk that traversed the protected dunes. After they abandoned the bikes, near the path, Dylan took her hand as he got his bearings. He liked the feel of her hand in his. Her skin was so perfectly soft, her hand so small and fragile. Even her feet were tiny, he noted as they walked side by side. The toenails peeking out of her leather sandals were painted pale pink, yet another tribute to the incredible femininity that had attracted him to Shelby that first night.

Only this was harder. He felt a weighty responsibility to find her son. If he didn't—or, God forbid, if it ended badly—he didn't think she would survive.

"What *exactly* are we doing?"

"We're going to the construction site," he said as they passed yet another palatial home.

"I still don't see why we didn't just drive on up and ask for their help."

"You will," he said, then mentally added, *I hope*.

The mansion was off what was considered the main road in the residential section of the island. Kiawah was a far cry from his humble beginnings. These were stately, individually designed buildings with landscaped lawns and perfectly pruned live oaks. He guessed even the Spanish moss needed permission to hang from the trees. The royal palms and evergreens on the road's median strip were identical heights, and evenly spaced. Even the wildflowers had an air of decorum.

Crossing the perfectly surfaced road, they came upon a dirt road covered in a thin layer of pine straw. The relatively undisturbed forest was thick with the smell of soldered metal and sawdust. Dylan felt at home with the scent of manual labor. It eased the knot of tension between his shoulder blades.

Sidestepping a makeshift barricade, he pulled Shelby behind him, down what had obviously once been a driveway. It was guarded on either side by overgrown oak trees. Portions of the brick-and-wood home were visible about fifty yards ahead of them. Workmen buzzed from place to place as they tended to the various responsibilities of renovating the dilapidated landmark.

"Tory would be like a kid in a candy shop here," she said.

"Why?"

"This place dates back to before the Civil War. It's the kind of preservation and restoration project she's been studying for years. Since these kinds of jobs are few and far between, she's after Rose and I to let her excavate and renovate the outbuildings at the Tattoo."

"She's definitely still in school, then?"

"Of course," she answered. "Rose and I try to help her whenever we can."

"Hey, you! Can't you read?"

The man coming toward them wore a hard hat and a frown. Dylan stopped short, and gave Shelby's hand a squeeze. "Go along with whatever I say."

"What do you mean?"

"This area ain't safe," the worker announced as he tugged up the tool belt surrounding his thick waist. "It ain't open to tourists."

Dylan extended his hand and said, "I appreciate that, Mr.... er..."

"Bo Halloday."

"Mr. Halloday," Dylan continued, "we don't want to disturb your work. My wife and I were just curious about something, and hoping you, or one of your men, might be able to help us."

Wife? she gulped.

"Help you what?" The man eyed him seriously. His weathered, leathery skin bunched at the corners of his mistrustful eyes.

"You see," he began, slipping his free hand into his breast pocket. "We think our nanny has been bringing Chad over here. We know how dangerous this area is, and we'll want to discourage her from placing him in any danger."

Nanny?

Halloday gripped the photo between dirty, honest fingers. "Cute kid."

"Have you seen him in his stroller? Perhaps you had to run them off in the past couple of days?"

Halloday yelled over his shoulder. A young man, lanky and shirtless, sprinted over to them. His T-shirt, which had been wrapped around his head, was grimy and damp. The stench of sweat was almost overwhelming.

"Tommy Ray? Is this the kid what was here with that lady yesterday?"

The boy took the picture and then bobbed his head. "I believe so," he said. "Nice boy. The man and the lady was real nice, too. Even when I had to tell them to move on."

"Man?" Dylan heard Shelby gasp.

"A tall guy, wearing a hat and sunglasses."

"What about the woman?" Dylan asked.

"Nice smile," the two men said in unison. "And she sure did dote on that baby," added Tommy.

Dylan gave Shelby's hand another squeeze, surprised at the amount of relief he felt on hearing that Chad was being well cared for. "Did you see them leave?"

"Watched until they got into their car."

"What kind of car?"

"American," the younger man said. "I'm pretty sure it was a black Taurus."

Dylan thanked them before tugging Shelby back in the direction of the bikes.

"Where are we going now?" she asked. "Do you think we'll be able to find them by just knowing the kind of car? I hope he was right. I hope this woman is taking decent care of him. I hate to think of my baby in the arms—"

He pulled her against him, cradling her excitement-flushed face in his hands. "Calm down," he told her. "I don't know if we'll be able to find them, but we've got a couple of leads. I think you ought to go back to town while I see if I can't get something more substantial."

"No," she said as her hands came up to close over his. "I don't want to go home, Dylan. I can't stand just sitting around and waiting. I need to keep busy."

He closed his eyes to wrestle with his misgivings. An intelligent man would send her packing. A smart agent would recognize the potential danger of having a private citizen involved in his investigation.

"I don't want you to go, either."

CHAPTER SIXTEEN

"LET'S HEAD BACK to the inn," Dylan suggested as they walked hand in hand toward the beach.

"What was all that stuff about a wife and nanny?" she asked.

She felt him shrug his shoulders. "Just playing it safe."

"Is this the same man who had nothing nice to say about the institution of marriage?"

"When did I ever comment on marriage?" he asked, stopping and tugging on her hand until she peered up into her own reflection in his glasses.

"You told me you'd been engaged. I believe your exact words were 'one arrest, no conviction.'"

His mouth curved into a sheepish half smile. "It was just an analogy, Shelby."

"But you made your point," she told him in a soft voice, her eyes dropping to the open V of his shirt. Dark curls peeked from the edges, set against tanned skin.

"I wasn't trying to make a point."

She could hear the frown in his voice, and his grip on her hand tightened fractionally. Tension enveloped her, and she refused to look up.

"If I remember correctly," he began, his hand stroking the faint stubble on his chin, "we'd been out maybe three or four times when I made that crack."

"It's not important," she insisted, forcing cheer into her tone. Turning, she pulled her hand free of his and began to walk. "I don't know how we got on this inane subject, anyway."

"I believe in marriage," Dylan said, very close to her ear. "When I made that comment, I was just trying to be cute."

"Fine," she said on a breath. "Let's drop it."

"Does this have anything to do with why you dumped me?"

"Dylan," she groaned. "I don't want to talk about it. It's ancient history."

"I suppose," he said as his hand snaked back to hers.

The sound of the surf acted as a tonic to her frazzled nerves. Why, she wondered, did walking with him, holding his hand, feel so right?

Her legs screamed in silent protest when she mounted the bike. Her spirits began to plummet. "What are we going to do now?" she asked as she pulled her bike next to his.

Dylan's legs were working at less than half the rate of her own. Leaning back on the seat, he guided his bike with only one hand through the damp sand at the water's edge.

"I'm thinking on it."

"Shouldn't we be scouring the island for a black Taurus?"

"Maybe."

"Well, I don't think we'll get much accomplished riding down the beach."

"Maybe."

Reaching out, Shelby swatted his sleeve before resuming her death grip on the handlebars. "Are you being intentionally obtuse?"

His chuckle was deep and throaty. The sound stroked her from the top of her head down to her toes.

"Obtuse?" he repeated. "Hardly. I'm simply devising a plan. The federal government prefers it that way. It's one of the first things they teach you in agent school."

"I'm just impatient, Dylan. I want my son back."

"I know you do," he said, touching the skin on her arm just above the elbow. "I'll find him."

The sincerity behind his words threatening to inspire tears, Shelby swallowed and lowered her eyes.

"Watch out!" Dylan yelled.

She looked up in time to see the blurred colors of a kite as it wrapped around her face. The next several seconds involved large quantities of sand and water, and a hard collision with Dylan's even harder body. They were a tangled mass of legs, spokes and wet paper.

She came up coughing, trying to expel some of the salty water from her lungs.

"You wrecked it!"

Blinking against the stinging water, Shelby braced herself upright as waves washed over her sodden form. The face of a very angry young boy came in to focus. "Wh-what?"

"You wrecked my kite," he yelled.

Before she could respond to the charge, Dylan reached around her waist and hoisted her from the surf. Her dress hung heavily from her shoulders, and she could feel her hair plastered to her cheeks.

"You okay?" Dylan asked.

"No," she groaned as she pulled the soaked fabric away from her legs. "I'm drenched and I have sand in my mouth."

"And you wrecked my kite."

"Sorry about that, pal," Dylan told the child.

Just then, a harried-looking woman with several ounces of white sunscreen lathered on her nose ran over to them.

"I'm so sorry," she began, her hand gripping the child's upper arm. "Are you two all right?"

Dylan answered for them both. "No harm done."

"I told you to keep the kite up near the dunes," the mother said to her son.

"It's okay," Dylan insisted.

The woman offered a weak, apologetic smile as she tugged the little boy up the beach.

"This is awful," Shelby groaned. But as she looked up

through her wet, clumped lashes, her annoyance abruptly melted.

"What?" Dylan asked.

Getting up on tiptoe, she extracted the bulbous strand of seaweed from the earpiece of his sunglasses with two fingers. She could feel the warmth emanating from his large body.

His eyes met and held hers. "Thanks."

The space between them filled with an electric current of awareness. His wet shirt clung to the etched definition of muscle, drawing her eyes like a magnet, and the tumble had caused it to work free of his jeans, exposing several inches of his firm, taut skin.

"Now what?" she asked, in a rather high-pitched voice.

"I think a pit stop is in order," he told her with a grin. "We'll see what we can do back at the inn."

He was smiling as he stood at the registration desk, his charge card in his hand. Shelby lingered near the doorway, half hidden by a large potted plant. After accepting a key from the clerk, he collected Shelby and led her to the elevator. They got more than just a few looks from passing vacationers.

"What good will a shower do?" she asked as he slipped the key into the lock. "I'll never get the sand out of my clothes."

"I'll handle it," Dylan insisted as he shoved open the door and stood aside. When she passed beneath his outstretched hand, he caught the faint scent of the ocean in her hair. He took a deep breath and reminded himself that he was here to do a job.

He left her and went across to the straw market. Discovering a trendy clothing shop, he selected some items for them and prayed his credit card could withstand the outrageous total. With the package tucked neatly beneath his arm, he headed back toward the inn. He didn't go directly to the room. Instead, he found the pay phone, dug into the soggy contents of his pocket and slipped a coin into the slot.

"Williams."

"Jay. Dylan," he began, cradling the phone between his shoulder and ear.

"Find anything?"

"Maybe. We might have a lead on the car."

"Really?"

"Didn't one of the neighbors say he'd seen a black car on the night Chad was taken?"

There was a brief pause, and Dylan could hear the sounds of papers shuffling before Jay said, "Yep. But he wasn't able to ID the make or model."

Dylan recounted their trip to the mansion, omitting the mishap at the end. "We're at the Kiawah Inn," he said, adding the room number.

"You two are together?"

Dylan felt his spine stiffen at the censure he heard in his boss's tone. "Just a home base while we look for the car."

"Why don't I send a car for Shelby? She's—"

"She won't budge," Dylan said, cutting in. "As long as there's a snowball's chance that we might find her son, she won't go anywhere."

"Are you sure it's Shelby and not you?"

Dylan drew his brows together and wondered why that remark should inspire such anger in him. "Meaning?"

"Look, Dylan," Jay began, "I know you had a thing for her last—"

"It's history," he said sternly.

"Yours or hers?"

An answer sprang to his lips—*hers*. But he kept it to himself. A silence ensued, a rather awkward one.

Jay relented. "I'll contact the management for the island and see if I can get any information on the car. I'll call you if I can find any residents who drive a black Taurus."

"Thanks, Jay."

"Speaking of calls—there have been three hang-ups here at her place. It's probably the kidnapper."

"Probably," Dylan agreed, a strange feeling settling in

his gut. Something disturbing, yet he was unable to give it a name or even guess at its origins. "He's slipping."

"How so?" Jay countered.

"He's usually pretty adept at making contact with Shelby, no matter where she is."

"You're right about that," Jay lamented. "It's like this guy has radar where she's concerned."

Anger surged through Dylan. He'd find this guy, and when he did, he'd make sure he paid. He suggested as much to Jay.

"Careful, Tanner," Jay cautioned. "I wouldn't want to see you lose your objectivity."

I lost it a year and a half ago, he thought. "I'm objective enough. I'll keep you posted."

When he returned to the room, he heard the unmistakable sound of the shower running. Depositing the package on the end of the king-size bed that dominated the room, Dylan battled to keep his thoughts on track. Unfortunately, his mind seemed intent on traveling beyond the closed door. The image of Shelby standing beneath the spray of water inspired any number of fantasies.

"Stupid," he mumbled as he separated the clothing into two piles. Letting out a breath, he frowned, remembering their brief conversation on the beach. When he told her about his short engagement, he hadn't meant her to take it as an indictment of marriage. He could only wonder how many other comments he'd made that she might have misconstrued. Could their breakup have been avoided by a simple conversation? That possibility darkened his mood.

"Why the scowl?"

His head whipped around at the sound of her voice. She gripped the top edges of the terry-cloth towel in white-knuckled fingers. Her dark hair was combed back, and her oval face held the rosy blush of the sun and wind. The scent of flowers filled the room, a fresh, clean scent.

"Scowl?" he repeated, forcing a smile to his lips. "I guess I was just deep in thought."

He watched as her features grew wide, frightened. "There haven't been any new developments, have there?"

He shook his head. The action caused a small cascade of sand to flutter to the floor. "Nothing new."

She visibly relaxed, her bowlike mouth forming a relieved smile. "Thank goodness."

He allowed his eyes to fall to the hem of the towel, where it grazed her legs at midthigh. She had great legs, firm but not muscular, perfectly delicate.

"Dylan?"

"Huh?" he managed over the lump in his throat.

"Clothes?"

"Right," he said as he reached behind him and grabbed one of the stacks. He thrust them in her direction, his eyes fixed on her tenuous hold on the towel.

"Thanks," she mumbled as she grabbed the items and held them against her. She slipped back behind the door, leaving him alone with his vivid imagination.

He didn't dare sit—not when he had a good portion of the beach in his clothes. It was just as well. The act of pacing allowed him a physical action to counter his emotional purgatory. Opening the sliding glass door, Dylan stepped onto the room's small balcony. His hands wrapped around the cool metal railing as he sucked in deep breaths and took in the panoramic view of the ocean. The sun was to his back, casting a long orange shadow on the high tide. He needed to get a grip, and fast. He just couldn't seem to get past this. He had been so sure that he was over Shelby, that she was just a painful memory.

"It's all yours."

He turned and felt his breath catch in his throat. Shelby looked like an angel, a vision in white. The dress he'd selected for her was simple. The clerk had called it a slip dress and insisted that it was appropriate. Now he knew why. Thin straps held the equally thin material against her body, leaving very little to his already overworked imagination. The stark contrast of the white silk against her darkly exotic coloring caused a predictable reaction in his body. Dylan very nearly ran into the bathroom, chased by his guilty conscience.

He stood under a punishing spray of cold water, berating himself for allowing his primal thoughts to get the better of him. He decided to concentrate on the case. He was still bugged by the inconsistencies. The idea that he was missing something crucial gnawed at him almost as much as the memory of Shelby in that dress.

Clearing a circle in the condensation on the mirror, Dylan smiled at the assortment of toiletries in a basket on the vanity. Of course, for what this place charged for a room, he felt it was almost fitting that the inn provided all the comforts of home. After shaving, he ran a comb through his hair and pulled on the khaki shorts he'd bought and shrugged into the shirt. Spotting a plastic laundry bag in the corner, he added his sandy offerings and pulled the drawstring.

"I feel much better," he announced as he strode from the bathroom.

She was on the balcony, her ebony hair floating off her shoulders in the breeze. She smiled when she spotted him. He found the action disconcerting.

"You look better," she teased.

"I thought women liked gritty, unkempt men."

"This woman doesn't."

He moved closer, until mere inches separated them. She rose slowly, her head tilted up toward him. Her eyes were wide, and so very blue.

"Now what?" she asked softly.

"Jay's checking on the car. He'll call when he has something. And he said they still haven't been able to trace the insignia on the ring."

Her lashes fluttered against her cheeks before she peered up at him. "That wasn't what I was talking about."

Dylan held his breath and went still.

"I..." she began softly. Her small hands moved to his chest, the palms flattening against him.

His body shivered involuntarily at her touch. He was afraid to move, afraid he might somehow break the spell.

"Tell me what you want, Shelby."

He saw the raw emotions in her eyes, everything from fear to desire. He prayed desire would win out.

"You," she said on a whisper. "I want you, Dylan. I know this is crazy, but I need to be close to you. I'm not quite as scared when you hold me."

He framed her face with his large, warm hands. He felt her shiver as the tips of his thumbs grazed her lips.

He kissed the corners of her mouth as his hands glided down her spine to her hips. When her arms twined around his neck, he lifted his head and looked into her eyes.

"Are you sure?" he asked.

"Very."

Urgency surged through him, setting fire to his blood. Scooping her up in his arms, he pulled her against his chest and carried her to the bed. He set her down amid the assortment of pillows. He settled next to her, arranging her hair to grant him access to the sweet skin of her throat. He kissed, nibbled and tasted. She responded by kneading the muscles at his shoulders and twisting her small body against his. Her actions turned his stomach to liquid and caused an unrelenting ache in his lower body.

Fanning his fingers against her flat stomach, he felt the effect his kisses were having. His mouth hungrily found hers. She made a small sound against his lips when his hand moved higher, until his knuckles brushed against the underside of her breast. His mouth moved lower, until he tasted the skin at her throat. Shelby caught his head between her hands and her fingers through his hair. He kissed the hollow, then stroked every inch of her collarbone with his mouth. Catching one strap between his teeth, Dylan smoothed it off her shoulder.

He heard her suck in her breath when his hand moved up to close possessively over her breast. He could feel her taut nipple straining against his palm. He squeezed gently.

Lifting his head, he felt satisfaction spill through his system when he saw the flush of desire on her cheeks. He captured her lower lip with his mouth, tugging gently as his hand slipped beneath the silky fabric. Cupping her breast in his hand, he kissed her hard as his thumb teased her nipple. Her response became more urgent as she pressed against him.

Her hands tore at his shirt, pushing the fabric down to trap his arms. Dylan lifted away from her long enough to shed the shirt and look and admire his prize. The dress had worked its way to her waist, and he caressed her with his eyes. It was a heady experience, looking down at her. Her erratic breathing and desire-glazed eyes were almost enough to send him over the edge.

Caging her with his arms, Dylan dipped his head and placed a hard kiss against her open mouth. His tongue teased hers, then moved lower.

She moaned in earnest when his mouth closed over one breast. He kissed the soft valley between her breasts, then moved his attentions to the other.

"Dylan..." She said his name on a rush of breath. "Dylan, please..."

He lifted his head, and she arched against him, communicating her need. Her fingers moved through the hair on his chest until she discovered his nipples. Lifting her head from the pillow, Shelby kissed him as he had kissed her. He watched her as her hands eagerly explored the contours of his body. They slipped around him, then moved lower. Shelby held his hips firmly against hers. Now it was his turn to moan.

Catching her chin with his finger, Dylan tilted her face toward his and kissed her passionately as he used his knee to spread her legs. He settled against her, feeling smugly male when she reacted to the unmistakable sign of his desire.

He wanted this moment to last forever. He felt her need, and it rivaled his own. Her hands molded to his hips, as she matched his rhythm. Slowly he slid his hands down her side, stopping briefly to explore the soft weight of her breasts.

"Dylan," she said against his mouth.

He brushed a kiss across her forehead. "Yes?"

Her hands began a frantic search for his zipper. Dylan accommodated her by rolling off to one side. He captured one pert nipple in his mouth as she fumbled with the snap. The rasp of metal on metal was followed by the relief of the intense pressure of confinement. When her fingertip slipped beneath the waistband of his shorts, Dylan tensed and silently begged for control. If she touched him, he knew, it would be over too soon.

Capturing her wrist, he brought her hand to his mouth and placed several kisses against her palm. Their eyes met in a long, silent dialogue of need. He placed her hand against his chest. She immediately began an exploration of the tense muscles at his neck. Balancing on his forearms, Dylan's eyes remained fixed on her as he slowly ground himself against her, reveling in the heat emanating from her body. She arched against him, her mouth seeking his. Dylan countered her actions, but maintained the slow gyration of his hips.

Her movements became more insistent. He felt her feet wrap around his ankles, joining their bodies and enhancing the intimate contact. Her fingers roamed over his biceps, squeezing and massaging the muscles.

He leaned down and kissed her with a thoroughness meant to leave her breathless. It worked. He found her flushed as he watched her take her lower lips between her teeth. He kissed the drop of perspiration between her breasts as he slowly eased off her.

The dress came off and was tossed mindlessly to the floor. Dylan stood and removed what was left of his clothing, his eyes remaining on her all the while. The sight of her wide-eyed admiration filled him with arrogant pride as he joined her on the bed.

He lay beside her, her head resting in the cradle of his

arm. He allowed his hand to rest on her abdomen. The heat of her skin nearly scorched him, and she tried to turn toward him.

"Don't," he said gently as he allowed his fingers to toy with the lacy top of her panties.

He could feel the small shivers of anticipation surge through her each time his fingertip slipped beneath the silk. He nuzzled her neck as the exploration continued. He called on all his control as he discovered every delicate inch of her body. Finally, when he could no longer bear the sweet agony, he whisked the panties off and positioned himself between her legs.

Shelby closed her eyes and lifted her willing body toward him. Dylan remained poised above her, but his lips found hers. The deep, demanding kiss lasted for several mind-shattering minutes. He lifted his head and said, "Open your eyes. I want to see your eyes when it happens."

Shelby complied, and he nearly dissolved when he saw his own searing heat mirrored in her expression. He thrust himself into her with slow, tender movements. He felt her nails dig into his shoulders as his body filled her. Together, they fell into the primitive rhythm. He felt her body building toward release as he increased the cadence of their lovemaking. When he at last felt the convulsions of her body around him he allowed himself to savor his own release.

SHELBY LAY watching the blades of the paddle fan spin above her. A myriad of emotions coursed through her mind. How could she have let this happen again? Guilt nudged at her conscience. How could she do this when her baby was missing?

"Is this a guilty silence?" Dylan's soft voice floated through the darkening room.

"A little," she admitted. "I... My son..."

"Don't," he said. He gathered her against him, gently stroking her hair as she rested against his chest.

She could feel the even beat of his heart against her cheek

as her hand instinctively rested in the thick mat of hair on his chest. "I've felt so alone since Chad was taken. I guess that's the only explanation for the way I behaved."

"It doesn't matter why we made love."

"Yes, it does." She was arguing more with herself than with him. "What kind of mother spends the afternoon in a hotel room with a man when her baby is missing?"

"One who needs comfort," he answered softly. "This has nothing to do with your love for your son, Shelby."

"I should be out there looking for him," she said as she shrugged away from his hold. She felt alone the moment his hands left her body. And she wasn't all convinced this little fall from grace was just the result of some need to be comforted.

That thought followed her into the bathroom. While she waited for the tub to fill, she stared at her image in the mirror. "Comfort?" she repeated, trying the excuse on her reflection. She frowned. "Complete loss of mental faculties?" She frowned again. "I'm still in love with him," she whispered. Then she nodded.

The long soak in the tub gave her enough time to banish the ghosts of her past. There would be time enough to sort through this mess when she had her son back. By the time she emerged, an artificial smile planted on her face, Shelby showed no outward signs of her inner turmoil.

Nor did Dylan show any signs of inner turmoil. He was seated on the balcony, his bare feet crossed leisurely on the railing. A bottle of beer dangled between his thumb and forefinger.

He turned when he heard her approach. His blue-gray eyes held just a glimmer of sadness that his faint smile couldn't hide. "There's all sorts of drinks and stuff in that cabinet next to the bed."

Shelby shook her head and said, "No, thanks. I'm not really thirsty."

"Jay called while you were in the tub."

"You didn't tell him—"

One of Dylan's brows arched reprovingly. "He's my boss, but I don't report everything."

"I just didn't want him to..." She allowed her voice to trail off.

"He's got three possibles on the car."

Her expression brightened, and she felt that familiar pang of hope swell in her chest. "Are we going to go see them?"

"Not we," he told her. "Me."

"But, Dylan!"

"But nothing," he said, then took a swallow of beer. "I called Rose. She's going to come out here and stay with you while I check things out."

Immediately her head turned to the bed. A blush crept up her cheeks when she realized that he had already taken care of the disheveled covers.

"But if you find him?"

"You'll be the first one to know."

There was an unmistakable tension in the room. Dylan's movements were measured and stiff. And he wouldn't look her in the eye. The knowledge brought the recent memory of their lovemaking to the forefront.

I want to see your eyes when it happens.

She stepped back into the room and found her waterlogged purse. Her wallet was limp, and her checks were damp, but she did manage to convince her ballpoint to work after a bit of coaxing.

"Here," she said, holding the check out to him.

"What's this?"

"For my clothes, and half the cost of the room."

His expression grew dark. "Forget it."

"C'mon, Dylan. There's no reason for you to pay—"

"I'm not destitute, Shelby."

"Neither am I," she countered haughtily.

"No," he admitted as he took another pull on the beer. "But I know you've got most of your money tied up in the Rose Tattoo."

"That doesn't mean I can't afford basic living expenses."

She placed the check on the edge of the chair. "We're actually doing okay," she rambled on. "The restaurant business is a lot different from what I used to do, but Rose and I are turning a profit. We've even hired an extra waitress to help on the days Tory is in class."

His brow creased in a series of etched lines. "Tory has day classes?"

"Twice a week," she explained. "She was going to sit this term out, but Rose and I convinced her to keep going."

"How'd you do that?"

His expression was hard, almost angry.

"She didn't have enough for tuition. Rose and I scraped together the difference."

"That's interesting."

"Why?"

"According to Oglethorpe College, Tory Conway isn't registered this quarter."

CHAPTER SEVENTEEN

"WHAT HAPPENED?"

Shelby shifted uncomfortably in the seat, beneath Rose's prodding eyes. "I don't know what you mean."

Rose grunted disbelievingly before gunning her car out of the parking lot. "Something happened. We were supposed to wait back at the inn."

"Well, we didn't. And nothing happened. Not really."

"Really," Rose said. "Tanner looked fit to be tied, and you—" she threw her hands up in the air for an instant "—you have that same look my son had when I caught him stealing a pack of gum from the Piggly Wiggly."

"I didn't steal any gum," Shelby said miserably. Irritably she shoved her hair off her forehead. "I made a terrible mistake."

"By not leveling with him about Chad?"

A heavy sigh escaped past her lips. "Among other things."

"You sleep with him again?"

"Rose!" she bellowed.

"That's a yes."

"I can't believe I could be so stupid again."

Rose jolted the car to a halt at a stoplight and turned in her seat. "You aren't being too objective about this."

"Oh, I'm objective," Shelby groaned. "I'm supposed to be looking for my son, but instead I...I..."

"You sought comfort from the man you love."

Shelby's eyes grew wide, and she was grateful for the shroud of darkness inside the car. "Don't be ridiculous. I can't love Dylan. We have nothing in common. We're practically strangers, for heaven's sake.''

"Strangers who made a beautiful baby together."

"You don't understand," Shelby protested.

"So explain it to me."

Wringing her hands, Shelby clamped her eyed shut briefly before beginning. "Dylan and I have this *thing*. It's so powerful, so consuming. It's like no matter what's happening around us, nothing matters but this...this..."

"Passion?"

The word brought with it the image of Dylan's handsome face at the very instant...

"I suppose." Shelby cracked the window. It had suddenly grown very warm inside the car.

"You're lucky," Rose commented after a brief, contemplative silence. "A lot of us go through life never finding that passion. You'd be a fool to walk away from it."

"It's sex, Rose. Dylan has never said he wanted anything more from me."

"Did you ever ask?"

"Ask?"

"You know." Rose waved her heavily jeweled hand in a circular motion. "Did you ever think to give the guy the benefit of the doubt? Maybe he's in love with you, too."

"I never said I was in love with him."

"And my hair's naturally blond," Rose said. "I know you, Shelby. You wouldn't have slept with the guy if you didn't have some strong feelings for him."

"But it's more complicated than that!"

"Because of Chad?"

"Among other things."

"I imagine Tanner will be a mite miffed when he first finds out he's that baby's father. But I think he'll warm up to the notion without a hitch."

"Right," Shelby said with a sneer. "Then what? Dylan once told me he couldn't imagine having a wife and family in his line of work. He even broke an engagement because of his feelings. And then there's the touchy matter of Ned."

"What's Nichols got to do with all this?" Rose queried.

"Dylan hates him."

"If the guy is running guns, he ought to. You, too, for that matter."

"I know I should," Shelby murmured. "But I owe Ned."

"Owe him?" Rose grunted, her disagreement apparent. "The man gave you a job, one you were right good at, I hear. Seems to me that's payment enough."

"But I need Ned," Shelby countered in a barely audible voice.

"I think you need Dylan more."

"But he doesn't need me."

"We'll see," Rose said, allowing those words to hang in the air between them for the remainder of the ride.

The Rose Tattoo was nearly empty when they arrived. Only a few tables were occupied by late-night diners. *Couples,* Shelby noted with distaste. Normal couples who didn't have secrets.

"Hey, Shelby," Keith called as she and Rose weaved their way through the kitchen. "Any news?"

Sadly Shelby shook her head. "Not yet."

"Anything I can do?"

The question came from Tory. Shelby stared at the young woman, her mind replaying Dylan's startling revelation.

"You can come up to my office," Shelby said. Then, turning to Rose, she added, "Give us a few minutes, will you?"

"I'm outa here," Rose announced. "Unless you want me to stay with you?"

"No," Shelby said, managing a small smile. "Thanks for picking me up."

"Think about what I said, Shelby. Ask Tanner what he wants. His answers might surprise you."

"Maybe," Shelby hedged.

USING THE MAP provided by the rent-a-cop at the gate, Dylan turned into a horseshoe-shaped drive in front of a huge house bathed in diffused light from a row of flood lamps. The muted sound of a small dog's yapping greeted him when he stepped onto the crushed-stone pavement.

Taking the steps two at a time, he rammed his shirt into the waistband of his pants and pressed the doorbell. Plastering a pleasant expression on his face, he let out a breath as he waited. He wasn't expecting this visit to be any more informative than the two that had preceded it.

A small white dog and a small white-haired woman peered out from a small crack in the door.

"Yes?"

Flipping open his wallet, Dylan offered his identification, as well as an introduction. "Are you Mrs. Carstairs?"

Surprise lifted her dark brows toward the mass of white-blue curls. "Yes."

He repeated the drill, asking if she owned a car like the one he was looking for, then asking to see it.

"Come in," she said tentatively as she scooped up the yapping dog and cradled it under her arm. The dog's black eyes watched him from beneath a crisp blue ribbon.

Dylan sneered at the annoying little creature. Foolish could eat it in one gulp.

Dylan followed the tiny woman through the expansive space, trying to figure out what such a small woman needed with so much room. It wasn't a house, it was a showplace. He could only imagine his mother's reaction to a place this size— *Too much to keep clean.*

"This way," she instructed as she led him through the kitchen.

Flipping a switch, she filled the garage with light. The black Taurus was parked next to a sleek white Mercedes, and there was still ample room for a third vehicle. In fact, he thought with a snide smile, the garage was bigger than his apartment.

Working his way past a collection of bikes, Dylan

checked the condition of the car, not expecting to find anything of consequence. He was right.

"Can you tell me what this is all about?" Mrs. Carstairs called from her perch on the steps. The dog whined, as well.

"I'm trying to find a car matching this description that *may* have been on the island yesterday."

"Oh, it was here," Mrs. Carstairs said with conviction.

Dylan straightened and tried to keep his surprise in check. "There are two other cars like yours on the island."

"Rebecca's and Grace's," she affirmed. "It wasn't one of theirs."

"How do you know there was a fourth car on the island?" he questioned skeptically.

"Angel," she said simply.

"Come again?" Dylan asked, feeling his hope dissipate as he regarded his elderly informant.

"Angel," she said more forcefully, holding the dog out and allowing it to dangle like a squirming dustball. "We were up at the straw market, and Angel took me to the wrong car."

Great, he thought disgustedly. His informant was a pedigreed pile of groomed white hair. "Explain what happened."

"I parked at the market, and when we came back, Angel and I went to the wrong car. It wasn't until I tried my key and set off the car alarm that I realized I'd made a mistake."

Dylan moved with such swiftness that the dog dived for protection beneath one of the cars. "I take it the owner came out?"

"Sure," Mrs. Carstairs said, a faint stain creeping up her thin neck. "She was quite nice about the whole ordeal."

"Did you get her name?"

Mrs. Carstairs sighed and began to stroke her chin with age-gnarled fingers. "I believe I did. Let's see. I know she called the baby Chad—"

"She had a baby with her?"

"Cute little thing, too," Mrs. Carstairs said with a fond

smile. "And her name was Katherine, I think. Yes. Katherine."

"Katherine what?" Dylan thundered. Mrs. Carstairs jolted at his tone, and Dylan uttered some sort of apology. "Did you happen to catch her last name?"

Mrs. Carstairs shook her head. "Afraid not."

"Tell me what she looked like."

"She was a handsome woman. Average height, fair complexion. Her hair was brown, as were her eyes."

"Anything else?" Dylan asked as he scribbled furiously in his notebook. "Anything you can recall that struck you about this woman?"

"Aside from her grandson, you mean?"

Dylan's nod was stiffened by the overwhelming anger boiling in his blood.

"She said she was glad the car alarm had gone off, because she had lost track of time."

"Time for what?"

"She had to hurry back into town for a meeting."

"What kind of a meeting? Did she say?"

Mrs. Carstairs's shoulders slouched forward. "Some society or another. I'm sorry, I just can't recall."

Jabbing the notebook between his teeth, Dylan extracted one of his cards from his wallet and handed it to her. "Please call me if you remember anything," he said.

He couldn't wait to get back to Charleston. Back to Shelby. He finally had concrete information about her son.

TORY'S SOFT FOOTSTEPS followed her up the steps and down the corridor. Shelby wasn't exactly sure how she would handle the situation, even as she took her position of authority behind the cluttered desk.

Any thoughts she might have entertained about Dylan being mistaken about Tory were erased when she looked at the nervous woman seated across from her. Tory's blue eyes were as big as the saucers she carted around. Her lower lip trembled, as did the small hand tugging on the short hairs at the nape of her neck.

"I need—"

"Wait!" Tory jumped to her feet, interrupting her. "I know what this is all about."

"Really?" Shelby tried to remain calm, tried to keep the disappointment out of her expression.

"The money." Tory barely managed to get the words out. "I know you and Rose meant for me to use it for school."

"That was our understanding."

"I was going to," Tory insisted, moving forward so that her hands rested, palms down, on the desk. Several papers fluttered on the breeze created by her sudden movement.

"Something came up, and I needed to use the money for something else."

"Are you in trouble?" Shelby asked.

"Trouble?" Tory blinked. "Oh, you mean like you were?"

Shelby winced, but didn't completely lose her grip on her self-control.

"I didn't mean it like that," Tory explained on a rush of mint-scented breath. "I didn't mean to insinuate there was anything wrong—"

Shelby lifted her hand. "It's okay, Tory."

The other woman fell silent as she slumped back into the chair. Shelby regarded her for a long moment before speaking. "Whoever has Chad wants one hundred thousand dollars."

Tory's gasp was audible. Her shocked expression dissolved, and was replaced by one Shelby could only categorize as a look of horror.

"You don't think I'm involved?"

"That's a lot of money, Tory. And if you're in financial trouble..." her voice trailed off.

"God!" Tory exclaimed, raking a hand through her short hair. "I could never do anything to hurt Chad. I can't believe you would even think I was capable of such a thing."

"Then explain to me what you did with the money Rose and I gave you for your tuition."

Tory surprised her by meeting her eyes squarely. "I gave the entire thirty-five hundred dollars to the Ashley Villas Rest Home."

"Ashley Villas?"

"My mother," Tory said softly. "She hasn't been, well, right since my daddy left us. She had a breakdown and never really recovered."

"I'm sorry," Shelby said feelingly. "When did all this happen? And why didn't you tell us?"

"Fifteen years ago."

Shelby's shock must have registered on her face, because Tory continued.

"Daddy used to own this place."

"The Tattoo?" Shelby queried.

Tory nodded and said, "This used to be my parents' bedroom." She punctuated the statement with a sweeping arc of her hand. "Of course, this was before Charleston became such a touristy place. When Daddy owned it, it was a townie bar. Kind of rough."

"And your mother?"

"Mama cooked burgers, served drinks and cleaned."

"And your father left?"

Tory's nod was a bit stiffer this time. "I was only eight. But he basically cleaned out the accounts and took off."

"And your mother couldn't handle it?"

"Nope. Daddy broke her heart and her spirit. She never recovered."

"If you were only eight..."

"My grandmother helped out," Tory said with a remembering smile. "Gran took real good care of my mama. Me, too. But she passed away two years ago."

"So now you're responsible for your mother's care?"

Tory sighed and clasped her hands behind her head. Her eyes went wistfully to the ceiling. "I don't seem to be as good at caring for Mama as Gran was. She's been going downhill ever since Gran died. But Ashley Villas is a great place for her. She's safe there."

"Safe?"

"Mama has it in her head that she doesn't want to live without Daddy."

Shelby felt a swell of compassion fill her chest. "Why didn't you say something, Tory? We would have done more."

"People don't usually take too kindly to the notion that you've got mental illness in your family." Tory's smile became wry. "I guess they think it's catching or something."

Shelby's expression matched her companion's as she recalled the way her neighbors had shunned her because she was an unwed mother. "How are things now?"

"Okay," she said with a shrug. "But it seems to me you have enough troubles of your own without worrying about mine." Tory leaned forward, her round face stiff with concern. "Where are you going to get the money to pay the ransom?"

Shelby sucked in a breath. "I'm working on it."

"I might be able to get some of the money back from the rest home—"

"Don't be silly," Shelby told her. "Thirty-five hundred wouldn't even make a dent, and besides—" she reached over the desk and patted Tory's hand "—maybe Dylan will find him first."

"Dylan? The guy who keeps coming by here, asking questions?"

Shelby nodded.

"He's Chad's father, isn't he?"

Shelby felt as if someone had kicked her in the stomach. "Why—"

"Chad looks just like him," Tory said sheepishly. "It's the eyes. Those vivid gray-blues are a dead giveaway."

"You didn't say anything to Dylan?"

Tory's pale brows drew together in a frown. "No. Are you telling me that he doesn't know? Is the guy blind?"

"He's never seen Chad," Shelby admitted.

Tory shook her head in utter disbelief. "I don't think you'll be able to keep your secret when he sees him."

"If he does," Shelby said, as pain gripped her chest.

"When," Tory insisted, coming around the desk and giving Shelby a much needed hug. "He'll be back in no time. You'll see."

"I hope so," Shelby groaned in a tight voice.

After soliciting Tory's promise that she would say nothing about the ransom demand, Shelby sat alone in her office. It was nearly two in the morning when she stepped over to the window. It was a black, starless night that seemed to mirror her bleak feelings of despair. Fingering the edge of the curtain, she closed her eyes and tried to envision her son, safe and sleeping in some unknown place. Warm, silent tears spilled over her cheeks. Anguish threatened to consume her.

"Shelby?"

Spinning away from the window, she found Keith lingering in the doorway, his head downcast.

"You okay?"

"Thanks, Keith. I'm all right."

"You don't look all right."

"I'm fine," she insisted as she dried her face with the backs of her hands.

"I was going to head out, but if you need someone to—"

"Go," she said with a forced smile. "I'm just going to do a little paperwork."

"I'm sure that stuff can wait."

"But I can't," she admitted softly. "I'll just work until I can't see straight."

"You sure?"

Shelby nodded and went over to him to give him a gentle nudge out the door. She listened until she heard the sound of his car starting. Wandering down to the kitchen, she frowned when she noted the metal pans stacked in the sink.

Rose would have a fit in the morning, one she would assuredly share with Keith.

Tugging opened the refrigerator, Shelby grabbed a bowl of sliced fruits and then collected a fork. She wasn't hungry, but she had the beginnings of a headache. Maybe some nourishment would keep it in check until she could exhaust her body enough to garner a few precious hours of sleep.

The dining room was a neat arrangement of tables with chairs perched on top. Josh and Tory had no doubt seen to it that this area of the building was ready for the next day's lunch crowd. Going to the jukebox, Shelby selected from the few non-Elvis offerings. Reaching behind the machine, she cranked up the volume so that she would be able to hear the music from her office.

With the fruit in her hand, she lumbered up the steps, the sound muffled by the music. "Exhaust the mind, exhaust the body," she told herself, repeating the words her mother often said.

The stack of mail, invoices and bills on the corner of her desk was moved onto the blotter in front of her. Using her fingernail, Shelby slit open the first envelope as she popped a strawberry into her mouth. She glanced over the text of the letter briefly before tossing it into the wastepaper basket. They didn't need any aluminum siding, even at half price.

She was in the act of reaching for the next item when the corner of one of the envelopes buried in the pile took her breath away. Carefully she eased it out.

CHAD'S MOM.

Ripping into it, she scanned the bold, concise block printing.

THE RULES HAVE CHANGED. BRING THE MONEY TO WATERFRONT PARK TOMORROW AT 9:00 A.M. SHARP. NO COPS OR CHAD DIES.

Shelby closed her eyes and took deep, purposeful breaths in an attempt to quell her panic. *Think!* her mind demanded. But there really was only one thing she could do.

Glancing at her watch, she grabbed the phone and dialed. Her toe tapped impatiently as she went through the process of placing an international call.

"Is this Mr. Chan?" she asked the semifamiliar voice.

"It is."

"This is Shelby Hunnicutt. We spoke yesterday. I need to speak to Mr. Nichols immediately. It's urgent."

"I'm sorry, Miss Hunnicutt. Mr. Nichols has checked out."

"Checked out?" she gasped. "How can I reach him?"

"I believe you should try the American State Department."

"Whatever for?"

"He was taken into their custody by the Turkish police earlier today."

"Why?" she yelled into the receiver. "Why would they be holding Ned?"

"Because I told them to."

Shelby's eyes collided with the angry, restrained figure of Dylan Tanner looming in the doorway.

CHAPTER EIGHTEEN

"YOU?" Shelby gulped.

"Miss Hunnicutt?" Mr. Chan called into the receiver.

"Never mind," Shelby said dully as she placed the phone back on the cradle.

Dylan strode into the room, reaching her in three thundering strides. His expression was hard, and his eyes were unforgiving. Menace fairly radiated from his large body as he loomed above her.

Shelby could feel his harsh breath wash across her face from between his tightly clenched teeth. She couldn't let him intimidate, not now. Too much was at stake.

"You'll have to do something to have him released," she told him.

Dylan grabbed her from the chair, his fingers painfully pinching the skin at her upper arms. "I can't believe you," he growled. "You've made quite a habit out of sleeping with me and then running to Nichols. What gives?"

Shelby looked into those angry silver slits, and her own eyes narrowed in response. "Let me go, Dylan. You're hurting me."

His eyes traveled to where his fingers bit into her flesh. Instantly his grip loosened, though he didn't release her. "Why?" he asked. It was a single strangled syllable.

"I need Ned's help."

"You think your gunrunning ex-lover is better equipped than I am to find your son?"

"No," she told him honestly. "And he isn't my ex-lover."

"Great!" he said, his voice grating. "It's still going on? What's the matter, Shelby—having trouble choosing between the two of us?"

"It isn't what you think," she insisted, trying vainly to twist away from him.

"I don't know," he told her, derision hanging on each word. "Seems to me you must get some sort of cheap thrill playing both ends against the middle."

"Stop it! You don't know what you're talking about."

"Then enlighten me," he said challengingly. "But I should tell you, I just came from seeing Jay. He played the tape for me."

"Tape?"

"Your heartwarming phone call to Nichols yesterday. You should have known better than to call him from your bedroom, Shelby. Not too bright."

"Jay knows?" she asked.

He nodded as his eyes roamed over her face, quietly studying the apparently visible signs of her fear. "Why would you ask Nichols?"

"I want your promise that you won't tell Jay."

He snorted. "No way."

"Then let go of me, and do whatever you have to for Ned to be released."

"Why should I?"

"Because if you don't, they'll kill my son."

Dylan's hands slid up and down her arms. She could almost see him thinking, hear the litany of arguments she felt sure were echoing through his brain. Soundlessly he stepped away from her, offering her his broad back as he stood at the window.

"Dylan?"

"Be quiet for a minute," he said in a hoarse voice.

Shelby stared at his back for what felt like an eternity. The music had stopped—not that she could have heard it above the pounding of her heart. Trepidation began a slow ascent up her spine, until it threatened total domination.

"Nichols isn't your lover."

It was a statement, not a question.

"No."

"Never has been, has he?"

It was a question, and an accusation.

"No."

Dylan's turn was slow, deliberate, measured. Shelby held her breath, bracing against the unknown. His eyes moved between Shelby and the framed photograph of the baby, his fists opening and closing at his sides.

Anxiously she watched the play of emotions in his eyes as the truth stretched between them like a wire. Dylan laughed harshly.

"He's mine." He said the words in a voice Shelby had never heard before. It was sarcastic, and very, very angry.

No longer able to stand the intense scrutiny of his penetrating eyes, she lowered her head and felt the burn of impending tears. She waited for the explosion. She reached for him with a beseeching hand. One he shrugged away from as if her touch were as repulsive as her lies. A sneering smirk marred his features as he stepped over to the bar and poured himself a glass of Scotch from the dusty bottle.

His mouth thinned as he swallowed the contents in one long drink. She could see the muscles of his jaw working as he ground his teeth. The silence became a deafening madness that felt as if it could go on forever.

"I never meant for—"

Dylan held up one hand to cut off her words while he poured himself another drink. "I had a feeling you were keeping a secret," he began, in a dangerously calm voice. "I just never dreamed it would have anything to do with me."

"I can explain, Dylan."

"Really?" he shot back, slamming the glass down in a thundering punctuation. "Can *you* explain why you decided to deprive me of the first year of my own son's life? Or maybe *you* can explain why you didn't tell me you were pregnant? Or maybe you've got some explanation for the way you've behaved since the night *our* son was taken.'' Dylan took two steps closer, but Shelby was having a difficult time seeing him through the glistening of unshed tears. "Now we've wasted God knows how many man-hours hunting for Nichols, when we could have been searching for Chad. If something's—"

"Don't say it!" Shelby screamed. Her head dropped, and she felt her whole body shaking with each gut-wrenching sob. "Please, Dylan..." she pleaded in a near whisper.

She fully expected him to storm from the house. Instead, she felt herself being dragged against him. She drank in the scent of his skin, but didn't react. Not until Dylan began to gently stroke his hand through her hair.

"Why didn't you tell me?" His voice was softer, calmer, but still held a slight edge.

Shelby went rigid in his arms, not certain she was capable of dealing with his recriminations. "The usual reasons."

"Being?"

His hand moved to her waist, his fingers kneading the tight muscles at the small of her back.

"I wasn't sure how you'd react. You'd already told me you didn't want a family. Not in your line of work."

"No," he said as his hands cupped her face, tilting it toward his. "I told you I broke my engagement because I wasn't ready for a family then. It was ten years ago, Shelby. You didn't listen."

His thumbs wiped away her tears, and his eyes held hers.

"I'm sorry. If what you said is true, I may have cost my baby his life—"

"Hush," he said as he brushed a kiss against her lips. "I was angry, Shelby. I shouldn't have said that."

"But do you think it's possible? How will I live with myself if I've done anything to jeopardize Chad?"

"You haven't done anything," Dylan insisted.

"I'm sorry about all the lies."

"I'm not thrilled that you didn't trust me enough to come

to me. I'm sorry I missed the first nine months of my son's life."

"I never meant—"

"For me to find out," he finished with a sad smile. "But I have, so we go from here."

"Go where?"

"We'll figure that out after we get Chad home."

Shelby reached up and grabbed a handful of his shirt. "You won't take him away from me, will you?"

"What kind of a man do you think I am?" His laugh was even sadder than his smile. "Of course not, Shelby. Give me some credit for being a decent guy."

"I do," she told him.

"Then explain all of it to me," Dylan suggested as he stepped back and leaned against her desk. "What's with you and Nichols? And when did the kidnapper contact you?"

"When we were searching Market Street for the woman and the baby. He called me on the cellular and set it up."

"What's the plan this time?"

Reaching behind him, Shelby tugged the ominous letter from the desk and handed it to him. He scanned the copy, a definite frown curving the corners of his mouth downward. She could almost feel the anger radiating from his large body.

"You can't tell Jay," Shelby said imploringly. "He'll kill Chad if the authorities are involved."

"Jay can—"

"I'm not willing to risk it," she told him as she moved to stand in front of him. They stood toe-to-toe, with Shelby craning her neck to meet his eyes. "Promise me, Dylan. Promise me."

"You don't ask for much, do you?"

"I can't risk my son's safety."

"My son, too."

"WE HAVEN'T SOLVED the problem of the money," Shelby told him as they entered her house.

"No," he agreed as his hand reached back for hers. "We haven't."

"You have to let me talk to Ned."

His hand tightened an instant before the rest of his body steeled in reaction to her statement. He pulled her in the direction of the living room.

After depositing her on the sofa, Dylan found the switch on the lamp. Soft light illuminated his features. Shelby felt the pangs of anxiety returning as she peered up into his troubled face. Shelby had the distinct impression that he was battling his temper. He hadn't managed to keep that spark of annoyance out of his glistening eyes.

"Tell me the rest of your secrets, Shelby." His voice was subdued, dangerously so. "Tell me why you left me and went running to Nichols. Especially when you knew you were going to have my baby."

"I—"

The shrill ring of the telephone prevented her answering. Automatically she reached over and grabbed the receiver.

"Hello?"

"Miss Hunnicutt?"

"Yes. Who is this?"

"Kurt Mitchell from down the street."

"Yes, Mr. Mitchell?"

"I know all about your little boy, and I just thought you'd want to know—"

"Yes?"

"That black car I saw on the night of the kidnapping?"

"Yes?"

"I'm pretty sure it's parked out front of my house."

"Thank you," Shelby managed to say before she hung up and filled Dylan in.

"Call 911. Tell them to come in quiet."

"Where are you going?" she wailed. Her eyes were fixed on the lethal-looking gun he now held in his right hand.

"I'll go check out our friend."

"Can't you wait for the police?"

Dylan looked down to where she had a death grip on his arm. His smile was slow and genuine. "I guess this means that you really care, huh?"

Her cheeks burned as she watched him leave. She tried to keep him in sight through the window as she called the emergency dispatcher. Dylan bobbed behind trees, slunk behind cars, until she could no longer see him in the hazy light of the street lamps.

Propping herself on her knees, she carefully put back the curtains and repeated, "Come on," as if it were a mantra. She could see no movement on the street, nothing to calm her growing concerns for his safety. Minutes passed like years, and she moved only when the painful tingling in her legs demanded it.

She paced. She prayed. She even cursed as she waited, feeling helpless and useless. "Don't let anything happen to him," she said in a whisper. If something happened to Dylan…

Her grim thoughts were blissfully halted by a loud and sudden disturbance moving toward the house. Shelby ran to the door and threw it open.

Dylan was dragging a struggling man up the sidewalk, flanked by a small group of police officers. Porch lights blinked on in a choreographed display of overt curiosity.

"Keith?" she gasped when she saw the culprit.

"None other," Dylan rasped, sounding winded and heartily annoyed.

He gave the smaller man a shove, so that Keith tumbled into the foyer with a thud. "Hey!"

"Thanks, guys," Dylan said as he slammed the door on the other men.

Instinctively Shelby stood behind him, peering around his shoulders as Keith slowly dragged himself to his feet.

"What are you doing?" she asked.

"Good question," Dylan added sarcastically.

"Just—watching out for you," Keith stammered, wiping his hands on the front of his pants.

"Peeping out for you is probably closer to the truth."

The two men glowered at one another.

"I'm not a pervert," Keith insisted.

"Then what have you been doing slinking though the neighborhood?" Dylan challenged.

"I was just looking out for her. With her kid snatched—"

"Wrong answer." Sneering, Dylan moved swiftly, anchoring Keith to the wall, his forearm against the smaller man's throat.

"Dylan!"

"We know you were out there the night Chad was taken," Dylan said.

"Keith," Shelby said imploringly. "Is that true? Were you here that night?"

His Adam's apple flickered just above Dylan's forearm. "I was parked down the street."

His evasive response earned him additional pressure from his captor. Shelby stepped forward and placed her hand on Dylan. Keith looked on the verge of collapse. "If you strangle him, he can't tell us anything."

Dylan snarled once, then loosened his hold. "Make it good, Keith."

"I was on the side, by the hedges."

"And?"

"And when I heard footsteps, I bolted."

"What footsteps?" Shelby nearly screamed. "Why didn't you tell me this before?"

"Because," Dylan began as he slowly released Keith, "then he would have had to admit that he's been staking you out for some time. Isn't that right?"

"I just wanted to be close to you," he said, in a pathetically soft voice. "I would never do anything to hurt you, Shelby. Chad, neither."

Shelby fell against the cool surface of the wall. "I know that," she managed to say.

"And if I'd really seen anything, I'd have told. Honest."

"What *did* you see?" Dylan asked as he stepped next to Shelby and placed his hand possessively at her waist.

The contact was enough to short-circuit her frazzled nerves. She could feel every inch of his fingers through the fabric of her dress. She was aware of the warmth of his body where it brushed hers. She was losing her grip!

"I only glanced back for maybe a second. There was this guy with a ladder coming through the back."

"What did he look like?"

Keith shrugged, glanced at Dylan and said, "Like you."

LIKE YOU. Dylan played the answer in his mind long after that little weasel left. He frowned, wondering why he had allowed Shelby to talk him in to letting the guy walk out of here. Keith and his little infatuation might seem harmless to her, but he knew better. He'd come across a few crazies in his time, and Keith had the makings of a true delusional.

"I could have fixed you something," Shelby said as she joined him in the kitchen.

His heart jumped to his throat when he saw the incredibly sexy little robe belted at her even sexier waist. He thought about bending her over the kitchen table. As much as he liked the idea, he knew it wouldn't solve anything. In fact, he was fast realizing that their strong physical attraction was one thing that seemed to scare Shelby into secrecy.

"Peanut butter on a piece of bread," he said, holding it up for her inspection. "Hardly an imposition on my limited culinary expertise."

She sat down in the chair and crossed her legs. The robe covered less than half of her shapely thighs, and Dylan nearly groaned when he allowed his eyes to caress the tanned skin. He had that same curious, guilty feeling he'd had in the eighth grade, when Marybeth Bartoli had gotten a conduct referral from the sisters from wearing her uniform too short.

"Is something wrong?"

Yes. "No," he assured her.

He watched as she lifted a bottle of water to her lips. His eyes remained fixed as she wrapped her rosy lips around the top of the bottle. He followed the path of the water, down her slender throat, down toward the deep V where the edges of the robe met. He could just make out the gentle swell of her breast—

"Dylan!" she said sharply.

"Sorry," he mumbled.

"We need to do something about the payoff. You have to get Ned to a phone, so I can talk to him."

The pleasant diversion of ogling her body evaporated under the instant steam of his temper. He didn't want any part of Nichols.

"You heard Keith. He said the guy looked like me. Nichols and I are similar in height and coloring."

"Ned does not have my son."

"Our son," he said deliberately. "And I'm not as convinced as you seem to be."

"Then just trust me on this."

"You tell me why you're so sure Nichols doesn't have the baby, and I'll let it rest."

He watched her expression falter. Saw the flash of uncertainty cloud her clear blue eyes. "Can't you just take my word for it?"

"Not without some rational explanation for your blind faith in that slimeball."

"He isn't a slimeball," she countered, crossing her arms defiantly in front of her small body.

"What would you call him?" Dylan taunted.

"My father."

CHAPTER NINETEEN

HE WAS ALONE in the kitchen. Shelby had left just after delivering her latest little bomb. It explained a lot, but left him with a whole slew of new questions. After discarding his half-eaten sandwich in the garbage, Dylan ran his fingers through his hair and let out a deep breath.

"It's family day at the Hunnicutt house," he grumbled. Learning he was Chad's father had brought with it a whole host of wonderful emotions. Finding out Nichols was Shelby's father made him want to spit.

He thought back to their conversation on the beach. She certainly hadn't grown up with Nichols in the picture. He wondered what rock the guy had crawled out from under to stake his fatherly claim. And why.

That ominous thought followed him up the stairs. He stopped outside Shelby's door, listening for sounds. He remained there for several minutes, debating. Finally emotion overruled common sense, and he grasped the knob.

"Dylan?" She said the name in the dark.

"I just wanted to make sure you were okay."

"I'm fine."

He could tell that was a lie. He could almost hear the tears in her husky voice, and he felt a surge of protectiveness surge up from deep inside his soul.

Slowly he walked to the edge of the bed. The room smelled faintly feminine, just like Shelby. Cautiously he took a seat, feeling her body move toward his weight.

He wanted to hold her, comfort her. He settled for ramming his fists in the pockets of his shorts.

"You don't sound fine."

"I'm scared."

"I know," he agreed on a breath. "I am, too."

"What if we don't get him back. What if—"

"I'll find him, Shelby. I promise you."

The room was silent, except for the occasional sound of her shifting beneath the covers. That inspired vivid memories of their passionate afternoon. He licked his lips, remembering the taste of her mouth.

"You'll like him," she said softly.

"I know I will," Dylan agreed. He wished he could see her face. "I'm sure you've done a great job with him."

"After seeing you with Keith, I know where he gets his violent streak."

"I'm not violent."

"Tell Keith that," Shelby said.

"I'd like to tattoo it across his forehead with an oyster fork."

"No, you're not violent," she said, teasingly. "Wonder how I ever got that impression?"

"When did you find out Nichols was your father?"

"The same day I discovered I was pregnant."

Hanging his head, Dylan sucked in air.

"The same day you told me you needed my testimony to put Ned in jail for the rest of his life."

The knot in his gut twisted and festered. "No wonder you bailed out."

"I didn't bail out," she said, after apparently giving his statement some consideration. "I just wasn't interested in letting the two of you tear me apart like two dogs going after the same bone."

"I wouldn't have pressured you, Shelby."

"We'll never know."

"What about Nichols? Did he back off?"

He heard a small decisive sound from the bed. "Ned was furious when I told him I wanted out. He didn't let up for a long time. That's probably why Chad was born a month early. My blood pressure went through the roof."

"I hope he rots in hell."

"He has basically the same wish for you."

"Then why didn't you help me put him away?"

"I would have," she answered immediately. "Until I realized the truth."

"Which was?"

"That Ned was manipulating me, and so were you."

"I never tried to manipulate you."

"Then how did I end up pregnant?"

Dylan tenuous hold on his self-control vanished. Blindly he reached out with both hands.

"What are you doing?"

"I'm about to show you how you ended up pregnant," he said against her open mouth. "And believe me, it has nothing to do with Nichols."

Despite his rather harsh tone, Dylan took infinite care in finessing her mouth beneath his. He savored, tasted and revered her with his kiss before gently laying her against the pillow. Wordlessly he rose and left her in the dark, silently praying she would see the light.

"WHERE HAVE YOU BEEN?" she demanded as soon as he slipped in the back door.

"Getting this." He held up a tattered gym bag and winked. "One hundred thousand U.S. dollars."

Relief washed over her as she flung herself against his solid chest. He smelled of soap and coffee.

"Where did you get it?"

"I wangled a few favors at the office," he said against her hair.

"You didn't tell anyone?"

Shelby backed up and searched his face. She could tell the deception weighed heavily on him.

"No."

"Thank you," she said as she reached up to trace one of the small lines by his mouth. "I know this is hard for you."

"Let's hope the ends justify the means."

"I should know in about two hours."

"*I?*"

"He told me to come alone."

"And he'll think you have."

"But last time—"

"Last time I wasn't calling the shots. This time I am."

She was torn between her fierce need for his support and her desire to follow the instructions explicitly. One glance at the tight set of his jaw told her all she needed to know. Short of hog-tying him in the basement, there was no way she could keep Dylan from accompanying her to the park.

"Take this and get going," he instructed.

"What about you?"

"I told you about my conversation with Mrs. Carstairs. We know there are at least two people involved here. I'll follow you in my car, from a safe distance."

With the bag of money in the trunk, Shelby negotiated the rush-hour traffic and arrived at the park a few minutes before nine.

Donning sunglasses, she nervously glanced around before retrieving the payoff from the car. "Now what?" she whispered.

Standing at the edge of the parking area, she scanned the grass and brick sections near the water's edge. A few joggers, a man reading the paper, a few young children—but nothing and no one resembling a kidnapper.

"What do you think he'll look like?" she said to herself. "Fangs and a hairy wart?"

Shelby meandered through the park, her eyes darting from spot to spot behind the shield of her glasses. She hoped for a glimpse of Dylan, then berated herself for the thought. If she spotted him, so might the kidnapper.

Glancing at her watch, she felt the first stirrings of panic. It was after nine. Shelby continued to walk slowly through the park, turning her head every few feet when curiosity and misgivings got the better of her judgment. She ended up at the pier, a walkway out over the muddy waters of the harbor, dotted with graceful white swings hanging every few feet.

She moved along the right side, one hand on the railing, the other tightly closed on the handle of the gym bag. The stale scent of rotting marine life wafted up from the calm brown waters. Stopping briefly, she watched the skeletal remains of a foam container float by.

"Miss?"

Shelby turned toward the child's voice, meeting an expectant pair of brown eyes. The young boy had skin the color of chocolate. His clothes told her instantly that he was from the well-hidden, little-discussed poor section of the city. The part of Charleston that never made it into any of the travel brochures.

"Yes?" she said, as she began to reach into her purse for a few dollars.

"I need the bag."

"Y-you?" she stammered as her mouth fell open.

"The man said to tell you to give me the bag and he'll be in touch."

"But you're just a child."

"Ten next month." He beamed proudly.

"What's your name?"

"The man said that I wasn't supposed to talk to you. Just get the bag."

Shelby closed her eyes and hoped for some sort of divine intervention. It seemed ludicrous to hand such an enormous sum of money to a mere boy.

"If I don't hurry, he won't pay me," the boy said urgently, glancing over one bony shoulder. "I can sure use that ten dollars, ma'am."

Thrusting the bag into his chest, Shelby watched helplessly as he struggled back down the pier under the heavy weight of the money. Every cell in her body screamed for her to follow him, to see if he would lead her to Chad. But the rational side of her brain insisted on some sort of calculated approach. God, she wished Dylan was there.

When the boy rounded the corner of Bay Street, Shelby damned reason and set off after him. Gathering the hem of her cotton skirt in her hand, she jogged through the park, her hair slapping at her back.

She reached Bay and looked right. Nothing. Without debate, she continued to follow the child's route, surveying each alley and driveway along the way.

She stopped short about three blocks from the park, nearly falling on her face when she negotiated an abrupt halt.

"Dylan!" she called.

Running up the uneven alleyway, she reached them, breathless.

Dylan straddled the subdued form of a man beneath the full weight of his body. The man's hands were crossed behind his body, limp, as Dylan slapped shiny metal cuffs on his wrists. Just beyond them, Shelby spotted the young boy, cowering against the wall. His eyes were wide, staring at some remembered violence.

Shelby stepped over Dylan's feet and went to see the boy.

"Are you all right?"

He gulped. "Uh-huh."

"He's great," Dylan managed as he wrestled the man to his feet and leaned him against the wall. "Greg was my partner. Right, son?"

"Uh-huh."

"Greg helped me catch the bad guy."

Shelby placed an appreciative hand on the child's shoulder, her eyes fixed on the back of the prisoner's head. "Where's Chad?"

"He was just about to explain that to me," Dylan said as he jerked the man so that his face was visible.

Shelby gasped. "Toby?"

"You know this guy?"

Looking past the trickles of blood from his nose and fast-swelling lip, Shelby nodded. "He's Keith's roommate. Toby Ballentine."

"Keith?" Dylan muttered, adding a few choice expletives. "I knew I should have turned that bozo over to the cops last night. At least now I understand how the guy had all your private telephone numbers."

"He doesn't know about this," Toby said between clenched teeth.

"Where is my son?" Shelby demanded.

He coughed. "I don't know."

Dylan placed his fist strategically in the man's rib cage. "Try again."

"I swear!" Toby yelped, clamping his arms at his sides in anticipation of another blow. "I don't have him."

"You just thought you'd pick up a few extra dollars?" Dylan said next to the man's ear.

"Keith and me were gonna open our own place. Until he started working for her." Toby cast Shelby a hateful look that rocked her in her shoes. "He's so hot for you, he changed his mind about our plan. Said he'd be happy to work for you for the rest of his life."

"You will be, too," Dylan snarled at him, his voice barely audible over the fast-approaching wail of a siren. "Only you'll do it as a guest of the state."

Shelby and Greg sat on the angled curb while Dylan and the local authorities worked out the arrangements to get Toby off the street. Knowing he would be incarcerated was of little consequence. Shelby still didn't have her baby.

"Let's go," Dylan said as he offered his hand.

She noted the knuckles were bruised and slightly swollen, but he didn't seem to notice the injury.

They walked arm in arm, Shelby resting her head against his chest, her hand on his stomach.

"Toby never had Chad, did he?" she asked when he got behind the wheel.

"Nope," Dylan answered. "But we still have the information Mrs. Carstairs gave me."

"Katherine Somebody, who attended a Something Society meeting yesterday?"

His hand shot across the car and captured her chin, forcing her to meet his eyes. "It's a start, Shelby."

"Can we stop at the Tattoo? I want to make sure Rose fires Keith when he shows his face this afternoon."

"I thought you were feeling charitable toward the guy."

"I'm fresh out of charity," she assured him glibly. "Besides, I left the pictures from the videotape in my office."

"We have more."

"I know, but they're close, and I want to memorize that woman's hand so that when I see it, I'll know."

AT ROSE'S INSISTENCE, they were seated in the dining room. They had pushed the plates of half-eaten food off to one side, to lay the pictures out in an arc.

A foot, a hand, and a ring. That was it. But something about the ring seemed oddly familiar to Shelby. She wondered if she hadn't seen the woman. Maybe she even knew the woman holding her son.

"Hi," Tory said as she came rushing into the room, fastening the top button of her blouse. "Rose filled me in. I'm so sorry."

"Thanks," they said in unison.

Tory leaned between them and ran her fingernail over the enlargement of the ring. "Your suspect belongs to the Sisters of History?"

"What?" Dylan bellowed, his massive hand clamped on Tory's wrist.

"Yeah," Tory said, startled. "That's the insignia of the society. Charleston blue bloods, mostly."

"What does this society do?" Shelby asked.

"Have lunch." Tory grunted. "Give out plaques."

"The plaque!" Shelby squealed, recognition dawning. "This is the same design that was on the doors of the homes in the Historic District. The small one beneath the historical markers."

"Right, those," Tory agreed. "And if Dylan would be kind enough to take his vise off my wrist, I'll go get a phone book so you can look these babes up."

"Sorry," Dylan said.

Shelby noted a small stain of red on each of his high cheekbones. "Why would a society matron take my baby?"

Dylan raked his finger through his hair, shaking his head. "I haven't got a clue. But I'm damned sure going to find out."

"THIS IS POINTLESS," he heard Shelby mutter as they tried the fifth and final window of the Sisters of History's office. It was locked up tighter than a drum and a sign in the window indicated that the society met only on the third Wednesday of the month.

"I think we've got enough for a warrant," he said as he stifled the urge to break one of the glass panes and save them all some time and trouble.

"We'll go to my place, and I'll call Jay to make the arrangements."

"What good will a warrant do? I doubt they have Chad stashed in their file cabinets."

"But I bet they have membership rosters. When we find Katherine, we find our son."

He liked saying that. Liked the way it felt on his tongue. *Our son*, he repeated as they went back to his car. *We just have to find him.*

"This is where you live?" Shelby asked not ten minutes later, when he'd turned into the small lot facing his building.

"What's the matter? Don't like the neighborhood?"

"It isn't that," she answered with a smile. "I looked at these places when I was pregnant. I thought an apartment might be easier to manage with a baby."

"It would have been," he said against her ear as they climbed the steps. "Because you would have had me, too."

His daily dose of patience dried up the moment he saw Miss Dog Expert perched at the top of the steps. She was snarling.

"It's about time, Mr. Tanner."

"Nice to see you, too, Mrs. James."

"Johns!" she fired back at him. "That dog of yours has been howling almost nonstop since right around midnight."

"Sorry," Dylan mumbled as he tried to steer Shelby around the hateful presence. "I'll take care of him."

"You'd have thought someone was breaking in down at your place, the way that animal carried on. It was almost as bad as last time."

"Down, boy," Dylan said as he caught Foolish in mid-leap. "Don't worry," he told Shelby. "He's harmless."

"Not according to your neighbor."

"My neighbor is a shriveled-up nag." He had to slap the dog's paws away at least a half-dozen more times just to get to the kitchen. "Get down!"

"Come here, puppy," Shelby said, going down on one knee to greet the dog on his own terms.

"Don't encourage him," Dylan growled, just before making the call to Jay to arrange for the warrant.

"Foolish!" he yelled, turning just in time to watch the animal tackle Shelby and plaster her against the floor. "I said *no*." Dylan gave a sturdy yank on the dog's collar, freeing Shelby and restoring some semblance of calm.

Bracing her hand against the wall, Shelby cautiously got to her feet. He was surprised to see the spark of laughter in her light eyes. "You think he's funny?"

"He's great," she said as she patted the dog's straining head. "He's just all wired because you left him alone last night."

"No, he isn't," Dylan countered easily. "He's always like this."

"Then he's lonely. You don't pay enough attention to the poor thing."

"Poor thing?" Dylan muttered, dragging the dog to the

back door and freeing him in the fenced courtyard. "I should have taken him straight to the pound that first night."

"Don't be so mean," Shelby admonished, slapping playfully at his arm as he walked in her direction. "Can I use your phone to let Rose know where I am?"

"Help yourself."

He tried not to watch her. Tried, but didn't succeed. There was just something about her that drew his attention. Part of it was looks. There was no question but that he thought she was beautiful. All that dark hair, and those big blue eyes. That small, perfect body of hers. But he knew it was more than just physical. He admired her strength. He appreciated her sharp mind, her quick intelligence. In short, he loved her.

"Really?"

The excited little edge to her voice focused his attention. He saw her scrounging around for something to write on and solved the dilemma by grabbing a grocery receipt and offering her his pen.

"Tory, I can't thank you enough." She twirled, her full skirt billowing out from her legs on the rush of air. "Tory called one of her professors and got the home telephone number of the president of the Sisters of History."

He lifted her off the ground and planted a loud kiss smack on her lips. Foolish barked wildly on the other side of the glass, while Dylan danced her through the apartment. He had a good feeling about this. And it certainly didn't hurt that she was plastered against him.

"I'll call," Dylan said as he took the paper from her hand.

In less than ten minutes, he had the woman agreeing to meet them back at the office for a full inspection of the files.

"Should we call Jay and tell him not to bother with the warrant?" Shelby asked.

"Nope. Best to cover all the bases. This broad may change her mind, and then we'll still have the warrant."

"I don't think Mrs. Pennington-Smythe is the type of

woman you call a broad," Shelby warned as they headed back to the car.

She stopped short, grabbing his hand. "You left the dog outside. Won't he bother the neighbors?"

"I sure hope so," Dylan said with a sly grin. "Then maybe she'll pay more attention when someone jimmies the lock on my door."

"That's not very nice," Shelby chastened.

"She wasn't very nice to me when she watched some dirtball—"

Dylan's voice trailed off as the gears of his brain suddenly cranked into overdrive.

"What?" Shelby asked, tugging his hand.

"Let me check something with Mrs. Johns."

"While you do that, I'll let Foolish back inside."

Grudgingly Dylan handed her his keys before bounding up the stairs. He knocked furiously, knowing full well the old bat was inside.

"Yes?" she said from the opposite side of the door.

"It's me, Mrs. Johns. Dylan Tanner."

"Yes?"

"I need you to tell me something."

She opened the door and eyed him cautiously from above the rims of her thick glasses. "What is it?"

"You thought the guy who broke...uh, who was 'working' on my door was me, right?" He waited for her uncertain nod. "Why did you think that?"

"He looked like you."

Keith's voice, reciting nearly the exact same words, filtered through his brain.

"And the jacket, of course," she added.

"Jacket?"

"The one you wear. The blue one with ATF painted on the back."

Dylan treated Mrs. Johns to a loud, damp kiss and a twirl. When he placed her on the ground, he noticed that she teetered and stabbed her glasses back up her nose.

"A simple thank-you would have been sufficient," she grumbled as she stumbled back into her apartment.

Dylan found Shelby waiting at the base of the stairs. He didn't bother sharing his suspicions, not yet.

Mrs. Pennington-Smythe was waiting for them at the entrance. Her perfectly styled blue-white hair seemed impervious to the heat and humidity of the afternoon. She led the way in her sensible, midheeled leather pumps, a flaxen handbag dangling from the crook of her arm.

"I can't imagine what interest you could have in any of our members."

"Just routine," Dylan assured her. "Do you know how many Katherines you have, offhand?"

"Let me see," she said as she tapped her blunt-filed nail against her even blunter chin. "There's Katherine Morrison, of Morrison Department Stores. Katherine Jenkins—her husband's family has organized the arts festival since its inception. And Katherine Williams. Her late husband—"

"I don't care if he was the Wizard of Oz," Dylan said, interrupting her. "Get me her application."

Shelby gasped behind him. "Is it possible? Or too much of a coincidence?" she whispered.

"Katherine isn't in trouble, is she?" Mrs. Pennington-Smythe asked as she nervously unlocked the file drawer. "I recall her being a rather reserved woman."

"Is she Jay's mother?" Shelby asked as she tugged on his shirtsleeve.

"Here we are," she said, opening a folder.

Dylan grabbed the whole thing from her trembling hand and sought the information with his own eyes. He found it on page two, item seven: "Nearest Living Relative, Jay Williams, nephew."

"What does this mean?" The pleading quality of Shelby's voice only served to shove the knife deeper into his gut.

Not Jay. They were friends. There had to be some other explanation.

"Thank you for your assistance, ma'am," Dylan said to the startled woman. "I would appreciate it if you could keep this visit confidential. We wouldn't want to sully any reputations needlessly."

"Of course not," she answered.

"Whose reputation? And is this Katherine Jay's mother?"

"Aunt."

"Jay is behind all this?" she managed to choke out.

Dylan wasn't much help to her. He was having a difficult time reconciling what he had learned with the man he had known and trusted.

"I don't know, yet. We'll see when we get there."

"Get where?"

"We're going to see Katherine Williams."

Dylan didn't speak to her as they drove across town. Shelby's nerves were knotted as tightly as Dylan's white-knuckled grip on the wheel. The rage emanating from him was almost palpable. Shelby knew exactly how he was feeling. If Jay was somehow involved in all this, the betrayal Dylan was experiencing would be similar to what she had gone through when Ned announced that his only reason for associating with her was to bring some respectability to his shady business. Shelby also knew he would get through it. She'd make sure of it.

Katherine's address led them down a tree-lined drive in North Charleston. The homes were older, with fences and wide, flat lawns. Katherine's was a brick rancher with rounded shrubs and a black Taurus parked in front.

"I'll go and—"

She didn't let Dylan finish the sentence. She was out of the car and at the front door like a shot. He reached her side as she depressed the doorbell.

"Chad! Baby!" she yelled, snatching the child from the woman before she even had an opportunity to react.

"Wait."

"Back up," Dylan commanded. Then she heard him ask, "Is he okay?"

"Perfect," Shelby said through tears of absolute joy. She hugged him, smelled him, and placed kisses all over his wriggling face. "I missed you so much," she cooed.

"There has to be some sort of misunderstanding," Katherine stammered.

"Not unless you've got a good explanation for kidnapping my son," Dylan told her.

"That isn't possible!" Katherine wailed. "That little boy is in the protective custody of the federal government. We can call my nephew, Jay—"

"Enough!" Dylan thundered. Then he read her the requisite Miranda warnings. They disappeared into the house briefly, with Dylan emerging alone a few minutes later.

"Care to introduce me?" he said, in a surprisingly soft voice.

"Dylan, meet Chad," she said, putting her son in his outstretched arms.

If she hadn't already told him the truth, Dylan would have known at this instant. Her tears resumed as she looked between father and son. Chad was a near-perfect replica of the tall man tossing him in the air. Her son's squeals of delight tugged at her heart, as did the beaming smile she saw on Dylan's face.

This magical moment was intruded upon by encroaching sirens. "Did you call?"

"Yes," he said, before placing a wet kiss on Chad's exposed belly.

"What about Jay?" She reached for his arm. "Don't you want to talk to him first?"

"He'll be here," he answered casually. "Called him, too."

His calm bothered her, but the arrival of a swarm of officers prevented her from delving too deeply. She also soon realized that nothing short of a crowbar could pry Chad away from Dylan.

Dylan cradled the baby against him as he stood, swaying, in the living room of the strange house. Shelby was on the sofa, and Katherine sat motionless in a high-backed chair. Several officers lingered in the kitchen, their conversation nothing more than a hum. Chad was nearly asleep, his tiny fist filled with a wrinkled wad of Dylan's shirt.

Her only glimpse of Dylan's emotional state was the dangerous glint in his eyes. When the sound of a car door closing reached her ears, Shelby stiffened.

Katherine's expression grew even more solemn.

Carefully Dylan extracted the groggy infant and carefully handed him to Shelby.

"What are you going to do?"

"Don't know," he answered under his breath.

Jay walked in, looking angry and flustered. Dylan was there to greet him. Or, more accurately, his fist was. Katherine cried out, Shelby sucked in an audible breath, and the officers came running.

Dylan simply shook his fist, turned and claimed his family.

EPILOGUE

"SHELBY!" he called, kicking at the dog as he balanced the three bags of groceries and tried to close the door.

"Foolish, sit."

The dog whimpered once, then skulked off into the living room and sat.

Shelby got up on tiptoe and planted a kiss on his open mouth. "Welcome back," she said sweetly.

"Da...Da...Da..." Chad sang from his high chair.

"Hi, sport," he called as he placed the heavy bags on the kitchen table.

Chad got his kiss first, Shelby noted with a dramatic frown. "I might get jealous if you keep putting him above me."

"No way," Dylan countered, pulling her into the circle of his arms and kissing her deeply and thoroughly. "You're a better kisser. Not as sloppy."

"Gee..." She sighed. "You sure know how to make a girl feel special."

"How about me?" he teased, stealing one of Chad's Cheerios, throwing it in the air and catching it in his mouth. Chad clapped. "It's very emasculating for me that Foolish hangs on your every command and I can't even get him to stand still long enough to put his leash on."

"He'd listen to you if you talked nicely to him," she said, with a taunting shake of her finger.

"I don't want to talk nicely to him. He's a traitor."

"No," she said softly, watching his eyes. "Jay was the traitor. Foolish is just a dog."

Dylan closed up and stalked into the other room. Wiping her hands on the dish towel, Shelby followed.

"Wait a minute," she implored, touching his arm.

Dylan rammed his hands in the front pockets of his jeans, his eyes distant and hard.

"It's been over two months," she began softly, her hand moving from his arm to his chest. She could feel the uneven beating of his heart beneath her fingers.

"And it is over," he insisted tightly. "Jay's admitted that he took Chad in the hopes of convincing you to testify against Nichols. He figured if he played the hero, you'd be so grateful, you'd turn on Ned without a look back."

"He was obsessed, Dylan. He lost sight of his priorities. And," she added more gently, "he'll pay for what he did."

"Not the way he should pay," Dylan countered.

"What do you want?"

"Nothing."

"Yes, you do," she said with a disgusted shrug. "You want to know how someone you trusted could betray you."

"Maybe."

"But Jay didn't know Chad was your son. He only left your medallion in the bushes so your office would be called. He didn't plan on you being involved."

"But I was involved."

"Jay didn't know that, not any more than you knew that Ned was my father when you begged me to help you to put him behind bars."

"Can't we just drop this?" he groaned.

"Not if you want to get married."

His expression darkened, and he gave her a wilting look. "Are you telling me you won't marry me now?"

"I'm telling you that I don't want to get married when you haven't come to grips with what brought us together."

Dylan raked his hand through his hair and turned his back. Foolish lifted his snout off the carpet and regarded him with disinterest.

Shelby felt as if she might explode with frustration. She glared at the steady rise and fall of his broad shoulders.

"You're right," he said, so softly that she almost missed it.

She went to him immediately, reaching around his waist and pressing her face against his back.

"Jay will be punished, and Nichols will probably trip up somewhere along the line. But none of that would matter to me if I didn't have you and Chad in my life."

"I love you."

"I love you, too," he said as he pulled her around to place a meaningful kiss on her lips.

"I knew there was a brain beneath all that brawn," she quipped, tapping her fingertip against his chest.

"Wrong," he said, setting her on the floor. "I just don't have the guts to call my mother and tell her there won't be a wedding in Loganville this Thanksgiving."

Shelby stepped away from him, her eyes carefully shielded from his scrutiny. "Stay right there," she instructed. She raced up to the bedroom and back in record time.

With nervous fingers, she held the small velvet case out for his inspection. One dark brow arched questioningly.

"What is it?"

"Open it."

His eyes grew wide as he lifted the thick gold band from the box. "Aren't you being a bit premature?"

"No," she managed to say, despite her tight throat. "We have to get married."

"I know that. November twenty-fourth, in—"

"No," she interjected. "I mean, we *have* to get married."

"Chad's nearly a year old. I think it's a bit late to be worried about proprieties."

"Fine," she snapped. "Then I hope your mother won't mind me waltzing down the aisle...let me see—" she stopped and made a production of counting on her fingers "—six months pregnant."

She held her breath, expecting something—anything but the long silence. Finally, when she couldn't stand it any longer, Shelby peered up at him through the veil of her lashes. Then she laughed.

"I believe that expression is referred to as 'dumbstruck.'"

"Again? Really? So soon?"

"Yes, yes and yes," she answered. "I'm beginning to understand why your mother had six children. You Tanners are a prolific lot."

He kissed her then. Allaying her fears and making her feel like the luckiest woman alive.

"Do you remember that day when we were looking for Chad and we took that god-awful bike ride on the beach?"

"Sure," he answered as his hands inched down to her waist.

"You asked me what I would tell Chad about his father."

His hands stilled. "You said you had the right child with the wrong man."

"I'd like to amend that," she said as she grasped his hand and slipped the ring off the tip of his forefinger. "Read the inscription."

The right man.

Heather MacAllister
Bride Overboard

Bride Overboard originally appeared as a Harlequin Temptation® novel. Four new sexy, sassy and seductive Harlequin Temptation® books by your favorite authors appear each month.

HARLEQUIN®
Temptation

CHAPTER ONE

TWITCHING HER VEIL aside so she could read, Blair Thomason opened her day planner and ran down the final wedding checklist. *Flowers.* Check. *Musicians.* She opened the door to the master stateroom of the *Salty Señorita,* listened to the flamenco guitarist and winced. Perhaps she could persuade the mariachist—mariachi man?—player?—to refrain during the wedding processional. Making a note beside *musicians,* she continued checking off various bridal elements until she reached the last thing on her list: groom. With a huge smile of satisfaction, she checked off Armand's name—all of it.

At precisely 8:17, as the setting sun cast its golden glow over the Gulf of Mexico, Blair would become Mrs. Armand Luis Jorge de Moura lo Santro Y Chiapis-Chicas Y Barrantes. Or was that Chicas-Chiapis? Blair made a note. Armand rarely used his full name, and when Blair asked him why there was so much of it, he vaguely alluded to a royal quarrel in his family history.

Royalty. Blair sighed. Armand could trace his lineage back hundreds of years. Armand had roots and by grafting herself onto his family tree, Blair would have roots, too.

There was a tap on the stateroom door. "Blair, my darling?"

"Armand!" Blair propped herself against the door. "You know it's bad luck to see the bride before the ceremony."

A richly accented chuckle sounded in the galleyway. "I saw you when we boarded this afternoon. I watched and admired as you most capably directed the catering staff."

Blair smiled at his praise. She'd hoped he'd noticed because she suspected hostessing elegant entertainments would be one of her future responsibilities as Armand's wife. "But I wasn't officially a bride yet. I didn't have on my wedding dress."

"My darling, you needn't have gone to so much trouble. This is merely the civil ceremony. In Argentina, we will be married in the de Moura family chapel by the priest who baptized me. You will wear the lace mantilla that generations of de Moura brides have worn before you."

As his words painted a future she desired with all her heart, Blair clutched her day planner to her chest and shivered. *Generations. Family.* She sighed, almost able to forget that none of Armand's extended family was present to witness the ceremony today. But she had no family present, either, and no friend close enough to ask to make the trip to Argentina with her.

"I will not have my bride touched by the fetid breath of scandal," Armand had declared. "Since you have no female traveling companion, we shall journey to Argentina cloaked in civil respectability."

Blair wondered if there was going to be a civil honeymoon as well as a religious one. She and Armand had not yet...well, Armand was very conscious of her honor. She would be able to face his family pure in heart, if not in actual fact.

"My darling," he said, "one of my cuff links has broken and I would like to retrieve another pair from the safe in the stateroom."

"Is everyone in the salon?" Blair asked.

"I believe so."

"Good. Then I'll be able to slip out and check on things one more time. Turn your back," she instructed.

When she opened the door, Armand, his dark hair just brushing his collar, stood with his back to her, as she'd known he would. Armand was a man of honor.

She was so very lucky, Blair thought, gathering the train

of her dress over her arm and climbing to the upper deck. Though neither of Blair's parents would come to see their daughter married, Armand had not even raised an eyebrow in disapproval. He'd simply suggested an early civil ceremony to avoid any implications of impropriety.

Blair felt cherished for the first time in her life. Someone cared about her. Someone cared *for* her.

Unbidden, her mother's oft-repeated advice drifted through her mind, "The first time marry for money. Then you can afford to marry for love. I got it backward and look what happened to me." Actually, Blair's mother had been married so many times, Blair couldn't remember if her current husband was love or money.

She reached the upper deck and surveyed the scene with satisfaction. It might be a civil ceremony, but a wedding was a wedding and Blair wanted it to feel like one. She needed the familiar bridal trappings to feel anchored to reality.

Anchored. She grinned. Six weeks ago she'd been an efficiency analyst with Watson and Watson Management Consultants in Houston. Now she was about to become the wife of Armand de Moura lo Santro y...etcetera. She really must remember the order. She'd actually written it down both ways.

Such sloppiness wasn't like her, but planning a wedding and preparing to live in another country all in two weeks had taxed even her organizational abilities.

Blair straightened a row of white folding chairs. Armand and his friends noticed details like crooked rows. She tugged on the white satin runner and refastened it. Two bouquets of white roses stood on either side of an arched trellis.

Blair frowned. The trellis, festooned with a huge white bow, didn't look quite right on the ship and it blocked the view of the sunset. The streamers from the bow flapped in the wind, which was much stronger than it had been earlier.

That's it. The trellis goes. Ugly silver duct tape secured the base to the deck. Blair peeled it away to find that a sticky residue marred the varnished surface. Oh, well, she'd position the justice of the peace there.

Once released, the trellis wobbled in the breeze. Now where was she supposed to put it? No one was around to help her. The guests, Armand's usual cadre of friends, would be in the salon eating canapés. The two-man crew had been pressed into service as waiters. The musicians were still below. Great.

She could not deal with her train, her veil *and* the trellis, so Blair simply lifted the construction over the railing and let the wind do the rest.

The trellis landed in the gulf, bobbing in the *Salty Señorita*'s wake.

Much better. Blair gazed out at the horizon. On the left, the Texas-Mexico coastline smudged into the edge of the ocean. Oil-drilling platforms spoiled the beauty, which was why the *Salty Señorita* was sailing so far out. Blair wanted nothing to mar her photographic memories.

She watched the trellis, a bright white against the muddy waters, and waited for it to sink. Her veil whipped across her face, stinging her eyes. This wind was really something. She'd have to check her makeup and figure out a way to fasten her veil, so it wouldn't go flying off during the ceremony.

Just as Blair turned to go below, a shape appeared from between the jumble of oil rigs and coastline. A boat. A small, ugly boat. Since it was ahead of them and traveling the same path, it was bound to be in the pictures, she thought ruefully. The ceremony was due to begin in twenty-two minutes. If the boat continued on course, it would be smack-dab in the middle of the horizon, a blot marring the matrimonial perfection she'd planned.

She couldn't have that.

Avoiding the salon, she returned to the master stateroom, half hoping to find Armand.

It was empty.

Blair retouched her makeup and pinned her veil tightly,

using so many bobby pins that the only way it was coming loose was if she was scalped.

Satisfied, she grabbed her day planner in case she needed to alter the timetable, and made her way to the pilothouse. She wanted to ask the captain to change course or hail that stupid boat and tell it to get out of the way.

Armand's dark head was visible through the open doorway. Maybe he'd noticed the boat and was conferring with the captain.

It would be just like Armand. He, too, was a detail-oriented person. That was why they got along so well together.

Blair, careful to keep her dress from touching any of the equipment bolted to the deck, edged forward, trying to hear but also trying to stay out of Armand's sight.

"—long until we're in Mexican waters?" he was asking.

"Not for another forty minutes," the captain replied.

"Perhaps you could go a little faster?" Armand suggested.

"It'll get mighty breezy up on that top deck."

"That is not my concern. My only concern is that we are in Mexico before the justice of the peace pronounces us man and wife."

"I'll see what I can do, sir." The pitch of the engines climbed.

Mexico. They were scheduled to stop for the night at the resort town of Sonoma Villa where they'd bid farewell to their guests and presumably begin their honeymoon.

Blair smiled. Armand must be rattled. It wasn't like him to make such a mistake. He meant to inform the captain that they should *not* be in Mexican waters when the Texas justice of the peace performed the ceremony. The JP wouldn't have jurisdiction in Mexico. Their marriage wouldn't be legal.

She took two steps toward the pilothouse, then stopped. Armand hadn't sounded rattled, though she saw him check his pocket watch.

"Do you think that boat belongs to the United States authorities?" he asked.

Feeling uneasy, Blair stepped into a stairwell and stayed out of sight.

"As far as I can tell, it's a lone fisherman," the captain replied.

"What is he doing?"

"It appears that he's watching us as closely as we're watching him."

"I don't like it." Armand's tone, while still accented, was clipped and devoid of the charming drawl with which he usually spoke.

"No one has reason to suspect anything. You staged the ceremony right out in the open—which is a nice touch, I might add. If this fisherman is with some law-enforcement agency, then he'll see a wedding as announced."

Blair stopped breathing. *Law?*

"Don't worry, Señor Varga. As usual, all is superbly planned."

Varga? The captain had called Armand Señor Varga. Blair might not be sure of the precise order of all Armand's names, but she knew which ones were there and which ones weren't. Varga wasn't. Was it?

Flipping open her day planner, she turned to the copy of the announcement she'd sent to the newspaper before she left. Armand Luis...it *was* Chiapis-Chicas, she noted—but there was no Varga.

Blair shook her head. She must have misunderstood. Her life had taken such an unreal turn so quickly that her mind couldn't absorb everything and had chosen now to malfunction, she told herself.

Blair liked things orderly and she'd been rushed to get ready for this wedding. She thought she'd handled everything, but...

"It's time," Armand announced with a heavy sigh. "If I do not signal the guests that it is time to leave the salon, my efficient bride will. Perhaps I can create a small time-consuming diversion...you will ring the bell when we cross into Mexican waters?''

Blair didn't wait to hear the captain's response. Gathering her train, she ran to the railing on the opposite side of the yacht and stared at the churning wake.

Varga? Law? Mexican waters? Superbly planned *as usual?* He'd done whatever he was doing before? Just how many faux brides were out there struggling to memorize the order of his names?

She could *not* have heard correctly.

She hadn't eaten since breakfast. That was it. She should eat something. Low blood sugar did funny things to the brain.

"Pondering the enormous leap you are about to take, my love?" Armand spoke from just behind her, his drawl in place, though not as charming as Blair remembered.

"Leap?" Blair whipped around, brushing the veil out of her face. "What leap?"

"Marriage," he replied lightly. "A leap of faith."

Apparently blind faith on her part. "Yes, it is a leap, isn't it? Because of you, I'm off to live in a country I don't know, among people I don't know, with a man..." She turned back to stare at the coastline.

"With a man who is grateful you've chosen to do so," Armand smoothly supplied. "You look lovely, my dear," he said, taking a step toward her.

Blair cringed against the railing, her veil billowing.

"Ah. I was not supposed to see you before the ceremony, was I?"

"No."

"My apologies."

She heard him pivot. "Armand?"

"My love?"

"It's so windy and this veil is being such a pain. Would you please tell the captain to slow down. Or better yet—" she turned so she could see his face "—ask him to drop anchor here until after the ceremony?'' Blair still clutched her day planner, her train and hope.

The small smile remained fixed in place. Armand's dark eyes gave nothing away. "Such a lot of trouble for a veil. Now, if it were my family's bridal mantilla, that would be understandable."

Blair gave him a brilliantly false smile. "Oh, but Armand, I want everything to be perfect." She linked her arm through his. "Let's go ask the captain together."

He allowed her three steps before she felt resistance.

Blair ignored it. "Oh, look!" She pointed and tugged him along. "That trashy little boat's going to spoil our pictures! We simply must speak to the captain—"

"I think we needn't bother the captain over trivialities, my dear." He patted her hand.

As unobtrusively as she could, Blair disengaged her arm. "Then it's time to direct the guests from the salon to the upper deck," she said. "We've timed everything so carefully. After all," she forced herself to add, "we don't want to leave Texas before we're married."

That's your cue. Laugh and agree. Then I'll know everything will be fine.

Armand didn't move. "Something troubles you, my love. The guests can wait a bit longer."

A small, time-consuming diversion...

Blair wanted to scream. Instead, she gazed at Armand, judging the man she thought she knew against the man she'd overheard. The long rays of the setting sun emphasized the furrows and hollows in his face. His jawline was soft. Bronzed skin from his neck lapped over the edge of his white shirt. Impossibly black hair and a pencil-thin mustache absorbed the light without giving any back.

How old is he? "You're not thirty-seven, are you?" she blurted out.

His face creased as he smiled—with relief, she suspected.

"I am thirty-seven in my heart." He placed both hands over the organ in question.

"So how old are you outside your heart? Forty-seven?" That would make him more than twenty years older than Blair.

At his raised eyebrow and elegant shrug, she felt chilled.

"My darling, I will answer your question, but do you truly wish me to?"

No, she didn't. Besides, she had another. "Are you in trouble with the law?"

She'd surprised him.

His black eyebrows arched, then he regarded her intently. "Someone has said something to you. What?"

Not, "No, what are you talking about?" or "Don't be silly, my darling." Blair's last doubts of his perfidy disappeared along with her dreams.

"No one has said anything," she snapped. "I overheard you talking with the captain. You were concerned that the feds were following you in that junky boat." She flung her arm toward it.

Armand glanced at her consideringly, then moved to stand next to her at the railing. "I could continue to maintain the masquerade by telling you that I was referring to customs officials and that I didn't want our wedding interrupted. But I think that would be pointless, would it not?"

"Pretty much." He'd always had just the right response to her questions. Blair began to see how she'd allowed herself to be manipulated. "And speaking of weddings, I gather that you didn't want our marriage to be legal."

Armand drew a deep breath and leaned against the railing, not looking at her. "I've found that life is so much more flexible without legal entanglements."

Blair paced. She'd been well and truly taken in. Armand was nothing more than a charming crook. "Well... congratulations, Armand," she said, coming to a stop in front of him. "You had me completely fooled. 'Lighten up,' my co-workers had said. 'You're so uptight, Blair,' they said. 'Seize the day. Relax. Be impulsive for once.' So I was impulsive and look where it got me."

Armand cleared his throat. "I hardly think two weeks of meticulous planning is impulsive."

"For me it is," she said dryly.

"My dear, you mustn't blame yourself," he said consolingly. It sounded like a speech he'd given before.

"Oh, I don't," Blair said. "It was a grand and glorious six weeks. You are a charming companion, Armand." She wasn't about to let him—or anyone—see that she'd been hurt.

"As are you." He bowed slightly and offered her his arm. "Come, my dear. It is time for the ceremony."

Blair laughed. "You aren't *that* charming. It won't be legal anyway. And now that I know, what's the point?" She started for her stateroom, yelping when her veil caught on something and pulled her hair.

Her veil had caught on Armand's hand. "The point is that we have guests who expect a wedding. And I want them to see a wedding." He tugged on the veil, causing her to stumble forward. "In particular, I want them to return to their homes and discuss the wedding."

"Why?"

Armand smiled his unctuous smile. "Because they surely do not expect me to conduct business when I am on a wedding journey with such a beautiful bride."

Blair thought of the twenty people accompanying them. Three couples were his "dearest friends" and fellow Argentineans, lovely people who made Blair feel as though she were one of them. Then there was the justice of the peace and his wife, while the others were part of the crowd that had grown around Armand during his stay in Texas, most of whom had invested in his beef-shipping venture. "What possible difference—" Blair asked this just as the answer occurred to her. "The investors—this is a scam, isn't it? There is no Argentinean beef-shipping consortium, is there?"

"There most assuredly is." This time, Armand's smile was one of extreme self-satisfaction.

"But..." Realization dawned. "You're swindling *both* sides, aren't you?" And a bride.

"Double the pleasure, double the fun and double the take," said Armand.

"And I provided you with the perfect cover, didn't I?"

"You are the most efficient woman I have ever met." He bowed over her hand.

Blair snatched it away. "Not so efficient that I saw through you."

Armand looked pained. "I cannot allow you to blame yourself," he repeated. "I am very experienced in these matters."

"So what were you planning to do with me after the wedding?" Blair asked, thinking she should have rephrased her question. "Leave me in Sonoma Villa? I'd awaken after my wedding night and find that my groom had run out on me?"

"Oh, no, my dear. People expect us to be on a wedding journey of some four months." Armand reached out and caressed her cheek. Blair recoiled and he let his hand drop.

"I'm not going anywhere with you for four months."

"I did not say I would be with you."

"You're darn right you're not going to be with me. As soon as we dock in Sonoma Villa, I'm outta here." She snatched her veil out of his hand and marched toward the stateroom, intending to lock herself in.

Armand grabbed her arm. "The ceremony, darling."

She jerked her arm away. "I am *not* going through with that sham. You're going to have to swindle those people without my help."

"Dear girl, you have no choice in the matter. The captain and crew are in my employ."

"So what are they going to do? Hold a gun on me? That'll sure give people something to talk about. And while I'm there, how about I tell everybody just what a crook you are?"

Armand didn't seem particularly bothered by her threat. "Crooks *we* are," he corrected.

"*I* haven't done anything."

Armand studied his nails. "That might be difficult for you to prove."

"Why?"

He shuddered delicately as though revealing his methods were distasteful. "There are documents, affidavits, loan papers and the like all bearing your signature." Smiling sadly, he continued, "It would not look good for you, my dear."

"I read everything I signed. I signed applications for residency, I had my money moved to a bank in Argentina..." Blair trailed off, thinking of the unexpected paperwork she'd encountered. There had been a lot, she remembered thinking.

"Do you read Spanish, dear one?" Armand asked softly.

"No, but I read the English translations."

He smiled.

In a heartbeat, she understood. "Oh no," she groaned and looked skyward. Armand had arranged for the English translations. She'd probably never find out what she'd really signed.

"Blair, I like you. Even in your chagrin, you are admiring my thoroughness, no?"

So help her, she was. What was the matter with her? She was in a hideous position, possible physical danger, her good name was ruined—and yet a part of her admired the way everything had fallen into place for him. Almost everything.

"I think I shall take you with me," Armand said after a moment. "I could make you my protégée. We would work well together." His eyes came as close to sparkling as she'd ever seen them. "Think of it. Planning grand schemes down to the tiniest detail."

"You've got to be kidding."

"Blair, Blair." He took her shoulders. "Cut yourself free from the anchor of morality and soar with me!"

"I don't think so."

The light went out of Armand's eyes and he sighed. "So be it. I must remind you that should you speak of this to anyone, I will have authorities waiting to arrest you the moment we dock in Sonoma Villa."

Blair backed away, nearly tripping over a metal cylinder. She grabbed at it to steady herself. "You think you've thought of everything."

"Because I have." Armand uttered the words with supreme self-confidence.

"I bet you haven't thought of this." Blair dropped her planner and yanked the pull ring on the metal cylinder. A life raft shot through the air, inflating as it fell.

"What are you doing?" Armand cried.

"Improvising." Blair grabbed her planner and climbed over the railing.

"Blair, people like us do not improvise well!"

"Goodbye, Armand." She scrambled down the metal ladder.

She'd counted on surprise to hold Armand immobile for a few seconds. She hadn't counted on her train.

With a very un-Armand-like howl, he grabbed it before it could slither over the railing after her.

It was detachable, held in place by a row of tiny satin-covered buttons. Blair jerked. Armand jerked back. The satin buttons held fast. The *Salty Señorita* sailed farther and farther away from the bobbing life raft.

Armand smiled.

Blair reached for the life preserver and jumped, pushing away from the side of the boat with her feet.

The train ripped free, but not before it shortened her jump. Blair felt the life preserver scrape through her fingers and braced for a watery impact.

The gulf was both harder and colder than she'd expected. The air left her lungs and she swallowed a mouthful of salty water before clamping her lips shut and kicking toward the surface.

Her veil dragged at her like bridal seaweed, but she couldn't rip it off. Blair was further hampered by holding on to her day planner as though it were a lifeline. To her, retaining possession of the details of her life was every bit as important as breathing.

Using the book like a paddle, she finally broke the surface and choked in a breath. Well, improvising certainly looked as though it was going to be a sink-or-swim operation.

Hampered by the slim sheath of her wedding dress, she could hardly tread water, much less swim for the life raft. There was no way she could keep afloat for long.

With her free hand, she tore at the veil, unable to get the sodden mass off her head and tread water at the same time.

She swallowed another mouthful of seawater, yet started paddling determinedly toward the now-distant raft. Someone called her name. Instinctively turning to look, her vision filled with white an instant before pain exploded in her head and she slipped beneath the cool, dark waters of the gulf.

CHAPTER TWO

"WHAT THE *HELL?*"

John Drake O'Keefe dropped the binoculars, blinked several times then squinted through them again.

"She jumped. I can't believe she jumped. What is she—nuts?"

He'd been keeping an eye on the big motor yacht for the last hour. The top deck was decorated with white froufrou and folding chairs. Obviously a wedding. He hoped they weren't planning to honeymoon on his island.

In the eight months since he'd moved to Pirate's Hideout, there had been instances of visitors who hadn't heard that the exclusive resort had closed due to hurricane damage and was now privately owned.

From experience, he'd found that it was better if he headed off boats instead of allowing them to dock. People had a tendency to disembark once they'd docked somewhere. It didn't matter what he said, they wanted to get off and have a look around, oohing and aahing at the damage and comparing how the place had looked when they were there last.

The first time it happened, Drake had still retained some vestige of polite, civilized behavior and allowed the folks to poke around. Trouble was, they didn't seem to understand the concept of private ownership. Or rather, they understood that he was now the owner, but they just couldn't accept that he wasn't willing—or able—to serve them a meal or put them up for the night.

Now he sailed out to head them off at the pass.

"Man, that must have been some lover's quarrel," Drake muttered to himself. He'd seen the struggle with the train and the bride's jump, veil trailing after her like a comet's tail. It was a long way to the life raft, too. He wished her luck.

Drake watched the churning froth of white until he saw the bride's head bob up through the surface. She didn't look as if she was doing all that great, but at least she— "No, you moron!"

The groom had let fly with the life preserver and had scored a direct hit almost as soon as the woman surfaced.

Drake stared hard at the ring as it flipped, then floated in the water. He couldn't tell if she was okay or not. He could still see white, which meant she hadn't gone under, but he didn't see her head or arms.

He was concentrating so intently that several seconds passed before he realized the yacht was sailing off. He jerked the binoculars to the railing and saw the groom—he assumed it was the groom—staring at the water, arms spread out across the railing. Then, as if the man knew Drake was watching, he looked directly at him. "Yeah, pal, you've got a problem."

But no alarm sounded. No activity indicated a rescue. And no rope materialized, attaching the life preserver to the yacht.

"Hey!" Drake actually stood and waved both arms above his head. "You've got a woman in the water! Your bride's overboard—get back here!" The yacht didn't slow down.

Stunned, Drake sat abruptly, expecting any moment to see the yacht turn around. Expecting somebody to jump in after her. Expecting...something.

"I don't believe this. You're crazy! Both of you have lost it. Haven't you ever heard of counseling? People make a nice living dealing with crazies like you. This is *not* my problem, people!" He berated the unknown couple even as he nosed his dinghy toward the life preserver and opened the motor full throttle. "My boat's too small for open water.

Who did you think was going to rescue you? Huh? Did you think of that before you jumped, lady?" he yelled. "The motor's going to blow any minute. And if it doesn't, I'll probably capsize and we'll both be in the drink."

Nobody could hear him, but Drake continued to rant and rave, steering with one hand, looking through the binoculars with the other. "I'm going to regret this." He cursed and braced himself as the wake from the yacht slapped his boat.

Miraculously, he rode it out and remained afloat, though an inch of water now sloshed around his feet.

Drake continued to plow toward the white blob, the motor protesting nearly as much as he was. Out of habit, he glanced down at his wrist to see how much time had elapsed since the woman had been beaned with the life preserver.

Tan obliterated all but the faintest outline marking the fifteen years where he'd worn his expensive graduation present. He'd kept the watch out of sentimentality, but timepieces were the first things he'd discarded when he'd come to live at the ruined Pirate's Hideout.

So how long had she been in the water? Two minutes? Three? His heart was getting as much of a workout as the engine. He hoped neither gave out.

Once he passed the protective barrier of his island, Drake bucked the waves of the open gulf. Currents were strong in this area and he'd already adjusted his heading as the woman drifted southward.

"Oh, man." When he got close enough to see her legs floating limply beneath the surface, Drake set aside the binoculars and grimly reviewed everything he knew about CPR.

He cut the motor and drifted the rest of the way toward her. "Hey, lady?" Maybe she was just dazed. He could see her veil, which meant her head had to be above water, didn't it?

Grabbing an oar, Drake maneuvered the boat closer and caught his breath.

The woman's veil had become twisted in the life preserver and its rope, keeping her head just above water. But occasionally, the ocean lapped over her face, so she'd probably inhaled a few snootfuls.

Drake prodded her with his oar, trying to bring her within reach without dislodging the floating ring. When he could, he grasped her arm, carefully sliding her closer. Something else, wedged beneath her neck and the ring, had helped keep her head out of the water, as well. A black book floated free when Drake pulled her toward the dinghy. He fished it out and tossed it into the boat.

"Okay, lady, let's see if your luck's held."

He leaned out as far as he dared and tried to disentangle her veil. When he couldn't, he tried unsuccessfully to pull it off her head. What had she used, superglue?

He placed her hands over the side of the dinghy and held them there to keep her from slipping away. Next he heaved the floating ring into the boat.

"You couldn't be a petite five-footer, could you?" He drew a couple of deep breaths, then began the battle of hauling her into his boat.

She was a good-size girl with some muscle on her. Probably had worked out to get ready for her wedding. Muscle weighed more than fat, which wasn't helping him any.

He wondered why she'd jumped. So help him, if he couldn't revive her, he'd never know.

He didn't care, he just wanted to know.

Drake braced his feet against the weathered wooden side of the dinghy and, with a mighty heave, pulled her most of the way in—at least to the point where gravity was finally on his side.

He fished her leg out and she half slid, half rolled into the boat. She was all caught up in the veil, so Drake had to unroll her before he could attempt to get water out of her lungs.

All the jouncing helped, and water drained out of her mouth. "Atta girl." He moved her arms over her head and pressed her back.

More water. He rolled her over, tilted her head back, checked her mouth for any obstructions, pinched her nostrils and puffed air into her lungs, watching to see if her chest rose and fell. It did, but only once.

"Come on, lady. I've gone to a hell of a lot of trouble here and I'd appreciate it if you'd make an effort to cooperate."

Drake thumped her back, willing water to drain out.

He tried mouth-to-mouth resuscitation again and again. He was feeling light-headed, when she jerked and coughed. Her hands clawed air as she choked, gasped, then rolled over and promptly threw up.

Drake had never been so glad to see anyone throw up in his life. He rubbed her back, his hand trembling.

She continued to cough and gurgle. He sat on the wooden seat and dangled his hands between his knees. A cold sweat covered him.

He'd saved her life. He'd never saved anybody's life before. Lifesaving was exhausting.

When at last the woman drew a shuddering breath and lay still, they both sighed.

She was curled on her side, her eyes shut. Her skin was unnaturally pale and the freckles on her nose stood out. Her dress was a tight white number, or it had been until she'd gone for her bridal swim and had been dragged over the side of his boat. There was a slit up the back that had torn, probably when she'd kicked.

And, though he tried not to be aware of it, the damp material was nearly transparent.

To distract himself, Drake gazed at her headdress, now sporting an aquatic theme. Twisting his head to one side, he read the yacht's name on the life preserver. *Salty Señorita.* How apt. He grinned for the first time today. Maybe for the first time this week.

The salty *señorita* wrinkled her nose and opened her eyes.

Drake prepared himself for an outpouring of gratitude.

She blinked a couple of times, then grimaced. "Oh,

gross!" She sat up and scooted toward the other side of the boat away from the mess. "I feel like garbage."

"You look like garbage," Drake offered. But considering what she'd just been through, she could have looked a lot worse.

She squinted at him. "You're that guy in the boat." Reaching up, she began pulling pins out of her hair.

"Yeah." There were a lot of pins. Drake was fascinated by the movements of her fingers as pin after pin dropped into her lap.

"What took you so long?" she asked. "I almost drowned out there."

"What do I look like, the Coast Guard?" She wasn't acting like somebody who had nearly drowned.

She glanced at him, then at his boat. "No. Definitely not the Coast Guard—" Breaking off, she coughed.

"Are you going to be okay?" Drake asked, refraining from adding, *since you wouldn't be breathing now if it hadn't been for me.*

Nodding, she visibly swallowed. "Yeah, probably."

"You don't sound all that thrilled at the prospect."

She managed a half smile and resumed pulling out the pins. "Is that your subtle way of asking if I was trying to kill myself?"

Drake had always found half smiles sexy, though why he should think so under these circumstances was beyond him. "Were you?"

"No." Her eyes widened, and she swiveled her head from right to left, looking all around them. "Where are we? Where's Armand?"

Must be the groom. "He sailed off while you were playing bride of the sea." Drake pointed southward where a small speck may or may not have been the *Salty Señorita*.

Blinking, she absorbed this development. For the first time, she noticed the life preserver. "What happened?"

"You jumped, surfaced and, about a second later, were

conked on the head by that." Drake toed the ring, still enshrouded in bridal netting.

Her eyes grew wide. "You mean, he tried to kill me?"

"I don't think it was intentional. Hitting you from that distance was a hundred-to-one long shot."

"It would have been a lot easier for him if I'd drowned."

"Oh, I don't know. You look like the type to haunt a guy."

"H-how long was I unconscious?" Her face paled even more.

Watching her carefully, Drake shrugged. "A few minutes."

She blinked at him. Her eyes were blue—the pale blue kind that made the pupils stand out. They'd dilated. "I could have drowned," she whispered through lips that were trembling.

"Hey, don't go into shock on me."

"I could have *drowned*," she repeated, sounding bewildered.

"Well, yes, but you didn't."

"But why? Why didn't I drown?"

Approaching her cautiously, Drake touched her clammy arm. *Oh, great.* He briskly rubbed both of them. "Your veil got caught in the ring and kept your head above water. If the ring had flipped the other way, it would have been a different story." One he shouldn't dwell on.

She shuddered.

"Look, it'll be dark soon and I'd better get us to shore. We've already drifted. Hope there's enough gas," he muttered and fired up the motor.

The woman stared dully at him.

"Put your head down." He pressed her forward, but her skirt was so tight she couldn't spread her knees apart. Drake lengthened the rip at the back of her dress.

She didn't even flinch.

Urging her head down, he increased the engine speed and the boat bounced over the waves.

"How're you doing?" he asked after a few minutes of silence.

"I think I'm going to be sick."

"You probably don't have much left to be sick with."

She groaned and resumed pulling out pins without lifting her head. When her fingers didn't find any more, she flipped the veil over her head and Drake saw why it hadn't come loose. Part of her hair was braided over a plastic ring. She fumbled with the rubber band, then jerked it off, bringing several strands of brown hair with it.

He winced.

At last, she pulled the veil from her head and sat up, finger-combing her hair until it hung in wavy strands to her bare shoulders.

Drake studied her. As far as he could see, her pupils were the same size and the zombie look she'd worn earlier was replaced by a pensive expression.

She stared out at the ocean, bathed in the orangy glow of the setting sun. "Thanks," she said quietly, without looking at him.

He understood. Nearly dying would make a person want to reflect for a time.

"What's your name?" he asked her quietly.

"Blair. Blair *Thomason*." There was an unmistakable emphasis on the last name.

"Is that *Mrs*. Thomason?"

She glanced down at a diamond the size of his thumbnail. "No." Holding out her hand, she wiggled her finger and watched the stone catch the light.

"So, Miss Blair Thomason, what happened? Counseling didn't work out?"

Her gaze swept over him as though she was aware she owed him an explanation yet didn't want to give it. "What's your name?"

He could answer anything. He could be anybody. "Drake," he said, deciding on the truth. Deception took too much effort.

"Well, Drake, it was like this. Armand wasn't the man I thought he was."

How intriguing. This Armand had definitely transgressed. Drake wondered how. Must have been a lulu. "Couldn't you have told him you'd changed your mind?"

"I did, but he wasn't taking no for an answer."

Drake waited, but Blair wasn't inclined to elaborate. He couldn't stand it. "And so you jumped ship in a remote area of the Gulf of Mexico? What the hell were you thinking?"

Her eyes narrowed. "It was important to Armand's plan that there be a wedding ceremony. I made sure there wouldn't be one."

"What are you, some kind of heiress?" He glanced at her hand.

"No." Following his gaze, she looked at the ring, then slipped it off. Drake thought she was going to offer it to him as some sort of payment and was preparing to refuse when she raised her arm and he realized she was going to throw the ring into the ocean.

"Hey!" He grabbed her arm. "If you don't want the ring, I'll take it."

"This diamond is probably as fake as Armand."

"But you don't know that for a fact."

She rolled her eyes, crawled toward his rusty metal toolbox and proceeded to pound and rub the big square diamond against the sharp corners.

Drake shook his head.

Blair tilted the ring toward the waning light and smiled grimly. "Fake," she pronounced, crawling back and handing it to him. "And not even a good one."

Gouges and chips scored the surface of the stone.

"Was he a good one?" Drake asked, handing the ring back to her.

She tossed it overboard, then sat on the wooden seat across from him. "Pardon me?"

"Was your Armand a good fake?"

"Triple-A quality."

"At least you found out in time."

"That's a matter of opinion. Look, can you slow down or make the ride smoother?"

"I wish I could. Running at max for this length of time isn't good for the engine, but I don't want to get caught after dark. Won't be able to find my way home."

Blair was gazing intently at the murky shoreline. "Where are the lights?" she asked suddenly.

"I didn't leave any on. Didn't plan to be out this long."

"No, I mean where are the *lights?* From houses and buildings. Streetlights, that sort of thing."

"There aren't any."

"Why not?"

"Because there aren't any people."

"What do you mean, there aren't any people? Where are you taking me?"

"To that island straight ahead and to the right. I live there."

"Alone?"

Drake nodded. "Just me and the gulls."

She recoiled. "I don't want to go to your island."

"You don't have a choice."

With her hands folded quietly in her lap, Blair tilted her head regally. "I demand that you take me to the nearest police station."

"Sorry. No can do."

"Well, you'd better!"

"Or what? You'll jump overboard? Be my guest... And while you're at it, take this with you." He tossed the life preserver with its attached veil toward her.

She glared at him. "You're as bad as Armand."

Unreasonably stung, he protested, "I am nothing like Armand."

"Yes, you are. All men are. You're all bullies."

Drake was beginning to sympathize with the unknown Armand. "Is this the way you show gratitude? By insulting me? Haven't you ever heard of the custom that the savee's life belongs to the saver?''

"Oh, so *that's* what this is about. It got a little lonely on that island, did it, Drake? And what better love slave than a woman who was left for dead?" She scorched him with a look. "You pervert."

"Love slave? *You?*" Drake laughed. The idea was so preposterous that he laughed more. In fact, he laughed until he was weak, then had to correct the boat's course.

Blair maintained a frigid silence and held herself with such queenly dignity that it set him off again.

"I believe you've made your point with insulting clarity," she said over his fading chuckles.

"Good." He grinned. "And I'm glad to see you aren't dwelling on what some people might see as an enormous debt to the person who saved their life. In fact, some people might even try to cooperate instead of issuing orders."

Her eyes narrowed. "I should have kept my mouth shut about the engagement ring and just given it to you as payment."

"You'd have done that? You'd give the man who saved your life a worthless piece of glass?"

"I wouldn't have known for certain that it was worthless, and material expressions of gratitude seem important to you."

"What gave you that idea?"

"You tried to keep me from throwing the ring away."

"That's because I thought it was a five-carat diamond. I mean, sentimentality aside, a real diamond that size would have netted you at least enough to pay for your dress."

She looked down at herself and grimaced. "You also asked if I was an heiress. I told you no, but it's obvious that you don't believe me."

Drake opened his mouth, then closed it and concentrated on the approaching shoreline. The woman's brains must have been pickled by saltwater. He'd cut her some slack.

"I'm telling you, I'm not an heiress and I'm not wealthy."

"Congratulations."

"So there is no point in kidnapping me. Please take me to the police and I promise I won't mention anything about your momentary lapse."

Drake's brief amusement had long since faded. "Believe me, it would give me the greatest pleasure to unload you onto somebody else, but I can't. The nearest town is San Verde, on the Mexican border, and it's a three- to four-hour boat trip, depending on the boat. And *this* boat can't make the trip."

That shut her up for a while, at least long enough for Drake to concentrate on the approaching shoreline. He just barely avoided running them onto a sandbar.

They were still south of his dock. He cut the motor's speed and rode parallel to the island, straining to find the marina.

"You don't understand." Blair leaned forward. "Armand is a crook—a swindler. A con man. For all I know, he tried to kill me. I've got to tell the police."

"You can tell them whatever you want, but you're not telling them tonight." She was getting on his nerves. *Really* getting on his nerves. Fortunately, he spotted the dock and pointed the dinghy toward it.

"You want details?"

"Not particularly."

"He ran a scam between people in Texas and Argentina. That's two countries. He's probably broken all kinds of international laws."

"And you were going to marry this guy?" Drake cut the motor and glided into the dock.

"Not after I found out."

"That would be when you jumped overboard." He climbed on to the dock.

"Yes."

Blair threw him the rope and he tied the boat to a wooden post with a No Trespassing sign nailed to it.

"Get your stuff," he ordered. "You can clean up the boat tomorrow."

Her mouth dropped open, but amazingly she didn't argue. She grabbed the life preserver and veil and held out her hand.

"Is that planner yours?" Drake pointed. "It was tangled in your veil."

"You found my organizer!" Blair grabbed the black book, a look of joy on her face.

Drake had had a Filofax once. The executive size. He hadn't made a move without consulting it. The fact that she'd jumped overboard with hers told him she felt the same way he'd felt. But those days were over for him, thank God.

Shaking his head, he held out his hand to help Blair out of the dinghy.

A rip accompanied her climb from the boat. They both ignored it, though Drake noted the well-shaped leg it revealed, and walked over what was left of the wooden dock. Here and there, boards were missing. After a few feet, the walkway ended and they trudged through sand until they reached the golf-cart track.

"This is perfect," Blair said from behind him. "I have notes in here that will prove Armand—"

"Nobody in San Verde will care one way or the other what Armand did or didn't do." Drake held a low-hanging branch out of her way.

She ducked under it. "He left me floating in the Gulf of Mexico."

"You jumped."

"He's swindled people."

"They should have been more careful."

She spluttered. "He *lied* to me."

"*You* should have been more careful."

The golf-cart track intersected with the main drive of the lodge and continued in a loop that would bring it by the six cabanas on various parts of the tiny island. Three of the outer cabanas had been flattened. All had suffered damage. The nearest one to the lodge wasn't as bad as the rest and Drake had spent a week or so living in it until he'd made sufficient repairs to the lodge to be fairly certain the place wouldn't collapse on him. He'd get Blair some supplies and point her in the direction of the habitable cabana.

"He told me he was going to hold me prisoner for four months." Blair was still whining about Armand.

Drake wished she'd drop the subject. "I thought he was going to marry you."

"But it wouldn't have been a legal marriage and then he—" She broke off as they approached the dark hulk of the Pirate's Hideout Lodge. "What's that?"

"That," Drake said, "is my home."

CHAPTER THREE

"THAT'S NOT A HOME. That's a pile of driftwood."

"Isn't it great?" Drake gestured to the doorway, which was permanently open, since the door was propped beside it.

"What are you, a squatter?" Gingerly, Blair stepped over the rough boards and into the dark interior. Drake had disappeared inside. She heard rustlings and stayed near the doorway.

"No, I own the place. All of it." Drake struck a match and a kerosene lamp dimly illuminated the interior.

Directly in front of her was a desk and telephone switchboard, though she didn't see a telephone. Drake was standing immediately to the left, at a bar.

Bottles still lined two of the mirrored walls, but the third section was bare and only a jagged piece of the mirror remained.

He hung the lamp on a nail in a post, and struck another match.

"There's no electricity?"

"Nope." Drake lit two more lamps. "Not tonight."

Blair could almost see the whole place. Chairs and tables littered the room. "So there *can* be electricity."

"There's a generator out back, but it's a noisy thing. I run it when I need to."

"Can I convince you that you need to now?"

He shook his head. "If you need more light, I've got another lamp around here you can use. And maybe a flashlight or two."

"How about a telephone?" Blair asked, thinking of the switchboard.

"No telephone. Electricity wouldn't make a difference for that, anyway."

"How am I going to call the police?"

He shot her a frustrated look, his bearded face forbidding in the lamplight. "I have a shortwave radio you can use *tomorrow*."

The tone of his voice warned her not to press the point. Well, too bad. "But Armand will be gone by tomorrow!"

Drake vaulted over the bar and ducked behind it. "By now he's in Mexico."

"Yes. We were going to spend the night in Sonoma Villa. If they hurry, the police can still catch him."

When he stood, Drake was shaking his head. "You think he's going to sit around in Sonoma Villa and wait to be arrested?"

Actually, Blair did expect Armand to make some excuse to their guests—probably that she was seasick—and let them off in Sonoma Villa as scheduled. She smiled grimly. She'd upset his plans, but he was the type to recover quickly. "No, but the police in Sonoma Villa can be alerted."

"To what?" Drake shoved a canned drink down the bar to her. "According to you, he hasn't done anything yet."

And he never intended to—that was the point. But when would Armand's inaction become a crime? Blair had no idea what he'd told the investors. Yet, surely there must be some law he'd broken. Unfortunately, until she could think of one, it appeared Drake had a point.

She needed time to organize her thoughts and think of possible courses of action. Obviously, if she couldn't convince this man of the urgency of her story, then what luck would she have with disinterested police in a tiny border town? They'd chalk up her story to the hysterical ravings of a woman in a wet wedding dress—as Drake was probably doing.

Blair eyed him as he took a long swallow from his drink. Time to drop the subject. She could deal with Armand's perfidy tomorrow.

Propping the life preserver against the wooden bar, she nodded to the can and asked him, "Have you got any diet drinks?"

Drake's mouth twisted in a mocking smile. "I think you can stand the calories this once."

She probably could. Anyway, her mouth had the most horrible taste. Blair sat on a bar stool and reached for the can. "It's cold!"

"Dry ice."

A cold drink. Suddenly nothing sounded better. From the first sip, Blair couldn't stop herself from guzzling the sweet liquid. It was all caffeine and sugar, but who cared?

"Hey, go easy on that." Drake's callused hand closed around her wrist.

"But I'm so thirsty," she complained. Her tongue seemed to swell in her mouth.

"See how your stomach handles this much." Sympathy flashed in the depths of his usually dispassionate gaze.

She closed her eyes as a sudden queasiness came over her, but it soon passed.

"How are you feeling now?" he asked when she opened her eyes to find him watching her.

"Hungry. I haven't eaten since breakfast."

"Let's see what we've got back here." Drake reached beneath the bar and brought out a box of crackers and spray cheese in a can.

"You're kidding."

He stared at her. "I like junk food. And if I want to eat junk food, I'll eat junk food. I eat plenty of fish. I grow vegetables. I pick fruit. My body can handle a little Jiffy Cheez." He ripped open the cracker box and mangled it in the process.

"I was only commenting." What a grouch. "It was unexpected, that's all."

Drake offered her a cracker. "I thought the crackers would settle your stomach."

"Thanks." She took one.

He held up the can.

In the interest of harmony, Blair nodded.

Shaking the can, Drake flipped off the top and squirted a perfect rosette onto her cracker.

She laughed. "You're good at that."

"Hours of practice."

"Just how many cans have you got back there?"

He squirted cheese on three more crackers. "I order it by the case."

"It's not bad," Blair admitted, though the cheese probably wouldn't have tasted so good if she hadn't been starving.

She studied Drake as she chewed. It was hard to tell how old he was. He wore a New York Knicks cap, and neither the scraggly locks of hair that hung beneath it nor his beard were streaked with gray. Squint lines around his eyes could be due to age or hours in the sun. He wore a knit shirt, which revealed tanned, muscled arms, cutoff jeans and holey deck shoes on his feet. Was he good-looking? Maybe, but the beachcomber look had never appealed to her.

No, you like suave, well-dressed fakes.

The thought sickened her. She and the others had been taken in by Armand largely because of the way he'd dressed and the lies he'd told. No one had looked beneath the surface.

What a snob she was. Here she was criticizing this poor man's appearance after he'd shared his Jiffy Cheez with her. She ought to be ashamed.

"Here you go," he said, pushing another cracker toward her.

A familiar form wiggled at her. "It's an elephant! How'd you do that?"

"Like this." With a few squirts, Drake fashioned an alligator.

"You're good." As she ate the elephant, Blair watched Drake sculpt a cat, a dog and a rhinoceros—or it could have been another elephant with a misshapen trunk. Blair doubted it, though. He was really quite skilled at cheese sculpture.

After eating half a dozen of Drake's cheese animals, she pronounced herself full.

"Better now?" he asked.

She nodded, feeling sleepy. Probably a delayed reaction setting in.

He came out from behind the bar. "Follow me, and we'll get you settled."

She slid off the bar stool. "What happened to this place?"

"Hurricanes. Three of them." He handed her a lamp. "Two early in the season and one at the tail end."

Blair accepted the lantern. She held on to her soggy planner.

"This place used to be a resort. This is the lodge." Drake gestured with his lamp. "We're passing through the lounge. Restaurant's through there. The kitchen, laundry, housekeeping and so on is this way." He swung the light to the left and indicated that she should turn.

"We're walking through the rec room."

Silently, careful of her bare feet, Blair followed Drake through the ruined lodge. At every turn, she expected to see signs of repairs in progress, but as far as she could determine, nothing had been done for quite some time.

The odor of mildew permeated the air. The night sky was visible through holes in the roof, and water had rotted several interior sections.

The only room that looked vaguely inhabitable was the rec room, and it appeared that this was where Drake slept.

It was a spacious room with Drake's bed against one wall. By shifting chairs around, Blair could have a little privacy. It wouldn't be the best accommodations, but she could stand it for one night.

"Come on." Drake gestured impatiently from a doorway

at the end of the hall. "This is the linen closet. We've got sheets, towels and spare uniforms in here." He pulled the items off the shelves and piled them into her arms. "You want a medium or large T-shirt?"

"Medium."

He started to take a yellow one from the stack.

"Yellow isn't my color," Blair said. "Could I have one of the teal ones?" She pointed.

Drake looked as though he was about to say something, apparently thought better of it and replaced the yellow T-shirt. "Here you go." He set a teal square on the stack in her arms.

Looking down at it, Blair could see embroidered writing above the pocket. "Pirate's Hideout. That's what the sign said out front. Is that the name of this place?"

"Good guess." He piled something khaki over the shirt.

"You don't have to be sarcastic. I was just making conversation."

"You don't have to make conversation. In fact, I'd prefer it if you didn't." Drake positioned a small rattan basket on top of the stack. Inside were the usual hotel toiletries.

This was working out far better than she'd expected when she'd first seen the building.

"I nearly forgot." He stood on a metal shelf and reached for an unopened clear plastic bag containing an off-white fabric. "Mosquito netting. I'd suggest you make hanging it your first priority." He scooted it under the rattan basket.

The stack was so high, Blair had to hold the little basket in place with her chin.

"If you think of anything else you need, you can poke around in here all you like. Food's in the kitchen next door. There's a whole pantryful of cans. Trouble is, the labels are gone."

"I bet that keeps your meals interesting."

"I've had some strange ones," he admitted, and led her back the way they'd come.

When they came to the rec room, Blair started to go inside.

"That's my room." Drake continued down the hall.

Blair stopped. "I assumed...it's big enough for both of us."

He turned around and stared back at her. Dark eyes looked her up and down, then held her gaze. "No." Pivoting abruptly, he continued down the hall.

The incident unsettled her. She couldn't read the look on Drake's face—probably because of his beard. Beards didn't appeal to her. Come to think of it, pencil-thin mustaches didn't appeal to her, either.

Blair struggled to keep up as the bare concrete floor scraped her feet. She could imagine what this place must have been like. There had probably been carpet here once. The bar-area floor had been a soothingly cool tile. She could picture lazy afternoons spent sipping iced drinks as ceiling fans circulated ocean breezes.

She wondered about Drake, living here all alone. A hotel like this had probably been his dream and he'd run out of money to repair it. And without repairs, no guests would ever come. She remembered the season of storms two summers ago. The second hurricane wasn't so bad, but people had just finished or were still making repairs from the first one. Several areas of Houston had flooded, and there were stories of people with carpet installed only two weeks before it was all ruined again. By the third storm, the government had stepped in and refused to allow home owners to rebuild in certain areas.

That must be what had happened here. Too bad.

She expected Drake to show her to a room in another part of the lodge, but he headed out the front door. "Where are we going?" She found it difficult to negotiate the treacherous steps with an armload of linens and a kerosene lamp.

"Cabana number one," he replied.

Blair stopped. "Wait a minute—I'm not sleeping in the lodge?"

"No."

It was dark now and she couldn't see much beyond the circle of light made by her lamp. Drake's lamp was bobbing farther and farther into the mass of vegetation at the edge of the lodge's overgrown front yard.

Reluctantly, she plodded down the golf-cart track after him. The cracked asphalt was still warm from the day's sun, but it was hard on her feet. She couldn't wait to return to civilization.

She couldn't wait to get even with Armand.

Within a couple of minutes, just long enough to walk out of sight of the main lodge, Blair saw Drake open the door to a small cabin.

When she stepped inside, she saw that he was carefully examining the walls and floor around the perimeter of the room.

"I don't see any scorpions, but check your shoes before—you don't have shoes. No problem."

"I happen to think it's a problem."

"Yeah, well, you can tie banana leaves or something on your feet." He held up the lantern and checked the roof.

Feeling the gritty coating of sand on the linoleum floor, Blair crossed the room and gingerly set her stack on the bare mattress of the bed. A low, square canopy frame stood guard over it.

"Looks like this place has stayed fairly waterproof." Drake lowered the lantern. "I lived here before I moved into the lodge."

Blair crossed her arms over her chest. "What's the point of making me sleep out here? Are you punishing me for the love-slave remark?"

"Punishing you? I fed you and gave you supplies. Then I took you out here and made sure there weren't any nasty old bugs to bother you. If you think that's punishment, then you've led a sheltered life."

"I don't want to stay out here by myself. If you don't want me sleeping in your precious rec room, then I'll sleep on the floor in the bar." She grabbed her stuff and knocked over the little rattan basket. Miniature bottles rolled everywhere. Muttering, Blair bent to pick them up.

"I don't want you in the bar, either."

"Why *not?*"

"Because I am not playing house for two weeks with a crazy woman. Hang the mosquito netting. Good night." He crossed to the door.

"Wait—what do you mean, two weeks?"

"That's when the next supply boat is due out. You can catch a ride into San Verde on it."

Blair grabbed at his shirt. "You can't possibly mean that I'm stuck here for two weeks!"

"That's exactly what I mean." He peeled her fingers off him.

"No."

"Yes."

"I can't spend two weeks here. You'll just have to take me to San Verde."

"I can't. The dinghy won't make the trip."

"You mean you're stranded here all the time?"

"Not all the time, but I am until I replace the carburetor in the launch."

"And when will that be?"

"In *two weeks* when the supply boat brings it!"

"Then you'll have to contact somebody to come and get me." Blair bit off each word. Honestly, eating all that Jiffy Cheez had affected his brain.

Drake rounded on her. "Let's get a few things straight, lady. I don't *have* to do anything. You can do whatever you want to this place to make yourself comfortable. I'll turn on the water pump so you'll have running water, but don't drink it. Either use purification tablets or drink bottled water. You'll find everything in the kitchen. You're going to have to catch your own fish and cook your own meals. But most important, you are to stay the hell away from me!" He jerked open the door. "And don't eat all the Jiffy Cheez!"

"I wouldn't dream of it!" Blair yelled after him and slammed the door.

The light wobbled as vibrations rattled the lantern.

She couldn't believe she was stuck here for two weeks. She would *not* be stuck here for two weeks. She would think of something.

And she wasn't going to stay alone in the cabana tonight, either.

Blair started to gather her things, then stopped. The sun had set and a high-pitched whine told her the mosquitoes were out. She was standing in a damp wedding dress in the middle of an island inhabited by a grumpy recluse. She was not in the best of negotiating positions.

Blair sank onto the mattress and wondered why she didn't feel like crying.

This was supposed to be her wedding night.

She thought of Armand—the Armand she'd seen in the waning light. The Armand who was who-knew-how-old. The Armand who'd planned to dump her, penniless—or pesoless—in a foreign country.

The Armand she could now admit that she'd never loved. She'd *wanted* to love him. She loved the whole idea of him and his family and generations of history. Was any of it true? Blair supposed she'd never know. She liked to think she would have made him a good wife and had looked forward to adding a few twigs to his family tree.

Now what? As she sat there, she slapped at a mosquito and decided to take Drake's advice about the netting.

Tomorrow she'd analyze her situation, organize her thoughts and plan what to do. All she needed was a plan. Fingering her agenda, she opened the rings and began spreading the damp pages on the floor to dry. The mosquito netting could wait.

Drake may have thought he'd won their encounter, but then he'd never come up against Blair when she had a plan. She'd get off this island, see if she wouldn't. She slapped at another mosquito.

Okay, maybe the mosquito netting *couldn't* wait.

CHAPTER FOUR

THERE WAS A WOMAN on his island.

It was his waking thought.

Drake hadn't seen her this morning. Drake didn't want to see her this morning or any other morning. But in the event their paths should cross, he wrapped a towel around his waist after his swim and shower rather than enjoy the feel of the sun and salty breezes on his bare skin.

But that was as far as he was prepared to alter his routine just because there was a woman on his island.

Slicking back his damp hair, he strode from the outside shower, intended for guests to rinse off sand before entering the lodge, down the utility path to the generator, concealed behind artful landscaping entwined in metal fencing.

Drawing his hands to his waist, Drake glared at the generator in its bower of vegetation, thriving without any encouragement from him, then in the direction of cabana number one. He hated the sound of the generator. To him, it represented the pulsing vibrations of the city—something he'd come here to escape. Forever.

But *she* wanted electricity.

Since this was the emergency generator, there wouldn't be any power in the cabanas, but the ceiling fans and window units in the lodge should run.

The coffeemaker would work, too. Drake hadn't been able to convince himself he liked the percolated coffee he brewed on the propane stove. There was just something about coffee made from freshly ground beans and a drip coffeemaker.

Probably leftover from all those years he'd spent guzzling the stuff at the office.

The thought of his former life sent a tremor along his spine and reminded him of the letters that Mario had brought on his last supply run. Drake hadn't opened the letters. It wasn't necessary. They'd all be variations on the same theme, the when-are-you-getting-over-this-nonsense-and-coming-home song and dance.

He wasn't coming home. This *was* his home.

Inhaling the muggy air of his island, he closed his eyes, stepped from the shade into the sunlight and willed the warmth to ease the knots forming in his neck and shoulders. In the distance, the ebb and swell of the ocean as it rasped over the beach was far more tranquilizing than any commercially-prepared relaxation tape.

Drake stood there until an unknown insect crawled over his foot and broke the mood, much the same way the woman had disturbed his serenity. And as long as she was here, she was going to keep disturbing him, too.

He fueled the generator and turned it on, wincing as the roar drowned out the subtle sounds of his island paradise.

He shot another look toward cabana number one. He hoped she was happy now.

Feeling edgy, Drake headed for the kitchen, intending to reward himself with a decent cup of coffee. On the way, he detoured to the fruit trees rimming what had been the back lawn and patio. Peaches were ripe now. Lots of peaches. All at once. He was getting sick of eating peaches, but maybe what's-her-name—Blair—would eat some, he thought as he picked a few.

But this was the absolute final thing he was going to do for her. He'd saved her life and given her food, shelter and clothes. How much more was a man expected to do, anyway?

Drake shoved open the screen door to the kitchen, set the peaches on the counter and dug around for the coffee beans.

Once he had the coffee brewing, he stared at the peaches

grimaced and thought about eggs and toast. He could use the toaster now. If he had to suffer with the noise of the generator, then he might as well reap the benefits.

He was feeling almost charitable, when he turned to get a plate out of the cabinet at the exact instant Blair appeared in the doorway.

She looked as startled to see him as he was to see her.

Her wide-eyed gaze flicked over his bare chest, blinked at the towel, then returned to maintain a determined eye contact. "You obviously aren't expecting company, so I'll come back later."

Involuntarily, Drake tightened the knot on his towel, annoyed with himself for responding to her prissy expression.

Still, she hesitated in the doorway, casting a longing glance toward the coffeepot.

He knew that look. With a grudging "Help yourself," he got two mugs out along with his plate.

"Oh, *thank* you." Blair had filled the mug and brought it to her lips before he'd shut the cabinet door.

Drake tossed a chunk of butter in the skillet and covertly studied her. She seemed okay this morning, which was a relief because getting medical attention would be a major hassle. Her voice had a husky edge that probably had more to do with the time of day than swallowing saltwater. Yeah, she was okay.

She looked different dry. Her hair had fluffed out and lightened and the Pirate's Hideout uniform suited her, though it was hard to beat the see-through wedding dress.

He wouldn't think about that.

And he wouldn't think about the long tanned legs revealed by the khaki shorts, either.

The butter melting in the skillet bubbled. He turned down the flame and cracked the eggs. Real butter. Real eggs. Real coffee.

"You've got enough fat in there to clog the arteries of a third-world nation."

And a real pain. "I like fat."

She poked at the loaf of bread. "White bread?"

"Yes, *white* bread." The sneer in her voice got to him. "It makes the best bacon, lettuce and tomato sandwiches. You see, whole-wheat bread has a rough surface and holds too much mayo. White bread will give you a smooth foundation on which to build your masterpiece." He held up a piece and ran his fingers over the surface. "After the mayo, you slap on a quarter-inch slice of the sun-warmed beefsteak tomato you've just picked and—here's where people usually go wrong—then comes the lettuce. And not iceberg lettuce. People use iceberg and it's too hard. Gouges the bread."

"No iceberg," she repeated in a wary voice. She took a step backward.

"No, ma'am. What you want is bib lettuce. Soft. Makes a perfect bed for the bacon. Baby bib is superb." He brought his fingers to his lips and kissed them. "After that, you add your four pieces of bacon, another slice of tomato and top it with the bread." He popped the bread he held into the toaster. "Nothing better."

Blair looked dazed. "What were you—the chef here?"

"No."

"Bartender?"

"No." He turned back to his eggs. Couldn't she just be quiet and drink her coffee? Or better yet, leave?

"Obviously you weren't working in a capacity that required you to be nice to the tourists."

"Obviously." Drake tilted the skillet and spooned hot butter over the tops of the eggs.

Blair moved closer—after pouring herself another mug of coffee. At this rate, there wouldn't be any left for him. But she'd poured a mug for him, as well.

He acknowledged it with a nod.

"So...you were a hands-off kind of owner?"

"What?"

"I'm trying to find out what you did around this place." She eyed him speculatively over the rim of her mug.

"I didn't do anything. I bought the place after it closed."

"And it looked like this?"

"Pretty much."

"How long have you been here?"

"Since last fall."

"You mean, you've spent all this time here and..." Her eyes narrowed. "I don't believe you. You *are* a squatter. *That's* why you won't let me contact the police, isn't it? Because nobody knows you're here!"

He could strangle her and nobody would ever know. No wonder Armand had just sailed off into the sunset.

Drake drew a deep breath and spoke in a carefully controlled voice. "The police department in San Verde consists of Jorge, who also runs a vegetable market, and Mario, his nephew, who was deputized solely because he has a boat and can keep an eye on the marina. Jorge's wife, Lupe, is the dispatcher, if you will, because the police radio is right by the cash register. The market closes at sundown, so most likely nobody would have been around to hear you whine about Armand. If you ask me—"

"I *didn't* ask you!"

"Of course not. That would have been the smart thing to do!" Drake's voice was louder than he intended. "Lady, you ought to be thanking your lucky stars that I'm nothing scarier than a burned-out commodities trader, because you have no brains. Not one single...solitary...cell!"

She smirked. "I'm not the one who bought the world's largest pile of driftwood."

He'd ignore that. He wouldn't forget it—he'd just ignore it for now. "Let's say I am a criminal on the lam. You've stumbled onto my hiding place, but for some reason I'm feeling indulgent and I decide to let you live. Whatever you suspected, wouldn't the intelligent thing be to play along and let me think I'm fooling you until you can get off this island? After all, nobody knows you're here, do they?"

Her eyes widened.

"Yes, that's right. You're all alone. With me. And nobody knows." He leered.

"A-Armand—"

"Armand?" He shook his head. "Armand is history. He won't even bother to report you missing."

The flash of uncertainty in her eyes sparked unwilling sympathy in Drake. Even a little guilt. After all, she *had* been going to marry the guy. His betrayal must have hurt and Drake shouldn't have rubbed her nose in it, no matter how much she got on his nerves.

He wasn't fit company for humans—especially females, which was why he wanted her off his island. He had to get her off the island. Mario could be bribed—if he had something to bribe him with.

The toast popped up. They both looked at it. The sound of frying eggs filled the silence between them. She was subdued now, and when she sipped her coffee, Drake thought he saw her lip quiver. He groaned inwardly. Not the whipped-puppy look. Anything but the whipped-puppy look.

"Are you hungry?" he asked, guilt roughing the edge of his voice.

She swallowed. "Usually, I don't eat anything for breakfast but fruit and coffee—"

"Fresh peaches right over there," he interrupted.

"But today, for some reason, I'm ravenous." She gave him a tremulous smile. A brave little I'm-doing-the-best-I-can smile.

Nuts.

"Where do you keep the silverware?"

Breakfasting together would set a dangerous precedent— but it would be the last thing he'd do for her. After that, she was on her own. "In the drawer over there." He pointed.

She may have sneered at his eggs, but she gobbled them up fast enough. The white toast, too.

Drake cracked two more eggs into the skillet.

"Why haven't you fixed this place up?"

She should have seen it when he first got here. "It's livable."

"Barely." Blair got up from the table and, without asking, ground more beans for another pot of coffee. She was making a serious dent in his supplies and she considered it barely living?

"You have clothes, food, shelter and some of the prettiest scenery around," he said. "What more do you need?"

She stuck out a foot. "Shoes."

Would she never be satisfied? He sent her a long look. "Watch the eggs."

Grumbling to himself about ungrateful castaways, Drake stalked toward the utility room, grabbed a net bag filled with the rubber thongs Pirate's Hideout had thoughtfully provided for its guests, and dumped it at Blair's feet. "There. Shoes. Now you have everything."

But was she surprised? Grateful? No.

He rescued his eggs and ate them directly from the skillet.

He was tense, tense in a way he hadn't been for eight months. He had to get away from her—couldn't she tell?

No, she kept jabbering and trying on thongs.

"What did you say you were before you came here?"

He didn't want to answer. "Commodities futures trader."

"In…?"

"New York." Stomach roiling, he clipped the words. *Go away.*

"Ooh, Wall Street. Sounds exciting."

Drake swallowed. He could feel the food sitting in a lump in his stomach.

"When are you planning to go back?"

Memories flashed. Caffeine-fueled marathons, staring at numbers until they swam, the roller-coaster ride of fortunes won and lost, and adrenaline rush when he hit big—the nausea when he didn't…the relentless pressure, the expectations… "Never." He stared at the last of his eggs, stood abruptly and scraped them into the trash.

Blair seemed oblivious to his inner turmoil. "Hey, I found a pair that fits." She paced back and forth. "Thanks."

Drake mumbled and filled the sink with soapy water.

"What is that hideous racket?" she asked after gathering the rejected thongs into their net bag.

"The generator." Drake held out a faint hope that she'd beg him to turn off the noisy thing.

Blair perked up. "You mean we've got electricity now?"

"In places."

"What places?"

"The lodge, mainly, but don't go plugging stuff into any old outlet. I've got a power strip in the rec room."

"I don't have any stuff."

"You wanted to use the radio."

"I'm not allowed in the rec room," she reminded him.

"I'll make an exception this once." He left the dishes soaking in the sink—something he never did—and pushed past Blair.

He heard her follow him to the rec room, feet slapping in the thongs. With each slap, his irritation and the need to escape grew. "Here's the radio." He plugged it in and set it to the right frequency, hoping that Lupe was at the cash register this morning. Maybe Blair would have luck persuading another woman to help her get off the island.

"How do I work the radio?"

Drake seated her in a chair, noticing the scent of shampoo in her hair. It was the same stuff he used, but the scent seemed different on her. Sweeter. "Turn the knob." The radio crackled to life. "Press the microphone button when you talk and release it when you listen. That's all there is to it."

He stood, desperate to escape Blair and her sweet-scented hair. "I'm going fishing."

She gasped and started to get up. "I haven't had a chance to clean the boat."

Drake gently pushed her back in the chair. Her shoulder

felt solid and soft at the same time. He let his fingers linger more than he should have. "I took care of the boat."

"You..." Blair glanced away then faced him squarely. "I think that's the nicest thing anybody has ever done for me." Her blue eyes were sincere. "I'm sorry I've been such a bother."

"No problem." What was he *saying?* She was nothing *but* a problem. One, big, irritating female problem. Drake backed away—away from the sincere blue eyes, the sweet shampooed hair and the long, tanned legs. Away from the brackets on either side of her mouth which she probably hated, yet gave her smile an attractive sophistication.

Away from the first woman he'd seen in eight months. "I'll be back. Late. Poke around all you like." *Run.* Run now.

"Drake?"

"What?"

"Wouldn't you like to get dressed first?"

THE FEEL OF HIS HANDS on her shoulders remained long after Drake collected his clothes and left. No matter how cranky he acted, there was caring in those hands.

He'd fed her, clothed her, sheltered her and saved her life and she hadn't really given him much thought at all. Last night, she'd dismissed him as a reclusive, ill-tempered beachcomber. She hadn't even considered him as a man, but she hadn't considered any man as a man since the suave Armand had come into her life. Men as men had ceased to exist. They had become people.

Drake, the person, had rescued her yesterday, but once she'd encountered him in his towel at breakfast, she'd become aware of him as a man. She'd tried not to be, since he seemed so laid-back about his attire, but after all, it was *only* a towel, and a low-riding one, at that.

He was better-looking than she'd first thought and probably younger. She still wished he'd lose the beard, but with his hair slicked back, she could see the elegant shape of his head and forehead.

But who cared about an elegant forehead when faced with a broad, bronzed back, impressive chest and flat stomach? Maybe doctors should rethink their warnings about high-fat diets. Drake's body certainly hadn't been adversely affected.

And the horrible thing was, after seeing Drake with his smooth, golden torso, she was forced to admit that she'd avoided considering Armand as a man at all. Or rather, she had, but preferred not to.

She'd never even seen his torso. Never imagined it. She'd convinced herself that the physical aspect of their relationship was not important. Being comfortable together and fitting into his life *was* important.

Had she been insane?

Resting her hand on her chin, Blair stared out the recroom windows to the dock, where Drake was loading a cooler and fishing paraphernalia into his boat.

He was still shirtless.

Blair sighed a little. She'd definitely been insane.

Not that being in her right mind now was going to do her any good, unless she got off this island in time to…to do something about Armand. The exact details would require some thought, but it looked as if she was going to have plenty of time to think of a plan.

Drake cast off and headed his dinghy out to sea, leaving her all alone just like every other man in her life—including Armand.

Drake had said he'd be back late. Blair would probably be gone by then. No matter what his opinion was, she knew the police would want to question her.

Tucking her hair behind her ears, she picked up the microphone. "Hello? I'd like to speak to the police, please."

Silence. She remembered to release the microphone button and there was still silence.

Maybe she needed to be more specific. "My name is

Blair Thomason and I'd like to report a crime to the police in San Verde.''

More silence.

She clicked the button. "Is anybody there? Hello?"

"Hello? Who's this?" asked an accented female voice.

Blair exhaled, unaware that she'd been holding her breath. She gripped the mike. "Blair Thomason. I'd like to report—"

"Where are you?"

That stopped her. "I don't know."

"Are you on a boat?"

"No. I'm on an island. There's water all around me."

"Sounds like an island, all right."

Blair wished she'd written a script so she could have sounded intelligent and calm instead of inane and scattered. "I'm on the Pirate's Hideout island."

"Ah, you're with Señor Drake, then. Let me talk to him."

"He's not—" She stopped and pressed the microphone button. "He's not here right now. He's fishing."

"Can you give him a message? Tell him the carburetor he wants isn't in stock and will have to be special-ordered."

Blair didn't care about any carburetors. "I need to report a crime—is this the police?"

"Yes, but hang on. I've got to ring up a customer."

Ring up a customer? When Blair had asked to report a crime? Weren't there rules about this sort of thing? Did the mayor of San Verde realize how lax the police department was?

Unfortunately, the silence gave Blair time to remember her last conversation with Armand. She had no doubt that she would look as guilty as he was, but she was counting on the fact that she'd jumped overboard to prove that she'd been a victim, not an accomplice.

"Okay, now, what was your problem?"

Collecting her thoughts, Blair told the woman about Armand's beef-shipping scam and how she'd jumped overboard when she'd discovered it. When she finished, there was silence. Too much silence.

"Hello?"

"You finally finished blabberin'? Lady, you gotta release that button once in a while. Listen, if this man is in Mexico—"

"But he's on his way to Argentina," Blair interrupted, forgetting that the woman wouldn't be able to hear her.

"—do anything."

She was going to assume the woman had just told her she couldn't do anything about Armand. "Can you alert the Mexican police then?"

"What for?"

Blair felt herself hyperventilating. "So they can catch him!"

"I don't know why they'd want him."

"To make him give back the money! My money!"

"Okay, okay. Do you know where he is?"

If Drake had let me call you last night, I would have. Maybe. "I believe he spent the night in Sonoma Villa."

"Okay. Is that it?"

"No! I think you should call the federal authorities, as well. American citizens are involved."

"That's a good idea. Let them take care of it. You finished now?"

"Aren't you going to send somebody to get me?"

"Sure. My nephew Mario takes mail and supplies there two times a month. You can ride in with him on his next trip."

Drake had said two weeks. "But I don't want to wait that long!"

"Well, lady, you're gonna have to. Mario'll be there about noon Wednesday after next."

"Ma'am, I can't stay on this island all that time. I'll pay your nephew or someone else to make the trip."

"What are you gonna pay with? You said this Armand took all your money."

Blair swallowed. "Credit card?"

The next sound she heard was laughter. From more than one person. Blair was obviously entertaining an audience. "Lady, we don't take credit cards."

If she'd still had her credit cards, Blair would have been more upset.

"Tell you what," the woman continued. "You want me to call your family or a friend for you?"

A friend or family.

Blair had plenty of acquaintances, but no friends. Certainly no one she could ask to get her out of this mess. As for family... "No," she answered shortly.

Something of her feelings must have come across in her last transmission.

"Hey, it's not so bad. Why are you in such a hurry to leave the island, anyway? Señor Drake is easy on the eyes, no? Eh, Rosa?" The mike cut off and the woman returned. "Rosa says you should forget this Armand. He's not comin' back." Blair heard murmurs of agreement in the background. "Señor Drake has been all alone for many months. A clever woman should be able to use that to her advantage."

CHAPTER FIVE

BLAIR HAD NO INTENTION of seducing Drake.

She was going to get off this island. The San Verde police might not be interested in rescuing her, but Blair expected representatives from some branch of federal law enforcement to arrive within hours. Maybe they'd send a helicopter. She'd never flown in a helicopter before.

At the very least, the Coast Guard should be paying a visit.

Turning off the radio, Blair returned to the cabana. The pages of her agenda had dried and thankfully, the writing had remained surprisingly legible. Blair stuffed the bumpy pages back into their binder and folded her ruined wedding dress. Within half an hour, she'd stripped the bed, removed the mosquito netting and was on her way back to the lodge. Only at one point during the walk was the beach visible and though she searched, Blair didn't see any sign of Drake—or the Coast Guard.

Good, she'd have time to wash the dishes before she left.

Blair had time for that and a lot more. Once she started putting away the dishes, she realized the kitchen hadn't been organized with any thought to efficiency. Frequently-used items should be stored in the most accessible areas, but pots and pans had been placed clear across the kitchen, far from the stove.

From the kitchen, Blair could keep an eye on the beach and the back veranda. If she stepped outside, she could see around the corner to the dock. Still no sign of anyone.

With nothing else to do, Blair couldn't help herself. She

switched the pots and pans to the cabinet near the stove and once she'd started, it was difficult to stop.

The contents of the drawers and cabinets needed cleaning, too. The humidity and salty air had left a film on the glasses, except for those few that Drake used regularly.

Blair washed them all, the entire time gazing out the window for any sign of an approaching boat.

Hours must have passed, though without a watch, she didn't know how many. It drove her crazy not knowing what time it was.

She got hungry and ate one of the peaches Drake had left on the counter. Then she ate the other one, feeling guilty. These were the best-tasting peaches she'd ever had in her life. In fact, they redefined her whole idea of what a peach should taste like. She hoped Drake wouldn't be angry that she hadn't left one for him.

The kitchen was in perfect order when Blair stepped outside to find nothing on the horizon. Maybe she should wait on the beach. What if her rescuers had missed her?

But a few minutes of relentless sun convinced Blair to turn back to the lodge. Waiting on the beach was a bad idea. She had no sunscreen and the short shadows told her that it was no later than midafternoon. Perhaps Drake had sunscreen, though his tan told her he foolishly didn't use it.

Blair entered Pirate's Hideout through the front, as she'd done last night. While she was waiting to be rescued, she'd snoop. After all, Drake had granted her salvage rights. Though she fully expected never to see him again once she left the island, she was curious—*mildly* curious—about a man who apparently had chucked his career to become a beach bum.

On a whim, Blair wandered through the ruined bar and dining room to the section of the lodge Drake hadn't shown her last night. The far side of glass walls had been broken. Someone had nailed plywood sheets over the openings, but had either given up, or another storm had ripped away the coverings. The side with the glorious view—the side facing the ocean—had borne the brunt of the storm and was now open to the elements.

And the elements hadn't treated this area kindly. Fine sand coated the black-and-white tiles, along with dead leaves and debris. Since no footprints marred the coating, Blair knew Drake didn't use this area.

She wished she had a flashlight as she passed the public rest rooms and found what must have been the hotel offices. The roof had caved in on this side and she hoped the manager's office was safe to enter, although she wasn't entirely certain about that.

Rusty file cabinets protected their mildewed contents. Silt stains marked the walls where the room had flooded.

Watching for snakes, Blair amused herself by rescuing still-usable office supplies until she found a packet of brochures. The middle ones were practically untouched and gave Blair an excellent picture of how Pirate's Hideout had functioned in its heyday.

Words like *secluded, private* and *discreet* illustrated lush photographs of the stately lodge. Pirate's Hideout had been a retreat for the working rich. It was a place to find some privacy. To unwind and recharge.

Blair had never heard of it, but she wasn't among the working rich. One had to "apply" to be accepted as a guest.

There was a picture of a manicured lawn with rows of chaise lounges. For gentle amusement, the brochure invited guests to wander the nature trails and provided a map. Shuffleboard and croquet were offered as alternatives.

The brochure mentioned a library, which Blair hadn't seen yet, and showed the rec room with a pool table, piano and gaming tables.

The place screamed, in a genteel way, old-fashioned stateliness. Blair saw no television sets or anything about computers and faxes. The world was kept firmly at bay.

Pirate's Hideout had been prized for the very isolation that frustrated Blair now.

She also thought she understood Drake now. He was obviously bitter. No doubt he'd had dreams of restoring Pirate's Hideout to its former glory and had run out of money.

He, alone, had refused to abandon the island. He was fighting the odds—and losing.

Picturing Drake as a tragically romantic figure, Blair sighed and wandered back through the dining room. As she reached the bar, she remembered Drake and his cheese animals, which pretty much negated the tragically romantic aspects of his personality.

Actually, that cheese stuff hadn't been so bad.

She could use a snack.

Walking behind the bar, Blair ducked below to search for the cheese and crackers and found a sign stuck over the box top.

"Off limits. This means you."

THE FISH WEREN'T BITING in the shady lagoon today, which suited Drake just fine. He wanted to be alone, though he'd definitely need to catch something soon with the way Blair was eating his supplies. Not that he minded particularly. When she was eating, she wasn't talking.

He hoped she'd convinced Lupe to send Mario out, but he doubted Blair had had any luck.

It was Mario's closely guarded secret that he got seasick. If Lupe knew, she pretended not to. Mario could stand the short jaunts around the San Verde Marina, but due to currents and land jetties, there was a stretch of rough water between Pirate's Hideout and San Verde that got him every time.

He was determined that no one would know. Anyway, once Drake got the hotel's launch running properly, Mario wouldn't have to make the trip anymore.

Drake spent the day fishing and napping and fishing a little more. By the time the shadows lengthened, he'd regained the serenity he'd sought by spending the day away from his unexpected refugee. Out of sight, out of mind.

He tossed back the two small fish he'd caught and nosed

the dinghy toward the north side of the island to check the crab traps. He was in the mood for boiled crab to go with the last of the French bread that Mario had brought on his last supply run. Lots of melted butter...whatever looked good from the vegetable garden...and the time to savor it.

This was life as he wanted to live it. A life without deadlines and people constantly yammering at him. A life where he wasn't responsible for other people's fortunes. Life out of the pressure cooker.

Drake cut the dinghy's motor and drifted toward the traps, admiring the way the evening sun colored the sky and enjoying the fact that he could gaze for miles and miles and not see another human being.

Hauling the first trap out of the water, Drake plucked two good-size crabs from the basket and emptied the smaller ones and debris into the sea. He repeated the process with the other traps, tossing crabs into the bucket of water at his feet. As their white underbellies flashed, he was reminded of a certain wet white wedding dress and the woman who'd worn it.

The thought had come out of nowhere. One minute he'd been collecting crabs for his supper and the next moment he'd been thinking of *her*.

Was the image forever burned into his brain?

He felt his serenity melt away. He didn't want to think about her. Certainly not in that way. He didn't want to think of *any* woman in that way because he didn't want a relationship, and women always wanted relationships. A relationship was work and Drake was avoiding work. Therefore, he'd avoid *her*. It was the only way he'd survive the next two weeks.

There was no sign of Blair when Drake returned to the lodge. Carrying his bucket, he walked around to the kitchen entrance, stopping to pick a tomato. Looked as if there was going to be a bumper crop. He'd staggered the planting, but even so, maybe he could learn how to make ketchup or fresh Bloody Marys or something.

He entered the kitchen, set the crab bucket in one side of the double sink and reached under it for the stockpot. His hand knocked over a bottle of something. Dishwashing soap. He stared at various cleansers, sponges and a can of bug spray.

There was no sign of the pot.

He opened another cabinet, then another. "What the hell happened to my kitchen!" *Nothing* was where he'd left it.

"Oh, you're back." A nonchalant Blair appeared in the doorway.

"What did you do to my kitchen?" He jerked open drawers, slamming them shut again in frustration.

"I rearranged it to maximize efficiency." She looked pleased with herself.

"You what?"

"I simply put the objects you use most often within easy reach and grouped similar tools together." She sounded like a damn training video.

"I liked where everything was."

Shaking her head, Blair advanced into the room. "Once you become accustomed to this arrangement, you'll see how much more practical it is."

"But I don't know where anything is! What's practical about that?"

"It's arranged logically." She absently folded a tea towel. "If you use something several times a day, such as the cleansers, you'll find it close at hand. If an item is seasonal—"

"Seasonal?"

"Like Christmas decorations," she explained, ignoring his ill temper. "If an item isn't used very often, you'll find it in secondary storage."

Drake didn't have Christmas decorations. "What's secondary storage and what did you put there?"

"Secondary storage are those shelves and out-of-the-way nooks that aren't easy to get to."

"I don't have *nooks*."

"Oh yes you do." She nodded her head.

Nooks shmooks. "I want my stuff put back the way it was." Drake was proud of the way his voice sounded, betraying nothing of the inner struggle he fought with himself to keep his hands from closing around her neck.

"No you don't. You're the type who is resistant to change, but once it's done for you, you'll like it."

Drake gritted his teeth. He'd been a teeth grinder in his other life and had been forced to wear a plastic device at night. He hadn't worn it since he'd arrived at Pirate's Hideout. Something told him he shouldn't have thrown the thing away.

"Watch. I'll set the table." She walked to the cabinets next to the kitchen table and positioned herself. Without taking a step, she was able to gather plates, silverware and glasses and arrange them on the table.

"There. Easy, efficient and quick." She'd set the table for two, he noticed.

He glared at her. "Where is the stockpot?"

She smiled complacently. "In secondary storage. Such a large object—"

He smacked his fist on the counter. *"Get the stockpot!"*

Blair scrambled to the pantry, dragging a kitchen chair after her.

Drake willed himself to calm down and followed her. She was standing on the chair as she stretched to reach the top shelf where she'd put the pot.

The chair wobbled and Drake braced it. All he needed was for her to fall and break her leg. Then he'd have to wait on her. He'd never get any peace and quiet if she did something stupid like break her leg...her long tanned leg, which was now mere inches away.

Drake hadn't been this close to a female leg for many a moon. It didn't matter that this leg was attached to the world's most irritating woman. After months of countering the ill effects of years of stress to his body, his body was letting him know that certain parts of it wouldn't mind a little stress again. As though he needed the reminder, his mind replayed the image of Blair in her wet wedding dress. It was the only erotic image imprinted in his brain recently, which was why it frequently came to mind, he supposed. It couldn't have anything to do with Blair personally, because personally, she annoyed the hell out of him.

To distract himself, Drake tried recalling images from his past without success. They were gone. All gone.

Blair looked down at him with her big blue eyes. "Thanks, but the danger's past."

He had a horrible feeling that the danger was just ahead.

"Let me get the stockpot," he offered and straightened, careful to avoid looking at her legs.

"I got it up here. I can get it down." Blair reached again, worked the pot off the top shelf and handed it to him. Then she casually propped her hands on his shoulders and jumped down.

It was a good thing he was holding the stockpot, or he might have done something stupid, like putting his hands around her waist and pulling her close.

She probably would have slugged him.

"I'm sure there'll be other adjustments you'll want to make," Blair was saying as she dragged the chair past him. "Since I don't know your personal cooking-utensil preferences, I had to guess—"

"I don't want adjustments. I want everything put back exactly the way it was."

The look she gave him was patient, the smile patronizing. "You're just saying that because you don't want to admit that you didn't arrange things in the best way."

He hadn't consciously arranged things at all. "No, I'm saying that because I don't know where anything is!" Drake punctuated his words by slamming the pot into the sink and turning the water on full blast.

She stalked over to the sink. "I can't believe you're being so stubborn. People pay me hundreds of dollars to organize their homes and businesses. It's what I do for a living. Naturally, I'd know more about ergonomics than you."

"But you don't know when to shut up." Drake turned off the water, carried the pot to the stove and lit the gas. It would be a few minutes before the water was boiling. Time for a snack.

Without another word to her, Drake left her in all her efficiently arranged glory and headed for the bar.

Flip-flops sounded behind him. "I organized the kitchen as a token of my appreciation. You can at least acknowledge the gesture, even if you intend to rearrange everything the instant I leave."

Drake stopped and stared back at her. "You're leaving? You found somebody to come out here and take you off my hands?" A broad smile creased his face.

Blair winced. "Not exactly."

"Bummer."

"As it stands, I'm still riding back on the next supply boat."

"Yeah, that's what I expected." He continued to the bar, with Blair flip-flopping her way right beside him.

"Unfortunately, no law-enforcement agency is interested enough to get me off this island. I'm neither rich nor famous nor related to anybody who is."

She looked so incensed he refrained from saying *I told you so.* "What about Armand?" he asked instead.

"Until one of the investors files a complaint, the Securities and Exchange Commission won't act. Not enough time has passed to determine intent. So I told them *I* was filing a complaint, since he took my money, too."

She seemed to have covered all the bases. "Did you?"

"Yes, but when they heard we'd been engaged, they told me they didn't get involved in domestic disputes."

Drake rubbed the back of his head. "Maybe I can talk Mario into coming early if they get that carburetor in."

"Oh."

"Oh, what?" They'd reached the bar and Drake turned to face her.

"The lady on the radio said to tell you that they didn't have the part in stock and it would have to be special-ordered."

A delay? "No," Drake groaned, then mumbled a few choice words concerning the cruelty of fate. "You mean, I might be stuck with you even longer?"

"Unless you can figure out someone to bribe, yes."

"Don't *you* have anyone to bribe?"

"No—and if I did, I wouldn't have anything to bribe them with, remember?"

Drake groaned again.

Blair bristled. "It may interest you to know that I want to be here even less than you want me to be here!"

"I seriously doubt that," Drake snapped, then noticed the bar for the first time. "It looks different."

"I alphabetized the liquor bottles."

"For the love of Mike, will you just leave my stuff alone?" He vaulted over the bar and grabbed for the Jiffy Cheez, ready to consume an entire can.

It wasn't there.

Drake looked all over the bar but couldn't find the can. "Where in the hell is my Jiffy Cheez?" He glared at her.

She glared right back. "I've hidden it where you won't find it."

"What?"

Blair drew a deep breath. "Since it now appears that I'll be staying a while—"

"Give it back. Now." Drake felt a murderous anger well up inside him.

"No."

"No?"

Something must have shown in his expression, because Blair took a step back, even though the bar was between them. "If anything happens to me, I'll carry the location of your Jiffy Cheez to my grave."

Drake pounded the bar with his fist. "Why are you torturing me like this?"

"Because ever since you brought me here, you've been rude and inhospitable."

"Rude? Inhospitable? I saved your life! I gave you the run of the place." He glared at her. "Obviously a huge mistake on my part."

"You banished me to a shack in the jungle."

"For privacy!"

"Too much privacy. I can't stand the thought of wandering around here day after day all alone."

"And so I'm supposed to entertain you now, too? You want entertainment? Talk to Lupe on the radio."

Blair swallowed and glanced away. "I did. She won't answer anymore."

"Oh, great." He looked skyward. "You've alienated our only contact to the outside world."

"I didn't mean to!"

Drake leaned against the bar and regarded his newly alphabetized liquor supply. If he started at *A*—Amaretto—how long would it take him to get drunk? He wasn't normally a drinking man, so he had a feeling he wouldn't get much past *B*—bourbon. "So what's the ransom for the Jiffy Cheez?"

"I move into the lodge."

"Why?"

"I don't like being all alone out there. I had trouble sleeping last night."

Drake thought about it. He could always move out to the cabana if she proved too distracting. "You can't sleep in the rec room."

"Okay."

"And I'm not running the generator like I did today. I don't have enough fuel for that."

Blair nodded stiffly.

"Is that it?"

"No." She drew a deep breath. "I want you to behave civilly toward me."

He scowled. "I'm not a civil person anymore. That's why I'm living all alone on an island."

"But I'm not responsible for whatever drove you here and I shouldn't have to suffer for it."

Drake skipped *A* and grabbed the bourbon. He supposed she was right, but he didn't want to admit it. Besides, she was aggravating enough to sour the sweetest of dispositions. Look what she'd done to the garrulous Lupe.

"I don't want to follow you around all day or interfere with whatever it is that you do, but perhaps we could eat breakfast and dinner together and…talk."

"Talk about what?" Drake had been twisting the bottle cap and it finally came off. He sniffed. Smelled like bourbon all right.

Throwing up her hands in a gesture of apparent frustration, she paced in front of the bar. "About our lives. About philosophy. Politics. Religion."

"What's the point?"

"To get to know one another."

Where were the glasses? "I don't want to know you and I don't want you knowing me."

She met his eyes, then turned to gaze out the back of the dining area.

The setting sun washed the room in an apricot light. It looked good on her. It would have looked even better if she hadn't stolen his Jiffy Cheez.

"I—I seem to have a talent for irritating people." She glanced at him.

"No kidding." Deliberately, Drake brought the bottle of bourbon to his lips and drank.

Liquid fire coated his mouth and throat. He gagged, but turned his back so Blair wouldn't see, and forced himself to swallow. Good God almighty, how could people drink this stuff?

"I don't know why I can't seem to make friends."

Drake would have told her if he'd been able to speak. Perhaps it was just as well that he couldn't.

"Except Armand," she added quickly. "Armand never lost his temper with me."

No, Armand was a swindler and a con man and he left you to drown in the Gulf of Mexico. Blinking his watering eyes, Drake saw her reflection in the cracked bar mirror. She'd wrapped her arms around herself.

"I know what he's doing is wrong, but I think, in his own way, he really liked me."

She continued to watch the sunset and Drake continued to watch her as the quiet poignancy of her words penetrated the wall he'd erected against the human race.

He'd only thought she was irritating to him—anyone would be while he was in his current state of mind—but he hadn't realized she affected everyone the same way. Or that she was aware of it.

Slowly, he returned the bourbon bottle to its place in the alphabet. He hadn't paid much attention to her, but he didn't think she'd mentioned someone wondering where she was or worrying about her. She'd been getting *married.* Weren't there bridesmaids or family or guests to notice that she was missing? And come to think of it, why should she have to depend on the police to rescue her? Wasn't there anyone else she could ask?

But Drake already knew that if there had been a single person Blair could have contacted, she would have. She was thorough that way. Instead, she was holding his Jiffy Cheez hostage in exchange for a little conversation.

He'd been a rotten, ill-tempered jerk.

But he didn't have to stay one.

He turned around and the movement drew her attention. "Blair," he said, deliberately using her name. "I've got a pot of boiling water and a bucket of crabs." He lifted a hinged section of the bar and walked under it. "Would you care to join me for dinner?"

She blinked at him suspiciously. "Are you sure?"

He nodded.

"Okay." Her smile lit up her face. It was a nice face, scrubbed free of makeup. "I'll get a can of Jiffy Cheez."

Drake reached for her hand and laced his fingers through hers, preventing her from pulling away.

When she looked at him in puzzlement, he smiled. He was out of practice, so it was a bit lopsided. "I don't need the Jiffy Cheez."

CHAPTER SIX

"DID YOU FIND the library while you were exploring?" Drake asked after they'd put away the last of the dishes.

"No," Blair answered, remembering that the brochure mentioned a library. "I'd like to see it, though."

"Then follow me." He hung up the dish towels, handed her a lantern, then led the way to the rec room.

During dinner, he'd been a pleasant companion—not exactly charming—but he barely resembled the grouch he'd been ever since she'd arrived. He hadn't talked much, but he *had* talked. She might have been fooled into thinking he hadn't minded her company, but she wasn't that gullible.

Blair was amazed to discover that he hadn't read a newspaper or magazine in eight months, and only seldom listened to the shortwave radio. She started to fill him in on recent current events, but he cut her off with a curt, "If I were interested, I would have listened to the radio."

She wanted to ask him what he was doing here, living away from everyone and everything, but knew he wasn't ready to tell her. Not that he'd ever be. She was a temporary interloper, only a few cans of Jiffy Cheez away from being ignored once again.

At least he'd stopped complaining about her arrangement of the kitchen. As they washed and dried the dishes, he watched without comment where she put everything, and though he stopped short of complimenting her, Blair got the impression that he wouldn't be rearranging things after she left.

Following him down the hallway, Blair admitted to herself that she was intrigued by Drake. She wouldn't go so far as to call it a full-fledged attraction, but now and then he showed her another glimpse of his personality—a personality that was far more appealing than that of the curmudgeonly beachcomber he portrayed.

When they reached the rec room, Drake pointed to a double door that Blair hadn't noticed before. It was painted the same celery color as the walls and the wainscoting continued uninterrupted, but when Drake drew it open, Blair stepped into another world.

"This room wasn't damaged at all," she said, noting the lush Oriental carpet covering the tile. Three of the walls were lined floor to ceiling with books. Small writing desks dotted the room, along with overstuffed chairs and side tables. The last wall was made up of French doors opening onto an enclosed patio.

"These windows were boarded up during the storms, but water did blow in through the cracks." He gestured to a far corner near the ceiling. "The roof leaked in that area. Rain dripped behind the shelves and warped them."

She searched for water stains and didn't find any. "Everything looks fine now."

"That's because I repaired the roof and rebuilt the shelves. I didn't want the books to be damaged any more than they had been." He walked to the shelves and ran his hand over the volumes in a revealing caress. "Some of the bindings are water-spotted, but I think that adds character."

His smile invited her to agree and she nodded, struck by the change in him. His movements were slower and more relaxed and he was no longer engaging her in verbal skirmishes. Obviously, this room was a demilitarized zone. "You spend a lot a time in here, don't you?"

"Every evening." He set his lantern on one of the reading tables and moved around the room lighting wall sconces and other lanterns. "I'm working my way through the classics by candlelight."

"Sounds like a program on public television."

He laughed and Blair realized it was the first time she'd heard him genuinely laugh because he was amused and not because he was mocking her. "My mother would tell me I'm ruining my eyes, but I get a pretty good light."

Her mother wouldn't have noticed whether Blair was reading or not. Actually, Blair had been a heavy reader. She and her mother had moved frequently and the library had been her one constant from city to city.

The room was silent except for a faint buzz from the lanterns and the tapping from bugs hurling themselves against the glass. Drake had turned off the generator before they'd eaten and Blair enjoyed the silence. She was beginning to think like Drake—electricity just wasn't worth the noise.

"What are you reading now?" she asked, trying to see the title on the end table next to a cushy leather club chair. She guessed this was where Drake read each night.

He grinned. "Anne Rice. I intend to read all the Shakespeare plays, but I need a break every now and then."

"From Anne Rice, or Shakespeare?"

He laughed again. "Both."

Blair wandered over to the shelves. "What will you do when you've read all the books?"

Drake pulled the gauzy drapes and gazed around the room. "I've got years of reading in here. You know how many people say they want to read *War and Peace?*" He tapped his chest. "I have. I didn't like it, but I read it."

"I hope I'm not here long enough to read *War and Peace.*" When he didn't respond, she glanced at him. "That's okay. I know you hope I'm not here long enough to read *War and Peace,* either."

"Depends on how fast you read."

Not fast enough. She scanned the shelves thinking about all the hours she'd spent reading as a child. Somehow, she'd fallen out of the habit. "Do you have something lighter?"

"Such as?"

Blair shrugged. "I don't know—mysteries?"

Drake crooked his finger. "Agatha Christie? Or—" he hefted a fat book "—here's the complete Sherlock Holmes. And don't forget the ever-popular island reading, *Robinson Crusoe*."

"I'll pass." Blair chose Agatha Christie and settled on the leather sofa, tucking her legs beneath her. Soon she forgot all about being stranded on the island and thwarting Armand.

Every once in a while, she looked over at Drake, engrossed in his own book, his long fingers carefully turning the pages. He was content and, for the moment, Blair was content, too.

Some time later, she roused enough to feel something soft whispering over her and being tucked around her shoulders. Then she burrowed into the sofa and went back to sleep.

DRAKE STARED DOWN at the sleeping woman, feeling a curious admiration. She wasn't so bad, he conceded. She'd actually gone hours without saying a word. He hadn't thought she was capable of it.

The room had that effect on a person—at least a person with any depth.

So Blair had depth. Who'd have thought it? He wondered what her story was, and not the Armand part, either. Maybe tomorrow he'd find out.

Drake extinguished the sconces and lanterns, one by one. When he reached the lantern next to Blair, he hesitated, then turned down the wick on that one, as well.

He'd leave the doors open in case she awakened during the night.

Climbing into his bed, Drake's last conscious thought was of Blair in that damn wedding dress.

BLAIR PEELED HERSELF off the leather sofa the next morning when a beam of sunlight caught her across the face.

Drake wasn't in the room.

Great. She'd fallen asleep. What if she'd snored?

After folding the white fleece blanket with the royal blue Pirate's Hideout logo embroidered on it, she checked her wrist, unable to break herself of the habit of looking at her watch.

No matter, it was breakfast time.

Blair peered into the rec room. Drake was already up and gone so she headed for the kitchen.

It was a bright morning that promised to become a hot day. Blair measured coffee beans into the grinder and pressed the button.

Nothing happened and several moments passed before she remembered that there was no electricity. Now she'd have to use the canned ground coffee and figure out how to use that old stove-top percolator she'd seen yesterday.

Blair was watching the water bubble, wondering if she was going to manage to make drinkable coffee at all, when a shadow crossed the doorway. Drake stepped over the threshold, caught sight of her and tightened the knot of his towel.

"Wearing your usual morning attire, I see," Blair said, dragging her eyes away from his golden torso.

"Usually I don't bother with the towel," he said, approaching the coffeepot. "You could say I'm being civilized."

Blair felt herself blush. That's right. She owed him Jiffy Cheez.

He leaned against the counter and watched her, too closely for her peace of mind.

"I'm fishing today. You want to come?"

The invitation caught her completely off guard. "I—really? That's not part of the deal."

"Forget the deal. You want to fish with me, or not?"

Uppermost in her mind was trying to figure out why he'd asked her. "Well, I...why?"

"We need food, for one thing. For another, I now know

it's possible for you to keep your mouth shut." He opened a drawer. "Hot pads?"

Blair pointed to the next drawer over.

"Coffee's done." Drake pulled the pot off the burner. "So, are you fishing with me, or not?"

Blair was cautiously pleased with Drake's invitation, but she didn't want to take advantage of him in a moment of weakness. "I had planned to try and mend fences with Lupe and see if she'd had any luck finding a way to get me off the island," she offered, waiting for his reaction.

"Fine. Suit yourself." He'd grabbed a mug, but forgot to use the hot pad when he reached for the coffeepot. When he jerked, coffee sloshed out of the pot. Drake drew in a sharp breath between his teeth.

Blair ran cool water and pulled his hand under the stream. They stood there for several seconds.

"You don't have to stand here and hold my hand."

Blair stepped back. "Do you think Lupe will speak to me today?"

"I have no idea."

"I probably ought to try and contact her, don't you think?"

"Fine. I said *fine*." He flung an arm in the direction of the rec room. "Stay here or fish. I don't care."

Blair hesitated. "I don't know how to fish."

"Everybody knows how to fish."

"Well, I don't."

He'd been staring at his hand. Now he stared at her.

"Would you teach me?" she asked.

"Nothing much to teach."

"I'm sure there're all kinds of techni—"

"You put a hook in the water! The fish either bite or they don't!" He glared at her, then at his hand again.

"Does your hand hurt?"

"Yes, my hand hurts!"

"Sorry. I was just trying to help."

"If you want to help, pack us a lunch." Drake turned off

the water. As he dried his hand, her silence must have registered. "What?"

"You're sure you don't mind me coming with you?"

His gaze swept over her. "I wouldn't have asked you if I minded."

She could tell he'd made an effort to keep his annoyance in check. A pleased smile touched her lips. "Then it's a date."

A wary look crept into his eyes. "Hey, this isn't a *date* date or anything."

"Well, technically—"

"Technically nothing."

Blair went directly to the coolers she'd packed away. "You issued an invitation and I accepted. I'd call that a date."

"This isn't a date!"

Blair was enjoying herself. "Then what would you call it?"

"I'd call it fishing, because that's what it is. We're going to catch some fish and then we're going to clean the fish and then we're going to cook the fish, because otherwise, we're going to run out of food!"

"Clean the fish?" Blair made a face as she scrounged for something to pack for lunch. The bread was nearly gone. "That involves knives and fish guts, doesn't it?"

"Yeah, and then we take the heads and put them in the crab traps." From the way his eyes crinkled at her over his coffee mug, she thought he might be smiling. A good sign.

"Oh, joy." She straightened. "Looks like it's peanut butter and jelly for lunch."

"Sounds okay." He rinsed the mug and set it in the sink. "Come on down to the boat when you're ready."

"You've never been fishing before? *Never?*"

Blair shook her head. "I told you I didn't know how."

Drake pulled his cap low over his forehead and squinted at her. "Your daddy never took his little girl fishing?"

"Not this little girl." She gazed back at him musingly. "I don't think he's the fishing sort."

Drake noticed she spoke in the present tense. He'd wondered, not that he wanted to, but it had begun to nag at him that she could disappear the way she had and nobody seemed to care one way or the other. Armand had his reasons for keeping quiet, but wasn't there anybody else who would be interested in knowing that she hadn't gotten married as planned?

Drake cut the dinghy's motor and they drifted into the shady lagoon where he did his best fishing. "Were you eloping?"

She'd been dragging her hand in the water. "Where did that question come from?"

"You talk about your dad as though he's still alive."

"Yes, why wouldn't he be?"

"He wasn't at your wedding?"

Blair laughed. "He and my mom split up when I was little. He surfaces every once in a while and offers to take me to lunch. Then he stands me up. I'm not even sure where he is right now."

"Your mother then." Drake handed her a fishing pole. "Wasn't she there?"

"Mother has been married so many times, herself, that weddings have lost their appeal."

So they weren't a tight-knit family. That wasn't necessarily a bad thing, Drake decided, thinking of his own interfering mother. "But this was *your* wedding. Or have you been married before?"

Eyeing the fishing pole, she shook her head. "How do I get the hook loose?"

Drake showed her how to work the simple reel, but he wasn't ready to drop the subject. "You said there were guests on the boat."

Her glance told him she didn't want to discuss it. "Armand's friends. Where are the worms?"

"We're using canned corn," he explained impatiently. "Didn't you—"

"I may not have been fishing before, but even *I* know you're supposed to use worms," she insisted.

"It's too much trouble to dig them up. Didn't any of *your* friends—"

"Well, how am I supposed to get corn on a hook?"

"Forget the hook!"

She blinked at him, her jaw set stubbornly.

He snatched the pole from her and shoved a few kernels of corn on the hook. "There. Cast it in and—not like that!" He ducked as the hook flew inches from his arm. "You'll catch the hook on me."

It plopped into the water. "But I didn't."

"Just remember for next time. Now, about your wedding..."

"I *don't* want to discuss my wedding." She gazed determinedly out at the lagoon.

"Why weren't any of *your* friends and family there?"

She had hunched over, her elbows resting on her knees. As he watched, she tucked a lock of brown hair behind one ear.

A tiny gleam drew his eyes to her earlobe where a chaste gold-ball earring shone. It was the only adornment she wore.

She didn't need adorning to look good. Her skin was the kind that tanned easily and the few freckles sprinkled across her nose contributed to her natural outdoorsy look. Some women could carry off the casual look and some couldn't. Blair could.

"It was just going to be a civil ceremony," she said with a sigh. "When we got to Argentina, we were going to be married in the de Moura family chapel where generations of de Moura brides have been married." There was still a remnant of anticipation in her voice. "Armand has a large family and they all live on..." She trailed off with an embarrassed glance at him. "I suppose that's all a lie, too."

Swallowing heavily, she turned away. When the hair fell from behind her ear, she didn't push it back.

"Armand is a jerk." Drake wanted her to believe that with an intensity that caught him unaware.

She lifted her shoulder in a small shrug. "I was stupid. Stupid to think anybody—" She interrupted herself with a shaky breath. "I was just stupid, that's all."

Drake had spent most of his adult life working with numbers. In commodities futures trading, there wasn't time for emotion. There wasn't room for emotion. His clients exhibited one of two emotions: elation or despair, according to the reckoning at the end of the trading day. Nothing in between.

Whether or not slowing the pace of his life was responsible for a heightened awareness of the feelings of others, Drake didn't know. He hadn't been around others, except for Mario, since he'd come to the island. But Blair was here now and he found himself sensing her feelings. That she'd been hurt was obvious. What Drake thought was more significant was her acceptance of the hurt. She got a little quiet, sure, but mostly she brushed it away.

She'd had practice, he realized with a new certainty. She'd been hurt before—so many times she expected to be hurt.

"Hey, it could have happened to anybody," he said, and awkwardly patted her shoulder. The gesture felt awkward because Drake wasn't used to comforting by touch and because he wasn't sure touching her would be a good thing for either of them.

She stiffened at first, then relaxed when he didn't pull away.

Drake moved his hand in slow circles, then rubbed the muscles in her back. He could feel them beneath the teal knit Pirate's Hideout shirt. Though he and Blair were in dappled shade, her shirt was warm. He was warm. He bet she was warm, too.

If he'd been by himself, he would have stripped off his shirt and not given it another thought.

It didn't seem fair that he could take off his shirt and Blair couldn't.

Of course, she could if she wanted to. *He* wouldn't mind. And her lacy bra would cover anything important. He wondered if it would be as transparent dry as it had been when it was beneath the wet wedd— He gave her shoulder one last pat and eased his hand away.

"Thanks," she said. "I'm okay."

He hated that tone in her voice. "No, you're not okay! Damn it, Blair, you've got two living parents and you can't call them for help?"

"Oh, I see." She straightened and glared at him. "You want me off your island." She inched away from him.

"No." He reached for her arm, feeling the need to touch her again. "Well, yes, but I didn't mean it like that. I'm curious to know why you didn't call them. If you'd asked Lupe to call your mother, she would have."

She gave him a look he couldn't read. "Mother would tell me to wait for the supply boat."

Before he could question her further, a movement in the water drew their attention. Blair's float bobbed and disappeared beneath the surface.

"Pull up!"

"What?"

"You've got a fish!"

"I do?"

Drake grabbed for her fishing pole and jerked it up. "Start reeling it in."

Giving the task far more concentration than it deserved, Blair worked the reel. "It's heavy. The fish must be huge."

She looked so pleased with herself, Drake watched her instead of the float.

Blair finally wrestled the fish out of the water, squealed and laughed, letting it swing until Drake caught it.

"I thought it would be bigger."

"It's at least a pound and a half. A keeper." He removed the hook and tossed the fish in the bucket of water he'd brought for that purpose.

"What kind is it?"

"I don't know—a little ocean perch, maybe. I don't introduce myself, I just eat them."

Blair laughed, her eyes now shadow free.

As he gazed into her upturned face, with the freckled nose and the blond-tipped eyelashes, Drake wished he could have just three minutes alone with Armand-the-sleaze-bucket.

And Blair's parents, too.

"THIS WAS the hotel's boat? I didn't even know there was a boathouse." "Boathouse" might be a generous description for the open-sided ruin she saw, but Blair could see that Drake, or someone, had been making repairs.

"Yes, the *Pirate's Lady*. It's visible from the dock, if you know to look for it," Drake said. He tossed the rope over the pole, climbed out of the dinghy and helped Blair.

After they'd caught enough fish, Drake had taken her the long way back around the tiny island. The coast had been cleverly landscaped with inlets and sheltered coves where hotel guests could swim or play in paddleboats. Debris now littered the white sand, but Blair could see how appealing the coastline once must have been. Actually, it was still appealing.

Now, as she climbed out of the dinghy, Blair guessed that this dock had been where the guests landed. A wide asphalt path led the way up a gentle incline. "That's where the golf-cart track leads, doesn't it?"

Drake nodded. "If you follow the main road, you'll get to the lodge." He walked over to the dry-docked *Pirate's Lady* and stood, hands on his hips. "She was banged up pretty good, but I thought I could fix her."

"Are you a good mechanic?"

Drake grinned. "I'm a terrible mechanic. Every time I get this thing running, something else goes wrong."

"So you are stranded a lot."

"More than I intended to be, that's for sure. Someday, after I teach myself enough about it, I'm going to take off in this boat." He looked back at her. "I was going to work on her this afternoon. If you stick around, I'll find something for you to do."

He was being so decent to her, Blair thought she'd reward him by leaving him in peace. "Tell you what. I'll take the fish back to the lodge and fix a fabulous dinner for you."

His face creased into a pleased smile. "What are we having?"

"Well, fish."

"Of course."

"And I thought I'd raid the cans."

"Ah. Chef's surprise. I'll look forward to it."

Blair stepped back into the dinghy and retrieved the bucket of fish. "Okay, it's a date then."

"A date?"

She met his eyes squarely. "Yes, a date."

"A *date* date?"

"A dinner date."

They looked at each other, the silence broken only by the water lapping against the dinghy, and some noisy bugs.

"Okay. A date." Slowly, a smile spread across Drake's face. "I'll bring the wine."

CHAPTER SEVEN

BLAIR HAD NEVER CLEANED a fish before and hoped she never had to do it again. Fortunately, the professional cookbooks she'd found gave explicit instructions. Normally, Blair appreciated explicit instructions. Normally, she wasn't cleaning fish.

She saved the fish heads for Drake's crab traps, wrapped the fillets and set them in the ice chest.

Baking a peach pie was infinitely more pleasant. Although the flour she found was of indeterminate age, it was in an airtight canister and appeared to be okay. The peach trees were loaded with fruit. If Drake were smart, he'd can some. She hadn't found any canning jars and made a note to suggest that he order some.

Deciphering the contents of the cans in the pantry was actually kind of fun. By shaking them, she guessed which ones held the same things and grouped them together. They were all a fairly large restaurant size, so once she opened one, they'd be committed to eating what it contained for several meals.

She wasn't ready for a long-term commitment so she headed to Drake's kitchen garden.

The plants were more or less in straight rows and the garden could stand a little weeding, she thought critically. Then she proceeded to do so. Only after she was hot and sweaty did she think about a change of clothing. She could probably scrounge another shirt and shorts from the linen-storage room, but she had a horrible feeling she was going to play hostess to Drake without wearing any underwear.

A DATE.

He shouldn't have encouraged her, but nobody likes to be shot down.

Drake put away the last of his tools and wiped his face with his shirt. Blair probably meant she was getting out a tablecloth and candles, so he should spruce up a little. He could do that.

A date. When was the last time he'd gone out on a date? Long before coming to Pirate's Hideout, that's for sure.

The last time had been with Pamela and then it was only to keep his mother quiet. But afterward, she'd grilled him and he knew that if he hadn't asked Pamela out a second time, his mother would trot out some other candidate for her future daughter-in-law.

So he'd asked Pamela out again. And maybe a third time. He couldn't remember actually asking her, but he'd attended some charity dinner with her.

Then there were a few times when he took his mother to one of her functions and Pamela always seemed to show up. Between the "Pamela's going, too. Why don't we all go together in one car?" times and the "Look who's on my committee!" times, it seemed he couldn't turn around without running into Pamela. He was careful not to encourage her, but then, she appeared to need no encouragement.

Drake neither liked nor disliked Pamela. She was one of those women who slyly watched, then molded herself to her surroundings. Pamela would always fit in. He just didn't want her fitting in with him.

Blair wasn't Pamela. He didn't even think they'd like each other very much. Pamela didn't irritate him the way Blair did. And Pamela wouldn't have decided to take a swim just before her wedding, either.

God, that took guts. Smiling to himself, Drake walked to the lodge, remembering that he'd promised Blair a bottle of wine.

SHE HAD NO IDEA what time it was or when Drake would be back. Blair wouldn't cook the fish until she knew he was ready to eat, but in the meantime, she'd prepared a salad and assembled a ratatouille of baby vegetables.

A lovely white tablecloth covered an unfortunately water-stained table, and Blair had selected the best two chairs from the pile of ruined furniture in the restaurant dining room. The upholstery was rotted, so she covered the seats with large dinner napkins and stapled the fabric in place.

She found about a million votive candles and liberally placed them around the room. Because the room was open and there was an ocean breeze in the evening, she wasn't sure how many candles would stay lit, but the more she had out the better her chances. The room looked great.

Blair, herself, was another matter.

She'd managed to find some white pants, probably part of a waiter uniform, that were a wee bit snug, and a white, buttoned shirt that was too big. She tied the tails under her rib cage and rolled up the sleeves. If she remembered to hold in her stomach, the pants looked just fine.

Her underwear was drying on a hook in the storeroom.

Oh, well, she thought, examining her reflection in the bar mirror. No visible panty lines.

Checking to make certain Drake wasn't around, Blair went to the hotel offices and pried open the rusty file cabinet where she'd hidden half the Jiffy Cheez. At least she knew Drake would like the hors d'oeuvres.

IT'S ONLY A stupid dinner, Drake told himself.

So why was he standing in front of a bathroom mirror with a razor in his hand? He hadn't shaved for months, but, hey, the weather was getting hot and he'd been meaning to shave off the beard anyway.

Once his beard was gone, Drake decided his hair was pretty shaggy. When he didn't wear his Knicks cap, his hair got in his face, so he'd just trim it a bit.

Okay, so he hacked off his ponytail. It got the job done and felt cooler, too.

He dressed in loose cotton drawstring pants and a matching overshirt he'd bought during the short time he'd spent in San Verde buying supplies, but not even for a date with Blair was he putting on hard-soled shoes. And the deck shoes were out of the question, so he decided not to wear shoes at all.

He stepped back and tried to see himself. "Not bad, O'Keefe," he murmured and grabbed the wine.

The wine collection had been one of the few pleasant surprises he'd come across during his stay here. The former owners had literally sailed away and never returned after that last hurricane. They'd given up and left everything behind.

Naturally, without electricity, the cellar wasn't kept at an optimum temperature and Drake was no wine connoisseur, but the few bottles he'd sampled had tasted okay.

This white one should be more than okay according to the prices on the laminated wine list.

He wondered if Blair knew wines. They could sample some and compare, he was thinking as he opened the kitchen door.

The kitchen was empty and the table wasn't set.

There was no sign of Blair.

Drake felt a prickle of alarm just before the heavenly smells of baking registered. He let out a breath. She was around here somewhere then.

Still carrying the wine, he walked the length of the lodge to the bar.

And then he saw her, sitting at a table, surrounded by papers, the glow of candles casting interesting shadows on her face.

She hadn't heard him approach and continued to write in her agenda, concentrating on who knew what.

The more he was around her the better she looked. He was going to have to be careful. She was vulnerable, no matter what kind of front she put up.

Everything was ready except the fish. Blair even tried sculpting a few Jiffy Cheez animals, then gave up. Drake made it look easy.

She was hungry. Hungry and bored and tired of waiting for Drake to finish fooling around with his boat.

She'd been stupid to place any importance on this dinner. He obviously hadn't.

And why should he? They were just marking time until she left. She should remember that—she'd had plenty of practice in her life.

Blair was always leaving. She'd learned not to make close friends because it hurt too much to leave them behind. Her mother moved from place to place looking for something Blair could never figure out. Even as an adult, she couldn't figure it out.

Sometimes Blair felt like a dandelion seed pod, drifting on breezes until she could finally land and set root.

But where would she drift now? She had no job, no friends, no home and no money.

On that depressing thought, she wandered over to the windows and gazed out at the ocean. The sun hung low in the sky and the whole view looked like something from a travel brochure.

There was a soothing sameness to the gulf's ebb and flow. People would pay—and had at one time—big bucks to have a view like this. It was a shame to let the lodge crumble. Rebuilding would be a huge task and, due to the island's remoteness, probably wildly expensive.

But it could be done with careful planning.

Detailed, methodical planning—the kind at which Blair excelled. She could do it, she knew she could. If Drake didn't want to bother, then Blair could be his agent. She *wanted* to be his agent. It would give her a job and a focus. Something she could do until she knew where to go next.

And if Drake needed money, he could take on a partner. Blair could help him there, too. If she'd learned anything from hanging around Armand, it was how to describe dreams in terms of profit-making potential.

The more Blair thought about it, the more enthusiastic she became. With the brochure to guide her, she smoothed her bumpy agenda-project sheets and proceeded to plan the resurrection of Pirate's Hideout.

She'd outlined a basic stage-one repair before she had to light the candles and then went right back to work.

"Good evening, Blair."

The deep voice startled her. She hadn't even heard Drake approach. Blair looked up, but the words of greeting died on her lips.

A stranger stood in the shadows by the bar.

She jumped to her feet, ready to run, when he stepped into the candlelight and she recognized him.

Drake. But a Drake she'd never imagined.

The loose, natural-colored clothes he wore glowed in the subdued light, imparting a cinematic heroic quality to his appearance. His hair was brushed back and the blond sun-streaks gleamed. He looked larger than life. He looked like something from her dreams. He looked nothing like Armand.

"You shaved."

Reflexively, he rubbed a hand over his jaw. "The beard was getting hot now that it's getting warmer."

With the beard gone, Blair saw that Drake had a strong, well-defined jaw and a well-shaped mouth.

Put it all together and he was handsome. Incredibly handsome. The kind of handsome that exists on a plane not inhabited by ordinary-looking people like Blair.

The kind of handsome that would never give her a second look—unless she was the only female on a deserted island, which she was.

Blair wanted to shrivel in embarrassment. She'd called this a date. How...presumptuous of her. Men such as Drake didn't date the ordinary.

And here she was in ill-fitting clothes, her hair all kinky and her face not covered in a speck of makeup.

Maybe she should extinguish a few candles, she thought desperately.

"And what is this?" Drake exclaimed mockingly. "Why, could it be...?" He stepped closer to the bar and set a bottle of wine on it. "Jiffy Cheez!" Holding up the can, he kissed it.

Blair smiled weakly.

"My favorite." Drake immediately began sculpting animals on the crackers Blair had arranged.

"I should have brought flowers," he said. "But this will have to do."

He held out a cracker with a perfectly formed rosette on it.

Just like the first time, so long... Okay, it was the day before yesterday. She felt sentimental anyway.

Blair stepped forward and Drake froze.

Puzzled, Blair stopped walking. When he said nothing, she nervously looked over her shoulder. "What is it?"

"Nothing." His voice cracked. He cleared his throat. "You look great."

"No, you look great," she corrected and accepted the cracker. "*I* managed to find a change of clothing." She popped the cracker into her mouth.

"I see that. Good job." He turned and concentrated on his animal sculptures.

Blair stopped chewing and just stared, stared at the newly revealed jaw of the gorgeous man she'd invited to dinner in his home with his food.

The same man who had appeared in the kitchen for two mornings in a row wearing nothing but a towel, and a skimpy towel, at that.

She squeaked.

He looked up. "You thirsty?"

She nodded, though she was content to simply drink in the sight of him.

"I have a lovely white wine here that should complement the Jiffy Cheez." Drake walked behind the bar. "Corkscrew?" he asked and Blair tried to remember where she'd put it.

"Never mind," he said. "There are only two drawers. Wait a minute, here it is," he said holding one up. Now, wineglasses could be a problem. The shelf holding them collapsed and I think they all broke."

"Not all." Blair found her voice. "I found some in the back of the kitchen cabinets." She walked to the table she'd set in front of the open window. "I put two on the table."

With a dramatic gesture, Drake pulled out the cork.

He was waiting for her to return with the glasses. Blair could hardly function. She reached for a wineglass and noticed that her hand trembled.

It was her left hand. Forty-eight hours ago, another man's diamond—a faux diamond from a faux man, as it turned out—had graced her fourth finger. She'd been ready to link her life with his. She would have been his wife and would have borne his children, which would have meant sleeping with him. She'd mentally glossed over the sleeping part and had convinced herself that this was what she'd always wanted.

And now all she wanted was for the man behind the bar to find her one-tenth as attractive as she found him.

"Blair," she murmured to herself, grabbing the glasses. "You are one shallow woman."

MAYBE IT HAD BEEN a trick of the light.

Drake concentrated on removing the cork from the corkscrew and not looking at Blair.

But he couldn't help himself. Those pants she wore might have been painted on. There wasn't room for a freckle underneath. Or lace. He was fairly certain lace would have been outlined.

There was no lace.

She was walking toward him.

Don't look.

But he did.

A revealing jiggle accompanied each step. Two dark shadows touched the white shirt, no matter what light she stood in.

How the hell was he supposed to sit across the table and make idle conversation with her? How was he supposed to maintain eye contact?

She arrived at the bar in a shampoo-scented cloud. "Here are the glasses."

"And here is the wine." How wonderfully witty he was.

Drake poured and they ate the cheese and crackers. He kept the bar between them until Blair moved closer and leaned her elbows on it as she talked. He caught himself losing eye contact.

"Shall I get more crackers?" she asked.

"No. If I want more cheese, I'll just..." He squirted an elephant onto the back of his hand.

Laughing, Blair held out hers. "I want a monkey."

Drake obliged, smiling. Then Blair licked off her monkey and he nearly lost it.

Remember her managing ways. Remember how she rearranged everything. Remember how much you craved your solitude. Remember that she's holding your Jiffy Cheez hostage. "This place looks great," he said. He'd have to order more emergency candles.

She perked up. "I hope you don't mind." She laughed self-consciously and tucked a lock of hair behind her ear. "I got carried away with the candles."

"It looks perfect." *You look perfect.*

She smiled. "I guess I should finish cooking dinner."

Drake gestured for her to precede him down the hall. Yes, it was so he could watch her walk. So sue him. "I smelled something wonderful as I came through the kitchen."

"I baked a peach pie. I hope it turns out."

"A peach pie?" He hadn't eaten a pie in ages. It had

never occurred to him to try to make one. "I'm being overrun with peaches, as I guess you noticed."

"But they're the best peaches in the world," she said.

When they got to the kitchen, Blair removed the pie from the oven and Drake wanted to kiss her. Just for the pie, of course. Not because they were very much alone and she wasn't wearing underwear.

He was just going to have to get past that. Maybe if he ate a lot of food, he'd be too miserable or too sleepy to think about Blair and her bouncy curves and her long legs and her blue eyes and her fresh face and the wide mouth with the sexy brackets.

And then again, maybe not.

HE WAS SO GOOD-LOOKING, he made her nervous. Blair found it very difficult to refrain from inane babbling, especially since Drake gazed directly into her eyes as though he was truly interested in what she said.

She drank her first glass of wine too quickly and forced herself barely to sip at the second.

"Don't you like it?" Drake asked, gesturing to the bottle in the champagne bucket standing next to the table. Dry ice and water bubbled and set a romantic fog swirling down the sides.

"Oh, it's lovely. I wonder if I've had it before. Armand liked wines and I wrote down the ones—" She broke off. *Babbling, babbling.*

"And I'll bet you've got the list with you, too."

Blair slid a glance to her saltwater-damaged planner on the table where she'd been working. "Yes," she admitted, staring at her hands in her lap.

"You'll have to bring it and take a look at the cellar here," he continued, apparently not thinking anything was unusual about Blair and her list of wines. "I haven't studied all the ins and outs of wines. The owners just left the bottles here and I have no idea what I've got."

"Okay." Blair looked up gratefully, but Drake was looking at his plate. She let her face relax for a few seconds.

He's gorgeous and he's still speaking to you. You haven't run him off yet and you haven't spilled any food. The night is going well. Then again, the night is still young.

"The fish is great, but these—" he held up a corn-bread muffin "—these are excellent, especially slathered with far too much butter."

She giggled. Ack. "Thanks. They're not hard to make."

"You'll have to show me how. I miss bread between supply runs. It doesn't last more than a few days because of the humidity."

"If you ordered yeast next time, you could make your own bread."

"Bread." He gazed out at the night just beyond the edges of candlelight. "Bread takes time. I've got time. Sounds good."

The smile he gave her, warm and approving, made tears sting her eyes.

This was not good. She was feeling things she shouldn't be feeling.

She was so easily manipulated, she thought with disgust. Let a man gaze intently into her eyes and ask her a few questions about herself and she was ready to…ready to…she didn't want to contemplate what she was ready to do.

She needed a break. "I'll go get the pie now."

NICE REAR CHASSIS.

Drake watched until Blair was out of sight, then slowly lowered his head to the table and closed his eyes.

His eyes hurt from staring into her eyes so he wouldn't start concentrating on his peripheral vision.

He'd talked about the most idiotic things. *Baking bread.* Although the more he thought about it, homemade bread might be the missing ingredient to his quest for the perfect bacon, lettuce and tomato sandwich.

Even the thought of the perfect BLT didn't squelch the things he was feeling that he definitely shouldn't be feeling.

She'd be gone in a couple of weeks and he'd never see her again. That could be a good thing, if all parties were equal and all parties were agreed.

But they weren't equal. She was here by accident and was dependent on him for everything. Therefore, the rules of love and war clearly stated that he shouldn't take advantage or indicate that he wanted to take advantage.

It was complicated when he tried to analyze his situation, but the main drift was "hands off." The "eyes-off" part he'd added all on his own.

He sat up and emptied the last of the wine into his glass. Good as it was, the wine wouldn't go with peach pie.

"It's still pretty warm." Blair had arrived, looking flushed and lovely and bouncy.

While he was waiting, Drake had cleared away the dishes, stacking them on the bar. Blair set the pie on the table and handed Drake the pie server. "How big a piece do you want?"

Drake looked from the pie, warm and waiting, to her. "I want it all," he replied.

She laughed and rested her elbows on the table. "You think you can handle it?"

"Oh, yes. It's been a long time since I've had pie. I didn't even miss pie until—" he gestured "—now."

"Go ahead. Have some." Her voice was breathy and eager.

"I'd like to. Believe me, I can hardly wait, but sometimes the anticipation is just as enjoyable." He smiled, allowing himself a quick lack of eye contact.

"I know," she said. "When it's cooking, I can hardly wait, myself. And you know the worst part?"

"*Is* there a worst part?"

She nodded. "It's when you've taken the pie out of the oven and you're waiting for it to cool. I'm ready for it, but I can't have it. Drives me nuts."

Drake gave her a slow smile. "That's why I always keep my pies warm. Cool pies aren't nearly as enjoyable."

"But if they're too warm, the juices run."

"Running juices has never been a problem for me," Drake told her.

Her lips parted. "You must have incredible self-control."

"I do," he assured her.

"Sometimes I just lose control." Blair broke off a piece of crust and popped it into her mouth.

"I know exactly what you mean." Drake leaned forward. "Just the thought of those warm, soft peaches in their sweet juice and the way they taste and feel on my tongue…"

Blair's eyes were glazed. Sweat beaded her nose. "I hope this pie lives up to your expectations."

"It would—will," he corrected. "It will." With a deep breath, he picked up the pie server and sliced into the pie. Cutting a wedge, he put it on a plate.

"I thought you wanted it all," Blair asked as he cut a second piece.

"I do, but I've found that…*pie* is much better shared." He speared a peach on a fork and offered it to her.

Blair smiled uncertainly before allowing Drake to feed her the fruit.

He was going to pay for this, he thought, watching her lick her lips.

MAYBE THE WAY to a man's heart really was through his stomach, Blair thought. He certainly liked pie.

"What happened that made you want to come here?" she asked.

Drake was midway through his second piece of pie and looking mellow, so she decided she had a fair chance of getting the answer to her question.

She knew at once she'd overestimated the quality of her baking. Drake dropped the fork and gazed hard at her.

"I don't want to talk about it."

"I can tell. Lighten up."

"Leave it alone, Blair."

"I've told you all about my stupidity with Armand. I'm entitled to hear your story." She sat back and crossed her arms.

"Why?"

She tried to think of a compelling reason. "Why not?"

"I'll tell you why not. Because I've had it up to *here*—" he slashed across his neck "—with trying to explain my reasons to people and having them tell me I'm crazy. I'm not crazy," he said, and Blair detected a wildness in his eyes.

"I'm not having a midlife crisis—or maybe I am, but it's *my* midlife crisis. For the first thirty-five years of my life I was a dutiful son, a great big brother and a valuable partner. But I was a hell of a husband."

"You're married?" Blair's eyes widened. She'd been lusting after a married man. Was still lusting, in fact. She'd sunk even lower than she'd thought.

"Not anymore and not for very long. But I married because it was expected of me. Don't get me wrong, I loved Tiffany—"

"*Tiffany?* You were married to a woman named Tiffany?"

"Hey, she's a terrific lady. I was the one who screwed up our marriage. Fortunately, she found somebody else, by all accounts a great guy, and she doesn't hate me. In fact, I manage, or rather I managed, their kids' college fund."

"Sorry."

He brushed away her apology. "I shouldn't have jumped on you."

"Do you still love her?"

He smiled briefly. "Not that way. The fires are out. We got married right out of school and I got a terrific job that sucked me in. She wanted me around more. She wanted to have a baby. Roger and I wanted to start a business. I chose Roger. Tiffany very wisely, but not very quietly, left."

Blair nodded, afraid to say anything in case Drake stopped talking.

"Roger and I decided we were going to make a potful of money, then chuck the business and live on the beach. Sounded great to me, so I lived the business. I thought Roger was living the business, too, but somewhere along the way, he found time to get married. We postponed our retirement. And Exeter-O'Keefe got bigger and the pressure got more intense and the only thing keeping me going was knowing that I could quit in a couple of years. Except—people depended on me now. Lots of people. I tried to cut back and guess what?"

Blair shook her head.

"I was trapped. I had no life. Stress was killing me. So I told them that the day I turned thirty-five was my last day as a trader. And it was."

"But why here?"

"I'd been here once and wanted to build a house on the other side of the island. When I tried to negotiate with the owners, I found out the whole thing was up for sale. So I bought it."

"Did they tell you about the damage?"

"They did and I didn't care."

"Why aren't you rebuilding?"

He finished the last of the pie before answering. "Right now, it isn't an option. I used my liquid assets buying this place and Roger refuses either to sell the business or buy out my half." Drake grimaced. "He's convinced that I'll be back, and I don't feel like getting into a legal battle at the moment." His voice dropped. "But I'm not going back."

"I-I've been thinking." Blair stood and retrieved the pages from her planner.

"Sounds dangerous." His words followed her across the room.

"I've formulated a plan where you can rebuild even without investment capital on your part." Blair deliberately chose words Drake would have used. She wanted him to take her seriously. "Repairs can be done in stages and you could take on a silent partner. When Pirate's Hideout becomes profitable again, you can gradually repay your partner, if you choose."

"Didn't you listen to anything I said? I don't want to rebuild. Why would I want to work so other people can enjoy themselves?"

"You wouldn't have to do anything. *I'd* do it for you."

"You? What about your own job?"

Blair cleared away the dishes and spread her plans in front of Drake. "I quit my job to marry Armand."

"You could get it back."

"No, I trained my replacement so she could do my job perfectly. And she's being paid less money."

"So find a new job."

"I did. This job." She tapped the papers. "I can organize anything, and I can organize the rebuilding of this resort. I bet I can even find you investment money. Or you, with your contacts—"

"My contacts are mad at me."

"Then I'll do it."

"No!" He stood. "I like things the way they are. I don't want people tramping all over my island. And if this place is rebuilt, people will come here to *visit*. Lots of people. People I haven't seen since second grade. Friends of friends. Cousins of friends. Oh, and clients. In-laws and bosses of clients. Even people jumping off passing ships."

Blair made a face at him.

"They'll come here whether or not they're invited, and short of running them off with a gun, there's no way to get them to leave. But leave it the way it is now, and nobody in his right mind would want to stay here. It's perfect the way it is." He placed his fists on top of the papers and leaned until he was inches away from her. "I want to be left alone!"

"I think you overestimate your charm."

Straightening, he visibly calmed himself. "Instead of

poking your nose into my business, you should occupy your time coming up with a plan for yourself. From what you say, you have no home and no money. Once Mario lets you off in San Verde, what are you going to do?''

With that, he stepped through the empty window frame and walked out into the night.

CHAPTER EIGHT

ONCE MARIO LETS YOU off in San Verde what are you going to do? In one sentence, Drake had forced Blair to accept the reality of her situation. And reality was not candlelight, a handsome man and a peach pie. Reality was burned bridges and no money.

What *was* she going to do?

Ever since she'd arrived, Blair had focused first on Armand, then the police, then Drake. It was time she accepted the fact that no one was going to help her out of this mess anytime soon. Until she could convince some government authority—or one of the investors—to investigate Armand's scam, she had to support herself. She wasn't going to talk herself into a job supervising the rebuilding of Pirate's Hideout, either.

It would have been perfect. Blair would have had a base of operations and a fancy title to impress those who were impressed by fancy titles. Her accusations against Armand would have carried more weight.

And it would have been an excuse to stay with Drake, though why she wanted to stay with a grumpy, if gorgeous, hermit was beyond her.

But he wasn't always grumpy—only when people interfered with him. Drake was a man who knew exactly what he wanted.

As she gazed into the darkness, straining to see a bit of bright moonlight on Drake's clothes, Blair realized she'd hoped he'd want her.

For a long time, she sat with the flickering candles, wishing that Drake would return, to tell her he'd thought about her plans and had changed his mind.

But he didn't.

From the look on his face as he walked out, Blair knew that he might never rebuild. With the size of the *Pirate's Lady*, he wouldn't have to. Blair could see him sailing away in the boat, drifting from port to port. That would appeal to him.

Drake was a man who'd checked out of society just as she was desperately trying to check in. A man who'd pulled up his roots when she was trying to grow hers.

Their lives were going in different directions.

So now what?

Now she needed a plan. Blair pushed the papers to one side and opened her agenda to a new, but equally bumpy, project page.

Goal, she wrote, then modified it with *short-term*. If short-term didn't work out, there wouldn't be a need for long-term. Short-term was to get a job. But before that, she needed a place to stay. And to get a place to stay, she needed money.

She started another column: *Assets*. Underneath that, she listed: ruined wedding gown, torn veil, small gold earrings, salt-stained leather agenda, one set of underwear, one life preserver, used. And one heart, bruised, but that probably wasn't an asset.

It was so hopeless, Blair's head dropped to her arms and she cried for the first time since she'd come to Pirate's Hideout.

But Blair never cried for long, and by the next morning she had a rudimentary plan, which unfortunately hinged on Lupe's assistance.

Blair had slept on the library sofa. She was pretty certain Drake hadn't come in to read last night. In fact, she didn't know where Drake was now and, frankly, she didn't much care, except that she wasn't sure how long the radio batteries would last and she didn't know how to turn on the generator.

If she had to, she'd figure it out.

Striding toward the rec room, Blair heard Drake's voice and decided to eavesdrop. Politeness and civility be hanged, her survival was at stake here. If he was talking to the dispatcher/market cashier, Blair needed all the hints she could get for ingratiating herself.

"Now, Lupe, I know you're there." Drake sounded amused, not frustrated. "Come on, I haven't talked to you in two days."

"Four," came the reply.

Drake chuckled. "You know how I lose track of time." His voice was low and caressing.

Blair bet Lupe was purring. *She* would have been.

"So what do you want?" Lupe sounded impatient, but there was no bite to her words. The woman must not be as gullible as Blair first thought.

"Have you heard anything concerning my refugee?"

"She still there?"

"You know very well she is."

"Ha. Figured you woulda strangled her by now."

"She's not so bad," Drake said.

Blair hadn't expected him to say anything nice about her, not that he'd exactly *raved*, but it was better than agreeing with Lupe.

"So have you heard anything?" he asked again. "Any missing-persons reports? Outraged investors screaming?"

Blair held her breath.

"Nope."

Drake exhaled, covering up Blair's sigh. "So how about the status on that carburetor?"

Oh, great. She was in the same class as a carburetor. Blair listened while he and Lupe discussed the part. She wanted to peer around the corner, but didn't dare since she didn't know which way he was facing.

"You want I should read your messages?" Lupe asked after Drake agreed to pay extra to have the carburetor shipped express.

"Anything new? Anybody dying?"

"No, mostly the same old, same old."

"Then don't bother reading them."

"Except there's more of 'em."

Blair heard a faint groan.

"This Roger, he's sent letters. Sent them registered and I had to sign."

"Thanks, Lupe. Sorry you were inconvenienced."

"Sent some express, too."

"Roger is impatient."

"And what about your mama? A mama wants to hear from her son."

"Then she should listen to her son when he speaks to her," Blair heard him say. "You know the cards I left you?"

"The ones that say, 'I'm fine. Leave me alone'?"

"Yeah. Drop one in the mail for me, would you, Lupe?"

"Okay. I only got two left."

"I'll send you more when Mario comes out here." There was a pause. "I don't suppose there's a chance Mario would make an extra trip?"

Please, Blair breathed.

"No. He's busy. He only makes the trips as a favor to you."

"He makes the trips because I pay him," Drake retorted.

"Well, that, too," acknowledged Lupe. "Hey, Señor Drake, if that part comes in early, you want Mario to come on out?"

"Sure."

"Then you got your order ready?"

Blair decided to make her presence known as Blake unfolded a piece of paper. She strolled into the rec room, as though everything was just peachy-keen between them, and propped a hip on the table.

Though he never hesitated as he read his list, his gaze traveled up and down her length. "A *case* of Jiffy Cheez," he said, looking directly at her.

"That stuff will rot your stomach. It's not natural," Lupe said.

"Right on, Lupe," Blair said.

"Make that *two* cases."

"Did you remember to order yeast?" Blair asked. "You could use more flour and sugar, too."

"Hey, Lupe," Drake said. "I want to bake some bread. What kind of yeast have you got?"

He could have asked *her,* Blair thought. "When you finish, I'd like to talk with Lupe."

Drake released the microphone button. "That's not a good idea."

"Excuse me?"

"I don't want you antagonizing her again."

"She's the *police dispatcher!*"

"Yes, but San Verde is a little more casual than most places."

"Oh, for—" Blair hopped off the table. "*Fine.* But you can tell her for me that she *is* representing the San Verde police and if she won't talk with me, then she darn well better find someone who will. Because if she doesn't, when I get off this island, I will blab my story to every newspaper, radio station and sleazy talk show in the country because *I have nothing to lose!*"

And that was as good an exit line as she'd ever delivered, Blair thought, stomping off to the kitchen. A person had her limits and Blair had reached hers. She'd tried to be honest and look where it had gotten her.

She reached the kitchen to find that Drake hadn't made

coffee yet. And he probably hadn't planned to. Why? Because no doubt he expected *Blair* to do it.

Blair, the rule follower. Blair, the good girl. Blair, who always tried to fit in and never got it right.

Boy, what a sap.

Blair jerked open the cabinet, grabbed the percolator and slammed the door shut. Armand had offered to make her his protégée. She should have taken him up on his offer. Obviously, honesty didn't pay.

She *would* go on the talk-show circuit. See if she wouldn't. She'd be bad. She'd be outrageous. She'd be the sound-bite queen.

Blair filled the coffeepot and fired up the burner. "Boil!" she snarled.

"Blair." Drake walked into the kitchen. "If you're not careful, you'll break something."

"Put it on my tab!"

"What's the matter with you?"

She glared at him. He had the nerve to look great this morning. "Do you think you're the only one entitled to a tantrum now and then?"

"No, but I think you're overreacting."

"Oh, really." Hands on hips, she faced him. "Did you give Lupe my message?"

He rubbed the space between his eyebrows. "She...had a line at the cash register."

At this rate, Blair's blood was going to boil faster than the water. "I hope she treated her customers well, because that's the only job she's going to have when I get finished telling my story."

"Blair—"

Blair spanned her hands. "Talk shows. Radio interviews. Tabloid sales. Maybe even a book deal. And I have nothing but time to plot it all. Lots and lots of time."

"I hate to burst your bubble... No, actually I don't mind

bursting it at all. If nobody cared about your story before, they're not going to care now."

She smirked. "It's called spin, Drake. It's all in the way I tell it. The media is a giant monster just waiting to be fed. And I'm offering a buffet!" She held up her hand and counted off her fingers. "I've got all the main food groups. Money, scandal, sex, small-town corruption, the little guy fighting against the uncaring government—"

"Back up. Sex? There hasn't been any sex. I would have remembered sex."

She gave him a pitying smile. "There doesn't have to be. After days alone on a tropical island, everyone will believe it anyway." Especially when Drake's picture was plastered all over the newspapers. No woman alive could resist him.

But Drake hadn't had any trouble resisting *her* and don't think *that* wasn't a sore point.

"I'll deny it."

She laughed. Then she deliberately tousled her hair and pouted. Grabbing a handful of her shirt and pulling it so her form was clearly outlined, she spoke in a breathy voice, "Well...what are two people to *do* day after day and night after lonely night..."

Drake stared at her. "I'll tell them there was nothing between us."

Blair wrung her hands. "He...he said that?" Her voice quavered. "But I thought he cared about me!"

"Blair!"

She covered her eyes. "I can't talk about it anymore." She broke into sobs.

"Blair?"

Blair dropped her hands, saw his expression and laughed. "Ha-ha. You see?" She continued to chortle. "This is going to be great!"

DRAKE GRITTED his teeth, his hands clenching and unclenching as Blair laughed and embellished her abandoned-damsel act.

BRIDE OVERBOARD

"I never thought I was the type of man who slapped hysterical women."

She thrust her chin up. "Good, because I slap back."

He stared at her, at the defiant chin and the mocking blue eyes, then grabbed her by the shoulders, hauled her against him and kissed her.

The kiss was hot and hard, born of frustration, anger and suppressed desire.

Especially suppressed desire. Drake had fought to keep from thinking about Blair ever since he'd pulled her out of the ocean. But consciously not thinking about her made him think about her even more. All the time, in fact.

He supported her weight as Blair hung limply against him. No doubt shock was keeping her immobile.

Drake didn't want her shocked. He wanted her arms around his neck so he could release her shoulders and let his hands roam over her body. He wanted to bury his fingers in her hair and angle her head so he could capture more of her mouth with his. He wanted his fingers free so they could unbutton her shirt, except she was wearing a knit shirt and he'd have to drag it over her head and they'd have to stop kissing for him to do that.

Abruptly, Drake set her from him. But not too far.

"What was that for?" she gasped, her lips parted.

"To find out what else you did back."

"Huh?"

"Never mind." Though she still looked dazed, he lifted her arms and put them around his neck.

Angling her head, he kissed her again. She still wasn't kissing him back, but that was okay. She wasn't pulling away, either. There was a lot to work with here.

Drake slid his hands down her back and cupped her hips, fitting her against him. She relaxed with a soft sigh that ended with a tiny moan in the back of her throat.

Drake felt it more than heard it. With one tug, he pulled

her shirt from her shorts. Skimming his hands over her waist, he lingered, enjoying the feel of her satiny skin.

Then he allowed the image of Blair in her wedding dress, accompanied by one of Blair in last night's outfit, to flood his mind.

He could touch her now. Drake unhooked the lace bra and splayed his hands over her back, sighing into her mouth.

Blair flinched.

Okay, he was going too fast. Drake rested his hands at her waist again and nuzzled the side of her neck.

He felt her draw a deep breath and began moving his hands.

"What's going on here?"

"I'm kissing you senseless." He nipped her ear.

"Not quite."

Smiling, he trailed kisses toward her mouth. "I'll have to try harder."

"Drake, stop."

He stopped, his eyes still closed, his lips a millimeter away from hers. "I thought I heard you say stop."

"I did."

"Did you mean *stop* stop or slow down?"

"Red light."

Drake swallowed. "When's it going to turn green?"

She didn't answer.

He lifted his head and met her eyes.

"Where are we going?" she asked.

He smiled. "I've always had fantasies about the beach, but my bed is big enough for two." He brushed his index finger across her lips.

"No, I mean after that."

"Anywhere you want. We've got almost two weeks."

She gave him a sad smile. "In other words, until Mario arrives, right?"

What she was asking finally got through Drake's lust-soaked brain. "Well, yes."

"I see."

"There's nothing for you here, Blair."

"There's you," she said, her gaze steady.

He shook his head. "I have nothing to offer."

She tilted her head, a half smile creasing the brackets by her mouth. "You offer clothes, food, shelter and some of the prettiest scenery around. What more do I need?"

He remembered saying the same thing to her.

Though the blood pounded through his body and desire weighted his movements, Drake unhooked her arms from behind his neck. "You need a commitment. You want to build. You want direction. I want to drift, unfettered, through the rest of my life."

"You won't always feel that way."

Drake put a finger over her lips. "You can't count on that and you can't count on me." Kissing the top of her head, he left her in the kitchen, just as the coffee began to boil.

SHE COULDN'T HAVE HAD her crisis of conscience a couple of hours later, oh no. Blair couldn't just feel, couldn't just be swept away. No, she had to think. Had to push for a pledge that she'd be a part of Drake's future.

Drake wasn't thinking of his future. He was living the moment and what a moment it was. Even now, three days later, she could recall the hot feelings he'd stirred within her.

Some things aren't meant to last. Blair's problem was that nothing in her life had lasted at all up to this point and she hated that.

Drake was right. She wanted to build. Wanted security. She wasn't the fling type. She should be grateful that he was the sort of man who wouldn't take advantage of her.

Even though three days had passed, she was still filled with regrets. Engaged in her daily ritual of gathering shells and throwing them into the ocean, she looked back at the lodge to see if Drake had left yet.

She saw him walking along the path toward the *Pirate's Lady* and turned her head so he wouldn't see that she was looking at him.

They'd been avoiding each other, coming together for stilted shared dinners.

Of course, after the debacle last night, she'd probably never see him again.

Sinking onto the sand, Blair relived her humiliation.

It was just that Drake had looked so handsome, sitting in the candlelight of the library and Blair was regretting her scruples and thinking that a couple of memorable nights might not be such a high price to pay for future misery, since she was miserable now anyway. She'd put aside the book she was reading and walked behind him.

She had to touch him and so she'd tried the old rubbing-the-shoulders ploy. For a while, she thought it worked. As she'd kneaded the strong muscles, Drake at first ignored her, then leaned his head back and closed his eyes.

And there was his mouth, just ready for the taking.

So Blair had taken it.

For the briefest instant, he'd responded, then twisted away.

"It's all right," she'd told him breathlessly. "I can handle it."

At that, he'd stood and shook his head. "I'm not sure I can. Please don't make any further physical overtures."

He'd actually said "physical overtures." Physical overtures? He'd sounded like a sexual-harassment lawyer. Embarrassment and something else she'd never felt before made her scream at him. Then she'd stormed off, unearthed all the Jiffy Cheez and thrown it at him, can by can.

Expressionless, he'd caught them all, thanked her and returned to his book.

Blair had returned to cabana number one.

"What an idiot I am," she moaned, imagining how she must have looked, shrieking at him and pelting him with Jiffy Cheez.

He'd be glad to see her go.

She sat on the beach, traced circles in the sand and gazed out at the ocean.

When her skin began prickling from the sun, she knew it was time to go inside. She was hungry anyway.

Standing, she brushed at her legs, then squinted at the horizon.

A black speck that she'd first thought was a bird, then an oil-drilling platform, had grown larger.

Heedless of the threat of sunburn, Blair watched the speck turn into a dot, then a lump, which bobbed up and down.

It had to be a boat.

The supply boat. Drake's carburetor must have come in early, after all.

Blair felt chilled in the midday sun. This was it. She was leaving and she'd never see Drake again.

Never see Drake again.

Never.

She wasn't ready for *never* yet. She couldn't leave now. She couldn't. She didn't have enough memories stored to leave. She needed memories—lots of memories to comfort her in the dark days ahead.

Memories of love. None of this imagination, either. She wanted specific memories and she wanted them now.

It would have to be now, judging by the progress of that boat.

Blair started to run toward the *Pirate's Lady*.

To save time, she peeled off her shirt.

"DRAKE!"

Drake heard Blair's breathless approach from inside the *Pirate's Lady* galley where he was checking the electrical connections. "Coming!" he called.

Hoping she wasn't hurt or hadn't set anything on fire, he scrambled up the steps and peered over the railing.

Blair jogged down the path.

Drake blinked. Damn, he had a vivid imagination. He'd undressed her in his mind so often his sense of sight had started doing the same. And doing it very well. He could visualize her lacy white bra as clearly as though she was wearing nothing else.

"Come down here," she commanded, breathing heavily.

Drake hesitated, enjoying the rise and swell of her barely covered breasts from this particular vantage point. "What do you want?"

"You."

Drake gestured. "Here I am."

"Okay, if you won't come out here, then I'm coming up there." She began climbing the ship's ladder. "In fact, this is a better idea. We'll be more comfortable here."

"Comfortable for what?"

"For sex."

He was hallucinating. He must have spent too much time in the hot sun—except he hadn't been in the sun.

And then she was standing beside him and he was still visualizing her without her shirt and wondering why, if he had such a good imagination, he couldn't visualize her without her bra, as well.

And then he didn't think, because Blair was kissing him and this time he wasn't going to push her away. Since this was all a hallucination, he couldn't get into any trouble. Right?

"Blair." He clutched her tightly to him.

"We've got to hurry." Blair wiggled her arms free and pulled off his shirt without unbuttoning the neck.

"Ouch—damn it, Blair, what are you doing?" In spite of his vow, Drake pushed her hands away and freed his head from his shirt.

"Memories. I want memories."

"Of what?"

"Of what happiness is." She planted little nipping kisses across his chest.

"That sounds oddly familiar."

She gave him a frustrated look. "Please, Drake."

"You're serious."

"Yes!"

"So you're really not wearing a shirt?"

Blair looked down at herself. "Um, no." Quickly she unzipped her shorts and tossed them. "Now I'm not wearing shorts, either."

Drake closed his eyes. Blair. Blair was here. Here and nearly naked. There had to be a catch somewhere, but damned if he could think of it.

His eyes still shut, Drake reached out and his hands found the curve of her waist. Moving his fingers lightly, he explored her shape. Gooseflesh rose on her skin and he smiled at her response. Desire zinged through him, but he deliberately tamped it down, wanting to luxuriate in the sensation of her body against his.

She was damp from her run along the beach and her rib cage rose and fell. He skimmed his hands lower and cupped her hips, which she rocked against him.

"Hurry," she whispered, her hands clutching him.

"Blair," he breathed. He bent his head, knowing her mouth would find his, savoring the moment, breathing in the heady scents of sun, sea and Blair.

His lips had barely touched hers when Blair unsnapped his shorts.

"Get with the program, Drake."

"I am, I am." He lazily traced a finger across her parted lips, feeling her breath puff against him. "Be patient." He gave her a heavy-lidded smile and bent his head once more. "We've got all the time in the world."

She turned her head away from his kiss. "No, we don't."

"Why not?"

Blair tugged on his shorts, but Drake tugged back.

"Because Mario is on his way—"

"Mario?" he asked sharply.

She nodded. "Yes, I saw the boat, so I'll be leaving soon. I'll never see you again and I—"

"Hold that thought." Drake stepped into the pilothouse, reached for his binoculars and trained them on the horizon.

Blair used the opportunity to pull off his shorts.

"Blair! Stop it. This boat might not be Mario and—"

"Holey-moley, I've hit the mother lode."

Drake snatched his shorts back up. "Behave!"

"If I'd known you weren't wearing underwear, I would have done that days ago," Blair said.

"Yes, knowing the one you're with isn't wearing underwear has that effect on a person." Without waiting to see her reaction, Drake peered through the binoculars again. "I want to make sure this is Mario. Not everybody who sails these waters is friendly."

"If it is Mario, can we have sex?" She wound her arms around Drake.

"You want to have sex with Mario?"

"No!" Blair swatted his arm. "With you."

"And have your only memories of us together be of some quickie? I have my pride." He didn't want *his* only memories of her to be a hurried coupling, either.

"Drake!"

"Hang on." Drake stared, trying to make out the details. "It looks like Mario, but...he's got people with him."

Blair stopped kissing his neck. "How many people?"

"At least two more, maybe another." He lowered the binoculars. Cupping her face, he kissed her gently. "Blair, I'm flattered, but..." He shook his head.

Blair's eyes filled with tears. "I'm not ever going to see you again, am I?"

Probably not, and the emotions accompanying that realization unnerved him. He'd miss her. But would he miss her enough to ask her to stay?

He couldn't answer, either her or himself, so he lifted the binoculars again and tried to blot out the sound of Blair's sniffling.

"No!" It couldn't be.

"What?"

"*Damn* it!" Drake looked around for something to kick.

"Drake? Are we in trouble?"

"Probably." He rubbed his eyes and looked through the binoculars once more. "Oh, great. You better get dressed. Mario's got my mother with him."

CHAPTER NINE

IT WAS WORSE than that.

While Blair searched for her shorts in the vegetation, Drake identified the others on the boat. "What the hell? She's brought *Pamela* with her."

Blair stopped her search. "Who's Pamela?"

"You don't want to know."

"Yes, I do."

He started swearing again. "It's Roger! Roger's with them."

"Who's Roger? Pamela's husband?" she asked hopefully.

"Exeter. My business partner."

"Oh, right, you told me." She found her shorts in a clump of sea grass.

"So who's making the trades? Who'd he leave in charge?" After that, Drake stomped around and only spoke in four-letter words.

Blair had her own problems. She'd left her shirt right out there on the beach. This was just great. She was about to flash Drake's mother.

Leaving Drake behind, Blair jogged along the golf-cart path, hoping she could retrieve her shirt before the introductions. First impressions were so important.

When she found it, her shirt was a sodden lump and she could make out people on the approaching motor launch. Fortunately, she couldn't see the whites of their eyes. Blair snatched her shirt, then escaped to the lodge.

By the time she'd put on the white shirt from the other night, Drake had arrived at the dock and was standing, feet apart, fists planted at his waist, his stance clearly stating, Don't mess with me.

He looked great.

Blair elected to remain in the lodge. Guessing that the visitors weren't going to stay on the boat, Blair boiled water to make ice tea. Tea was such a civilized drink and she had a feeling civility was going to be in short supply.

Drake didn't have any lemon, but she picked some of the fresh mint that was threatening to take over his garden.

Then she stood at the kitchen window and watched the drama unfold.

As she suspected, Drake was not welcoming. And as she also suspected, about the time she added the tea leaves to steep, Drake was leading a small procession toward the lodge.

One man remained on the boat and unloaded boxes. That must be Mario.

Blair had no trouble identifying the hatted woman in navy and white as Drake's mother, or the younger woman as the mysterious Pamela, but there were two men. Drake hadn't mentioned two men.

Looking murderous, Drake stalked up the cracked asphalt drive and stomped inside.

The little group stopped outside. "Oh, Drake!" Blair heard an older woman's voice. "You can't possibly live here!"

"I can, quite comfortably, as it happens," Drake replied. "Are you coming in or not?"

"Is it safe?" a man asked.

"That depends on why you're here," Drake said.

"I think we should accept Drake's invitation to go inside," said the other man. After some hesitation, the others followed his suggestion.

Blair was still in the kitchen, and they were now out of her sight. She decided to eavesdrop a little more.

"Drake, buddy, this place sure took a hit." Must be Roger.

"Three hits."

"I told you it should have been inspected. It's not like you to invest blind."

"This is not an investment, this is my home."

"Whatever you say, buddy."

The tone of Roger's voice was so patronizing that Blair braced herself for the sound of a fist striking flesh.

Amazingly, Drake restrained himself.

"Mrs. O'Keefe, let me find you somewhere to sit." This was a younger female voice, faintly accusing. Pamela.

Blair's eyes narrowed and she moved closer to the door.

"Drake, there isn't any furniture," Pamela said.

"In here."

Blair guessed they were moving into the bar and restaurant area. Now she wouldn't be able to hear.

She diluted the tea and added chunks of dry ice to the metal pitcher. Unorthodox, but effective. Blair set the pitcher on a tray with glasses and mint leaves, then walked down the hall, trailing fog behind her.

"...situation intrigued him," Blair heard. "And Dr. Farnham would like to talk with you."

"About what?"

A throat was cleared. "What would you like to talk about, Drake?" Blair assumed this was the doctor's voice.

"I don't want to talk."

"Then you don't have to," the doctor said agreeably.

"But, Dr. Farnham—"

He interrupted Drake's mother. "We've only just arrived. Drake must become comfortable with us after these months alone."

Blair hesitated. What an odd thing to say.

"Drake, you haven't said a word to Pamela."

"What are you doing here, Pamela?"

"Drake! Do you see how hostile he is, Dr. Farnham?"

"It's what we expected, Mrs. O'Keefe."

"Just what kind of a doctor are you anyway?" Drake asked.

Yeah, what kind of a doctor?

"Well, Drake, I'm a psychiatrist."

"Mother!"

"Just think of me as a friend," the doctor continued in a voice that made Blair want to shake him.

"Shut up!"

Evidently, Drake felt the same way. Blair decided to make her entrance.

Whether it was the surprise factor or the frothing pitcher of tea, her entrance was more dramatic than she intended.

Mrs. O'Keefe squealed and clutched her chest. A blond woman about Blair's age immediately went to the older woman's assistance. After the first shock of surprise, a knowing gleam entered the eyes of a balding, potbellied man whose hairy white legs extended from a pair of relaxed-fit Docker shorts. The other man, thinner and grayer, alternated his gaze between Blair and Drake.

Blair crossed the room and set the tray on the table where she and Drake had eaten their last wonderful dinner. Then she glanced uncertainly toward Drake, hoping for some sign of whether he wanted her to make herself scarce or offer her support.

Drake looked awful. His jaw clenched and unclenched as though he was grinding his teeth. He was breathing shallowly and was standing rigidly at the bar.

He was furious. Livid. And something else. Fear? Panic?

He looked as if he were about to explode. Blair grabbed a chair and carried it over to him. His eyes locked onto hers.

She took that as a sign. "Sit down," she whispered. When he didn't move, she rubbed her hand over his arm, urging him downward.

"Pamela—Pamela, darling, don't look. He's taken up with a native woman." Mrs. O'Keefe continued in a stage whisper audible to all.

Blair opened her mouth to protest, but Drake grabbed her hand and sat in the chair.

He wanted her next to him. Blair was so happy she forgot what she'd been going to say.

"Well, Drake," said Dr. Farnham as though he were speaking to a child. "Why don't you introduce your friend to us?"

"Why don't *you* tell me what you're doing here?"

Mrs. O'Keefe glanced at Dr. Farnham, who nodded. "Drake, we've been worried about you."

"I've sent word that I'm fine." He tugged on her hand and Blair landed awkwardly on the arm of the chair. Drake slid his arm around her waist. "You'll vouch for that, won't you, sweetheart?"

Okay, she'd play sultry island girl for him. It was for a good cause. Blair nodded and gave him a smoldering look.

"But you haven't answered any of our letters," Mrs. O'Keefe said.

"I quit reading them. Found something else to occupy my time." He gave Blair a look that made her heart beat faster.

Boy, he really had great faith in her ability to play the femme fatale, not that anyone else had shown up for the casting call.

Dr. Farnham removed a small black notebook from his pocket and scribbled in it.

"You haven't returned our telephone calls." Drake's mother was beginning to whine.

"There's no phone here."

Drake was still looking at Blair. The touch of anxiety she'd seen in his eyes was gone.

"I figured as much," Roger broke in. "That's why I

brought you this." He crossed the room and handed Drake a black object. "It's a cellular phone."

Drake gave him a look. "I know what it is."

"You can hit the Brownsville cell from here."

"I don't need to." He tried to hand the phone back to Roger, but Roger backed away.

Blair hated the way they were acting around Drake, as though he were a wild animal that they didn't quite trust.

She caught Dr. Farnham looking at the liquor shelved behind the bar, then apparently making notes about it. Uneasily, she wondered if alphabetizing the bottles was a sign of a personality disorder for which Drake would be blamed.

"I would like to hear your voice occasionally," Mrs. O'Keefe said.

"But you don't listen to what I have to say, Mother."

"Not if you continue to insist that you're not coming—"

"Mrs. O'Keefe," Dr. Farnham interrupted with a slight shake of his head. "Tell me about your days here, Drake."

"I fish, I eat and I sleep," Drake snapped.

"Do you cook the fish first?" Pamela asked.

Blair gaped at her.

"If I feel like it," he answered.

Pamela gasped. Mrs. O'Keefe and Roger exchanged looks. Dr. Farnham made a note.

Drake regarded them with contempt. "Oh, come on, Pamela! Even you've eaten sushi before!"

"Sushi and raw fish aren't the same thing at all," she said. Now that Drake's mother had apparently recovered from the horror of Blair's appearance, Pamela stood and glided to a chair.

She was very pretty in her white shorts, pink-and-white-striped shirt with matching pink socks, wristbands and visor. Blair could have hated her, but since Drake didn't seem glad to see her, it wasn't worth the effort.

Blair caught Roger's eyes on her. Him she could hate. Tugging at her midriff, she inched closer to Drake.

"I notice that you have an extensive liquor supply here, Drake."

The doctor's unctuous voice grated on Blair's nerves almost as much as the implication.

"The previous owners stocked the bar."

"That must have been convenient for you."

"If you want to know how much I drink, then ask."

The doctor obliged. "On average, how many drinks per day do you consume?"

"Depends on if you count a bottle as one drink or not."

Blair nudged him. Drake nudged back.

Mrs. O'Keefe gave them a look of disapproval. "Dear, this is a family matter. Perhaps you could go brew something else."

"She's fresh out of eye of newt, Mother."

Pamela whispered something to Mrs. O'Keefe, who leaned forward. "Do—you—speak—English?" she asked loudly, her lips exaggerating the words.

Blair snaked her arms around Drake. "I speak ze language uf luv."

"And she speaks it fluently," Drake added before capturing Blair's mouth in a kiss designed to let everyone there know it wasn't the first they'd shared.

But it was by far the best one. He was solid and warm and his hands were roaming where they shouldn't be. Blair would have been happy to kiss Drake as long as he wanted, but she was bent at an awkward angle. She straightened to find Dr. Farnham writing, Roger grinning, Mrs. O'Keefe averting her eyes and Pamela gazing malevolently at her. Blair left her arms around Drake's shoulders and tried to imitate the smile of a sexually satisfied woman—a good trick, since she wasn't.

"I made ice tea for you. Pleez help yourself." Her accent was less island girl than gypsy fortune-teller, but no one called her on it.

"I'll have some tea," Roger announced. He poured a glass as the women looked on warily.

He downed the glass and poured a second.

"Be careful, Roger," Mrs. O'Keefe cautioned. "Do you feel quite well?"

"It hit the spot," he said.

"Good grief. Do they think I've poisoned it?" Blair murmured to Drake.

"Don't you wish you had?" he murmured back.

"I'll have some iced tea." Smiling at her, Dr. Farnham approached the table.

He was a little late demonstrating his trust, Blair thought. The women apparently decided Roger was going to live and accepted glasses of tea from the doctor.

While everyone was occupied at the other end of the room, Blair whispered to Drake, "Why do you think they're here?"

"This is a competency hearing, Blair. I'm surprised you didn't pick up on that."

"If that's true and you know it, then why are you being so antagonistic?"

"Because they've already made up their minds. Nothing I say will matter. It never did."

The defeatist tone in his voice alarmed her. "Yes, it will. Be nice to Dr. Farnham and he'll tell your mother she's full of beans."

"Then she'll be back with another doctor. And another. As many as it takes."

At that moment, Blair understood Drake perfectly. She knew why he'd come to live here and why he didn't want to go back. It was extraordinary that he'd put up with these people for as long as he had. What did they want from him? Why couldn't they just leave him alone? "Couldn't you tell Mario not to bring her?"

"She'd find somebody else."

"Good luck. I couldn't find anybody else."

"You don't have as much money as she does."

"Iced—tea—very—good," shouted Mrs. O'Keefe.

"And you called *me* irritating," Blair muttered.

"I'd like to see your house, Drake," Pamela said with an encouraging smile.

"Yes, Drake. We'd like to see how you live," Dr. Farnham seconded Pamela.

"Oh, I don't know if I can bear it," moaned Mrs. O'Keefe, yet she stood with the others.

With ill grace, Drake waved around the room as Blair wiggled off him. "Bar. Dining room. Damaged offices that aren't structurally sound."

He stalked off down the uncarpeted hall, which even Blair had to admit didn't make a positive first impression.

The others looked at one another. Blair smiled and gestured for them to precede her. "I'm unarmed."

An impatient Drake waited at the entrance to the rec room. "My bedroom," he said.

Everyone's eyes were riveted to the rumpled bed.

The library doors were closed and Blair knew they might go unnoticed. She looked questioningly at Drake and he shook his head.

He ought to show them the library. It was the only fully restored room in the whole lodge.

Drake's mother entered the rec room and stared at the furniture piled against the walls. She and Dr. Farnham exchanged another glance.

Roger wasn't saying much of anything in support of his friend and partner. Blair wondered whose side he was on.

"And where's your room?" Pamela asked Blair, a hint of challenge in her voice.

"I leeve in a hut in ze jongle."

"Oh." Pamela smiled brightly.

"But I get lonely in ze jongle."

Drake grinned. "That's why she doesn't sleep in the jungle."

"Drake!" his mother snapped. "There is no need to flaunt your affair in front of your fiancée."

Wait a minute. Blair raised an eyebrow at him.

He glared at Pamela. "She's not my fiancée!"

She better not be. Blair, along with everyone else, now looked at Pamela.

Pamela blinked, then clasped her hands together. "Drake? I...I can't believe you said that."

"It's true and you know it."

"But..." Pamela looked from Drake's mother to the psychiatrist. "I thought he cared for me!"

"He does, my darling girl. He doesn't know what he's saying." Mrs. O'Keefe patted Pamela's hand and sent a glance toward Dr. Farnham, who was dutifully making notes.

"Bravo." Blair clapped. "*Myself* couldn't have done better."

Both women sent her murderous looks.

DRAKE STRODE out of the room. "It's uncanny. Is there some script you women pass down from generation to generation?"

"Drake, *what* are you saying?" Mrs. O'Keefe said. "You see, Dr. Farnham? He's speaking utter nonsense. While they weren't formally engaged, there was certainly an understanding between Drake and Pamela."

"Yes, a *mis*understanding," Drake said.

"If you hadn't...had your breakdown," his mother said, "you and Pamela would have been married by now."

He hadn't had a breakdown, but he would have if he'd continued his old way of life any longer. "You're delusional." He turned to Dr. Farnham. "They're both delusional. I hope you're making a note of *that*."

"I'm making notes on many aspects of this situation," the doctor said. "Please proceed."

How was he going to get rid of them? Drake wondered.

The situation had gone from absurd to annoying. He could feel his blood pressure inch up notch by notch.

He grabbed Blair's hand and started down the hall. "Thanks for your support back there, *buddy*," he said when he passed Roger.

Roger spread his hands. "Hey, I don't know what sweet nothings you whispered in Pamela's ear."

"Empty nothings." Drake hooked his thumb toward a door on their left. "That's the storeroom. The kitchen is this way."

"And organized superbly, if I do say so myself," Blair murmured. "Be sure and point that out."

Drake grinned at her. She was being great and he was a rat to use her to fend off Pamela, but if Pamela and his mother thought he was living with someone, maybe they would finally leave him alone.

They piled into the kitchen.

"Here's another good *buddy* of mine." Drake walked over to a greenish-looking Mario, who was sitting on a stack of two boxes and fanning himself with a straw hat. "How ya doin', Mario?" He accompanied his greeting with a whack on Mario's back.

Mario grinned weakly. "Oh, hiya, Señor Drake."

Don't "hiya" me, traitor. "How was the trip out? Smooth and boring, or was there a little rough water?"

Mario grimaced. "It was a pretty rough trip."

"Ah, but there's nothing like the movement of a ship as she rocks with the waves. Back and forth, back and forth." Drake moved from side to side. "And you've got the return trip to look forward to."

The last vestiges of color left Mario's cheeks and he closed his eyes.

"I see you've got my supplies."

"Yes. Two cases of Jiffy Cheez."

"That's all you eat?" Drake's mother wore a horrified expression.

"Don't forget the raw fish," Pamela reminded her.

His mother sank onto one of the kitchen chairs and brought a hand to her forehead. "Have you seen enough, Dr. Farnham?"

The doctor joined her and Pamela at the kitchen table and began to murmur soothingly.

With a wounded look toward Drake, Mario scuttled out the kitchen door.

Roger eyed the trio, then ambled over to Drake. "This is killing your mother."

Drake's jaw set. His mother, he could understand. Even Pamela, he could understand. But Roger? How could Roger be a part of this?

Blair linked her fingers through his and he smiled at her briefly. She'd been so supportive. And she was in for a miserable trip back with this bunch.

"How did Mother talk you into this charade, Roger?"

"She didn't have to talk me into anything. I was wondering if you're crazy, myself."

"That's the same thing I wonder about you."

The two men stared at each other. Roger, with his forty pounds of extra weight, pasty skin and circles under his eyes reminded Drake of where he'd been headed. "What about our plans?" he asked.

"We were kids dreaming kids' dreams," Drake said. "And part one of those dreams was Exeter-O'Keefe. This is part two."

Roger shook his head. "Man, how could you walk away from it? We had a gold mine."

"I made enough gold."

"*I* haven't!" Roger jabbed at his chest. "I've got kids."

Yeah, and where do you find the time for them? Drake refrained from asking. "That's why I stuck around another five years."

"Look. I understand that you needed a break. But you've

been gone for months." Roger gazed at him intently. "You've got to come back now."

"Back to sixteen fun-filled hours of stress a day?" Drake shook his head. "I'm happy here."

"Happy? How can you be happy? You're living in squalor with—" he gestured toward Blair "—her."

Blair flinched as though she'd been struck. Drake squeezed her hand, then brought it to his lips and brushed them across her knuckles. He could have punched Roger for the hurt he saw in Blair's eyes. He might still punch Roger before the day was over.

"Pamela's waited all this time for you." Roger leaned forward and lowered his voice. "I think you've still got a chance there."

"You mean I haven't completely alienated her yet? Thanks for the tip. Blair, think of something."

"Drake, show them the *Pirate's Lady* and the li—"

Drake stopped her with a finger to her lips and a plea in his eyes. He couldn't stand the thought of these people contaminating the sanctity of the library.

He saw the understanding in her eyes and dropped a light kiss on her mouth. "Pamela isn't even in your league," he breathed next to her ear.

"Drake." Roger glanced over at the whispering trio. "Come back. It can be part-time."

Drake gave a short laugh. "There's no such thing as part-time."

"Did you read the prospectus I sent you?"

"No."

"Have you read *anything* I've sent you?"

"Not in the last six months."

Roger made a fist and the breath hissed between his teeth. "Well, here's the deal. I brought a computer with me. A primo laptop."

"That's not the deal I want to hear."

"You can work from here," Roger continued.

"No electricity." The generator didn't count.

"It's got batteries."

"For how many hours?"

"It doesn't matter." Roger's breathing quickened. "I'll send you cases of batteries. I'll have them airlifted to you. Anything. But you've got to help me."

For an instant, Drake considered doing as Roger wanted, but they weren't working toward a common goal any longer. Roger wanted more. Drake wanted less. "Find somebody else, Roger."

"But you're the best. The clients want you."

"I'm not available. You were supposed to bring in some hotshot to replace me. I assume he or she is handling my former accounts."

Roger looked grim. "I thought you'd be back."

Drake gave him a long look. "I'm not coming back. Either you buy me out, or we sell the company. That's what we agreed."

Sweat beaded Roger's upper lip. "I need more time."

"You've had time!" Drake was out of patience. For months he'd kept a countdown calendar in his office. Roger had known exactly how many days he had to make plans.

"What if you'd changed your mind? Huh? What if I'd shut everything down and then you'd come back? We would have had to start all over again."

"I gave you fair warning."

Roger rubbed his hairline. "Everybody talks about chucking it all and becoming a beachcomber. Sane people don't!"

This time, Blair squeezed Drake's hand. He squeezed back.

"You know, Roger, when you and Dr. Farnham first got off the boat, I actually thought he was a lawyer and you were bringing papers for me to sign. It almost made up for the fact that you brought my mother with you."

Roger looked back at Drake's mother. The group at the

table was watching them and had probably been listening for some time.

Roger lowered his voice, "I've got a liquidity problem, Drake. A pressing problem."

Drake was disappointed but not surprised. "Then sell the company."

"I can't." He spoke through clenched teeth, his lips barely moving. "Understand this. If you won't come back, then you're going to be declared mentally incompetent and I'll petition the court to make me trustee for your half of the business."

"Thus solving your liquidity problems." Which must be enormous.

Roger nodded. "I see you still have a grasp of business fundamentals."

"Go to hell."

"I warned you." After a moment, Roger raised his voice, "Okay, okay. Don't get violent on me, buddy." He backed away, hands held outward.

Rage welled up within Drake. He stared at the man he'd thought was his friend as Roger gave the trio at the table some embellished story.

"Drake?" Blair tugged at his hand. "Can he do that? Can he take over your share?"

Drake exhaled. "Probably."

"Then you've got to stop this."

"Don't worry about it. Let them do what they want. I'll refuse to come with them, so they'll have to return with reinforcements. By then, I'll be sailing away on the *Pirate's Lady*."

"In other words, you'll let them drive you away from your home."

She looked so aghast that he traced the curve of her cheek with his fingers. Maybe she could come with him.

Maybe he *was* nuts.

Dr. Farnham cleared his throat. "Drake, Roger tells us

you have no interest in returning to the firm you two founded.''

"No, I don't."

"Yet this firm was a significant portion of your life for years."

"Yes."

"In fact, you worked long hours up until the day you quit."

Drake nodded, waiting for him to get to the point.

Dr. Farnham cleared his throat. "Drake, this sudden change in your behavior and life-style, coupled with your antagonism toward the people closest to you, tells me that you're a victim of depression."

That wasn't what he'd expected. "I'm not depressed."

"He isn't depressed," Blair said at the same time.

Dr. Farnham's smile was both patronizing and superior. "Oh, but I believe you are. You exhibit all the hallmarks." He pointed his pen toward the cases of Jiffy Cheez. "Eating disorders, alcoholism, and, uh, the lack of fastidiousness in your personal appearance, the squalid living conditions—"

"They're not squalid!" Blair argued loyally. She'd dropped her accent.

"Not to mention the low-class company he keeps," Pamela added.

That was it. "Get out!" Drake ordered. "All of you, get out of my home."

"Drake." His mother regarded him sadly.

"I'm recommending that you undergo therapy," Dr. Farnham said.

"You can recommend all you want, but I'm not going back with you." Drake couldn't stay in the room with them any longer. "I'll be at the dock helping Mario unload."

He tugged at Blair's hand, but she shook her head. "You go on," she said, facing the group. "I have a few things to say."

He probably should stick around, Drake thought, then decided against it. "You sure you'll be okay?"

She smiled. "More than okay."

THEY IGNORED HER.

She might as well have gone with Drake.

"He's not cooperating," Mrs. O'Keefe fretted.

Dr. Farnham turned to Drake's mother. "I warned you that we might have to use restraint."

Restraint? What were they going to do? Tie him up? Shoot him with a tranquilizer gun?

Drake's mother nodded, a pained expression on her face. "Anything that will bring him back to us, Dr. Farnham."

"The business is suffering without him," Roger added. "You'll have to move quickly. I don't know how much longer I can keep it going."

What a scuzzball, Blair thought. While Drake was working those sixteen-hour days, what exactly had he been doing?

Drake's mother gripped Roger's arm. "You know how grateful we are for your patience, Roger."

He nodded and patted her hand.

Blair stepped forward. "As I understand it, Mr. Exeter, you weren't supposed to keep the business going at all unless you bought out Drake's half."

Pamela's head jerked toward her. Mrs. O'Keefe's eyes widened. Roger's narrowed and Dr. Farnham blinked.

"Isn't that correct, Mr. Exeter?" Blair prompted.

"Drake wanted me to buy him out, yes. But you don't just dissolve a business partnership on a whim."

"This was no whim, as you well know."

"Who *are* you?" Mrs. O'Keefe asked.

Blair smiled. "Come with me and I'll show you."

CHAPTER TEN

BLAIR WAS ABOUT to give the most important presentation of her life.

She'd shepherded the group back into the dining area because she wanted the spectacular view as a backdrop. A quick trip to cabana number one for her notes and she was ready to begin.

"Usually, I have more notice when I give a presentation." She handed an old Pirate's Hideout brochure to Dr. Farnham and to Drake's mother. "And I naturally would have made sure everyone had a copy of the materials, but we're being informal today, so if you wouldn't mind sharing?" she asked brightly.

Walking back to the bar as though she was wearing her favorite presentation suit—the fire-engine-red one—and expensive pumps, Blair pivoted and offered them her most confident, professional smile. "I'm Blair Thomason, formerly with Watson and Watson Management Consultants in Houston. I've recently started my own agency—" *very, very recently* "—and am still waiting for business cards."

"So give us one of your old ones." Roger snickered.

Blair opened her abused planner and pried a stained business card from the front pocket. "I'm afraid my materials met with an expected dunking," she said, handing him the card. "As you can see, the roof leaks in several areas." Of course that wasn't what had happened, but Blair didn't see how her unexpected arrival on the island would add anything to her presentation.

Roger's snide smile vanished. He stared at the card, then at Blair. Without comment, he passed it to Pamela, who snatched at it.

"I thought you were some island girl," Pamela said accusingly.

Blair gave her a pitying smile. "I know you did, because that's what you wanted to believe. Much more face-saving than the truth. I'm certain there's a psychiatric term for persistent self-delusion, isn't there, Dr. Farnham?"

"Yes. It's—"

"But that's not why we're here," Blair said quickly.

"Why *are* we here?" Roger asked.

"Well," Blair said, using a pseudoconfiding voice. "I'm hoping to avoid an expensive and protracted legal battle. Unfortunately, I'm having a difficult time persuading Drake that it won't be necessary. To do so, I'll need your help—all of you." She made a gesture encompassing everyone in the stunned group. "But especially you, Mr. Exeter, as you have the most at stake."

Roger sat down.

"Drake is becoming very impatient and is ready to throw the whole mess to the lawyers. After having met you and listened to your opinions, I can understand why he feels that way." She paused, and Drake's mother glanced at the others uncomfortably.

Roger was sweating. Good. He deserved to sweat.

"Now, I don't want to wait on the outcome of a court fight."

Roger quickly shook his head.

"I don't know how long my schedule will remain as flexible as it is now and I would hate to turn over this project to someone else."

Dr. Farnham murmured in agreement until Mrs. O'Keefe quelled him with a poisoned look.

"So let me tell you what our plans are and then see how

far we are from reaching a mutually beneficial solution to our problem." She paused to smile at them again.

Dr. Farnham smiled back, but no one else did.

"I'd like to draw your attention to the picture on the front of the brochure. That's the lodge as it appeared before the storm damage. Inside the brochure, you'll see the interior of the lodge, including this room. I think we can agree that Pirate's Hideout was a very exclusive resort. It catered to the burnt-out captains of industry. It offered elegant simplicity, quiet and—" Blair swept her arm toward the broken-out windows "—breathtaking scenery."

Everyone turned to view the breathtaking scenery.

A shadow appeared in the doorway. "The boat's unloaded and Mario is waiting." Drake took in the group. "What's going on here?"

"Drake, please sit down and be quiet," Blair said. "You know how I hate to have my presentations interrupted." She held her breath and hoped he'd let her proceed.

To her shock, he did.

Without a word, he took a seat behind the others. "Carry on," he said, and leaned back in the chair.

She was nervous with him sitting there watching her. She wanted to do well, not only for him but for herself.

"Having toured the lodge, you'll agree that extensive renovations are necessary." Blair outlined the damage and what areas could be salvaged and what couldn't. "Though without the report from the structural engineer, I'm only guessing, you understand."

Then, using the notes she'd prepared for Drake, she outlined four stages of construction. She mentioned the *Pirate's Lady,* too, and the cabanas.

She did not mention the library. For some reason, Drake didn't want them to see the library and, although the brochure referred to it, no one asked where it was. But, then again, no one was saying much of anything.

Blair didn't give them a chance. She deliberately overloaded them with the tiniest details, many of which she made up as she went along. She spoke until her throat was dry and their eyes were glazed. At last, Drake's mother asked the question Blair had been waiting for.

"But why hasn't any of this begun?"

"Naturally, Drake has made extensive repairs, but—" Blair moved in for the kill "—Mr. Exeter is holding up funding."

Everyone stared at Roger.

"I am not!" he protested.

"Drake, correct me if I'm wrong, but as I understand it, you purchased this island using cash to achieve a favorable price."

Drake nodded.

"And assumed that proceeds from your interest in Exeter-O'Keefe would be forthcoming. They have not and, therefore, there are no funds to begin construction. Drake has expressed his desire to have the island remain a private holding and so we are at a standstill." Blair closed her planner. "I've tried to get him to explore alternate methods of funding, but he refuses." She spread her hands. "There you have it."

"Well." Mrs. O'Keefe didn't appear to know where to look.

"Thank you, Blair." Drake stood. "I realize that you were at a disadvantage without your normal equipment and I appreciate your willingness to wing it today." His amused eyes met hers.

"I must stress that these are only preliminary plans, since there are so many variables." She looked pointedly at Roger.

He was staring at the brochure, his face devoid of expression. At her silence, he looked up.

"But I think everyone here can see the possibilities," Drake said. "Along with the obstacles."

"Well, Drake, if you'd only told us," his mother began.

"I did. Repeatedly." He drilled her with a look.

"He never discussed it with *me*," Pamela said.

"No one close to me could have been in doubt of my intentions to retire from commodities trading," Drake informed her.

He showed great restraint, Blair thought.

A grim-faced Roger stood and the two men stared at each other. Without a word, Roger left the room.

Dr. Farnham also stood. "Mrs. O'Keefe, this appears to be a legal matter, not a psychiatric one. I admit that initially I might have given more weight to your concerns than was perhaps justified, but I'm confident that after a few sessions, I would have discovered that Drake is of sound mind."

"*Thank* you, Doctor," Drake said.

"Not at all," Dr. Farnham replied, either oblivious to, or choosing to ignore, the sarcasm in Drake's voice.

"But...but none of this explains his hostility toward me and dear Pamela."

"I'd be delighted to explore possible reasons for your son's antagonism, Mrs. O'Keefe," Dr. Farnham offered. "And with counseling, we can devise strategies for effective interaction between you. Please call my secretary for an appointment."

Blair turned toward the bar because she was afraid she'd burst out laughing. In the mirror, she caught Drake's eye as he made his way to her.

He slipped his arm around her waist. "You were magnificent," he whispered, and kissed her temple.

Blair didn't feel like laughing any longer. She stared at their reflection in the bar mirror, at the handsome man standing next to her in an "us-against-them" pose, and wished everything she'd said about rebuilding Pirate's Hideout was true.

"How did you know the plans would appease them?" he asked.

"I showed them what they wanted to see, since they *re-*

fuse to accept reality." She was having trouble with reality herself. Perhaps it would be best if she moved out of Drake's hold, which she did. "My strategy wouldn't have worked if Roger had already bought you out and you were sitting on a potful of money. So be careful. It won't work again."

"Thanks." He looked down at her, staying close, even though she'd reluctantly moved away. "I'm grateful that one of us kept a clear head."

And one of us is going to have to keep a clear head now, Blair cautioned herself.

Drake was looking at her as though she were Jiffy Cheez on a cracker. He made her insides feel like Jiffy Cheez, too.

No man had *ever* made her insides feel like Jiffy Cheez before.

"I had to do something," Blair said, trying to keep the thread of conversation going. "I couldn't stand the thought of you being forced to give up your library before you finished Shakespeare."

He laughed, but it was an intimate laugh, accompanied by an intimate look.

"Anyway, I owed you," she said a bit desperately.

"Not anymore." Drake's voice was low. "We're more than even."

Blair looked at him, very aware that she would be sailing out of his life in a very few short minutes. That was *her* reality. Words that would have to remain unsaid clogged her throat.

Drake stroked her hair and tucked a strand behind her ear. The feel of his fingers on her neck sent prickles racing along her skin. She leaned into his palm, savoring his last touch.

"I want to go home," Pamela announced. Ignoring Drake, she made an elegant retreat.

"I think my work here is done," Blair said. She and

Drake shared a smile as Pamela was followed by Dr. Farnham.

"Mario's ready to leave anytime," Drake said.

Blair swallowed. That was a hint if ever she heard one. "I'd better get my things, few though they are." She hesitated, hoping Drake would ask her to stay, but his attention was claimed by his mother and Blair slipped away before she started to cry.

She cried anyway as she stuffed her wedding dress and veil into a pillowcase so Pamela and Drake's mother wouldn't see them, cried as she slung the *Salty Señorita*'s life preserver over her shoulder and cried when she snuck back into the kitchen to snitch food because otherwise she didn't know where her next meal was coming from.

Of course he wasn't going to ask her to stay. She'd made her conditions very clear and he'd made his equally clear.

The fact that she'd fallen in love with him didn't change anything. She'd just fall *out* of love with him.

Then Blair saw the cases of Jiffy Cheez and cried even more. But she didn't take a single can.

Disgusted with herself, Blair splashed water over her face at the kitchen sink. She didn't even have sunglasses to hide the blotches. Everyone would know she'd been crying and they'd guess why. She'd better start preparing a speech about the evils of mixing business with pleasure.

Watching from the kitchen window, Blair saw Drake give his mother a brief hug and then she and Pamela stepped onto the boat. He didn't hug Pamela and Blair felt cheered.

He didn't hug Roger, either. The two of them spent several minutes talking, and judging by the rigid postures of both men, they weren't patching things up. That would be a mess, but it wasn't her mess.

Blair couldn't delay her departure any longer. There was no future for her here.

Of course, there wasn't a future for her anywhere.

How had she, who planned each detail of her life so carefully, found herself in this situation? She'd learned a lesson, though. She'd never completely trust anybody ever again—not even herself.

Blair trudged toward Mario's boat, wondering if she'd have the opportunity for a private goodbye with Drake. One last opportunity for him to...

Honestly, she was as bad as Drake's mother and Pamela, wanting things to be a certain way when the facts indicated otherwise.

Blair stopped a few feet from the arguing men and dropped her pillowcase and life preserver in the sand.

"Thirty days," Drake was saying.

"You don't know what you're asking," Roger insisted with a glance at Blair. "Don't tell me she's coming with us?"

Drake stared at her, an arrested expression on his face.

"Mario is giving me a ride into San Verde," she said to Roger.

"But I thought...I mean, I assumed you two..."

"There's been a lot of that going around lately," she said.

Belatedly, Drake stepped over to her and slipped his arm around her waist.

Blair removed it. Continuing the charade hurt too much.

"Blair?"

"I wanted to say goodbye, Drake."

Without looking away from her, Drake said, "I'll be in touch, Roger. Now, give us a minute alone."

Roger was already walking backward. "Sure, buddy."

"Don't worry," Blair told Drake wearily. "I won't blow your cover. I'll tell them I'm coming into town to shop and meet with contractors and so forth. I'll think of something convincing."

"You can't leave like this," Drake said.

"And how am I supposed to leave? You've been counting the minutes until the supply boat would come. It's here. It's leaving. It's time for me to go."

Emotions Blair couldn't read flickered across Drake's face. Slowly, he raised first one hand, then the other and cupped either side of her face. "You don't want to leave."

With the way he was looking into her eyes, Blair could only tell him the truth. "No."

"Then stay."

Stay. He'd said stay. "Here?"

"Here."

"W-with you?"

"With me."

He'd asked her to stay with him. *Stay with him.* It was exactly what she wanted to hear. Hoped to hear. Joy flooded her with breath-stealing intensity.

And then, as though she needed convincing, Drake slowly lowered his head and kissed her in full view of the group on the boat.

Blair instantly forgot about their audience. There was something different about this kiss. It was a kiss of promises, not merely a kiss of the moment, the way his other kisses had been.

It was a kiss of commitment.

Stay here with me.

Blair wanted to lose herself in the kiss and the promises and the commitment—especially the commitment. She pressed her body against his, longing to feel his arms around her.

She felt a chuckle deep in the back of his throat before he lifted his head. "Is that a yes?"

"Yes," she breathed, and tried to kiss him again.

"Patience," he whispered. "Now, let's wave goodbye or my mother will never leave."

Arm in arm, they walked to the edge of the dock. "You can shove off, Mario!"

"Okay, Señor Drake!"

As Mario chugged toward San Verde, Drake and Blair

waved. Only Drake's mother seemed to wave back, but Blair couldn't be sure, since her eyes were blurry.

"I guess they're really gone," Blair said when they couldn't make out the figures on the boat any longer.

"Yes." Drake picked up Blair and spun her around. "They're gone and I have you to thank."

"I can think of many ways you can thank me, but they all involve the same thing."

He lowered her, sliding her down the length of his body. "What's that?"

"Taking off your clothes." Blair tugged at his shirt.

Drake tugged back. "Oh no. Let's make this nice and slow. We've got all the time in the world."

"Okay. That's a great idea." It was a stupid idea. "A fine and wonderful idea." Blair untied her shirttails.

"What are you doing?"

She unbuttoned a button. "We've been standing in the sun and I'm just so…hot." She pulled the fabric away from her body.

"Yes, I can see." Drake's eyes glinted in amusement and more.

"Blair unbuttoned another button.

Yes, there was definitely more there.

But before she could learn how much more, Drake spun her around and swatted her rear.

"Hey!" She spun back around. "Just so you know, I'm not into that."

"I'm not, either. Neither am I into rotten food, which is what I'll have unless I pack away the supplies Mario brought."

Pack away supplies? She was undressing on the beach and he wanted to put away the groceries? "How romantic." Blair had obviously overestimated her charms.

"You'd rather I left the food sitting in the sun?"

"Well…yes." She fluttered her eyelashes.

Drake laughed and grabbed her. Bending her backward

in a silent-movie clinch, he kissed her. "Oh, my sweet, I've been so terribly foolish. We don't need food. We can live on love." He kissed her again.

He'd said the "l" word. Blair quivered. It wasn't precisely in the right context, but getting a man to say it at all was half the battle. That meant he was thinking about love.

Well, of course he was. Wasn't that why he'd asked her to stay?

Wasn't that why she'd stayed? She already knew she loved him. He just needed time to get used to the idea.

Drake finished unbuttoning her blouse, kissing the skin exposed by each button. "Blair," he murmured against her, "I hope you like fish. Lots and lots and lots of fish."

She started laughing and couldn't stop. "All right! Go put your food away." Drake let her up. "This is the most inept seduction I've ever experienced!"

"I thought you were doing the seducing."

"I was trying to, but you keep spoiling the mood."

"I'll make it up to you."

"And I'll let you," Blair said as they walked back to the lodge.

CHAPTER ELEVEN

SHE HAD NO IDEA what she was doing to him.

Drake could hardly think as he packed away the meat Mario had brought—or rather, he *could* think and his mind was filled with Blair.

When he'd stepped into the dining room and had seen her effectively skewering the whole lot of them, he'd wanted her more than he'd ever wanted any woman. She'd managed to discourage Pamela, placate his mother, neutralize the doctor. And Roger—damn, she'd made Roger sweat. As he deserved to.

Drake had let his frustration overwhelm him, but Blair had handled everything. She was brilliant and sexy and strong and he wanted her.

And she'd chosen to stay with him when she'd had the chance to get off the island. *Chosen.* She hadn't been forced here by circumstances and she'd known exactly what the situation was.

She accepted his life as it was and, for the time being, was going to share it with him. She wasn't going to try to change him.

And he was going to do his best to see that she didn't regret her decision for one minute.

They were about to embark upon a fantasy interlude others only dreamed about. Time would stop. Neither had any responsibilities or deadlines or end-of-vacation timetables.

Their affair would end when it ended.

Blair was the perfect partner for him, Drake acknowledged. Nothing and no one was waiting for her. She was completely free to choose to do whatever she wished.

She'd never have to hack at the roots of an old life the way he had. He envied her. She was free in a way he wanted to be.

And he would be. He was closer than he'd ever been.

Blair was just coming out of the pantry. Drake caught her and kissed her a moment before she walked past him.

"Now?" she asked breathlessly.

"No. I'm only reminding you what you have to look forward to."

"How about reminding me in more detail?" she asked.

He grinned. "By the end of the evening, I'll have made love to each of your five senses."

"How about best three out of five?" Blair offered.

"How about you trust me?"

"I do." She gazed up at him and he wanted to change his mind about going slow.

"So." Blair backed away and looked around. "Shall I carry this into the bar for you?" She hefted a case of Jiffy Cheez.

Drake grinned. "Can I trust you with it?"

"Maybe." She threw him a grin back and sashayed down the hall.

"Ohhh, Armand," Drake murmured, watching her. "You made a biiiig mistake."

BLAIR WAS NERVOUS. The hand-trembling, butterflies-in-the-stomach, have-I-lost-my-mind nervous.

She'd hoped for mad, passionate, spontaneous-combustion type of sex that wouldn't have given her time to be nervous. She'd tried that, what? Three—four times today?

Most women would kill for a long, slow seduction and a man like Drake doing the seducing. They'd look forward to it. But Drake was a woman's fantasy and Blair didn't have any experience being seduced by fantasies.

Nightmares, yes. Fantasies, no.

Speaking of fantasies, where was Drake?

After they'd packed away the food, Drake had shooed her out of the kitchen. Blair had raided the storage closet for a change of clothing, had showered and ever since had been hanging out in the library pretending to read.

She couldn't stand waiting any longer and intended to find Drake and tell him so.

She headed for the kitchen. On the way, she passed Drake in the hallway.

He'd changed into the loose cotton clothes that looked so wonderful on him, and his hair, still damp from a recent shower, was combed back from his face.

He was incredibly, heart-stoppingly handsome.

"Hi," she chirped.

"Hello," he murmured in a seductive voice. "You're wearing my favorite outfit."

Blair looked down at herself. "Pants and a shirt?"

"Yes, but it's the way you wear the pants and the shirt."

Blair looked at him uncertainly. She hadn't been able to find another shirt in the right size and this one was too big. It had a tendency to slip off her shoulder.

She tugged at it now. "Uh, when are we going to get this seduction thing going?"

He studied her. "You're nervous."

"What, me nervous?"

"You, nervous." He put his hand on the back of her neck as his fingers slid under the loose collar. "Come with me."

They walked to the bar and Drake stepped behind it. He reached into the tiny refrigerator and withdrew a bottle of white wine. "The dry ice is mostly gone, so this won't be very cold, but—" he quickly removed the cork "—I want you to *slowly* savor this. We're not after drunken revels here."

Blair giggled nervously.

Drake gave her a look. "We missed lunch today, didn't we?"

She nodded and he brought out the crackers.

Watching him fashion his cheese animals calmed Blair. He gave her several and she gobbled them. "Feeling better?" he asked.

She nodded.

"Liar," he said softly. "But a very pretty one."

"I'm not pretty," she mumbled through the crackers.

"You're absolutely right. I should have said beautiful." He propped his elbow on the polished wood of the bar and gazed into her eyes.

Blair brushed cracker crumbs off her shirt, which slipped to one side, exposing her shoulder.

When she reached up to reposition it, Drake stopped her. "I like looking at your bare shoulder."

"Oh, stop. I feel like I'm in an ad for wine coolers."

"Hmm." Drake tapped his fingers. "Yes, I've noticed things are a little cool. Relax. Have some more wine."

"You're not drinking wine."

"I will." He poured a glass for himself, but didn't drink any of it. "I have plans for us. Do you want to hear my plans?"

"I don't know—do I?"

"Perhaps I won't tell you, after all. I'll surprise you. Do you like surprises, Blair?"

"Sure," she squeaked, draining her wineglass.

However, when she held it out for more, Drake took the glass from her cold fingers and set it on the bar.

"Come with me, Blair." He came out from behind the bar. "This is an evening for the senses."

He led her through the dining room, where he'd set the table, and stepped out the windows.

With his hand at the small of her back, Drake directed

her to the overgrown hibiscus bushes that had been planted next to the walls.

Picking a bright pink flower, he tucked it behind her ear.

"They're beautiful," Blair said.

Drake smiled and picked a yellow one, which he trailed across her cheek. "What are you thinking?" he asked, his voice low and intimate.

What she'd been thinking was that yellow wasn't her color, but she couldn't tell him that. "I'm wondering what you're going to do next."

Drake picked more of the flowers, filling her arms with reds, oranges, pinks and yellows. "At first I was thinking we'd put the flowers on our table, for the sense of sight. But now I'm thinking touch and scent."

"Scent? They don't really smell."

"Ah, close your eyes and breathe."

Blair did so.

"That heavy musky scent is used in perfumes. It's very earthy and elemental."

But not very pleasant. She inhaled harder, then sneezed.

"You have pollen on your nose," Drake said, and flicked it away with his fingers. "I'm thinking of how you would look as you lay naked on a bed of hibiscus blooms."

Blair sneezed again.

"Perhaps not," Drake murmured as he led her back up the gentle incline.

Great. She'd bombed out on touch and smell. But she did think the flowers were pretty.

Drake arranged them in the glass bowl he'd put in the center of the table.

Blair laced her fingers together and cast covetous glances toward the wine.

Pulling out a chair, Drake indicated that she should sit. "I will serve you dinner," he announced. "I will cut each bite myself and feed it to you."

He leaned down, but instead of kissing her mouth the way

she expected, he pushed her shirt off her shoulder and kissed the side of her neck.

This was it. Any moment his fingers would begin to work their magic and she wouldn't be nervous anymore.

But Drake stepped away. "I'll bring dinner."

Blair waited until he was out of sight, then she leaped from the table and ran to the bar. Pouring a glass of what was undoubtedly expensive wine, she drank it all at once, which was the way she wanted it to hit her.

She wanted to feel soft and fuzzy and romantic.

What she felt was queasy. She was eating more cheese and crackers when Drake brought in a tray.

"What's this? Don't you trust my cooking?"

"I was just...hungry."

He struck a match and lit the cluster of candles at the edge of the table. "Come here then."

"Shall I bring the wine?" she asked hopefully.

"Only if you don't like the red I've opened." Drake indicated the tray. "It's been breathing."

"Has it caught its breath yet?"

"Yes." Drake chuckled. "I found myself in a steak mood this evening. Mario brought potatoes."

Blair slipped back to her place and stared at the grilled meat. She wasn't hungry. Probably due to her nerves and too many crackers.

But Drake had gone to so much trouble. He moved his chair next to hers and was cutting into her baked potato. "What do you like on your potato?"

"Oh, everything."

"I have butter and fresh chives, but no sour cream," he said.

"Okay."

Drake set down the knife and gave her a considering look. She gazed back, wondering what he was going to do next. He leaned forward and stopped.

Blair braced herself.

Drake closed the gap between them and kissed her. He raised his head, looked at her again, then kissed her harder, parting her lips.

Blair closed her eyes and leaned into the kiss.

This was it.

Only it wasn't. But she could pretend until it was.

Drake stopped kissing her, but he didn't stop looking at her. Sitting back in his chair, he leaned his cheek on his fist. "You're not with me, are you?"

"I want to be," Blair said miserably.

"So...what? You don't like the way I kiss?"

"I adore the way you kiss."

"You *adore* the way I kiss. I like that." He leaned forward and kissed her again.

Blair waited for desire to well up within her. She kissed back.

Drake stopped. "You're still nervous."

She nodded.

"This isn't like you—oh, Blair." Drake's face cleared and he took her hand. "Don't worry. I've got plenty of little foil packages."

"I know, I saw them with the toiletries in the supply closet."

"So you aren't worried about that."

She shook her head, feeling incredibly embarrassed.

"Hey." He stroked her hair and tilted her chin up. "Just relax and enjoy dinner."

"Okay." He was being so decent and understanding.

What was the *matter* with her?

Drake handed her the wineglass.

"I should warn you, I already had another glass and you said you didn't want drunken revels."

"I'm ready to take my revels any way I can get them."

Blair laughed in spite of herself.

"There. That's better. You haven't smiled all evening." He cut a piece of steak and offered it to her.

She ate it, meeting his eyes and concentrating on the taste, trying to feel sensual.

She felt silly, and after a few bites Drake could tell.

"Damn, I'm trying all my best material here and none of it's working."

"I'm sorry."

"Don't be." Drake cut into a peach. "I look on this as a challenge."

"I don't want to be a challenge!" Blair stood. "I want to be...spontaneously wanton."

"Spontaneous? But you like plans. Detailed plans." He offered her a peach slice, then popped it into his mouth when she refused it. "I was wooing you with plans."

"I know." Blair paced in frustration. She reached the bar and turned to face him. "It doesn't make sense, but I feel...*stifled* by the plans. I've *never* felt stifled by plans of any sort. I don't know what's wrong with me."

She grabbed the white wine and poured a glass. It was actually pretty good.

"I guess this place is rubbing off on you. Plans aren't necessary here." Still eating slices of peach, Drake wandered across the room. "I was a plan-everything person like you once, except my organizer was the executive size."

"I figured as much." She watched, mesmerized as he slowly demolished the fruit. "Could I have some of the peach now?"

Drake cut a slice and held it out. When she tried to take it, he jerked it out of the way. "Open your mouth."

She did so and he placed it on her tongue. "Taste. Savor."

She did, conscious of his eyes watching her.

"Have you ever looked at a peach before?" he asked. "Looked at its shape? It has a very erotic shape."

As Blair swallowed, she tried to think of peaches as erotic. "You don't give up easily, do you?"

"Nope." Smiling, he leaned against the bar.

Seeing his smile, Blair began to breathe easier. She expected him to be angry and he wasn't.

Lord, but he was gorgeous.

She sipped her wine and he finished the peach, then idly began fiddling with the Jiffy Cheez.

When he handed her the cracker, there was a heart with an arrow through it.

"Oh, Drake," she murmured. It was absurd, but she didn't want to eat it.

"I'll make more." He squirted hearts on the last two crackers.

"Now you're out of crackers."

"Hold out your hand."

Blair did, laughing as he put an orange cheese heart on it. She licked it off as Drake fashioned something on his hand.

"What are you making?"

"People, but I'm better at animals." He showed her.

"Well, if that's the way you sculpt people, no wonder. They're out of proportion."

"Says who?"

"Says me. That woman would never be able to stand upright. And as for the guy, well, in his dreams." She laughed.

"You think you can do better?"

"I couldn't do a whole lot worse."

"Is that so?"

She held out her hand for the can.

"Oh no." Drake reached over the bar. "I'm getting you your own can."

He brought out two more cans. "You're going to need a lot of practice."

"Oh yeah?" Blair grabbed one of the cans and shook it.

"No, don't do that, it'll—"

But Drake's warning was too late. Blair pressed the nozzle and a glob of cheese shot through the air, landing on Drake's cheek.

After a moment of shocked silence, Blair started laughing.

"You think that's funny?" He wiped it off and licked his finger.

She immediately stopped laughing. "No, no I don't."

"Maybe you'd like a Jiffy Cheez mustache."

She struggled, but he squirted a line across her upper lip. He watched as she licked it off.

"Hey, some got on my shirt!" She wiped off the cheese.

"Sorry," Drake said. But he didn't look sorry.

Then Blair pointed her can at him and sprayed cheese all over the front of his shirt. It was spontaneous, all right, but it was also stupid.

"Blair—you're wasting it." He pulled off his shirt.

Hey, not so stupid, after all. His torso was golden in the candlelight. Blair was so caught up in the sight that she failed to anticipate his retaliation, and seconds later she was wearing a Jiffy Cheez necklace.

"I thought you didn't want to waste it."

"I have no intention of wasting it," Drake murmured, and proceeded to nibble his way around her neck.

Blair held her breath at the unfamiliar sensation of his tongue against her skin. Her head lolled back.

"Much better than crackers," Drake whispered.

"Much," she agreed breathlessly.

The cheese must have sprayed in a much wider area than she thought because Drake found it necessary to kiss and nibble all the way out to her shoulders, her earlobes and into the vee of her shirt.

"Your turn," he said.

She couldn't. But he stood there, patiently watching her. Slowly, she positioned the tip of the can over his chest and drew a cheese heart over his. Then she stepped forward.

The rise and fall of his chest quickened. His eyes glowed with an amber light.

Blair touched him with the tip of her tongue.

He flinched and dropped his can of cheese.

She stopped to look up at him.

"Go on," he whispered, his hands resting on her shoulders.

Blair licked off the cheese, tracing the outline of the heart. Drake's skin was warm and smooth beneath her tongue and she could feel the muscles beneath.

She wished she'd drawn a bigger heart, but since she hadn't, she'd concentrate on making certain she removed every trace of Jiffy Cheez.

"Blair..." Drake clutched her shoulders.

When she finished, Blair looked up to find his head back and his eyes closed.

She'd aroused him. She, Blair the ordinary, had aroused this lion of a man. And she'd barely touched him.

For the first time, Blair felt the power of a woman who was desired by a man.

He wanted her. Maybe even more than she wanted to be wanted.

She was so amazed that at first she didn't notice Drake looking down at her.

His thumbs slipped beneath her collar and worked the shirt off her shoulders.

Her heart pounded so hard she thought the fabric must be quivering.

As the garment slid lower and lower, Blair's mouth grew dry and she handed him the can of cheese.

Without taking his eyes from hers, Drake slowly removed the can from her grasp and set it on the bar.

Another tug and Blair's shirt dropped to her waist. Drake's lips parted. "You can't possibly imagine how many times I've dreamed of you like this."

The expression on his face banished any qualms she felt

about pleasing him. Warmth coiled within her and she drew her shoulders back. "You dreamed about me?"

"Constantly. Incessantly." He closed his eyes and inhaled. "In your wedding dress."

"That's kind of kinky."

"It was wet."

"Oh. Oh!"

He opened his eyes and she was stunned by the desire she saw there.

"You're beautiful." He nuzzled the side of her neck. "Incredibly beautiful."

And he made her feel beautiful. As his hands caressed her back, his tongue made circles around her collarbone.

Blair clutched at him as her body shot its entire supply of mating hormones into her bloodstream all at once.

"What about the cheese?" she gasped, not at all sure she could survive the onslaught of sudden desire. Did people have seizures from this sort of thing?

"Forget the cheese. I want to taste you."

And he did, licking a meandering swath to her breasts until Blair felt boneless.

When her knees buckled, Drake scooped her into his arms and carried her across the dining room, out the windows and down the slope to the beach.

"See the moon?"

To heck with the moon. "Yes." Blair hadn't opened her eyes. She'd take his word for it that the moon was there.

"There have been nights like this when the moon is big and full and I've sat on the beach, listening to the ocean and wishing I could share it with someone."

"I thought you wanted to be alone."

"Not lonely alone."

"Oh, Drake." She sighed his name. "You're not alone anymore."

"I know." He set her gently on her feet. "I'd hoped we'd make love for the first time here."

Make love. Love.

He did love her, Blair thought. Though he hadn't said the actual words, everything he'd done had been showing her that he loved her.

He'd carried her to a nest of blankets and pillows he'd arranged at the edge of the line of beach grasses. Now he knelt and brushed away sand.

Then he stood and loosened the drawstring on his cotton pants and they fell to his feet. He stepped out of the pool of fabric.

Blair was speechless. The brief glimpse she'd had of him on the boat didn't begin to compare to the Drake who now stood before her. The Drake who very obviously wanted her.

"I want to see the moonlight on your skin."

But Blair could only stare dumbly at him, so Drake kissed her once, hard, then unsnapped her pants.

"They're so tight, you'll have to peel them off," she managed to say.

"No problem," he said, and demonstrated that it wasn't.

And then he was staring at her in the moonlight. Blair could only marvel that he wanted her.

"Touch me," he whispered hoarsely.

And she did, running her hands over his torso and down his lean flanks, thinking that if she hadn't stayed, she never would have had these memories. And her imagination could never have done justice to this moment.

Then Drake touched her and she stopped thinking.

He pressed her back onto the pillowed sand and covered her body with his, his murmurs mingling with the rush of the waves and the whispering sea breezes.

Blair lost her mind to the feel of his hands and mouth and the hardness of his body against the softness of hers. And always, there was the spiraling heat.

She loved the way his muscles bunched when she drew her fingers across his back, loved the strength in his arms when he supported himself above her and loved wrapping her legs around him.

She loved him.

And when Drake finally joined with her, Blair knew that at last she'd found a corner of the earth to put down roots.

CHAPTER TWELVE

BLAIR MIGHT HAVE STAYED on Pirate's Hideout forever if it hadn't rained.

But it did. Three days of hard, steady, tropical showers.

Three days of endless dripping. Three days of dark rooms and dodging puddles on the floors. Three days of water, sand and debris blowing into every open window.

And also, three days of fabulous sex and a couple of nude walks in the rain. But despite the wonderfully sensual experience, Blair longed to feel completely dry again.

The library was the only room safe from the wind and rain, but because of the books, they had to keep the French doors closed and the room became stuffy.

Making love on the leather sofa didn't help and only made the room warmer.

Drake didn't seem to mind and Blair hated to complain. He couldn't control the weather, but...

It was when she was between books that Blair got her idea.

Drake didn't want to restore the lodge because he didn't want to attract people to it, so why not leave the outside in a shambles and restore the interior?

Blair wandered through the rooms, grimacing at the sandy sludge that coated the floors. Cleaning it out would take hours, especially the dining room.

All Drake needed to do was build a wall between the bar and the dining room. Passing boats would still see the yawning black windows and the overgrown banana trees, but the inside would be protected from the weather.

After that, Blair couldn't help herself. She listed all the repairs—minimal, in her opinion—to make the lodge truly livable.

And after the roof and windows were fixed, maybe Drake would consider some modest redecorating. For instance, the rec room could be made more "bedroomy," Blair thought, and happily dabbled in color schemes and curtains.

On the fourth day, the sun came out and the lodge turned into a sauna.

"I'm going to work on the *Pirate's Lady* today," Drake told her. "I've nearly figured out the carburetor installation. You want to join me? Maybe we can take her out later."

Blair had a pretty good case of cabin fever, but she resisted. "Tell you what. I'll bring you lunch. I'm going to spend the morning drying out sheets and towels before we start growing mushrooms."

"You don't have to. I send the laundry in with Mario."

"We can't wait for Mario. The storeroom ceiling cracked and rain leaked inside. You've got a lot of wet laundry."

"Okay." Drake seemed unconcerned. "Then I'll see you at lunch."

Blair tried not to feel resentful as she hauled out stacks of sodden, dirt-speckled linen. If Drake had known the size of the job, he'd have offered to help her.

As it was, Blair found herself bent over a washtub that had probably never been used for its original purpose.

With a little electricity and a new washer and dryer, life would be a lot simpler.

After stringing a clothesline and wrestling with wet, king-size sheets, Blair was ready for a break. She used that break going over her argument for hiring a carpenter. And as long as the carpenter was out here, Blair could think of a few more things he could do.

Drake wouldn't have to be bothered at all.

Blair would take care of everything.

Armed with her plans and her lists and a can of Jiffy Cheez in the lunch basket, Blair practically danced down the path to the *Pirate's Lady*.

"Drake!" she called.

Within moments, his head appeared. "I wondered when you'd get around to helping me christen the boat." He waggled his eyebrows.

"Mmm, maybe after lunch." Blair climbed partway up the gangplank and handed the basket to Drake.

He'd already dived into lunch by the time she'd reached the upper deck.

"Your BLTs are almost as good as mine." He handed her the other sandwich and bit into his.

"Thanks." Wincing, Blair sat in a plastic deck chair. "My back is sore from bending over the washtub."

"Makes you admire those pioneer women."

"Yes, but I never saw myself as the pioneer type," Blair said. "I still didn't get all the things washed. The leak in the storeroom is pretty bad."

"I'll have to take a look at it." He found the Jiffy Cheez and held it up, a question in his eyes.

Blair shook her head. "There are several leaks you'll need to look at."

He shrugged. "Or I can find somewhere else to store the linens."

"That might be more difficult than you think," she warned.

"Don't worry about it," Drake said, tossing the can back into the basket.

"I'm not *worried*." Blair set her sandwich aside. "I did walk around and make a list for you."

"That's my girl."

"It's…a long list."

Drake held out his hand and Blair handed him the list of repairs.

She'd save the other list—the one with alterations—for later.

"You weren't kidding when you said there was a list. We'll have to put out more buckets." He grinned and returned the paper to her.

Blair tried to smile back, but she couldn't.

"What's wrong?"

"The lodge is a mess."

"It gets that way when it rains. Then the sand dries and I sweep it out."

"If you'd fix the roof and put glass back in the windows, that wouldn't happen."

He shook his head. "It's not worth the hassle. And I'd miss the salty breezes."

Yeah, the salty breezes that left grit everywhere. "We could leave the windows open," Blair offered.

Drake laughed. "Then what's the point of putting in glass?"

"*I* would be more comfortable."

"So hole up in the library."

"The library is...cozy." She knew better than to criticize the library.

Drake popped the last of the sandwich into his mouth and brushed his hands together. "Want to see the engine housing?"

Obviously she wasn't going to get anywhere with her improvement campaign at this precise moment. "Okay." But Blair wasn't abandoning her campaign for a carpenter.

She followed Drake below and half listened as he recounted his adventures installing the carburetor.

"Sounds like you're about to get the *Pirate's Lady* seaworthy again." She crouched next to the opening in the deck where Drake had climbed down to the engine.

Drake nodded, his sun-streaked head below her. "One good thing about making these repairs myself is that I'll know what to do should I ever have a breakdown at sea."

"Look, since you've got enough to occupy you here, why don't you hire a carpenter to make repairs to the lodge?" She spoke casually, as though the idea had just occurred to her.

Not casually enough. Drake shot her a look. "A carpenter?"

Blair nodded. "I'll just hand him the list and you won't have to be bothered."

"I don't want a carpenter here."

"If you hired a good one, he wouldn't have to be here long."

Drake shook his head and grabbed some long silver tool. "I'll take a look at the storeroom leak, since you're so bothered by it."

"Yes, I am bothered by it!" Blair found herself bothered by more and more things. "Drake, I spent *hours* this morning hand-washing all the things that got soaked and I'm not even halfway through."

"I *said* I'd take care of the leak."

"But why not fix all the leaks? And add glass to the windows, while you're at it. Why not make the lodge weatherproof?" She should have stopped, but once she got started, she couldn't. "Then you could have the wiring fixed and run electricity from the main generator. You told me it wasn't nearly as noisy as the emergency generator."

"I don't need electricity."

"I sure could have used some for a washer and dryer this morning."

His mouth tightened. "I didn't ask you to do the laundry."

"No, but it needed to be done." Blair thumbed through the papers. "I haven't made radical plans. Nothing that will compromise your lifestyle, but living here will be more comfortable."

"I'm—comfortable—now," he said between pulls to tighten a nut.

"I'm not," Blair said. "At least not when it rains." She couldn't even contemplate winter. The climate was mild in the South Texas area, but the temperature had been known to dip to freezing during the night.

"Sorry." He glanced up at her, then went back to fiddling with the engine.

Why wouldn't he listen to her? "Drake, I even found a way to completely renovate the lodge without anyone ever knowing from the outside!" She shuffled through the papers. "You'd have to build a wall—"

"Hold it. I don't want to renovate. You know that."

"The place is falling down around our ears. You're going to have to do something sometime."

"No, I don't. I've got plenty of space and I can live on the *Pirate's Lady* if I have to."

Blair fought down rising anger. "What about me? What about the way *I* feel? I can't live like this forever."

"Nobody asked you to."

Drake's words froze her heart. "What do you mean?"

"I MEAN THAT when you're tired of me and tired of living here, you'll move on." Drake was angrier than he let on.

He couldn't believe that after the incident with his mother, Blair—*Blair*—was trying to interfere with his way of life. "Hey. Why don't we stop arguing about leaks and go check the crab traps?"

"We're not arguing about leaks. You're explaining about me moving on."

Drake was disappointed. He'd hoped she'd be around longer, but it was obvious that the end was in sight. "Blair, we both know this isn't permanent. It's great for as long as it lasts and then it's over."

She stared at him. "Apparently," she said with a catch in her voice, "only one of us knew it wasn't permanent."

They stared at each other and Drake saw the hurt in her eyes.

Damn. "Blair." He reached out and she flinched away from him. "I never said..." Had he? "I never meant—"

"You asked me to stay!" she cried.

"Blair..." Drake felt about as low as a man could feel. He wiped his hands on a greasy rag.

"But you didn't mean you wanted me to stay forever, just to stay and play." Her voice was filled with contempt.

"I thought you understood," he said quietly.

"I didn't then, but I sure do now."

"Blair, I'm sorry." There wasn't anything he could say that would make it right. "I wouldn't have hurt you for the world. But we want different things from life. I'm not willing to live the type of life you want and you obviously aren't content on Pirate's Hideout the way it is." Mutely, he gestured to the crumpled papers in her hand. "You've only been here a couple of weeks and look at all the changes you want to make."

"Not changes. Improvements." Blair stared at the plans. "I can't believe you don't want to repair the lodge just for yourself. Just for yourself, Drake. You can do that without reopening for business."

He shook his head. "That would only be the beginning. Say I let you go ahead. After a while, you'd want more. Then it would be, 'Can't we have so and so come to visit?'" He shook his head again. "No."

"I don't know any so and so's."

He half smiled. "Anyway, I want to sail around on the *Pirate's Lady* now that I've got her running. If I had a big fancy house, I'd be worried about it while I was gone."

"Fixing the roof would hardly qualify the place as fancy. But if it bothers you, there are plenty of people who'd be willing to keep an eye on the lodge in exchange for living here for however long we—you'd be away."

Drake recoiled at the thought. Changes. He didn't want any changes. He'd finally arranged his life the way he wanted it. "You don't get it, do you? And I thought you, *you* of all people, were willing to accept me the way I am."

"So it's your way or no way, right?"

Drake nodded. He'd waited too long for his freedom.

"There's something called compromise," Blair continued. "Each person gives a little and both people get some of what they want."

"I don't want some, I want it all. I've had a lifetime of compromises. I'm ready to be selfish. I want to do what I want when I want and how I want. And I want to do it by myself."

"I see."

He could barely make out the words.

"So you want me to leave now?" Blair asked.

No, honestly, he didn't. But she was unhappy and he didn't want to be responsible for another person's happiness. It was over and they both knew it. "I don't think we'll be able to get back what we had."

"No," she answered shortly.

He gestured to the engine he'd finally fixed. "I'll be able to take you to San Verde tomorrow."

Instead of saying a frigid, "I'll be more than ready" or some variation on that theme, Blair's lower lip quivered and she burst into tears.

Drake was caught completely off guard.

"What's wrong with me?" she said, sobbing. "Why can't any man love me?"

Oh no. "It's not you, Blair. It's me."

Shaking her head, she hiccuped out something that sounded like, "Ar-mand."

Nuts. He should have remembered she was on the rebound. Now he felt worse than ever. What was the matter with him? Just because she was strong on the outside, he'd overlooked the fact that she was emotionally vulnerable on the inside. "What happened with Armand could have happened to anybody."

She sniffed. "You do realize how stupid that sounds."

"I meant that a lot of women get taken advantage of by men."

"Men are scum."

"Yeah, looks like you're right." He wasn't in a position to argue.

"Quit agreeing with me."

"Okay, most men aren't scum."

"Except you. You're scum. In fact, you're worse than Armand. *He* never slept with me."

"I resent being lumped together with scum like Armand."

"Oh yeah?" Blair scrubbed at her eyes. "Well, now that playtime's over, you're going to dump me in a strange town knowing that I don't have any money, no credit, no job, no place to live, no prospects—and I don't even have any real clothes. I could starve and you wouldn't care. If that isn't scum, I don't know what is."

"I care," he protested, horrified at the picture she'd painted.

"Scum."

"I wouldn't have left you without any money." How could she think that?

"I don't want your money!" She flung the papers at him, then ran down the gangplank.

Drake let her go. When she calmed down, he'd apologize and keep apologizing, not that it would do any good.

This whole situation just proved that he was better off alone. Look how he'd hurt her. He didn't deserve a woman like Blair. She had a lot going for her and she shouldn't waste her life with him.

He sat on the deck and let his legs dangle in the stairwell. For a while there, he'd considered taking Blair with him as he sailed. The *Pirate's Lady* was an awful lot of boat to handle and he would have been glad to have an extra pair of hands during its maiden voyage. He planned to hug the coast until he polished his sailing skills, and Blair could have hopped off anytime she felt like it.

Apparently, he was being as unrealistic as Blair. He knew how she craved a home. She was the perfect candidate for a life in the suburbs, not living on a tiny, isolated island.

Drake stared in the direction of the lodge. Somehow, he was going to have to convince her that even though the two of them weren't destined for a life together, she was still a desirable woman and would make some other man a wonderful life mate.

"I *am* scum," he muttered, and gathered the papers she'd thrown at him.

He read snatches of lists and time lines. She *was* thorough, he thought, and then his attention was caught by another list. *Flowers, musicians, trellis, groom.* Drake smiled. This was Blair's wedding list. Looked as if she'd marked groom off too early. He flipped over the page and saw more Pirate's Hideout plans. She was running out of paper and was writing on the backs of other lists and plans.

Her whole life was lists and plans and organizing. She'd be a great PTA president. He pictured her as a mother. Any less than three kids wouldn't keep her busy enough.

Yeah, he'd miss her, but it was time for her to go. She wanted to put down roots and this wasn't the place.

Idly, he looked at the backs of other lists. Hello? What was this? A list of traveler's-check numbers—Blair was incredibly thorough—but other numbers, as well. Account numbers. Drake had seen enough account numbers in his lifetime to recognize them when he saw them.

According to Blair's notations, they had to be Armand's accounts. She'd never mentioned having this kind of information. What else had she recorded in that planner of hers?

He considered the possibilities as he finished working on the engine. So she had Armand's account numbers. The more Drake thought about it, the more he itched to see what he could find out.

He gathered the remains of their lunch and started up the path.

"Blair!" Drake called as soon as he was within earshot of the lodge. "Blair, I want to ask you something."

He listened but couldn't hear a response.

"Blair!"

"I'm in the library." Her voice was muffled.

The library. Drake's heart started pounding and he ran down the hall. *Not the library.*

"Oh, for pity's sake! I wouldn't hurt the library," she was saying even before he appeared in the doorway. He felt ashamed that his first thought had been so obvious.

"Since I'm leaving tomorrow, I wanted to make sure I finished the mystery I started."

Her eyes were red, but she was pretending she was over her hurt. Drake exhaled. "Blair, I'm sorry. For everything. But I might be able to redeem myself."

She closed her book. "Not that it's possible, but how?"

"The back of these papers you left on the boat—"

"The ones I threw in your face?"

"Yeah, those. These numbers—" he pointed "—they're accounts?"

Blair nodded. "That's my old one and those are Armand's. They're probably phoney."

Drake studied them. "I don't know. They look genuine. What does chocolate mean?"

"That's the Swiss account."

He grinned. "Very good, Blair. Do you have any other notes about Armand?"

Blair shrugged and showed him her planner.

"Mind if I borrow this?" he asked.

"Why?"

"I'm going to fire up that laptop computer Roger left and see what I can see."

She stood. "Then I'll be in the cabana."

"No, Blair, you don't have to go."

"Meaning I don't have to go to the cabana."

"Right. I'll turn on the generator and run power to the rec room. You can stay here."

"Stay here *temporarily,* you mean."

Drake nodded, feeling scummier by the minute.

"I just wanted to clarify your invitation," she said in an icy voice.

Drake briefly shut his eyes. "Blair, I've already apologized."

"I'm only making certain there aren't any further miscommunications between us," she said, settling back onto the leather sofa.

She'd be singing a different tune when he managed to access Armand's accounts, Drake vowed.

In the end, it was almost too easy.

Drake was filled with contempt—both for Armand and for the investors he'd fleeced. Didn't anyone make basic inquiries?

He walked to the library doors and stuck his head in. "Did you know Armand's last name isn't in this string of names you wrote down?"

"Yes." Blair's voice was clipped. She didn't look up from her book.

So she was going to play it that way. "Just wondered," Drake said.

By using the cellular phone and the laptop, he was able to poke around in any number of financial institutions.

The first time he was asked for a password, Drake called out to Blair, "Did Armand tell you his passwords or ID codes?"

"No," she answered.

Obviously Blair wasn't going to help him try to guess Armand's password, so Drake typed her name and, to his utter astonishment, discovered he'd guessed correctly on the first try. What's more, Armand had used "Blair" as the password for all the accounts—except the Swiss one. Drake didn't have any luck there.

Drake used his own Exeter-O'Keefe authorization codes, which were still active, as he'd suspected, and promptly drained Armand's accounts. Then he created a new one for Blair and funneled all the money into it.

Triumphant, he marched into the library to tell her, but she'd fallen asleep.

It was then that he noticed it was dark outside.

Drake went to turn off the computer, but instead began cruising the financial web pages on the Internet, catching up on the news.

By the time the foreign markets were open, Drake couldn't stand it. He took a hunk of the money he'd recovered from Armand and bought currency futures with it.

Then he sat back and watched.

By dawn, he'd made a tidy profit. "I've still got the touch," he gloated to himself.

Drake got up and made coffee. Blair was still asleep. He couldn't wait to tell her what he'd done. She had a healthy nest egg now. She could make a fresh start.

Though he'd been up all night, Drake wasn't sleepy. How many other nights had he done the same thing and hated it?

Now he felt...exhilarated. And a lot less guilty.

Setting his coffee mug beside the keyboard, Drake logged on to the Exeter-O'Keefe computer.

Just how much trouble was Roger in, anyway?

Within minutes, he had the answer: serious trouble.

Drake scrolled through the accounts one by one. How had Roger managed to run a successful business into the ground in only eight months?

He'd made huge speculative trades, then had made the mistake of trying to make it back too quickly. He'd panicked.

Clients had been pulling out. The business was worth far less than what it had been when Drake left.

Dreading what he'd find, Drake accessed his personal account.

It was all but empty. Drake reviewed the transaction history, saw that Roger had frequently used the funds to cover margin calls, but that he'd replaced them. And then one time he hadn't, except for piddling amounts to cover the transfers Drake had made to the bank in San Verde.

Stunned, he watched the sun rise.

It was obvious he'd have to return to New York and do what he could to stop the financial hemorrhaging. It would be a long time before he could return to Pirate's Hideout.

If ever.

"I smell coffee," said a sleepy-voiced Blair.

"In the kitchen." He didn't turn around to look at her. He didn't dare. He was afraid he needed her, but he couldn't let her know that. Not now.

"Have you been up all night?" she asked.

"Yeah."

"And?"

"And I'm going back to New York."

"BUT I TOLD YOU I don't want your money!" Blair insisted.

Drake ignored her and propelled her outside San Verde's tiny bank and in the direction of the bus station.

"It's not my money, it's your money. I got it back from Armand."

"How?"

"I transferred it out of his accounts, that's how. The man used your name as his password."

"Really?" She looked pleased.

Women. "Here." He handed her the checkbook, account papers and an envelope of cash.

Blair ignored the cash and was looking in the checkbook. "I wonder how much of my money he spent—" She gasped, then clutched Drake's arm. "There's way too much here."

"I didn't know how much was yours, so I took it all," Drake said. "Justice, don't you think?"

"But, Drake, all the investors' money must be here, too."

"Then give it back. You've got a list of their names."

"I will." She looked up at him. "Thanks."

He shrugged, wondering what she'd think if he told her that she was now worth more money than he was.

"How long are you going to be in New York?"

Drake glanced away. "A while."

They walked in silence for a time, then she said, "Roger messed up big time, huh?"

Drake only nodded, hoping she wouldn't ask how big.

"Where will you dock the *Pirate's Lady* while you're gone?"

Drake thought about not telling her. "I'm selling her."

Blair stopped walking. "You're selling the *Pirate's Lady?*"

"Yeah, it's easier." He tried for casual eye contact. Mistake.

Blair was looking at him with far too much understanding in those blue eyes. Fortunately, she also understood not to say anything else.

"So." Drake shoved his hands in his pockets to keep from touching her. "The bus station is right down the street." He didn't trust himself to go any farther.

"Yes, I see it."

They stood in the middle of the sidewalk, both dressed alike in khaki shorts and knit Pirate's Hideout shirts as though they'd been to an exclusive summer camp.

Blair gazed at him steadily. He knew she wanted him to ask her to come to New York with him, but he wasn't going to ask and she knew that, too.

In the end, he gently kissed her cheek. "Goodbye, Blair. Have a good life."

AS IF SHE COULD HAVE a good life without him.

Within a couple of weeks, Blair had tracked down each

surprised and pleased investor and had returned the money.

She still had a hunk left over. A hunk she decided to invest. In a boat. How convenient that she knew of one for sale.

Drake hadn't told her much of what he'd discovered about Roger's activities, but what he had said let her guess that Roger had really blown it and Drake was riding to the rescue.

So Blair was going to rescue Drake.

She'd planned to give him plenty of time to take the money he'd get from the *Pirate's Lady* sale and start remaking his fortune. Drake was brilliant. She knew he could do it. But in the end, she only lasted two more weeks.

So, a month after Drake had left her at the San Verde bus station, Blair, wearing a new red suit, followed Drake's receptionist to his office. She'd given her name as the former Mrs. Armand Varga, figuring that would get Drake's attention, since she hadn't made an appointment.

"Blair!" he said when he saw her. "You have a wicked sense of humor." But he was smiling. "You shouldn't be here."

"But I am." And just in time, too. He looked horrible. Very classy in his suit, but his tan had faded and his hair was shorter.

But his eyes were dead. She shivered when she looked into them.

He came around from the desk and took her in his arms. "Am I allowed to say that I've missed you?"

"Only if you mean it."

His kiss nearly broke her heart. It was more desperate than passionate, as though he was trying to transport himself back to Pirate's Hideout.

"Oh, Drake." She sighed against his mouth. "Are you rich enough to go back yet?"

"I'm getting there." She felt him chuckle. "How did you know?"

"Because you were selling the *Pirate's Lady*."

"Yeah, that hurt. But I needed seed money."

"*I* had money you could have used."

Drake drew his finger down her nose. "That's *your* money. You should invest it in growth stocks and not speculate in risky futures trading or wild schemes involving slick foreign gentlemen."

She tossed her head. "Too late."

His face froze and he gripped her arms. "What happened?"

"I bought a boat," she announced, and watched his face to see how long it took him to figure out which boat she'd bought.

Not long. Leveling a stern look at her, he leaned against the desk and crossed his arms over his chest. "You bought the *Pirate's Lady*."

She nodded. "Paid cash. Got a great deal."

"You bought my boat," he repeated.

"It's not your boat anymore. It's my boat. *Blair's Boat*. That's what it says right on the side."

He shook his head. "You shouldn't have told me you bought my boat."

"Why not?"

"Because now when I tell you I'm in love with you, you'll think it's because of the boat."

"You're in love with me?" She felt a goofy grin spread over her face.

He nodded. "Yeah."

"It's because of the boat, isn't it?"

"Come here." He opened his arms and Blair stepped into his embrace. "I suppose you want to hear me confess that I've been a blind idiot and all that."

"You betcha."

He sighed. "I...can't live here. I can't live like this. But I can't live without you, either."

"So let's go home."

"Home?"

She smiled. "Pirate's Hideout. I already put down roots. I couldn't help it. That's what happens when you fall in love with somebody. Home is where the heart is."

Drake ran his knuckles over her cheek. "You think you can be happy there?"

"With you."

"Exactly the way things are?"

"Certainly not," she said coolly. "I want full-time electricity, telephone and repairs to the lodge. I see no reason to be uncomfortable, but if you want to go native, there are six cabanas scattered over the island."

He blinked. "Is that all?"

"No. I have a list."

She unfolded a paper and he laughed. "I knew you would."

He scanned the list. "I can live with this. But what about you? Won't you get bored and lonely?"

"If I do, I'll just sail into San Verde. I've got my own transportation, you know."

Drake burst out laughing. "Oh, Blair, I do love you. But," he said, dangling the paper in front of her, "you're slipping. You left one very important item off the list."

"What?"

"Our wedding."

"Well, actually..." She held up a brand-new planner. "I wanted to be prepared in case I needed it."

"You need it," he said just before he kissed her.

"I need you," Blair said.

"I need you, too." Drake sighed. "But I've got to get back to work."

"Not until after lunch."

"Blair, I can't leave now."

"You don't have to. I brought lunch." She reached into her purse and withdrew a can of Jiffy Cheez.

"That's lunch?"

"Yes." Blair hopped onto the desk and tossed him the can.

"Where are the crackers?" Drake asked.

Blair smiled and began unbuttoning her suit. "I didn't bring any."

Deborah Simmons
The Squire's Daughter

The Squire's Daughter originally appeared as a Harlequin Historicals® romance. Four new Harlequin Historicals® books appear each month to sweep you away to the past and deliver unforgettable heroes and heroines who are fated to share their destinies.

Harlequin® Historical

CHAPTER ONE

CLARE CUMMINGS GAZED about the room, her yawn of boredom cut off as an ivory fan suddenly poked her in the ribs. Its owner, an elderly lady wearing a purple turban, appeared to be gouging her way through the crowd, Clare noted. Now she knew why the most successful London balls were called squeezes.

Lady Lynford's vast reception hall was packed with people, a mass of brilliantly colored silks and satins moving to and fro like wind-tossed wildflowers, and about as substantial as them, too, Clare mused. Rows of candles in shiny chandeliers and sparkling candelabras lit the scene brightly and glittered off a vast array of diamonds and priceless gems worn by the ladies. Glancing up at the seemingly endless columns of marble that rose to the vaulted ceiling, Clare wondered how she would ever grow accustomed to London.

Feeling another yawn coming on, she moved, weaving in and out of the mob until she reached one of the tall windows. Some fresh air might rouse her, she decided, but she changed her mind as soon as she breathed in the town's fumes, heavy with sewage and smoke. Oh, for the country... Clare was struck with a sudden, heart-piercing longing for clean breezes and green grass and rolling hills.

"There you are," warbled a voice at her elbow. "Where have you been? Now don't be difficult tonight, my dear. You know how that confuses me."

Aunt Eugenia always looked confused. She had pale yellow hair that frizzed about her white face as though she had lost her comb and brush, and since she was farsighted but refused to wear her spectacles in public, she was perpetually squinting her watery blue eyes. A full head shorter than her niece, Eugenia disdained to look up, and so contributed to her air of bewilderment by rarely meeting her niece's gaze.

"With Mr. Farnsworth absent tonight, it's a perfect chance for you to catch the eye of all the other eligible men," Eugenia said. Unable to stifle the yawn that threatened this time, Clare raised her fingers to cover her breach of etiquette.

"Now, Clare," Eugenia said. "I called upon the good graces of some old friends to procure an invitation for us, and I don't see how you can be bored! Every girl longs for a London season! I admit I'm a bit on in years for such doings, but when your father asked me to usher you into society, even I looked forward to all the excitement."

Eugenia sighed, obviously exhausting herself with the effort of trying to comprehend her stubborn niece. "Yawning like a country bumpkin is not going to bring you favorable attention!" Her aunt's hair was sent flying with the strength of her vehemence. "You simply must present yourself well, if you are to make a propitious match. I might remind you, Clare, of your duty to wed advantageously."

Clare, who had heard this many times before, smiled gently and placed a hand on her aunt's arm. "Excuse me, dear, I'm going to get an ice. Would you like one?"

"Oh, heavens yes, but child, you can't go get it yourself!" Eugenia's words were lost on her niece, who smiled heedlessly at the warning. The refreshment was purely an excuse to escape, of course, and she moved as best she could about the rooms, watching the scenes that played out around her.

The dancing was very pretty. Clare admired the swirl of the ladies' skirts and the grace of the gentlemen as they stepped to the minuet or whirled across the room in a waltz. Perhaps a turn about the floor would enliven her, Clare thought with a brief surge of interest. She had little chance of receiving an invitation, though, because her circle of acquaintances was still so small, and having no desire to stand at the side, looking gawky and awkward again, she walked wistfully past the dancers.

In the card room, the play was pretty tame, limited mostly to elderly guests and a few young couples flirting over their hands. A lovely rendering of a hunt graced most of one wall. Clare's eyes followed the scene to its conclusion near one of the marble mantelpieces, and there her gaze remained, arrested in front of the fireplace. No fire burned there, but heat rose in her cheeks as she recognized the figure that stood before the empty grate. Her breath lodged in her throat, her limbs froze and she stared.

He was slightly taller than most men, and of medium build, but otherwise far from average. He leaned casually against the mantelpiece, a wayward shock of straight mahogany hair falling over one eye to make him look a little disreputable. Dressed all in black, he wore a perfectly arranged white cravat that set off his face. That face...Clare thought dizzily before being transported back in time.

She was fourteen again, and the groom had told her not to go out riding that soggy spring day, but as usual, she rebelled. She ignored his warning of fog and raced away on Phantom. The boy had been right, of course, and a thick blanket of mist rolled in, obscuring all landmarks until she knew she had gone too far and had left her father's, the squire's, property. Then, suddenly, she crested a hill and saw it, tucked into a valley and rising out of the fog like something from the fairy stories she loved so well.

It was an enchanted castle, with a square tower in the center standing proudly over the adjacent roofs, their medieval battlements intact. Without a second thought, Clare sent Phantom down the slope toward the vision—or so it seemed. When she neared the stone walls, the silence became eerie. No barking dogs marked her arrival, no grounds keeper shouted a greeting, just thick, white silence met her as if she were adrift in a dream.

She approached from the side, only to find her way blocked by water, dark and still in the mist, which told her the castle was moated. Following the water's edge, Clare found the bridge leading to the tower. The sound of Phantom's hooves echoed loudly against the stone walls. At the huge, arched entrance, Clare slid off her horse and tentatively put a hand to the worn wood of one door. She did not even blink in surprise when it swung open beneath her hand, as if by magic.

Clare secured Phantom's reins to an iron post near the door that looked like it had once held the family crest, then peered inside. No servants bustled busily to her side, and no horns sounded a greeting as in days of old. All was quiet, but for the noise of her footsteps across the tiled floor into a cavernous hall. Light spilled in from high, mullioned windows cut into the thick walls that rose to a vaulted, timbered ceiling lost in darkness above her.

High-backed Tudor chairs and side tables stood along the bare stone walls, and in the center of the room a massive dining table was surrounded by heavy chairs, the largest of which sat at the head like a shadowy sentinel. Clare stopped and waited a long, silent moment, certain of nothing but the tingle of anticipation beneath her skin until a movement in the great chair drew her attention.

"Good God," said a voice. "It's a pixie!"

Clare glanced at the enormous seat, where a pair of legs, sprawled across most of the chair and part of the floor, took shape. Expecting to see a ghostly apparition in her enchanted castle—or at the very least, a prince—Clare was a little disappointed when the figure evolved into an ordinary man.

"Well, come closer, pixie," he drawled, and Clare stepped forward, her gaze taking in the empty bottle on the table and the disheveled state of the speaker. He was not only a man, but a drunken one at that. He seemed young, although a stubble of beard lent a rakish cast to his boyish features. His straight, dark hair fell into eyes that stared rather morosely from his very handsome face.

His white shirt was open at the neck, and he wore light-colored breeches that clung to his thighs above mud-stained top boots. Were it not for the glass of liquor still clutched in the fingers of his left hand, she would have thought him a lost traveler like herself, seeking refuge in this mysterious place.

Too enchanted to be afraid, Clare stepped forward without hesitation when he held out his right hand to her. Trustingly, she placed her fingers in his, surprised by the pleasant feel of his firm clasp. She realized then just how much she missed the touch of another, for her father was not given to displays of affection.

"Have I imagined you, my lovely little sprite?" the man asked, rubbing his thumb absently along her hand, and Clare had the impression that perhaps she wasn't dreaming, after all. "I must have drunk more than usual." He peered down into his glass with the most melancholy air, his grip on her fingers tightening.

Perhaps it was his touch, or perhaps it was the sad look in his eyes, but Clare felt as though he were reaching out to her. She decided then that whether this was dream or reality, the castle was enchanted, and the prince—her prince—was laboring under an evil spell. And she knew with the certainty of a lonely, romantic fourteen-year-old, that she, and only she, could save him....

Clare shook her head as if to deny the memory. It was not 1808, but 1812, and she was eighteen now, dressed elegantly in a silk gown of Bishop's blue, and moving among the sparkling ton of London. She was no longer a lovesick child entranced by fairy stories. Clare's breath came back to her as she returned to the present and realized she was staring—at him. Turning away abruptly, she ran smack into someone else.

"Whoa!" a voice said, and Clare recovered herself sufficiently to apologize to the lovely young woman who was steadying her.

"I beg your pardon!"

"No need to," the girl said with a smile. "I can see why you're dazed, but if you'll take a bit of advice, don't get caught under that one's spell." She tilted her head toward the mantelpiece, where *he* still lounged negligently.

"Oh, I don't intend..." Clare mumbled something incoherently as she assessed the young lady before her. She was beautifully dressed and had shiny, auburn ringlets that were the height of fashion. The freckles that dotted her nose made her look friendly, and Clare returned her smile. "I'm sorry. You must take me for a great oaf."

"Ah ha! So you've been teased about your height, too," the girl said conspiratorially. She did stand taller than Clare, which was a fair bit more of a height than any other female around, or so the squire always claimed. Clare nodded and grinned then, finally shaken out of the mist of memory by the refreshing young woman. "I'm afraid we haven't been properly introduced. I'm Felicity Shaw."

"Clare Cummings. It is a pleasure to meet you." Stepping out of the flow of traffic, they found a pair of vacant seats, and Felicity sank down with a sigh of relief.

"Oh, I vow I've been standing since I came in. Chairs are harder to come by than spun gold tonight," she complained. "Is this your first London season?"

Clare nodded.

"Mine, too," Felicity said, pulling out a fan to ply the air gracefully, "though I'll dare swear that because of my sisters, I've more knowledge than most. And that's how I can tell you to stay away from that one," she said, nodding again toward the mantelpiece.

Clare refused to spare *him* another glance and told herself firmly not to blush. "He reminded me of someone—someone I once knew," she said softly, angry with herself for the catch in her voice.

"Ah, I see," Felicity said, looking as though she didn't believe a word of it, but was too nice to admit it. "Well, that just happens to be Justin St. John, the Marquis of Worthington. Don't let his handsome looks and winning ways snare you. He is a notorious rake who will only ruin your reputation—definitely not the thing for girls in their first season!"

"He drinks quite a bit, too, I gather," Clare said, surreptitiously eyeing the glass in his hand. At the sight of his lean, masculine fingers, her mouth went so dry that she longed for a swallow herself.

"Well, yes, he does have a reputation for the bottle, but also for holding his liquor," Felicity whispered behind her fan.

Clare nodded. He would. Of course, once she got to London, she had heard the rumors about him. Outlandish, she had called them, and had told herself she didn't care. She didn't, she swore again. Then, as if to prove her thoughts a lie, his low, husky voice sounded in her ear, and Clare nearly leapt from her skin.

"If it isn't the youngest Miss Shaw," he drawled. Thankful that he had not addressed her, Clare tried to appear inconspicuous, but she lifted her head ever so slightly to see him. He was leaning toward them gracefully, the same shock of hair falling over one eyebrow, and she realized that he was so close that she could almost reach out and touch him—for the first time in two years.

He was drunk. She could tell by the glassy, distant look in his eyes as he bantered with Felicity. "Now how many sisters are there?"

Clare felt like landing him a facer. She could see that it concerned him not a whit how many sisters Felicity had, but then he didn't care about anything, did he? Clare's breath raced, and her heart banged in her chest as she wished herself part of the woodwork. Oh, please, don't let him notice me, she thought desperately. But her prayer went unanswered.

He glanced at her, and Clare, holding her breath, let it out slowly when the dark eyes, minus their sparkle, moved back to Felicity. He didn't recognize her! Clare couldn't decide whether to be relieved or insulted.

"Now you must introduce me to your lovely friend," he coaxed. Relief won out, and before Felicity could utter a word, Clare spoke up.

"I don't care to be introduced," she said, rising so abruptly that she nearly knocked him aside. She could hear Felicity's gasp, and could see the dazed look of surprise in his eyes that told her she had caught his interest. She didn't want it.

Turning her back on him, she spoke to Felicity. "Excuse me, won't you?" Without waiting for an answer, she walked away, nervously hoping that no one else had heard her insult a marquis so blatantly. She didn't dare look back to see if the whole room was staring, however, because she knew if she had to look at him again, she might knock him flat.

Weaving her way through the crowd once more, Clare slipped out the nearest door and found a quiet corner in the garden. Once there, she took a deep breath, and another and another until her heart finally slowed. Of course, she had hoped never to see him again, but it was to be expected that she would. Ever since she had arrived in London two weeks ago, she had wondered when and if she would run across the notorious marquis.

Well, now that she had seen him, she would know to avoid him, and since he hadn't recognized her, that made it all the easier. If he heard her name, he might remember her, so she must stay away. She didn't want him to remember. *She* didn't want to remember. She wanted to forget, but the past wouldn't let her. Even now, it was taking her back again to that day four years ago....

"What's your name, sprite?" her prince had asked.

"Clare Cummings," she'd answered simply.

He started and pulled her closer for a good look. "By the devil, you are real. And just a child."

Clare, who had not yet gained her height, did not dispute his assessment, but she bristled, nonetheless. "And how old are you?" she asked.

He laughed, and she smiled, though she had no idea why. Perhaps it was the crinkles at the corners of his eyes or his infectious grin. "Twenty-one," he said, and Clare decided that was a fine age.

"How long have you been here?" The fog, the castle and the handsome character holding her hand created such a magical setting that they all seemed caught in time. In fact, Clare would not have been surprised if he told her he had been drinking from the same bottle for the past hundred years.

He sighed. "Got here this morning," he said with a careless frown. Clare gasped, a bit disappointed that her prince had not been doomed by a spell to reside here forever. "Rode here all night on a bet. Lucky I didn't break my neck, too."

"But whatever are you doing here?" she asked.

"God only knows," he answered. He reached up to put his glass on the table and push it away. Perhaps he had forgotten that he still held her fingers in his other hand. "It's been awhile, as I'm sure you could tell from the grounds."

"Been awhile?" she asked, puzzled.

"Since I've been here," he said. "Oh, I suppose I should show some manners. Would you care for a seat, Clare?"

She giggled at the adult treatment. "No, thank you." I'd rather hold your hand, she thought.

"Oh, well, I tried, didn't I?" He swung his feet to the floor, stretching his long legs out before him. "Where were we? Oh, yes. It's been years since I've been...home," he said, flinching with distaste.

Clare stared at him in awe. "This is your home?" she asked.

He nodded. "Ghastly, isn't it?" He pretended a great shudder, and she giggled again.

"But no! It isn't ghastly," she protested. "It's wonderful! It's beautiful. I thought...that is, it rather looks like an enchanted castle."

Her prince gave a disgusted snort. "Cursed is more likely." He reached for his drink, then caught himself and pulled his hand back.

"But where are we? I had no idea this place existed," she said, still uncertain whether it did, indeed, exist anywhere but in her vivid imagination.

"Oh, it exists all right, probably closer to your home than you think," he answered, then paused. "Are you related to Squire Cummings?"

"Why, yes! He's my father," she answered, startled by his knowledge.

The young man groaned. "He's been after me for years to clean up the place. For heaven's sake, don't tell him you were here, or he'd have an apoplexy."

"Oh, I won't!" Clare answered. "It will be our secret, but only if you let me find my way around or give me a tour," she said cheerfully.

"You want to look about this old haunt?" he asked skeptically.

"Oh, yes!" she answered, and then she saw he was teasing her. His eyes sparkled. Were they brown? Yes, a deep, rich color, she thought giddily.

"Well, I can't vouch for our safety if we wander about," he warned.

"Oh," Clare said in disappointment. "Might the castle fall in?"

He snorted again. "No hope of that. The thing will be

here after the apocalypse. No, I was referring to the various mysteries it holds," he said, lowering his voice dramatically. "What are children reading these days? Oh, I imagine there are gnomes and elves and—"

"And secret passages?" Clare asked breathlessly.

"At least a dozen."

"And...ghosts?" she asked, her eyes wide as saucers.

"Well, we'll leave them out of it," he said, standing up. The well-built young man towered over her, and still holding her hand, led her through the labyrinth that was Worth Hall. Although he claimed it was only a medieval manor house, Clare was unconvinced, and she whispered, "Worth Castle," reverently, which made him smile.

Whatever its true title, the building obviously had been shut up for some time, but to Clare that only added to its allure. Some rooms were empty; others held furniture covered with great cloths, gray with dust. Once in awhile, she would discover open treasures of massive oak pieces under the musty cloths.

Clare was entranced, and thought as she pinched herself that she would never live to see a better day. In the great chamber, she raised a hand to touch the fringed edge of the heavy bed hangings, where light spilling in from the oriel windows caught the once-brightly colored fabric. She breathed in the lingering smell of old wood and spices, along with the fresh scent of her prince, a mixture of mud and liquor and man. With a piercing longing, Clare wished that the enchantment would pass to her, keeping her bound here with him forever.

But it did not. A glance out of the many-paned glass told her that the fog had lifted a little, and that she had tarried too long on her adventure. "Oh dear, I must be going. Will you be here tomorrow?" she asked with the boldness of youth.

He shook his head slowly, then stopped as disappointment dissolved her eager smile. "Well, I suppose I could stay a few days, just to get the place in order. It is looking pretty frightful...." His voice trailed off as if he were still reluctant.

"Yes! You simply must stay!" Clare insisted with all the forcefulness of a lonely little girl desperate for excitement and company.

He didn't refuse. He led her out to her horse, and told her how to find her way home. "I'd take you myself, but I fear your father would have an attack," he said dryly as he helped her into the saddle. He told her how to come round the back way, through the old gardens. "Now run along like a good little thing, my pixie," he said, waving.

"Goodbye! Oh," Clare said, turning Phantom so that she could see the young man's face again. "And what shall I call you?"

"You may call me whatever strikes your fancy," he said with a grin that flashed his white teeth. "But Justin will suffice." Of course, it was some time later that Clare discovered her spellbound prince was nearly that. Her friend, her confidant, her simple Justin, turned out to be a marquis, and an infamous one, too.

He had stayed for a few days, as promised, and later, he returned. He even opened up some of the rooms, brought in a housekeeper and half-heartedly turned some attention to the overgrown grounds, but he never saw the castle as she did. He didn't even know any tales about the place, so she made some up, and soon he was begging her for more. The more fanciful the story, the better, for he would smile at hairy goblins and laugh delightedly at purple dragons with golden wings....

"Go away!" Clare said aloud. She put both hands to her head, trying to stop the flood of memories that washed over her. They didn't heed her, but crowded around her, waiting their turn: fishing with Justin on the river, digging with Justin in the old gardens, buying a Christmas present for Justin, feeling the excitement when he would be in residence, however brief it was. He was her friend, her big brother, her prince—until she had the misfortune to grow up, and that was the end of that fairy tale.

HORRIFIED, FELICITY STARED openmouthed after her new acquaintance. No matter what the man's reputation, one could hardly insult a marquis. Good heavens, the girl must be as green as grass! For once in her voluble life, Felicity was at a loss for words, and she glanced up in trepidation at the man leaning toward her, expecting to see an angry visage.

She need not have worried. Worthington was gazing down at her with a quirky smile on his face. "Good heavens, Miss Shaw, what did you tell her about me?" he asked in mock horror, and Felicity was immediately at ease again. He was such a charmer.

"Oh, truly, my lord, I think she's just in from the country and didn't at all realize what she was doing," Felicity said by way of apology.

"I see," the marquis said softly. "Perhaps you can enlighten me as to her name, and I'll present myself to her at some other date when I'm not wearing two heads, or is it horns I've sprouted?"

Felicity dissolved into giggles, flattered by his attention, for he was, truly, a very handsome man, and oh, the things they said about his ways with women. Just recalling some of them made her blush.

"Well, my littlest Shaw?" he prodded.

"Her name is Clare Cummings." Felicity was going to say more, but his reaction caught her totally by surprise. The perpetually bored and apathetic young marquis looked as though someone had punched him in the stomach.

Although she was dying of curiosity, he obviously had no intention of enlightening her about the cause of his reaction. "Very interesting," was his only comment as he returned his attention to her. When Felicity opened her mouth to speak, he cut her off, firmly closing the conversation. "It has been a pleasure, as always," he noted, bowing gracefully. "Give my regards to your dear sisters." And then he moved casually away.

Felicity craned her neck to watch his exit, anxious to see if he followed the girl, but the crowd soon swallowed him. With a sigh, she fanned herself rapidly. Then her frustrated frown was replaced by a smile, for she knew how much her sisters liked to share odd bits of gossip. Just wait until she related this incident!

Had Felicity seen the marquis's path, she would have been disappointed, for Justin St. John did not search for anyone. He grabbed a bottle of his host's best brandy, slipped inside the deserted study and sank into the nearest chair—quite alone.

In the silence of the dim room he tugged at his neck cloth, effectively ruining the elaborate design his valet had tied, and pulled out the chain that hung around his neck. He had replaced the original with one of shimmering gold, but the piece it carried remained the same, and Justin held the small charm in his fingers.

The candlelight glinted on the wings of a tiny golden dragon that ignited his memory as surely as if it breathed fire into his hand. Closing his eyes, he leaned his head back, his fingers closing around the bauble as he remembered....

"Open it, Justin!" Clare urged, her shining face eager. She clutched the book he had given her to her chest and smiled up at him, all the love in the world brimming in her hazel eyes.

Justin grinned and opened the box to reveal his Christmas gift: a chain with a small golden dragon. He laughed with delight until he realized that she must have purchased the present. "Clare, I thought I asked you to make me something," he said, eyeing her critically.

"You did," she answered with a grimace, "but I'm not

very good at making things, and besides, Papa gives me an ample allowance."

Justin shook his head, aware that ample to her was probably a pittance meant to help spruce up her wardrobe, not to buy presents for profligate neighbors. But he was also aware that Clare cared more about stray dogs and toads than pin money. He took his gift from the box and held it up.

"Don't you like it?" Clare asked, her expressive eyes taking on that wide, sad look that made her seem so fragile. His fragile little pixie.

"I love it," Justin said, hugging her tightly. "And I shall wear it always." Was that the only promise he had ever kept? Stepping back, he'd slipped it around his neck, where it had remained, a source of curiosity and amusement for all his lovers. Yet despite their prodding, he had never told anyone why he wore it. It was no wonder, for he wasn't quite sure himself....

Justin let the chain slide through his fingers and reached for his host's bottle. He tried to picture Clare as she had been tonight, but he simply had not taken a good look at her. He had seen a pretty female, vaguely familiar, staring at him from across the room, and he had assumed that, like so many others, the lady wanted him. For a moment, he had thought her one of his past lovers! The notion wrenched his stomach, for he could never view Clare in that light.

Clare. Whenever he thought of her, all Justin could see were those limpid eyes gazing up at him adoringly. Blast it! He slammed his fist into the wall and blamed himself, as he usually did.

He didn't even bother to glance up at the sound of the door opening.

"Demolishing the house, Justin?" his friend Fletcher Mayefield asked. Taking the brandy, Fletcher grabbed a couple of glasses from a nearby table and poured them each a serving. "I don't think Lynford would care for it."

Justin grunted. He could feel Fletcher's gaze on him, but ignored it.

"Well?" Fletcher walked around the host's desk and eyed his friend expectantly. "When I saw you pass, white-faced and clutching a bottle for dear life, I admit I was curious. I haven't seen you this agitated since you seduced those two actresses from the same company, and they were calling for your blood, or was it testicles?"

"I do believe they intended castration," Justin said, smiling. "But I talked them out of it."

"So what is it tonight? Have they changed their minds again?" Fletcher asked.

Justin sighed. "I saw a ghost from my past."

"Is that all?" Fletcher scoffed. "I imagine you must run into them daily! I know I do. What's so special about this one?" The young man seated himself comfortably in a chair and propped his feet up on the desk.

"She's not one of *those* ghosts," Justin said glumly, disgusted at the thought of classifying young, innocent Clare with his lovers. And then it struck him, with piercing, paralyzing horror: his Clare was no longer a child. She was a woman now and, as such, was prey to all the other rakes and schemers and charmers that haunted London society. Justin gazed at Fletcher warily. "Do you know a Clare Cummings?"

Fletcher leaned his head back as if mulling over the question, his golden hair shining in the glow of the candlelight. "No," he finally said. "Should I?"

"No," Justin said, a little too forcefully. Blast it, now he was going to start worrying about her.... No, he wasn't going to think about her at all. He'd go home—not *there,* but to the estate in Devon—take a party with him and hole up until the end of the season. And then the devil take her, he would never have to know what happened to her. "What is she doing here in London?" he asked aloud. "I thought she would be married to some dreadful village idiot by now, and the mother of ten children."

"Who *is* this woman?" Fletcher asked.

"Clare Cummings," Justin repeated, flinching. Just saying her name hurt, and he stopped to rally his resources with a long swallow. "She was a little girl I befriended back home, at the hall, a few years ago."

"And?" Fletcher prodded.

"And she grew up," Justin answered before downing his drink.

"Girls have a way of doing that," Fletcher said, tongue firmly in cheek.

Justin ignored his comment, and held out his glass for a refill, which Fletcher poured obligingly. Justin shook his head at the recollection. "One day I went home, and it had happened," he said, waving his free hand in the air. "She was a foot taller, I'll swear, and had developed these... curves. Naturally, I suspected that she was too old to be trailing along after any young man, let alone me, but I did nothing, and then the whole thing came to a head."

"Ah," Fletcher said softly.

Justin sent him a quelling glance. "Her father found out and charged over to the hall in a veritable fury of outraged paternity, bellowing that I had better leave his daughter alone."

Fletcher grinned. "You're lucky he didn't force you to marry the chit."

Justin frowned. "He did his best, but...I prevailed. It would have been hard for him to prove anything." He moved restlessly in his seat, the memory of their encounter not a pleasant one.

"Well, she was neither the first nor the last to set her sights on your name and fail," Fletcher commented dryly as he swirled the liquor in his glass.

"She wasn't like that," Justin snapped, glaring at his friend. Fletcher lifted his brows in silent question, but he did not answer. He looked down into his brandy, seeing Clare's eyes in the depths. She was the only woman who had *not* thrown herself at him, who had *not* angled for marriage, and yet... He shut his eyes against the memory of those golden pools, shot with green, looking up at him, so trusting, so innocent and so full of love.

Maybe that was what had scared him, or maybe it was the strength of his own attachment to the girl-child she was, or maybe he was just a coward, taking the easy way out. Whatever the reason, he had told the squire that he would never see her again. Of course, it had not been that simple. But, in the end, he had cut the ties that bound them together with stunning finality.

Justin sighed, shaken by the images of the past, and took a swallow as the sound of his friend's voice pulled him back to the present. "So you broke the girl's heart," Fletcher said with a shrug. "You've broken too many—before and since—for it to matter."

"Yes," Justin agreed softly. "But that was the only time I broke my own as well."

CHAPTER TWO

FLETCHER SWUNG HIS FEET to the floor. "I must meet this woman! Is she here tonight?" he asked, rising from his seat behind Lynford's desk.

"No, you don't," Justin said, sending his friend a warning glance.

"What?" Fletcher asked innocently, halfway out of his chair.

"Leave her alone, Fletcher."

"I just want to see the girl," he said, sinking back down. "What does she look like?"

"I'm not sure," Justin answered gloomily.

"You're not sure?" Fletcher repeated with a laugh.

"I haven't seen her in years. How should I know what she looks like now?" Justin tried to reconcile his little pixie, dressed in boyish clothes, her dark hair cropped below her ears, with the elegant woman he had glimpsed in the card room. He could not.

"All the more reason to find out. Aren't you curious?" Fletcher asked, eyeing his friend speculatively.

"Yes. No." Justin shook his head. Yes, he was desperately curious to see her, but he did not want to face the look in those eyes ever again. And Clare, with her fine bones, her wide eyes and her dainty mouth, had always held the promise of beauty. What if she had fulfilled his expectations and been transformed into a lovely butterfly? Then he would worry about her all the more. The thought of a fragile treasure like Clare loose among the jaded London types made him cringe. He took a drink. "Oh, give it up, Fletcher. It's complicated."

"How complicated can it be? We leave this stifling study, we find her and we discover just how much she's grown. Then you introduce me," Fletcher added with a grin.

Justin snorted. "Not bloody likely," he said, draining his glass.

"Why?"

"Because she doesn't want to see me, that's why," he mumbled. "She just gave me the cut direct—the worst setdown I've had in years," he explained with a scowl.

Fletcher laughed. "Probably the *only* set down you've had in years," he amended. "Justin, you are simply too spoiled. The ladies all adore you, gushing and drooling over you in a manner the rest of us find most disgusting. You're probably the only man alive who manages to remain friends with his former lovers, with the possible exception of the aforementioned actresses."

"Clare was *not* my lover," Justin said angrily. He caught himself when he saw Fletcher's raised eyebrows and took a deep breath. "She was a child, blast it, and I promise you that she will never gush or drool over me."

"Why?" Fletcher asked.

"Because when she refused to believe that I was a worthless bastard who didn't care about anything, I..." Justin's words trailed off and he put the glass to his lips.

"You what?"

"I proved it."

JUSTIN WAS STILL in his dressing gown when Fletcher bounded into his bedroom at the unholy hour of eleven o'clock. Justin's butler, accustomed to Fletcher's unorthodox entrances, could only close the door behind the guest with a sigh.

"Blast it, man, it's before noon," Justin grumbled, eyeing his friend suspiciously. When Fletcher possessed this much energy this early, it usually boded ill. Justin knew that many an escapade—dares that ended in hard riding, hard drinking or other exhausting pursuits—began with just such a morning visit. "What are you doing here?"

Fletcher ignored the question to glance at Justin's valet, who was moving among several open trunks and valises. "Are you going somewhere?"

"Yes," Justin said, waving away the servant with a hand. "I just told my man to pack. I'm taking a party to Devon. Care to come along?"

"No," Fletcher said, "and neither do you."

Justin rolled his eyes heavenward. "Fletcher, whatever you're planning, deal me out of it. I've a mind to visit the country, and I'm planning on a long stay." Resolved not to become involved in Fletcher's latest scheme, he set his mouth firmly and shook his head.

"Oh," said Fletcher slyly. "Then you wouldn't be interested to know that your Clare—"

Justin cut him off with a glare. "She is not *my* Clare."

"Well," Fletcher said, nodding, "you are right there. According to the latest gossip, the beautiful young thing—and I do mean beautiful—is nearly betrothed to Richard Farnsworth."

Justin could feel the blood leave his face at the mention of the name. "You're hoaxing me, of course," he said softly.

"Sorry, my dear fellow, but I most definitely am not. Would I make something like that up?" Fletcher raised his eyebrows in question.

"Yes," Justin answered snidely as he lifted a hand to rub the back of his neck. He prided himself on never feeling the aftereffects of liquor, but his head was starting to throb at the thought of Clare and... "Farnsworth," he repeated. "Why Farnsworth, of all people?"

Fletcher seated himself casually in one of the gray Louis XVI chairs scattered about the room and propped his feet on another. "It's been rumored for some time that he is looking for a wife."

"Who would have him?" Justin asked with a shudder.

"Well, face it, Justin, "There's never been any real scandal attached to his name. For someone in need of funds, as I assume her father must be—"

"You're serious, aren't you?" Justin asked, the appalling reality of the news finally sinking in. At Fletcher's nod, he sank down in a chair, setting the blood to throbbing in his temples. "Good God! I was at Eton after him, and the stories they told about him.... He's some kind of—of..." Justin sought vainly for the right word, his head pounding.

"Fiend?" Fletcher supplied calmly. "I was at Eton, too, Justin—a year behind you, certainly, but they still talked about him, of how he used to strangle cats and leave them in the beds of the new boys. His name alone was enough to scare us when we were little! And from what I gather, he's still up to his bizarre tricks, although he has the sense to keep them quiet. He has a penchant for a certain type of woman from Old Westminster—"

"All right, all right!" Justin said. He raised his hands, unwilling to hear more. His heart was racing, and he realized with a kind of dull surprise that he was frightened for the first time in his life. Just the thought of his Clare with that maniac Farnsworth was enough to scare him. "All right," he said more quietly. "I'll take care of it. Who is she staying with in town?" He paused to stare at his friend accusingly. "I assume you've been extremely thorough in your inquiries?"

"But of course!" Fletcher said, grinning guiltlessly. "She's staying with an aunt, Eugenia Butterfield—a featherbrained sister of her dead mother, so good luck."

Justin scowled. He'd had no idea Clare had any relatives, let alone someone with enough wherewithal to present her to society. He sighed. Now he was getting himself fully embroiled in it, wasn't he? He scowled at Fletcher, who smiled serenely, unaffected by his black looks.

"I assumed you would want to know," his friend explained innocently as he unfolded his long limbs and stood.

"Thank you so much," Justin said sarcastically.

Fletcher laughed. "They've hired a house in Carlisle Square," he said breezily as he showed himself out of Justin's bedroom. "Let me know what the old lady says."

When the door closed, Justin leaned his head back and sighed. His heart was still pounding apace, making him feel a bit foolish. All right, he thought, trying to steady himself. There was no reason to panic; the solution was quite simple. He would have a word with the aunt, explain to her that Farnsworth was not exactly the kind of man she would want her niece to marry, and that would be it. Then he would head off to Devon as planned, and the devil take Clare Cummings.

IT TOOK JUSTIN all afternoon to find a suitable female and cajole her into going with him. Lady Berkeley, of an age and temperament designed to appeal to an elderly aunt, was finally prevailed upon to do the deed, especially after he told her that Clare was a special friend of one of her granddaughters. Although he could never keep them straight, Justin thought it was Prudence.

"Well, any friend of Prudence's should be rescued from that horrid fellow," Aurora said forcefully. "There have always been odd rumors floating around about him. Of course, there are rumors concerning everyone, but the man does give me the shivers," she admitted. "Something in the eyes, I think."

Tall and beautiful despite her advanced years, Aurora patted Justin's arm as he led her from the carriage. "I shall be happy to put this lady to rights concerning Farnsworth," she said. Smiling sweetly, she paused in her progress toward the rented town house, her fingers lingering on his sleeve.

"Oh, Justin, you will bring your friend Fletcher Mayefield to my little soirée Saturday, won't you?"

"I really can't speak for him," Justin said, accustomed to denying all requests for his friend's presence.

"Oh, do say you will prevail upon him," Aurora urged as she clung to his arm. "You know the man is one of the most sought-after bachelors in London, and I have several granddaughters who are still unattached. Think what a coup that would be for me, if one of them snared Mayefield!" She paused again, meaningfully, and gazed at him with her lovely gray eyes. "Naturally, I've already told *them* that Farnsworth is not a suitable suitor."

She smiled slyly, and Justin tried not to scowl at what he perceived as a bit of blackmail. "I'll do my best to persuade him. And I can assure you that I will be there," he added, mentally postponing his journey to Devon again.

"Oh, yes, dear, we would love to have you, though no one wants to marry you, of course. You're far too disreputable," Aurora said mildly.

"Thank you for your vote of confidence," Justin said dryly, sending Aurora into soft peals of laughter as she clung to his arm.

Clare was not at home. Having no desire to see her, Justin had made sure she was out before he even approached the town house. They had sent round a note, so Miss Butterfield was expecting them, and from the looks of her, Justin suspected that Fletcher had been right. She appeared entirely featherbrained.

After the introductions, Justin sighed and moved to the window, where he stood gazing out to the street with his hands clasped behind his back. From that position, he could listen without participating in the conversation, for he was there, ostensibly, only as the widowed Lady Berkeley's escort.

It soon became clear, however, that his carefully laid plans were going awry, and Justin struggled to keep his temper in check. Featherbrained was hardly the word for Eugenia Butterfield. He was certain that birds possessed far more sense than the little woman perched on the flowered settee.

She simply refused to acknowledge Aurora's subtle hints concerning Farnsworth. She looked confused, rattled on about other topics and generally ignored the lady's gentle prodding concerning her niece's suitor, until Justin could stand it no more.

"Blast it, Miss Butterfield," he said, turning from his position at the window. "Lady Berkeley is trying to give you some good advice. Believe me, you do not want your niece to marry Lord Farnsworth! The stories I could tell you about him would turn your stomach."

Aurora frowned at him for interfering, while Miss Butterfield squinted at him. "Stories and rumors," she said, waving her hands in dismissal. "Mr. Farnsworth has shown himself to be a perfect gentleman to me and my niece. And if you'll pardon my saying so, my lord," she said, screwing up her face into a pout, "your reputation is far worse!"

Justin could have cheerfully wrung her silly neck. "My reputation, whatever it may be, is not the topic of discussion," he said quietly, "for I am not the one offering for your niece. I believe we all have Cla—Miss Cummings's best interests at heart and are concerned that she not suffer because those close to her have made an uninformed decision."

The woman looked so bewildered by his words that Justin wondered if perhaps she were foreign and suffered from a poor grasp of English. He started to speak again, but she shook her head as though overwhelmed, and turned to Lady Berkeley. "I appreciate your interest, Lady Berkeley, and I do so enjoy a visit, but my niece's father has already made the decision. I believe the banns are to be posted any day now."

Justin felt as though someone had kicked him hard in the

THE SQUIRE'S DAUGHTER

stomach. He actually struggled for breath while trying to gather his composure under Aurora's concerned gaze. Finally, he forced himself to speak. "All right," he said softly. "I'm sorry we have troubled you, Miss Butterfield. Lady Berkeley?"

He could see Aurora eyeing him worriedly as she said goodbye to Clare's aunt, and he felt the gentle squeeze of her fingers on his arm when they walked out to the carriage. He ignored both, hardly daring to talk.

"Justin, my boy, are you all right?" Aurora asked.

"Yes," he answered stiffly, although his blood was boiling. He didn't know whom he longed to strangle the most, Farnsworth, that pea-brained aunt or Clare herself. And while he was planning a massacre, he decided to include Fletcher for getting him involved in this little fiasco. He could have been happily getting drunk in Devon when, instead, he was involved up to his neck cloth in Clare Cummings's nuptials. The irony of it all did not strike him as amusing.

"I'm sorry. Truly I am, my dear," Aurora said softly. "I honestly wouldn't wish that Farnsworth on any decent young girl, but perhaps he isn't as bad as the rumors have it."

"He's worse," Justin said, tight-lipped. The thought of his little Clare in the hands of Farnsworth made him forget his irritation at becoming embroiled in her affairs. He saw her in his mind, perpetually a young pixie with limpid hazel eyes, midnight hair and flawless skin.

Unthinking, he reached for the chain around his neck, absently running his fingers over the gold. Little Clare, who lived so wholly in her imagination, in a world peopled with dragons and enchantment, would be broken by a man like Farnsworth.

"Justin?" Lady Berkeley said. "She will be all right."

Justin nodded. Yes, he thought firmly, she will be all right because she is not going to marry Farnsworth. If he had to trot up to Yorkshire and throttle the good squire himself to prevent it, by the devil, he would.

JUSTIN STARTED HAVING MISGIVINGS when the countryside became familiar: green, rolling hills, valleys patterned with low stone walls and a mist that crawled around his feet just to tweak his memory. He had a couple of bottles stashed in his bag, and he resolved that when he finished with his little chore, he'd crack one open and have it emptied by the time he reached The Red Lion at Rillford.

He rode past the fork to Worth Hall without giving it a glance. There were other ghosts there besides Clare's, and she had been the only reason he ever returned. Instead, he rode straight on to the squire's property, halting in the long drive to view Clare's home for the very first time. The neat brick house was more than a cottage, but definitely modest in size, Justin noted, and from the activity around the grounds, it made no apologies for being a working farm.

Justin had talked to the squire once before their final confrontation, when the man had ridden over and made noises about cleaning up the hall, as if it were a blight on the neighborhood. For Clare's sake, Justin had not laughed in his face. He remembered the fellow as being the typical robust, rustic type, far more concerned with his hunting than with raising an ethereal daughter.

Memory had served him well, for Squire Cummings, if he had changed at all, was only rounder of belly and redder of face than the last time they had met. "My lord," the older man said gruffly, his head tipping slightly in acknowledgment. His lips were grimly tightened in a firm line, making his greeting nothing more than the barest of civilities and telling Justin, in no uncertain terms, that the task before him would not be easy.

When the squire spoke again, he asked so many questions about the journey from London that Justin nearly shouted in impatience. He never shouted. This business with Clare, he decided, was driving him mad.

Finally, he was shown into Cummings's study, a tiny, untidy room filled with guns, papers, maps and fishing equipment. Justin nearly sat on a lure. Holding it up and eyeing the barb critically, he assumed it to be an omen of a thorny conversation to come.

The squire heaved his great bulk into a sturdy armchair and gave Justin an appraising look. "So here you are, my lord," he said as he filled a pipe from a jar of tobacco. "I was surprised to get your note. I can't say I'm happy to receive you, but if you are planning to work on that eyesore next door, I'll lend my support."

Justin declined to point out that the alleged eyesore was at least three miles away and tucked into a valley off the road, but he smiled in what he hoped was a neighborly fashion. "I'm sorry if my message misled you, Squire," he said. "But I've come on another matter."

"Oh?" Cummings's wide mouth curved down at the corners and bristly blond-gray brows moved low over his eyes. He did not look pleased.

Gazing with fascination at the squire's ruddy complexion, fair hair and fat lips, Justin decided Clare must take after her mother. He also decided the portent had been correct: things were already not going well. "No. I've come about something else. You see, I'm acquainted with a friend of your daughter."

"Clare?" the squire asked, looking up with a startled expression.

Justin smiled reassuringly and nodded. He could well understand the man's panic after what had gone on before. To be associated with Justin was enough to destroy any young girl's standing, so he quickly distanced himself from Clare, emphasizing instead his connection with her female acquaintances. "Yes, and I promised Prudence and her grandmother, Lady Berkeley," he said, lying smoothly, "that I would speak to you about your daughter's suitor, Mr. Farnsworth."

The squire was positively glaring now, but Justin continued calmly. "As I well know, life in the country can be insulating, and those in the city hear things that one cannot possibly hear when he is away. To be frank, Squire, Mr. Farnsworth is not what you would want for your daughter. He has a reputation for cruel and bizarre behavior."

The squire was turning red. He looked ready to "blow up," as Clare had often described it, and as Justin himself had witnessed before. Justin revised his assessment of the proceedings: events were swiftly moving from bad to worse. Then the squire slammed down his pipe on the desk, sending ashes across the paper, and Justin had the wild notion that the heedless action might send them, and all conversation, up in flames.

"How dare you come down here and disparage a man who has offered for my daughter?" Cummings growled.

"Squire Cummings—" Justin began in his most soothing voice.

"You young scoundrel! With a reputation like yours, you dare come down here and lecture me?"

Justin's anger flared. He might be careless about his rank, but he was not used to being addressed in such a fashion by a country bumpkin. "Yes, I dare," he said evenly, "because people are worried about your daughter. You have no idea what this man is capable of. *I* have no idea what he is capable of! Perhaps my own sordid reputation gives me insight into another's.... I'm here to enlighten you because I know you want to do what's best for your daughter."

"I told you to stay away from her!" Cummings shouted.

"I have, and believe me, I harbor no wish to become the slightest bit involved with you or your daughter," Justin said tersely. "But with no one else to advise you, I felt it my duty—"

"Your duty! You don't know the meaning of the word,

you rakehell! Get out of my house, and stay out. What I do for my daughter is my own business!"

"Then make it your business to know what kind of man you're selling her to!" Justin leapt from his chair, more furious than he had ever been in his life. He was suddenly, keenly frustrated by his blackened reputation, which was not serving him well, and by his idiotic concern for Clare, which had brought him to this impasse. Stepping back, he took a deep breath as the squire watched him warily. "Reconsider, Squire, for her sake."

"I will not," the squire said, raising his fat chin to glare at Justin. "And I fail to see what business it is of yours."

Justin caught the man's eyes and stared into them. They were hazel, too, but that was certainly all of him that was in Clare. I know you, Justin thought grimly as he gazed at Cummings. I know you for the stupid, narrow-minded, greedy rustic you are.

"Then I'll make it my business," Justin said calmly. "I don't know what Farnsworth has promised you, but I can tell you that it's a pittance compared to what I can give you." Justin smiled as he saw the play of emotions on the older man's face. The vivid blotches of anger were replaced by surprise and then an eager pleasantness.

"Just what are you saying, my lord?" the squire asked, showing his teeth.

"I'm saying, Squire," Justin said, "that I can offer you a very healthy settlement, a fat allowance, the consolidation of our adjoining properties and a title for your daughter—if I may have her hand in marriage."

JUSTIN ARRIVED BACK in London with the bottles intact. In far too great a hurry to return, he had never taken the opportunity to drink them. He wanted the banns posted immediately, so Farnsworth would back off, and Clare would be safe. She would be unhappy, he was certain, but safe.

He told himself it was for her own good, but he was

acutely aware that while once he had refused to marry her, and had worked to destroy any desire she had to wed him, now he was forced by circumstance to persuade her to do just that. He felt sick. He reached for a bottle. He put it back. He rubbed his neck.

If Clare could just be made to understand that even an empty marriage was better than life with Farnsworth, Justin thought grimly. She would be angry, yes, but once she realized that she would have her freedom, that he would make no demands of her, she would be relieved.

They would live the life of so many London couples, each going their way, independent of the other. She would never even have to see him after the ceremony, so how could she fault him? Justin closed his eyes against the memory of Clare hurting, her hazel eyes awash with tears, and he poured a drink.

It sat untouched beside him as he tried to compose a note to her. After spending an hour at this unsatisfying chore, he finally just sent round the letter he had carried back from her father, along with his hastily scrawled message begging leave to call upon her at the earliest opportunity to discuss this turn of events.

"TURN OF EVENTS!" Clare's screech brought her Aunt Eugenia running into the front parlor as fast as her age and eyesight permitted.

"My dear, what is it?" Eugenia asked, squinting at her niece.

Clare crumpled up the note and threw it into the fireplace. "Nothing, Aunt," she said, taking a deep breath. "Nothing. I'm sorry to have bothered you."

"Bad news from your father?" Eugenia placed a dainty hand on Clare's arm. "Is he ill?"

"What? Oh, no," Clare said. "He's just lost his mind."

"I beg your pardon?" Poor Eugenia appeared more confused than ever, and Clare took pity on her.

"Oh, it's nothing, really. I'm sorry, Aunt. All my life I thought my father had no imagination, and now..." She snapped her fingers in the air. "Apparently, he has dreamed up some scheme to marry me off to our neighbor." Clare giggled, even though she knew it further bewildered her aunt. She couldn't help it. The whole thing was all too ridiculous.

"Oh, dear," Eugenia said. "Not some village boy, I hope."

Clare burst out laughing at that. "No, no. He's definitely not a village boy. He's no boy," she said softly as her laughter died away. She smiled unhappily. "He's the Marquis of Worthington."

"No! You don't mean it!" Eugenia gasped, dropping onto the settee and flapping her arms about her like a crazed fowl.

"What is it, Aunt? Are you all right? Should I get the hartshorn?" Clare asked as Eugenia struggled with speech.

Finally the lady shook her head vigorously, her hair frizzing wildly about her pale face. "No, no, my dear, but this is too bad, just too bad! Oh, Clare, the man has a dreadful reputation. You simply cannot marry him."

Clare sat down beside her aunt and gently took her hand. "Believe me, Aunt Eugenia, I am not going to marry Justin." If only his name hadn't caught in her throat, she would have sounded totally unaffected. But it did, and Clare fought vainly against the memory. It swelled and coalesced around her until she was back at home....

On that day two years ago, the squire's face had been beet red, and Clare cringed away from him, although he had never before raised a hand to her. He had never seemed to be interested enough in her to bother—until now. And now he looked mad enough to beat her. If he did, Clare decided, she would run away for good. She would run to Justin and never come back.

As if by just thinking about him she had revealed his

presence in her life, Clare heard her father mention Justin's name, and she reeled in dismay. "I've spoken to the marquis," the squire said between gritted teeth, "and you are never, *never,* to see him again. Do you hear me, Clare?"

She felt herself going white, felt the breath leave her. How had he found out? She shook her head, unable to believe that her long, secret friendship had at last been discovered.

"Don't deny it, Clare!" her father warned. "I saw you with my own eyes, riding from the hall—that unholy den of depravity. Has he touched you, Clare? He swore not, but the devil has no honor. The St. Johns have never amounted to anything, and he's the worst of the lot!"

Clare wanted to cover her ears against the lies, but the squire grabbed her chin and looked into her face, his own still flushed with fury. "Well? Answer me, Clare! Has he touched you?"

She wished violently that she could answer in the affirmative, but she only shook her head feebly, tears wetting her lashes. Even though she had come to adore her prince, he still treated her with the fond affection of an elder brother, and the only time he ever touched her was in her dreams.

The squire stared at her for a long minute, then dropped his hand, sighing. "Well, I'm thankful for that, at least. I told him if he had touched you, I'd be back to get a piece of him." He eased himself down into a chair, his fevered flush fading.

"These blackguards...haven't known a decent day's work in their lives, but they think that money and a title give them free rein to terrorize the countryside." The squire was mumbling now, lost in his own musings. Just when Clare thought she might leave without him noticing, he sent her a piercing gaze under bristling brows. "You are sixteen, Clare, and you aren't to be alone with any man, especially not a rakehell like Worthington. Do you understand? If anyone saw you with him, you'd be ruined! No man would ever marry you."

Clare was a bit startled by that pronouncement. Having no thoughts for anyone but Justin, she found the notion of wedding another slightly alarming.

"Justin is not a rakehell," Clare said, finally summoning the strength to defend him. Although she was not certain exactly what the term meant, she suspected it was bad, and Justin, she knew, was not bad.

The squire snorted. "I won't sully your young ears with reports of his misdeeds, but he is a dissolute, unprincipled libertine."

"That's not true!" Clare protested. "Justin has never been anything but the nicest of friends, nothing but a gentleman."

Her father nearly choked on his resurging rage. "A *gentleman* does not entertain innocent young girls alone. A decent man, if caught in such a situation, would offer for the lady, which, by rights, is just what the marquis should have done. Of course, the black-hearted devil would have none of it. He refused to marry you." The squire scowled. "Though if I thought he had touched you, by faith, I would force him at the point of my blade."

Clare felt her already spinning world whirl out of control, and struggled to right herself. "Justin refused to marry me?" she managed to ask.

"Of course. And it's not the first time he's refused to wed a young girl—and that when there was a bit more evidence at hand," the squire said before clearing his throat loudly.

Clare clenched her hands together, rubbing one over the other as she sought to justify her friend's action. Naturally, Justin had been unprepared for the squire's demands and would not be forced into anything. Still, she had always assumed that she would marry her prince someday. Wasn't it her destiny? That's the way all the fairy stories ended—living happily ever after.

"Since he referred to you as a child and said you had only been there a few times, I didn't pursue it. Bloody difficult, anyway," the squire muttered.

Clare looked up, startled by Justin's lie. She had been to the castle many times during the past two years, but perhaps he wanted to save her reputation....

"And since he swore never to see you again," the squire continued, "I will let it go at that, though I still think the devil needs a good thrashing."

Clare felt her father's words descend upon her like a black cloud, blocking out the sun. She was hurt over Justin's refusal to marry her, but that was nothing compared to the thought of never seeing him again. Surely it was a mistake, another little lie just to placate her father, for Justin would never simply abandon her, would he?

"What is it, child?" A soft, feminine voice interrupted Clare's thoughts. Clare flinched, but it was only Aunt Eugenia. Had she sobbed aloud? Oh, go away, stupid memories!

"I guess I don't feel well," Clare said quietly. "I think I'll go lie down. No!" she said suddenly, changing her mind at the thought of closing her eyes and envisioning the past. "Let's go out! Fresh air would be good for me.... Oh, plague the city. I want to go home." Clare heard her voice breaking, and she took a deep breath. Justin was reducing her to a weeping ninny!

"Oh, dear," Aunt Eugenia said, more confused than ever. She patted Clare's hand, then brightened. "A step out might be just the thing. We shall do some shopping, buy some trifles. Then you will feel better."

"Yes, I feel better already. Let's go out." Clare stood up and crumpled her father's letter, which he explicitly had requested Eugenia read, and tossed it into the fireplace after Justin's missive.

Her father could write whatever he wanted, she thought with grim determination, but she was never, ever going to marry Justin St. John. As for Justin, he could wait to discuss this turn of events until the end of time!

CHAPTER THREE

"MY LORD!" Justin tried to ignore the summons and rolled over, but he could not escape the tug on his arm. Finally, he opened his eyes to see Harris, his butler, bending over him impassively.

"What time is it?" Justin grumbled.

"It is ten o'clock, my lord."

Justin groaned and shut his eyes, but Harris did not go away. "What is it?" he finally asked, unmoving. Unless the house was ablaze, he had no intention of leaving his bed this early in the morning.

"I beg your pardon, my lord, but there is a young lady here to see you."

That got Justin's attention. He opened his eyes again to glance at his butler. Harris had seen just about everything in his years of service, so the arrival of a young lady, unescorted, at the unfashionable hour of ten o'clock left him unfazed. His countenance, therefore, revealed nothing. "Who is it?" Justin asked.

"She says her name is Clare Cummings, my lord, and might I add that she is brandishing the morning paper in a most agitated manner."

"Blast." Justin sat up, fully awake in an instant. "She must have seen the announcement of our betrothal." He swung out of bed.

Harris stepped neatly out of the way. "Shall I tell her you'll be down then, my lord?"

"Yes, yes," Justin snapped impatiently, waving the servant away.

"Oh, my lord?" Harris asked from the doorway.

"Yes?"

"You'll be marrying her, then?"

Justin smiled grimly. "Yes. This time, I'm marrying her."

HER BACK WAS TO HIM when he entered the red drawing room, giving Justin a moment to collect himself. He wasn't quite sure what he was expecting. Although he knew she was eighteen, whenever he thought of her he saw a young scamp, dressed in boyish clothes, her dark hair cropped under her ears and her slight frame a little gangly—as though she had not grown into herself.

Yet one glance at her back and Justin could see she was so tall now that the top of her head would probably reach his nose, instead of barely coming to his chest. She would be different, he told himself, and he took a deep breath as he tried to prepare himself for the sight of his Clare as an adult.

It did no good. When she turned around, his breath lodged in his chest, stopping his very heartbeat.

The woman standing before him was definitely no scamp and no pixie, either. Rather, she was an enchantress, tall, elegant, and beautiful—exquisitely beautiful, Justin realized dimly. Her glossy, dark locks had grown. They were piled atop her head in an intricate fashion and topped with a dainty hat. They looked so thick and luxurious that he longed to see them tumble down about her shoulders. Oh, her shoulders, smooth peach curves that were bared by the green gown she wore. And that was not all that was bare....

Justin's gaze traveled lower, to where the fashionable cut of silk revealed a good portion of creamy breasts. Startled, he raised his eyes to her face again. Her skin was still flawless, and the wide hazel eyes, rimmed with thick black lashes, were the same. Or were they? Right now they were flashing with a fire he had never seen in his pixie.

"What do you think to mean by this?" she asked, advancing upon him with the *Morning Post* in hand.

Involuntarily, Justin took a step back. "Clare?" he asked stupidly.

She ignored the whispered question. "Did my father put you up to this?" she demanded, while Justin just stood there, staring.

Her gown was a lovely color, shot with sprigs of darker green that clustered like vines around the bodice. Unfortunately, his eyes seemed drawn, against his will, to that particular bit of fabric. Ashamed, he forced his gaze back to her features, and there it remained, transfixed, until she was but a few inches from him and shouting into his face. Clare never shouted, he thought, dazed.

"Well, Justin?" she asked furiously. "Why?"

When he didn't answer, she struck him across the shoulder with the paper. Justin didn't even feel the edition make contact with his jacket, yet he reached for her arms to prevent her from throttling him. It was a mistake.

Her bare skin felt smooth and warm and alive beneath his fingers and sent heat surging through him as though he had never touched a woman before. And that was not the worst of it. When he looked down at her and saw the gentle curve of her flushed cheeks, and her moist, sweet lips, Justin nearly lost control of himself.

He wanted to pull her close, bend his head and taste her, he realized with dismay. He stood there for a long moment, gripping her arms, while the urge to kiss her struggled against a hearty disgust with himself. Finally, sanity won out, and he released her abruptly.

"I did it to save you from Farnsworth," he blurted out.

Clare felt as if he had struck her. She wasn't quite sure what she had been expecting. She had imagined the paper's announcement was some kind of mistake, and had suspected her father was behind it, perhaps in a misguided attempt to urge Farnsworth to offer for her.

And yet...Clare realized that in her still-childish heart of hearts, she dreamed that her prince had seen the light.... That when he had encountered her the other night, she had finally become a woman in his eyes—maybe even a desirable one. His answer crushed all her foolish fancies in an instant.

"So you are sacrificing yourself on the altar of matrimony for my sake?" Clare asked, her voice thick with sarcasm.

"Yes—no, Clare. I couldn't stand by while you married that man. He's some kind of fiend. I tried to reason with your father, but you know him. He would have none of it." Justin grimaced, acutely aware that he was again putting things badly. What was it about Clare that reduced him to a yammering idiot?

"Spare me your noble attempts at martyrdom, Justin," she said with real venom. Then she threw the folded newspaper at his head. It brushed his ear as it flew past.

"Clare!" Justin was shocked at her behavior. What had happened to the ethereal child who never raised her voice?

"You and Papa can say and do whatever you like," Clare said, her face pink with fury, "but I will never, ever marry you, Justin St. John!" She turned and stalked out of the room.

"Clare, wait!" Justin called after her, but the tall, elegant woman stepped past his butler and out the door.

Justin leaned back against the wall, feeling, oddly enough, as though he had just been run over by a team of horses. He glanced at Harris, who still held the door open, an almost imperceptible smile on his face, and scowled. The day had not arrived when he would go chasing down the street after a woman.

"Well?" Justin asked, eyeing his butler blackly. "What are you waiting for? Close the bloody thing!" Then he turned on his heel and marched back to his study. The devil take the early hour; he needed a drink.

Clare reached the waiting carriage without crying, but once she was shut inside, the tears came in great awful gushes, terrible, wrenching, unladylike sobs that would have horrified her aunt. Justin, she was certain, would have been revolted.

Justin. Try as she might, she could not be rid of him, for the memories were too vivid. And it was no longer the pleasant ones, but the bitter recollection of their last encounter that haunted her....

Although her father had ordered her never to return to the castle, Clare managed to sneak away the following day. Stricken with the fear that Justin had left, she relaxed when she realized he was still in residence. The slim waft of smoke that rose above the castle told her a fireplace was lit, Justin was home and all her fears were for naught.

Her prince had stayed. Clare breathed in deeply with pure happiness, for she knew Justin was not anything like the man her father described. He was warm and wonderful, and he would never give her up, no matter what the squire said.

As always, Clare let herself in through the rear and walked into the back rooms, calling his name. Dead silence met her in the kitchens and the great hall and even in the parlor, until finally she made her way upstairs.

There she found him—in bed with her maid.

Actually, Amanda wasn't her personal maid, but she did do upstairs and downstairs work for them at the cottage, and her wages were paid by the squire. The youngest of Widow Green's daughters, Amanda was a beautiful girl, but the squire, long past being interested in nubile villagers, had never given her a second glance.

Apparently Justin was not so blind, for he seemed all too happy to be entangled with her, and Amanda appeared to be enjoying herself, too—until she saw Clare. Then she squealed and hid under the covers, either ashamed of her nakedness or afraid that Clare would recognize her.

Justin had been drinking, Clare noted, for she could smell it in the air. Since the very first day she had met him, she had never seen him intoxicated, but something must have changed him, changed everything irrevocably. Like an animal sniffing danger, Clare sensed the change and longed to flee from it, yet she could not.

"Clare!" Justin shouted from the bed. Although she wanted to turn and run, she couldn't seem to force her legs to move. "I thought your father told you..." Justin didn't finish, but paused to prod Amanda from underneath the blankets. Obviously, the maid would not budge, for he swore softly and rose himself.

When he climbed from the bed, all smooth skin and lean muscles, Clare got a view of her prince that she had never seen before. She gasped aloud, her eyes wide at the sight of him, stark naked until he wrapped a blanket around his waist. Clare probably would have remained firmly rooted to her spot forever if it had not been for Justin, who grabbed her arm and dragged her from the room.

"Come on, young lady," he said. "This is no place for you." Once in the adjoining room, he shut the door, crossed his arms on his bare chest and glared at her. "I had a unpleasant little chat with your father just a few days ago, and he swore that you would never be coming here again."

Clare felt tears threaten at his cold manner. "But Justin, you know I wouldn't agree to that! And you can't mean to abide by his orders!"

"I do," Justin said. "I had a devil of a time escaping from the encounter unmarried, and I don't intend to have him breathing down my neck again or bringing along a sword to prove his point more forcefully."

Clare stepped back, stunned by his words. It was as if the Justin she knew had disappeared, replaced by this flint-eyed creature who tossed off hurtful remarks as easily as he jumped into bed with strange women. Clare swallowed hard.

"I don't care what Father says. I know you. You're not like he says you are. You're a good person. I know you will never turn your back on me, Justin, because we're… friends," she finished softly, a sob choking her. There was so much more to say, but she couldn't go on.

"Stop it, Clare," Justin said, his voice oddly thick. He turned around, took a deep breath, then faced her again. "We were friends, yes, but now you've grown up. Your father has spoken his piece, and the game is over. You don't belong here, Clare," he said very slowly. "You don't belong with me."

"But, Justin…"

"Can't you see? My God, child, you have only to look about you—at the grounds, at the house, at my life," he said, waving an arm to encompass the bedroom and his near-naked state. "I don't care about anything!"

"I don't believe you," Clare said defiantly, her lips trembling as she held back the tears.

"Believe it," Justin urged softly as he leaned against the doorpost, his face hard as stone. "I don't give a damn about anything, Clare Cummings, and that includes you."

She found her legs then, and ran out of the castle and out of his life—forever, she had sworn. A forever that had lasted until she had read in the *Post* that she was engaged to marry him.

"HE THINKS to wed me!" There was a desperate note in Clare's voice, even as she tried to make light of the situation to her aunt.

"Oh, this is too dreadful, too dreadful," Eugenia squeaked, sinking down onto the settee. "Oh, the scandal of it all! I had no idea he was looking for a wife, but then, as I told your father, I am not clever about these things."

She picked up the offending paper and fanned herself briskly with it.

"I warned you, my dear, that it was all too much for me—the ton and all the gossip surrounding its members. It's just too confusing. There are too many of them, for one thing, and you can never be too sure who is related to whom." Eugenia paused to take a breath, her cheeks pink with the strength of her emotion.

"Aunt Eugenia," Clare said, "this is not your fault. It has nothing to do with you."

Eugenia ignored Clare's words and continued chattering like a wounded magpie. "But I should have known. And that business about Farnsworth! I suppose I should have known that, too.... But Farnsworth, Farley, Farmington," she gasped wretchedly, "oh, who can keep them all straight?"

Clare stopped frowning long enough to look at her aunt, whose squint was made more pronounced by her frustration. "What business about Farnsworth?" Having no intention of marrying anyone, Clare had never given much thought to the man. He seemed pleasant enough, but she had never taken his suit very seriously.

"Oh!" Eugenia's bosom heaved with indignation. "To think that *he* had the audacity to come here and preach to me about you—with the kind of reputation he has! Well," she announced with a huff, "I might not remember the Farnsworth gossip, but I am certainly well aware of the marquis's soiled mantle! Who isn't?"

"What marquis? Justin?"

"Why, Worthington, of course. Naturally, I had to receive him, but I certainly didn't—"

"What are you talking about?" Clare asked impatiently. "Justin was here? When?"

"Why, just the other day," Eugenia answered. "He came here and told me that Farnsworth was an unsuitable match for you! Quite a case of the pot calling the kettle black, I'd say."

Seeing that Eugenia had worked herself into such a state that she was now totally incomprehensible, Clare decided to change tactics. "I'll call for some tea, Aunt, and then we'll sort this out," she said calmly.

After ringing for the refreshments, she sat down cozily beside her aunt and tried to be patient. Once the cups were brought and tea poured, Eugenia was breathing a little easier, and Clare began again. "Now, Aunt, I don't want you to upset yourself. Just tell me calmly what Justin said when he was here."

"Justin? Really, dear, it's quite improper to call a man by his first name," she said, shaking her head, sending wisps of hair flying about her face. "Especially that one. Oh, he is the height of impropriety!"

Clare smiled sweetly. "Yes, Aunt. Now, what did he say?"

"Well, Lady Berkeley was very nice about it. She came with him. I believe she was trying to set me against Farnsworth, too. It was a bit confusing, and *he* stood there the whole time like some great dark hawk."

Clare tried not to smile. "Yes?" she prodded.

"Lady Berkeley says you're a friend of her granddaughter, although which one I'm sure I don't remember. I think she has dozens of them."

Clare thought for a moment, then smiled. "Felicity, but I would hardly call her a friend. We just met."

"Well, they are all lovely girls, I'm sure. I couldn't find any fault with Lady Berkeley, mind you, but *him!*" Eugenia squinted ferociously. "He turned around and glared at me. Just why he is thought so handsome and charming is beyond me.... He even tried to blame me for your betrothal to Farnsworth!"

"My what?" Clare asked.

"Well, I know it wasn't official, but your papa wrote me

that it was all but done, so that's what I told the marquis. He looked as though he were having a collapse, and then rushed out the door with hardly a civil goodbye. He's a very haughty man," Eugenia declared. "Oh, dear, to think of you marrying him!"

Clare sank back against the embroidered cushions, puzzling over the story, especially the notion of Justin appearing upset about her engagement. Her engagement! How could her father plan to marry her off to not one, but two different men, without so much as asking her opinion?

Clare sighed. She had given up on the squire long ago—and on Justin, too, she reminded herself firmly. Whatever was he about? She sat up suddenly. "What did he actually say about Farnsworth?" she asked her aunt.

"Oh, rumors," Eugenia said, waving her hand in dismissal. "Rumors and stories, and I can't remember a one of them."

"Justin told you rumors and stories?"

Eugenia looked thoroughly bewildered as she searched her memory. "Oh, yes, I have it!" she said, proud as a child recalling a snippet of poetry. "He said that the stories he could tell me about Farnsworth would turn my stomach! Can you imagine? Using such language with me! I tell you the man is simply impossible." She clicked her tongue in disgust.

"I must say, my dear," she added, "when your father asked me to present you to society in the hopes of securing a husband of means, I had no idea that you would end up marrying the most notorious rake in all of London!" She paused as if in thought. "Of course, he does have an enormous fortune, that much I do know...."

Clare was no longer listening. She was staring pensively across the room and wondering what would possess Justin to interest himself in her future when he had made it abundantly clear that he cared nothing for her. Clare found it difficult to imagine him calling on Aunt Eugenia simply to say horrible things about Farnsworth. On second thought, hadn't he called the man a fiend this morning? Perhaps she ought to investigate these "rumors and stories" herself.

Whether or not there was something to the gossip, she was not going to marry Justin, Clare resolved grimly. Still, she did not know how she was going to evade the nuptials when both her father and Justin seemed determined to see them occur. She listened absently as Eugenia rattled on about Justin's money, which didn't interest her in the slightest, and tried to think of a means of escape.

"It's obvious that his wealth and title have not aided him in securing a bride, and I'm not surprised," Eugenia fussed. "Why, no decent girl would have him! That is, except you, of course, but no one will think ill of you, I'm sure," she hastened to add. "After all, a girl has a duty to marry advantageously."

Clare smiled slowly. If no decent girl would have him, why should she? Although she couldn't cry off herself, she could put it about town that she was not at all happy with the betrothal. Then perhaps Justin would drop the whole ridiculous thing.

SHE REFUSED to see him. When Justin came to the door, Clare had her servant turn him away. She returned his notes unopened, and peacemaking efforts such as flowers or gifts were sent back with whoever delivered them. Clare did not feel a bit guilty, nor was she troubled any longer by recurring memories. Her revenge, such as it was, tasted sweet.

Of course, she knew that Justin was not sobbing his heart out over her little irritations. Still, she was grateful for the opportunity to annoy him in any way she could, and she had no intention of agreeing to his ridiculous proposal. If she ignored him long enough, Clare assumed, he would lose interest in his noble offer and romp off to one of his estates, where he could bed all the maids without interruption and drink himself to death.

One of his invitations, to go with him to Lady Berkeley's soirée, managed to sneak by her vigilant eye only because it was addressed to her aunt. Eugenia, of course, insisted that it was her duty to attend, and Clare agreed complaisantly, fully intending to become ill at the last minute. Her imaginative mind came up with a more wicked scheme, however, and she decided that she would go, simply to give Justin the cut direct all evening. If the man had a shred of pride left by the end of the night, Clare was certain he would break the engagement.

As she dressed for the soirée, Clare remembered her other reason for attending. She wanted to ask Felicity about the rumors surrounding Farnsworth. It wouldn't hurt to be informed about her former suitor, in case he made a reappearance once Justin was persuaded to drop his claim on her.

Not that she really expected to hear from that quarter again. Clare suspected that Mr. Farnsworth was so angry with the squire for accepting another proposal that he had lost all interest in her. If she had been more aware of the rumors surrounding the man, she might not have dismissed him so casually.

While her aunt stood waiting, Clare took a good look at herself, and for the first time since arriving in London, she assessed her own physical worth. She gazed into the glass and decided, defiantly, that she was pretty.

Maybe she wasn't all the rage this season when delicate blondes were popular, but she wasn't plain, either. Maybe she was too tall, but she had curves in all the right places, didn't she? She wore her best gown, a pale violet-striped overdress that fell past her knees to reveal a deeper purple below. The darker color was echoed in ribbons round the high waist and the neckline accentuated her full breasts.

Clare stood back and frowned. She made a lovely picture, but what did it matter? Whatever she was blessed with, obviously it wasn't enough. London's most notorious rake, who had his way with the town's most beautiful women, wouldn't look twice at her, she thought gloomily. And then she told herself she didn't care.

Still, she jumped at the sound of his arrival, and when he stepped into the parlor, looking breathtakingly dashing in a midnight blue dress coat, a striped waistcoat and a pair of buff pantaloons that hugged his form like a second skin, Clare began to think twice about her plan. It was hard to ignore someone who took your breath away, she noted as she sought to inhale.

Justin and her aunt exchanged but the stiffest of greetings, and Clare realized that only Eugenia's deep sense of duty prevented her from forgoing the soirée. For his part, Justin looked as though he would rather be anywhere else on earth, and Clare was heartened. So far, her scheme was working; Justin was miserable. Now, if she could only keep him that way.

He turned to her, his gaze traveling down her body in a most unsettling fashion, and Clare struggled with her breath again. Oh, dear, perhaps this was a mistake...

"Clare," he said softly, his voice strangely tight. "You look beautiful." She ignored the compliment, which she suspected was part and parcel of Justin the polished flirt, and eyed him as coldly as she could.

"Shall we go?" she asked. Eugenia, who normally would have been shocked by such poor manners, held her tongue, her dislike for the marquis apparently overcoming her usual devotion to proper etiquette.

Seemingly undisturbed by her directness, Justin smiled serenely. "Certainly."

The carriage ride was a disaster, to Clare's delight, with the three of them closeted together in tense silence. She met Justin's efforts to engage her in conversation with terse answers, preferably of one syllable, and she refused to look at him. It was better that way, she discovered; it was hard enough to hear his voice after all these years, without seeing him leaning back but a few feet from her, an errant lock of hair falling over eyes, which glinted darkly in the lamplight.

To Clare's disgruntlement, Eugenia finally took pity on him, her naturally talkative nature overcoming her disapproval of rakes in general and the marquis in particular, and chatted on blithely during the final minutes of the journey. Then, suddenly, they were freed from the closeness of the carriage and thrust into the brightness of Berkeley House, where Clare proposed to ignore her escort in earnest.

It was not as easy as she expected, for when they were announced, Justin took her arm. The warmth of his hand above her glove startled her, and she shook off his grasp. "Don't touch me!" she hissed, glaring at him. Let those who watched think what they liked, Clare decided; she had no intention of allowing his fingers, lean and familiar, to remain at her elbow. They were unsettling, as if they had the ability to reach something deep inside of her, only vaguely remembered.

"For pity's sake, Clare!" she heard him whisper back. Justin could hardly take her arm again without drawing more attention, so he walked along beside her. She could see he was angry. Good, she thought, maybe he was angry enough to cry off.

He wasn't, but he was angry enough to firmly grab hold of her again once they were no longer the center of an audience, and start dragging her across the room.

"Justin St. John, let go of me this instant!" Clare said. She stared up at him in surprise when he didn't, for he had never behaved this way before. Who was this strange man with the steely gaze and grim visage? He was certainly not the friendly, careless Justin she had known.

"Not until I've had a word with you," he answered, his dark eyes flashing.

"Justin, if you don't release me, I swear I'll scream my head off, right here and now," Clare claimed.

Her threat did not appear to alarm him in the slightest,

for his grip did not falter, and his mouth moved into a determined line that she did not recognize. "Fine, Clare. Do so, and ruin yourself," he said disgustedly. "If you think to hurt my name, think again," he added with a hard smile. "It's beyond blackening."

Clare scowled. She was tempted to scream anyway—for all she cared for her reputation—but instead returned his furious stare silently.

"Good," he said. He proceeded to haul her outside.

The scent of roses drifted up to greet them from the gardens of Berkeley House. Neat hedges and perfumed beds lined paths lit by lanterns that cast only a dim glow into the secluded spots where a stone bench, a marble figure or a sparkling fountain was tucked under the trees. It was in one of these darkened places that Justin finally halted.

"Let go of me!" Clare repeated.

"I won't until you spare me a moment's speech," Justin said. "And stop acting so indignant. You brought this upon yourself by refusing to see me, returning my notes and all that other childish nonsense. Now, I'd like you to tell me why everyone is talking about how unhappy you are with the betrothal," he said seriously, still grasping her arm.

Clare felt a certain smug pleasure at the question. "Probably because I *am* unhappy. I have no intention of marrying you, Justin St. John."

"Clare!" Justin, exasperated, sighed and rubbed the back of his neck, giving Clare some small satisfaction. She hoped he had one devil of a headache. "People are talking enough already. Don't add fuel to the flames. By faith, consider your own reputation!"

"I for one don't care what people say," Clare said. She realized that this conversation was getting her nowhere. How could she ignore him when he'd physically towed her out here, and who would see her disdain for him when they were alone?

He sighed. "Clare, marriage to me can hardly be as bad

as you imagine. You will have a title, position and wealth. You can travel, indulge yourself, buy whatever you want. Choose whichever estate you fancy, or take up residence anywhere you like. You won't even have to see me. I'm asking you only to take my name, for your protection.''

The words struck her like a slap in the face, an insult beyond anything she had anticipated. So that was his game: he planned to force her into a loveless union. Was she so repugnant to him that he would not even consider a real union with her, a real life together? Clare felt the thin threads of her control threatening to break.

"Blast you!" she shouted. "I don't want your protection!" She slammed her fist into his chest, where it thudded ineffectually against his lapel.

He grabbed her hand then, his voice low and strained when he spoke. "Let's not make this more difficult than it is already."

Clare fought back the impending tears and lifted her head. "I've got a suggestion," she said evenly. "If you think it's so difficult, why don't you break the engagement?"

"I can't, Clare," he said.

"Don't try to act the noble savior with me," Clare snapped.

"I know it seems a bit out of character, but don't deny me the one benevolent inclination I have ever had," Justin answered, bitterness creeping into his tone.

Good! She had struck home with that barb, and she decided to pursue it further. "I do deny it," she said. "But if you feel that strongly, Justin, become a missionary or join a monastery! Oh, I suppose it's much too late for that," she added, her voice heavy with sarcasm. "Then just go spread your newfound philanthropy somewhere else, on someone else—anyone else." Her words got a reaction, though not the one she had hoped. Instead of stalking off in a rage, Justin reached out to grasp her other arm and pull her to him, so roughly that she gasped.

"Oof!" Clare said dazedly. She looked up, startled, into his face, and saw a wild look in his eye. She realized that she must have truly enraged him. Before she could imagine what the consequences might be, Justin bent his head and put his mouth on hers.

She was held so tightly against him that she could barely breathe, and his lips were hard and ruthless upon her own—all in all, not what she had envisioned for her first kiss. But then his grip loosened—allowing her to take in air once more—and his mouth moved against hers softly, catching first her upper lip and then her lower in a sweet rhythm that set her heartbeat racing.

Just as Clare decided that this tender play was the most wonderful feeling she could ever experience, Justin's tongue traced her lip and brushed against her teeth, seeking entrance. Confused, she opened her mouth, and in it swept, sending sharp, breath-robbing sensations through her.

Oh my, oh my, oh my, Clare thought dimly. She had so often dreamed of kissing him, yet her dreams could not even begin to touch the head-spinning reality. She heard Justin make a sound deep in his throat that sent another wild quiver shooting through her. Then he released her, so abruptly that she nearly fell. She stepped backward, grateful to feel the steadying support of a marble bench against her legs.

The cool evening breeze chased away the lingering warmth of his body and brought her back to her senses. The giddy excitement she had known in his arms was replaced by a fearful suspicion that grew with the length of the silence that stretched between them. When she could speak, she all but threw her words in his face.

"If you think plying me with kisses will change my mind, you are more conceited than even I imagined!" Clare said with as much contempt as she could muster. "Give it up, Justin, for I am immune to your infamous charms."

Justin made no response, but whirled on his heel and stalked off—a reaction for which Clare was immensely grateful. As soon as his back was turned, she dizzily sank down to the bench, her weak knees no longer able to support her. Gingerly, she raised a finger to trembling lips that gave lie to her words.

CHAPTER FOUR

CLARE TOOK one deep breath after another, and tried to forget the feel of Justin's lips against her own. Of all the low, underhanded, cruel tricks! She expected little enough from Justin, but she'd never guessed he would try to seduce her simply to gain her hand. Considering his reputation, she should have anticipated it, Clare thought bitterly, though why he was so determined to marry her was still a mystery.

Farnsworth, indeed! Clare stood up, gathering her wits about her and pushing Justin's kisses firmly from her mind. She did not believe for one minute that his fierce desire to wed her stemmed from concern for her. In fact, she nearly laughed aloud at the notion.

Whatever his reasons, Justin had made it clear that her efforts to see him embarrassed, miserable or shunned were not going to change his mind. The realization was disappointing, yet she felt some measure of relief that she no longer need remain at this silly soirée, waiting for him to try some new, shabby deception. Picking her way back into the house, Clare decided on an abrupt exit, while she still had her dignity. She went in search of her aunt.

Before she could find Eugenia, however, she was snared by Lady Crawley, with whom she was only slightly acquainted. A snide young widow, Lady Crawley took the opportunity to bait her about her betrothal. "Oh, my dear girl, I couldn't quite believe it when I heard! You and Worthington!" she said, moving her fan languidly. "An odd pairing, that is it not?"

"One must abide by one's family's wishes," Clare said tersely.

"Oh, I see! Not looking forward to a night in his arms, are you? Good for you. I fear that females these days are all too eager for a romp in Worthington's bed. Of course, his skills in that quarter are...legendary, shall we say?"

Clare felt herself blush crimson, which only encouraged Lady Crawley to further nastiness.

"But to be forced into marrying him, that is another situation entirely, isn't it? Why, it's simply dreadful! A young innocent like yourself thrust into a world of depravity." Lady Crawley made a show of shuddering, then smirked.

"I would hardly call Justin depraved," Clare said, her eyes darting around the room, searching for an excuse to depart from Lady Crawley's company.

"Oh, really?" the widow asked. "Then you must sanction his activities." She leaned forward to whisper behind her fan. "Drunken orgies at some old castle, I hear. Is it true?"

Clare, a bit startled by the words, looked wide-eyed at Lady Crawley, who smiled smugly. Realizing she was being teased in a decidedly unpleasant fashion, Clare sent her companion a scathing glance. "Drunken orgies? Really, Lady Crawley, you seem so knowledgeable, one would think you speak from experience."

The grin promptly left Lady Crawley's face.

"But as one of the few women whom Justin has not seen fit to pursue, you are unlikely to know what you're talking about, are you?" Clare asked, amused by her companion's speechless fury. "In the future, please save your gossip for someone who is interested. Justin suits me perfectly just the way he is."

Leaving the woman to fume silently, she glided serenely away. It wasn't until she was nearly across the room that she stopped dead, suddenly aware of what she had just said. Instead of appearing unhappy, she had managed to tell one of the ton's most malicious gossips that she was pleased as punch with Justin.

Clare felt like beating her head against the wall, and she might well have done so if Lady Berkeley had not waylaid her. Taking both of Clare's hands in a friendly greeting that prevented her escape, her hostess smiled graciously. "Congratulations upon your engagement," she said.

"It is none of my doing, my lady," Clare said, determined to set at least one person to rights about her betrothal.

Lady Berkeley, nearly as tall as Clare and looking very elegant in a claret gown that matched the handsome ruby necklace she wore, nodded knowingly. "Unhappy about his reputation, are you?" she asked. "Don't give it another thought, my child. Haven't you heard the old adage? Reformed rakes make the best husbands."

Clare was not comforted. "But he doesn't want to reform," she protested. "He doesn't even want to be my husband," she added without thinking.

"Nonsense, child," Lady Berkeley said, giving her a pat. "Justin has never wanted anything more." Her gray eyes sparkled with such warm reassurance that Clare was tempted, for a moment, to believe her. Dismayed, She opened her mouth to question her hostess more closely, but the lady waved over a young girl with fashionable blond ringlets.

"Prudence! Have they laid out the buffet yet?" When the girl shook her head firmly, Lady Berkeley sighed. "The household has been directionless since Mrs. Fields left. Prudence, here is your friend, Clare. You two must entertain each other while I make sure we have some food." Before Clare could mention that she was not acquainted with the young lady beside her, Lady Berkeley was gone, moving gracefully among her guests.

Prudence, another of Lady Berkeley's granddaughters, took the mistaken identity with good grace; apparently she was quite used to being confused with her sisters. A friendly girl, she insisted upon helping Clare find Eugenia, so they set off together through the crowd.

They were delayed by the appearance of Fletcher Mayefield, a highly eligible bachelor with whom Prudence was enthralled. As soon as Prudence caught sight of him, she kept up a continuing stream of whispers about his appearance, his address and his wealth, which failed to impress Clare one whit. When he approached them, Clare spared him little attention; her only concern was that Prudence might swoon. She hoped that Mr. Mayefield would be prepared to catch her.

"Miss Shaw." His address and smile sent Prudence into a fluttering fit behind her fan. Clare glanced up at the tall, blond man and wondered what the fuss was about. He had that air of dissipation she did not like, but which she had noticed in so many of the men in London, including Justin. She suspected most of these town fellows could use a healthy dose of fresh air and exercise in their indolent, perfumed lives.

His manners smooth and practiced, he tilted his head toward Prudence as though she were the only woman in the room. Despite his charming ways, Mr. Mayefield seemed a bit detached. Watching him closely, Clare realized that his fine smile did not quite reach his eyes—until he turned to her, and then they sparked with interest.

They were emerald-green, shining like the deep color of a multifaceted gem, and Clare caught herself staring. Then she smiled in gracious surrender, for it appeared that even she was not unaffected by Mr. Mayefield.

"Miss Cummings," he said, bending low over her hand. "You must pardon my boldness, but even though we haven't been introduced, I feel that I know you. I'm a friend of your future husband." He paused, awaiting her response, and seemed a bit taken aback when Clare looked at him blankly. "Worthington?" he prodded, his eyebrows raised.

Clare gave him a sickly smile. "Yes, of course. Where

is...his lordship?" she asked, realizing that in all the years she had known Justin, she had never once addressed him properly.

"Oh, he's here somewhere," Fletcher said carelessly. "The devil told me you weren't coming. How like him to try to keep such a beautiful woman all to himself."

Assuming that Mr. Mayefield was teasing, Clare smiled nervously at the compliment. She had not mastered the arts of light banter and flirtation so practiced by the ton, and the knowledge that Justin spoke of her to his friends made her stomach flutter. She felt his marriage proposal tightening about her like a noose.

Mr. Mayefield turned back to Prudence, his easy grin gently apologetic. "You will excuse me, Miss Shaw, if I steal her away, won't you? I do so want to get to know the lady who won Justin." He held out an arm to a startled Clare, who wanted no part of his attentions. She saw the disappointment Prudence tried valiantly to hide, and demurred softly.

"I'm afraid it is I who must beg your leave," Clare said. "Why don't you two have a nice chat?" Although she won a smile of thanks from her new friend, Mr. Mayefield was not so pleased. His eyebrows rose in wry annoyance, forcing Clare to choke back a chuckle. The man would never want to see her again, but that was just as well; she had no intention of ever moving in Justin's circles.

Leaving the two of them together, Clare silently hoped Mr. Mayefield would be gracious enough to stay with Prudence awhile, no matter what his feelings. Although she had planned to leave the soirée, her meeting with Prudence had reminded her that she wanted to talk with Felicity about Mr. Farnsworth.

Clare decided to risk searching the card room, in the hope of seeing Felicity—and not Justin—but she had not gone very far when a servant appeared at her elbow.

"Excuse me, Miss Cummings?" the man said. "Your aunt asked me to fetch you."

"What is it?" Clare asked, her search immediately forgotten by concern for Eugenia. "Is she ill?"

"I don't know, miss, but she wanted me to take you out to the carriage straightaway."

"Oh, dear," Clare said. "She must have one of her headaches." Eugenia's headaches, though infrequent, were severe, and she liked Clare to rub her temples with lavender water when they occurred. Without a second thought, Clare followed the waiting man outside, where they were met by another servant.

"Miss Butterfield went on ahead," the second man told them. "She said for you to follow her on home, miss."

"All right," Clare said. Suppressing a stab of annoyance that her aunt had not waited for her, Clare turned back to the house servant. "Please inform Lord Worthington that we have gone home," she said tersely. At the man's nod, she let him help her into the carriage, then leaned back against the seat, sighing over her aunt's incomprehensible behavior.

Clare had not met her aunt until after the occasion of her eighteenth birthday, when the squire had taken a good look at her and announced that, although he was deuced as to how it had happened, she had turned out middling pretty. He had gone on to swear that she ought to "fetch a nice purse in London if we can figure out a way to present you."

The solution was her Aunt Eugenia, who, albeit living on the extreme fringes of society, was nonetheless prevailed upon to do her duty by her niece. So Clare had been sent off to town with enough money from her father to purchase "some new finery so as to appear to her best advantage" and instructions from him to keep her "willful streak" to herself when dealing with the dandies. Clare found herself thrust into a London season, attending parties in the evenings and walking or making calls during the afternoons.

THE SQUIRE'S DAUGHTER

Her initial excitement faded soon after she'd taken in all the sights, and her life, as orchestrated by Eugenia, became a boring routine. The fancy balls revealed themselves to be deadly dull "squeezes," and whatever hidden hopes she might have harbored for finding romance were dashed by the realization that as a penniless daughter of a rural squire, Clare had very little to offer in a marriage market bursting with beauties of title, money, consequence or connections.

Then, just as she was sinking into ennui, Justin had appeared to turn her world upside down again. She had no interest in renewing their acquaintance, and she knew, from Justin's own words, that he did not care about her. And that was what made this whole engagement so utterly ridiculous.

What was his game? Clare decided that he must truly think her green to swallow his humbug, until she was struck with an abrupt realization. She *was* still green—green as a peasant girl—for why else would she have gotten into this coach?

With a sinking heart, Clare peeked out the window and saw the town going by at quite a pace. Although she had been lost in thought, she knew that her vehicle had been traveling long enough to reach the town house twice over. Had the driver simply received the wrong directions in the rush, she wondered hopefully, or had she fallen prey to the city's sinister element?

Kidnapped. The word formed soundlessly on her lips, and Clare's vivid imagination immediately conjured up a vision of being sold into white slavery to some eastern potentate. Or perhaps her destination was a London brothel, or a filthy waterfront prison where horrible things occurred! Clare was not exactly sure of the details, but according to the village women's whispered warnings, those who strayed from home were often better off dead.

In Yorkshire, where she could ride and shoot—as well as a man, thanks to a father who had treated her as male for most of her life—Clare had never given much heed to such cautionary tales, but here in London, a city rife with crime and filth, they made her stomach twist into knots.

Clare told herself to calm down and investigate the situation before jumping to conclusions. She took a deep breath, leaned up and knocked loudly on the box above in a determined fashion. There was no answer. Perhaps the driver hadn't heard her, she thought with a touch of desperation, and she banged louder. When she still received no response, Clare stuck her head out the window. With a gasp of surprise, she realized they were leaving London.

"Stop this coach at once!" she shrieked. She banged her hand against the smooth surface and shouted until she was hoarse. If the driver heard her, he made no sign. The coach did not slow down; instead, it traveled faster as they hit the open road.

Clare sank back into her seat, fear and frustration making her hands tremble. She could, of course, try to leap from the moving vehicle, but even if she were lucky enough to escape injury, her abductors could quite easily retrieve her. She leaned her head back with a sigh. She had no gun, no weapon of any kind, not even the point of a parasol with which to defend herself. Her only hope was to flee the moment the conveyance slowed, and disappear into the darkness before she could be discovered.

CLARE AWOKE SLOWLY as the motion of the coach ceased, her cheek warmed by a patch of sunlight. Stiff and aching, she stretched herself warily as she opened her eyes, coming alert in an instant. She had slept the night through, and the carriage was stopped! Cursing herself for her lack of attention, Clare looked out the window. She saw a small, rustic inn, and although no people were in view, she heard voices. Jolted when the vehicle made a sudden lurch, she realized they must be changing horses.

It was morning, which meant London was miles and long hours behind her. Her heart sank at the thought. Yet at least they were somewhere. An inn meant people—perhaps someone who might help her get back to the city—so she opened the door as stealthily as possible and stepped down. As soon as her toe touched ground, a short, stocky man moved in front of her.

Before she could open her mouth, he thrust a basket into her hands. Clare gazed down stupidly at a brightly colored napkin laid across hot rolls, which steamed in the early morning coolness. Annoyed to discover that she was hungry despite her predicament, she ignored the growling of her empty stomach.

"I demand that you move out of my path at once," she said, pushing the basket back at him.

"Sorry, miss, but we've orders to take you to Gretna Green."

"Gretna Green?" Clare stood frozen, certain she must have misunderstood. A prison, a ship, a brothel—all those sordid destinations had crossed her mind, but Gretna Green?

"Yes, miss," he said with a broad grin.

Just across the Scottish border, Gretna Green was famous for providing quick and legal marriages for those who did not have parental leave to wed. Heiresses were often cajoled, seduced or downright forced into such unions, but Clare couldn't imagine why anyone would take *her* there.

She had gotten into the wrong vehicle. This was all Aunt Eugenia's fault, she thought, her temper snapping. Obviously, the carriage her aunt had countermanded in her usual confusion had already been pressed into service. Clare had been mistaken for the bride-to-be...but where was the groom?

"There's been a mistake," she said. "This is not my coach, and I am not going to Gretna Green. Now I suggest you step out of my way before I call the authorities." She started to move around him, but he closed the space. She dodged; he dodged. Grinning, he seemed to be enjoying the game. Clare changed tactics. Standing stock-still, she screamed as loudly as she could.

The sound was cut off almost as soon as it began by the fellow's hand closing over her mouth. He picked her up neatly and tucked her into the coach as though she were light as a feather. "Off we go, miss," he said with a smile. Then he closed the door.

The coach pitched forward, and Clare threw herself at the door, where she pushed and worked vainly at the latch. The horses were moving at a good clip, leaving the inn behind, when she leaned out and yelled for help. It did no good. The only response was the friendly wave of a stable boy disappearing into the distance. Clare leaned back against the seat and seethed with frustration.

Gretna Green, of all places! She smiled grimly, imagining the look of surprise on the bridegroom's face when he discovered his bride missing and an unknown woman in her place. He would be shocked, but Clare would be free to return to London. Unfortunately, she had an unchaperoned night to account for, which, through no fault of her own, might ruin her.

Clare sighed. It was better than being sold into white slavery. Yet a nagging uneasiness stole over her. The marked absence of the bridegroom bothered her. And what kind of wedding party forcibly restrained the bride in her coach? Such characters might not be amused to find they had the wrong lady, she realized.

She pushed the thoughts aside. They would hardly murder her in cold blood, and even if they dumped her by the side of the road, it would be a great deal better than being abducted. She glanced down at the basket that the man had thrust into the coach with her, and the smell of breakfast made her stomach rumble anew. At least they were keeping her fed, she thought dismally.

Clare was halfway through a tender roll when she thought of her aunt. Eugenia would be frantic! A warm piece of the sweet bread dropped from her fingers at her mental picture of the lady, undoubtedly more bewildered than ever by her disappearance. How long would Eugenia wait for her before becoming worried? Clare imagined her aunt lying on her bed, waiting for lavender-scented fingers to rub her brow and, later falling asleep. She groaned as she realized that her disappearance might go undetected until Eugenia rose in the morning.

Justin! Surely he would notice her missing.... Clare dismissed the idea as soon as it formed. She had left Justin among friends at the soirée, where he had undoubtedly drunk and gambled and flirted until the morning hours. He would think her early departure simply another example of her angry contempt for him.

An odd sadness swelled within her as she saw Justin in her mind, and she wished she had been kinder in her dealings with him of late. She suppressed the vague hope that he would somehow come to rescue her; Justin had long ago thrown off the mantle of knight errant that she had tried to thrust upon him.

And yet, didn't he claim he was going to save her from Farnsworth? Clare grew suddenly cold, her fingers closing over the forgotten roll and crumbling it in her lap. Farnsworth. The name lodged in her brain, raising an ugly suspicion that refused to be vanquished.

I could tell you stories that would make your stomach turn. Justin's words flashed by with a sudden, wild lucidity. Farnsworth. No, Clare told herself, no man could be so enamored of her as to thwart a betrothal to a marquis. Yet Clare realized with a certain sickening feeling that she had made it known that she was unhappy with her engagement to Justin. If Mr. Farnsworth believed the gossip, he might think her grateful for an alternative....

Closing her eyes, Clare tried to remember all she could of Mr. Farnsworth, but it was precious little. He was of average build, average height, and had sandy blond hair and blue eyes. He had always seemed polite and rather bland, and she could not imagine him kidnapping anyone—let alone a penniless nobody like herself.

Rumors and stories. What rumors and stories? she wanted to scream. She had suspected Justin was stuffing her full of nonsense, but what if he were not? Uneasiness settled over her like a funeral pall.

He's some kind of fiend, Clare heard Justin telling her, and fear, plain and simple, sent little shivers down her arms, raising bumps along her skin. What if this Farnsworth had taken it into his fiendish head to elope with her? Surely he couldn't force her to marry him in front of a clergyman and witnesses, could he? Clare felt her stomach twist into knots.

She would reason with him first, Clare finally decided. No matter what odd gossip was flying around about him, Mr. Farnsworth had always seemed a gentleman to her, and if he were behind this abduction, then she would try to talk him out of it. The plan calmed her racing heart, and Clare settled back in her seat, her anxiety eased somewhat. If she couldn't reason with him, then she would steal the nearest horse and take off into the hills, finding her way back to the main road eventually.

Since that option was not very attractive, Clare hoped that she could prevail upon him to simply take her back to the city. Her reputation would be ruined, but she could go home to Yorkshire without marrying anyone. Gathering some comfort from that notion, she turned to her breakfast again.

AN INTERMINABLY LONG DAY in the coach had driven most of Clare's fears away, but added to her frustration. After more vain attempts to stop the vehicle, she had shouted a string of her father's curses to the wind. Trying to use a chamber pot in a moving carriage did nothing to improve her frame of mind, and she tossed the contents out the window, sincerely hoping they would land in someone's face.

THE SQUIRE'S DAUGHTER

By the time darkness settled upon the countryside, she was in no mood to reason with anyone.

When the carriage stopped, she waited silently for her guard to open the door, fully intending to kick him in the teeth. Her plan changed when she faced, instead, a young postboy who helped her down solicitously. She made her first bid for freedom. "I'm afraid there has been a mistake," Clare told him firmly. "I have no desire to go to Gretna Green, and I insist you return me to London immediately."

The boy gave her a wink and a grin, as if he didn't believe a word, and vanished into the darkness behind the carriage. They had drawn up before an inn, whose welcoming lights promised people inside, and this time Clare was not going to let anyone force her back into her traveling prison.

Glancing back at the dreaded conveyance, she saw a figure drop down from the driver's box, and she felt fear return, working a knot into her belly. Even in the darkness, Clare could tell the man was too tall to be her former guard. Trying to calm her racing heart, Clare turned her back on him and hurried toward the inn.

She did not get far before a hand on her arm stayed her steps. Anger, despair and pure fright washed over her. She had meant to reason with her kidnapper, but now that the time had come, Clare found herself unable even to speak. Her tongue stuck uselessly to the roof of her mouth and her blood pounded in her ears as Clare turned slowly to face her abductor.

CHAPTER FIVE

CLARE TURNED in trepidation, and what she saw stunned her so forcefully that she nearly fell to her knees.

"Justin St. John, you bastard!" She swung her reticule at his head as hard as she could. The bag, which carried precious little weight, fell away without bruising him in the slightest, and Clare wished she had had the opportunity to fill it with rocks. Despite its negligible effect, she swung it again and again, while Justin held up an arm to protect himself from the rapid blows.

"Clare, what the devil?"

"How dare you?" she said, seething with anger. Dropping the reticule to her side, she attacked him with her fists, pummeling the soft surface of his elegant velvet jacket until tears formed behind her eyes. "Do you have any idea how terrified I've been, locked in that coach?" Seeing genuine surprise on his face, she finally stopped hitting him. "Well?" she asked, a bit more calmly. "Well?"

"I had some things to take care of before I joined you, and when I finally caught up on horseback midday, I saw no reason to spend the afternoon arguing with you in the coach," Justin explained tersely. Then he eyed her curiously. "You were frightened of me?"

"Of course not!" Clare said. "I thought...how was I to know it was you?" she whispered angrily.

"Who in blazes would be taking to Gretna Green if not me?" he asked, frowning.

Feeling her spirits lift slightly at the question, Clare thrust her chin up and lied brazenly. "Any number of people. Believe it or not, Justin St. John, I am considered attractive by some members of the male population!" When Justin stared at her stupidly, Clare took his response as disbelief. She longed to slap his handsome face, and might have done it, too, but he grimaced and grabbed her by the arm.

"Come on, let's get some supper," he said, dragging her into the inn.

The trip was going to be worse than he expected. And he had expected it to be pretty bad. Impatient with her refusal to see him, and anticipating no end to the deadlock, Justin had taken the bold step of planning her abduction, even though he knew Clare would not like it. Although he'd nearly abandoned the plan when she joined him for the soirée, her reckless behavior at Lady Berkeley's party had immediately changed his mind.

His own reckless behavior, he admitted, had also influenced his decision, for Justin cringed as he remembered the last few minutes they had spent together in the gardens of Berkeley House. He felt like a base beast for kissing Clare. It was not at all what he had intended, but there in the moonlight she had looked so precious, like a pure, radiant diamond....

Justin dropped that line of thought. Although there was no excuse for his actions, they confirmed his opinion that the sooner this wedding took place, the better for all concerned. Once Clare had his name, he planned to remove himself from her vicinity so that he would no longer be tempted by familiar rosebud lips or her womanly face and form.

An elopement would cause gossip, to be sure, but he preferred it to a protracted engagement consisting of scenes like the one at Berkeley House. Left to her own devices, Clare would probably ruin her reputation just to spite him, Justin thought. She had no idea of the ramifications of her rash conduct, or of what had awaited her with Farnsworth.

When they were married, he told himself, Farnsworth wouldn't dare seek her out, and that, he knew, was the most important thing. She might be unhappy, but she would be safe. And she could go her own way, while he... Well, he could return to his old life without the increasingly annoying complication that was Clare.

Justin glanced around the common area, where a few small groups of diners were gathered at the tables. Although the place was relatively quiet, he bespoke a private room, for he suspected that this unpredictable, adult Clare might rouse herself into a new fury and either start shouting or pounding him with something. Either way, he didn't care for an audience.

Justin glanced at her, his gaze taking in the fine sheen of her dark hair, her flushed cheeks and the firm set of her dainty mouth. She did not look at all pleased, but he would rather see her angry than tearful. If she started crying, God help him, he didn't know what he would do. He needed a drink, he thought grimly, but then decided against it, for he would have to keep his wits about him on this trip.

"Justin, is that you?" a voice called sweetly. What the devil else could go wrong, he wondered as he turned around. The answer came to him in the person of Marie Summerville, one of his former lovers, who was approaching from across the room.

Marie stepped toward them, her auburn hair gleaming, her red lips curved in a seductive smile, and she placed her bejeweled fingers familiarly on his arm. "Why, Justin, what are you doing this far north?"

"Marie, you look lovely, as always," he said, gently taking her hand and removing it from his arm. Then he nodded towards Clare. "Marie Summerville, I would like you to meet Clare Cummings, my betrothed."

Marie couldn't have looked more startled if he'd said he had joined the Scottish hussars. Her violet eyes grew wide and her red mouth slack, but she recovered herself nicely.

"Justin, you scoundrel, you're off to Gretna!" she said gleefully.

Then she turned her attention to Clare, and Justin could see each woman taking the other's measure. Marie was obviously wondering what Clare possessed that all his other amours had lacked, while Clare...God only knew what she was thinking.

"My dear child," Marie said, "how in heaven's name did you manage to snare this one?" She grinned at Clare's weak smile. "In case you didn't know, there are at least fifty women in London who would love to take your place!"

Justin could anticipate several snappy retorts that Clare wouldn't hesitate to make, and he maneuvered himself gently between the ladies. "You'll have to excuse us, Marie, we are dead on our feet from the journey." He pushed his sputtering bride-to-be toward the private dining room and nodded at Marie over his shoulder.

"I'll let you go only if you promise to visit me and give me all the details," Marie said as they moved away. "Clare, I want to hear all about the wedding!"

Taking a seat at the table, Clare looked decidedly disgruntled. Justin couldn't help smiling at her. She was so beautiful, even after the long trip, that she put the renowned Summerville in the shade. It amazed him, really, how she could look so pure and piercingly lovely at this late hour.

"Take that grin off your face, Justin St. John. I have not agreed to marry you!" she said, scowling at him. "What possessed you to abduct me?"

Justin's grin grew wider, his brown hair falling into his eyes, and Clare could see how the female population, or at least fifty London ladies, found him irresistible. She told herself she was immune to his charms.

"It seemed like a good idea at the time," he answered, shrugging carelessly. "You wouldn't see me, and I wanted to make sure the ceremony took place as quickly as possible."

"To save me from Farnsworth," Clare added snidely.

"To save you from Farnsworth," Justin agreed.

Clare felt sick and tired, worn out from worry and the jostling carriage ride. She no longer cared about the Farnsworth stories. In fact, she heartily wished she would never hear the name again. When the food came, she ate in silence. Although she felt Justin's dark eyes upon her, she ignored him, and he said nothing.

After supper, she excused herself to freshen up, then returned to the common area. Seated at a table with an elderly lady and gentleman was Miss Summerville, who raised a wineglass in salute and then waved at her coyly. Clare smiled thinly. At least Justin wasn't drinking, she thought gratefully as she passed by the group.

He was waiting near the door to their supper room, looking tall and handsome, his wide shoulders filling out his jacket to perfection, his thighs still tightly encased in the buff doeskin that he'd worn to the soirée. Would she ever get used to seeing him this close again, after all these years—after everything? Just the sight of him brought on a mixture of pleasure and pain. How could she possibly marry him?

She couldn't. Clare had known it all along, of course, ever since the banns were posted, and nothing had changed since then. Although unsure of the reasons behind Justin's proposal, she was certain of one thing: she could not bear being locked into a loveless marriage with the only man she had ever loved.

Taking a deep breath, Clare walked over to him, determined to end the charade once and for all. When he turned to her, the dark thatch of straight hair fell into his eyes, and she nearly reached up to smooth it back into place. Angry with herself for harboring such a desire, she snapped, "Justin St. John, you can turn around and take me back to London this minute."

He did not look at all surprised or hurt, but simply exasperated. "Blast it, Clare, why couldn't we have discussed this privately?" he asked, rolling his eyes heavenward.

Clare felt like screaming. She wanted to slap him or conk him with a nearby bottle—anything to jar him out of his casual manner until he felt something, some semblance of the emotional turmoil that raged within her. But then, he didn't care about anything, did he? Not even whom he wed, apparently. "I mean it!" she warned.

"Your reputation is so besmirched now, you have to marry me, Clare!" he whispered.

"I don't have to marry you!" she denied loudly, and Justin decided the evening had reached a new low. A glance around the room told him they had everyone's attention, including the man who had just entered and who stood by the door looking smug.

"You certainly do not have to marry him, Miss Cummings," the man said, and Justin amended his assessment. The evening was descending into farce, resembling one of those badly acted productions in the seedier sections of London. He could tell that most of their audience, including Marie, was eagerly awaiting the next act of this gratuitous entertainment.

"Mr. Farnsworth!" Clare said in surprise, stepping toward the door.

Justin gave a sigh of disgust, expecting the fellow to any minute now brandish a sword or start beating his breast. Oh, the drama of it all! How in God's name had he ended up in this situation? He was bone tired from riding all night and day—too tired to take to this impromptu stage. The only thing that gave him comfort was the idea that when it was all over, he would throttle Clare, whom he held responsible for the whole, ludicrous mess.

"Miss Cummings." Farnsworth bowed elegantly. "When your aunt discovered you missing, she seemed to feel you might be in some jeopardy." His thin smile was nearly a smirk, and Justin longed to wipe it from his face.

Along with renewed desire to strangle the aunt for sending Farnsworth, of all people, Justin felt a surge of animosity toward Fletcher, who had been assigned the sole task of keeping the old lady busy. Knowing Fletcher, the careless, irresponsible bachelor probably had run off with some delectable young thing, forgetting all about aiding his friend's elopement.

"I immediately suspected that you might be found in this direction, and luckily, I was able to cover the ground quickly on horseback," Farnsworth said. "I am at your service."

"She doesn't need your service," Justin snapped. "She's marrying me."

"I believe it is customary to let the lady decide," Farnsworth said smoothly. "I'm just offering her a choice, in case she feels *constrained* to do something she would rather not."

Farnsworth moved closer, so that Clare stood an equal distance between them.

"How can the lady make an informed decision unless she knows more about you, Farnsworth?" Justin asked. "Or have you given up your bizarre tastes? I was up to Eton after you, and they still told stories of your brutal antics—the animals you mutilated for amusement, for example."

"Ha!" Farnsworth said, waving a hand in dismissal. "Schoolboy stories. I would have thought you a little more adult, my lord, than to believe in that nonsense."

"But there's more. Shall I give her the details?" Justin asked grimly.

Watching the two men as if she were part of a tableau, Clare saw sparks fly from their eyes, and she noticed a muscle move in Justin's jaw. So he was alive, she marveled. Farnsworth had shaken him out of his complacency and into a full battle stance. She wondered if an old quarrel existed between them, for she had never seen Justin so angry, never realized he could contain so much rage underneath that negligent exterior. *He cared about something.*

"Say what you want, Worthington," Farnsworth said scornfully. "It's all crude innuendo. My name has never been attached to scandal...unlike yours, my lord." He spoke the address like an insult, then smiled slyly. "How old were you when you killed that girl? Oh, I'm sorry, she fell, didn't she? Or at least that's what the official version was. The lovely young thing dropped from the battlements of that crumbling relic you call a hall and drowned in the moat." He paused for effect before uttering the last, damning slur. "Carrying your child, too, wasn't she?"

Clare heard Marie's gasp, but her eyes were on Justin. She saw the color leave his face and the muscle in his jaw twitch violently, and without even thinking, she walked over to stand beside him. Silently, she took his hand in hers. The long, slim fingers felt strange, yet familiar, in her grasp. Clare squeezed them tightly, in just the way Justin had reassured her when she was young.

Then she looked at Farnsworth, who waited expectantly, like a dog that has scented blood, and she was sickened. He had dropped his blandness, replacing it with something disquieting. Although he had cast himself in the role of rescuer, Clare found nothing of the hero in him. Perhaps it was his eagerness, his obvious pleasure in slandering Justin, or maybe it was the startling change in him. She had to wonder what he was really like, when he had hidden so much of himself from her. Then Clare decided just what it was that bothered her: it was his eyes. Something in the pale blue depths was deeply disturbing.

"I think this has gone far enough," she said evenly. "Mr. Farnsworth, I appreciate you making such a fatiguing journey simply to assure my aunt of my safety. And I thank you for your concern, but I'm afraid there has been some misunderstanding."

She could hear Justin breathing hard beside her, could

sense his taut nerves, and she willed him to maintain control of himself. Farnsworth, too, was struggling with his temper, Clare could tell, and she desperately hoped that the two men would not come to blows.

"You see, I'm the one at fault," Clare said, smiling in a self-deprecating manner. "I persuaded Justin to elope, and he agreed, simply to indulge my romantic fancies."

Her words, however sweetly pronounced, were a rejection, and Farnsworth's pale skin became blotchy and red in response, his lips a thin, grim line. Feeling for the first time truly afraid of the man, Clare stepped closer to Justin, but Farnsworth made no move toward them. "I beg your pardon, then, Miss Cummings, and wish you well," he said, bowing stiffly. "My lord," he added with a nod, his nostrils flaring. Then he turned on his heel and left the inn.

Clare and her audience uttered a collective sigh of relief at his exit, with only Justin remaining silent and rigid next to her. He pulled his fingers from hers. "You'll excuse me," he said, his voice sounding odd and strangled.

Clare put a hand on his arm to detain him. "You're not going after him, are you?" Justin didn't look at her, but shook his head stiffly, and she let him go, her hand slipping from the smooth velvet of his jacket a little reluctantly.

As she watched him, a riot of emotions churning in her breast, she felt fingers close over her wrist. She turned to find Marie at her elbow, squeezing her hand familiarly. "You chose the right one," Marie said simply.

Clare nodded slowly, although she knew that she had never really had a choice. Her decision had been made one foggy day long ago when she'd chanced upon a castle in the mist.

"You won't regret it," Marie said. Then she leaned over to whisper conspiratorially in Clare's ear. "My dear girl, you have yourself the best lover in all of London! Why, his hands alone are magical. Just ask anyone who has known him. Enjoy him, you lucky thing," she added wistfully. "Would that I were in your shoes!"

Clare, who blushed scarlet at Marie's pronouncement, gazed diligently at the worn wood of the counter. From the woman's tone, she guessed her worldly words had been brought on by wine and a genuine feminine fellowship, not by jealous sniping. Still, Clare found it difficult to listen calmly. "Of course, that necklace of his is a pesky thing," her confidant continued, sighing heavily. "That pointed little charm nicks you in all the wrong places, if you take my meaning, and he *never* takes it off."

Clare jerked her head up to stare at the woman, her attention caught forcibly by her last words. "What did you say?" she whispered.

"I was complaining about that charm Justin wears around his neck," Marie said. "Don't tell me he's taken it off?"

Clare reached over to grasp the lady's arm, her chest suddenly so heavy and full she could hardly draw a breath. "What is it, this charm?"

Marie paused as if in thought. "Some sort of exotic animal...a dragon, I believe," she answered. "Yes, it's a dragon. Perhaps it has something to do with the Regent. He does love all things Oriental, and there are dragons hanging at his Brighton Pavilion, you know." Marie shook her head at the mystery. "No use asking Justin about it, though. No one I know has ever got him to explain it. He won't take it off, and he won't say why. Has he told you?"

Clare could only shake her head. Throwing off her puzzled look, Marie smiled wickedly and leaned close. "Then don't let it bother you. It's a small price to pay for Justin's attention!" she said. Squeezing Clare's hand again, she moved, a little erratically, back to her table, and Clare was left staring off into space, memories swamping her.

As if it were yesterday, she saw herself back in Yorkshire, years younger....

She'd found it at one of the late-autumn fairs that moved

through the countryside, in a little booth that displayed watches and fobs and other jewelry. Among the charms was a beautiful, little gold dragon, and Clare knew she must have it for Justin, who loved her stories, silly, made-up stories that she had never told to anyone but the village children.

Of course, the little ones loved her tales, but she had never dreamed that an adult would treat them with anything but scorn. Her father didn't even read books, let alone listen to such nonsense, so she had been astonished when Justin liked them, when he wanted to hear more, when he told her to write them down and gather them together into a volume.

Clare raced home from the fair and ransacked her room for her pin money and the coins she'd been saving to spend on books, not fripperies. She rode back to the fair, her heart pounding with the fear that someone else might have bought the dragon charm, and she couldn't hide her eagerness from the old salesman, who drove a hard bargain. He claimed the piece was real gold, so it cost her dearly. She had him throw in a chain, too, and then she had clutched Justin's Christmas gift tightly in her hand.

"Clare!" The sound of Justin's voice—real, not imagined—drew her dizzily back to the present. He was standing by the door, and she moved shakily toward him. She had to fight an impulse to unbutton his waistcoat, to discover for herself if Marie spoke the truth, for the woman's revelation had left her more unnerved than the confrontation with Farnsworth had. *Are you wearing my dragon, Justin?* Clare longed to ask him, but she couldn't summon the words, her throat having gone thick with some emotion she thought long buried.

They walked silently to the carriage together. After helping her up, Justin stepped in, too, and sat across from her, leaning back against the cushions. Although he moved with the easy grace that he always did, Clare could tell he was tired. She realized suddenly that he must have ridden all night and all day, courting exhaustion, only to face a recalcitrant bride and a furious interloper. She opened her mouth to suggest they stay at the inn, but closed it promptly, for she had no desire to go back there or to spend the dark hours lying sleepless in a strange bed. The arrangements, she thought with a blush, did not bear consideration.

Justin closed his eyes. He'd had a drink, perhaps more, she could tell, but at least he hadn't brought the bottle along with him. She watched the dark hair slip over his brow, the lashes dip against his cheeks. He deserved sleep, she knew—the rest and the forgetfulness it would bring—but she could not let him go just yet. "Tell me about it, Justin," she said softly.

"Clare, I'm tired, and we have a long way to travel," Justin answered without moving.

"Tell me," she repeated. There was a long moment of silence, and she held her breath, waiting. Then he opened his eyes, stared out the window and spoke.

"Her name was Elizabeth Landrey," he said. "She was sixteen—" the last word came out roughly "—and I wasn't much older. I was eighteen, but I had been shifting for myself since my parents died. I thought myself quite the young lord, part of a certain crowd that favored wild parties, such as the one that night...the night she died." Justin paused. "I didn't push her, but she didn't fall, either," he said evenly. "She threw herself off because I wouldn't marry her. She was carrying my child." The last words were spoken coldly, without emotion, but Clare knew better.

"So you blamed yourself," she said. Justin didn't answer, but closed his eyes again, his head resting against the cushions. And drank to escape your guilt, Clare thought. And perhaps used women for the same reason—to forget something that shouldn't really be laid at your door. Irresponsible males of all ages were always getting foolish young women in the family way. It was a scandal, but it was not a matter of life and death, not a matter of suicide and lifelong torment. And Justin was tormenting himself, of that Clare was certain, yet she said nothing as the full import of her discovery settled over her.

So this is the curse, my prince, Clare thought with sudden clarity. After all these years, she had uncovered it. Not laid by any witch or devil, it had been woven by the prince himself. And like the enchanted castle in which she'd found him, he was doomed to fall to ruin unless someone intervened.

Clare eyed Justin surreptitiously under her long lashes. The thatch of hair fell across his forehead, and an unshaven stubble darkened his face, making him look much the same as he had that first day she'd met him, when she had sworn to free him. Clare sighed, long and low. Having failed once before, she didn't see how she could possibly save him now. But she was determined to try, for she was certain—again— that it was her destiny. She'd never really had a choice. She had to marry him.

GRETNA GREEN WAS A LITTLE VILLAGE where everyone from fishermen to blacksmiths officiated at the weddings of runaway lovers. Justin declined to ask the vocation of the fellow smiling at him from across the room, for it was all legal as long as the bride assented of her own free will.

Justin caught himself glancing over at Clare nervously, waiting for her refusal. She had been quite adamant about not marrying him, even before Farnsworth's revelations. Now that she knew his sordid past, Justin was sure she wanted nothing more to do with him. Yet she had not argued with him again, nor had she tried to bolt when they finally took lodgings at an inn, although he could probably lay that down to exhaustion. Still, her apparent acceptance of the impending nuptials puzzled him. Perhaps she was waiting for a dramatic moment to renounce him, he thought painfully.

Watching Clare's serene features, Justin realized that she must be up to something, for all the fire and fury had left her. She had to marry him now or her reputation would be destroyed. Basically, she was stuck with him, a man she hated for past hurts and now despised anew. His good intentions seemed for naught as guilt pressed down on him; he had botched this one good.

The "parson" nodded to him, but Justin hesitated, still uncertain what his bride-to-be might do. "Clare," he said, drawing her aside. "I want to assure you again that you'll have your freedom. You can choose an estate in the country or a town house in London—wherever you want to live— and you'll have more than enough money at your disposal. You won't ever have to see me again."

Although he spoke earnestly, the words were harder to get out than he had anticipated, and his plan to give her his name and casually walk away seemed unappealing. But it was her reaction that left him truly surprised. A blaze returned to her eyes, and her calm countenance was replaced by one of sharp, swift anger. "Take me home, Justin," she said. Then she turned to go.

"Clare!" He reached for her arm, but she flung off his hand.

"I won't submit to this...travesty!" she hissed. "You think to buy me off with a building, with money, with your indifference?"

Justin saw the pain in her hazel eyes, and he was appalled—and genuinely bewildered. He heard a witness clear his throat and glanced over at the man, who looked deuced anxious to get started. Justin smiled at him reassuringly and turned back to Clare.

Why was it so hard to speak to her? When he looked into the swirls of green and yellow in her eyes, reminding him of fallen leaves and golden meadows, his normally glib tongue became tied in knots.

Justin looked down at the floor instead of at Clare. "I thought, after last night, that you would never want to see me again," he said stiffly. It came out sounding like a childish whine, and he felt like kicking himself.

"Don't be ridiculous," she snapped.

Justin's eyes moved back to hers, where sparks flamed in the amber depths. He was totally confused. As a girl, Clare had been so straightforward, so easy to read, but now he hadn't the slightest notion what she was thinking. Who was this unpredictable woman? "All right," he said softly. "What is it then?"

"I don't want that kind of marriage, that's what it is," Clare answered, "and if that's what you're offering me, then you can just turn around and take me home." She faced him, arms folded across her chest, and glared.

"No," Justin said, with sudden, definite firmness. "I'm not taking you home." The words came out roughly, but at least they came out. And he hoped she got the message, for by all that was holy, he was not leaving here until they were married. "All right," he said again, more evenly. "What do you want?"

"I want to go back to the castle and live there with you," Clare said. The anger left her eyes, replaced by that pure, clear light that was hers—and only hers. "I want to rescue it from ruin."

Her answer stunned him, and he gaped at her, speechless. After all that had happened there, in his past and in hers, she wanted to go back? Justin was so used to thinking of Worth Hall as repugnant that it took him a moment to realize he wasn't repulsed at the notion of living there. Instead, he felt an odd tingling of excitement, as if by returning with Clare, he might recapture the companionship they had shared at one time—a friendship that had made the bleak hall the only bright spot in his world for a while. "All right," he said with a nod.

"And I have two other conditions," Clare said, looking up at him seriously.

"Go on," Justin urged. He was afraid to say more, fearful

that this sudden, strange mood of hers might turn, banished by rage or, worse, a painful sadness he could not bear to face.

"No more drinking, Justin, and no more women." Clare paused, dropping her gaze while her creamy cheeks took on a definite blush. "No *other* women."

Justin's heart nearly stopped in astonishment. If her previous requirements had startled him, nothing could have been more unexpected than this insinuation that she wanted to live with him as husband and wife. He stared at her, shocked, for he had never thought of his innocent Clare in that fashion. She had never sought such attentions from him. She wasn't now, either, for that matter. Justin knew when a woman wanted him, and he would never have suspected Clare of harboring such desires. Since she was grown, there was no reason why they shouldn't consummate the marriage, but he had hardly expected her to want him after all that had passed between them.

His gaze roved over her in wonder, taking in her downcast eyes, her flawless skin, her glorious hair—great locks of which were falling from their fancy arrangement—her pale shoulders and the smooth curves of breasts. As he looked at her, Justin felt desire rock through him so fast and so furiously that he shuddered where he stood. His Clare, he mused, his heart pounding. To touch his Clare... The thought was too hot to hold on to.

"Yes, of course, Clare," he managed to whisper. Watching those hazel eyes rise to his, Justin wanted nothing more than to clasp her to him right then and there.

"Uh hum." The sound of someone clearing his throat made Justin turn his attention back to the room. With what he was sure was a rather baffled grin, he presented his arm to Clare, and they walked over to where the parson stood.

The ceremony was short and simple. They gave their names, spoke their vows, and then Justin pulled out a thin gold band. It seemed odd to him that a ritual he had long mocked and shunned now had the power to affect him. When he slipped the ring onto Clare's slender finger, he felt as though he had to steady his own hand lest it tremble.

"What God joins together let no man put asunder." The words held a strange and moving finality that made Justin's throat go tight. Before he could consider the ramifications, he was moving to kiss his bride. Intent upon giving her only a perfunctory kiss, Justin was unprepared for her gentle response. Soft and warm, Clare's lips moved under his, and the longing to taste her defied control. His tongue swept into her mouth, and he pulled her against him, felt her arms slide up over his shoulders and groaned in pure pleasure.

Instead of a jaded rake who had sampled the delights of innumerable beautiful women, Justin felt like a monk who had just escaped from the abbey. His blood raced, his heart pounded, and he would have never let her go but for the gentle cough of the supposed clergyman.

He released her then, reluctantly, and when he saw her shy smile, he reached up to cup her cheek. He knew he ought to be relieved now that this beautiful woman-child faced no threat from Farnsworth or any other man, but all he felt was a reckless joy at his own good luck in somehow managing to marry the only person who had ever made him happy.

CHAPTER SIX

WHATEVER JUSTIN HAD EXPECTED of his wedding day—and that had never been much—he had never anticipated that he would be this happy. He felt rather silly; most of his friends had married for profit, position or some other reason of convenience. But while his could hardly be called a love match, he was possessed of a quiet delight that he had not known since...well, probably not since he had known Clare before.

Although they did not share the same friendship they once had, Justin was glad to discover there was more between them than past hurts. Clare had said she wanted a real marriage, by faith, and when he had kissed her, she had melted against him like so much warm honey. The memory sent a fire raging through him again, and Justin tried to ignore the pain in his loins.

As if in answer to his most fervent wish, one of the witnesses suggested they obtain a wedding chamber, which Justin suspected was a euphemistic term for any room with a bed. He turned to Clare. "Shall we stay?" he asked, as noncommittally as he could.

"Oh, no," Clare answered, dashing his hopes in one fell swoop. "I want to go straight home—to the castle. May we, Justin?" she asked.

With those hazel eyes, so pure and bright, raised to his, how could he say no? "All right," he answered, despite the fact that it would be a long, exhausting trip to Worth Hall.

It was. Justin sat next to Clare in the carriage, thinking to get a little closer to her during the journey, but he suddenly felt as inept and idiotic as a schoolboy. The woman beside him was not one of his many lovers, ecstatic simply to be in his company. This was Clare, who, in a sense, knew him better than anyone else ever had. Justin had the unsavory feeling that if he used any of his standard approaches, she would turn and laugh in his face.

So he sat there and tried to think of the right words, the right actions, but instead found himself tongue-tied, as was becoming usual in her presence. She finally fell asleep, her head against the corner cushion, while Justin stayed awake, frustrated.

Why he should suddenly lust after Clare with the ferociousness of a raging bull puzzled him immensely. Normally, he chose his lovers quite calmly, with a discerning eye for beauty. They also had to have enough experience to know what they were about; virgins need not apply.

Casting an honest look back over his many liaisons, Justin could not recall one single instance where the lower part of his anatomy had figured in the decision to begin an affair. His head had always chosen the lady, and his body had gone along willingly. Certainly, he had healthy appetites, but he had never wanted anyone with such nearly uncontrollable desire in his life.

He tried to focus on what was left of the girl he had known, but found little about her unchanged. Her hair was too long, too artfully arranged, despite its current disarray, to remind him of the child she had been. His gaze moved to the long, dark lashes resting against her cheeks, the luscious rosebud mouth and the slightly turned-up nose that stopped her face from being too remotely perfect and lent it warmth, instead. Justin knew that she was more beautiful, more intelligent and more…everything than any of his lovers had been.

"Clare," Justin whispered suddenly, brushing his knuckles against her cheek. "My pixie."

THE GROUNDS WERE in horrid shape. Several large bramble bushes had encroached onto the path to the house, and Justin knew his driver was probably swearing under his breath while trying to maneuver past such shrubbery. Leaning out the window, Justin directed him toward the stables at the rear of the hall that had been owned by his family for centuries.

When he stepped out of the carriage, Justin's view of the formal gardens told him that nature was rapidly overtaking the once-prized beds. He sighed. What Clare saw in this overgrown ruin was a mystery to him.

"Clare," he said softly, turning to help her out. "We're home." The simple words stuck in his throat, lodged there by an odd burst of emotion. Had he ever called any place home?

Clare smiled and gazed out past Justin's outstretched hand, catching her breath as she did. Mist hung over the tangled gardens like a sorcerer's spell, rising from the grounds to meet the dusk in an eerie twilight tableau. She clasped Justin's fingers and stepped down, as awestruck and entranced as she always was by his castle. It rose tall and noble before them, its central, square tower reaching to the heavens, its battlements silent and beckoning.

Justin was certain she would change her mind about living at Worth Hall, and her wide-eyed stare confirmed his opinion. Perhaps she had forgotten just how ghastly it was. "Pardon me, sir, are we staying here?" he heard the postboy ask the driver. "The heap o' stones makes me feel devilish queer!" He could hear Bodesby shushing the boy, but Justin could hardly fault his opinion.

Although he himself felt immune to its "queerness," the sight of Worth Hall did not strike Justin as pleasant. It stood dark and forbidding, like a sentinel to the past, hiding its secrets. It was filled with too many ghosts, and the only good memories Justin could recall were those shared with the woman beside him. "Shall we go on to London or Rillford?" he asked her.

"What?" Clare asked, dragging her gaze from the castle to Justin. "Neither! Oh, Justin, isn't it beautiful?" she breathed softly.

Certain she was either joking or trying to gloss over the truth, Justin took a good look at her face, but those hazel eyes were moving lovingly over the hall as if she were greeting a treasured friend. Justin shook his head. "All right. Bodesby," he called to the driver, "see to the horses. We're staying."

Justin took her arm to lead her, in the gathering darkness, over the old wooden bridge to the enormous rear door, until he realized suddenly, stupidly, that he couldn't get in. "Oh, blast it, Clare," he said before he could even think. "I don't have the key!" He could see the bloody thing in his mind's eye, an ornate old piece of iron as big as a fist. Presumably it was in the possession of his steward in London, for he certainly had never expected to need it.

"Scale those vines and climb in the kitchen window," Clare suggested. She pointed a gloved finger at some heavy growth leading up the stone wall to a window that had to be a good twelve feet from the ground. Unable to recall the last time he had scaled anything, Justin shot her a look heavy with skepticism. "I've done it before," Clare explained, giving him a smile that nearly buckled his knees.

Justin thought about calling the postboy. What else were youths good for but emergencies such as these? Unfortunately, Clare was looking at him so expectantly, as though he were a prince from one of her fairy stories, that he would be hard-pressed to get out of it. He sighed and wondered for the first time if he was going to regret this marriage.

He was halfway up when he heard Bodesby yelling, "My lord, what are you doing?" He nearly lost his grip then, and swore under his breath as the dried stems cut his hands.

"I'm breaking into my own home, of course," he called

back. "Any objection, or do you plan to summon the authorities?"

"No, my lord," Bodesby answered, suitably chastened. Justin realized that had he half a wit in his head, he would have asked the driver to come closer, to break his fall should he take a tumble. If the vegetation did swing loose, he'd better kick out from the wall, he decided. Better to land in the moat than on the ground, for then he might come away wet but with all his bones intact.

Presumably, Clare had chosen this means of entry because this particular window opened easily. Yet when Justin finally reached it, the thing wouldn't budge. Letting loose a string of obscenities, he swore he was not going down the same way he'd come up, and that it had better open or else.

As if realizing its own peril, the pesky casing finally moved, and Justin swung one leg into the darkness. He tried to imagine exactly where he was, but couldn't remember a thing about the kitchens. Had he ever even been in them? He knew that, should the drop inside be as far as that on the outside wall, he would more than likely break his neck just trying to get down.

Cautiously slipping his head inside, Justin let everything else follow. He slid down the wall to a tall cupboard, where he managed to knock over a variety of cooking utensils before gaining the floor. Sundry copper and pottery vessels banged to the stones and rolled over and over, making enough noise to wake the dead.

He decided right then and there to give up gambling, for if he ever lost his vast fortune in deep play, he could never turn to a life of crime. At burglary, he was obviously inept.

"Justin! Are you all right?" He heard Clare's worried voice calling.

"I'm fine," he shouted back, then leapt backwards as a mouse ran over his boot. Apparently, it had made a nest in the kitchens and did not care to have Justin disturbing the peace. Sighing long and low, he lit a lamp to help him find his way to the huge arched doorway in the rear hall. He still had a devil of a time getting the massive oaken door open, and by the time he did, he had a scowl on his face.

It was wasted on Clare, who swept past him toward the great hall with a look of rapture on her lovely features. Justin followed, lamp held high, while Bodesby and the postboy trailed behind. Watching her tall figure, Justin felt an odd ache in his chest. He knew that the place would be as he had left it some two years before, not long after... He couldn't finish the thought. When Clare had gone, there had been no point in returning.

Despite the pleasant summer weather outside, the hall was cold as a tomb, and their footsteps echoed in the gloom, kicking up years' worth of dust. Justin took in the cobwebs, the furniture cloths, the chill, bare walls, and realized what folly it had been coming here, trying to recapture something that had never been. He turned to Clare for confirmation of his own dismal thoughts.

But Clare didn't see things as he did. She saw the vast great hall with its vaulted ceiling rising into the darkness in majestic grace, and she was blind to the dirt. She saw the castle as it should be: the walls decorated with bright tapestries and antique ornaments, the furniture uncovered and refurbished, everything brought out of storage and fires burning brightly in all the hearths.

Standing by the massive old table that still graced the center of the great hall, Clare glanced over at Justin and realized that he looked much the same as he had that first day she had come upon him in this very spot. His face sported the same dark stubble, the same thatch of mahogany hair fell into his eyes as he glanced morosely around him and his clothes were travel stained as they had been years ago. He still filled them out quite nicely, too, though he no longer could pass for twenty-one, she mused. Too much drinking had aged the formerly smooth-faced youth.

Welcome home, Clare thought, a smile playing across her

lips, and she was seized with a feeling of completeness. Everything had come full circle, destiny having brought her the enchanted castle and the prince she had loved from that very day. She was suddenly so happy that she threw herself into his arms.

Justin was so surprised that he nearly dropped the lantern. He set it down on the table so that he could enfold her in his embrace. "Welcome home, my prince," she whispered in his ear, and Justin, strangely overcome by both her words and her gesture, buried his face in her hair, and for some odd reason felt like crying.

An eternity—or perhaps only a moment—passed until Clare stepped back. It dawned on Justin then that Bodesby and the post boy were still standing behind them, and that they had a lot to do yet this night. He released her reluctantly.

"I'll send for some of my staff tomorrow," he said, "but for now, we are on our own. Bodesby," he said, turning to his driver, "I want you to go over to Squire Cummings's house and pick up some of my lady's clothes. Oh, blast it, I suppose I ought to go myself to give him the news," he said, glancing at Clare for confirmation.

She smiled, but shook her head. "Don't bother. We'll make a formal call later. I'm sure father will not be alarmed that we eloped."

Justin grinned gratefully. He did not think he could quite stomach the squire tonight. It had been a long, difficult week, he had to admit. "All right," he said to Bodesby. "Go on over to the squire's, tell him that we are in residence and request that someone pack up a trunk for my lady. I'll tell you how to get there. It isn't far. Then you might as well go on down to the village and pick up some supper for us—and for yourselves as well."

"Oh, no. Don't go to all that trouble," Clare said. "I'm sure if you ask father, he can spare something from our kitchen."

"All right," Justin agreed. "Clare, I'm going to find some wood and get a fire going. It's deuced cold in here." He lit some candles, then made his way back to kitchen, where he took the servants aside. "While you're over there, ask the squire if he can spare a housemaid to get our rooms suitable to sleep in. Look in on the stable quarters, and if they aren't acceptable, which I suspect they aren't, then you two will have to hie down to the village inn for tonight."

"No, my lord," Bodesby said, shaking his head. "I ain't leaving you alone in this place. I've slept on the ground before, and I can do it again."

Justin smiled. "Well, I hope it won't come to that, but here's something for your trouble," he said, slipping some coins into his driver's hands.

"Not necessary, my lord, but thank you!" Bodesby said, grinning. "Come on, Thad!"

Left alone, Justin discovered plenty of wood, well-seasoned by now. He toted it up to his chambers, and soon had fires blazing in his bedroom and in the adjoining room for Clare. She had found a broom, and was sweeping up great clouds of dust that set him to coughing. "How about a bath?" he asked, hoping to distract her from further house-cleaning.

"Oh, that would be heaven, Justin!" In her dressing room was an ornate brass tub, and he nearly killed himself dragging it across the floor to the fireplace. Justin cursed his lack of foresight for not keeping the postboy here for such chores.

He was cursing even louder after he hauled several buckets of water from the ground floor up to Clare's room. Innovations had been long in coming to Worth, and just having water pumped to the lower floor was an enormous improvement over centuries of fetch and carry. His parents, who had not favored the old family seat either, had not seen fit to pour much money into it, a problem that Justin proposed to remedy immediately.

"Baths, and water piped to them," he resolved after a few trips up the stairs with buckets he set to heat on the fire. The heinous task confirmed his previous resolution to give up gambling, for should he lose his fortune, he had no desire to become a servant, either.

Justin looked at the low level of liquid in the tub, thought of making one more trip and groaned. "This is it, Clare," he said, calling her over.

If she thought the amount of water woefully lacking, she did not say so, but smiled at him gratefully, as though he had just slain ten dragons for her. Justin felt good as he stood back, enjoying her warm gaze, until with sudden, unexpected ferocity, he was again struck by his desire—no, his need—to have her. It was a tangible thing, this longing to touch her and to feel her move beneath him. He inhaled sharply and stepped toward her.

"Out, out!" Clare said, shooing him away with a hand to his chest. Oblivious to his raging lust, she obviously wanted to take her bath in privacy, and Justin gritted his teeth and went, the sound of the door closing behind him grating on his temper. He scowled, then grabbed the broom and finished sweeping, coughing loudly all the while.

Clare slipped down in the tub as far as she could go and sighed. Even though it barely lapped at her thighs, it felt wonderful after her days on the road. She closed her eyes and didn't move for long minutes, luxuriating in the warm water. The sound of Justin moving in the next room roused her, and she soaped herself thoroughly, washed her hair, then finally, reluctantly, got out.

Donning one of Justin's old dressing gowns, she rolled the sleeves up several times and cinched it tightly at the waist. The heavy satin felt delightfully sinful against her bare skin, and the thought that it was Justin's made her flesh tingle even more. Ignoring the way her heart tripped, Clare found a brush, which she hoped had belonged to his mother and not one of his other women, and sat by the hearth, drying her hair.

"Clare, are you finished?" Cozily curled up by the fire, she had been lulled nearly to sleep by its quiet warmth and started at the sound of Justin's voice.

"Yes," she answered, wrapping the robe tightly around her. Although it covered her from neck to toe, Clare still felt indecent, since she had nary a stitch on underneath.

"May I come in?" Justin asked from behind the door separating the rooms.

"Yes," Clare answered, standing up nervously. She thought of all the time she had spent with him, often alone in the deserted castle, and yet things were so different now. This physical tension had never existed between them then, had never crackled in the air like sparks from the blazing fire. She had been but a child before, and now she was grown. Now they were married.

Anxiety knotting her stomach, Clare stepped back awkwardly as Justin set down more towels and clothes of his own. Uncomfortable with him for the first time since the ceremony, Clare fled to the other room. There she searched frantically for the broom, intent on finishing her sweeping, only to discover that Justin had finished the job for her. She swallowed hard, then heard a voice downstairs.

"My lady, I've got some clothes for you." Clare relaxed as she recognized the voice of her father's housekeeper.

"Up here, Mrs. Sutton," she called, stepping into the hall. She ducked back in when she saw Bodesby bringing her trunk, and moved out of the way, trying to look inconspicuous in her robe. Apparently well trained, he did not even glance her way before leaving, but Mrs. Sutton gave her a toothy smile.

"Oh, Clare! My *lady*," she said, beaming. "Who would have ever thought you'd be living here in this great, fancy manor and married to the marquis himself? Oh, but don't you deserve it! I always said you were the most beautiful girl this side of Rillford, and not just outside pretty, either,'' she said, her cheeks pink with excitement.

"Thank you, Mrs. Sutton," Clare said, smiling herself. "You are a dear, and am I glad to see you! Thank goodness Father sent you over. I'm afraid the castle's been closed up for years, but I made Justin bring me straight here anyway, so now we are here with a bit of...dust."

"That I can see," Mrs. Sutton said with a nod. "And Mr. Bodesby explained as how you needed beds made up and all that, so don't you worry your head about it. Oh, you've got the clean things laid out already," she said. "Now that you're a marchioness, Clare, you shouldn't be doing such things. Now, run off and get dressed, while I do them up, and I've got some hot supper down in the kitchen that I'll bring up to you, too."

Clare smiled happily and picked out her things from the trunk. She didn't remember shutting the door to her room, but she was already thinking of a quiet dinner in clean clothes, so she gave it little thought. Closing it behind her, she laid her things on her bed and slipped off her robe.

Ensconced in the tub, Justin lifted his head when he heard the door open. Surprised to see Clare walk right in and put something on the bed, he nonetheless admired the way she looked in his dressing gown. He saw that her hair reached her shoulders and a little beyond. And it was lovely—shining smooth and dark, and still damp from her bath.

Bodesby must be back, he noted idly, because she had some fresh clothes. Good, perhaps he had brought some food, Justin thought—before he lost his train of thought completely. As he watched her, his attention turned to another appetite, for as if she were totally unconcerned or unaware of him, Clare undid the belt of his dressing gown and dropped the garment to the floor.

Justin got a delightful view of a smooth back of flawless skin gently curving into a softly rounded derriere, followed by two incredibly long, gracefully shaped legs. He sucked in his breath and desire rocked through him so powerfully that he grasped the sides of the tub.

Clare apparently heard the noise, for she turned her head to glance at him, then whirled in surprise. Lifting a hand to her mouth as she gasped, she gave him a lovely look at her full, high breasts, slim waist and swelling hips, convincing him quite thoroughly that he should never think of her as a child again. Raising his eyes to hers, he hoped to see a longing as fierce as his own, but he found only startled confusion and embarrassment.

"Justin, what are you doing?" she asked. Grabbing up the robe and draping it in front of her, she managed to hide her most appealing parts from his perusal.

For a minute, Justin couldn't even answer, having gone beyond tongue-tied to a state of speechlessness. He was so hard he ached. "I was taking a bath," he managed, surprised at how easily the words came out.

"Well, take it somewhere else!" Clare cried. Clutching the satin to her shapely form, she edged toward the adjacent dressing room, never taking her eyes off of him. "Justin St. John, a gentlemen wouldn't look!"

The comment annoyed him for some reason, perhaps because he was beyond such silliness. He had seen any number of women in various states of undress, flaunting their bodies, and yet he had never felt compelled to watch them as he did now. He couldn't have taken his eyes away if he tried, and he was both irritated with himself for such lack of control and disappointed in Clare for not showing herself to him willingly.

"I'm your husband, for pity's sake," he said as she slipped out of his sight. "And I was not about to carry up any more water or move this tub. Not for the Regent himself!"

Clare leaned back against the wall, holding the robe against herself and breathing heavily, her mind filled with the image of Justin naked. He was so well formed, broad shouldered and lightly muscled...it was too bad that the sight of his body brought back such bad memories.

Jarred out of the present, all Clare could see was Justin getting out of that bed in the other room—out of bed with her maid. All over again she heard him tell her with painful bluntness that he didn't care about anything—least of all her. Clare's fingers dug into the satin as she tried to banish the memory.

Justin did care about her. He cared enough to marry her, even if it was only to save her from Farnsworth. But what if he didn't? All Clare's doubts, momentarily discarded in the heady excitement of her destiny-fulfilling wedding. What if his vows had been motivated by some old rivalry with Farnsworth? Clare felt her stomach wrench at the thought of herself as a pawn in some dreadful game. No, no, she couldn't bear to consider such a possibility. How could she live with him then?

He did care, Clare told herself. He had agreed to all her conditions, hadn't he? No drinking, no women, and he had assented to living at the castle. Here they were, so that proved something.

But what if he did not hold to his promises? She swallowed hard, and unable to answer, pushed her fears back down inside her, where they lingered, dark and murky around her heart.

Taking a deep breath, she put on the robe, wrapping it around herself tightly as if it were a shield that could somehow protect her from Justin—and his power to hurt her.

"Clare?" She heard his voice, sounding a bit disgruntled, coming from her room and felt anxiety grip her again. "I'm going back to my chamber now. You can come out and get dressed."

"Oh," she said faintly. "Mrs. Sutton is laying out supper there, I believe," she added, just in case he planned to stroll about with nothing on. He didn't, for she crept out of her dressing room in time to see him leave, encased in a fine white shirt and brown doeskin. She relaxed slightly. At least he was dressed.

After putting on her own clothes, Clare joined him for supper, more subdued than she had ever been in his presence. She glanced at the bed, made up now and turned down, and she lost her appetite. All she could see was Amanda there, and Justin, drunk and uncaring.

"I'll be downstairs if you need me," Mrs. Sutton said. "Henry brought me over, so he'll be taking me back when you're finished." She paused to eye the marquis. "My lord, you'll be needing some help here, I'm thinking."

"I'm having some of my staff sent round as soon as possible," Justin replied.

"Well, till then, I've got a sister with two strapping girls who could come and get started on a good cleaning," she said. "If you'd be wanting them."

"Are they pretty?" Clare asked before Justin could answer. She ignored their startled expressions to fiddle with her silver.

A bit taken aback by the question, the housekeeper seemed at a loss for an answer, then she smiled broadly. "Well, to me, mayhap, since they're my kin, but to the rest of the world, I expect not."

"Good," Clare said. "Then send them over."

She refused to glance at Justin, who she knew was eyeing her from across the table. "All right, Mrs. Sutton," he said. "That will be fine."

Once the housekeeper left, they began their meal in silence. Clare was sure the food—hearty meat pies, boiled potatoes and thick slices of bread—was not of the sort Justin was accustomed to, and she felt suddenly rustic and backward, which only added to her discomfort. She ate quietly, without even looking at him, until finally he laid down his fork to gaze at her.

"What is it, Clare?" he asked gently.

She wasn't going to answer, had no intention of telling

him the truth anyway. But he asked so nicely, so much like his old self, that it came out of its own accord. "It's this room," she said. "I don't like it."

Clare saw surprise flash across his face, but she didn't explain. "Are there any other chambers we can move into instead?" she asked.

"Certainly," Justin answered. "I've always kept these rooms out of habit, for they are in the best condition. But there are others—the great chamber, in fact."

"If you don't mind, I'd like to stay somewhere else, after tonight," Clare said.

"All right," Justin answered. "The great chamber is larger and more appropriate, I'm sure." He watched her downcast eyes, the frown tugging at her beautiful mouth, and knew the reason for her odd request. He pictured the past just as well as she did, and he liked it just as little. He felt like swearing, and he wished he had thought to pick another suite.

He couldn't bear to see Clare's bent head, couldn't bear to sense her sadness, but he didn't know what to say. He hesitated to speak of that other time at all, for neither of them ever mentioned the past, as if by an unwritten rule. Would breaking it end the fragile truce between them?

"I'm tired, Justin," she said softly. "It's been such a long journey. If you'll excuse me, I think I'll go to bed."

Justin nodded and stood up. What else could he do? "If there's nothing else you need, I'll have the woman clean this up and go home," he said, gesturing to the table.

"That's fine," Clare said. "Good night."

When she went into the other room, Justin opened his door and called for Mrs. Sutton. The housekeeper had the supper things cleared away in no time, and bobbed her head in farewell. "I'll send my girls over first thing tomorrow," she said.

"Well, maybe not first thing," Justin amended. Mrs. Sutton grinned from ear to ear.

"Just as you say, my lord," she noted before exiting.

Justin closed the door with a sense of relief. They were finally alone: he, his bride and the ghosts of Worth Hall. Although ordinarily he had an entourage of servants attending to his every need, Justin had often come alone to Worth before, so it felt like old times. A shiver of excitement ran through him at the knowledge that the best of those times had been shared by the woman who lay waiting for him in the adjoining room.

As if on cue, desire surged through him like rampaging wildfire, and he took a deep breath as he pictured her dark hair falling around her shoulders and her creamy skin bared from head to toe for him. The very idea of having Clare, his Clare, set his heart hammering in his chest and his loins ablaze in a way he did not even attempt to define.

Justin could hardly get his clothes off fast enough, and he tossed them haphazardly about before donning the dressing gown she had worn earlier and unrolling the sleeves with a grin. Should he give her a few more minutes or should he go to her now? He stepped toward the door to her room, then turned around and walked away. He would have to keep a tight rein on himself to govern the nearly uncontrollable passions she aroused. It had been a long, long time since he had bedded a virgin. A vision of Elizabeth appeared, unbidden, in his mind, and he cursed the haunted walls around him.

Stepping again toward her chamber, Justin vowed that tonight had to be perfect for Clare. A long, slow seduction was in order, one that lasted all night, though how he was going to manage that in his present condition was beyond him.

Justin whirled and paced back across the floor. By faith, he felt like a young, untried boy, instead of a man who, he had been told often enough, could make most any woman forget herself. Blast it, he was skulking in his room, afraid to go pleasure his own wife! With a grim determination that bore little resemblance to his usual carefree seductions, Justin moved to the door and flung it open.

CHAPTER SEVEN

CLARE JUMPED in her bed. "Justin, what are you doing here?" she asked, her voice unnaturally high. The fire lent a glow to the room, and he saw her sit up, clutching the blankets to her chin and gazing at him wide-eyed. He decided this was not going to be easy.

Walking slowly toward the bed, Justin watched her sink back farther into the pillows with his every step, and he wanted to cringe. "I thought you..."

He realized he was tongue-tied again and nearly cursed under his breath. He used to talk to Clare effortlessly, but he looked at the grown woman before him and he wasn't sure he knew her at all. Perhaps it was that odd combination of the familiar and the unknown that twisted his tongue into knots. Whatever caused it, he didn't speak again until he reached her side. Then he formed his words carefully, softly. "You said you wanted us to have a real marriage."

Clare gazed up at him as if he were an ogre from one of her fairy stories. Justin sat down on the edge of the bed next to her. She inched a tiny bit away, farther into the middle of the bed, since she could hardly get any closer to the carved and painted headboard. Justin smiled in what he hoped was a reassuring manner and resisted the urge to touch the silky hair that fell about her face.

"Clare, it's just me, Justin." His words came out huskily, as they sometimes did when he was with her. It was almost as though she could pull emotions out of unknown recesses within him.

"I know," she answered. He saw her relax a bit, and he did, too. She looked down at the covers. "I know I said that about the marriage, but I didn't think...I forgot that...I really wasn't sure what was...Justin, I just don't feel ready yet for whatever..." Her words trailed off.

And he thought *he* was tongue-tied! Justin would have grinned, if the message she was sending weren't so painful. She looked up at him, and he saw panic in the amber depths. "All right," Justin heard himself say. "I know the wedding was rushed." And I know you did not want to marry, he thought sadly.

"Maybe you need some time to get used to the idea. Take your time. Take all the time you need, Clare," he said gently. He was rewarded with one of her genuine smiles, her rosebud mouth curving until he was dazzled. Clare smiled from the inside out, he had always thought, and it was still true. It took his breath away before it faded.

"Justin?" she said, turning pensive again.

"Yes?"

"You won't be coming in here every night... unexpectedly, I mean, will you?" Clare asked, looking down at the wretched blankets again.

"No, I won't ever come in again, if you don't wish it," Justin heard himself say. "I'll stay in my own room, and when you feel you're ready, you come in to me."

Clare smiled gratefully, while Justin longed to kick himself. Her dark hair flowed down around her shoulders, and he wanted desperately to bury his face in it before moving on to the rest of her, now well hidden under the bedclothes.

Justin started to rise and then leaned over her. A kiss, after all, was not too much to expect, he thought. And if it led elsewhere, who was to blame? He felt her lips, soft and warm under his own, but only briefly. Unlike the one that sealed their marriage, this kiss was broken by Clare, who managed to scoot halfway up the headboard to get away.

"Good night, Clare," Justin said, his words sounding disgruntled even to himself.

Back in his own chamber, Justin looked at the empty bed strewn with his clothes, and started toward the hallway. What he needed was a bottle—no, several of them, he decided. Then he stopped dead in his tracks and smacked his forehead in disgust. Hadn't he promised her that he wouldn't drink? Cursing a blue streak, he climbed under the cold covers, knowing sleep would be a long time in coming.

Justin eyed the ceiling suspiciously, half expecting a piece of crumbling plaster to drop down upon him from between the ancient beams during the night. If only it would knock him blissfully unconscious.... He sighed deeply. That morning he had thought himself the victor in this marriage. Now he wondered morosely if Clare weren't exacting some form of torture for his past treatment of her. Here he was in a house he despised, with a fire in his loins that would not be quenched by his wife, who was lying in the next room—or by any other woman, for that matter—and without even a bottle to give him comfort.

Somehow, he did not think this a wedding night to remember.

CLARE WAS UP bright and early. Glad to have some of her clothes again, she donned one of her old working gowns and prepared to tackle the castle. Her castle. The fact that it was her own came to her in sharp little bursts of happiness. Of course, that thought led to her other recent acquisition, and she grew curious to peek in on Justin to see how he looked sleeping. But he was in *that* room, in *that* bed, so she slipped out into the hall and made her way to the kitchens.

She had already started cleaning the great hall when Mrs. Sutton arrived with her relatives. By the time Justin came wandering down around noon, they had already been working for hours.

"Clare," he said from the doorway, and she nearly jumped at the sound of his voice. Wiping her hands on her dress, she walked over to him. He was wearing a dark green coat with light breeches, and he was clean shaven. Even his errant thatch of hair was in place. He stood tall and elegant, from his head down to his top boots a strikingly handsome man, and Clare realized that she must look a mess.

Raising a hand to the hair falling free past her shoulders, Clare tried to pat it down. "Good morning," she said, a little nervously.

"Your hair—" Justin began.

Clare wouldn't let him finish. "Oh, I'm sorry," she said. "I guess I'm not acting like a marchioness, but I so want to get the castle in shape and to poke around in all the rooms." She felt silly and unappealing and woefully lacking in the proper graces.

"No, you definitely don't look like a marchioness," Justin said with a slow smile, "but you do look beautiful. I like your hair down. You've let it grow."

Clare laughed, a low, clear sound that seemed to dance along his skin. "Yes," she murmured, grinning at him so impishly that he saw the scamp she once was. "I no longer cut it myself with gardening shears, if that's what you mean."

Justin's short burst of laughter joined the soft sound of her own. He had forgotten the story behind her previously short locks. As Clare had explained it, she became sorely vexed with her long tresses. *So much trouble,* she had said. *Always in the way!* So she trimmed them herself, horrifying the housekeeper, who ran to her father with the tale. The squire, as usual, didn't care a whit what she did with her hair, so she felt her actions sanctioned, and continued to keep it short.

"I'll make sure all the scissors are kept under lock and key," Justin teased, "for I would beg that you never cut it again." He spoke the words with a wistful smile, and she returned it shyly.

"Then I shall let it grow, as you wish," Clare said softly, "as long as you don't mind if I don't look like...like a real lady."

She was sincere, he could tell, but Justin couldn't help laughing all the same at the thought that her appearance might be lacking in any way. "Clare, you look like a real, beautiful lady, all the time. Just be yourself. That's all I want." *That's all I've ever hoped for*, he thought. He was rewarded with a dazzling smile that pierced his heart, and his tongue threatened to tie in knots again. He changed the subject.

"As to the hall, do whatever you wish. If you like, I'll get someone up from London, and you can redecorate the whole place from top to bottom—carpets, wall coverings, chandeliers, furniture, whatever your heart desires." It was not a magnanimous offer. He had ample funds for such a project, so he was not prepared for the look on her face. Joy and warmth swept over her features like sunshine, and she threw herself into his arms.

It reminded him of years past, when his spontaneous Clare would suddenly give him a quick, tight hug and he would laugh. Justin didn't feel like chuckling at this moment, however, for things had changed too much since then. When he folded his arms around her now, he had hold of a soft, shapely body, with firm breasts pressed into his chest. He rubbed his cheek against her silken hair, which smelled faintly of roses, and waited for it—the swift onslaught of desire to which he was growing accustomed.

It was immediate, and so forceful it nearly robbed him of breath. Though he felt like a cad since she was embracing him solely in happiness, he moved his hands down her back to the delightful curves below and pulled her up against his hardness.

He groaned, and she gasped, moving her head back to

look up at him in surprise. Justin took advantage of her parted lips, covering them with his own and sweeping his tongue inside. She tasted warm and sweet and...Clare. Feeling her stiffen in his arms, he told himself to slow down, but couldn't. His tongue was too busy exploring her mouth, while his fingers were trailing across her back.

Then, just as he told himself he would have to release her, it happened. She melted against him again like honey, and Justin thought he would lose his footing. He pressed her tightly against his loins once more and groaned again. He had never desired a woman so strongly in his life. Where years ago, weeks ago, even days ago, such a thought would never have crossed his mind, he now found that he could not banish it. He wanted her, his pure and sparkling Clare, his special girl in a grown-up body. He wanted her in his bed—now. "Clare, I need you. I need you," he whispered.

Justin felt her start of dismay, but her head fell back as he kissed her earlobe and her throat, and he could hear her breath coming low and quick. Seeing her response as agreement, he decided to pick her up and carry her upstairs to bed, some other bed, any other bed—somewhere soft where he could ease himself into her tenderness.

Just as he was about to lift her, a door slammed and Clare jumped back as if she had been burned. She smoothed her skirt and her hair nervously as the squat figure of Mrs. Sutton approached. Justin found himself trying to breathe again and he swore softly while the housekeeper, who obviously thought they were taking up where they had left off this morning or last night, grinned at him. Just wait until you change the sheets, old woman, Justin thought. Then you'll know why I'd like to strangle you.

"Will you be wanting breakfast, my lord?" Mrs. Sutton asked.

Justin glanced at Clare, who was studiously looking at the floor, her face bright red. "Not yet, Mrs. Sutton. I believe I have some pressing business with my wife." *Wife.* The word sounded strange to his ears, but it moved him.

Apparently not so Clare. Her eyes flew to his in something like panic, and his hopes fell. "No! No, Justin, you go on ahead and have something to eat. I'm afraid I—I should really finish in the other room, but you...you haven't even had breakfast yet, so please do."

"All right," Justin said with a sigh. He refused to look at Mrs. Sutton, and nodding to Clare, walked toward the dining hall. Clare was not used to servants constantly at one's elbow, privy to one's every move, he told himself, and so she had been embarrassed by Mrs. Sutton's entrance. The alternative—that she did not want him to make love to her—was too gruesome a thought to contemplate.

Watching him gracefully exit, Clare reached out to lean against the table for support. She let out a long breath and raised a hand to her throat. What had just happened? She still felt dizzy and giddy and weak in the knees. Of course, she had always dreamed of Justin's kisses, had always known they would be wonderful, but the reality was so breathtaking, so mind-numbing, so incredibly *incredible* that she could never have imagined it.

Did he feel the same way, or was kissing her ho-hum for a man who was renowned for his skills as a lover? Clare frowned at the thought. Justin had said she was beautiful. And he had whispered that he needed her. Was it true? Then perhaps he had wanted to be with her last night, and had not simply felt obligated by their vows.

Clare blushed at the memory, and turned pinker still as she recalled him in the bath. The other vision of him naked—when he'd gotten out of Amanda's bed—intruded, and she forced it aside, concentrating instead on the picture of him yesterday, all lean and smooth and shining wet.

The image made her swallow hard as she savored it, and then she suddenly realized that Justin had been wearing something, even in the water. She had been too distressed yesterday to remark on it, but she saw it in her mind now as clearly as she saw the drops glistening on his chest. Around Justin's neck had dangled a glimmering golden chain, and on it hung the dragon she had given him.

Clare clung to the table again, as though the discovery threatened to unbalance her. So he did wear it, as Marie had claimed, and never took it off, not even in the tub. Why? If she'd meant nothing to him all these years, why would Justin wear her charm?

Clare poked her head into every room in the castle, pulling cloths off the furniture and leaving great piles of them in the hallways. She shouted for Justin whenever she found a real treasure, like the stained glass of the chapel windows or a lovely tapestry hidden under layers of dust. He would grin and shake his head at her wonder, while she went on to the next item.

The great bedchamber was opened for cleaning and airing, and Clare made her way along the upper floor to the end of the west wing, peeking in here and there until she was faced with a stout door that would not budge. She tried all the keys on the ring she had found in the servants' quarters, but nothing seemed to turn in it.

Frustrated, she called for Justin, who by now was used to her frequent interruptions. He came ambling along the narrow hall, but when he saw where she was, he stopped dead, his face cold. "That door stays shut," he said harshly. "As does the one at the end of the other wing."

"But where do they lead?" Clare asked.

"They go to the roofs," Justin answered, his dark eyes hooded.

"Oh, Justin! The battlements! The view must be magnificent. Can't we go up?" Clare asked. She had always wanted to walk along the high walls, but Justin had told her before that there was no way to get to them.

"No, we cannot go up," he said with a fierce scowl. "No

one goes up there, and the doors stay closed. And stop trying your keys, Clare, because the bloody thing is nailed shut,'' he added, turning on his heel to depart.

"But shouldn't we have the roofs checked before we start any improvements?" Clare asked. "Maybe you should have someone brought in to take a look."

Justin didn't even glance back at her to answer. "When the ceilings cave in, we'll know there's a problem," he said as he stalked off.

Clare sat down in the nearest chair, bewildered until the reason for his grim mood came to her with sudden, heart-wrenching clarity. She had forgotten about the girl who'd jumped—or fallen—into the moat. In the excitement of the wedding and the return to the castle, the curse upon her prince had totally slipped Clare's mind, and she felt a surge of guilt at her carelessness. How was she supposed to lift the spell when she didn't even spare it a thought?

Now that she had been reminded, Clare resolved that she would not be so remiss again. She reviewed what little she knew about the incident. She still found it hard to believe that the young woman, Elizabeth Landrey, had killed herself over Justin's perfidy, but then she had never dreamed of such a solution to any problem. Perhaps if she learned more about what had happened, she could throw more light on the girl's motives.

She sought out Mrs. Sutton, who was attacking the great bedchamber with vigor. "Oh, it's lovely, isn't it?" Clare asked as she looked over the room, its timbered ceiling gleaming darkly and the oriel window, stripped of its aged draperies, glowing brightly upon the thick carpet. Once the musty air was removed, the smell of old wood and lingering spices drifted to greet her.

"It surely is that, my lady," Mrs. Sutton said, sweeping out the neighboring dressing room.

Clare eyed the huge, richly carved oak bed, her heart thumping. No bad memories lingered here to distract her, so she should be able to join Justin in it, shouldn't she? She reached out to touch the gold fringe of the bed hangings, stirring recollections best left undisturbed. If only there wasn't so much hurt yet to forget and forgive... Clare sighed and turned her thoughts back to her purpose. "Mrs. Sutton, have you been here before—to the castle, I mean?" she asked.

"Good heavens, no," the lady answered.

"I just asked because I know Justin has been in residence before, and I wondered if any of the local people were employed then." Clare was careful to leave herself out of it. She had never mentioned to a soul that she'd been to the castle before, and besides Amanda, whose lips had been firmly sealed by Justin, no one had ever connected the squire's young daughter with the dissolute marquis.

"Oh, my, but that was awhile ago," Mrs. Sutton said, stopping to lean on her broom. "But no one I know was working here, even then. Being a marquis and all, he usually brought his own servants from London or other places. We thought the St. Johns had houses everywhere," she said with a smile.

"I do remember when the old marquis was in residence," the housekeeper went on, her eyes looking back into time. "That was always exciting, seeing him drive through the countryside or the village. But the family has always been more associated with Rillford and probably hired help from there, as it's a mite closer to the hall."

She paused as if to mull over the question. "Now that I think of it, I do believe one of Mrs. Calder's girls was taken on as a housemaid. But of course, when the family moved on, she went with them—on to new and exciting adventures, we all thought."

"When was that?" Clare asked, smiling encouragingly.

"Oh, my, fifteen or twenty years ago, I imagine. It has to be ten years or more since the old marquis and his wife were killed," Mrs. Sutton said sadly. "A carriage accident right near here, and the young boy left all alone. He has grown up a fine man, for all of it, though.'' She straightened and grasped the broom handle again.

"Then he wasn't here much after he came into the title?" Clare asked, prodding gently but deliberately for the information.

"Oh, we would hear the odd story of wild goings-on once in a while, but that wasn't too often," Mrs. Sutton said while she swept, a little too busily, past Clare.

"One party in particular?"

Mrs. Sutton stopped immediately, her broom stilled in her big hands as she eyed Clare solemnly. "You know about the girl who fell?"

"Yes," Clare said. "I know about it, but not as much as I'd like to. What can you tell me?"

Mrs. Sutton shook her head. "Sad. Sad, it was. Some young lady from London fell from the top," she said pointing a strong finger toward the beams overhead. "Landed in the moat, she did. My cousins in Rillford talked about it and little else at the time, for all that it was hushed up." She glanced again at Clare, her blue eyes shrewd. "Seems the young people here were feeling a bit of their oats and such."

"Then Rillford people might have been working here at the time and might remember that night?"

Mrs. Sutton shook her head. "That I can't tell you. I could ask my cousins, but I doubt that they would be able to tell much, and what they would pass on might not be the Lord's own truth but a lot of silly gossip," she said, clucking her tongue and taking up her broom again. "They are a superstitious lot, you know, and when the girl died here, well, it just set them in mind of the old talk—about the Worthington curse."

"The curse?" Clare started in surprise at the word she had so often used to describe Justin's fate.

"Oh, old wives' tales—you know the stuff and nonsense

that grows up about these old families," Mrs. Sutton said, shaking her head. "A sensible girl like you shouldn't pay any heed to such silliness. You're the lady of the hall now, and no one better suited, either."

"What exactly is the curse?" Clare asked, undeterred by Mrs. Sutton's swirling broom and retreating back.

"Oh," Mrs. Sutton answered over her shoulder, "naught but that each generation would come to no good."

"But that can't be true," Clare protested. "His parents—"

"Some folks claim their accident was the fulfillment," Mrs. Sutton said as she moved away. "Some folks will claim anything."

Stunned by Mrs. Sutton's words, Clare wandered out into the hall, almost giddy at the irony of the situation. She had thought to save Justin from his own melancholy, and now she was faced with a real curse—not that she had much faith in anything so vague.

Her dismay was increased by her own ignorance. She was annoyed that Mrs. Sutton knew more about Justin's family than she did. Of course, by the time Clare had discovered the castle, it had been quiet and overgrown for years. The only time the squire mentioned the place was to complain about its neglect.

Clare did not recall the villagers talking about it, nor had she ever spoken of the hall to them, for she silently hugged her secret visits to her heart. Perhaps tongues wagged more in Rillford, since the town appeared to be more closely linked with the Worthington fortunes, she mused.

Still, there was one person who could have told her about the curse, and that person had specifically denied knowing any stories at all about the castle. In fact, he had told her to make some up of her own! Frowning blackly, Clare went downstairs in search of her husband.

She found him in the study going through old account books and papers in a general housecleaning. She stood in the doorway, her hands on her hips, eyeing him accusingly. "Why didn't you tell me about the Worthington curse?"

"The Worthington curse?" Justin repeated. He rose from his seat, his dark eyes flashing ominously, his quick surge of anger calming Clare's own irritation. "Blast these rustics! That's why I never hire any of them!" He looked as though he would turn Mrs. Sutton and her relatives out upon their ears, until Clare stepped toward him and put a hand on his chest.

"That is no answer," Clare chided softly. "I asked you why you didn't tell me before. You claimed you didn't know a thing about the castle's history and forced me to entertain you with my own imaginings," she reminded him, a smile teasing the corners of her mouth.

Clare saw him relax. "I didn't want to scare you off, I suppose," he grumbled. "And your stories were a vast improvement over the real history," he said with a smile. "I loved to listen to them."

Clare's heart leapt into her throat at Justin's use of the word *love,* even though it was applied only to her tales, for they were a part of her, weren't they? If he loved them, he had to care for her, didn't he? Suddenly conscious of her fingers on his waistcoat, Clare wondered just how it would feel to slip them into his shirt and touch his skin. She stepped back, dropping her hand to her side, and tried not to blush.

"But turnabout is fair play, Justin St. John," she said. "I want to hear everything you know about this place, and now, if you please. Why don't we go into the gardens, like we used to do, and you can tell me the whole story?"

At the mention of the mess of undergrowth that had crept up to the moat, Justin eyed her a bit skeptically. "Certainly. I'll get my scythe and hack us a path," he said dryly.

"Justin!"

He grinned. "All right. I suppose we might be able to get through some of it if we follow the old stone walkways. But unless you are still wont to dangle out of a tree or perch upon an old stump, I suggest we take something with us on which to sit.''

Justin put a hand to her back as he walked beside her and realized with a jolt that, for the very first time, they had spoken of the past. They had broken the unwritten rule, and nothing untoward had occurred. In fact, quite the opposite, he decided, as he basked in the warmth of Clare's smile. Perhaps, he thought hopefully, it was the first step toward more than a truce.

CHAPTER EIGHT

THEY ABANDONED THE GARDENS to move through the tall grass that rose behind the castle. Justin laid out a blanket on a small hill overlooking the river and stretched out in the sun, his arms behind his head.

Sitting down beside him, Clare felt a haunting familiarity, for they had done this so often before. Yet, as she watched Justin under her lashes, she recognized how very different things were today. This time it was not she who spoke, weaving tales of knights and dragons and evil spells, but Justin. He began his account of Worth Hall with the first Marquis of Worthington, Guy de Fiennes, who had built the castle in 1341. By the time he reached the life of the third marquis, Clare was thoroughly exasperated.

"How could you?" she asked, tickling his chin with a long stalk of grass. "You lying beast! Swearing to me that you knew nothing of the place, when you knew every detail of its history from the first ostler on up."

Justin laughed. "I guess I didn't want to think about the hall then, and, besides, the real story is such dry, dull stuff. How could it compare with Clare's imagination?" he asked.

"But it's the truth!" she protested.

Justin looked at her skeptically. "Who knows? It all happened long ago, and time has a way of changing the facts. Now, do you want to pummel me with greenery or hear about the curse?"

Clare smiled. "Go on." She watched Justin's warm

brown eyes as he spoke, and felt a betraying warmth of her own, surging up from deep inside her.

"Supposedly, it came upon the family through the third marquis, Roderick de Fiennes, who was under retainer to the rich and powerful Lord Moleyns. Lady Moleyns had a very famous necklace made specifically to show off two monstrous rubies known as 'The Sisters,'" Justin said, glancing at her. "The huge gems were surrounded by pearls and lesser jewels set intricately in gold."

"You're making this up!" Clare accused.

Justin laughed softly. "I am not! It's the truth, or so the story goes. Anyway, it just so happened that the duke and duchess came for a visit. All went well until they prepared to leave the hall, and then the incomparable necklace was discovered missing."

"Oh, no," Clare said, wide-eyed.

"Oh, yes," Justin noted with a grin. He was enjoying himself. Although he had never displayed anything but contempt for the ridiculous tale, he found that Clare's reaction made it seem different somehow, like a piece of romantic legend rather than an annoying bit of chaff.

"Naturally, they blamed the marquis and his family. Roderick, being a hotheaded sort, took exception to being accused of thieving from his own lord in his own home. The two men drew their swords, and the marquis ended up lying bleeding on the floor of the great hall." Justin smiled at Clare's shiver.

"He wasn't dead, so the duke stood over him and said, 'Be that as a lesson to you, Worthington, and to all your heirs—that all of you will come to naught until what is mine is returned to my household,'" Justin intoned.

"The duke's entourage left in a flurry, and the marquis was taken up to bed, where he died a week later. The marchioness, totally distraught, took the children and fled to her family in London, closing up the hall for the first but not last time in its rather dismal history," Justin said. He paused to look at Clare, who was hanging on to his every word, her perfect rosebud mouth agape in a perfect O shape.

"The duke, a very powerful man, set out to destroy what was left of the family, and he nearly did," Justin continued. "The two children died young, victims of one of the fevers that swept through the town, so the title passed to a cousin, William St. John, a man ill-prepared for the enmity of Lord Moleyns. The Worthington fortunes were so badly reversed that they were not regained until a century later."

"Good heavens, Justin," Clare breathed, enthralled. "But what happened to the necklace?"

Justin shook his head. "No one knows. Some thought that the marquis did steal the thing and died before he could reveal its whereabouts. There are also stories of his later descendants knocking holes in the walls and other nonsense, claiming they had clues that led to the priceless heirloom," he said with a snort.

"The prevailing opinion of the family, however, is that the duke stole the necklace himself, pried out the gems, perhaps even cut them down, and sold them separately for profit, having used the marquis as a scapegoat," Justin said, echoing his own view on the fate of the jewels.

"No!" Clare whispered, her face crestfallen. "How awful! But then the necklace will never be found, and nothing will ever be proved."

Seeing her disappointment, Justin wished for a moment that he could actually provide a different denouement, the happy ending that Clare always craved. But that was just it, wasn't it? Life itself rarely ended happily. "That's my guess," he said. "It is long gone, my dear, romantic Clare."

The endearment felt like a caress, and Clare, suddenly giddy, looked down at the blanket to hide her reaction. "But all that nonsense about the family being cursed. People don't actually believe that, do they?"

"I'm afraid that the simple people of the times, who still burned witches, mind you, were very eager for such stories of retribution to last the centuries. The fourth marquis never had much of a chance, fighting an uphill battle to retrieve the family fortunes and honor, and people died young then, of diseases of every description," Justin noted. "Life was hard, and I'm sure that every misfortune was attributed to the curse, just as some of the villagers deemed it responsible for the death of my parents."

"I'm sorry," Clare said, sensing his outrage. Justin's handsome face was turned up to the sky, and he did not answer. "But that must be why the castle was never looted," she said suddenly. "I wondered how you dared leave it unattended." She sat back on her heels, a long piece of grass still dangling from her fingers, and when Justin did not return her gaze, she felt a twinge of suspicion.

"Justin St. John, as if you cared!" she said, tickling him with the green blade. "You probably would have let robbers knock it to the ground without a qualm. Oh, how could you?"

Justin turned to her and grinned. "Oh, my romantic Clare. I swear I will never harbor a bad wish for the place again." He reached up to brush his knuckles along her cheek.

"I should hope not," Clare said. She was a bit miffed at his blasé attitude toward her enchanted castle, but his touch made her forget her resentment and set her heart racing. She longed to take his hand in her own, to hold it tightly, to hold *him* tightly. But she couldn't, not yet. *If only he meant it.*

Clare rose shakily. Looking down over the castle and the river that fed into the moat, she sighed at its beauty. "And to think of all the stories I dreamed up about the hall, when all along there was a real curse."

"A curse, yes. Real, no," Justin said, rising to stand beside her. He took her hands in his, and she felt their warmth cover her fingers like an old friend she had sorely missed. "You won't take it into your whimsical head to swallow such nonsense, will you, Clare?" he asked. He grinned at her teasingly, but she could see the earnest question in his eyes, and she smiled.

"No, I do not believe in it. I suppose your curse has about as much substance as my tales of dragons and knights and sorcerers," she assured him. And she spoke the truth, for she did not believe the words of a 400-year-old duke or the fate of a missing necklace could affect the life of her or her husband.

No, the Worthington curse was just an old story, but the real curse, the curse of brooding melancholy that enveloped her prince more often than not, still held sway. Clare knew that to break its spell she would have to delve into the more-recent past, specifically a night when a young pregnant girl had drowned in the moat.

Realizing that Justin still held her hands, Clare lifted her gaze to his. His eyes, dark and deep, held something she had not seen before, a promise that both drew her and frightened her. One step, one lift of her head, and perhaps... Her usual boldness fled, and pulling her hands from his, Clare turned her eyes from his, missing the bitter disappointment there.

EACH DAY, Clare worked on her castle, and Justin, to his distaste, was coaxed into moving furniture, lugging in wood and hauling things out of storage until he felt more like a workman than a nobleman. Although he complained, he actually felt better than he had in a long time, and it didn't hurt when Clare turned those wide hazel eyes upon him as though he had just completed some magnificent feat.

Justin felt her gaze on him often, and he sensed she was warming toward him. Sometimes it even seemed like old times between them. But her laughter was missing. He longed to hear the throaty sound that had echoed so often in the hall years ago. And he longed to touch her.

Every night, Justin lay alone in his bed, awake for hours, cursing his promises to her. Truly, he did not long for another woman. Nor did he really miss his liquor, which surprised him—but then, he had never drunk around Clare before, either. It was the promise not to go into her room that made him want to kick himself nightly. He was certain that if he could just get her into bed, everything else would proceed naturally. But during the day, Clare was wary, and he never could seem to catch her alone, while during the night, she was safe behind the door that separated their chambers.

After a few days, the servants arrived, bringing some sort of normalcy with them, and then came the modiste he had requested from London to fit his wife with gowns appropriate to her station. He was afraid Clare might give him some trouble over that, but she seemed to have outgrown her careless disregard for clothes and to enjoy ordering a new wardrobe.

Soon after came Mr. Clifford Brown, also of London, who was to provide Clare with whatever she might want to refurbish the hall. As Justin watched the two go through one room after another, planning renovations and admiring existing decor, Justin wondered how in the devil he had ended up actually living at Worth Hall. He suspected that he was going mad when he found himself growing to like it.

Clare loved it, but she was so busy she hardly had a chance to breathe. The swarm of servants rather unnerved her, but she tried to adapt, recalling with amazement how Justin had done without all these people just a few days before. Now there were cooks and scullery maids and footmen and upstairs maids, and even Justin's butler from the London town house. She passed these people in the hallways, hardly knowing who was who, and once tried to engage Justin's valet in conversation, thinking he was a visitor.

She herself had a personal maid now and a seamstress who planned a vast array of gowns: dresses for carriage, dinner, evening, morning, garden, riding, walking, and on and on until she was bewildered, and needed the maid just to tell her what was what. For a girl raised mostly as a boy in the Yorkshire countryside, it was overwhelming. But Clare was enough of a dreamer to want to be dressed for her part as the woman to save Justin from his demons.

Unfortunately, she was too busy to do much saving. She had hoped to find some servants who had been here at the hall the night of the accident, but Mr. Brown and the modiste took up so much of her time that she had no opportunity to question anyone. As much as she enjoyed renovating herself and the castle, Clare found that she was not spending much time with her prince, and that irked her far more than she cared to admit.

Already a week married, they seemed no closer to burying the past than on their wedding day. Nor had Justin kissed her again, which made her worry that he did not find her beautiful or desirable. She knew she had requested some time to grow accustomed to his touch, but if he wasn't touching her at all, how was she to do that?

This afternoon would be different, Clare vowed, as she stood waiting for her husband in a new dark green gown with matching spencer. Today they were going over to her old home to make a formal call on the squire. Clare admitted that she would enjoy the ride and the time alone with Justin, if not the visit itself.

She smiled when she saw him approach, so handsome in a claret jacket and pale yellow breeches that fit him very well. Running her eyes over him, she thought she detected a new robustness about him. Perhaps all the work she was thrusting upon him was building new muscles. The thought made her eager to discover them, and she looked down at the ground.

"Well, I suppose we can't put it off any longer," Justin said with a disgruntled grin, and out they went to mount their horses.

As they rode, Clare was very conscious of Justin by her side. Aware that she had always taken these hills alone at breakneck speed to reach him, she enjoyed the leisurely pace, and the presence of the prince she was taking home as her prize.

The squire greeted them gruffly, slapping them each on the back in congratulations, and ushered them into the parlor. The room seemed tiny after the spaciousness of the castle, and Clare realized just how little she had in common with the enormously wealthy marquis she had married. Yet she had so often felt more comfortable there at the hall than here in her own home. Justin had made her welcome, had made her feel wanted and appreciated and special. The memory raised a lump in her throat.

And now? It wasn't the same, Clare knew. She wouldn't let her guard down long enough to trust him, to let him into her heart, for she wasn't sure she wanted him there again. More than anything, she couldn't bear to be hurt again. Blinking back unexpected tears, Clare asked Mrs. Sutton for a glass of water and tried to compose herself.

She saw Justin eye her closely and then glare at the squire as though he blamed her father for her discomfiture. That telling action made Clare smile tremulously. It didn't matter that Justin was responsible for her sadness; the notion that he was out to avenge whatever was disturbing her warmed her heart. Her prince was protecting her again.

Watching him uneasily engaged in conversation with the squire, Clare told herself she ought to be happy simply to have her prince, past hurts notwithstanding. How many times had she come home to this house, wishing instead that she could stay with Justin forever? And now she could. It was eerie to recognize all the hopes and dreams that had been formed here, and to know that somehow they had, for the most part, come true.

She caught Justin's questioning glance and nodded reassuringly, then smiled at her father, who appeared oblivious to any undercurrents in the conversation. "Well, I can't say that I'm sorry you eloped," the squire announced. "I think all that expense and ceremony a lot of unnecessary hogwash."

You would, Justin thought uncharitably. He had always felt an odd sort of antagonism for the squire, perhaps for not loving Clare the way the man should have when she was growing up. Instead of allowing her to tear around the countryside alone, the squire should have seen to her education, encouraged her creative bent and generally taken a bit more of an interest in the ethereal creature with whom he had been blessed.

Yes, Justin thought grimly, he harbored a lingering disappointment in the thoughtless man before him, which was exacerbated by the fellow's recent threat to give Clare to Richard Farnsworth. Justin eyed the man coldly. The squire didn't flinch.

"Well, I hear that you've got some big doings over there at the hall," the squire said, leaning back to fill his pipe. "All sorts of work to fix it up as it should be, eh?"

Justin nodded and listened while Clare told of her plans for the place, and he had to marvel at the change in her face. She had seemed uncomfortable to be in her old home, and who could blame her with the squire for a father? he thought churlishly. But when Clare spoke of her new abode, her eyes shone and her voice trembled with excitement. Justin found delight simply in watching her. She was so bright and lovely she took his breath away, and he felt a small bit of pride in causing her current enthusiasm. At least he had gifted her with the hall, which obviously gave her more joy than he himself ever could.

"What about the stables, my lord?" the squire asked, and Justin reluctantly stopped admiring his wife. "Ought to tear down that old mess and put up some new ones."

So you can come over and borrow my best stock, I suppose, Justin thought, eyeing him shrewdly. "Perhaps," he answered. Then he was forced to sit through a lengthy discourse on horseflesh that wearied him so considerably he felt like nodding off. Finally, Clare managed to turn the conversation, and he could again take pleasure in listening to her talk.

It wasn't until they were ready to make their farewells that the squire shook Justin from his lethargy. "Ah, Clare, I got a note from your aunt," her father said to her. "She seems to be in quite a state over your elopement and was determined to head down here straightaway to check on matters. Naturally," the squire added, clearing his throat, "I couldn't have her here, so I told her she could stay with you, to see for herself that you were perfectly fine and all." He smiled shamelessly.

"You what?" Justin asked, horrified at the mere thought of Clare's aunt.

The squire grinned wider, this time with real pleasure. Apparently Justin's marriage had done little to improve the squire's attitude toward him. Otherwise, how could the man subject his own son-in-law to such torment?

"Now, my lord, you aren't going to prevent my poor daughter from seeing her relatives, are you?" he asked slyly.

"I certainly would not be so ungracious. Any time Clare wishes to visit her aunt, I will be happy to go to London with her and put up at the town house," Justin answered.

"Too late, my lord. Eugenia's already on her way," the squire said, slapping him heartily on his back. "Let me know when she's gone, and I'll drop by myself to have a look at the improvements."

"I'LL NOT HAVE THAT WOMAN in my home!" Justin said heatedly as soon as they left the squire's land.

"Now, Justin," Clare reproved. "She's an old lady, and she's a little confused some of the time. Have a heart."

"A little confused? She's hen witted, and rude besides," Justin answered. He remembered all too well the foolish woman's refusal to heed his warnings about Farnsworth.

Her treatment of him still rankled. Although well acquainted with his own unsavory reputation, Justin was not used to having it thrown in his face, especially by a silly woman of no consequence.

Clare smiled. "It's a big castle, Justin. You'll never even have to see her." Then she sent her mount galloping onward, and Justin was forced to follow. He didn't bother to try to shout an answer. Clare was bloody well right, he decided; he wasn't going to see her aunt. As soon as the twit arrived, he planned to discover some pressing business in London.

Justin kept that bit of information to himself, however, and smiled carelessly when they reached the Hall. "I see they've finally managed to hack a place for us out of the wilderness," he said, noting with approval that the grass had been trimmed. The gardens stretched out before them, a mass of overgrown vegetation, but at least they could walk the paths without struggling through knee-high growth.

"I want to revive the formal gardens," Clare said. Pointing this way and that, she began to outline her plans, and Justin saw her light up with animation. Her hazel eyes shone brightly, and she spoke with the same joyful tone she used when talking about the hall. Justin watched her in wonder, admiring her tall, shapely form, her beautiful, brilliant face, while she...she lovingly eyed the weeds.

Feeling a strange stab of something akin to jealousy, Justin tried to dismiss it, but couldn't. "This is why you married me, isn't it?" he asked. Clare turned to him, her expression showing only puzzlement, but he searched her features keenly, probing those hazel depths for any hint of dissembling. "For the castle?"

Clare smiled and put up a hand to the dark hair being tossed about her face by the breeze. "Partly, yes," she said. "You know I've always loved it. I wanted to save it."

"And the other part?" Justin asked, feeling momentarily stricken and tense. It didn't matter what his own motives for the marriage had been. He suddenly needed to hear Clare's reasons, and he didn't want them to be as passionless as his own.

She looked away, delaying her answer, and a darkness descended upon him. Perhaps he didn't really want to hear, Justin thought. But when she opened her mouth to speak, he strained to listen. "Maybe to save you from yourself, Justin," Clare said lightly, and the world brightened again. He relaxed, letting out the breath he had been holding. Although it wasn't precisely the answer he wanted, it was more than he'd expected.

She turned back to him. "Admit it, it's not so bad living here with me," she teased, and for a moment he caught a familiar light in her gaze. "Just look at you. Now that you aren't drinking all the time, you look so much better."

"As opposed to last week when I was repulsive?" he asked dryly.

Clare laughed, the sound drifting through the air to him like sunshine. "As you know all too well, Justin St. John, you are too handsome for your own good. But all that liquor does something after a while. I would hate to see you end up all puffy faced like Mr. Cobb."

"Or the squire," Justin said simply.

"Or the squire," Clare repeated. Then she smiled. "Though I certainly cannot picture you ever getting fat." Justin watched Clare's eyes travel over him, from his hair, down past his shoulders and chest to his waist, and finally to his thighs, and he was hard-pressed not to reach for her.

"And all this activity that I've been forcing upon you has only made you look...healthier," she said, her voice huskier than normal.

Justin, who had grown hot under her perusal, could think of another activity he would easily submit to under her direction.

"All that lying around, drinking and gambling," Clare chided, raising her eyes to his. "It could hardly be good for you. Fresh air and riding, isn't it much better?'' she asked hopefully.

"Much," Justin said slowly. Riding was just what he had in mind, he thought as he let waves of desire for her rise and flow over him. "All right," he said, with a grin. "I am suitably prettified. You've improved my looks, my health and my...appetites. Now what?" The not-so-subtle insinuation sailed right over her dark head, and he smiled at her sweet innocence.

"Well..." Her words trailed off as she looked away, her hand lifting again to keep the dark locks from whipping across her face.

"Kiss me, Clare," Justin said softly, without even intending to. He saw her surprise as she whirled back to him. "Just a kiss," he urged, "since I am so much better looking, owing to my wife's new regime."

She looked embarrassed, as though she was going to try to deny the request, but she smiled nervously and stepped toward him. "I'm afraid I'm not very good at this," she said, and he could see the dismay in her eyes. Didn't she want to kiss him?

Clare wanted to kiss him very much. She had always longed to caress her prince, and now that she knew what would happen, she was more than willing to melt in his arms like so much candle tallow. But she had no idea how to begin, and the vision of all those who came before her returned to mock her. How could she compete with the elegant London ladies who knew what they were about? Justin, she decided, would be sadly disappointed with her. She swallowed hard.

"You'll do fine," he said. He raised a hand to brush back her hair and left it cradled against her neck, where it sent shivers throughout her entire body. She took a deep breath, and placing her hands on his lapels, leaned up and pressed her lips against his. They felt good, she thought, her heart hammering in her chest. But Justin remained still. Perhaps...

She traced his lips with her tongue, and suddenly he groaned and pulled her against him until she could feel his hardness. His tongue swept into her mouth, and she slipped her arms around his neck, clinging to him for fear her knees would buckle as she dissolved into his heat. Justin, oh my, Justin...

His lips moved over hers, clinging and caressing before opening her mouth again to delve inside, and she lost her breath. When she tried, tentatively, to kiss him in return, he inhaled sharply, and when she met his tongue with her own, he groaned anew, pulling her closer. "Clare, I need you," he whispered against her cheek as he cupped her to his body. "Let's go in, upstairs."

Clare, who had forgotten they were standing on the rear lawn in plain sight of anyone in or out of the castle, whimpered agreement. She ran a hand along his face, and slipped her fingers into his hair. Justin, Justin, hers at last, holding her, kissing her. Justin in the flesh was so much more than she had ever dreamed, and she didn't want this soaring euphoria to end. She wanted to lie down and be done with this standing, which was so difficult when the warm dizziness threatened to overwhelm her. Such a nuisance was this balancing, and by lying down, perhaps she could get closer to him, feel his strength, touch him....

It was all Justin could do not to pull her down into the grass with him. If it had still been tall, he might have, but he knew that the ground was hardly the place to ease one's wife into the joys of marriage. Still, she was so pliant—eager even—that Justin hated to break the spell.

He slipped a hand between them, sliding it under her spencer and over her breast, encased in the soft cloth of her gown. He heard her gasp and knew that soon he wouldn't give a damn where they were. His thumb worked the sweetness lying under the silk as his mouth moved down her neck. "Clare, let me take you upstairs," he whispered. "Let me...Clare, let me love you."

Justin felt her stiffen immediately. What the devil? She pulled back, taking her arms from his neck and actually pushed on his chest to make him release her. Then she turned and fled across the bridge into the castle. He leaned over, resting his hands on his thighs as he tried to calm his raging desires. "Clare," he shouted. "Blast it!"

She was too far away to hear him, Justin realized, swearing softly. He straightened to go after her, and then thought better of it. After all, he had promised to give her time, and yet here he was pressing her—pressing her because he was so bloody needy. Justin did not care for the feeling, and his pride refused to let him beg for any woman's favors, even Clare's. After stomping around the grounds in a fit of frustration, he decided the squire was right. He ought to tear down the whole blasted stables.

CHAPTER NINE

CONCIOUS OF THE WATCHFUL EYES of the servants, Clare slowed her pace inside the hall. She slipped upstairs, heading toward her chambers, apprehensive of Justin trying to corner her there. She stepped into one of the empty rooms and made her way to a window to look out upon the drive and the old gardens.

Justin was not in sight. Just as well, she thought, as long as he did not come in search of her. Her face heated at the memory of his embrace and his kisses, and she raised her hands to her head as if to banish her confusion. She longed for his touch, melted under it, and yet it meant total *surrender*.

The word appeared out of nowhere to describe her distress. If she let herself be carried away by his passion, just how far would Justin take her? Would she lose herself in the process? Clare pushed a fist against her mouth, stifling the fear that welled up in her, for she knew she was unwilling—unable—to give him her heart again.

An image of Amanda and Justin, naked and entwined, swam before her eyes, and she realized how much better suited the maid had been for Justin's bed. Together they had shared intimacies that meant nothing to either one of them, but for Clare it could not be that easy. When Justin kissed her, she felt herself being sucked into his very being, where she was afraid to go.

BY THE TIME Justin had calmed down enough to go in and change for dinner, Clare was nowhere to be seen. As he was dressing, a commotion outside drew his attention to the window, and he found her. Justin groaned aloud, and this time the sound had nothing to do with pleasure. Down below, stepping from a carriage, was Eugenia Butterfield, and his wife was greeting her.

He decided not to leave for London immediately, on the extremely slim chance that Clare might come to his room tonight. Tomorrow would be soon enough, he mused. He would find out just how long her aunt planned to stay, and would schedule his return for when the hen witted woman was gone.

London would be a welcome diversion after his quiet stay here, Justin told himself. He would find Fletcher and berate his friend for not keeping the aunt at arm's length during his elopement. Then he would look in at one of the clubs and play a little... No, he had sworn off gambling. Impatiently waving his valet away, Justin tied his neck cloth with sharp tugs that grew more vigorous as the full import of his situation sunk in. What the devil was there to do in London when he had forsworn gambling, drinking and women?

"JUSTIN THINKS you don't like him," Clare said to her aunt, determined to smooth over things between the two before Justin came down for dinner.

"I don't," Eugenia answered bluntly.

"But you don't even know him," Clare said.

"I suppose I don't, but even someone as far from the center of society as I am has heard of him. Such a reputation! I had no idea the man was looking for a wife, but, of course, now that he's your husband, I'm sure he'll mend his ways." Eugenia turned her face to Clare worriedly. "Won't he?"

"Of course," Clare assured her aunt with a smile.

"Well, then I suppose I shall have to change my mind

about him, though I can't say I care for the way he bullied me when he came to the house."

"I'm sure he was just worried about me," Clare explained. "I know he can be a bit abrupt, but usually he's most charming."

"Well, that's what they say about him, but I never saw it myself." Eugenia paused to squint at her niece fiercely. "I must say that you didn't appear to be too happy with his suit, either, Clare, and that's why I was so terribly concerned when you eloped."

"I'm sorry," Clare said sincerely. "It was dreadful of me to go off without telling you, but Justin can be so persuasive. I was not quite sure I wanted to marry him at first, but then he...then I decided that it would be best," she finished lamely. How could she explain the complex tenor of their relationship, spanning the years with a wide range of love and hate and friendship?

Eugenia frowned a little worriedly. "I know your father was determined that you marry, and, of course, the only consideration should be that the match was advantageous. A woman must do her duty, you know," Eugenia said, nodding so that her pale hair bounced about her face. "But I wouldn't want you to be unhappy, child. You aren't, are you?"

Clare laughed. "No, dear aunt, I am perfectly happy," she replied, and she proceeded to explain all her plans for improving the castle and the grounds while they waited to go in to dinner. She only stopped when she caught sight of Justin out of the corner of her eye. He was dressed all in black but for the white of his cravat, and looked so utterly handsome, she didn't see how even Eugenia could remain unaffected.

"Justin," Clare said. "You remember my aunt, Eugenia Butterfield?"

"Of course," Justin said in his most charming voice as he bent low over Eugenia's hand. "It is such a pleasure to see you again." Clare's heart pounded just watching him emit elegant allure from every inch of his tall, well-formed frame, and she waited anxiously for her aunt's reaction. Although Eugenia did not flutter in response, as most women would have, she did unbend a little, and Clare released her pent-up breath. One small battle won.

For his part, Justin hardly claimed it a victory. He had no desire to add Aunt Eugenia to his list of conquered females, but it would, he knew, make things decidedly more comfortable for them all if she felt more charitably toward him. Still, he fully intended to leave for London tomorrow, and not long after the first course, he decided to break the news to his wife.

The announcement was made difficult by the fact that Clare was beaming at him proudly, just as though his small graciousness toward her aunt was a splendid feat. In the candlelight, her flawless skin glowed like honey, the deep blue gown she wore exposing so much of it to his gaze that he found it hard to concentrate on his dinner.

"Clare," Justin said finally. "I've decided that tomorrow I'm going to—" She eyed him expectantly, a soft smile curving her lips, and he wished he were close enough to gaze into her hazel eyes. "—to tear down the stables."

Justin sat there, feeling stupid but relieved, while Clare nodded enthusiastically. He realized with sudden certainty that he had no desire to leave his wife as yet, even for a brief trip to London. The things that had lured him to town before seemed but trifles in comparison to the woman who held him here at the hall. And as for the aunt, well, he would be busy with the stables, and out there he was certain he would rarely have to see the woman.

"YOUR AUNT, my lady," Harris said tonelessly, and Clare looked up to see the butler gesture for Eugenia to enter the parlor. From Harris's stricken expression, she guessed Eugenia had annoyed him, too, but how she had managed to do so this early in the morning, she had no idea.

"Oh, Clare, these large country houses are so confusing," Eugenia said, sinking into a brocaded chair. "I don't know how you find your way from one end to the other, I truly don't," she added, yellow curls flying frantically about her face.

"Thank you, Mr. Harris," Clare said, giving the butler a look that told him he ought to be ashamed of himself. "It is quite large. Small for a castle, of course, but huge in comparison to my home or the town house we shared," Clare said. "If you need direction, you have only to ask one of the servants."

"There are quite a few of them, aren't there?" Eugenia asked. "I hardly know what to do with myself, there are so many willing to do for me."

"Just relax and enjoy your stay," Clare said with a smile.

"Oh, I wish I could, but I feel as though I was remiss in my duties toward you, child," Eugenia replied with a sigh. "I should have insisted on being involved in your upbringing, but you know your father was never very cordial, and I could hardly argue with him. He is such a forceful man."

Clare cut her off. "Oh, Aunt, don't worry about that," she said. "I know how papa can be. Look at these old drawings I found of the castle." She held up a depiction of the hall, but her aunt would not be deterred.

"So, of course, I could hardly argue with him about his choice for your husband, either. After all, Clare, it is a woman's duty to marry advantageously," Eugenia pointed out again.

"And so I did," Clare answered, dropping the sketch back onto the table. She was wondering if the tapestries shown in it might be found in one of the storage rooms.

"And so you did. But now, Clare, your duty is to your husband, and although he might not have been your choice, it is your responsibility to be a good wife," Eugenia said.

Her voice sounded so odd that Clare looked up. Her aunt was squinting ferociously, her bosom heaving with emotion, and Clare could only wonder what she was getting worked up about. "I know that his reputation is...unsavory, but Clare, you must do your duty," Eugenia said firmly.

"I will," Clare said soothingly. "Now, don't take on so, Aunt."

Eugenia took a deep breath. "Clare, I mean it," she said, her head bobbing.

"So do I," Clare answered calmly. "I don't know what is distressing you. Papa said you were upset about the elopement, and I can understand that, but everything is fine now. I promise you that I will take good care of Justin, if that's what has you worried," she added with a smile.

"But, my dear, there is simply more to it than that," Eugenia said. "When I refer to your duty, I mean that a woman must take care of her husband and—and give him an heir." She finished the words on a strangled note, and looked anywhere but at Clare, who glanced over at her in startled surprise.

Eugenia was now pink with embarrassment. "I might not have married myself, but I was brought up to know the responsibilities of a gentlewoman, and one of them is—is—Clare, you must do your duty."

Clare stared, stunned, while her aunt continued, "Personally, I can't see why you are not already engaged in this *task*. Although I must admit I didn't care for the marquis at first, he is rather personable and handsome. Not being privy to London gossip, you might not be aware of it, but he has quite a reputation for being talented at that sort of thing. If I recall correctly, rumor always had a number of fashionable ladies all wanting to be his paramour," Eugenia whispered.

Clare frowned. As if she needed that thrown into her face. "Thank you, but I've already spoken to one of his references," she snapped. She slapped the drawings together firmly and stood up.

"Now, dear, don't be difficult. You know how that confuses me," Eugenia said.

"I do not wish to discuss this."

"But Clare, you said you would take care of him. You said you were happy, and that he's all that he should be. What more do you want?" Eugenia asked.

"I want him to love me!" Clare shouted. The words escaped before she even realized she had opened her mouth to speak. Stricken, she raised a hand to her mouth, and choked on a sob. Blast it, why couldn't her aunt just leave well enough alone?

"Oh, dear, I must be going," Eugenia said, rising from her chair.

"No," Clare protested. "Please don't, Aunt. I didn't mean to yell at you."

Eugenia smiled as she stepped toward Clare. "Now, Clare. I just came to see for myself that you were fine, and you are. But I'm here much too early for a long stay. You and your husband need time to be alone together, without a guest in the house," she said, reaching up to pat Clare's cheek. She turned to go. "I'll just have one of those nice servants get my things."

"Aunt Eugenia, wait," Clare called, walking after her. "This really isn't necessary. Now that you are here, you might as well have a comfortable visit. Justin and I will have plenty of time to be together," Clare protested. If the truth were known, she was not certain exactly how much time she wanted to spend alone with her husband anyway.

Eugenia brushed off her words as she flitted down the hallway like a bird in flight. "You two need time to work things out, and you don't need me getting in the way. I do so want everything to turn out for you, dear," she said, pausing to eye Clare warmly. Then she promptly turned in the wrong direction.

Setting her to rights, Clare walked along with her, still trying to convince her to remain. "Really, Aunt, everything will be just fine. I'll consider your advice," she said, swallowing hard. "And as for that other bit of business back in the parlor, it doesn't mean a thing. I was just being foolish."

Eugenia paid no heed, but stopped in the upper hallway to look around. "Now where is my room?" she asked. "Do keep it ready for me, and I'll return later—after you two get to know each other."

Clare cursed her own tongue for its betrayal and her aunt for her prying as she walked back downstairs. The problem was that she already knew Justin far too well! Glaring at every servant she saw, she wondered just which one had informed her aunt that she wasn't "doing her duty."

She was going to send one of them for Justin, so that he would come to see Aunt Eugenia off, but the fresh air beckoned her, so she went to look for him herself, ordering up a coach and driver for her aunt while she was about it. Some local men were already at work tearing down the stables, and Clare had to pick her way inside to find her husband. She had to look twice before she realized the figure before her was him, and then she gulped.

Justin hardly looked like a marquis, for he had stripped off his shirt and his muscular chest gleamed with sweat. She had no idea what sort of physical labor he had been doing, but he looked so very good that she could only stare in dismay. The same disreputable thatch of dark hair fell over one eye, but her gaze was drawn to his chest, smooth and broad and shining, and tapering down to his narrow waist. His doeskin breeches clung to his thighs, and he had one leg up, resting on a pile of rubble, his expensive top boots layered with dust.

He was so absolutely beautiful it was no wonder that women fought for his favors, Clare mused. She felt herself grow warm at the very sight of him. The thought of touching him, of exploring that perfect body, of being on the receiving end of Justin's skilled passion, made her weak.

Then she noticed the chain around his neck, her dragon

charm dangling against his skin. The sight of it made hope flicker in her heart for just a moment before memory flooded her, and she was drowning in the past. Suddenly, there was Justin without his shirt again, younger and leaner, telling her he didn't give a damn.

"Clare," Justin said, bringing her back to the present. He grinned in greeting, but she could not answer in kind.

"Please put your shirt on," she snapped.

"Why?" Justin asked, glancing behind her for signs of her aunt. He found it hard to believe that the harridan had followed Clare into the stables.

"Because it brings back bad memories," she said curtly.

Justin laughed, certain she was teasing him. "By faith, Clare, how are we ever going to consummate this marriage if the sight of me with my shirt off brings back bad memories?"

"Oh, no! Not from you, too!" Clare shouted. "I'm sick to death of hearing about it, Justin St. John. You would think that nothing in the entire kingdom was more important, from the way the servants are gossiping about it. I don't even like servants. I don't want any servants, if that's the way it's going to be!"

Justin stared at her dumbfounded. What the devil was she yelling about? Her eyes lighted on his shirt, then she grabbed it up and threw it at his chest, where he caught it with one hand. "If you can't wait another minute, then don't!" Clare practically screeched.

She found his jacket next and launched it at his head. Not as quick this time, Justin found he did not care for the indignity of wearing one of his best brown superfines on his hair. He pulled it down with an oath. "Blast it, Clare! What is the matter?"

"Go find one of your other women, if you have to. Go please them all, for all I care. Perhaps I can read about your exploits in the *Post,* with hundreds of ladies attesting to your virility—in spades! Go on,'' she said with a sob, ''I release you from all your promises!''

She whirled and walked out, leaving Justin totally bewildered. ''Clare!'' He called after her and stepped forward, nearly pitching headfirst onto the rubble at his feet. Swearing a blue streak, he pulled on his shirt so hard that he nearly put a fist through the fabric. The coat he tossed onto the ground in a heap as he stalked after her.

Outside, he found Eugenia Butterfield climbing into his coach. What the devil? ''Where are you going?'' he growled. Eugenia didn't even flinch, but looked daggers at him.

''Aunt Eugenia is going back to London,'' Clare said brittlely as she stood by.

''What did I do?'' Justin asked in frustration. Having lost all sense of decorum, he raised his palms to the heavens to give him strength. ''Did I do something?''

''No, my lord,'' Eugenia said stiffly. ''It's what you didn't do.'' She shook her head, so that yellow hair flew everywhere.

''What?'' Justin asked. ''What?'' He ground his teeth wondering how Clare managed to thrust him into these situations that resembled nothing more than poorly acted farces. And he…he felt like one of the amateur players.

''Nothing, Justin,'' Clare said, scowling. ''Aunt Eugenia will be back for a longer stay later. Perhaps next month?'' she asked, stepping toward the coach window.

''Perhaps,'' Eugenia answered. ''But now, Clare, I'm expecting you to do your duty,'' she said firmly. Then she eyed Justin meaningfully, although exactly what meaning she intended, he had no idea. Perhaps the woman's confusion was contagious, he thought, momentarily diverted by the notion. Having first spread to Clare, now it was turning his own brain to mush, and so on throughout the country. Justin raised his hand, trying to wave as cordially as he could. Reining in his anger and frustration, he tried to think positively. At least the woman was leaving.

As soon as the coach rolled down the drive, Clare turned to walk back to the house, but this time Justin was determined not to let her go. He put a hand on her arm, gently restraining her, and looked down into her face. Clare's eloquent features were awash with distress, and he felt as though someone had kicked him in the ribs. Oh, Clare, don't cry, Justin prayed fervently.

"What was that all about?" he asked softly. She shook her head and tried to turn away. "Clare, It's me, Justin. Tell me what has happened, what I've done to anger you so much." She only shook her head, as if she couldn't speak, and he longed to hold her, so much that he ached. "Oh, Clare," he whispered, finally giving in and pulling her close. To his surprise, she did not resist, but rested her head on his chest.

"Are you upset because your aunt is leaving?" he asked. "If you are, I'll go after her. I'll try to talk with her, to make her feel more welcome." Justin could hardly believe what he was saying. Clare had definitely put one of her spells upon him. Either that or he was a real glutton for punishment.

"No, that's not it," Clare said brokenly. "It's just that everyone's talking about how I'm not a proper wife, and I just...I'm so embarrassed and ashamed. But it's of no consequence, Justin."

He tried to make sense out of that muddle. "Who's talking about you?"

"The servants. They told Aunt Eugenia that we weren't...sharing a bed."

Justin felt a quick surge of anger at the pettiness of others, especially that harridan aunt. "I find it hard to believe that the members of my staff, who are quite accustomed to keeping their mouths firmly shut amongst the intrigues of London, are bursting to tell everyone that we aren't sleeping together," Justin said dryly. "My guess is that your aunt was trying, in her backward way, to find out if all was as it should be, and the end result was, of course, confusion."

She lifted her head at his words, and he was rewarded with a tremulous smile that made him long to kiss her tender lips. Keep out of this, he ordered the lower part of his body.

"You are being sweet, Justin, but it's unfair of me to hold you to all those promises when I can't... I release you from them all," Clare whispered, looking down at his shirt.

He put a finger under her chin to raise it, so he could look into her face. Her eyes were so beautiful he thought he could lose himself in them, lose himself in Clare. He held her gaze calmly. "But I don't want to be released."

Again he wanted to kiss her, but he willed the primal lust that so often overcame him to stay away, and hugged her to him gently instead. "You're just upset because I took off my shirt," he said wryly. Bad memories. And he knew just which ones. The past lay between them like a deep, black crevice that they tried to dance around with little or no success.

"Clare?" he said softly. "I know there are bad memories, but don't you have some good memories, too?" he asked, hardly daring to wait for the answer. "I do," he said quickly. "Oh, Clare, I have so many of them, all of you." Justin felt his throat grow oddly constricted, and he couldn't finish. He rested his chin on the top of her head. "Maybe we should try to recapture some of the good ones," he added finally.

"I know," he said, suddenly struck with inspiration. "Let's go fishing, just like we used to! I wonder if that old tree trunk is still there."

"That was the best spot," Clare said, her voice muffled against his shirt.

Justin felt his heart pound in response. She looked up at him, her flawless skin all peaches and cream, and smiled tentatively.

"I'll have to change," she said.

"I'll tell the cook to pack us a picnic," Justin said. He felt her move in his arms, and he let her go, reluctantly, but kept close to her as they walked into the hall. For the first time in a long time, he felt his spirits lift. Perhaps there was a way across the dark ravine of the past.

ALTHOUGH THE AREA was a bit more overgrown, they found the spot much the same as they had left it several years ago. The huge old tree straddled the river as it always had, and the tall oaks and hemlocks along the bank spread their branches over the water, making the surface a brilliant blend of light and shadow. The only sound was the rustle of the leaves overhead, the creak of the branches and the songs of the ever present thrushes.

Seating himself on the edge of the log, Justin tugged at one boot, then looked up at Clare with a grin. "Would the sight of my bare feet offend you?"

"No," Clare said, making a face at his teasing.

Justin breathed a sigh of relief. It was bad enough that he could not remove his shirt in her presence. "Good," he said. "Then I'm going to take off my boots."

He tossed them aside just in time to see Clare remove her stockings without the slightest hint of modesty. *Oh, Clare, you are such a bewildering, bewitching creature,* he thought as he caught a glimpse of a shapely ankle. Then she stepped right past him, her toes gripping the bark as she walked along the giant log. He was up behind her in a moment, and soon they were both balancing on it, and laughing like children when they nearly lost their footing.

In the middle of the natural bridge, they sat down and tended to their poles. Justin watched Clare push a fat worm onto her hook without a moment's hesitation, and realized just how much a part of this world she was. She didn't belong back in glittering London. She could shine there, too, but not as brightly as here at home. *Their* home, he thought grudgingly, for the hall was a perfect setting for this radiant beauty who was such an odd mixture of fairy stories and tomboy, of dreams and common sense.

As if aware of his perusal, Clare glanced up and gave him a wry look. "As I recall, you were more often on the shore, fast asleep," she said.

"Untrue! I was focusing all my immense concentration on the fish, so that they would be drawn to my line."

Clare laughed, the throaty sound dancing across the river like sunshine, and Justin stared at her. She was laughing again, and there was hope for the world—at least his small corner of it.

By faith, he felt good. And she had wanted to release him from his promises! Over his dead body. He didn't want to be released. He didn't want a drink, didn't need one to escape from himself, because he was happy right where he was. Even though he wasn't sure if he would be pummeled one minute or hugged the next, he was content. And he certainly didn't want any other woman on earth. He wanted the one right next to him, the one dangling her dainty toes in the water in delightful abandon.

Better not let his thoughts move in that direction, Justin told himself as he felt the hot surge of need run through him. Even in one of her old gowns, a faded muslin dotted with pale flowers, she looked beautiful. Her dark hair was flowing loosely around her shoulders in a thick, shining mass, and her sweet mouth was upturned at the corners in just a hint of a smile.

Justin tore his eyes away and looked at the sun, sparkling through the leaves above, while he tried to think of something else besides running his hands over Clare's silky skin. "It's beautiful here, isn't it?" he finally said.

"Yes," Clare breathed as she gazed about her. The water was dappled with bright, glittering light, the shadows under the trees a cool, dark contrast. The air was fresh and sweet with the scent of primroses, and the river ran gently beneath them, singing its patient song.

"Peace and quiet, that's what I think I liked most about coming here," Justin said. "God knows I rarely caught any fish," he added with a grin.

"That's because you were always asleep," Clare chided, smiling at him. He was much more beautiful than the scenery, she decided. His white shirt was open at the neck, showing some of his smooth, tanned chest, and his thighs, encased in their snug breeches, looked as hard as iron beside her. "That's probably why you found it peaceful, too," she said. "*I* happened to catch some delicious fish here, but then I was not usually napping."

"I was not always asleep, for pity's sake!" Justin said with mock indignation. "I seem to remember wading into this icy water to retrieve a blasted hat of yours at one time."

"Oh!" Clare said softly as the memory flooded back, and in her mind's eye she could see Justin, younger and more carefree, walking through the stream to reach her old straw bonnet. "I do remember that," she said, suddenly feeling a lump in her throat. "You were always so gallant," she said, looking down at the water with a tremulous smile. "Just like one of the heroes from my stories."

Beside her, Justin sighed. "Unfortunately, I turned out to be a real man, with real failings," he said.

"No, Justin," Clare corrected. "You're a real man, with *more* than your share of failings."

Justin looked wholly insulted. "Why, I ought to..." he growled, pretending to push her from her seat, and Clare shrieked, kicking at his legs. He released her, yet she kept her toes where they were, running them absently along the firm muscles of his bare calf. It felt nice.

"But you are reforming me, Clare, and soon I mean to have but a normal number of failings," Justin assured her. Then he turned his face toward her, his eyes serious. "Don't set standards too high for me, Clare, for I can't meet them."

Clare could tell that he meant what he said, and perhaps he was right to warn her. Before, she had made him over in her mind into all that she had wanted him to be, and maybe, just maybe, he had collapsed under the weight of her expectations.

"Nonsense," she said lightly. "Why, look at how much you've improved already, since you haven't been drinking and have been doing all that heavy work," she teased, "building muscles." I can even feel them, she thought a little giddily as she slid a toe along his leg.

"If I'm such a fine specimen, why don't you make love to me, Clare?" Justin asked, his voice oddly tight.

Angry that he would bring up the distressing topic again so soon, Clare glanced over at him with a frown, but his dark eyes were neither taunting nor demanding. She had the feeling that he simply wanted an answer, but she didn't know what to say, for she wasn't certain herself. This morning she had given her aunt a reason, yet it was not one that she wished to share with Justin. She looked down at the water and gripped her pole nervously. "I wouldn't know a thing about it," she whispered finally.

"I should hope not," Justin answered, his tone lighter. "But you grew up in the country, Clare. You must have an inkling of how it's done."

"What's that supposed to mean?" she asked, glaring at him.

Justin grinned. "I mean, the squire's been breeding horses for years, and didn't you help deliver a foal at one time?"

Clare stared at him and gasped. "You don't mean it's like breeding horses!" She frowned in distaste, certain he was teasing her.

Justin chuckled. "Well, not exactly, but I do believe that animal and human mating are based on the same simple principles."

Horrified, Clare could no longer even look at him. She turned her gaze to the river, but she saw a stallion at stud instead. She could not reconcile the memory of Justin's kisses with the animal's behavior until she recalled the image of him naked in the bath, a certain part of him rising ramrod straight from the water. With a hot blush bathing her cheeks, she stole a glance down at Justin's lap, where the body part in question was nestled, dormant, between his legs. She looked away immediately.

"The devil take you, Justin St. John, for if that's how it's done, I want no part of it," she said. "I imagine that it's most uncomfortable, and ridiculous appearing besides."

Justin laughed so hard that he nearly dropped his fishing pole, while Clare continued to mull over the import of his explanation. "And why those London women line up waiting for you to do *that* to them, I cannot imagine!" she added in dismayed accents. She looked over, to see if he was paying attention to her words, only to find him doubled over in amusement. How dare he laugh at her? Outraged and embarrassed, Clare decided one nudge in the right direction should do it.

She pushed him right off the log.

CHAPTER TEN

JUSTIN WAS STILL LAUGHING when he came up from the water. He shook his head, his dark hair flashing drops across the sun's path, and stood up, the water lapping around his chest. Clare giggled at the sight of him, her anger and tension melting away, until he reached up to close his fingers around her ankle.

"Justin, no!" she protested, but before she could scramble out of the way, he tugged on her leg and she slid forward. She hit the river with a smack, her rage dissolving in the deliciously cold, clear water. Knowing the stones could be sharp, she didn't put down her feet, but threw her arms around Justin instead.

He fell back, nearly going under again. "What, Clare, would you drown me?" he spluttered.

"Are you insinuating I'm heavy?" she asked, grabbing a handful of his wet hair and pulling on it.

"Ouch! Of course not, my dear wife," Justin said. "I like having you clinging to me," he added with a devilish grin.

"If you think I'm going to put my bare feet down on these rocks, you're mad," Clare said, careful to explain the reason behind her embrace. "You can get your feet cut in this river, in case you've forgotten."

"Afraid of a few rocks, are we?" Justin teased as his arms closed around her. "I thought it was the snapping turtles."

"Justin St. John, there are no snapping turtles in this river!" Clare said, laughing.

"Just trying to keep you hanging on to me. I like it," he growled, sliding a hand up under her skirts to her thigh.

"Justin!"

"I believe, my dear Clare, that I have you right where I want you," he said wickedly.

"You do not," she protested airily. "I shall simply swim away."

"I won't let you go," Justin responded, and she felt his arms tighten pleasantly around her. He leaned back until only their necks were above water, as if threatening to take her under with him, and she shrieked, securing her hold around his neck. While he grinned at her, she felt his hands underneath her skirts again, lifting her legs until she was straddling him in what was, she was sure, a most indecent fashion.

Then he stood up, and as the water fell away, Clare found herself pressed against his body, tighter than she had ever thought possible. She noted with dismay that her gown was plastered to her breasts, and through the thin fabric she could feel Justin's chest, hot against her nipples.

She looked at his face, only inches from her own, and she could see the amusement leave it, see the change in his eyes. Though she wasn't sure exactly what it meant, she felt her heart leap in response.

"I could love you right here, right now, like this," Justin said huskily.

"Justin—" she began.

"Is it so bad, Clare?" he asked, his dark gaze serious and full of longing.

"No, but I—"

"It's not like you to be afraid, Clare."

"I'm not afraid," she answered heatedly. And truly, it was not the physical closeness that scared her. The warmth of his arms, the touch of his body to hers was exciting, tempting her to discover the delights that he promised her.

"Then what is it?" They stood eye to eye, their bodies locked together, their hearts racing in unison as her breasts pressed into his broad chest.

I want you to love me, just as I always dreamed you would! The words formed in her head, but Clare couldn't say them. She could only blink helplessly at his dark stare.

He cupped his hands underneath her and moved her against him. She gasped as she felt him, no longer dormant, but hard under the thin material of his breeches. "Clare, I want you so much I hurt. I admit that I always thought of you as a child, but then, when I saw you grown-up, more beautiful than ever—more beautiful than any woman I have ever known—I wanted you. I want to touch you, to be inside you," he said in a hushed, yet fierce voice.

Clare dropped her head to his shoulder, unable to hold his gaze as she blushed with embarrassment. "It will be good, Clare, better than anything," he whispered into her hair. She shivered at the words that promised so much, for her body was ready and willing and eager, and she knew it. And what would be wrong? He was her husband, for God's sake!

But he doesn't love me, her mind answered. He left me. He abandoned me....

Justin moved her against him again, and Clare lost all train of thought. "Kiss me, Clare," he urged, and she couldn't fight that beckoning voice any longer.

With a cry of pain and longing, she entwined her fingers in his wet locks, lifted her head and kissed him. It was as if the river exploded around them, though she felt nary a ripple. Justin's tongue swept into her mouth, and she met it with her own, tasting and savoring as her hands curved into fists in his hair.

Their lips met and broke apart and met again hungrily, and Clare pressed herself against him, rubbing her hips against his arousal until he groaned. All the longing she had ever felt for him seemed to burst forth like a cannon shot, and suddenly she could not stop herself or pretend to contain it. How long they stayed there, soaking wet in the middle of the stream, Clare had no idea. She only knew she wanted Justin to kiss her forever.

Finally, he leaned her back into the water, and she felt it slosh around her as his mouth moved down her throat to her shoulders. Then he was tugging impatiently at the wet fabric of her gown, until he had bared her breasts. Cold water moved over them, making Clare shiver, but Justin's hand brought warmth, his lean fingers cupping and caressing. When the air hit her wet nipples, she cried out at the sensation, wanting, needing some kind of surcease, and Justin answered her plea, covering one with his mouth. She whimpered as he suckled, the water playing in her hair, his wet locks smooth against her neck.

It was too much. Clare felt overwhelmed by everything—Justin's touch, his lips, the river, the rhythm of his hips against hers, and her own unforeseen, ungovernable desires. For someone so steeped in dreams, Clare suddenly decided she didn't like the way she seemed to be slipping away from reality.

"No bad memories, Clare. I don't have to be naked," Justin whispered, his voice so hot that she leapt against him at his words. Clare felt like a slave to her body, held in thrall by the passions he aroused in her. Awakened to the potent power of him, she was sinking—not into the water, but in the unbelievable, exquisite sensations that he created. She was on the brink of giving him everything, trading her very soul for the feel of his hands upon her, his mouth against her.... But what would she have to call her own if he put her aside again?

It was all happening too fast, everything careening out of control, and she wasn't prepared. How had their nice, tame fishing jaunt turned into this? Suddenly, inexplicably,

Clare's mind took over, and she didn't want to feel these feelings anymore. "Justin, stop," she gasped. "I'm afraid."

He immediately lifted her head, his eyes, dark and brimming with a wild look, rising to hers. She couldn't meet his gaze. "I won't drown you, love," he whispered, misreading her concern.

"Don't call me that," Clare said, lashing out at him. She struggled to right herself, and Justin did it for her, but she was still locked in his embrace, her gown down to her waist. "Blast it," she sobbed.

"Clare, what is it?"

She didn't know how to answer, feeling awkward and embarrassed and resenting him for making her body respond so passionately. "I can't do it," she said. "Not here, not like this. Maybe not ever. Maybe there's something wrong with me."

"There's nothing wrong with you," Justin said firmly. "It's my fault. I'm not used to...I was going too fast. I got carried away," he said, grinning crookedly, as though it were difficult for him.

She could feel his heart thumping against his ribs, and added guilt to her roster of confused emotions. She felt guilty for not being a proper wife, for binding him to promises she herself couldn't keep. Surely she would just go mad, and to the devil with everything.

While she stewed, Justin managed to return her wet gown to its proper place with one skillful tug, and Clare could only wonder suspiciously how he had learned that little trick. Then he picked her up in his arms and began wading toward the bank.

"Well, I must say you're the most delightful catch I've ever gotten from this stream," Justin said cheerfully, pausing before they reached the grass. "Shall I throw you back?" He swung her from him as if to fling her into the river. Clare didn't laugh, but he managed to wring a smile from her. Good. He was glad she didn't realize what a struggle it was for him to make light of a situation that had promised to be the best sexual experience he had ever known, and he had known quite a few. Now it was nothing but a sweet memory, an ache in his loins, and he had only himself to blame. What was it about Clare that made him lose whatever good sense he had, along with his self-control?

She's a virgin, and yet you try to take her in the middle of a river, for God's sake. What's the matter with you? It had seemed like a good idea at the time, Justin thought dismally. Someday, he swore, someday when Clare was wholly comfortable with lovemaking, he would bring her back here and finish what they had started.

"TELL ME A STORY, Clare," Justin asked lazily as he stretched out on the quilt spread over the grass. They had dried off in the sun, then shared their picnic, and now Justin wanted a tale.

The familiar words seemed strange but comforting, and Clare rolled over onto her stomach to get a better look at him, to see if he was teasing. He was not. His hands were tucked behind his head comfortably, while his long, muscular legs were crossed at the ankles, his bare toes curling absently. Justin was definitely relaxed.

Clare smiled in genuine relief at his lethargic state, for she had no wish to begin their sexual battles anew. She was a bit wary when they were alone together because Justin's moods seemed to shift suddenly, and without preamble, in that direction. She had expected him to try to carry her back to his bed after the episode in the river, but he had made no more mention of the embraces that had almost turned the water to steam with their heat, and she was grateful.

Resting her elbows on the quilt and her chin in her hands, Clare appraised him silently. His dark eyes were nearly closed as he looked up at the sky, and she wondered just how long he would remain awake. It would not be the first time her stories had put him to sleep, she thought with a smile. Kicking her bare legs up behind her with total disregard for the fact that she was no longer fourteen, and was now the marchioness of Worthington, Clare began her tale. "Once upon a time, long, long ago, there lived an evil overlord, Baron Blackmoor by name," she said.

"Suitable," Justin commented with a grin, and she was forced to jab him in the arm for his interruption.

"Now Baron Blackmoor had a heart as black as night. Have you heard this one before, Justin?" Clare asked, suddenly unable to recall if she'd told it before.

"No," he answered, still grinning. "I don't believe I have. I'm certain I would have remembered such a disreputable character."

"Good." Clare nodded. "Now Baron Blackmoor kept his people virtually enslaved. He forced them to build a huge stone wall around his lands, and they worked day and night, until they dropped. Ten feet high, and up hill and down dale, around and around it went, and each day he inspected it, to make sure the surface was perfectly smooth and impossible to scale, for this wall was not to protect his lands from attack, but to keep his people inside...."

Although Clare fully expected Justin to fall asleep, he did not. His eyes remained fixed on the sky above or moved to her face, making it hard for her to concentrate as she spoke. Then he smiled in encouragement, and she went on, pleased that he still liked to listen. When she finished, he grinned with pleasure, praised her and turned onto his side, the open neck of his shirt revealing a glittering bit of gold, caught by the sun.

Her mouth tightened against the sudden lump in her throat, and Clare reached out for it, her fingers brushing against the warmth of his chest as she freed the chain to fall into her hand. She looked down into her palm, knowing what she would find there: the dragon charm she had once given him for Christmas. The years slipped away, sweeping her up in the love she had once felt for him, and she tried to steady herself. She lifted her eyes to probe his searchingly. "Why?" she asked as steadily as she could.

The dark gaze that greeted her was hooded, hidden, and held no answer. Justin shook his head as if he couldn't speak, and the silence stretched out between then until his lips finally moved. "I wanted to keep something of you with me always," he said hoarsely.

Clare felt like weeping at the words, for sweet as they were, they held little comfort. You could have kept *me* with you always, she thought bitterly, but you chose not to. Unable to meet his eyes, she looked down at the charm and let it fall from her fingers. Like everything else between them, it was bittersweet.

Justin's admission wrenched his gut. He himself had never known why he wore her gift, and yet, why *not* keep something of her? Would that it was more, that he could bottle her laugh or catch her sunbeam smile in glass, its brilliance captured forever. Justin shook his head at his own whimsy. By faith, he was growing positively silly, he thought with chagrin.

He forced himself to admire the fleecy clouds above him, but his glance soon strayed back to Clare, stretched out beside him. Her silken hair had dried as smoothly as if she had put a brush to it. Her gown was tangled around her knees, allowing her long, shapely legs to swing free as she pointed her dainty toes up in the air. The stance, if not the expanse of bared bosom, was familiar. She looked as fragile and delightful as she had four years ago. Now he just had to add "provocative" to the description.

"You weaved a spell upon me from the first moment I saw you," Justin said. "Do you remember?"

"Of course," Clare whispered, her wide hazel eyes gazing at him solemnly. "How could I forget?"

Justin smiled to himself. "There you were, boldly walking into the hall, the most beautiful, winsome child. I thought at first you were a product of my drinking too much, and even after you spoke, I still doubted my senses," he said fondly. "It wasn't until I touched you that I was sure you were real." And from that moment on, he thought, I loved you....

Justin sucked in a breath, startled by the realization. Unwilling to believe it, he tried to gather his wits to deny it. How could he have loved a fourteen-year-old girl? Feeling an overwhelming urge for a drink, he sat up abruptly, determined not to think about the wild conclusion that threatened to disturb his hard-won peace.

Clare watched the play of emotions on Justin's face and wondered what had distressed him. The memories, she assumed. Feeling the heavy pressure of tears behind her lids, she stood up and looked away. Would the two of them ever be at ease again?

"It's getting late," he said. Even his voice sounded shaky, and she found she didn't want to listen to it.

"Yes," she agreed without glancing at him, and she started back toward the castle. Behind her she could hear Justin picking up the basket and blanket, and soon his long strides had caught him up with her. They walked in silence, Clare musing that their attempt at recapturing good memories this afternoon could hardly be deemed successful.

Just as their efforts at lovemaking had been bitterly frustrating, she thought dismally, the recollection bringing a blush to her cheeks. Oh, how easily she had succumbed to his kisses! In all her youthful dreams and all her womanly suppositions, Clare had never imagined that Justin could do such things to her, such unbearably wonderful things, or that she would so desperately want him to continue doing them.

Clare was uncomfortably aware that, like Pandora, she had unleashed something that would do her no good, for knowing just what pleasures were to be had in Justin's arms would make it even more difficult to deny him. Even now, she longed for his kisses, his touch, his voice whispering of his desire.... But she had struggled so hard to be strong, the thought of being vulnerable again made her ill. To be naked before him, not just physically, but emotionally as well, scared her to death.

Justin moved beside her, suddenly impatient to be back at the hall. He still craved a drink—no, a bottle, he decided, suddenly resenting Clare for the foolish promises he had made to her. What was the harm in a little claret, for God's sake? It was not as though he was mean or morose when he drank. He was not one of those fellows who cast up his accounts or behaved in an embarrassing fashion, and his women never complained that it hampered his technique in any way.

His women. Justin suddenly regretted that promise, too, and longed for enough bottles to send him blissfully to sleep. He was sick to death of lying awake half the night, alone in his bed, listening like a hopeful child for the slightest sound from the next room that might signal his wife had taken pity on him and was coming to join him.

Justin's mood blackened with his thoughts. He was not used to exercising forbearance, not skilled in gently wooing a maid. The women who wanted him knew what he was about, and begged him for his attentions. He was unaccustomed to being spurned, for whatever reason, and try as he might to ignore it, it was beginning to wear upon his pride. He hadn't realized he had any of that left, but apparently he did, because it was goading him now that his wife found his lovemaking not to her liking.

Justin schooled himself to patience, but Clare's rejection just seemed to heighten his desire. By faith, he had always laughed at the kind of men who were attracted to women who teased and pretended disinterest. Now he found himself driven to the brink of madness by the sight of his wife's shapely ankle. Madness, he thought grimly. Married only weeks and he was losing his mind, probably an advanced stage of the disease of confusion that Eugenia Butterfield had brought upon his household.

Eugenia Butterfield. Justin felt a momentary horror that she had returned when his eyes lighted on a shiny new phaeton in the drive. Then he saw a familiar figure and groaned. He felt like grabbing Clare's hand and turning back the way they had come, but it was too late. Sauntering around the corner of the demolished stables was Fletcher Mayefield, grinning from ear to ear in a most annoying fashion.

"Oh, we have a guest!" Clare said, appearing immediately discomforted. "I don't look at all as I should," she said, her gaze flying to Justin's.

"It doesn't matter," Justin said with a frown. "Fletcher won't care." Fletcher probably would take one look at the rumpled pair and think they'd been snatching a little love in the out-of-doors, he thought with irritation. *If he smirks at me, I'll wipe his face with my fist.*

"Greetings, my lord, my lady!" Fletcher said, making a courtly bow. He bent over Clare's hand and kissed it.

"What are you doing here?" Justin asked in a surly tone.

"Justin! Is that any way to greet your old friend?" Fletcher asked, laughing at Justin's scowl. "Can't a man bring a wedding gift to your wife?" He waved his hand at the phaeton, and Clare gasped.

"For me?" she asked. She was obviously delighted, which further darkened Justin's mood.

"But of course, my lovely lady," Fletcher said with that spurious charm of his, and Justin felt like gagging—or strangling—the man. The gift was wholly inappropriate, of course, but then most of Fletcher's behavior was inappropriate, Justin thought sourly, forgetting that he himself usually acted in much the same manner.

"Oh, it is beautiful, Mr. Mayefield!" Clare said. "I can't wait to give it I try. Shall I drive you?" she asked.

Justin wondered if steam was rising in great clouds from his skin or simply shooting out his ears. Apparently neither, because no one paid the slightest heed to him. "Perhaps you would care to change before going on an outing," he suggested smoothly. He saw Clare blush and felt like a cad.

"You're right, of course. I do look a fright."

"Nonsense, Clare...may I call you Clare?" Fletcher asked. "Justin and I have been friends for so long that I could hardly stand on ceremony with his wife." He grinned at her nod. "Good. But you look beautiful, Clare, utterly charming, and I shall never forgive Justin for stealing you from under my nose!"

"You are teasing me," Clare said. She seemed to throw off the compliment, but Justin could see the faint blush in her cheeks. "You must join us for dinner, Mr. Mayefield. I hope you have planned to spend a few days at the hall."

"I'm sure Fletcher has pressing matters in London that require his attention," Justin said, giving Fletcher a look that suggested agreement would be a wise course.

Fletcher ignored the glance and smiled innocently. "Truly, Justin, I happen to be perfectly free, and I was hoping to have a nice visit. Don't believe I've ever been to the hall, have I?" he asked. Justin barely grunted a reply.

"You must let me show it to you," Clare said, brimming with enthusiasm.

Justin, unable to bear the byplay for another moment, stalked past them into the house. Blast it, promise or no promise, he was getting a drink.

DURING DINNER and afterward Justin watched Fletcher flirt with Clare so outrageously that only a rigid control kept him from erupting into violence several times. He cursed the sort of low, despicable characters who would intrude on a newly married couple, Eugenia Butterfield and his former friend Fletcher included.

Sorely tried, and longing for a brandy, Justin nonetheless kept a rein on his emotions until Clare finally excused herself, leaving the two men alone in the parlor. Then he called for a bottle and got down to business.

"By all the devils in hell, stay away from my wife!" he warned, eyeing his guest in a way that gave no doubt that he meant what he said.

Fletcher raised his brows innocently. "Really, Justin, I can see marriage has changed you. I wonder if it's for the better or worse?"

"Don't parry with me, Fletcher," Justin said. "Clare is not one of those loose-moraled ton wives that we know so well. She is mine, and mine alone." The words came out with more force than he intended, and he saw Fletcher assess him deliberately. He downed his drink in one long swallow and poured another.

"You love her, then?" Fletcher asked.

"Love her?" Justin snorted. "Of course I love her. I've always loved her." He sat down and drained his glass. "I fell in love with her when she was fourteen." He looked up at Fletcher, expecting a scathing reply, and when none came, he prodded, "Well? What think you of that, my dissipated friend?"

"That would depend on how old you were at the time," Fletcher said smoothly as he found a seat himself.

"Twenty-one, by faith," Justin answered. "Old enough to avoid an attachment for a child!"

"Did you take her?"

Justin slammed his glass down in response. "Of course I didn't take her! Clare was radiant, as pure and lovely a girl as you would ever see. Do you think me that base, man?"

Fletcher shrugged. "Then what's the problem? Seven years is not a tremendous age difference. If you'll pardon my saying so, I've known tender things of sixteen to marry old goats of sixty," Fletcher said, leaning back in his chair and propping his feet up on another.

"It seems to me to be a case of beating a dead horse, Justin. She was fourteen, and you fell in love with her, and you're still in love with her. Great. Wonderful. Isn't it? From your glowering expression, it certainly doesn't appear to be. No wonder I refuse to succumb to the dreadful emotion,'' Fletcher drawled.

"You don't understand," Justin said as he tossed back another drink. Then he stared at the bottom of the glass, feeling as empty and hollow as the clear container in his hand. "It is great. It is wonderful—sometimes," Justin clarified. "But it requires a bloody lot of work, and I don't think I'm up to it. I wasn't before. Oh, blast." He reached for the bottle again.

"Well, just be glad that she's with you and not Farnsworth," Fletcher said, sipping his own brandy casually. "By the way, this is not solely a social visit. I wanted to let you know that one of your old paramours has been spreading quite a lurid tale about your elopement, which has made Farnsworth a laughingstock. Did he really think to save Clare from you?"

"Oh, don't bring up that farce," Justin said with a shudder. "I'll give you fair warning, Fletcher, Clare has a tendency to create situations that resemble nothing but bad drama, and before you know it, you're suddenly one of the actors." He lifted his glass and then paused as Fletcher's message sunk in. "And of course the little tableau you're referring to had to take place in the presence of Marie Summerville. Still, I didn't believe she would have the nerve to tell it," Justin added, shaking his head.

"Well, she has told it, to anyone who would listen, and Farnsworth cannot be pleased. Knowing his reputation for bizarre behavior, I just thought I'd give you notice to watch your back."

Justin eyed him appraisingly. "You don't actually expect the fellow to come after me?" he asked, his voice heavy with skepticism.

Fletcher shrugged. "Will he sneak into your room and slit your throat? I doubt it. But he'll want revenge, and there are many ways to go about it. In his case, I'm sure he's more creative than the average man."

"Oh, stop, or you'll have me shivering in my boots," Justin said scornfully. "Richard Farnsworth is a strange one, capable of many cruelties, but he is also a coward. He only bullies those who can be bullied. He's never fought a duel or even come to blows with anyone."

Fletcher raised his brows. "Then you have nothing to worry about, do you?"

Justin noticed the tone in his friend's voice, but ignored it. By faith, he had enough on his mind without Farnsworth giving him the bugaboos. He stared at his empty glass again. If Fletcher only knew… "Oh, blast," he said. Then he threw the glass into the fireplace, smashing it to pieces while Fletcher watched, unflinching.

One promise broken, Justin noted, but what did she expect?

CHAPTER ELEVEN

"Mr. Mayefield," Clare said, walking over to greet her guest. She was pleased to find him up and about. It was past noon, and still she'd seen no sign of her husband, causing her to suspect the two had made a very late night of it. "Would you like some breakfast?"

"No, I never take any, thank you," he said. "But if your offer still stands, I would love to have a ride in your new phaeton."

"But of course! That would be delightful," Clare said, eager to try out her gift. "I've never had anything so lovely," she added, smiling up at Fletcher, "but you really shouldn't have. And the horses! They look to be fine specimens, too fine for you to part with, I'm sure,"

"Nonsense. Nothing is too fine for Justin's wife, and besides," he added, giving her a grin, "I came out very handsomely in the deal I made for them."

Clare laughed, delighted at his effort to deflect her thanks, though she was certain that such prime animals had cost him dearly. She was glad Justin had such a personable friend. Although she would hardly concur with Prudence's opinion of Mr. Mayefield as godlike, she had grown to like him, and she would enjoy his company on the drive.

They went outside together, walking across the old wooden bridge that spanned the moat behind the castle. Although the sky was somewhat overcast, the air was warm and Clare was eager to be out. Still, her steps halted in the gardens as she thought of Justin. He had not been in the best of spirits yesterday and had scowled throughout dinner and beyond. Thinking it was her presence that distressed him, she had excused herself early, so that he could enjoy the companionship of his old friend. Perhaps he would not care for her stealing Fletcher away this afternoon, either, she mused.

"Do you think Justin will mind if we leave without him?" she asked with real concern.

"I don't think Justin will even notice," Fletcher said dryly. "I imagine he will still be abed when we return."

"Oh? Were you two up till the dawn?" Clare asked teasingly, before realizing that her words might give her away. She moved a little ahead, so that Fletcher would not see the blush rising in her cheeks, and hoped fervently that he simply thought her a heavy sleeper. How else would she not be aware what time her husband came to bed?

"No," Fletcher answered casually, and she could not tell from his tone whether he guessed her shameful secret. Perhaps Justin had confided in him, telling his friend of his frustration with a wife who did not jump eagerly into the marriage bed. The thought horrified Clare, until she told herself firmly that Justin would not be that cruel.

"I imagine the amount of liquor he took in last night should keep him dead asleep for a while longer, for I've never known Justin to drink that much and then rise early," Fletcher said.

Clare stopped in her tracks, uncertain if she were hearing correctly. She whirled to face him. "Justin was drinking?" she asked.

Fletcher raised his eyebrows in surprise. "Yes," he answered. He paused, as if awaiting an explanation for her odd question, but Clare could not speak. She could hardly think, in fact, as the pain of Justin's betrayal seeped through her.

"Oh," she said softly, willing herself not to cry in the presence of her guest. So Justin had broken his word last night. Last night only, or had he been drinking all the time and hiding it from her? And what of his other promise? Clare's mind quickly flew to all the maids in the castle, and she felt ill.

I cannot live like this, she thought as her heart beat wildly against her chest. Yet hadn't she released him from his promises? Oh, dear heaven. She raised a hand to her cheek. The words had flown from her lips so quickly, so carelessly, but the consequences...they would not be so easily suffered.

"What is it, Clare?" Fletcher said. "Are you unwell?"

"No, no," Clare denied. "It is nothing, really. Some fresh air will do nicely," she said, forcing her tone to be bright. "I can't wait to drive my new phaeton."

The horses, two beautifully matched bays, responded eloquently to the lightest of touches, and Clare was able to make them the focus of a long conversation. When she exhausted that topic, her mind turned again to her husband and the muddle that was their marriage. How had everything turned out so badly? she wondered desperately. Why had she ever agreed to wed Justin?

Destiny. Clare was losing her faith in it, and quickly. She had dreamed of saving Justin from himself, and yet she had done nothing but make demands, giving precious little in return, and Justin was back on his old path to ruin. She sighed, as if the weight of the world pressed down upon her.

"That was a mighty sigh," Fletcher said, his mouth curving up at one corner. "Too heavy for such a beautiful and charming lady as yourself."

Clare tried to smile back. "I'm sorry."

"Don't be," Fletcher said. "I'm afraid I'm not very good with damsels in distress, but if I can help, I am yours for the asking," he said, nodding his head toward her.

"How very gallant of you," Clare said, "but there is

nothing you can do for me." She paused then, struck by an idea. Perhaps there was something. "Fletcher, you've known Justin for a long time, have you not?"

"Longer than I care to admit," he answered wryly. He rested one hand on a long leg encased in pale blue superfine.

Clare eyed him intently. "Were you here the night the girl fell from the roof?"

She saw his eyebrows lift in surprise, and thought perhaps she had been too forward, but he held her gaze. "No, I was not," he answered, "though I heard of it, of course."

"Justin blames himself," Clare said softly.

Fletcher shrugged. "If he does, he has never spoken of it to me. I thought it an accident—a party of young people, all a little too young, a little too wild and with a little too much to drink. Unfortunate, but hardly unusual."

Clare didn't care for his matter-of-fact approach. "Perhaps," she said, unconvinced.

"My dear Clare," Fletcher said, "I fail to see what that ancient bit of history has to do with anything." He crossed his arms across his chest, his blue jacket dark against the silver threads of his waistcoat.

"And I must admit that although I feel rather responsible for your unhappiness, since I had a hand in forcing your union, I don't understand why you two are having difficulties. Justin spoke in riddles, so perhaps you could enlighten me." He looked at her calmly, as if he had just asked for another jaunt in the phaeton and not the key to her soul.

Clare swallowed hard, unwilling to share her marital problems with a man who was nearly a stranger to her, but feeling that she owed him some answer. "It is complicated," she finally said. "Far too complicated for me to unravel," she added with an unhappy smile.

"More riddles," Fletcher said.

"More riddles," Clare agreed.

FLETCHER TOOK HIS LEAVE as soon as the drive was done. "But you must at least wait to see Justin," Clare said, distressed. "He will be most unhappy."

"In his current mood, he will not miss me." Fletcher gave a crooked grin, laughing off all her efforts at persuading him to stay. "I have one thing for you to ponder," he said. "What's a rake to do when he's no longer a rake? Use that bit of whimsy as you see fit."

Clare was not sure what he was implying, but she nodded. Then he bowed over her hand, brushing his lips against her skin, and released her with a smile.

"Good luck, Clare. I've a feeling you'll need it."

She watched him go with a sense of abandonment. It seemed as though everyone who came to the hall took one look at the deteriorating marriage of its inhabitants and fled like leaves before a storm. Putting a hand over her eyes, Clare gazed up at the darkening sky, which reflected her mood, and frowned. It appeared that a tempest was brewing both inside and outside the castle.

What was a rake to do, indeed, Clare wondered as she mulled over Fletcher's words. She knew very well what Justin was famous for doing. His prowess in the bedroom was renowned, she recalled with a shiver, and no wonder.... Clare felt herself go warm at the memory of their tryst in the river: Justin's mouth on her breast, his hands on her thighs, the heat of his hard body amid the cold water, and his voice, low, tantalizing, whispering of what he wanted....

With a start, Clare realized that her heart was pounding just at the thought of him—Justin, master of movement and touch, the virtuoso of lovers and her own fantasy prince. She could feel the pull of him even when not in his presence, the heady yearning for him that tempted her to cast aside the past, forget about love and surrender to the passion that was just a pulse beat away.

And yet, he had broken one promise. Had he betrayed her, too? If he had, Clare knew she could not bear it, and sighing, she forced her thoughts away from her husband's bed. Although too vulnerable to succumb to that lure as yet, she had to do something to save their faltering marriage.

With an effort, she turned her attention to Elizabeth's death, for she was still determined to find out more about the night of the accident. She decided to question the staff—delicately, of course. Some retainers, such as Harris, she dared not speak to because of their loyalty to their master. Others, lower on the household ladder, she hoped to coax into telling her anything they knew.

Clare started in the kitchens, asking the cook how long he and each member of his staff had been with the household. She claimed she was looking for someone who had worked at the castle before, who was familiar with it. She hinted at a promotion for anyone with an intimate knowledge of the place, but her inquiries got her nowhere.

Although he had been with the marquis for ten years, the cook couldn't, or wouldn't, tell her anything himself. Finally, he directed Clare to a scullery maid named Mary, who fidgeted and squirmed as she was questioned. Yes, she had been to the castle before, but she didn't know about anything except the kitchens. She remembered when the old marquis and his wife were killed, but it was all too long ago to recall any details. Yes, she had been here the night the girl fell, but she knew nothing about it.

It would be easy to give up—too easy, Clare decided. On to the chambermaids, she thought with a sigh. But just as she meant to stand, she heard a voice. "My lady," it called, and Clare turned to see a gnarled old woman in a heavy apron standing in the doorway to the cellar.

"Yes?" Clare asked, straightening in her chair. The woman's white mane was flying down her back, and she beckoned with a bony hand that made the hairs on the back of Clare's neck stand upright. Now, Clare, stop being so imaginative, she admonished herself. The woman was a servant, not a witch.

Clare followed the woman into the old butler's pantry.

"My name's Dorothy, my lady. I'm the laundress," she explained. Her lips stretched tightly together in an odd smile, and her gray eyes bored into Clare. "I heard you asking Mary about the girl what fell into the moat."

Clare nodded, trying to appear nonchalant, but the woman intrigued her. She had the strangest feeling that she might finally learn something important, and her heart raced in anticipation.

"I was here that night," Dorothy said. Then she paused dramatically, as though waiting for Clare's reaction.

"Were you?" Clare asked, as coolly as she could.

"Aye, but I was snug in my bed, like the poor girl ought to have been," the old woman said, cackling at her own wit. "But I'll tell you who might be able to give you an earful," she added slyly. "Addie McBride. She was one of the kitchen girls and was seeing a lot of Bob, the cook's assistant, if my mind serves me correctly. Now Addie had a habit of meeting her man up on the roofs, is why I happen to think of her," Dorothy said, her eyes narrowing.

"The day after they found the girl and all, Addie was white as could be. And weren't more than a week later when Addie up and quit, just like that," Dorothy said, snapping her bony fingers in Clare's face. "Now, you can think of it what you like, but I always wondered if Addie knew more than she was telling."

Clare felt heavy with disappointment. It was obvious the old woman knew nothing herself and could only offer the name of someone else who might be just as ignorant of the incident—and who no longer worked for Justin. "But if she quit, how can I find her?" Clare asked.

The laundress smiled widely, revealing a missing tooth. "She still lived in the village, last I knew," she said. "If you're as interested as you make out, my lady, you might want to pay her a visit. Now, there's no call to let on who sent you, but don't be taking no for an answer. You get her to tell you what she knows, and my guess is you'll find what you're seeking."

Clare didn't like the way Dorothy's gray eyes were assessing her shrewdly. "What about this Bob? Where can I find him?"

The old lady cackled again. "Well, I can tell you where to find him, but he won't be sharing anything with you."

"Why?" Clare asked, frowning impatiently.

"'Cause he's dead, that's why. Took to his bed one day and never got back up," Dorothy explained.

"Oh," Clare said softly. "Well, thank you for your information, Dorothy." She put a coin in the woman's hand and watched the long fingers close over it tightly.

"Thank you, my lady," she said. "You just go see Addie," she advised with a knowing nod. Then she left Clare alone in the pantry.

Although Clare's curiosity was piqued, one look out at the black clouds racing across the sky made her decide to forgo the journey until tomorrow. Determined not to give up, she fully intended to talk to the chambermaids next, but she caught sight of Justin in the parlor.

Although he was sitting with his back to her, she could smell the liquor and see the drink in his hand. Oh, Justin, Clare thought dismally. She nearly turned to go, but forced herself instead to step toward him. Leaning down, she slipped her arms around his neck. "Good day," she whispered softly.

Clare heard his sigh and watched him put his glass on the table. "I've let you down again, Clare."

"Nonsense," she said, forcing her tone to be light. She stood up. "I released you from your promises, remember?"

Justin pulled her onto his lap, and she opened her eyes wide in surprise, but he only buried his face against her neck. "Oh, Clare," he whispered. "It's all slipping away, isn't it?"

"Nonsense," Clare repeated, cupping his face in her

hands. His great dark eyes were filled with melancholy, and she wondered if that might be part of his appeal. Like Byron, he had the look of a lost soul, waiting for the right woman to claim him. "I'm here. I'm not slipping away," she reassured him, her voice husky with emotion.

One corner of his mouth curved up, as though he didn't believe her words, but appreciated the effort. "I'm glad Fletcher left," he admitted, brushing his knuckles against her cheek. "I find I am a most jealous husband." Clare smiled at his teasing, but his frown soon reappeared. "I want to know, Clare, if you are attracted to him," Justin said.

Clare's lips parted in surprise. "To Fletcher? You can't be serious, Justin," she said with a laugh. His dark gaze remained intent, however, and she shook her head in amazement as she realized he was waiting for an answer. "There's never been anyone but you, Justin," she answered, with a tinge of bitterness.

"Then show me, Clare," he said, his face only inches from her own. "Prove it." Before she had a chance to react, his mouth came down on hers. Not a gentle kiss, it was a demanding one, marking her as his possession. His tongue plunged into her mouth, entwining with hers until she felt light-headed and her heart hammered in her chest.

When Clare responded in kind, Justin softened the kisses, catching her lips and releasing them in a sensuous rhythm, his tongue playing havoc with her senses. Her arms tightened around his neck of their own accord, her hands clutching his hair as if to keep her steady. She felt his lean fingers, smooth against her neck, then gliding down her shoulder to slip under the edge of her sleeve. *Oh, my, he's going to take off my clothes right here in the parlor,* Clare thought wildly.

She tore her mouth from his, but Justin simply moved his lips down her neck to her bare shoulder in a hot, wet, path that made her head fall back. Wasn't she supposed to be putting a stop to this?

Clare started in surprise at the feel of his warm fingers along her leg, and she knew she had to end this now. But his touch was so smooth, so gentle.... Then his hand slid under her chemise to cup her derriere. "Oh, my...Justin!" she murmured heatedly.

"Yes, oh, yes," he whispered, and in one fluid motion, he stood, cradling her in his arms like a limp rag.

"Justin, please," Clare pleaded, hiding her face in his shoulder. "Put me down."

"Why?" he asked.

"Because this is not the time or place." Clare breathed, still unable to look him in the eye. She was unceremoniously dumped on her feet in an instant.

"Just when is the right time, Clare?" Justin asked. "I came to my wedding expecting nothing, but you said you wanted ours to be a real marriage. And yet you treat me as though I were a leper."

"That's not true!" she said indignantly, mindful of how she had clung to him, returning his kisses, but a few moments before.

"Very nearly so!" Justin snapped back. "And then you would escape from my loathsome attentions by releasing me from my promises! But it is too late for that. Did it ever occur to you that I don't want any other woman now and probably never will? I want you, Clare, you and only you, and every time I touch you, I am rebuffed," he said, shaking his head. "By faith, I have never in my life been so humiliated! Am I that repulsive, that repugnant to you?"

"Of course not," she said, her throat swelling with emotion.

"Then what is it?" Justin asked, rubbing the back of his neck.

Clare couldn't answer, couldn't even speak, as guilt and unhappiness threatened to overwhelm her. It was all so complicated she didn't quite understand it herself, but she was determined not to burst into tears. How dare he, she thought, righteous anger surging to the surface to replace her self-reproach.

Justin had a lot of nerve promising her time—all the time she needed—and then turning around to shout at her for not rushing into his arms. After all he had done to her, how could he expect her to fall into bed with him whenever and wherever he wanted? How dare he, Clare thought again, when everything was his fault? "I didn't seek this marriage, you know!" she cried. "I never asked for this!"

Justin looked at her, his dark eyes distant and pained. "We can get an annulment, if you wish," he said, his voice deadly quiet and serious.

"You would like to get out of it, wouldn't you?" she screamed, disregarding all logic. His words hurt her so much that she lashed out with her fists as well, punching him in the chest.

Justin ignored her feeble efforts. "Then what do you want, Clare?" he asked, his voice weary.

"I want you to love me!" she shouted, pummeling his chest until she collapsed in sobs against his waistcoat.

Justin stiffened in response to her startling words. Of all the reasons he had imagined, this was not one of them. He took her wrists in his hands to still her blows, then lifted her tear-stained face so that she might see his dull surprise.

"But, Clare, I've always loved you," he said softly, gazing into the amber pools of her eyes. "I've loved you since the moment I saw you. Why else would a grown man dally in a forsaken manor house with a fourteen-year-old?"

She didn't believe him, he could tell, and that knowledge tore at his very heart. "I love you, my Clare, my own," he repeated. Although the words acted as a balm to him, they had no affect on his wife, who pushed out of his embrace to turn away from him.

When she whirled around again to face him, her features

were stricken with pain, her voice full of accusation. "If you loved me, you never would have abandoned me!" she said. The charge sliced through the air like a saber that had hung too long and too precariously over their heads.

Justin sighed, relieved that it was finally out in the open. What lay between them would be resolved, for good or ill, this day, and he would be heartily glad of it. "Your father gave me no choice," he said.

"Ha!" Clare snorted. "He gave you a choice! He gave you the chance to marry me, and you refused. You refused! And yet, here we are." She waved a hand in irony.

"I didn't realize then that I loved you," Justin said, immediately aware of how lame that excuse sounded. His mind a jumble, his tongued tied, he knew that the right words could make or break his marriage, but they seemed to elude him. "I thought you could do better than me," he finally said. "You had everything—beauty, intelligence, creativity—"

Clare didn't let him finish. "As though any other man would appreciate my stories! Don't make me laugh."

"All right, so maybe another man might not have loved you for that talent, but another man could have offered you stability and respectability, for pity's sake. You were just a child, with a whole glorious future ahead of you, while I was a man with a poor reputation and worse prospects."

He saw the desolate expression in her amber eyes and felt a surge of anger such as he had never known. He clenched his hands at his sides. "All right, so I took the easy way out," he admitted. Forcing himself to look her directly in the eyes, he ignored the pain there as he told the bitter truth.

"When your father suggested I marry you, I said no without even thinking. I never even considered it, because I was so accustomed to refusing such offers," he said slowly. Clare flinched as if he had struck her, but he continued, unable to stop the torrent that he had held back for so long.

"Just what did you expect, Clare?" he asked nastily.

"You with your narrow, innocent world, with all your dreams of knights in shining armor and honorable princes. You think I didn't know that you tried to make me one of them? Well, you couldn't, because I wasn't honorable or noble or any of those things." Justin was amazed to find himself shouting. He took a deep breath and lowered his voice.

"All you saw was a charming young man, but I was so much more than that…so much less," he said softly. "It wasn't until a day or so after your father confronted me, when you came upon me with the girl, that I discovered just how far apart our worlds were. I saw myself then with—with disconcerting clarity—" Justin's lips curled humorlessly "—and I didn't like what I saw. I knew you wouldn't like it, either."

He couldn't go on, couldn't explain that after viewing himself through her eyes, he had gone back to London and proceeded to prove to himself and the world just how unworthy he was, never suspecting at the time how much his defection would cost him.

Clare made no response, but just stood there, as though the world had collapsed around her. "Blast it, Clare. I was not one of your bloody heroes! I never will be!" Justin said. He gazed at her with an odd mixture of damnation and hope in his eyes as the long silence stretched between them. He wanted her to see him, truly see what he was, and yet he still wanted her to love him. It was an impossible combination, but Justin had always known that.

"Yes, you were, whether you willed it or no," Clare answered softly, her anger having finally worn itself out. "I'm sorry it was a burden too heavy for you." Turning her back on him, she walked out of the parlor. She didn't have anything more to say, nor did she have the energy for more screaming, more shouting, more dredging up of the old pain. It felt like a fresh wound, newly opened, and she wanted to tend to it—alone.

Justin watched her go, hopelessness overwhelming him at the sight of her set mouth and her straight back. He picked up his abandoned glass, thinking to drink the last of the claret, but he stared at it instead, suddenly sickened by the smell. He threw the glass into the fireplace, sending a stream of red liquor like a trail of blood across one of Clare's new carpets, and cursed himself loudly.

"Harris!" he yelled at the top of his lungs. Then he moved to the doorway and stuck his head out, waiting for his butler.

"Yes, my lord?" Harris asked, without batting an eye at his master's unusual and unseemly behavior.

"The wine cellar," Justin said. "Pack it up and..."

"Yes, my lord?"

"Send it all over to the squire, with my compliments," Justin added, through clenched teeth.

"Very good, my lord," Harris said. He nodded and left without commenting on the bizarre request or on Justin's demeanor.

Leaning his hand against the door frame, Justin rested his head against his arm and sighed. It was going to take a lot of work, and maybe he wasn't up to it, but, blast it, he was not about to give up on this marriage—not yet, anyway. Once before he had turned away from the only woman he had ever loved. He would not do it again.

CLARE SAT IN HER ROOM a long time, listening to the rain whip against the stone walls and watching the moat boil and churn with the force of the tempest. She had always enjoyed a good storm, an invigorating, majestic display that struck a chord in that part of her nature that was wild and free. But now it seemed only a sad reflection of the events inside the castle—gray and dismal. Instead of cleansing, it was eroding her marriage, her happiness and her very life.

Justin still might ask for an annulment, and maybe she should agree, Clare thought sadly, but her heart rebelled.

She had her prince and her castle, just as she had always dreamed, and she was superstitious enough to dread altering her destiny. If she threw it all away now, she most assuredly would be interfering with the Fates themselves. No, her place was here.

That decision made, she still had choices before her, choices that would determine the course of their lives. The easiest path would be to turn away from Justin. Too burdened by past hurts to let herself love him, she could shut him out permanently...but then why remain married to him? If she were going to continue as his wife—and she was—then this marriage deserved her best efforts, which, Clare realized, she had not given it so far.

She had allowed her old pain to distance her from her husband, to prevent her from trusting him. She had closed her heart and, though outwardly cordial, had actually longed to punish Justin for leaving her before. The feelings that should have been expressed physically between them became a weapon for her to use against him. She was suddenly ashamed at her own behavior.

All along, she had resisted him, struggling against the sweet, hot pleasure of his mouth, his touch, his seductive whispers. And in doing so, she had punished not only Justin, but herself, for she had longed for nothing more in the past four years than to kiss him, to run her fingers through his hair and along his chest, to feel him against her, to share his passion. To let him work his magic....

Clare grew breathless at the thought, light-headed with relief that her surrender would no longer mean defeat. Justin had married her, he'd said he loved her, and he was usually more than willing to please her. Now it was her turn to please him. What was it Fletcher had said? "What was a rake to do when he stopped being a rake?" Clare had made Justin give up his way of life, and for what? She needed to replace what he had lost with something more precious.

It would be easy to do, she knew. If she opened her heart

for an instant, she would adore him with all the fervor she once had, and more. For now she would love not a dream, but a flesh-and-blood man, with failings, yes, but much more substantial than an imaginary hero. Clare sighed. The time had come to accept the past and embrace the future, if she were to have one, and that meant loving her husband in every sense of the word.

CHAPTER TWELVE

CLARE TOOK DINNER ALONE in her room, afraid that if she had to face Justin before it was time for him to retire that, she might lose what little nerve she possessed. She lingered over a warm bath, brushed her hair for an eternity, dawdled over her toilette and cast one nightdress after another aside in indecision.

She was nervous. It would not be easy to walk through that door into Justin's room, knowing that this time she could not back down. It was not the act itself that frightened her; she had only to draw on Justin's reputation to realize that it couldn't be that bad. Fifty London woman couldn't be wrong, she thought with a slightly hysterical giggle.

No, it was not so much her body that she feared to give him, but her heart and her soul, for she suspected the three would be wound intricately together during the night ahead. And Clare knew from her experiences in Justin's arms that he had the power to make her lose control of herself, a rather uncomfortable feeling. "Stop worrying," she told herself as she paced the room, listening for the sound of his movement behind the door, of his bed creaking as he settled in for the night.

When it finally came, Clare waited a few minutes longer, putting off the moment of reckoning until she realized that she was cowering. She picked up a candle and stepped toward the door that stood between them, trying to concentrate on how much she cared for him and how much she had always longed for his caress. She had wanted him to love her, and he said that he did. She was not too sure if she believed him, but Justin had said it, and that would have to do, she thought as her hand closed on the handle.

Justin heard the door open and wondered what servant was wandering about at this hour. When he looked up and saw Clare standing in the doorway, his heart thudded against his ribs in a jolt of surprise and pleasure. Tonight of all nights he had not imagined she would come to him, but there she was in a lavender robe, looking tall and beautiful...and damnably nervous.

In fact, she resembled a woman with eyes wide open walking toward a precipice, and Justin wasn't thrilled by the look. It was not the sort of response he was used to engendering in females. "Clare, you're not here because you feel pressured, are you?" he asked, needing some confirmation that she did, indeed, want his attentions, and feeling the fool for it.

Moving gracefully toward the bed, Clare put the candle down beside it and faced him. "I'm here because I want our marriage to be real. I want to forget about the past and begin anew," she said firmly.

Justin felt relief surge through him and realized just how tense he had been, waiting for her answer. She was staring at his chest, and he hoped the sight was not bringing up bad memories. "Come to bed then," he said, pulling back the cover for her.

Clare watched him anxiously, twisting the tie knotted around her waist. "All right," she said finally. Undoing the knot, she opened her robe slowly, then let it fall to the floor. Justin sucked in his breath, for she had nothing on underneath. Clare stood before him, her breasts high and heavy, their peach nipples hard from cold or anxiety, her slim waist curving gently to hips that ended in those incredibly long and shapely legs.

Justin couldn't speak. He motioned for her to join him instead, and she slid in beside him, pulling the blanket up to her chin. Observing her sudden modesty with amusement, he regained the power of speech—and coherent thought, which told him that he had better go slowly this night, very slowly. It was not going to be easy.

She wasn't looking at him, but up at the ceiling, with rapt interest. "Clare," he said softly, trying to find the words that would put her at ease. "It's just me, Justin."

She turned to gaze at him, her hazel eyes wide and so full of love that they took his breath away. It was a sight he hadn't seen in many a year, that unguarded, wholehearted gift of her love, and Justin felt his throat tighten and a strange pressure build behind his own lids. "Clare, my own, I love you. I do," he whispered, brushing a knuckle against her cheek.

Oh, my, he's going to cry, Clare thought dizzily as she considered dark eyes that appeared to be swimming in liquid. Perhaps it was only a trick of the candlelight, she decided, but Justin had never looked at her with such tenderness. This was not at all what she had expected.

She had imagined that he would clasp her to him and kiss her until the world spun out of control, and that that wild look that had always frightened her a little would appear on his handsome features.... Clare had prepared herself for that; she was not prepared for tears. "What do we do now?" she asked, trying to turn his attention back to the business at hand. Good heavens, she had never thought she would have to do that.

Justin smiled slowly, his lips curving into a seductive grin that made her heart pound frantically. "I want to explore every inch of your luscious body," he said. "May I?"

"Well, I..." Clare was at a loss as to an answer, for this was *definitely* not what she'd expected.

"I'll touch you, and then you can touch me—unless you'd rather not," he said, his voice so matter-of-fact he gave her pause.

For one of the ton's most infamous rakes, he looked oddly

unsure of himself, Clare thought. "No, I would like that," she said. "I've always wanted to touch you...." Her words trailed off and she blushed furiously.

Justin ignored her discomfiture. "All right," he said.

Although she didn't dare look at him, she noticed that he sounded much happier. Surely the man didn't need reassurance? The notion that he might require just that made her feel better.

"Why don't you roll over?" he suggested. Then he nudged her until she moved onto her stomach.

Clare smiled, for she was actually feeling much better about the whole thing. Her arms seemed stiff and awkward at her sides, so she crossed them and rested her head on them, sighing softly.

The sigh caught him unawares, and Justin gritted his teeth against the desire that shot through him. He closed his eyes and struggled with it for a moment, wishing he had drugged himself into insensibility with several choice bottles. Then perhaps her slightest sound wouldn't threaten his tenuous self-control, and his proximity to her naked, woman's body wouldn't make his groin ache so painfully.

Unfortunately—or fortunately, depending on one's point of view, Justin reflected—he was not only cold sober, he was more alert than he had ever been, every sense alive with the wonder that was Clare. Every other woman he had ever held seemed a pale shadow, a lifeless imitation, compared to her, bright and beautiful and stretched out before him.

Justin knew instinctively that if he handled this right, tonight would be like nothing he had known before. Like a skittish horse, Clare had a tendency to bolt when pressed too quickly into unknown territory, so he was not going to rush. In fact, he hoped to turn the tables on her tonight, so that *she* would press *him,* wanting and needing desperately what he could give her. Justin grinned. He was going to enjoy it thoroughly—if it didn't kill him first.

Clare never knew what it cost him. She only knew that his touch on her arms was feather light and teasing, not at all what she had anticipated. Her prince possessed wonderful hands, she decided as they traveled along her shoulders and down her back in gentle whispers.

Justin's long, slim fingers moved with such grace, caressing the curves below her spine just as sweetly as the rest of her, that she forgot to be embarrassed. Oh, she could grow to like this, she thought as she felt herself relax. His fingertips trailed down her legs, tickling her behind her knees, and she smiled when they wandered past her ankles and even onto the soles of her feet.

He made his way back up her body, gently smoothing her skin this time, instead of barely making contact. Clare still was at ease, but a new feeling came over her, an intriguing longing for more. When Justin brushed the side of her breasts, she moved restlessly against the bed, realizing that she wanted him to do it again.

He didn't. Instead, he prodded her onto her back. Clare rolled over, but she couldn't look at him, disconcerted to be lying naked before him. She grew tense again as he lightly traced her forehead. "When do I get to touch you?" she asked.

"Maybe after you open your eyes," Justin said. "I don't know if I care to have you groping blindly for me."

Clare caught the humor in his voice and gazed up at him. He was leaning over her, the thatch of dark hair falling free, and his mouth curving up at the corners. She couldn't help smiling in return. Justin was teasing her; he was the same old Justin, with or without his clothes. Clare sighed and closed her eyes, this time in sweet pleasure, as his caress moved along her hairline, down her throat and across her shoulders.

She drifted in sensation: the warmth of Justin's strokes on her arms; the scent of him, masculine and familiar; the candle glow lighting his well-loved face, edged with his dark hair; and this feeling inside her, wonderful and new. She was wholly comfortable, yet tingling and alive—until his palms stroked her breasts.

"Oh," Clare whispered, surprised at the strong reaction of her body. She was struck by a wave of excitement and something else. She wasn't quite sure what it was, but she was certain of one thing: she wanted him to do it again.

He didn't. Justin's fingers moved lower, circling her stomach and trailing down her legs to her toes. They returned, however, to softly fondle the inside of her thighs, and Clare caught her breath again, longing to lean into him to prolong this gentle caress, too.

When his hand cupped her mound of curls, she knew she ought to be mortified, but it felt so good, all other thoughts were banished by her bliss. All too soon his tender pressure had moved on, his palms reaching her breasts again, making lazy circles, and Clare gasped with a mixture of frustration and ecstasy. She wanted Justin to kiss her, wanted him to press himself against her in that wanton way he usually did. But he didn't.

Clare gulped back her disappointment. She realized, finally, that Justin wasn't going to kiss her, but her body was filled with such a restlessness that she couldn't lie still any longer. "It's my turn now," she said when he traced her ear. Sitting up, she watched him turn onto his stomach and rest his head on his arms just as she had done.

Clare was surprised that she didn't feel the least bit awkward. It all seemed so natural now, sprawling in bed with Justin, both of them naked. "I used to dream about how your skin would feel," she whispered, unaware of the grim struggle that passed across her husband's face at her unintentionally provocative words.

She moved her fingers along his strong arms. He was smooth and warm, and Clare liked the feel of him. She spread both hands over his wide back, reveling in the suppleness of his skin and the hardness of his muscles. She pressed lower, over his taut buttocks and down his legs, tickling the hairs there, then up his body again, in slow motion.

With a tremble of surprise, Clare noticed her breath coming faster, and she realized just how much she was enjoying this. It was exciting to touch him, but doing so had the same effect on her as his ministrations did. She wanted *more*. She wanted to kiss him, to rub against him, to have him press his hot mouth upon her as he had in the river. Her thoughts made her warm and she fidgeted, prodding Justin to turn over.

He was a glorious sight, Clare discovered, when he rolled to face her. He put one arm behind his head and threw the other carelessly against the sheets as he settled onto his back. His eyes sparkled with delight as he watched her. Clare let her gaze travel over the length of him from his wide chest down to the part between his legs that was hard and tempting.

Her heart leapt. She knew she ought to be apprehensive, but she wasn't. She wanted to touch it. She glanced back up at his face. Justin was trying to smile encouragingly, but looked as though he were having difficulty taking in air. Perhaps he was impatient for her to begin, she thought, turning her attention to the arm that was flung out beside her.

She trailed her fingers up the inside of it to his shoulder, then along his chest and around his nipples. His stomach muscles contracted at the contact, but Clare did not linger there, moving instead along his hip. Her interest was focused elsewhere, to that part of him that seemed to draw her to him, and finally she dropped her hand between his legs, then up to boldly touch him.

Justin groaned. Glancing at his face, she saw that wild look in his eyes, and for once it didn't scare her. She slid her hand along his hardness, tracing the contours there, until she saw that he was rigidly clutching the sheets. Was he in pain?

"Are you all right?" she asked. Justin shook his head, his hair moving softly against his cheek, but Clare snatched her fingers away. "I didn't hurt you, did I?" she asked.

Justin wanted to laugh, but he was still in the grip of a desire so strong that all he could think about was spreading her legs apart and pounding into her. How much longer could he stand this torture? He gazed up into her eyes, saw the wonder and need there, and had his reward. He took a breath and trusted himself to reach up and brush a knuckle against her breast.

Clare leaned toward him and sighed. He raised both hands to her breasts then, rubbing the nipples with his thumbs as he caressed the flawless skin. Clare moved restlessly, making his groin ache painfully again. He was suddenly stricken with the fear that he might lose his seed across the bed like a schoolboy, and the thought spurred him to action.

Justin rolled her onto her back, pressing his body down upon hers, and groaned at the feel of her warmth under him. Clare entwined her fingers in his hair, dragging his head down to hers, and kissed him with the fervent abandon that he did not know she possessed. He groaned again at her boldness, at the sweet taste of her, and told himself firmly to hold on, even as he felt his command ebb.

Apparently unaware of his struggles, Clare became more demanding. She rubbed her hips against his hardness and sent her tongue playing in and out of his mouth in a natural rhythm that made Justin realize his ploy had worked all too well. His innocent wife was actively seducing him.

In the throes of a passion such as he had never known, Justin lost all semblance of his usual finesse. Lust overwhelmed him as his hands swept down her length, smooth and creamy in the candlelight. This was Clare, pure and radiant and writhing beneath his touch. He put his lips to her breasts, running his tongue around the buds as she arched against him. Taking one into his mouth, he heard her moan, and he nearly lost control at the sound.

When she grasped his locks, pulling him closer and inducing him to suck harder, Justin knew he couldn't delay any longer. He slipped his fingers to the junction of her legs, and he shuddered as they met moist slickness.

"I can't wait, Clare," he whispered shakily. "I can't wait." He moved between her thighs, bracing his arms at her sides while he watched her lovely features. Her swollen lips were parted, her high cheeks flushed with pleasure and her hazel eyes clouded with desire.

"Then don't wait," Clare whispered as she gazed up at him. Justin needed no further urging. Groaning, he entered her with one rapid thrust that nearly burst his heart. Then he paused, his breath coming fast and hard, as he sought to gain mastery over himself. He had been right: this was like nothing he had ever experienced before. It wasn't only that she was so hot and tight around him, it was that she was Clare, and Justin realized shakily that he had never really made *love* to anyone before. With a kind of dazed surprise, he looked down at the only woman who had ever affected him this way, engendering such deep emotion and such overpowering sensation.

Clare had bitten her lip so hard that she had drawn blood, and Justin was horrified to notice tears, too. "Oh, Clare," he whispered, his throat constricted with love and sorrow. "I'm so sorry."

His words seemed to comfort her, for she smiled and bestowed upon him the same gift she used to give him. She blinked her eyes, and Justin saw all the love in the world shining from those hazel depths. Shaken to the core, he kissed her brow, licking the moisture from the corners of her eyes, whispering to her all the while. "Clare, my love, my light, my own."

Clare slipped her arms around Justin and squeezed him tightly to her, glad she had braved the pain without crying out. Even the horrible, piercing hurt had faded before the look in his eyes, a look that told her more forcefully than any words he might utter that he loved her. He truly did. Her prince really, truly loved her.

She said his name, once, softly, and suddenly his mouth was on hers, his tongue seeking and invading, even as he moved inside her. Clare braced herself against the ache, but it receded, and her heart began to race again. She throbbed, not just with the pressure of Justin's intrusion, but with a fiery need that drove her to arch against him and run her hands along his smooth back. She couldn't seem to get close enough to him as he continued his slow, gentle strokes.

"Better?" he whispered into her ear.

Clare wound her fingers into his hair and pulled his face toward her. "Yes, better," she answered huskily, gazing at his familiar features in wonder. He was breathing in low, shallow bursts. A mahogany lock hung over one brow, and his lips were parted, inviting her. Clare thought that he had never seemed more handsome, more exciting.

"I love you," she confessed. "I've loved you since the first moment I saw you, and—and I always dreamed of this, but I never dreamed it would feel so...good." Justin groaned at her words, then grasped her hips, driving into her, faster and deeper.

Clare gasped as a knot of longing grew with the strength of his thrusts, and then, suddenly, she couldn't inhale. She dug her nails into his shoulders and pushed toward him, harder and harder until pleasure flooded over her in wave after wave of intensity, obliterating all else. Dimly she was aware of Justin making a sound, a final movement, and then the shuddering of his body before he, too, was still.

They remained entwined in silent exhaustion for a long time before Clare finally spoke. "Justin, if I had but known..." She hesitated. "If I had known, I would have surrendered sooner."

"Surrendered. That's an odd word for a wife to use," Justin said softly, leaning on his arms to look down at her. He traced her lips with a finger as she gazed up at him. "If

I had but known," he repeated, "I would have tried a lot harder to persuade you to my bed."

"But you knew what it would be like," Clare protested. "You've done this so many times before." She found she didn't like to think about that and shut her mind against the image of Justin and countless others.

Justin shook his head. "I've never done this before. I've never known anything like this before," he whispered, his eyes dark and serious. "Because I've never loved anyone but you."

"CLARE, are you awake?" She felt Justin nuzzling at her ear, his tongue tracing delicate patterns on the back of her neck that made her shiver. "Clare, tell me you aren't too sore," he whispered, his voice a soft, cajoling caress in the night.

Clare smiled into the darkness, then gasped as his fingers trailed over her breast. She arched toward his touch, and Justin made a low sound of pleasure, his palms moving tantalizingly over her skin. She sighed as his hand slid down to her stomach and even lower, until it nestled between her thighs. Then he worked some kind of magic there, cupping and stroking her until she moaned. All the while his hardness pressed to her backside. She squirmed against it until finally she felt it slip between her legs, rubbing against her slowly in a rhythm that made her wild with desire.

She reached for Justin, but he was still behind her, his kisses spreading moist heat along her neck and her shoulders. She found herself clenching the sheets in her fist instead. "Justin," she urged, and he answered her plea, grasping her hips and slipping inside her from behind.

The sensations were wholly different this time, for she felt no pain, only pleasure, slow and gentle and maddening. She heard his groan and felt the pace increase as his fingers roamed over her. When they settled between her legs again, she exploded against him, gasping for breath and clutching the bedclothes as release rushed over her in great pulsing waves. She heard Justin groan again, then felt his final, driving thrust before he, too, gasped and shuddered.

"Clare." Justin's breath whispered against her tresses like the barest of breezes, and she turned in his arms to see his face, shadowed by the night. No fire burned in the grate, but inside her one lay banked, waiting for his caress to ignite the flame that had become her body.

As if echoing her own thoughts, he spoke. "Who would have thought my little pixie would become such a temptress? So hot, so tight." His lips were against her ear, and Clare felt herself grow warm again at his words. She put a hand to his smooth chest and moved against him. "Ah ha! And so greedy, too," Justin said silkily, his fingers smoothing her hair back over her shoulder, his heart still racing under her hand.

In the blackness, he seemed wholly dangerous, a true rake, dark and seductive. "You have only yourself to blame," Clare said breathlessly as she searched his features, "if you keep saying such things."

Justin grinned, showing the white of his teeth, so slowly and so sensuously that Clare felt her body shiver in response. "Then I will be sure to always describe my... sentiments most thoroughly, my pixie," he said.

"Oh," Clare said softly, a bit shaken by the force of his promise—a promise she knew to be real, that assured her surrender over and over and over.

"Don't worry, my Clare, my own," Justin said, grinning even more broadly, "for it is the same with me." He trailed a long finger across her breast and she pushed against it, sighing. "All I have to do is look at you and I want you. I shall never give you any rest," he promised wickedly.

"I have waited a long time, long, wasted years for you, but you are mine now, at last," he whispered thickly, his hand rising up to knead one breast. "And I shall have you, again and again, writhing underneath me, your mouth locked to mine, your long legs wrapped around me." He casually thumbed a nipple while he held her with his compelling voice, weaving his own sultry spell around her.

Clare could not move, trapped beneath that dark regard and that magical touch. She lay still, her breath coming faster until she sobbed with desire. His hand traveled down to cup her mound then, his fingers stroking and pressing until she was throbbing with need, yet he did not move to kiss her, did not pull her close. She was held not by any grip of his flesh but by the slow seduction of his words.

"And your sweet opening will be wet for me, my Clare—warm and wet and waiting...." Clare was choking, unable to inhale, unable to take her eyes from the shadows of his face. "Waiting for me to fill you, to shove my hard, hot sex deep into your womb." He slipped a finger inside her and pressed, and Clare finally closed her eyes, rising off the bed with a strangled cry, her hands reaching for his arms, her nails digging into his skin. She fell back with one final shudder.

It took her a long time to return to the room, to the pale glow of moonlight that danced through the oriel window onto their bed and to the strong body of the man who still leaned over her. Knowing that her face was probably crimson, Clare was glad of the night that hid her blush. "Oh, Justin," she whimpered. She took a deep breath before she spoke again. "Your reputation is not undeserved."

Justin laughed softly and lay down, gathering her close. "It's all for you now, Clare, only for you."

She felt him tense suddenly as if struck by an ill thought, and his fingers closed about her upper arm tightly as he pulled his head back to stare at her fiercely.

"You are mine, Clare, mine, and no one else's. You've had my promise. Now I'll have yours—that you will take no lover but me to your bed."

"Justin!" Clare murmured in surprise. She nearly laughed at the very suggestion that she might be unfaithful.

By all that was holy, who would need anyone else but Justin? Yet the serious look on his face told Clare that he would not welcome her amusement. She shook her head gently and raised a hand to his cheek. "Just you, my prince," she whispered softly, and kissed him to seal the pact.

CHAPTER THIRTEEN

ADDIE MCBRIDE LIVED with her brother James and his family in a small cottage at the east end of the village. The door was opened by a stout, red-faced young woman who gasped with pleasure at the sight of her visitor. Although she was unknown to Clare, the woman obviously remembered the squire's daughter or recognized the elaborate coat of arms emblazoned on the side of the coach that waited outside the gate, for she greeted Clare with a friendly smile.

"My lady! Come in." Dressed in a plain cotton gown and balancing a baby on one hip, she hastily stepped back and thrust the infant into the arms of a young girl, one of several children clustered around her whom Clare recognized from her storytelling days.

"I'm Corliss McBride, and I'm pleased to welcome you," the woman said, ushering Clare into the cozy room. "Best wishes to you in your marriage! We heard you're living up at the hall now and fixing it up. Oh, I would dearly love to see it. Like a king's palace, I expect it is."

Clare smiled. "When it is all finished, we'll have a great celebration, and you shall see it."

The girl holding the child eyed her curiously, then frowned with disappointment. "But it's just Clare," she complained, obviously wondering why her mother was getting all out of breath over the squire's daughter.

Her mother gave her a fierce look. "She is the Marchioness of Worthington now, Kate," Corliss said. "She married the marquis, so you must curtsy and speak respectfully to her."

Kate puzzled over that news and shifted the gurgling baby in her arms. Then she smiled shyly and looked up at Clare. "Oh, I see. It's just like one of your stories, isn't it?"

"Yes," Clare said, feeling an odd lump in her throat. "It's just like one of my stories."

"Can we come see your castle, Clare?" asked Eric, one of the boys lingering on the periphery of the excitement.

"Oh, no, I wouldn't want to go there. It's cursed!" said Kate solemnly.

"Kate, Eric, Mary, all of you," Corliss said, pushing the children toward the door. "Take the baby out into the garden, so I can have a proper visit with the lady." Her tone brooked no resistance, and after a few complaints, the younger children were racing off across the damp ground, Kate following with the baby in her arms.

"Here, my lady, sit down," Corliss said, pulling out her best chair, an armchair with a faded embroidered seat.

After a pleasant chat, a glass of cold lemonade from the cellar and a piece of strawberry pie, Clare finally mentioned the purpose of her visit. "Your sister-in-law, Addie McBride, lives with you, doesn't she?" she asked.

"Yes," Corliss answered, her tone hinting that the arrangement was none too pleasing.

"I heard that she used to work at the hall," Clare said casually. "I wondered if I might talk to her."

"You'll never get her to go back," Corliss blurted out. Then she turned a little pink at her quick words and eyed Clare apologetically. "Although I can't say I would mind if you did," she added with a rueful smile. "But she won't even talk about the place. Now, if you're looking for help, I know Molly Williams's girls are looking to take up with a good household. They're to go to Rillford next week to try for something there."

Clare smiled. "Thank you, Corliss, I'll keep them in mind, but I would still like to talk to Addie."

Corliss nodded. "Well, she went to market for me this morning, but she should be back soon." The woman stood up and moved to the door. Clare heard her call for Eric and send him toward town to hurry up his aunt.

Clare refused another glass of lemonade and was just about to suggest a story for the children when Addie, a thin, white-faced woman past the first blush of youth, appeared at the door. She gazed at the visitor with such a look of horror that Clare was taken aback. So, apparently, was Corliss, for Clare noticed a disgusted frown on the face of the young matron. "Addie, this is Lady Worthington, down from the hall. She would like to have a word with you."

Clare stood up and smiled warmly. "Addie? Perhaps you've seen me around the village. I'm the squire's daughter," she said reassuringly, "though my name is now Clare St. John. I wondered if I could take a moment of your time to speak to you privately?" Clare could see Addie relax somewhat, the look on her features shifting from total terror to simple fear.

Nudging Addie into a chair, Corliss hesitated a moment, obviously dying to stay and listen, but then she smiled broadly. "I'll leave you two alone for a visit. If you need me, I'll be in the garden out back," she said, more to Clare than to her relative.

"I didn't mean to startle you," Clare said soothingly once they were alone. Although she had hoped to put the woman at ease, Addie's pale blue eyes darted anywhere but at her.

"I understand that you used to work at the hall," she went on.

The blond head nodded jerkily.

"I was curious about one specific night in particular," Clare began, "the night Elizabeth Landrey—"

She didn't finish, her words cut off as Addie emitted a strangled cry and grasped her throat.

"You were there, weren't you?" Clare asked, hardly daring to believe her good fortune. Addie closed her eyes, and Clare felt a momentary misgiving for troubling the woman, but she couldn't give up when she was so close to learning something about Elizabeth's death. She leaned forward, trying to hide her eagerness.

Addie nodded, her face pale and stricken, and Clare felt a surge of relief that she was not going to deny she'd been at the castle that night. She certainly wasn't talkative, though, for her mouth remained grimly shut. Taking a chance, Clare prodded her. "You were on the roof?"

Addie met her eyes then, her own wide with shock at Clare's words. "Tell me," Clare said softly, trying to calm her own frantic heartbeat. She knew from the woman's reaction that there was something here beyond the simple story of seeing Elizabeth jump.

Corliss's aunt sighed shakily. "I knew it—I knew you would come someday," she finally said. At Clare's puzzled look, she said, "Oh, I didn't know it would be you, but I knew someone would come." She sighed again, the fright on her face giving way to a bitter resignation, and gazed down at the floor. "I was up on the roofs," she admitted.

"Yes?" Clare asked.

"Bob, one of the cook's assistants, and I used to go up there to catch us a bit of privacy," Addie said, still gazing downward. "Everyone used to sneak up there, guests and servants alike, for the view and all," she explained. Then her eyes darted up to Clare's face. "I've kept it to myself all these years, you understand, though it does bother me sometimes. Sometimes I have dreams about her, that—that she's wanting me to tell," she finished, looking down again at the floor.

Clare felt the skin on her arms rising into little bumps. "Tell what?" she asked, her voice a hoarse whisper.

"What really happened." Addie stared past Clare, unseeing. "The hall was filled with people that night. Scores of guests were down for a house party, with local gentry and others adding to the crowd, and no one keeping track of the comings and goings." As she talked, Clare could picture the circumstances of that one wild evening....

The lord and his friends had been gaming and carousing so loudly they could be heard even on the roofs. Bob was late, and Addie had cursed him under her breath, wondering if he was off with that tavern wench instead of coming to meet her.

Addie saw the woman, young and sad, walk out of the shadows, and knew her for one of the marquis' light-o'-loves. *Them's what plays, pays,* she'd thought as she watched the forlorn little thing. Then she heard other footsteps and stepped back, hoping that if it was Bob, he'd have enough sense to keep out of the lady's sight.

"Elizabeth. How delightful to find you alone," a man's voice said, and Addie pushed herself closer to the stones, scowling at the appearance of another guest. Why didn't they go back down and join the rest, or do their wooing in those fancy bedrooms? she'd wondered.

But it soon became apparent that this fellow did not have wooing on his mind. The two began to argue, and she heard the young woman's voice, high and plaintive. "Stop, Richard, you're hurting me." Addie dared to peer out then and saw that he had hold of her arms.

"But I thought you liked it that way," he said, almost snarling at her, and Addie got a good look at his face. It gave her the shivers, and she slipped into the shadows again. She had never seen the like before, she told Clare, on a gentleman, leastways.

"Well, I don't," the girl said in a trembling voice.

"You did until you thought you could snare a title, is that it? And give another man my child?" The man's tone turned deep and mean then, and Addie peeked out once more. These were juicy occurrences, even for the ton.

She saw he had the girl right up against the parapet, much

too close to the edge, and wondered if he was trying to scare her into coming back to him. But he only laughed. "Take the babe and be damned," he said, just as cool as you please. Then he pushed her off, laughing quietly all the while...."

Addie shivered, trying to shake away the recollection like the remnants of the nightmares that she confessed had plagued her since. "The party was so loud that you could hardly hear the girl screaming," she said dully. "I couldn't have moved then if I wanted to, and when I finally left, I took the other stairs straight to my room."

They both sat still and silent for a long moment, Addie lost in her memories, and Clare haunted by the vivid, frightening picture that Addie had painted. The faint sound of children's laughter drifted in from outside, returning them both to the cozy cottage room, and Clare felt her racing heart begin to slow down. "Why didn't you tell the marquis?" she asked softly.

Addie appeared surprised at the suggestion. "Even if I had the courage, I couldn't have talked to him. The marquis locked himself up in his rooms after and wouldn't see anyone."

"But why didn't you come forward and tell someone?" Clare asked, shocked that any person could keep such a thing as murder a secret.

Addie eyed her with the look, singular to her class, that held a mixture of hopelessness and amusement at Clare's naïveté. "My word against a gentleman's? I probably would have got myself locked up," she said, her lips curving faintly at the corners. Then the ghost of a smile faded, and she seemed to lose even more of her color. "I was too scared. When a man kills someone that easily, he won't think twice about doing the deed again."

"And now?" Clare asked. "Won't you tell your story to the marquis?"

Addie shuddered. "Please don't ask me, my lady. I've

lived in fear of this day coming and of that man returning to kill me, too," she whispered, her eyes pleading. "Please don't ask me."

"All right," Clare said, reaching out to pat Addie's arm. "Don't worry. That man, Richard..." She paused. "You don't know who he was?"

"No, my lady, I don't." Addie spoke sincerely, the blue pools of her eyes guileless. "I never had much to do with the guests, you understand."

Clare nodded. Although she believed the woman, she felt a sharp stab of disappointment. How could she discover the man's identity? "Can you describe him?"

Addie paused and then spoke haltingly. "He was of medium height and build. He had kind of an ordinary face, not too handsome, nor plain either, but I'm sure he was a gentleman."

Clare felt her heart sink at that woefully brief description. "His hair?" she asked.

The woman frowned. "Light colored, I think. It was too dark to see much," she said, shrugging in apology.

Clare swallowed hard. "Thank you, Addie," she said. "If you think of anything else, send word to me at the hall." The directive was wasted, for she could tell, as soon as she had spoken, that Addie would never contact her. Still, Clare was thankful to have the truth, and she pressed a purse into the woman's hand.

"Oh, I couldn't take that, my lady," Addie said, looking slightly alarmed.

"I insist," she said softly. She rose and headed toward the door, then turned to say goodbye.

Addie remained seated, clutching the coins, her face still grim. She sighed, a painful, wracking sound in the quiet cottage. "Thank you, my lady, for the money, and for coming," she said. "Maybe—maybe now she will leave me alone."

"Who?" Clare asked from the doorway.

"Elizabeth Landrey," Addie answered with a shiver.

SINCE SHE WAS already abroad, Clare decided to travel on to visit her father. He welcomed her with his big, booming voice, but would not abide a kiss of greeting. Clare smiled, thinking how different the squire was from Justin, who had reached out for her hand the moment they'd met.

After a hearty luncheon laid out by Mrs. Sutton, Clare spent a surprisingly pleasant afternoon in the squire's company, listening to him boast of his hunting skills and the quality of this year's crops. She refused an invitation to go fishing with him on the grounds that the jonquil silk gown she wore was not suited to such rigorous use. The subject of fishing turned her thoughts toward her husband, and Clare blushed, suddenly anxious to be home.

"Father," she said hesitantly, "have you ever been to the castle before, when Justin was in residence?"

"Castle? Oh, you mean the hall?" the squire asked, rubbing a hand across his bushy eyebrows. "Well, now, yes, I was there a few times when the old marquis was alive, though they didn't spend a lot of time there. They were always in London," he said with a snort of disgust, his usual response to any mention of town. "And then the boy, too—Lord, he was never there. Let the place fall to ruin. I'm surprised it's livable."

Clare smiled. "It's fine, Father." She paused, not quite knowing how to broach her subject. "I've heard that Justin was here when he was younger, and, in fact, had quite a few parties at the hall," she said.

The squire frowned and eyed her warily under his gray brows. "Now, Clare, what a man's done in the past shouldn't concern his wife," he said, and Clare had to suppress a smile of surprise. Was her father actually defending Justin?

"What about the night the girl fell into the moat? What do you know about that?" she asked bluntly.

"That was a long time ago and should be better left alone." The squire paused and reached for his pipe awkwardly, as if searching for the right words. "I know the man has a bad reputation, but he came about in the end, and he seems to care for you, doesn't he?" From his terrific scowl, Clare knew it pained him to even discuss such things.

"Yes, he cares for me," Clare said, "but what—"

"Well, then!" said the squire with a snort. "I see no cause for you to complain about the marriage or the man," he said, standing up in his haste to be rid of the topic. Clare realized with amusement that he thought her disenchanted with her husband. She laughed aloud.

"Father, I am not complaining about Justin. I'm just trying to find out exactly what happened that night," she explained.

"Well, ask your lord, then, and leave me out of it," he said gruffly. He tossed his pipe back down upon the desk, unlit. "Come out to the stables, and I'll show you my new pride and joy."

Clare frowned as she rose to follow him. *And if I were to complain about a husband, I would find no sympathy here,* she thought, briefly bitter at the discovery. Thank God for Justin, her savior, her prince.

The squire had a fine new bit of horseflesh to show her, so Clare dutifully trooped into the stables to view the handsome stallion. She did not tell him that a friend of Justin's had carelessly gifted her with two beauties that far outshone this acquisition, but exclaimed graciously over the new purchase.

"And what of your husband's stables?" the squire asked with interest.

"He has taken your advice," Clare said, "and is tearing them down. And," she added with a frown of reproach, "Aunt Eugenia has left, so you may visit the hall at your leisure."

"Already?" the squire asked with a grin. "What did the boy do to scare her off?"

"Nothing," Clare said. To her annoyance, she blushed scarlet at the reason for her aunt's prompt departure as her thoughts turned in that direction. She seemed to want to linger on the pleasant fulfillment of Eugenia's instructions to "do her duty."

Clare wished her father goodbye hastily, gratefully accepting his offer of a horse to ride home and disdaining the coach in favor of a gallop over the hills. During the ride, she debated whether to tell Justin what she had discovered about Elizabeth's death. She knew he was too steeped in his own guilt to relinquish it lightly, and she imagined him scoffing at Addie's story.

Perhaps she ought to gather more information on her own. But Justin might know who else had been close to the murdered girl, or he might remember a light-haired Richard. If so, Clare would have the killer's identity in a thrice. Unable to make up her mind, she decided to wait and see, gauging Justin's mood before determining a course.

Clare found him sooner than she'd expected. She led the squire's horse into the half-ruined stables, and there was her husband. Although the workmen had left for the day, Justin was standing amid the crumbling walls, surveying the wreckage. He must have been working again, because his shirt was off, and Clare admired the muscles of his back, the line of his shoulders and his trim waist. The thought of their lovemaking returned, to make her blush again. She realized with a sigh of relief that any painful memories she had harbored of Justin's body had been banished last night.

In fact, when she saw him now, all she remembered was the feel of that sleek skin under her fingertips, and how she had gripped the flesh of that back while he created sensations she had never before imagined. Clare felt a piercing longing for him to repeat them all, and as soon as possible.

Justin turned at the sound of a sigh and smiled in genuine

pleasure to see his wife. She looked beautiful, of course, in a yellow gown, her dark hair windswept, her cheeks flushed. She had an unusually intent look on her face, her hazel eyes warm and bright, and he suddenly remembered that his shirt was gone.

Blast it, he hoped she wasn't going to run in fright or pummel him in rage every time she saw him without it. It would make for an inconvenient marriage, he thought grimly. The errant piece of clothing was hanging across one of the fallen beams, and he reached out a hand for it, but the gentle pressure of fingers on his arm stopped his progress. He eyed Clare quizzically, and when her lips curved seductively, Justin felt desire sweep through him, rampaging in his blood.

"It's all right, Justin," she whispered, stepping closer. "You can leave it off." He read the intent in her eyes and it made him grow hard in an instant. When her palms slid down his chest, her fingers softly tracing the line of muscle to his navel, Justin inhaled sharply. Then she ran her hands along his arms and pressed kisses to his chest.

"Is there something you want, Clare?" he asked, grinning with pleasure. His voice was husky even to his own ears, for the pressure of her lips threatened to rob him of speech. She looked up then, and smiled provocatively. Her fingers slid to the waist of his breeches. With slow deliberation, she began unbuttoning them.

"Yes," she answered breathlessly. "There is something I want. You," she whispered as she met his gaze. "Like last night. Inside me. Hot and hard and—"

Justin didn't let her finish, but grabbed her with a groan, his mouth devouring hers in answer to her demands. They fell back among the straw still mounded in one of the empty stalls, into a patch of fading sunlight.

He pulled impatiently at her gown, his hands freeing her breasts to stroke them, his thumbs drawing the nipples to attention, and he heard her gasp against his cheek. Then he pushed up her skirts, and tested her with his hardness.

She was wet, Justin discovered, without any stroking from him, so he didn't wait, but took her hips in his hands and penetrated with a single thrust. He heard his own groan as he plunged deep inside her, then paused as the sensation he could only describe as "Clare" spread through him like fire, and he looked down into her face.

Her lips were red and swollen, her cheeks flushed, her eyes swimming with passion, and the sight of her sent feelings rushing through him. Love, lust, joy…Justin struggled to regulate his breathing, which had gone ragged the moment she had tugged at his breeches. "Is this what you wanted?" he managed to whisper.

"Yes, oh, yes," Clare answered. Her hands, entwined in his hair, tugged him downward. He found her mouth again and began to move inside her, out of control in an instant.

WHAT WAS IT ABOUT CLARE that made him lose the finesse for which he was so widely known and abandon himself to pure sensation? Justin smiled in chagrin, gaining comfort from the knowledge that Clare did not seem a bit disappointed in their hasty coupling. She was curled up against him, eyes closed in languid repose. He tightened his arms around her as possessiveness, that still new, but increasingly fierce emotion, settled over him.

"Justin," she whispered against his chest. "I was just thinking—"

"About me, I hope?" he teased, running a finger down her arm. She looked up and smiled, but not as brightly as she might have. What was on her brilliant mind now? Anything but the past, Justin hoped. Not once in their long night of lovemaking had they discussed it, and, as far as he was concerned, it was a dead issue, resolved by the passion that raged between them.

"I was thinking about Elizabeth Landrey."

Justin started, his body tensing in surprise while he stared down at his wife. As if dredging up their own past had not been difficult enough, she presumed to discuss Elizabeth! Releasing her abruptly, Justin sat up and began to fasten his breeches. He wished now that he had never told her about the girl. Not trusting himself to speak, he glared at her silently while he stood and brushed the straw from his clothing.

Clare returned his gaze calmly. "If we're going to free all the ghosts from the castle, we might as well start with Elizabeth," she said. Justin snorted. He did not plan to let Clare take that bit of Worth history to heart. He turned away and reached for his shirt. "So we must find out who killed her."

He dropped the garment and turned to her, trying to rein in his fury. What was it about this new, adult Clare that made him feel so wild? "Who killed her?" he growled.

"Yes," Clare said. She straightened her gown and looked up at him, her wide hazel eyes bright and sincere. "I spoke with someone who saw the whole thing. Elizabeth was pushed off the roof, Justin, by a man named Richard. So you see, it wasn't your fault."

"What the hell are you talking about?" he asked. Clare saw the muscle throb in his jaw, a telltale sign of his anger. She guessed that he did not like to be reminded of the curse that hung over him, but how else was she to remove it?

"Someone named Richard pushed Elizabeth into the moat—and pretty cold-bloodedly, too. And she was carrying *his* baby," Clare added.

Now he was really riled. His face was even turning red. "And how did that happen, immaculate conception?" he asked through clenched teeth.

"Well, I—"

He didn't let her finish. "Since Elizabeth was only sixteen and untouched when I bedded her, I find it extremely difficult to believe that she left my side to go to another man, only to return to me, telling me she carried my child in but the briefest span of time."

Clare stood up and dusted off her own clothing as she puzzled over this piece of information. The way Addie had related the story, Elizabeth had already been with this Richard fellow, having thrown him over for Justin. "How do you know she was untouched?" Clare asked.

Justin answered with a look that was part rage and part exasperation. "Well, in your case, Clare, I had only to glance at the sheets," he said dryly.

"Oh," Clare said. "Was there a lot of blood then?"

Justin stared at her as though he could hardly believe the question. "Blast it, Clare, I don't remember. For pity's sake, drop this whole thing," he said impatiently. "You've been dreaming." He bent to pick up his fallen shirt.

"I have not been dreaming," Clare assured him calmly. "Do you remember who was here that night? He had light hair, and Richard was his name.... How about Richard Farnsworth?" She seized up on the familiar name. "You said he was some kind of fiend. Perhaps Richard Farnsworth killed her. Was he here that night?"

Justin straightened, surprising her with the look of cold fury on his face. "Richard Farnsworth has never been in any home of mine!" he snapped. "Where did you get this fantasy?"

"Oh," she said, disappointed.

"Clare," Justin said, walking toward her slowly. He took a deep breath and spoke more calmly, as though he were addressing a child. "Elizabeth was not pushed. She jumped. She killed herself. Don't try to make up a better solution from your own stock of tales."

With that, he turned on his heel and walked out of the stables, leaving Clare alone in the ruins, feeling annoyed and sadly disappointed with him. The least he could do was believe her, she thought with a sigh. Lifting this curse was going to be deuced difficult.

CHAPTER FOURTEEN

CLARE WAS ABLE TO COAX Justin from his ill mood at dinner, and, as if regretting his earlier angry words, he lavished attention on every inch of her body when they lay together in the great bedchamber, loving each other until late into the night. The issue of Elizabeth's death had been swept under the rug for the time being, but Clare knew that sooner or later they must come to terms with it, just as they had with their own turbulent past.

Since Justin knew about her interest in the murder, Clare felt free to question the rest of the servants, but no one could add anything of interest. Nothing, at least, that could compare with Addie's story, which Clare kept to herself.

Finally, she called an obviously uncomfortable Harris into the parlor. "Mr. Harris," she said, smiling graciously. "Please, sit down." Although the butler looked rather alarmed at her request, he balanced on the edge of one of the Gothic oak chairs.

"As you know, Mr. Harris, I am interested in restoring the entire castle—" she paused significantly "—including the battlements." If the butler was surprised at her words, he did not show it.

"The marquis seems to have difficulty opening the doors to the roofs again because of the unfortunate incident that took place seven years ago, when Elizabeth Landrey was killed," Clare continued. "Are you familiar with that incident, Mr. Harris?"

The butler said nothing, but coughed uncomfortably.

"I'm interested in finding out exactly what happened. Could you please tell me what you remember?"

Harris eyed her painfully. "My lady, that was a long time ago. I'm afraid that I cannot help you. I remember nothing."

Clare forced herself to smile in the face of his blatant lie. "Surely you recall something, Mr. Harris. Who was here, for instance?"

The butler simply shook his head.

"Perhaps if I prod your memory, Mr. Harris," she said, her voice rising. She would prefer to prod his thick skull with one of the fireplace tongs, yet in the face of his obstinacy, Clare was helpless. She could threaten to dismiss him, but Justin would never agree to it, especially when he found out the reason for her displeasure. More than likely, her husband would side with his butler, rewarding the man for keeping his mouth shut.

Clare tried one last time. She abandoned the smile and the ingratiating manner for the stern voice she used on recalcitrant village youngsters. "Tell me this, Mr. Harris," she said, her gaze boring into him. "Who was here that night by the name of Richard?"

She waited, her expression set, for she was not going to let the man leave until he gave her an answer, and she was prepared to wait all day.

Harris looked ill at ease, but after the silence dragged on between them for what seemed like an eternity, he finally spoke. "I remember that Richard Kingsley was here, and Lord Wilmington—yes, Lord Wilmington also." He paused as if in consideration. "I don't know if there were any other guests named Richard, but there was quite a crowd that night, and not all those present were invited," he noted with a sniff.

"Is either man fair haired?" Clare asked.

"Mr. Kingsley is very dark, but Lord Wilmington is blond," Harris said. His patience with her questioning, Clare could see, was wearing thin.

"All right. Thank you for your help, Mr. Harris," Clare said graciously, while her mind raced ahead. Bowing briefly, he was almost to the door before Clare thought of one more little thing to add.

"Oh, Mr. Harris, you needn't mention this to Justin," she said with a smile. "We don't want him to get upset."

JUSTIN WASN'T UPSET. He was furious, more furious than Clare had ever seen—or heard—him. She was dressing for dinner when the sound of his bellow rang out even before he threw open her door.

"Clare!" He called out her name again loudly, even though she was sitting but a short distance from him.

Frowning as she turned to face him, Clare could easily guess what had irritated him, and she could just as easily imagine how he had found out, too. That perfidious butler, Harris, had run to his master like a spoiled child anxious to tattle on her. Silently, she vowed to have revenge upon the man when she got a chance. For now, she only wished to diffuse the anger that had transformed her husband's stunning features into a grim scowl.

Clare waved away her maid, who needed no further encouragement to flee the scene. The door closed with a bang behind the girl as Clare looked up at Justin.

"What the devil do you think you're doing?" he shouted.

Justin had never used to shout when she was a girl, Clare noted. Perhaps he reserved his best behavior for youngsters—which would bode well for their children. She smiled happily at the thought.

"Blast it, Clare, I'm yelling at you!" Justin declared, stating the obvious. "Why are you smiling beatifically at me?"

Despite his words, Clare knew she had robbed him of his rage, and she was glad. She had no wish to war with her prince. In fact, her inclinations were quite the opposite.

"I was thinking of our children," Clare said. She saw surprise cross his face.

"You're deliberately turning the topic," Justin said, though he didn't appear to be too disturbed at the prospect. He stepped closer.

"Sorry," Clare said. Although she was clad only in her chemise, she no longer felt any constraint with her husband. Far from it, for the sight of his passionate gaze made her heart pound and her breasts ache with a longing to shed what little she wore. She rose from the chair and put a hand up, curling it behind his neck. "Shall we go back to arguing?"

"No," Justin said gruffly as he pulled her to him. "I have no wish to quarrel, but I want you to drop this nonsense about Elizabeth. For pity's sake, stop bothering my servants with it."

"All right," Clare said softly as she pulled his head down. What harm was there in agreeing, when she had already finished her questioning of the servants? She kissed him, slowly, her hands slipping underneath his shirt.

Justin tried to keep his mind on Elizabeth's death, although he had no desire to think of her, not when his wife, his love, his Clare, was tracing his ribs with her fingertips. And yet...he definitely did not want Clare's interest in the dead woman to continue. Unfortunately, he knew Clare well enough to realize that once she took an idea into her head, it was fairly difficult to dislodge, except by drastic means.

What he needed was a distraction. The activity they were engaged in leapt to mind, but as much as he would like to, Justin knew he could hardly make love to her every moment of the day. The situation called for a different sort of distraction.

Clare was too involved with the hall and its renovations, he decided. He knew, all too well, how the old building could prey on one's mind. Sometimes it had even seemed a dark, foreboding presence to him, and Clare had enough imagination for an army of storytellers. He couldn't begin to fathom what the place did to her. A change of scenery, Justin resolved, would be the solution.

"I have some business that needs to be taken care of in London," he whispered against her cheek. "We can take your new phaeton, and you can show it off, do some shopping, throw a party...visit your aunt." The last words were spoken with enough reluctance to make Clare giggle against his chest.

"That sounds lovely, Justin, especially the visit to Eugenia. You are so thoughtful," she teased, smiling into his shirt. Privately, she was amazed at her good fortune. A trip to London! She could hardly have planned it better herself, she thought as she snuggled against him. Although she did not care much for town life, she was nonetheless thrilled, for in London she would be able to pursue her investigation into Elizabeth's death. It would be the perfect place to find out more about her most likely suspect, Lord Wilmington.

"Good," Justin said, his fingers playing in her hair. "We'll leave the day after tomorrow."

"Oh? Why not tomorrow?" Clare asked, looking up in surprise.

"Tomorrow," Justin whispered seductively. "I would like to go fishing again. Care to join me?"

Clare smiled slowly. "You want to catch the one that got away, I presume?"

"Definitely," he answered, grinning wickedly. "Think I shall?"

"Definitely."

A LIGHT DRIZZLE the next morning prevented their jaunt to the river, so Justin decided to head for London, and Clare was in agreement. She looked forward to pursuing her investigation, visiting her acquaintances there and seeing Justin's town house.

Justin's London residence was beautiful. But it was a far cry from Worth Hall. A palatial, modern building filled with gleaming new furniture and perfectly displayed works of art, it lacked the sense of history and warm familiarity of the castle. Clare found no cause for complaint in the spotless and luxurious atmosphere, for no bits of plaster fell from the ceilings, no paper peeled off the walls and no sense of an unhappy past lingered in the rooms. It was a chance for a fresh start, she thought as she eyed the elaborately painted ceilings. Nonetheless, she missed her castle.

When word circulated that they were in town, they were inundated with invitations. Clare thought back on all the effort Eugenia had gone to just to garner them but a precious few. Despite his reputation, or maybe even because of it, Clare thought churlishly, the Marquis of Worthington was assured his pick of entertainments.

Seated at the shining desk in his study, he handed invitations to her with careless indifference, along with the announcement that she might choose whatever function met her fancy. After sifting through the stack, Clare chose a reception at Lady Lynford's. Although it promised to be a dreadful squeeze, Clare suspected that most of the ton's finest would be in attendance. "What would you think of Lady's Lynford's fete?" Clare asked.

"By faith, Clare, the place will be packed," Justin said, looking up from his correspondence.

Clare tapped the invitation against her chin thoughtfully. "Yes, but everyone will be there. Do you think Lady Berkeley will come?" Clare asked the question as guilelessly as possible, for she did not care to reveal just how interested she was in seeing that particular lady.

"I imagine so, yes," Justin said, glancing back down at his papers.

Clare smiled to herself. The event presented a perfect opportunity for her to further her acquaintance with Lady Berkeley, a preliminary step in her inquiries into Elizabeth's death. She was counting on Lady Berkeley to help her. The woman obviously knew Justin very well, because she had gone with him to Aunt Eugenia's. And as a ranking member of the ton, Lady Berkeley presumably could give her information about Lord Wilmington, too. Things were proceeding quite well, Clare thought happily.

Justin watched his wife's face and wondered what had come over her. He felt a twinge of disappointment in Clare's eagerness to see and be seen at the most exclusive function, for he had never put any stock in such things. Now he wondered if perhaps the distraction he'd provided might prove too diverting, and he frowned as he realized he had liked it better when they were alone together and he was the center of Clare's world.

As they prepared to leave for the party, Justin looked so handsome in his evening finery that Clare had a momentary twinge of regret. She could picture the ladies swarming about him, eager for his attentions, and she swallowed hard, already feeling jealous. Clare didn't really expect Justin to betray her, but she was uncomfortably aware that those who would be seeking him out had no knowledge of his promise to forswear all others. She suspected that even if she took out a notice in the *Post,* they would not believe it.

Clare ran her fingers over the embroidery on his white swansdown waistcoat, ostensibly to straighten it. "I'm going to be jealous, you know," she advised as he took her arm to step into the brightly lit reception room crowded with London's elite. He glanced at her in surprise, his grin warm and appreciative.

"I shall be, too, so don't dance with anyone else too often," he warned. Based upon her previous experience in London, Clare could hardly imagine men lining up to take a turn with her, so she smiled up at him with amusement. Although she was now gowned in the most stylish of dresses, a deep burgundy, with matching elbow-length gloves and a necklace of sparkling sapphires about her throat, Clare was too unsure of herself yet to imagine that she was very appealing.

She was not prepared for the change in status that her marriage brought her.

Men, young and old, swarmed about her like flies to a honey pot, while Clare flushed with a bewilderment that resembled Aunt Eugenia's. Finally, she recognized that she was a marchioness now, which made her infinitely more interesting than an unknown country miss, and a perfect target for those males who wanted a lovely young lover without legal entanglements.

More important than her marriage, however, was the identity of her husband. One of the city's most infamous rakes had forgone plenty of attractive, eligible women—and countless others who were not—to choose her, and the rest of the world wanted to find out just what made her so special.

They discovered that she was tall, darkly beautiful, and that her hazel eyes were brilliant with life and intelligence. She could be dryly amusing, but to their disappointment, they also discerned that she was in love with her husband. More to the point, they found Justin quite possessive of his new bride, for he glared at any man who danced with her more than once.

Since the libertine had never exhibited the slightest concern over his previous paramours, being content to drink the night away, do a little gambling and flirt with anyone that caught his notice, his friends were dismayed when he could not be coaxed into gaming, refused anything stronger than water and smiled with strict politeness at any lady who tried to capture his interest.

"What did she *do* to him?" Lord Maplethorpe asked in wonder while he watched the marquis dance with his bride.

"It'll pass," commented an elderly roué standing nearby. "Just the odd thrill of marriage, I'll warrant."

"Don't be too sure," said Lady Berkeley, who watched

the couple happily. "Justin's in love, and you know what they say about reformed rakes.…"

"Making the best husbands, you mean?" Prudence asked, as she walked up behind her grandmother. The lady nodded gently. "Oh, dear, I do hope so," Prudence said breathlessly as she spotted Fletcher Mayefield across the room.

"Humph," Lord Maplethorpe snorted, obviously disbelieving, but Lady Berkeley only smiled to herself. When the dance ended, she stepped forward, catching Justin's attention, and he walked toward her, his fingers on his wife's elbow in a careless, perhaps even unconscious, gesture that announced to all that she was his.

Don't tell me this will pass, Lady Berkeley thought. She had seen Justin St. John lose his temper for the first time in her life over Clare, and now he couldn't keep from touching her, even in public. Lady Berkeley had seen him with many a female, and she had never seen that quiet look, that tender regard, that fierce possessiveness that he bestowed upon his wife.

"Justin," she said warmly. "Since you deprived me of a big wedding reception, you must let me hold a small ball in honor of your marriage," she said.

"If you feel you must," Justin said with a wry grimace.

"Justin, don't be rude," Clare said, scolding him with a squeeze of his arm and a glance. Lady Berkeley marveled at the way they looked at one another, his dark eyes and her hazel ones caressing like a kiss. Over soon? What prittle prattle, she thought. Their grandchildren would find them still in love.

"It is a pleasure to see you again, Lady Berkeley," Clare said. "And we would be honored by any celebration in which you are involved. I would like to plan a party myself, but I'm afraid I have little expertise in such things. Could I call on you for advice, sometime this week, perhaps?" Clare held her breath, trying not to let her eagerness show, for she intended to question Lady Berkeley on far more than social arrangements.

"Why, of course, dear. I would love to have you, but you must call me Aurora, as everyone does," Lady Berkeley answered, reaching out a hand to touch her arm. Clare felt herself relax with relief. She looked up at Justin, who smiled unsuspectingly, and decided he need not know of her plans. One step at a time, she thought, and then, when she had all the answers, she would present them to him—as her gift.

"Clare!" Her thoughts were interrupted by Felicity, who greeted her warmly. "You slyboots!" she accused, glancing at Justin. "All the time I've tried politeness, when I see that you must insult a man to gain his attention!"

Clare laughed and Justin scowled, obviously not caring to be the butt of such jokes. "If you ladies will excuse me," he said, and Clare nodded, watching him walk toward Fletcher, who was grinning from across the room. She hoped that whatever jealousy Justin had harbored for his friend had ended, for she did not want to see anything come between the two men, especially not herself.

"Lord Wolsey appears lost without his wife," Lady Berkeley said, her eyes on an elderly man across the room. "Excuse me, my dears." Moving away gracefully, her head high, her throat and arms draped in jewels, she looked like a fairy queen, Clare thought.

Her granddaughter was much more earthbound. "Oh, he's so handsome, Clare! How did you manage it?" Felicity asked, leaning close.

Clare opened her mouth, uncertain how to answer. "We had met before, you see," she began lamely. "But I..." Clare was well aware that Justin had offered for her only to prevent her marriage to Farnsworth, no matter what existed between them before—or since—yet she could hardly admit as much to Felicity without casting Farnsworth in a bad light.

Having no wish to unfairly malign anyone or initiate titillating gossip, Clare shut her mouth again, while Felicity waited anxiously for her explanation. "It's all so very complicated," she said with an apologetic smile. "Suffice to say that I am quite pleased with the arrangement, and I think Justin is, too."

"I should say so," Felicity said. "Goodness, you've only to look at him," she marveled, gazing over at Justin, who was lounging casually against an archway, deep in conversation with Fletcher. "A month ago I would have said he was handsome, yes, but now he positively...glows. Oh, I don't know how to describe it," she said.

"I know what you mean," said Clare, beaming with pride at her prince. She knew what it was: the absence of drink and the presence of, she hoped, happiness. "His eyes are sparkling again."

"Look at them," Felicity urged. "One golden-haired, the other dark, yet both undeniably handsome. I would have told you before that I thought Mr. Mayefield the more favored of the two, but now...it's as though the marquis is drawing women to him from across the room, like moths to a flame."

A good description, Clare thought wryly as she glanced around, for the attention of more ladies than she cared to count was focused upon her husband. She told herself they were admiring Fletcher, and turned to Felicity. "Have you the same appreciation for Mr. Mayefield that your sister has?"

"Goodness, no!" Felicity said, with a laugh. "Prudence is positively silly over the man. He is quite good looking, I will admit, but I have less lofty ambitions," she said, with a teasing grin, "or perhaps more realistic ones. Mr. Mayefield has been most determined at avoiding the altar. I cannot imagine the lady he would wed," she said, shaking her head.

Clare watched Justin's friend appraisingly. Although he treated women with a disarming warmth, she sensed again a distance that suggested he held a part of himself aloof from them all. She wondered, too, what lady might capture his heart.

"But then I would have said the same, and more, for the marquis." Felicity said. "And here you are, married to him, when the last time I saw you together, you refused even to accept an introduction. At the very least, you must tell me about your romantic elopement," she demanded, leaning close.

Clare hesitated. She could hardly admit that Justin had abducted her against her will or that she had not made up her mind to marry him until minutes before the ceremony. "Justin can be very...persuasive," she said. The soft smile that unknowingly came to her lips added a wicked note to her words, and Felicity giggled gleefully.

"I can see that he lives up to his reputation," she whispered behind her fan. "You have the look of a satisfied bride!"

Clare felt a blush rise to her cheeks. "Felicity! You shouldn't know about such things."

Felicity laughed. "I have too many sisters *not* to know, and I have learned quite a bit from them," she assured Clare. "Yet as nosy as I am, I am not asking for the details of your marriage bed, you goose, only your elopement!" She shot a probing glance at Clare. "Is it true that Richard Farnsworth fought a duel for you and lost?"

Clare gasped in astonishment. "Good heavens, no!" she said, gazing at Felicity in disbelief. To her dismay, her friend did not appear to be joking, but eyed her expectantly. "Where on earth did you hear that?" Then she remembered the presence of Justin's old paramour.

"Well, I heard it from Prudence, but I do believe it originated with Marie Summerville," Felicity said, "who claims to have been there. Wasn't she?"

"Yes, she was there, but no duel took place," Clare answered. "Mr. Farnsworth was sent by my aunt, who worried that I might have been abducted. When he discovered that

Justin and I were eloping, he was most gracious and left.'' Clare did not feel the need to mention Farnsworth's fury or his spiteful tactics in throwing Justin's past in her face.

"Well, isn't that just like Prudence to embellish something out of all recognition," Felicity said with annoyance.

"I don't know how the story got so garbled, but I would appreciate it if you would set people to rights, given the opportunity," Clare said.

"Of course," Felicity declared sincerely. Then she paused. "No wonder Mr. Farnsworth is so angry over all the talk. He hasn't been *anywhere* lately."

Clare nearly dropped her fan. She swallowed hard at the thought of the "fiendish" Mr. Farnsworth's reaction to the rumors. It would not be pretty. She looked at Justin, still chatting amiably with Fletcher, and fought with the worry that swept over her.

"Nonsense, Clare," she told herself. "Don't let your imagination run wild. Mr. Farnsworth is a civilized man, not some ogre from one of your stories," she assured herself. He might not like what was being said, but he would bear up under it, knowing it would soon be forgotten.

Still, Clare could not shake the niggling fear that seemed lodged in her spine like an unwanted burr. If she saw her former suitor, she decided, she would greet him warmly, as though nothing had happened, and that would soon put the tale from people's minds. The plan eased her concerns somewhat, but if he were too angry to show himself, how was she going to see it through?

Her thoughts were interrupted by the appearance of Justin and Fletcher, both apparently in good spirits. Whatever jealousy that had divided them seemed to be at an end, to Clare's relief.

"Miss Shaw, how delightful to see you again," Fletcher said, bowing low over Felicity's hand.

Clare decided that her friend was not as immune to the man's charms as she pretended. Felicity bent her head flushing slightly, while Fletcher moved closer with practiced grace, his smile warm and alluring. Yet Clare could still see that he held himself a bit distant. It was as if the smooth exhibition of his charms did not extend to his eyes—until he turned to her.

To her surprise, Clare saw his emerald gaze brighten with pleasure as he greeted her. A bit dismayed, she wondered what that signified. She could not imagine Fletcher feeling anything but friendship for her, but the discovery that he treated her more cordially than other women made her uneasy just the same.

"Clare, your husband is claiming that you have promised this dance to him, when I know he's just trying to keep you all to himself," Fletcher complained. His brows rose in silent question.

Clare smiled and glanced at Justin, who grinned in graceful surrender. "Oh, I think he was teasing you, Fletcher. I'll be glad to dance with you, if you wish."

"My fondest wish," Fletcher said softly, and Clare found herself coloring. Unaccustomed to the practiced flirtations of the ton, she was uncomfortable with the words and with Fletcher's attentions.

It must have showed, for while he whirled her about the floor in a graceful waltz, she felt his probing assessment. "What is it, Clare?" he asked gently. Glancing up, she found him appraising her with bold directness. Clare stared past his shoulders.

"Justin seems to be over his fit of jealousy, if that is what is bothering you," Fletcher said. "In fact, I think you've managed the impossible. The man seems to be quite happy." Clare reluctantly lifted her chin then, to see his white teeth shining in a wide grin.

"Fletcher," she began, glad to turn the topic from herself. "About Justin...remember when we talked before, I was interested in discovering more about Elizabeth's death?" She waited for his nod of acknowledgment. "Well, I have found something out." She ignored his raised eyebrows and frank look of disbelief. "Fletcher, I don't think she threw herself off the roof. I think someone pushed her."

"Clare—"

"Hear me out, Fletcher. What if someone did kill her? Shouldn't the culprit be brought to justice, even after all these years? Admit it, wouldn't Justin quit blaming himself? You say he's happy—well, I think he would be happier to know that whatever happened that night was not his fault."

Fletcher eyed her skeptically, but said nothing.

"Tell me this," Clare urged, "what do you know of Lord Wilmington?"

Fletcher's brows rose even higher in shocked surprise, then he studied her in that calm manner of his. "Well, he's a member of the House of Lords, and from what I gather, he takes his duties quite seriously. He has proposed a number of bills, and is quite interested in increasing foreign trade."

Clare frowned. She had to admit the man did not sound like a murderer. "What if I said I would like to meet him? Could you arrange it?"

She glimpsed the alarm that crossed Fletcher's features. "I could," he answered, "but I don't know if I would."

Clare nodded. Fair enough. She would need more information before she confronted the man, anyway. "All right," she answered. "I'll let you know when I find out more."

They continued dancing, their conversation a heavy counterpoint to their light movements. "Clare, if you want a bit of advice, which I'm sure you don't, please drop this whole thing. I know you think you are doing what's best for Justin, but even if your outlandish story has some merit, do you think it's safe to chase headlong after a killer?"

She glanced up at him in surprise. To be honest, the thought of danger to herself had never crossed her mind. Fletcher obviously read her reaction, and shook his head.

"You mean far more to Justin than some old skeleton in

his closet. He will be happier just to have you at his side than he would be receiving exoneration for a several-years-old accident. Let it go, Clare," Fletcher said seriously.

She swallowed hard. "Perhaps you are right." She would have to think about his words, but for now she wanted a promise from him. As much as she appreciated his concern, she did not want it prompting him to run to Justin with the tale of her doings. "I'll consider your advice, but you won't tell Justin, will you?" she asked.

Fletcher frowned, and she could see his hesitation. Finally, he sighed again. "I won't tell Justin," he promised, "not yet, anyway."

"Oh, thank you, Fletcher, you are wonderful!" Clare said, smiling up at him brightly before she realized what she had said. Then she blushed rosily, and stared across the room again while her partner chuckled softly.

CHAPTER FIFTEEN

"I DO SO APPRECIATE YOUR ADVICE, Aurora," Clare said. She had come prepared with pen and paper, much to Lady Berkeley's amusement, and had taken many notes on the finer points of entertaining the ton, from putting on a small soirée on up to a ball for two hundred or more.

The topic was a serious one for Clare, for she realized that her new position required a few skills she lacked. Unfortunately, the talents she did possess, those for hunting, riding, fishing, and above all, storytelling, were hardly in demand by Justin's set. She needed to be able to oversee a large household and handle social responsibilities that suddenly seemed very heavy, indeed.

Lady Berkeley was patient and kind, though, going over seating arrangements and menus and protocol with gentle humor. If she could hardly imagine a young woman of decent birth being unschooled in such subjects, she did not say so, but was generous with her time and knowledge.

Glancing at the clock, Clare realized that she should not impose on the woman any longer, yet she still had not broached the subject of Elizabeth's death, and she had no idea how to work it into the conversation. "How can I thank you enough for all your help?" she asked. "I honestly never intended to take up so much of your time."

Aurora made a soft sound that dismissed her gratitude. She was dressed in a pink gown that matched the glow in her cheeks, her white hair piled high upon her head, and

Clare was again struck by how regal she looked. "Seeing Justin happy is thank-you enough," she said.

Clare seized the opening. "You seem to be fond of Justin. How long have you known him?" she asked.

"My goodness, forever," Aurora said, sighing as if in thought. "I knew his parents. You see, I'm his godmother."

"Really?" Clare could hardly dare believe her good fortune. Aurora must have kept an eye on her godchild since his birth. "You are well aware of his poor reputation then?" she asked, a little hesitantly.

Aurora laughed. "Goodness, how could I not be? Someone was always running to me with new tales of his scandalous behavior." She shook her head. "The boy needed a father. My husband was already gone, and I had four girls. I tried to have *their* husbands set him straight, but Justin always ended up intimidating anyone who tried to right him."

Clare smiled wryly. That was only too true.

"I must say that I despaired of ever seeing him married," Aurora added.

"Did you...did you not think he might marry Elizabeth Landrey?" Clare asked, trying to steer the discussion closer to the subject that haunted her—and Justin.

Aurora looked at her intently, as if trying to gauge how much to say. "No," she said finally. "There was never any hint that he might, from Justin, anyway. I'm sure Elizabeth, like many who followed her, hoped otherwise."

So Aurora would be blunt. Clare felt herself relax a little, and realized that she had been sitting tensely on the edge of her chair, hoping to gain the information she sought without losing the lady's goodwill. So far, so good. "Then you remember Elizabeth's death?"

Aurora made a soft sound of regret. "I do indeed." She shook her head again. "It was fodder for the gossips for weeks and blackened Justin's reputation so much that mamas warned their daughters away from him, and still do."

Seemingly lost in thought, she offered no details of the incident.

"Were you there the night she died?" Clare prodded.

"Goodness, no!" Aurora answered, looking up as if shocked by the question. "No one with a decent reputation would be caught at the hall in those days," she explained. "Justin ran with quite a loose crowd, and the house parties were known to be wild affairs, with young men drinking themselves into a stupor and losing fortunes on the turn of a card."

"Sounds just like London to me," Clare said dryly.

Aurora laughed. "Well, yes, but more so. Ladies of quality did not attend, though I'm sure others did," she added, eyeing Clare meaningfully.

Clare smiled. "I'm sure they did, but what about Elizabeth? Wasn't she quality?"

"Well, yes, but she was there with her guardian, who didn't always seem to have her best interests at heart. What was his name? Clevindale? Cavendish? Well, no matter. He was the one who introduced her to Justin and supposedly acted as chaperon during her visits," Aurora said, with a frown of distaste.

"I see," Clare said softly. "Do you think that was the first time he threw her into harm's way?"

"What?" the older woman asked in surprise.

"Well, I mean, perhaps he had introduced her to another man before Justin," Clare finished, trying to choose her words delicately.

Aurora's lips thinned. "I really couldn't say. I know Justin felt terrible after her death and put an end to the wild parties, even going so far as to close up the hall. For a few years, he seemed to tone down his ways—or at least he was more discreet—which gave me hopes for his ultimate reformation. But then something happened. I never could discover what it was," she said softly, as though to herself. "He had been running off to Worth again, and then he returned to London a madman, intent upon ruining himself." Seeming to catch herself, Aurora looked up and smiled reassuringly. "But that is all behind him now that he is happily wed."

Clare's thoughts were diverted from her goal as she considered Aurora's meandering memories. Following Elizabeth's death, Justin had calmed down, only to launch himself into renewed dissipation a few years later...after visiting Worth again. Could it be that the past had returned to haunt him, or was it as Justin had claimed, that he was as devastated by their parting as she herself had been? Clare closed her eyes against the old ache. What a waste the years of separation had been, years that had made her hardened, and Justin dissolute.

"Clare?" Aurora's soft voice brought her back to the present and to her mission.

"So Justin withdrew after Elizabeth's death?" she prompted.

Aurora hesitated as though considering her words. "He blamed himself," she finally said.

"But that's just it!" Clare said. "What if there was someone else to blame?"

"Who?" Aurora said simply.

"Aurora, what do you know about Lord Wilmington?" Clare asked.

"CLARE!" She could hear the shout from clear down the gallery of the town house and frowned. She was accustomed to shouting from her father, but not from Justin. When had he acquired this annoying habit? And did he plan to continue it indefinitely?

"Clare!" Justin threw open the door with such force that it thudded against the wall, sending reverberations through the room. She sat at her secretary, where she had been composing a list of prospective guests for the ball she knew she must sooner or later arrange. Putting down the paper, Clare eyed her husband calmly and wondered who had given her away.

"Clare!" Justin shouted. He struggled with the urge to beat some sense into her, but she looked up at him with such bright-eyed expectancy that he decided to slam his fist into the wall, instead. When he did, Justin realized why he hadn't done such a thing since he was a scrawny youth: it hurt like the devil. "Blast it," he said, cursing under his breath.

He received no sympathy from his wife, who sat staring at him with a look of dismay on her beautiful features. "Honestly, Justin, why would you want to that? You'll ruin the silk hangings—"

Justin didn't let her finish. "Clare," he said angrily, "I thought you had agreed to forget all about Elizabeth Landrey."

Clare had the audacity to appear surprised, and Justin nearly smashed his other hand into the wall. "I did no such thing," she protested. "You might have asked me, but I certainly did not agree. That would be lying, Justin, and I've never lied to you—at least not intentionally."

Justin raised his hands to the heavens for assistance and groaned in frustration. "No?" he finally said, glaring at her. "What would you call it when you go behind my back, pursuing a bit of history that I asked you to leave alone?"

Clare thought for a moment, and he could almost see the wheels turning in her head. Too intelligent, that was the problem, he decided. Clare was too smart for her own good. "I refuse to equate failure to mention something with lying," she said with extreme dignity.

Justin snorted. He rubbed the back of his neck. "Clare, have done with this wild notion of yours. People will talk, if they aren't already," he added, with a frown of disgust.

"And when did you start caring about gossip?" Clare asked.

Justin's eyes narrowed. "When it involved you! Blast it,

Clare, people are going to think you're foolish at best, a lunatic at worst. And to cast Lord Wilmington as the villain in your little drama! Lord Wilmington is a peer in the House of Lords, for pity's sake!''

Clare was scowling now, and Justin was glad to see it. Perhaps he was getting through to her. He felt himself unbend a little as he waited for her apology.

"No, it might not actually be Lord Wilmington," she admitted.

Justin nearly sagged with relief. At last they were getting somewhere! He held a smile of triumph in check as she opened her mouth to speak again.

"But he does have blond hair, and his first name is Richard, so he seemed the likeliest candidate," she said guilelessly.

Justin nearly choked. He was obviously not making the slightest impression upon her. He took a deep breath. "Clare, of all the sordid incidents in my life, why did you have to pick this one, the only one that still has the power to bother me?" he asked, annoyed by the catch in his voice.

She had the grace to look contrite then, but only for a moment. "But Justin, when you realize that none of it was your fault, then it won't bother you anymore. I only want you to be happy." She stood up and put her arms around his waist, pressing her cheek against his chest, and Justin felt his anger ebb under the warmth of her touch.

"I'd be *happy* if you left it alone," he said firmly.

"Yes, Justin," she whispered against his waistcoat.

He sighed, for he knew her too well. Her easy acquiescence was unconvincing. What would she do next? He didn't care to guess.

"FLETCHER MAYEFIELD! Isn't this the second party you've attended this week?" asked the aging Earl of Greyhaven.

Fletcher smiled and nodded at the older man. "Yes, I believe it is," he said, making light of the fact.

"I thought you detested these things as much as I did," Greyhaven said with a grimace.

Fletcher shrugged. "Sometimes I find them amusing," he said.

"Ah," the earl answered, with a glimmer in his blue gaze. "So it's a lady that's brought you here."

"Not precisely," Fletcher answered, grinning. "It is a lady, but the situation is not what you think, you old lecher. The lady, you see, is Worthington's wife, and I've a mind to keep an eye on her."

"What? Isn't Worthington up to the task?" the earl asked.

"Perhaps," Fletcher answered cryptically. "Perhaps." Privately, he thought not, but he hesitated to voice his opinion. His attention was caught by the very subject of their conversation, and Fletcher was tempted to answer, "Definitely not," for she was glaring daggers at him from across the room. Now what?

Clare saw him coming. She smiled sweetly for the sake of the crowd and hoped that none of Fletcher's considerable female following would descend upon them before she finished her diatribe, for a diatribe was exactly what she planned. She intended to tell Fletcher Mayefield in no uncertain terms just how little she thought of him for breaking her trust.

He approached her with a rather wary look that seemed to denote guilt, and as soon as he was close enough, she let him have it. "Fletcher Mayefield! I thought you promised not to tell Justin!" Scowling at him accusingly, she realized there was no reason why she should have believed the man except for a certain intuitive feeling, which had obviously proved to be wrong. His engaging candor aside, Fletcher was no different from most of the other men Clare encountered in London—vain, superficial characters she did not care to know.

"If you are referring to your persistent interest in Elizabeth Landrey's death, although it goes against my best judgment, I did *not* tell Justin," Fletcher said, his green eyes sincere, his mouth curving up teasingly at the corners.

"Oh," Clare said softly, her face coloring. "I'm sorry to have blamed you unfairly." Her mind raced from Fletcher to Lady Berkeley, the only other person she had taken into her confidence.

Clare had thought Aurora interested in Justin's welfare, but apparently the lady was not concerned enough to join Clare in her quest for his exoneration. Clare felt a twinge of disappointment, for she liked the older woman, and now she would have to guard her tongue around her, which would do little to foster a friendship between them.

"Come along, Clare, and you may make your apologies in private," Fletcher said, drawing her out of her thoughts and toward the garden. Clare glanced across the room to find Justin deep in conversation with Lady Berkeley, of all people. They were probably planning to muzzle her next, or sweep her away to the Continent, Clare thought grimly. She let Fletcher lead her out the tall French doors into the cool night.

He found a small bench and they sat down together, the scent of roses heavy in the air. "So someone has carried a tale to Justin," Fletcher said. "It wasn't me, Clare. I gave you my word that I would not speak of it as yet, and I do hold myself to my word," he said, subtly scolding her for her faithlessness. "Do you know who else might have told him?"

Clare nodded with a frown. "Oh, I'm sorry, Fletcher," she said, reaching out to pat his arm. "I just assumed it was you, and that was wrong of me." His hand gently covered her own.

"You are forgiven," he said. Clare thought she detected an odd note in his voice, but then he spoke in his usual bantering style. "Pardon my curiosity, but what did Justin have to say about your pursuits?"

Clare smiled at the memory of Justin's reaction. Reluctant to admit to his fury, she gazed down at her hand, only to find it still in Fletcher's grasp. She casually extricated her fingers and placed them in her lap. "He was not pleased," Clare admitted. Then she looked up at Fletcher, eager to share her discoveries. "But I found out that Elizabeth had a guardian who was not at all what he should be. Cavendish or Clevindale or something like that was his name. Do you remember the man?"

"No," Fletcher drawled, his brows rising in skepticism.

"Oh," Clare said, disappointed. She looked up again, with new hope. "Can you find out for me who he is?"

Fletcher rubbed his chin thoughtfully, his eyes like emeralds glowing in the light of the garden lamps. "Clare, you are a most persuasive lady, but as Justin's friend, I can hardly go against his wishes and aid you in this pursuit—a pursuit, I might add, with which I disagree."

Clare watched her hopes being dashed. Without help, how was she, unfamiliar as she was with the ton, going to discover anything? And who else could she turn to? Lady Berkeley had already betrayed her confidence. Clare felt the pressure of time, too. The more quickly she completed her task, the better, for Justin's patience with her defiance would surely wear thin sometime soon.

"Clare, don't look so heartbroken," Fletcher said.

She glanced up, surprised to see indecision flicker across his face. Not having mastered the employment of feminine wiles, she wasn't quite certain what had brought about the shift, but she immediately seized the opportunity to change his mind. "You know that I shall just ask someone else to help me," she said softly.

"I'm sure you will, and that will get you into more trouble," Fletcher said, with an exasperated frown. "Very well, then, Clare. I will find out about this guardian for you, on the condition that you don't do anything foolish, or more foolish than you have done already."

Clare nodded quickly, a smile of triumph lighting her features.

"And for the love of heaven, leave Lord Wilmington out of it."

"I have no intention of bothering his lordship, as yet," Clare said truthfully.

Fletcher rolled his eyes and stood up. He took her arm to lead her back into the house, gazing at her with an odd mixture of fondness and dismay. "Justin, may God have mercy on him, has his hands full," he announced.

ALTHOUGH CLARE SAID NOTHING to Lady Berkeley about her betrayal, she had found a way to exact retribution from Harris for tattling on her. It was an old tactic, really, one she had used on her father until he became so furious that he forbade it. Clare had discovered that men who think they are omnipotent, such as the squire or Justin's butler, do not like being taken unawares. It was simple, really. She just sneaked up on him.

The first time, he was overseeing the silver polishing, and she slipped into the room until she was directly behind him, then spoke his name softly. He jumped nearly a foot, but could hardly do anything, for Clare simply smiled innocently and sent him on some trifling errand for her. She then made a habit of suddenly appearing and startling him, anywhere, anytime.

Although Harris no longer visibly started when he heard her voice, her constant harassment did little to improve his composure. The poor man's eyes darted everywhere, and Clare noticed that he had taken to standing with his back practically against the wall, so that he might see his tormentor approach.

He took such a stance this afternoon, hovering by the front entrance as if it were the only place where Clare could not be expected to pop up. Seeing him there, she considered leaving the town house by one of the other exits and coming back through the front door, directly behind him, but she decided that was simply too petty. Instead, she gave him a brilliant smile as she swept past. "Please tell Justin that I've gone to visit my aunt, Mr. Harris," she said sweetly, noting the brief flash of relief that passed over his features at the thought of her absence.

AUNT EUGENIA, still living in the house the squire had rented, welcomed her niece with an excited flutter. "Clare!" she said with a happy gasp. "I never expected to see you in London so soon."

Clare hugged her aunt with pleasure. "Justin had some business in town, so I came along," she explained.

"As well you should," Eugenia answered. "It can't hurt to keep an eye on him," she added, nodding sagely.

Ignoring the comment, as she did so many of Eugenia's non sequiturs, Clare seated herself on the familiar settee, while Eugenia called for tea and cakes.

"Although I am surprised to see you, I couldn't be more pleased," her aunt said. "I've been staying on in the hope that you would visit, though I do miss my place in Bath. London is far too busy and noisy for me, Clare," she complained as she sat down beside her niece, her yellow hair moving gently about her face. Clare smiled and nodded in sympathetic agreement, although she suspected that Eugenia was quite happy to be enjoying the comparative luxury of her new lodgings and the bustle of London—at least for a while.

"Now, Clare—" Eugenia paused to pat her skirts absently, then turned to root among the cushions "—I do hope that you're getting along well with your husband."

"We're doing fine," Clare answered. "May I help you find something?"

"My spectacles! Oh, here they are." Eugenia slipped on the eyeglasses and immediately lost her habitual air of confusion. "Now, Clare, what I mean is…" Eugenia looked at her seriously and took a deep breath. "Are you doing your duty?"

Clare smiled. "Well, I wouldn't exactly call it that," she said, stifling the giggle that threatened. "But, yes, you needn't worry your head about it anymore."

Eugenia sighed. She did not appear to be as pleased as Clare anticipated, considering that not long ago she had harped on little else. Clare waited patiently for the explanation that appeared, from the struggle that was passing across the elderly woman's features, to be forthcoming. She sighed again.

"I must tell you, child, I have often wondered since my visit if I gave you the wrong advice."

"Good heavens, why?" Clare asked, genuinely puzzled.

"Oh, the things I've been hearing about your husband," Eugenia said. Fussing with an errant bit of loose thread on one of the cushions, she seemed to be ill at ease with the conversation. "At one point, I almost wrote to ask that you consider an annulment."

"Whatever are you talking about?" For a woman who had always considered duty to father and husband before anything else, what Eugenia was advocating was nothing short of heresy.

"Oh, the things I've heard, Clare!" Eugenia shook her head, so that her hair flew this way and that. "It is not at all good. Not at all good."

"What have you heard?" Clare asked calmly, expecting the usual prattle about Justin's scores of lovers, wild parties, feverish gambling and prodigious drinking.

"Well, for one thing, I was told that your husband attacked Mr. Farnsworth when I sent the poor man out with the sole purpose of securing your welfare," Eugenia said indignantly.

"Aunt, that is nothing but a Banbury tale," Clare said, growing angry herself. "The most ridiculous rumors are circulating about our elopement, but the truth is that Mr. Farnsworth found us, assessed the situation and departed without incident—certainly without violence of any kind."

"Well!" Eugenia said. Although her bosom was still heaving, she appeared to be somewhat mollified. "I was also reminded of an incident several years ago in which a young woman died at his home—the very hall where you are living—under very odd circumstances."

Eugenia lifted her chin, as if daring her niece to deny that story. Clare couldn't, but she swallowed to keep from gasping in surprise. Although she was interested in Elizabeth, she could not see why anyone else would be, nor why the story of a death that had happened seven years before was being resurrected now. Was it simply part of the general uproar over Justin's marriage, which stimulated people to drag out every sordid tidbit from his past, or was it something more sinister? Clare could not believe that her own discreet inquiries had reopened the incident for society's approbation.

"Who told you this?" Clare asked.

Eugenia paused, and she held her breath, only to release it when a look of bewilderment settled over her aunt's face. "Oh, dear, I can't recall, but it will come to me. And, of course, I remembered the incident, which caused quite a scandal at the time! And there was talk—" she paused to lower her voice "—that the girl was in the family way. Wild parties and loose morals," Eugenia said, shaking her head. "I certainly hope you won't stand for such nonsense."

Curiosity battled with outrage as Clare, determined to find out all she could about Elizabeth's death, also felt compelled to defend her husband. "Really, Aunt, that happened a long time ago, and Justin hasn't had a party there since. He hasn't even lived there in years." Then Clare paused as her own words sunk in, giving her an idea so daring that she caught her breath. A party hadn't been held there since Elizabeth's death.... "Perhaps it's time to open up the hall again," she said softly. "Aunt, do you remember anything else about the night, any other gossip?"

"Well, I..." Eugenia hesitated, looking even more confused by Clare's sudden eagerness "...I don't really know."

"Was there talk about the girl's guardian? Do you know what happened to him?" Clare knew she was risking a lot by trusting in Eugenia, despite her loose tongue, but if people were already talking about the incident, then what did it matter if she stoked the fires? "Do me a favor, Aunt, and find out everything you can about this bit of gossip."

"But—but, Clare!" Eugenia protested dazedly. "Whatever for?"

"I'm curious. And while you're at it, find out all you can about the evening and just who was there. I have been working on a guest list, but now I wonder..." Clare didn't finish her thought aloud, but smiled slowly. Yes, perhaps it's time for another party at the castle, she thought slyly.

HARRIS CLEARED HIS THROAT, and Justin looked up to see his butler proffering a letter as though it were a dead fish. Although it did not emit the same unpleasant smell, the missive was heavily scented. Justin immediately recognized the perfume—and the reason for Harris's disapproval.

"Thank you, Harris, that will be all," Justin said, glaring at his servant until he disappeared. He opened the letter, and as he expected, Elaine's barely legible scrawl darkened the white pages. Elaine Long, his last lover, was a tall, buxom beauty with fine bones and red-gold hair. A handsome stipend from her deceased husband made it unnecessary for her to marry again, but she had not forsworn the company of men by any means.

Yes, Elaine had diverted Justin for a spell, but though a gorgeous and lustful bed companion, she ultimately had lacked the intelligence necessary to hold his interest. She was not Clare, Justin thought with a grim smile.

They had parted without acrimony not long before Clare

made her appearance in London; in fact, Justin had been grateful that he had no relationships from which to extricate himself in order to wed. Now he found himself irritated with Elaine for writing. What did she want? She could hardly claim he had thrown her over for his wife, when the affair had already been ended, and those who played with him knew the rules. There were no second chances—except where Clare was concerned.

Justin lowered his eyes to the page and scanned the missive. What the devil? She wanted him to meet her in Bagnigge Wells. The old pleasure gardens were decidedly unfashionable, and he could hardly imagine someone with Elaine's taste electing to go there.

The sound of footsteps made Justin glance up, and Clare was standing before him, her very presence erasing the image of Elaine Long. Unfortunately, the lady's scent was not as easily banished. "What is that smell?" Clare asked, wrinkling her nose.

Justin laughed. "Elaine Long's perfume," he answered, tossing the letter across the table toward her.

Clare picked it up gingerly and read, her brow furrowing when she gazed up at him. "One of your old paramours?"

Justin nodded. "The last one," he said, stretching his legs out before him.

"What do you suppose she wants?" Clare asked.

Justin eyed her significantly. He was fairly certain what any former lover of his might want, but he declined to discuss it with his wife.

She looked at him askance. "My, you're awfully conceited, aren't you?" she asked. "Hasn't it occurred to you that the woman might really have something to talk to you about?"

"Such as?" Justin asked, with a sarcastic tone.

"Well, I don't know," Clare said, dropping the letter, "but it might be something important." The mysterious message put her in mind of Elizabeth's death, but she realized she was leaping to conclusions. All of London was not as obsessed with the seven-year-old incident as herself.

"Are you going?" she asked.

"Lord, no," Justin answered carelessly. His hair was falling in his face again, and he looked handsome enough to devour from head to toe. No wonder his old lovers couldn't get enough of him.

"I think you should," Clare said primly.

"By faith, why?"

"Because she really might have something to say, and it would be impolite of you to refuse."

Justin frowned at her logic, then he grinned wickedly. "Do you want to come along?"

"Of course not!" Clare said, starting at the invitation.

Justin reached for her and pulled her into his lap. "We could both go, and then she will be quite certain I'm serious about my marriage."

Clare smiled and smoothed his hair back into place. "But she wants to see you alone."

"That's what I'm afraid of," Justin said with a sigh.

"Well, she can't mean to leap upon you right in Bagnigge Wells, can she?" She was met with one of Justin's more engaging glances, which told her that nothing was outside of his experience. "I don't want to know!" she said, rolling her eyes. "What a *hard* life you've led, wanted by every woman in town." Clare shook her head with mock sympathy as she felt his long fingers thread through her hair. In spite of herself she leaned back and sighed.

"And when all I ever wanted was you," Justin whispered against her ear. She shivered and raised her hands to his shoulders as his touch moved lower, into her gown, pushing it down and freeing her breasts. She could smell the scent of perfume lingering on his fingers, feel the gentle brush of his lips against her cheek.

"Justin," Clare said, willing him to stop. Polite conven

tion told her that such actions did not belong in the drawing room, but she didn't have the strength to leave his embrace.

"Yes, love?" he asked, his mouth trailing over her breasts.

"Stop! Not here..." Clare protested, as one of his hands found its way up under her skirts to run along her thigh. She arched against him, gasping when his fingers met the sensitive point between her legs. "Upstairs—"

"No." Justin cut her off. "Right here."

Clare felt a wave of panic, and struggled to glance at the double doors leading to the gallery. They were both shut, but what if one of the servants walked in? The thought formed and dissolved as his finger slipped inside her, and she leaned back, her head falling over his outstretched arm.

She felt as helpless as a trapped bird, unable to take flight. "Justin, please..." In answer, he leaned over to kiss her, and Clare opened her mouth for the sweet thrust of his tongue, which matched the rhythmic movement of his fingers. She wriggled in his lap, grasping his hair and clenching the dark locks in her fists as pleasure surged through her. "Justin!" she cried as her body vibrated with sensation.

Clare opened her eyes to gaze dreamily at the carved and gilded ceiling. She was dimly aware of a shift in position, as Justin scooted her across his legs and unbuttoned his pantaloons. Then she was being hoisted over him, her gown pushed up to her waist as she nestled down onto his hot arousal. "Oh, Justin," she whispered, her heart still pounding in her chest.

"Oh, yes," Justin agreed. She heard his inrush of breath, felt his hands cup her curves as he settled her firmly upon his lap. "Right here, right now," he whispered. "With you, Clare, I can never wait."

CHAPTER SIXTEEN

ELAINE WAS LATE, and Justin stalked impatiently along the rustic bridge where he was supposed to meet her. Although Sunday was traditionally a busy day at the gardens, few people were in attendance. Justin remembered hearing a rumor that the establishment was destined for bankruptcy, and he could see why.

Elaine's choice of location was puzzling, unless she hoped to go unrecognized among the middle and lower classes that frequented Bagnigge Wells. Another reason for her selection sprang to mind when Justin's gaze was caught by one of the honeysuckle-covered arbors, well-known as trysting spots, nearby.

Groaning, he cursed his wife for talking him into coming alone to meet with a woman he had no real desire to see. Then the absurdity of the situation struck him, and he leaned his hands on the rail and laughed softly as the image of his beautiful, brilliant, sometimes foolish wife formed delightfully in his vision.

"Justin?"

Elaine's deep voice surprised him, and he turned to smile at her, his mood improved by thoughts of Clare. Dressed in a dark blue gown, cut low over her ample bosom, Elaine presented a pretty picture with her flushed cheeks and her heavy hair piled atop her head. Justin remembered the feel of it in his hands, thick and rich, but the memory of a darker head and shorter locks, glossy and smooth, filled his senses.

"Yes, Elaine?" he asked.

"I'm so glad you came," she said, her voice curiously high-pitched and fast, "but I knew you would."

For a moment, Justin thought his naive wife might be right, and Elaine might actually have an errand. Her violet eyes were curiously bright as she stepped closer to stand beside him. "Yes, I'm here," Justin said. "What is so important that you would arrange a rendezvous in the gardens for a man newly married?"

Elaine laughed, her warm tone betraying a trace of nervousness, which puzzled Justin. "Yes, well," she drawled, reaching out a finger to trace the bones of his hand, still gripping the edge of the bridge. "Your marriage. That is a bother, isn't it? Why did you do it?" she asked, glancing up at him with sincere inquiry.

"I love her, Elaine," he answered bluntly.

Her finger halted in its path, and she pulled back her hand. "Really?" she asked a bit scornfully. "I would never imagine you falling prey to such childish sentiment."

Justin ignored the gibe. "What do you want, Elaine?"

"Well, what do you think I want?" she asked, eyeing him seductively.

Justin remembered that look and felt an answering surge in his blood, which he quelled firmly. He leaned his arms on the railing to look out over the Fleet River. "I love my wife, Elaine."

"Well," she said with a sniff. "I guess that answers my question, doesn't it?"

Justin grinned, but did not even glance toward her. "I imagine it does," he said lightly.

Elaine stiffened as though insulted. "I expect that you will soon change your mind, when you become bored with her as you always do. And when you do, Justin, let me know. I might fit you into my schedule...if I haven't found someone else more interesting by then." She moved away from him, stepping back to survey him with disdain.

Justin turned to face her. "I appreciate the offer, but don't save anything for me, Elaine," he said. "You are too beautiful to waste your time waiting."

She smiled, a genuine smile that reminded him of lazy afternoons in her bed, and shrugged good-naturedly. "I hope your wife realizes what she has. Goodbye, Justin." Elaine held out her hand, and he bent to kiss it, nearly overpowered by her scent as he brushed his lips against her skin.

Taking in a deep breath to dispel the lingering fragrance of her perfume, Justin watched her walk away. Then he turned to stare out over the glittering water. It reminded him of Clare: clean and fresh and without the cloying aftertaste of artifice. And that made him realize just how mixed up Elaine's words had been. *He* was the one who should be well aware of the prize he had in *Clare*.

"My lord?"

Seated alone in his study, going over some accounts, Justin glanced up to see a stricken look on Harris's face. Justin's thoughts immediately flew to Clare, who seemed to take great pleasure in tormenting his butler. What was his wife up to now?

"Yes?" he answered wearily.

"My lord, there is a Mr. Dunn to see you." Harris cleared his throat, a painful expression on his features. "He claims to be a Bow Street runner."

"A Bow Street runner?" Justin asked in some surprise. The police force that had taken its name from its Bow Street office was well-known for solving crimes, but what a member of that elite group would want with him, he was at a loss to guess. "You may usher him in," Justin said.

Perhaps they are soliciting for funds, he thought, though he could not imagine the men making personal calls for such a purpose. More likely they were investigating one of the burglaries that occurred every so often in the neighborhood.

Justin did not have long to wonder. Mr. Dunn, although a burly man, moved swiftly and silently into the room. He was impeccably dressed, and Justin realized that he had seen the man before, guarding the Prince Regent on occasion.

"Thank you for receiving me, my lord," he said. "My name's Dunn, and I'm with the Bow Street office. I'm investigating the death of Mrs. Long," he explained bluntly.

Justin stared at him blankly. "The death?" he asked, stunned. "Are you telling me that Elaine Long is dead?" Even when the man nodded, Justin still found himself denying the news. He had talked to Elaine not more than a day before, and she had been alive, alive and well and glowing with seductive promises. "When did this happen?"

"That's what I'm trying to find out, my lord," Dunn said. "Someone came upon her body downriver. She washed up from the Fleet, you see."

"Elaine Long drowned in the Fleet River?" Justin asked. If it weren't for the fact that he recognized Dunn, he would have thought this all some sort of lurid joke perpetrated by Fletcher or one of his cronies.

"No, my lord," Dunn answered. "From the look of her neck, she was strangled and then tossed into the water."

"My God!" Justin said, starting forward in his seat. He was as familiar as the next man with the increase of violence in town, though it didn't usually happen in the better sections.

Even Justin had survived brushes with the criminal element. His pocket had been picked more than once when he was younger, and one evening a few years ago he had fought off a couple of footpads, an experience that suggested to him he might choose his routes home more judiciously.

The episode had shaken him, but it had involved men only, not an attack on an innocent woman! The thought of beautiful Elaine, her violet eyes closed forever by brute force, made Justin wince in horror. He felt an overwhelming urge to avenge her before getting himself under control.

Then he turned his gaze steadily upon the investigator. "How can I help you?" he asked evenly.

"It appears that you were the last person to see her, my lord," Dunn said, his dark eyes dull and hard.

"Me?" Justin said. "You mean at Bagnigge Wells?" he asked a bit incredulously.

"Yes, my lord." Dunn was watching him gravely. "Mrs. Long told her servants she was to meet you there, and that was the last anyone saw of her, except you, of course... assuming that you did meet her."

Something in Dunn's tone struck Justin as peculiar, and a quick glance at the man's face reaffirmed his suspicion that all was not as it should be. A man who has gambled long enough and well enough becomes attuned to the subtle nuances of expression and voice, and Justin had done more than his share of both. He felt the hairs on the back of his neck stand alert, warning him that he was in as much danger as if a man with a losing hand had a pistol tucked in his boot.

Just as though they were engaged in a game of cards, Justin returned Dunn's stare calmly. "Yes, I met her there, on one of the bridges," he admitted, his gaze never wavering. "We talked briefly, and she left. I remained there awhile longer and did not see her again."

Dunn nodded. "Pardon my saying so, my lord, but that's the problem. Since you were the last one spotted with her, and being on the bridge..." His words trailed off, his woolly brow rising just a bit, as if urging Justin to explain further.

Justin's first reaction was relief that he had not denied the rendezvous. Someone had noticed them together, or at least Dunn was insinuating that they had. So what did this mean?

He had only to look at Dunn's face, polite but skeptical, to know the answer. Still Justin asked anyway, to hear the words—to have the cards laid out on the table in full view. "Are you suggesting that I killed her?" he inquired, a mixture of disbelief and disgust in his voice.

"Well..." Dunn let the word linger in the air. "Seems to me, my lord, that you were involved in another incident when a young lady met her death. At your estate, I believe, although that one drowned, or so I gather from the report...." Dunn waited for a reaction, and he got one.

Justin rose from his chair, his eyes flashing with anger. Elizabeth's death, though he had always suspected it a suicide, had been ruled an accident by the local authorities. How the devil could anyone compare the two, let alone link them together? If Justin read the man aright, Dunn was intimating that Elizabeth might well have been strangled, too, and tossed into the water afterward, just like Elaine.

"You cannot be serious, Dunn."

Dunn shrugged. "I have to investigate all possibilities, my lord, though I am aware of your *position* in the world." Although presumably referring to his title, Justin thought Dunn could have easily replaced "position" with "black reputation."

"Are you arresting me, Mr. Dunn?"

"No, my lord."

"Then I suggest you leave," Justin said, keeping a tight rein on his rage. He could feel the muscle in his jaw throb, and he knew in a moment all his fury and horror would unleash itself, with Dunn as the target.

"Very well, my lord," Dunn said. "If you think of anything that might help us find her killer, you will let me know, won't you? It's a shame, it is, for such a beautiful lady to end up as naught but fish food."

Justin simply stared at the man, too livid to trust himself to speak.

"Good day, my lord," Dunn said. "I'll see myself out."

JUSTIN FOUND CLARE out in the garden, cutting flowers for the house. He stood for a long moment, simply watching her. She was kneeling, her gown yellow as the irises that surrounded her. Her breasts rose, round and flawless, from the curve of her neckline as she bent over to snip a bud, her smooth hands hidden in a pair of faded old leather gloves.

The day was hot and the garden a mixture of scents. Lavender, dianthus and the heady perfume of roses drifted toward him, along with the dull droning of bees. An idle breeze wafted bits of glossy, dark hair from Clare's face as the early afternoon sun kissed her features. Justin knew them all, intimately—the high cheekbones, pink with exertion or heat, the long, dark lashes draped over her eyes as she looked down and the tender mouth, berry red and sweet as the finest claret.

A drink—that had been Justin's first thought after his interview with Dunn. But he was more intoxicated with the sight before him. Clare. He wanted her, needed her, more than he ever had any liquor. "A servant could do that, Clare," he said gently.

She turned her head to look at him, a surprised smile on her face, that bright, priceless source of his happiness. He felt an overpowering urge to press her to him, to hold her so close that nothing, neither Dunn's subtle threats nor death itself, would have the power to separate them.

"I know, but I love to do it myself. Is it a total breach of etiquette for a marchioness to cut her own flowers?"

"No, Clare. You may do whatever you please," Justin answered, stepping toward her. "As marchioness, you are mistress of your own domain and may dig and *frolic* in the garden as you wish."

Clare looked up, suspicious at the language Justin used, and found him squatting down beside her. He reached a hand up to smooth a lock of hair from her face, his grin so poignant that her heart stood still. "What is it?" she asked softly.

"I love you, Clare," Justin whispered huskily. His eyes, dark and deep, were more serious than she had ever seen them. She felt, oddly enough, that something was wrong, but her fears were banished by the touch of one long finger tracing the outline of her lips. Clare sent her tongue darting out to taste him, forgetting, in the delirious spell of the moment exactly where they were. Justin spread his hand across her cheek, and she turned to take his palm and press it to her lips.

"Clare," he whispered. "My love, my own…" His words trailed off in a groan as he pulled her toward him and suddenly she was sprawled on top of him as they lay in between the bright beds of bobbing flowers, and he was kissing her so intensely that she thought she might swoon.

Justin rolled her on her back, and Clare felt his hands travel behind her neck and down below, clutching her to him with a fierce possessiveness. His mouth moved over hers in wild communion, his tongue touching the center of her being, and it didn't stop, this luscious assault, as if Justin could not get enough of her.

Finally, his lips moved to her cheeks, her eyelids, her hairline, and Clare gasped for breath. "Justin! We really shouldn't be rolling about in the garden," she protested faintly, even as he sapped her strength by nibbling on her earlobe.

"Why not?" Justin whispered wickedly.

"Because… Oh!" She gasped as his mouth moved along the curve of her breast. "Because someone might see us," Clare answered before arching toward him.

"Nonsense," he assured her as he sat up to strip off his jacket. "The hedges will hide us from prying eyes, and my servants are most discreet."

When he tossed his waistcoat aside, too, and followed it with his boots, Clare felt a dim panic. "But Justin," she said, unconvinced.

"But Clare," he mocked, a devilish smile on his face. He picked up her hands and slipped off her gloves, then placed her fingers under his shirt. "Touch me," he whispered.

She needed no further encouragement, but spread her

palms over the smooth lines of his chest, sighing in pleasure at the feel of his skin. Forgetting her reservations, she traced his muscles, and Justin leaned over her, taking her mouth again.

"Clare, you taste so good, so sweet," he whispered. He clutched her to him so tightly that she couldn't inhale, and Clare again had the vague sense that something was wrong. But then his fingers slid under her skirts and found her center, caressing with infinite skill, and she thought no more.

"Justin!" she cried, sensing that his growing impatience matched her own. She struggled with the buttons on his breeches, freeing him from their confinement. Justin groaned at her touch, but Clare did not stop, stroking him until he gasped and she was panting herself.

"Clare, Clare," he said urgently. He breathed her name, over and over, as he lifted her gown, his hardness sliding against the wetness between her legs. "Oh, my Clare," he murmured. Cupping her to him, Justin entered with one swift stroke, and she wrapped her legs around him in response.

As he thrust into her feverishly, Clare dug her nails into his skin, gasping at the surprisingly swift whirl of sensation that heralded waves of pleasure. "Oh!" she said softly, her head falling back onto the ground. The scent of grass and garden and Justin intermingled in a dizzying coil, then she saw his face before her, his dark gaze drawing her back to him.

"You're mine, Clare, now and forever. You've always been mine—from the minute you walked into Worth Hall—and you shall always be mine," he murmured.

She watched him wide-eyed, for she had never seen him like this. Justin usually made love with a careless ease, sometimes with a passionate abandonment, but never with such ferocious intensity. Before she could respond, he pounded into her, seeking his own release, and she felt sensation take over again, spiraling into such sharp, throbbing liberation that she called out, tears wetting her eyelashes.

Justin couldn't let her go. They remained entwined among the flower beds, their clothes in disarray as he held her tight, her cheek pressed against his shirt. He thought his gut-wrenching release would never end, and yet, he found himself wanting her again, wanting to bury himself in Clare as if to banish the power of death, for in making new life, man had his only revenge on his immortal enemy.

"What is it, Justin?" she asked, interrupting his thoughts. She lifted her head, and he saw her hazel eyes were awash with concern. What was it about Clare that allowed her to look inside him?

Despite her perception, Justin longed to hide today's grim news awhile longer, and he brushed away her worry with a smile. "What is it? Only look what you've done to me, my pixie," he said, drawing her hand down to touch his rigid arousal. "You must truly be the enchantress that I first suspected you of being."

"I may not be a sorceress, but I have a remedy for what ails you," Clare whispered.

Justin groaned as she pushed aside his shirt to press kisses along his ribs, then down into the open fall of his breeches. "No," he said, lifting a hand to rest upon her hair. "I've a mind to take you up to bed and spend the afternoon more comfortably engaged."

"What? Is the ground too hard for you? Afraid of a few grass stains?" Clare teased.

When her lips touched him, he breathed deeply in sharp, clear pleasure. Lying on his back among the flowers, gazing up at a cloudless, blue sky, Justin let the afternoon's interview with Dunn finally recede from his mind. He felt the warmth of the sun upon his chest, where his shirt was pushed aside, and the heat of his wife's mouth, where his breeches were open, and surrendered himself to pure sensation.

EVENTUALLY, he couldn't delay any longer. As much as Justin would prefer keeping Dunn's accusations to himself, he knew he had to tell Clare before she heard the vile charge from another source. And even he could not summon the energy for one more sweet union with his wife this afternoon. She was wrapped around him, her head resting on his chest, and he pressed a kiss to her hair, trying to find the words to begin.

She inched back to look at him, her breasts pressing into his chest. "What is it?" she asked again. Her eyes searched his for a clue, making him realize that he could hide precious little from her.

Clare knew something was wrong, that something was bothering him. Don't deny it, Justin, Clare silently urged. *Tell me.* She held her breath, suddenly certain that this sharing between them was as vital to their marriage as lovemaking.

"I had a visit from a Mr. Dunn of Bow Street," Justin said softly, his eyes dark and hooded. "Elaine is dead. Someone killed her, and Mr. Dunn insinuated, none too pleasantly, that I might be a suspect."

"You!" Clare started, gasping in shock. "Why?"

Justin smiled grimly. "Apparently, Mr. Dunn shares your interest in Elizabeth's death."

"Oh, my God," Clare said dully as Justin's words became clear. "He thinks you killed them both?" At Justin's nod, she sighed and looked out over the lavender bed sending out its sweet scent at her feet. So cheerful and pleasant only a moment before, the garden now seemed a forbidding place. She felt Justin's fingers, strong and warm, cover her own, and she returned the caress. "But Justin, how in the devil could the man accuse you?"

"He stopped short of accusing me," Justin said, "although he made it abundantly clear that my title would not protect me from further investigation."

"Dear heaven." Clare felt dizzy as a frighteningly detailed vision formed in her head of Justin being hauled off to prison—or worse....

"Now, don't let your imagination run wild," Justin said, as though he could see right into her skull. "More than likely, nothing will come of it. I didn't want to tell you, for I know your creative brain can conjure up all sorts of horrible denouements, but I didn't want you to hear talk from someone else." He paused, rubbing a thumb across her hand gently. "Hopefully, Mr. Dunn will be discreet in his inquiries, but we must be prepared that he might not, and should the ton get wind of it..."

Clare looked at him. "We will be social outcasts."

Justin paused, as if in consideration. "Perhaps, perhaps not. I've been in their black books before, so it means naught to me, but you, Clare—I don't wish for you to suffer."

"As if I could care what those ninnies say," Clare answered, scoffing at the notion. She was reminded sharply, however, that she did not like the stories that were already circulating about Justin. Frustration welled up in her as she longed to defend him against the outrageous allegations. And if they were truly ostracized? London with its crowded, smelly streets and fancy, superficial balls had never held much allure for her, but Justin might think differently.

"We can always retire to the castle," she suggested hopefully. Justin groaned in disgust, his mouth curving up at the corners in a teasing grin, and Clare smiled for the first time since he'd told her the news. She felt a stray breeze stir her hair, and tipped her head back, hoping that the sun's heat might drive away the chill that had settled over her.

It didn't. Clare's thoughts kept returning to Justin's bleak, tight-lipped announcement, and her initial shock gave way to sorrow. Although she had never felt charitable toward any of Justin's former loves, she was filled with sadness for the woman she had never known and would never know. "Poor Elaine," she whispered.

"It's unfair, isn't it?" Justin asked huskily.

Clare looked up at dark eyes stark with pain and dismay, and suddenly she knew why he had been so serious, treating her as if she might break, or disappear.... Perhaps the horrible uncertainty of death, normally kept at bay, had been let loose to taunt him. Clare put a hand to his forehead, smoothing back his errant hair in an effort to comfort him. Grieving for a woman he once had held dear, haunted by the specter of death, or imprisonment... The thought made Clare gulp.

"And what happens if they arrest you?" she asked, even though she shied from the answer.

"They won't arrest me," Justin said lightly. Although he squeezed her fingers and smiled carelessly, Clare felt a bitter dread. If his title would not protect him, then what? She caught her breath as the truth finally hit, and remorse overwhelmed her. She stared at Justin intently. "It was the meeting, wasn't it?" she asked. "It's all because I made you meet her?"

"Yes," Justin said, returning her gaze calmly. "But nothing will come of it. Don't worry, Clare. They are chasing phantoms, that is all." His dark eyes bored into hers, willing her to accept his reassurance. "Let's forget it."

Clare wanted to, and yet...she disliked this raw, new feeling of guilt that clung to her. For the first time, she had an inkling of what Justin lived with, and she didn't care for it at all. How easy it was to make a misjudgment, a wrong step, and then regret it.

CLARE WALKED OUT into the garden, trying to regain the peace of the day before, but it eluded her.

Justin had told her not to be concerned, but she couldn't help envisioning the worst—Justin holed up in a tiny cell in conditions she could scarcely conceive of, or Justin dangling from the scaffold. As her husband had suspected, her vivid imagination was a mixed blessing. Clare could weave wonderful stories that enthralled her listeners, but she also pictured things much more vividly than others might.

Focusing on the flowers, she admired the scene before her. The grounds of the town house were laid out beautifully, but the neat and tidy beds made her miss the wild disarray of Worth. She wondered how the gardener was progressing there, wanted to oversee the replanting and reorganization, and suddenly her heart ached with longing for the castle.

It was all her fault. She had been naive, just as Fletcher said, in trying to lift a curse. Wiping impatiently at the tear that slid down her cheek, she berated herself for believing in such nonsense. The fantasies of a fourteen-year-old! And now... She wished fervently that they had stayed in Yorkshire. If they had, then none of this would have happened.

Craving the calm presence of her husband, Clare headed back to the house, where Harris informed her that Fletcher had arrived and had been ushered into Justin's study. As she walked down the gallery, she didn't intend to eavesdrop, but something made her stop right outside the door, which was slightly ajar. Perhaps it was the seriousness of the voices that drifted out, when the two men usually bantered lightly, but for some reason, Clare halted and listened.

"If it comes to that, you'd be tried at the Old Bailey," Fletcher said.

"And wouldn't they love to see a nobleman hang!" Justin replied, his voice bitter.

"If you live that long," Fletcher said mildly. "Considering the cases of jail distemper at Newgate, the pleasant guards, the bleak cells of the condemned..."

"Please don't go on," Justin said in an annoyed tone. "You are cold comfort, Fletcher!"

"Because I don't want you to end up dangling from a rope! Do something, Justin! Don't just sit here waiting to be torn from your wife and from the only happiness you've known! Use your influence to nip the investigation in the bud right now, and if that doesn't wash, then go to the West Indies, to America—anywhere where you can begin again.''

"Run?" Justin said in a shocked voice. "Blast it, Fletcher, I may be a lot of things, but I'm not a coward."

"Then take your noble values with you to the gallows!"

Clare could listen no more, and turned away, putting a fist to her mouth to hold back her cry. She leaned against the wall and breathed deeply, trying to gain control of herself. She had never been the type to weep and wail, but this situation threw her off balance. She straightened resolutely, knowing that she had to do something—anything—besides stand here fearing what the future might hold.

She forced her limbs to move, to take her somewhere where she did not have to hear such dire predictions of Justin's fate. She was halfway down the gallery when Fletcher hailed her. Freezing in her place, she swallowed hard, then she pinched her pale cheeks and turned toward him, holding out her hands to his. His touch was warm and reassuring. "Oh, Fletcher, you will talk some sense into him, won't you?" she asked.

He smiled. "Clare, there is absolutely nothing to worry about," he said in that maddeningly calm manner of his.

Cringing at the condescension in his voice, Clare felt like admitting that she had just overheard their conversation and that it had been anything but comforting. She withdrew her hands from his.

"Don't frown at me, Clare," he said. "And when I have been doing your bidding, too," he complained with a teasing grin. Clare could not be coaxed from her mood, however, and only gazed at him solemnly. "I guess you don't care to hear what I discovered?"

Her enthusiasm for the seven-year-old mystery having declined sharply, Clare almost told him to forget whatever he might have found, but then, suddenly, she realized what she could do to help Justin out of the predicament she had forced him into. She needn't wait in tearful panic for the worst to happen, because she had an idea that, if successful, might exonerate her husband. If she could catch Elizabeth's killer, then perhaps the Bow Street runners would drop their interest in Justin. Certainly, they could no longer link the two deaths together. Her eyes flicked to Fletcher. "Well?"

He smiled. "I found out the name of the girl's guardian. It was Clevindale, Matthew Clevindale."

"Where is he? Did you find him?" Clare asked, her eagerness returning with this bit of information. If she could only talk to Elizabeth's guardian, the man might tell her who, besides Justin, Elizabeth had been seeing.

Fletcher nodded, but his smile faded. "Yes, I found him," he said, "in the cemetery."

"He's dead?" Clare asked, her voice rising with frustration.

"Quite so," Fletcher confirmed. "And he has been for some time. It seems that not long after Elizabeth's death, our man fell prey to footpads, who robbed and killed him."

"Blast," Clare said softly, her momentary excitement banished by frustration. Every new avenue only led to a blind alley. She glanced up at Fletcher. "Now what?"

"Now," he said, taking her arm to walk back down the gallery, "I want you to drop your pursuit of this matter. Since Bow Street is involved, they will investigate the girl's death themselves, if they truly believe it looks suspicious. My guess is that they don't, but were just trying to bluff Justin into admitting something. They are used to dealing with another class of people, mind you, who squeak loudly when pressure is applied." He looked down at her, his face serious. "Leave it to the professionals, Clare."

"But it's not a question of suspicion, Fletcher!" Clare protested. "I *know* Elizabeth was murdered. I talked to someone who saw the whole thing."

"What's this?" Fletcher asked, halting his steps. His green eyes were bright with interest.

"It's true," Clare answered with a measure of vindication

in her tone. Suddenly she felt weary, weary of no one believing her and of every clue turning to naught. She slumped down into one of the white satin chairs lining the gallery. "I talked to a former servant who was up on the roofs that night. She saw a man, a man with fair hair, throw Elizabeth off the parapet. His name was Richard."

"Did you tell Justin this?" Fletcher asked.

Clare nodded dully. "He didn't want a thing to do with it. He just wanted to leave Elizabeth's death alone, but now... Oh, Fletcher, now it could really be vital to discover the killer."

"Hmm, this puts a new light on things," Fletcher mused. He sat down beside her. For a moment they were both quiet, lost in their own thoughts, then he spoke briskly. "I'll do what I can, Clare, to find out who was there, but you must promise me that you won't do anything yourself." He stopped her protestations by holding up a finger. "Now that I know there is a murderer to be found, I definitely don't want you getting in his way. I have access to sources you would never even imagine," he added with a wry look. "Let me take care of it, and then maybe I can convince Justin."

His last words swayed her. If only Justin could be made to see... Clare nodded her head.

"Good," Fletcher said. He stood up and took her hand, raising her to her feet before pressing his lips against the knuckles. It was a formal salute, nothing more, but something in Fletcher's green eyes gave her pause. Confused, Clare stepped back, then, gathering her composure, she watched him walk down the gallery. Recent events had unnerved her, she decided. Still, she suddenly found herself wishing that she didn't need Fletcher Mayefield's help.

CHAPTER SEVENTEEN

JUSTIN WAS STILL SEATED at his desk, mulling over his conversation with Fletcher, when he heard his wife's gentle voice at the door. "Come," he called, and she stepped in, looking as beautiful as ever, tall and lovely, her cheeks flushed. The longing for a drink that had been pressing down upon him vanished abruptly at the sight of her.

"Clare," he whispered. Then it came, that hot surge of desire for her, catching him by surprise with its ferocity and scattering his thoughts. Justin opened his mouth to speak, surprising himself even more with what came out. "Let's go home," he said.

Once uttered, the words did not seem as foreign as they once might have, for right now London, with its sparkling sheen that covered dark layers beneath, disgusted him—and perhaps it always had. No wonder he had found his ease in Yorkshire with a fourteen-year-old. Wake up, man, that is where you want to be, that is where your heart lies—at Worth with Clare, he thought.

Maybe it was the cold reality of Elaine's demise or the specter of his own death or imprisonment, but suddenly life, which he had used up so carelessly, seemed very, very precious. Justin wanted to clutch it close to him, making every single minute with Clare last forever. The idea of siring children, something that he had always looked upon with a jaundiced eye, now took on an appealing aspect as he pictured them gathered around their mother, as eager as he to hear her stories.

With a jolt, Justin recognized that life as he had lived it was, for all intents and purposes, over, and he felt not a wit of regret. Let his friends snigger behind his back; he didn't care. He was going to savor each moment that remained of his existence, and he was going to do it with Clare—at the hall. The thought of lazy summer days in the country, fishing or plunging into the cool river for more than swimming, tightened his groin with delightful anticipation.

Clare stood watching her husband in puzzlement. Knowing Justin's feelings about the castle, his suggestion was a bit unusual. She wondered what the move would mean to her investigation—before she remembered that it was in Fletcher's hands now. She should let him do his job, presumably far better than she could.

With that weight lifted from her shoulders, Clare felt free to agree, wholeheartedly, to return home. She closed her eyes in anticipation, her longing for the castle engulfing her, then she lifted her lids to nod happily. "At least we won't have to hear the talk then, if it starts," she said.

Justin snorted. "Let them talk. I've a desire to go fishing," he said, that wild light coming into his eyes. Clare backed away with a wary smile. She knew that look, and knew that when it appeared, location was of no consideration to her husband. She shut the study doors firmly and locked them.

"Now?" she said softly. "What's this about fishing?"

He moved swiftly, with the same urgency as yesterday, as if the only ease he could find was in her body. Clare was eager to comply, although she paused to speculate upon just how many odd places for passion she might discover during her married life.

Her thoughts were lost in the searing pleasure of Justin's touch, in the hot length of him, and the rhythms that joined them together. Then, when both of them were relaxing in the sweet aftermath, Clare curled up against him, weary from a night of worry, and nodded off, without a thought that she was lying naked on the study floor.

Justin heard her breathing change, telling him she was asleep, and he sighed. All too soon, his mind turned back to Elaine's death, and the threat to his happiness that it entailed. Although he did not blame Clare for her ill-fated urging to meet with his former lover, he wondered if her bizarre interest in Elizabeth's demise had not stirred up a hornet's nest that had been better left undisturbed.

Elizabeth. Justin sucked in his breath and closed his eyes against his natural inclination to avoid all thought of her. If he really meant to start anew with Clare, the time had come to exorcise his own private demons, for the sake of their future and, perhaps, to save his own neck. He had delayed the reckoning long enough.

Satiated, his reason for living lying warm across his chest like a shield, Justin struggled with memory, trying to recall all that he could from that wild night seven years ago.

How long had he known her? A month? Young and bursting with his own virility, he had taken her without thought to the consequences. He had just ended a very discreet affair with the wife of one of England's most-famous politicians. He had been eager to thrill more than unsatisfied married women and peasant maids, though, and with the benefits of the society matron's tutelage… He was cocky and careless and uncaring, and he cringed at the memory of taking Elizabeth Landrey in the parlor of her own town house.

Had she bled, as Clare had asked? Justin tried to remember, but he'd been so very drunk that night. Clevindale had pressed the invitation on him, providing him and a few cronies with some excellent Bordeaux and some deep play in the town house he shared with Elizabeth and an elderly woman, a hired chaperon, Justin believed. He tried to remember, but the evening, like so many from that time, had been clouded with liquor. Before he had learned to modulate it and control it, it had controlled him.

He had known her a month, caught her admiring glances and talked with her briefly when they were thrown together by Clevindale. Clevindale... Justin shook his head at the sudden appearance of the man on the London scene. The old man had been smart enough to see that he had a gem in his beauteous young ward, but he was too stupid to present her to society, and so the poor girl had ended up rubbing elbows with all the wrong sort, such as himself, Justin noted ruefully.

And that night there had eventually been no one left but Clevindale and himself, so drunk they could barely see the cards in the candlelight, but having a whooping good time. Justin had gone in search of the water closet, and after relieving himself, had sought to relieve his other needs.

He frowned grimly, clutching Clare more tightly. No, it had not been like that. He had heard a noise from the parlor, had peeked in, and there she was in her nightdress, a thin robe barely hiding her curves, her long blond hair shimmering in the light of the fire burning in the grate.

Clevindale had a bizarre turn for weapons, claiming to have hunted in Africa and such, and in front of the fire was a huge bearskin. Justin had always thought it would be an interesting place to make love, and there she was, standing upon it, which naturally turned his thoughts in that direction. When he walked in, she didn't shrink away, but welcomed him....

"Oh, Justin," Elizabeth had said breathlessly. "I'm so glad it's you. I heard the carousing and came down to investigate. Sometimes my guardian needs a bit of help to bed, and the servants being asleep..." She left off the words nervously, and he stepped toward her.

The devil only knew what he'd said, probably, "You're beautiful," or perhaps, "You shouldn't be here in your nightclothes." Yet she had showed no alarm, only a sweet breathlessness.

"Oh, Justin, I could never be afraid of you," she whispered. She'd stepped forward, or had he? He could swear it was she who had moved, and then he had her in his arms and was kissing her. She did not demur, but opened her mouth to him, young and tender. Her hair gleamed, long and loose, in the firelight, and he was down on his knees on the bearskin rug, his hands seeking the softness underneath her nightgown.

Elizabeth never denied him, never whispered a word, but Justin knew he had an unfair advantage: the trust of a young girl who didn't know what she was doing, and the skills to make her melt. And melt she did. Only when he entered her did she balk, wriggling and crying, as though he had hurt her. He made it good for her, or thought he did, but afterwards she cried in hurt or shame, and he was appalled at his own behavior.

He tried to comfort her, and then she clung to him. Afraid that he might pass out or fall asleep, only to be found with his breeches down in the morning, Justin struggled to his feet. She kissed him then and ran up the stairs, back to her room. Feeling dazed and guilty, Justin wandered back to the drawing room, where her guardian was slumped over the cards, fast asleep.

He did not see her again until the house party at Worth. He was shocked to find that Clevindale brought her, but neither she nor her guardian acted as though anything was amiss, until late that night when she came to his room, slipped into his bed and opened herself to him. Only afterward did she divulge the reason for her visit. She was pregnant and loved him, and expected him to marry her.

Angry at her tactics, Justin told her he would never marry her, that she was beneath him and that he had no affection for her. She wept and pleaded, whining of her shame, blaming him for taking her virginity. Finally, he offered to set her up in a household. He could spare the funds, and he liked her body, though she was far too shallow to be anything other than a receptacle for his passions. Feeling nothing for the mother, he could muster up no emotion for the child, but said he would pay her well to keep the bastard.

The next day she spent closeted in her room, while Justin drank, putting off the inevitable meeting with Clevindale. Then, sometime during another long night of revelry, she'd gone up to the roofs and thrown herself off because of his treachery.

Justin felt the unfamiliar trail of tears on his cheeks, and put up a hand in surprise. He had never cried for Elizabeth, never wept for his own guilt, but now his cheeks were wet with the hot, shameful memory. He didn't bother to wipe them, but pulled Clare close, burying his face in the warm darkness of her hair.

"Do you think Fletcher will be at the party this evening?" Clare asked as carelessly as possible. She breathed in deeply, then poured herself a glass of water from the pitcher that stood on a side table near her bed. Tonight Lady Berkeley was holding a ball in their honor, their final engagement before leaving for the castle, and Clare did not feel up to it.

Although they'd heard nothing more from Mr. Dunn, Clare's sense of foreboding weighed so heavily upon her that it made her ill. She was weary and listless most of the time, and nausea dogged her constantly. Swallowing a sip of water, she frowned sourly. Warm. Before they left for the ball, she would have someone fetch her some ice water. It was the only thing that made her feel remotely better.

"Fletcher? I doubt it," Justin said. He stood in front of a mirror, involved in the intricacies of tying his neck cloth. Normally, she would tweak him about his vanity, but tonight she was too tired.

Anxious to find out how Fletcher was progressing with his investigation, Clare had forced herself to go to several social functions where she hoped to see him, but he was never there. Finally, in desperation, she had sent a note round to his house, only to have her servant return with the news that Mr. Mayefield was out of town.

Had Fletcher just been humoring her, with no intention of following up on her suspicions, or had he simply been sidetracked by some pretty face or bit of fine horseflesh? Either way, he hardly seemed to be honoring his promise to pursue Elizabeth's killer, Clare thought, and his apparent disregard for his task made her even more out of sorts than she had been lately.

"Why not? Shall we not see him before we leave?" she asked her husband, unable to hide the edge in her voice. She caught the dark glance sent her way and swallowed. Had she said too much?

"I thought you were not attracted to him." Although Justin's tone was teasing, Clare felt the blood rush to her face.

"I'm not," she reaffirmed.

"He's attracted to you," Justin commented, resuming his toilette.

"He is not!" she said, a bit startled. Justin finished his creation with a flourish, turning to show off the fine knots with a wave of his hand. Clare looked at the white silk dispassionately. "Very nice," she said flatly. "Your friend Fletcher is *not* attracted to me."

"Of course he is," Justin said, stepping close. He brushed his knuckles against her cheek, and Clare sighed softly, her momentary annoyance at his words slipping away under his touch. "You are not only beautiful and intelligent, but you are highly unavailable—just Fletcher's cup of tea." He turned to his manservant, who stood waiting with his coat.

"What do you mean?" Clare asked, her irritation returning.

"I mean that Fletcher never lets himself get too close to anyone, especially females seeking matrimony," Justin explained lightly. "So his few women friends are those who are no threat to him, like yourself."

"The devil you say!" Clare exclaimed, still unbelieving.

Setting her glass back down upon the table, she scowled in disgust. "If so, he's even more conceited than you are," she added.

Justin laughed. "Maybe, but count yourself lucky, Clare," he said. "Fletcher may be a bit erratic, and he has led me into some wild escapades, but he is a solid friend." He slipped into the dark blue evening coat, which fell over his shoulders very nicely, but she was too disgruntled to give his figure more than a cursory nod of appreciation. "As long as that's all he remains," Justin added with a wry look.

Clare ignored the warning, implicit even in his light banter. Solid friend, indeed, she thought miserably. If Fletcher was so reliable, where the devil was he?

He was not at Lady Berkeley's ball, and no one seemed to have any idea of his whereabouts.

"Oh, but you cannot expect to see Mr. Mayefield at every squeeze such as this," Prudence informed her seriously. "I believe he holds crowded parties in abhorrence."

"Oh," Clare said, with a sigh of dismay.

"Although, since we have seen so much of him lately, I had hoped..." Prudence let her words trail off. "That is, I had wished that he would make an appearance."

Clare scowled. Wishing being a little too vague for her, she had sent Fletcher a letter asking, in no uncertain terms, for a report of his progress, and she had requested that the missive be forwarded to wherever he might be. Her ill health made her glad she had turned over the investigation to him, but she hoped that she would not have cause to regret it.

"Clare, my dear child." Her thoughts were interrupted by Lady Berkeley, who took her hands in her own. Clare had greeted her hostess earlier with sincere, but reserved appreciation. Although Aurora had been kind enough to plan the entertainment in their honor, she had also run to Justin with the tale of his wife's doings, and Clare did not feel wholly comfortable with her.

"I've been searching all over for you! There's someone I would like you to meet," Aurora said with a warm smile, as if nothing had occurred to put a breach between them. Turning, Aurora slipped her arm around Clare's waist and nodded to a man standing beside her. "Lord Wilmington, I would like you to meet Lady Worthington. Clare, this is Lord Wilmington, who has made quite a name for himself in the House of Lords. I'm sure you've heard of him."

Clare nearly gaped at the figure before her. *Richard,* she thought dully as her gaze moved over him. He was of medium build and height, and his sandy hair was shot with a bit of lighter blond, or gray, perhaps. But it was his eyes that drew her. They were a bright blue and sparkled with friendliness. Clare stood stock-still in a rather horrified trance, for they were not what she expected. They were not the eyes of a murderer, and yet she knew they must be.

"It is a pleasure to meet you, Lady Worthington," he said, bending over her hand. She nearly snatched it from his gentle fingers, but restrained herself. His lips brushed her knuckles with a simple salute, then he released her and smiled, revealing even, white teeth. "Aurora," he said, with a self-deprecatory grin, "not everyone follows politics as you do. Perhaps Lady Worthington has other interests."

Yes, I'm interested in murder, Clare thought grimly. Do you indulge? It was but the first of a number of giddy responses that flew to mind before she finally reined in her panic and remembered her manners. "It is a pleasure to meet you," she said.

"The pleasure is mine," Wilmington answered smoothly. "I have been prodding Aurora all night for an introduction. You see, I knew your husband in my younger days, and having heard that he'd settled down, I must admit I was curious as to the reason. Now I can easily see what has changed him."

Clare nodded at the compliment, trying to force her lips to curve into a smile, but she felt as though she were having a conversation with a snake. She couldn't have been more appalled if the gilded reptile that decorated one of Lady Berkeley's ornate Oriental tables rose up to speak to her, couching its inherent coldness in genial warmth.

Lord Wilmington spoke with the ease of someone accustomed to giving speeches, yet Clare sensed a genuine concern for people and a gentle humor in his words. How could her impressions be so at odds with reality? Thinking that continued discourse with him would give her an answer, Clare kept him talking long after Aurora had abandoned them.

She listened to his views on trade, the bills he planned to present and the general state of the economy without falling into a stupor at what she would normally consider deadly dull topics. It was all to study him, to find some clue to his true nature, some hint in his words or expression of a darker side, yet she could find none.

Still, Clare refused to be fooled. As much as she wanted to accept Lord Wilmington as the congenial, thoughtful man that he seemed, she believed Addie McBride's story. And the man before her, despite his appearances, fit Addie's description as no other did.

How could she break through the pretense that surrounded him? They had gone on to chat about improvements to the hall, and Clare saw her opening gambit. Her nerves were stretched until she could stand no more. The lemonade in her hand tasted sour and rancid in her mouth, and her stomach hinted that it might toss up her dinner. Clare knew it was now or never, so she gazed at him directly and asked him.

"If you knew Justin when he was younger, you must be familiar with the accident that took place there, when Elizabeth Landrey...died," she said.

Lord Wilmington did not blink or flinch, but his features showed a trace of sadness. "Yes," he answered softly. "I remember it well. It was a difficult time for your husband.

We were all a bit young and careless then. We were carousing too much, perhaps, but one can hardly blame Justin for the incident. And it disturbs me, Lady Worthington, to see it all dredged up again."

Clare glanced at him piercingly, for his tone of voice finally suggested something. Was he warning her to cease her efforts to expose him? "Perhaps a renewed assessment of the episode would be of benefit to all concerned," Clare said coolly.

Lord Wilmington appeared to be rather taken aback by her words. "I hardly see how," he said. "It can only be painful, and perhaps...dangerous."

Clare felt herself go cold, cold and hard as flint. If he thought to threaten her, then he must be growing nervous, she thought, with a sense of triumph. "Oh?" she asked calmly. "Dangerous to whom?"

Lord Wilmington's brow furrowed as if in indecision, then he leaned toward her. Nothing but Clare's iron resolve kept her from leaping away as she watched his face, expecting the blue depths to turn black with hate and blood lust. They did not. Lord Wilmington's eyes were bright with concern.

"I'll be blunt, Lady Worthington," he said. "In my position, one is privy to a lot of information, and I have heard that Bow Street has taken an interest in the case, which, I can assure you, does not bode well for your husband."

Lord Wilmington took her hand, while Clare stared at him, her lips parting in surprise. His words were not at all what she had expected, just as the man, himself, was an anomaly. "For your sake, and his, I will do my best to see that all is resolved quickly, for upon meeting you, his lady, I am most charmed. Justin is a lucky fellow."

The man she suspected of murder then bowed low, excusing himself with a nod, and Clare was left to puzzle after him until she saw the tall figure of her husband approaching.

Justin did not appear to share Lord Wilmington's sentiments. At this moment he did not look as though he felt at all lucky to be married to her. Drawing her close, he whispered none too tenderly in her ear. "What the devil were you doing with Wilmington?" His face held a cordial smile, presumably for the public, but his eyes, focused upon her, were ominously dark.

Clare lifted her chin. "Discussing the latest import taxes," she said airily.

Justin was not amused.

She put a hand on his arm and closer. "He knows about Dunn," she said.

Justin sighed low and long. "And just how did that work itself into the conversation?" he asked. The muscle in his jaw throbbed, letting her know far better than his speech just how angry he was.

"I happened to mention Elizabeth's death, but I did not accuse him of anything," Clare added quickly.

The eyes that met hers were black with fury. "I hope to God you did not," he said, taking her arm.

"Where are we going?"

"Home," Justin declared with grim finality. "Where you can stay out of trouble. Perhaps I'll lock you in your room, or, better yet, chain you to my bed!"

"Lady Berkeley introduced us," Clare said in her defense, her stomach whirling at the sudden movement as she struggled to keep up with him.

"The poor, misguided woman probably thought that one look at Wilmington, or a few minutes of conversation with him, would convince you that your suspicions are unfounded," Justin said with some exasperation. "Unfortunately, she does not know you as I do. I assume that vivid imagination of yours will have its way, with total disregard for such a mundane triviality as the truth."

Clare bit her tongue to keep from arguing. Blast the man, and blast that Fletcher, who was supposed to be helping her convince Justin that she did possess the truth. Where was he?

WHEN THE TIME CAME to leave for Worth, Clare still had not heard from Fletcher, but she was feeling so poorly that she could not summon the energy to care. She didn't see how she could possibly travel without the chamber pot that had become her ever present companion. She eyed it critically as she sat on the side of the bed, feeling like crying for no reason at all.

"Better take it along, don't you think?" Justin asked, reaching for the pot. Clare's eyes darted to his in surprise, since she had been doing her best to hide her illness from him. As far as she was concerned, the man had enough to worry about without expending his concern on her bodily distress.

"A minor upset, that is all," Clare said defensively. "It will pass."

"I'm sure it will," Justin said dryly. "In about nine months, and right between your lovely legs."

Clare's head jerked up. "Whatever are you talking about?" she asked.

Justin shook his head, a wry smile on his features. "You really don't know, do you, my innocent Clare?" He stepped toward her and cupped her face in his hands in a gesture both tender and fierce. "My love, my own, I believe it's our babe that has made you ill. Are you sorry?"

"Our babe?" Clare looked into dark eyes that were questioning, probing hers, and she finally realized what he was saying. "Justin! Do you think so?" she asked. And suddenly, it was all right, the sleepiness, the nausea, the fits of temper. Anything would be endurable for a child. "Is it true? You and I...we're having a baby?" she asked tremulously. Despite the confirmation in his gaze, Clare was afraid that he was wrong, that they could not be so blessed.

Justin's mouth curved up crookedly, and he put a hand

to her smooth, but churning abdomen. "Oh, Clare, I know you so well, and yet sometimes I forget just who you are."

"What?" Clare whispered, too overjoyed to make sense out of his words.

"I knew, of course, when you became sick, what caused it, and I waited for you to say something, but when you hid it from me..." Justin paused. "I thought you didn't tell me because you were unhappy to be pregnant so soon, and irritated at the illness, and perhaps resentful of me for planting the seed."

"Justin St. John! How could you?" Clare asked, in horrified accents. She pulled back to search his face, offended that he could think such things of her.

He grinned, and pulled her close so he could press his lips to her dark locks. "Yes, scold me, Clare," he whispered, "for forgetting that you are not mortal woman, but my own, sweet pixie," he added, his smile disappearing into the glossy sheen of her hair.

A PROPRIETARY AIR of approval seemed to settle over the hall as word of mouth relayed Clare's condition throughout the household, and the servants whom Clare once thought viewed her with disapprobation now seemed to go out of their way to be kind. Even Harris unbent somewhat, although Clare was not sure whether this change could be attributed to her pregnancy or to the fact that she had stopped tormenting him.

At first, Clare watched the butler's new behavior with wariness, for fear he planned to begin another battle, but his changed attitude seemed genuine. And any doubts she harbored were dismissed one day when Justin was out surveying the lands and she was alone in the parlor, struggling with plans for her party.

"My lady," Harris said, clearing his throat.

"Yes?" Clare said absently.

THE SQUIRE'S DAUGHTER

"You once asked me about a certain incident at the hall...." The butler's words trailed off.

Clare looked up quickly, for he had her full attention now. "Yes?" she said again, hardly daring to breath.

"You asked about those in attendance that night."

She nodded urgently.

"Although I could not recall exactly who was here, it has occurred to me, my lady, that perhaps you would be interested in the guest list itself."

Clare gripped the arm of her chair. "A written list exists?"

"I am not certain," Harris said. "But I believe that all such records were put away when the hall was closed afterwards."

Only the utmost control prevented Clare from leaping to her feet in eagerness. "And these records would be..."

"In the storage rooms, my lady," Harris said softly. He looked at her, really looked at her for the first time, and she noticed his eyes were deep blue.

"Thank you, Harris," she said, resisting an urge to hug the man. "Thank you very much. I think I shall have a look through the storage rooms right now."

"Shall I accompany you, my lady?" he asked, inclining his head.

Clare smiled, a genuine smile of pleasure. "Yes, indeed, Mr. Harris."

They found the guest list an hour later in one of the hall's record books. Barely breathing, Clare scanned the names as she searched for Richards. There was Lord Wilmington and Richard Kingsley, but, apparently, no others. Then Clare's eyes were caught and held by something at the bottom of the page, and her heart began pounding with such suddenness that she felt dizzy. There was one more name on the list: Richard F. Mayefield.

She reached out toward Harris, her fingers closing over

his arm as she sought to find her voice. "Who—who is this?" she asked dazedly.

Harris looked surprised. "Oh, that is Mr. Mayefield, my lady. Although his first name is Richard, he goes by his middle name of Fletcher." Clare heard Harris, digested the information he gave her and then felt the room reel.

"MY LADY, my lady, are you all right?"

Clare wondered why the butler was disturbing her slumber. *Give me just a few minutes more sleep,* she thought, before coming fully awake and realizing that she was not in her bedchamber. She was lying on the floor of a storage room, her gown in the dust, with a horrified Harris bending over her.

"I'm all right," she managed to say. Then memory returned, and she closed her eyes against it. Fletcher. Fletcher, who had denied being at Justin's party. Fletcher, to whom she had entrusted all her knowledge. Fletcher, who had volunteered to hunt for Elizabeth's killer. His real name was Richard.

"Oh, thank heavens. My lady, his lordship will surely think ill of me," Harris said, and Clare finally came around. *Think ill of him?* Clare knew as well as Harris that should Justin get wind of this afternoon's work, the butler might be out of a job—and she might be locked in her room.

"I'm fine, Harris, really. It is just part of my condition, that is all, and no fault of yours, to be sure." The butler's white face seemed to gain some color with her reassurances. "There is no need to mention the exact circumstances to his lordship," Clare added as she let Harris help her to her feet. "If you just see me to my room and send for my maid, I shall lie down."

Their progress was interrupted by one of the footmen. "My lady," he said, "there is a boy from the village at the entrance, and he claims to have a message for you."

Harris, immediately resuming his usual implacable facade, drew himself up beside her, his hand placed protectively under her arm. "Her ladyship—" he began.

Clare cut him off. "Now, Mr. Harris, I'm fine, really. And I promise you that I shall lie down as soon as I see my visitor." She didn't know who was more surprised, Harris at her decision to see a village urchin, or the footman, who was obviously thrown by the sight of the butler coddling his mistress.

Although she was nauseous, as usual, Clare no longer felt light-headed, and she saw no reason to avoid the messenger. Still, she let Harris and the footman attend her while she walked down the steps, grimacing at their treatment of her as an invalid.

When she entered the great hall, she saw him immediately, a small boy dwarfed by the huge room and another footman, who looked down at the lad with not a little contempt.

"Eric! Have you come to see the castle after all?" Clare asked, approaching him with a smile. He was relatively clean, although his nose was running. He wiped it with the back of his hand and shook his head, a frown forming on his round face.

"No, my lady. My mum sent me to tell you something important," he said. At his words, Clare felt her heart begin tripping again, panic rising in her chest. She wanted to hold up a hand, to stop him, but even that small gesture was beyond her, and she had to listen, could not avoid hearing him when he spoke again. "It's my aunt, Addie McBride...she's dead, my lady."

Clare eyed him openmouthed, a gasp dying on her lips, and then, for the second time in her life, she fainted dead away.

CHAPTER EIGHTEEN

WHEN CLARE CAME AWAKE AGAIN, it was to the stinging smell of hartshorn, a restorative she had never needed before, but for which she was now heartily grateful. The rushing, dizzying panic that had seized her was gone, replaced by a calm she likened to that felt by a cornered beast when all avenues of escape had been exhausted. She waved off the servants who hovered over her nervously, sent a maid to the cook with instructions to pack a basket of food for the McBride family, and told Eric she would be taking him home in the coach.

The minute the words left her mouth, Harris stepped in front of her. "My lady, I cannot allow you to leave the hall in your condition," he intoned seriously.

Clare felt a bubble of hysterical laughter rise in her throat. The absurdity of a servant attempting to impose his will upon her, combined with the thought that only a few weeks ago Harris would have gladly seen her depart, ill or not, threatened to make her swoon again. She swallowed hard. "I appreciate your concern, Harris, truly I do, but I must go where I am needed," she said. Then she stepped right past him.

"My lady!" Harris cried. Clare ignored him to move toward Eric, who stood on the periphery of the group biting his lip. "Mr. Moore!" Clare heard Harris call one of the footmen sharply to attention. "Send out the stable staff in search of the marquis, and tell him his presence is desired at the hall immediately."

Clare rounded on Harris just in time to see the footman back out of the room. So it had come to this, had it—a battle between the butler and herself for supremacy in the household? Clare shot Harris a glance that told him he was overstepping his bounds, but when she saw real concern in his eyes, she faltered. Dropping her gaze, she turned back to Eric. Let Harris do what he must, she thought grimly, just as she, too, must follow her own conscience.

"Come, Eric," she said, holding out her hand, and they walked out the door.

CLARE COULD DO LITTLE at the McBride home. Although her gifts of food were greatly appreciated, the family was surrounded by villagers and relatives, so had no need of her small comfort. In a way Clare was grateful, for she was sure she could not hide her remorse from their eyes. Grief stricken and guilt ridden, she knew that Addie's death was her fault almost as surely as if she had wielded the knife that had slit the woman's throat.

He had waited until they returned to the castle, Clare realized, so that Justin would be blamed for the murder. And the killer had chosen this day well, for Justin was riding around his lands without witnesses to account for his whereabouts. The hopelessness of the situation weighed down upon Clare like a stone on her chest, and only the dread certainty of an even-worse future kept her from crying. Tears were pointless now.

The murder had terrified the village folk, including Corliss, for none of them knew, as Clare did, that they had no cause to fear. This was no lunatic on the loose, preying on random households, but a man with a cold-blooded plan, bent on one particular person. Addie had been right in the end: he had finally come back for her.

Stepping outside the stifling heat of the cottage, Clare noticed that a crowd had gathered in the yard. She was nearly startled out of her dazed state by an angry glance and a loud accusation, both seemingly directed at herself. "It's the curse," someone said, "the Worthington curse."

The Worthington curse. For one fanciful moment, Clare almost believed the old warning. *All of you will come to naught.* If the killer had his way, it would be too true, she thought, for Justin would be hanged, and she...

Clare finally faced the truth. The murderer could hardly allow her, with her special knowledge of his crimes, to go free. He had come back for Addie, and someday he would come back for her.

As she walked toward her waiting coach, Clare watched the murmuring group warily. Although she did not really expect violence to come to her from that quarter, she knew that fear could make them lash out, and it was best to keep her distance. Intent to do so, she hardly noticed the large, burly man who moved to her side.

"My lady, I believe you and I have a few things to discuss," he said smoothly.

Clare eyed him dispassionately. He towered over her, a well-dressed man with dark hair and eyes that told her he was not the one responsible for Addie's death. She was so sunk in despair by now that almost nothing but a knife suspended over her own throat could move her, so she said nothing and continued her steps until he spoke again. When he did, his words brought her up short.

"My name's Dunn," he said.

"Clare!"

Her lashes fluttered helplessly at the harsh tone in Justin's voice. At least he wasn't shouting, as had become his custom, but Clare suspected that his restraint was due to her condition, and not because he wasn't furious. She peeked at him from under lowered lids, saw the muscle in his jaw throbbing and closed her eyes again.

It had been hours before she could fulfill her promise to lie down, but now, finally, she was doing just that, though she admitted that her reasons for doing so had little to do with her physical needs. She was hiding from Justin. When she had returned to the castle in the company of Mr. Dunn, her husband had been quietly enraged. Obviously, his own interview with the Bow Street runner had not improved his disposition.

"It appears that Mr. Dunn has taken a liking to you," Justin said.

Clare peeked again, to see him leaning against the mantelpiece in a rather casual stance, but his negligent attitude was belied by his hands, which were balled into fists. She shut her eyes once more. "You're angry," she said.

"Blast it, Clare! Of course, I'm angry!" Justin answered heatedly. "I'm angry because you talked to Dunn behind my back, because you made plans with the man, because you dredged up this entire mess and because today you senselessly endangered yourself and our child! If I had my way, I would ship you off to the Continent, to the Colonies—anywhere to keep you safe from your own wild schemes!"

Clare didn't hear the desperate concern in his voice; she heard nothing but his words of blame. She *had* dredged up this entire mess and well she knew it. "Don't you think I know it's all my fault?" she whispered, her mouth dry. "I sought to absolve your guilt and instead...instead Elaine is dead and Addie is dead, and I killed them." And if you should die on the gallows... Clare couldn't finish the thought. She couldn't bear to know she might be responsible for Justin's death, too. Turning on her side, she rolled away from him, her hand moving instinctively over her stomach in a protective gesture.

She heard his deep sigh then his footsteps as he approached the bed. "Stop it. Stop it, Clare," he said. His voice was soft now, soft and soothing and calm. Clare felt the bed dip beside her and his hands, smooth and gentle, stroke her hair. "You are not responsible," he said. "Whoever is behind this wants me, not you, and with or without your interference, he would have come for me, sooner or later."

"But you said yourself—"

Justin cut her off. "Don't listen to me. I'm a fool," he said. He lay down beside her, curving his body against her back, and put his arms around her. "If I weren't, I would have married you two years ago or, better yet, four years ago!"

Clare found herself smiling in spite of her distress. "I don't think my father would have let me wed at fourteen," she murmured.

"Don't be too sure about that," Justin said dryly.

"Oh, Justin, what shall we do?" Clare whispered.

THREE WEEKS LATER, Clare stood nervously on the threshold of the hall, welcoming her guests. The party had been her idea. Even before Addie's murder, she had imagined that recreating the scene on the anniversary of Elizabeth's death might very well lure the killer back to the castle. He was toying with them; Clare felt it in her bones, and she suspected he was sporting with her particularly. She had been the one to open the Pandora's box of Elizabeth's death, and she had been the one he thwarted at every turn.

When Clare had suggested her plan to Mr. Dunn, in a desperate attempt to clear her husband's name, he had agreed, to her surprise. Justin had not been so easily swayed, but faced with the prospect of his own arrest, he had been convinced.

So here they were, greeting the odd collection of visitors who had accepted their invitations. The pressure of maintaining the charade was putting a strain between them. "Don't let any of them get you alone," Justin whispered heatedly in her ear as several smooth-talking charmers swept past her.

"I won't," Clare answered with a smile.

"I mean it, Clare," he warned.

"They don't look so bad," she said.

Justin groaned. "Most of them are worse now than they were years ago," he said as they watched a tall fellow being helped from his coach by his servant. Although it was still afternoon, the man appeared to be too foxed to stand on his own.

"That's not true," Clare said, although she eyed the newcomer with a grimace of distaste. "Lord Wilmington, for one, has distinguished himself."

Justin nodded grudgingly. "Yes, a few of my old companions have abandoned their youthful excesses, but…" His words trailed off as he moved to assist the drunken fellow up the steps. "Edgemont, how good to see you again," he said, giving Clare a pained look over his shoulder.

Clare would have laughed had her stomach not been tied in knots. Although only about half of the hall's previous guests had accepted, she was convinced that the murderer was among them. Would they be able to trap him?

Before she could pursue her thoughts, Justin was back at her side, hovering like a watchdog as he glanced down the empty drive. "I think that is everyone but the locals," he said of the guests who had been arriving in a steady stream since yesterday.

"Everyone except Fletcher," Clare noted.

Justin turned to her in surprise. "I don't believe Fletcher was here that night," he said.

"Really?" Clare asked, trying to keep the edge from her voice. She had confided her suspicions to Dunn, who'd advised her to say nothing to her husband. She was tempted to ignore that dictate, however. She knew they must all act as normally as possible, yet she wanted her husband to be prepared—and to watch his back. "Fletcher was invited," she said slowly.

Justin shrugged. "As I've told you, not all those invited were here."

"His first name is Richard," Clare said softly.

"Don't be ridiculous, Clare," Justin said, dismissing her insinuation with a sigh. "Come in now, and stay by me," he ordered. "You may preside at dinner, but then you are to go up to your chamber without delay. I have arranged for your maid to spend the night on a cot in your dressing room, and I have given her instructions to unlock the doors for no one but me."

"Oh, Justin, you don't really think—"

"I think I was a fool to agree to this scheme," he answered sharply, rubbing the back of his neck. "I should have sent you off to London, with or without our precious Dunn's approval."

"Hush," Clare whispered, taking his hand in hers. "You know what he said. It would look too odd to have me missing entirely." She did not add her own suspicion that if the killer got wind of her absence, he might not make an appearance himself. Although she tried not to think of herself as the lure needed to reel him in, it was always at the back of her mind.

CLARE HEARD SHOUTS from below and tensed in her chair, but it was only the racket of drunken revelry. She leaned back again, trying to relax. Although it was late, she sat up by the bedroom window, still fully dressed in the midnight blue silk gown she had worn at dinner, and listened.

The noise died down for a moment, allowing her to hear something else in the relative silence, and the hairs rose on the back of her neck as she recognized the sound of footsteps in the hallway. Clutching the arms of her chair, she stared at her door, following the path of rustling to the floor, where something pale was being slipped into her room. Forcing herself to stand, she walked toward the heavy oak panel until she stood before it and looked down at the sheet of paper that had been shoved underneath it. Then, with trembling hands, she picked up the message and unfolded it.

"If you would find out all that you seek, meet me on the roof. Come alone."

It was unsigned, but Clare knew the author. She flung open the door in the hope of catching him as he fled, but nothing greeted her except the soft glow of a lamp down the dim hall. If she had not held the evidence in her hand, Clare would have suspected she had imagined the entire episode. But it was there, in her fingers, its message taunting her.

Closing the door again, she leaned back against it and swallowed hard. She darted a glance at her maid, who was peacefully sleeping in the dressing room, and made her decision.

She was surprisingly calm, perhaps because she had expected this invitation. Something stood between her and Elizabeth's killer, something that ultimately must be resolved, and Clare had begun to see it as part of her destiny. She reached into a drawer for the pistol she had hidden there in preparation for this night, for she knew that the time of reckoning had come.

She walked silently along the hall to the door that, until a few days ago, had been nailed shut. She opened it, moving into the inky blackness of the stairwell. For a moment, she was overwhelmed with the fear that he might be waiting here, in the close darkness, but she forced her limbs to move up and up until a warm night breeze met her face and the light of the moon cast a glow on the battlements.

It was dangerous enough just walking up here, where pieces of stone had worn away and years of leaves and debris had piled up against the walls. Clare watched her steps carefully and wondered if Dunn could see her. Silently, she willed him to stay where he was until the killer approached. Too recognizable to make an appearance at the party, the Bow Street runner was hiding somewhere among the chimneys and the shafts that topped the house, hoping that the flamboyant murderer could not resist a return performance. He would not be disappointed.

"Clare!" Her heart froze at the sound of her name, her hand tightening on the pistol as she turned to face the man who had caused so much pain and grief. "You little idiot!" he said.

The moonlight gleamed on Fletcher's golden hair, casting his handsome features into relief, and Clare wondered how Addie could have described him as average. "I couldn't believe it when I returned home to the invitation," he whispered as he stepped toward her. "How could Justin let you go through with such a foolhardy scheme? Doesn't he know what you are doing?"

Clare brought up the weapon level with his chest as she searched for her voice. "Stop right there, Fletcher," she finally said, more firmly than she felt.

She saw his eyes take in the gun and noted his startled expression. Did he think her a total fool?

"Clare! What madness is this?" he asked.

"Stay where you are, or I shall be forced to shoot you, Fletcher. Or should I call you Richard?" she queried.

"Richard?" He paused, his eyebrows rising in startled surprise. "By faith, Clare, you don't actually think I did it, do you?"

Clare watched him through narrowed eyes. He was doing a credible job of playing the outraged innocent, but she knew better. Suddenly, his gaze darted to a spot behind her, and his expression changed. "Clare!" he cried, and then he surged forward. Without hesitation, she pulled the trigger and saw him stumble, a dark stain spreading on his chest before he fell.

She looked down at his body, unfeeling, unmoving, until she heard a noise behind her. Then a chill danced up her spine.

"Very well done, Clare," said a soft voice.

A tremor passed through her, a shiver of horror and dread, as Clare turned to find herself facing a man of medium height whose features were obscured by shadows, but who more accurately fit Addie's description than Fletcher ever would. At the sight of him, her heart, already close to bursting, seemed to pop loudly within her chest. Clare willed herself to stay on her feet, but the night gathered around her in a rushing, whirling frenzy, as Elizabeth's killer stepped forward.

It was only the wind, swirling the leaves into the air, that made the roof spin, and Clare took a deep breath as the world righted itself. She was not going to faint, thankfully. Her head clearing, she found the strength to respond. "Would you care to see me do it again, using you as the target this time?" she asked, even though she knew the weapon was useless. She had not the time nor the ammunition to reload it.

The figure laughed softly. "Very brave, Clare. You are quite a prize: brave, clever and yet soft as lambskin, aren't you? We could have dealt well together."

Clare's stomach gave a sickening flop as she recognized the voice, calm and light and deceptively bland. It was Richard Farnsworth, proving himself to be more fiendish than she could possibly have imagined.

"Your mistake, but I must admit it has provided me with some entertainment and given me the chance to tie up some loose ends," he added.

Clare stepped back, but Farnsworth moved swiftly to close the space between them. He wrested the empty pistol from her hand. It fell to the stones beneath their feet, and Clare felt panic seize her. Where was Dunn? She stalled for time. "But you weren't invited," she protested.

Farnsworth laughed. "No, but I came anyway. It was easy to slip into one of Worthington's drunken routs in those days, a little more difficult this evening, but not impossible, especially when I knew it was all for me. You did want me to come tonight, didn't you, Clare?" he asked softly. He was so close she could feel his breath, and she turned her face away, frightened by eyes that glittered malevolently.

"Step away, Farnsworth. I have a gun aimed at your head," called a voice. Low and smooth and decidedly not Dunn's, it made Clare draw in a sharp breath of fear for her husband. Oh, dear God, save us all, she prayed desperately.

"I vow this is a busy place, Worthington!" Farnsworth called back. "Someone behind every chimney! Mayefield, your wife and now you, too. Oh, and there was another fellow I met when I first came up. Perhaps you know him—a big, burly chap?" He let his words linger in the air and then he laughed softly. "Really, Worthington, you didn't actually think yourself smart enough to entrap me, did you?"

Clare's breath left her lungs in a rush as all her hopes for a rescue from Bow Street slipped away. She felt giddy again, but she fought it and the wave of nausea that followed. Although she knew the fainting was brought on mostly by her condition, she still felt furiously ashamed of herself for the two instances when she had succumbed. Now, dear heaven, was not the time to fall prey again to the engulfing blackness.

She tried to inhale evenly, focusing her attention on Justin, in case he wanted her to do something. But what could she do? Farnsworth had her arm pulled behind her back in a viselike grip now, and he pushed her forward to where Fletcher had fallen. With a grunt of careless indifference, he stuck a boot under the prone man and kicked him over. Fletcher rolled lifelessly onto his back, blood smearing his chest, and Clare sobbed aloud, knowing that she was responsible. Farnsworth laughed in her ear and shoved her onward.

"Farnsworth! Let her go, and I won't blow your brains out," Justin said calmly.

"Are you that good a shot, Worthington?" Farnsworth

jeered. "I doubt it. Would you risk your precious wife, the love of your life, the woman who carries your child? Or is it yours? Are you certain? Perhaps it is mine, just as Elizabeth's was!"

"Move away, Farnsworth, and I'll let you live," Justin said.

"I think it's only fitting, don't you? This woman!" Farnsworth wrenched her arm painfully, and Clare had to bite her lip to keep from crying out. "This woman betrayed me, too! Thought she could throw me over for a title, just as Elizabeth did. But her fate will be the same, Worthington." Slowly, Farnsworth was moving toward the edge. "Come out now and maybe I won't toss her into the moat," he taunted.

"It was easy enough to bribe Elaine to do my bidding. She was a greedy wench. A little florid for my taste, but this one..." Farnsworth's words trailed off as he moved. With sudden, brutal force, he twisted Clare so that she was bent over the parapet, and she gasped, the night spinning around her. Drawing a deep breath, she tried to fight the dizziness. Then she caught a glimpse of movement, and something flew through the air towards Farnsworth.

With a surge of sweet relief, Clare felt his hold on her slacken. She dangled for one brief moment over the castle's edge before falling like a stone.

Justin saw Farnsworth drop her, and a scream tore from his throat. He pulled the trigger, sending a ball into Farnsworth's chest, before he flew out of his position behind one of the old privy shafts and leapt to the edge. Farnsworth was lying in a pool of blood, while Clare...Clare was gone.

He stood there, staring into the darkness below, for what seemed like an eternity before his senses returned. Then he spun on his heel and charged down the steps, taking them two at a time, past Lord Wilmington, who stood white-faced at the bottom, surrounded by the other guests who were still sober. "See to Mayefield!" Justin shouted as he ran by them.

Then he was racing down again into the great hall, through the lingering revelers to the main entrance, where the door stood open. He sped through it into the night, and across the stone bridge to the bank, slowing only when he saw them—two figures in the darkness that resolved themselves into his butler and his dripping wife.

With a gasp of relief so heady that he nearly crashed to his knees, Justin took her in his arms, uncaring that he was wetting her further with his own hot tears of joy.

"I'M SORRY, Fletcher," Clare said softly as she looked down at her husband's friend. The ball had passed through the muscle below his shoulder. The wound had been dressed, and he was leaning back against the huge tester bed in the green chamber, looking surprisingly good.

"Thank heavens you are a poor marksman," he said wryly.

"I am not!" Clare denied. "It was dark...." Her words trailed off as she found three pairs of male eyes gazing at her with varying degrees of alarm. "Oh, dear Lord. Thank goodness it was dark," she said, knowing that she might well have shot him through the heart. She reached out to grasp Fletcher's hand, comforted by the warmth of his fingers, reassuringly alive in her own. "I thought I had killed you," she said softly.

Fletcher smiled and shook his head. "I know when to keep quiet," he explained. "Fully aware that I was in no position to take Farnsworth on, I decided to lie low, lest he finish the job."

"You saved my life," Clare said.

Fletcher grinned even wider. "I did, didn't I?"

"And you said you were no good with damsels in distress," Clare chided gently.

"I fail to see why you are lavishing such praise on

Fletcher for throwing your pistol at Farnsworth," Justin said. "All Fletcher succeeded in doing was knocking Farnsworth off balance so that he dropped you into the moat, which, I might remind you, was his intention all along."

Clare smiled and took Justin's hand, too, grasping tightly to both men, while Lord Wilmington looked on. "Yes, but falling is one thing, being strangled or struck and then thrown in is quite another."

Justin sighed deeply. "That anyone could survive that fall..."

"I am a good swimmer—you know that, Justin—and I was not hampered by heavy clothing. *And* I had so many heroes coming to my aid," Clare added. Beaming at the three surrounding her, she turned to include an anxious-looking Harris, hovering near the door with Mr. Dunn, whose own head was bandaged from the blow that Farnsworth had dealt him. "Thank you all," Clare said. Then she leaned over to kiss Fletcher's forehead.

"You may shoot me anytime you wish, Clare," he whispered.

She released his hand and put both arms around her husband, who was still a bit pale.

"Just as long as you and the baby are both all right," Justin said, his voice still laced with uncertainty.

Clare lifted her head. "I am not easily gotten rid of, Justin St. John. Don't you know that by now?"

CLARE GRABBED THE OLD TRUNK, stirring up a cloud of dust as she hauled it across the floor. Putting the night of terror and the death of Farnsworth behind her, she had attacked the castle again in earnest, going through all the storage rooms, cleaning and sorting and searching, particularly for nursery items.

The various cradles and books and toys she had assembled were gathered lovingly into the chambers next to their own, giving her plenty of time to decide just how to furnish the rooms. Although only a slight swelling of her slender waist gave testament to her condition, Clare was eager to have everything in readiness for the baby's arrival.

She plopped down in front of her latest find, an old wooden trunk that had been wedged with a few other items behind some wardrobes. Her curiosity piqued by the age of the chest, Clare lifted the lid in anticipation, sending more dust swirling around her. She sighed in disappointment as she viewed the contents: old linens and gowns.

Clare removed a handful of ancient material, the threads long ago having given way, and watched them crumble in her hands. Then she saw a tiny, beaded cap that had somehow weathered the years, and smiled. Children's clothing.

Digging deeper, she found a wooden doll, a set of tin soldiers and a ball whose painted finish had long since worn away. Too large for hockey, it must have been used for ninepins, Clare thought, but the weight seemed oddly at variance with its size. She hefted it in one hand and eyed it quizzically. When a tap upon its surface produced a hollow sound, Clare smiled and found the seam, which told her it must open somehow.

She tugged, turned, twisted and cursed, but the ball would not budge. Clare told herself that the aged wood had swollen shut and could not be freed, but she kept trying. What began as the conquest of a clever children's toy now assumed epic proportions as she swore to open the thing or see it sawed in two. Finally reaching the limit of her endurance, Clare flung it against the hearth as hard as she could.

It struck one of the irons and popped apart easily, revealing a shiny bit of color. Mollified, Clare thought a ribbon or some beads might have been preserved, and she stooped to look. Picking up the now-infamous ball, she poured the contents into her hand and stared in astonishment, her heart leaping into her throat.

Gold, heavy and old and encrusted with pearls and gems, spilled across her palm. Hardly daring to breathe, Clare lifted the piece slowly, to hold the burnished metal up to the light. Draping it over her fingers, she gasped at the sight of two magnificent jewels that still glowed warm and rich and red. *The Sisters.* The huge table-cut rubies told her in an instant that she held no ordinary necklace.

She held *the* necklace.

Clasping it to her chest in giddy excitement, Clare wondered how it had ended up here. Perhaps a child "borrowing" a sparkling trinket, then too frightened to admit it, had brought down the Worthington name for generations. She shook her head, for she would never know the true story, but would have to weave one of her own.

Still stunned by her find, Clare spread out her treasure to admire it anew and smiled in rapt wonder. She wiped absently at a tear as she looked down at the eerie evidence of her destiny. Now she could well and truly lift the Worthington curse.

CLARE STOOD BESIDE HER HUSBAND, looking out over the lawns surrounding Worth Hall, her heart filled to bursting. Villagers mingled with townspeople from Rillford as they milled around tables laden with food that scented the crisp autumn air. A wandering juggler made his rounds, followed by a trail of youngsters, giggling and tossing apples in imitation.

Behind them the stone bridge led over the moat to the entrance of the castle, thrown open during the celebration for everyone to see. Although Clare had not finished with it yet, she was pleased with her progress, and eager to show it off to those who had been estranged from it for too long. Of course, the excitement of the hall's renovation had been eclipsed in the public eye by another item on display, for who could resist a priceless necklace imbued with a hint of magical powers?

"It's time," Justin whispered, and Clare turned to see Harris, surrounded by a small guard of armed men, walk forward carrying the case. He handed it to Justin with a dignified nod.

"My friends," Justin said, and a hush fell over the crowd. "You all know my lovely wife, Clare." A cheer rose from some quarters and Clare blushed. "She has rescued my family seat, Worth Hall, from the ravages of time, and in her endeavors, she found something that people have talked about for centuries—" he opened the case and lifted it high, so that the afternoon sun glittered off the red depths of The Sisters "—the famous Moleyns necklace, tucked away in a child's toy. We cannot know whether it was placed there by accident or design." At this point Justin had to shout to be heard above the murmuring crowd. "But it has been found, and now it shall be returned to its rightful owner."

The current duke, a rotund, jovial man who had laughed when they had first contacted him about the curse, stepped forward happily, while the crowd roared. "I hope he doesn't sell it," Clare whispered.

"It is no longer our responsibility, Clare," Justin reminded her under his breath. Louder, he said, "Lord Moleyns, may I present to you the famous necklace of your ancestors, with my compliments!"

The crowd cheered, and Lord Moleyns mumbled something about goodwill between the two families, thumped Justin on the back and kissed Clare on the cheek. Then he gave the case into the safekeeping of the armed guards and made his way back to his meal with a hefty burp. The man was obviously enjoying himself, Clare noted.

She felt a tug on her skirts. "Hello, Kate, are you having a good time?" she asked of the young girl standing beside her.

"Yes, Clare. I mean, my lady," Kate answered, a bit nervously. "But we were wondering. That is…"

Clare lifted her gaze to notice several village children clustered not far away. She smiled as Eric broke away and ran to her. "Clare! Tell us a story!" he shouted without preamble.

With easy grace, Justin swung the youngster into his arms and grinned at her. "Yes, Clare, tell us a story," he coaxed, and she laughed happily.

"All right," Clare said. And then the Marquis and Marchioness of Worthington sat down upon the grass in front of the hall, she with her skirts tucked beneath her, he with his long legs stretched out before him, while a swarm of children climbed over them and curled between them. When one was settled on her lap, pillowed by her rounded stomach, and two were nestled beside her, and three were resting against her husband, she began.

"Once a long, long time ago, there was a beautiful castle called Worth...."

* * * * *

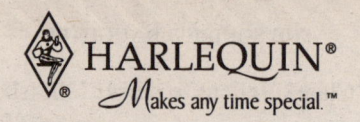

HARLEQUIN®
Makes any time special.™

HARLEQUIN® AMERICAN ROMANCE® — Upbeat, all-American romances about the pursuit of love, marriage and family.

HARLEQUIN Duets™ — Two brand-new, full-length romantic comedy novels for one low price.

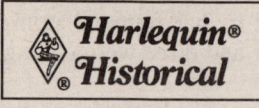

Harlequin® Historical — Rich and vivid historical romances that capture the imagination with their dramatic scope, passion and adventure.

HARLEQUIN® Temptation® — Sexy, sassy and seductive—Temptation is hot sizzling romance.

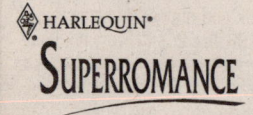

HARLEQUIN® SUPERROMANCE — A bigger romance read with more plot, more story-line variety, more pages and a romance that's evocatively explored.

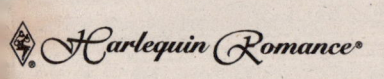

Harlequin Romance® — Love stories that capture the essence of traditional romance.

HARLEQUIN® INTRIGUE® — Dynamic mysteries with a thrilling combination of breathtaking romance and heart-stopping suspense.

HARLEQUIN PRESENTS® — Meet sophisticated men of the world and captivating women in glamorous, international settings.

Look us up on-line at: http://www.romance.net

HGEN99

If you enjoyed what you just read,
then we've got an offer you can't resist!

Take 2 bestselling love stories FREE!
Plus get a FREE surprise gift!

Clip this page and mail it to Harlequin Reader Service®

IN U.S.A.	IN CANADA
3010 Walden Ave.	P.O. Box 609
P.O. Box 1867	Fort Erie, Ontario
Buffalo, N.Y. 14240-1867	L2A 5X3

YES! Please send me 2 free Harlequin Superromance® novels and my free surprise gift. Then send me 6 brand-new novels every month, which I will receive months before they're available in stores. In the U.S.A., bill me at the bargain price of $3.57 plus 25¢ delivery per book and applicable sales tax, if any*. In Canada, bill me at the bargain price of $3.96 plus 25¢ delivery per book and applicable taxes**. That's the complete price, and a saving of over 10% off the cover prices—what a great deal! I understand that accepting the 2 free books and gift places me under no obligation ever to buy any books. I can always return a shipment and cancel at any time. Even if I never buy another book from Harlequin, the 2 free books and gift are mine to keep forever.
So why not take us up on our invitation. You'll be glad you did!

135 HEN CQW6
336 HEN CQW7

Name _____ (PLEASE PRINT)

Address _____ Apt.# _____

City _____ State/Prov. _____ Zip/Postal Code _____

* Terms and prices subject to change without notice. Sales tax applicable in N.Y.
** Canadian residents will be charged applicable provincial taxes and GST.
  All orders subject to approval. Offer limited to one per household.
® is a registered trademark of Harlequin Enterprises Limited.

6SUP99 ©1998 Harlequin Enterprises Limited

Back by popular demand are
DEBBIE MACOMBER's

Hard Luck, Alaska, is a town that needs women! And the O'Halloran brothers are just the fellows to fly them in.

Starting in March 2000 this beloved series returns in special 2-in-1 collector's editions:

MAIL-ORDER MARRIAGES, featuring
Brides for Brothers and *The Marriage Risk*
On sale March 2000

FAMILY MEN, featuring
Daddy's Little Helper and *Because of the Baby*
On sale July 2000

THE LAST TWO BACHELORS, featuring
Falling for Him and *Ending in Marriage*
On sale August 2000

Collect and enjoy each MIDNIGHT SONS story!

Available at your favorite retail outlet.

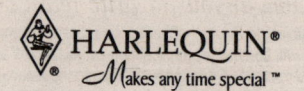

HARLEQUIN®
Makes any time special™

Visit us at www.romance.net

PHMS

HARLEQUIN®
Makes any time special™

This *Series Sampler* was a special collection of four Harlequin series,

**Harlequin Temptation,
Harlequin Intrigue,
Harlequin Historicals &
Harlequin American Romance**

If you enjoyed these titles,
you are sure to enjoy more of what
Harlequin has to offer.

Pick up more of these titles at your favorite retail outlet.

50¢ OFF!

the purchase of any **HARLEQUIN TEMPTATION, HARLEQUIN INTRIGUE, HARLEQUIN HISTORICAL OR HARLEQUIN AMERICAN ROMANCE** series book.

RETAILER: Harlequin Enterprises Ltd. will pay the face value of this coupon plus 10.25¢ if submitted by the customer for this specified product only. Any other use constitutes fraud. Coupon is nonassignable, void if taxed, prohibited or restricted by law. Consumer must pay any government taxes. Valid in Canada only. Nielson Clearing House customers—mail to: Harlequin Enterprises Ltd., P.O. Box 880478, El Paso, TX 88588-0478, U.S.A. Non NCH retailer—for reimbursement submit coupons and proof of sales directly to: Harlequin Enterprises Ltd., Retail Sales Dept., 225 Duncan Mill Rd., Don Mills (Toronto), Ontario M3B 3K9, Canada

**Coupon expires December 31, 2000.
Valid at retail outlets in Canada only.**

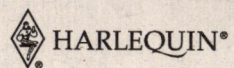

HARLEQUIN®

52602333

Visit us at www.romance.net

PHSERIES50CAN

HARLEQUIN®
Makes any time special™

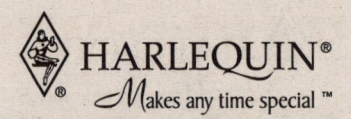

This *Series Sampler* was a special collection of four Harlequin series,

**Harlequin Temptation,
Harlequin Intrigue,
Harlequin Historicals &
Harlequin American Romance**

If you enjoyed these titles,
you are sure to enjoy more of what
Harlequin has to offer.

Pick up more of these titles at your favorite retail outlet.

50¢ OFF!
the purchase of any **HARLEQUIN TEMPTATION, HARLEQUIN INTRIGUE, HARLEQUIN HISTORICAL OR HARLEQUIN AMERICAN ROMANCE** series book.

RETAILER: Harlequin Enterprises Ltd. will pay the face value of this coupon plus 8¢ if submitted by the customer for this specified product only. Any other use constitutes fraud. Coupon is nonassignable, void if taxed, prohibited or restricted by law. Consumer must pay any government taxes. Valid in U.S. only. Nielson Clearing House customers—mail to: Harlequin Enterprises Ltd., P.O. Box 880478, El Paso, TX 88588-0478, U.S.A. Non NCH retailer—for reimbursement submit coupons and proof of sales directly to: Harlequin Enterprises Ltd., Retail Sales Dept., 225 Duncan Mill Rd., Don Mills (Toronto), Ontario M3B 3K9, Canada

**Coupon expires December 31, 2000.
Valid at retail outlets
in U.S. only.**

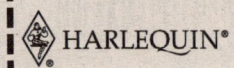

HARLEQUIN®

5 65373 00050 2   (8100) 1 06841

Visit us at www.romance.net

PHSERIES50US_R

HEART OF THE WEST

Every Man Has His Price!

Lost Springs Ranch was famous for turning young mavericks into good men. So word that the ranch was in financial trouble sent a herd of loyal bachelors stampeding back to Wyoming to put themselves on the auction block!

July 1999	*Husband for Hire* Susan Wiggs	January 2000	*The Rancher and the Rich Girl* Heather MacAllister
August	*Courting Callie* Lynn Erickson	February	*Shane's Last Stand* Ruth Jean Dale
September	*Bachelor Father* Vicki Lewis Thompson	March	*A Baby by Chance* Cathy Gillen Thacker
October	*His Bodyguard* Muriel Jensen	April	*The Perfect Solution* Day Leclaire
November	*It Takes a Cowboy* Gina Wilkins	May	*Rent-a-Dad* Judy Christenberry
December	*Hitched by Christmas* Jule McBride	June	*Best Man in Wyoming* Margot Dalton

HARLEQUIN®
Makes any time special ™

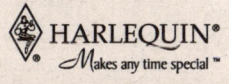

Visit us at www.romance.net

PHHOWGEN

Return to the charm of the Regency era with

GEORGETTE HEYER,

creator of the modern Regency genre.

Enjoy six romantic collector's editions with forewords by some of today's bestselling romance authors,

Nora Roberts, Mary Jo Putney, Jo Beverley, Mary Balogh, Theresa Medeiros and Kasey Michaels.

Frederica
On sale February 2000

The Nonesuch
On sale March 2000

The Convenient Marriage
On sale April 2000

Cousin Kate
On sale May 2000

The Talisman Ring
On sale June 2000

The Corinthian
On sale July 2000

Available at your favorite retail outlet.

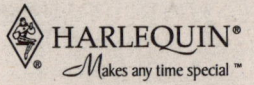

HARLEQUIN®
Makes any time special ™

Visit us at www.romance.net

PHGHGEN